1

"I don't feel good." Jay stood in the
was red, flushed with a fever, and I
with sweat. He wore a white short-sleeved pajama shirt with teal
sleeves. A brown baseball mitt was in the center of his shirt catching an
oversized baseball. His orange pajama shorts were from a different set.
Jay seldom matched his clothes. The white shirt and orange pants were
soaked with sweat, clinging to his thin five year old frame.

Todd and Emily were packing to leave Raleigh. It was early in the
morning, 6am. The sun was already up. Emily put her arm around Jay,
and gave him some soothing words. She talked to him about going to
the couch downstairs, and watching a movie. Jay nodded. Todd looked
at the television in their room. It showed an exodus, a traffic jam of cars
fleeing their city. Dozens of news helicopters cast black shadows on the
ground while filming the government checkpoints on every road.
Workers in yellow hazmat suits examined people before letting cars
pass.

Todd walked downstairs. He told Jay to feel better, and went into the
kitchen to pour his son a dose of cherry flavored medicine to curb his
fever and make him comfortable. Emily tucked Jay into a snuggly bed of
blankets and pillows on the couch in front of their living room television.
She checked the kids' networks for cartoons, but even those channels
showed images of cars stuck in traffic with the scroll "Residents Flee
Raleigh, North Carolina." Emily switched to their DVR recordings and
started a movie.

Todd wanted to be one of the cars being filmed on the road. His plan
was ruined. Jay was sick. They would not make it through the
checkpoints out of Raleigh. The helicopters showed infected people
being ushered to government vehicles, separated from their families.

Todd would not risk Jay being taken from them.

He handed Emily the red syrupy medicine before stepping outside onto their deck. Todd was in a daze. He sat down on the extra wide steps their contractor built two summers before. The steps were stadium sized, and took up an entire corner. They flowed into the yard, allowing anyone to sit on the steps comfortably. The contractor sold them on the idea of a "party deck," with the stairs doubling as extra seating for guests.

Todd and Emily watched the kids play in the yard from the steps. The kids ate their lunch on them too. It was a great deck.

He heard the door open and close. Emily sat next to him, and put her arm around him, the same way she soothed their son a few minutes ago. "What now?" She whispered.

"I guess we wait." He told her as she rested her head on his shoulder. "And hope."

Matthew Boone, Todd's neighbor, was a road warrior salesman for a technology company. Boone travelled everywhere and all the time. The Boone children were similar in age to Todd's, and played together almost every day. Two weeks ago the Boones came down with a summer flu. They had fevers, were lethargic, and had no appetite. It was not unusual to have a flu in the summer, but after what happened in Sao Paulo, Brazil, people were on edge.

Matthew Boone died three days ago.

The people in the yellow Hazmat suits removed the rest of the Boone bodies yesterday, one mother and four children.

The Boones were part of a growing number of dead in Raleigh, more than 1,500 bodies in three days. Panic was everywhere. People fled the city. Todd and Emily planned to take their two children to New Hampshire, riding out the epidemic at their family cottage. Now that

The Last Tribe

Brad Manuel

All thanks to my wife, Carolyn, for her love, unwavering confidence, editing, and support.

Book One

Jay was sick, they needed a new plan.

"You don't think we can get through?" Emily asked her husband. They began to sweat under the strong Carolina sun. It was already 80 degrees at 6:15 in the morning.

"You saw the T.V. They have checkpoints on every road. If you're sick, they want you to stay in Raleigh. It's not a recommendation. They are going to keep us here, or worse, they'll take Jay and send us away." Todd shut his eyes. "Dammit." They sat on the steps together trying to make sense out of their situation.

He turned and looked at his wife. "How much food do we have?"

"Why?"

"How much food do we have? The stores are closed, there won't be any more food coming into Raleigh. We need to make sure we have enough to last a few weeks, maybe a few months. Let's take an inventory." Todd got up. "I'm not going to die, and neither are you or the kids. Let's plan on making it through this plague, whatever it is. The first thing we need to do is make sure we have food."

Two hours later Emily and Todd stood in the kitchen with all of their food categorized on the counters and table. They had short term perishables and long term non-perishables. Todd assumed the power would go off if enough people left Raleigh. He suggested they eat everything in the fridge immediately.

"Meals are going to get smaller and more interesting. We waste nothing. If the kids don't finish something, it gets bagged and they have it at the next meal, or for a snack. Same goes for us." Todd paused. "I'm going to sneak over to the Boone's later and see what they have in the fridge. I'll go behind the houses, not on the street."

"Are you crazy? Why are you going to steal their food?"

"They're dead, Emily, they aren't going to eat it. If this gets any worse,

I'm going to steal everyone's food, but I'll start with the Boone's before someone else gets the same idea." Todd surveyed the counter and looked at Emily. "This is bad. Look at the news reports out of Brazil, and China, and Germany, and Australia. This isn't a passing flu that happened to kill our friends. We're in it, and the best way to survive is to plan to survive."

Todd took Emily's trembling hands. She was scared, and he could see despair in her eyes.

"We have to plan to survive, and our first step is to get as much food as we can. The Boones are gone. I'm taking their food, today. We have two rain barrels. I'll clean them out, sanitize them with bleach, and we can collect rain water."

"You really think we're okay?" Emily asked hopefully.

"I have to, and so do you."

2

The last neighbors in their cul de sac, the Williams, pulled out at noon. Todd waited an hour before he walked behind the two houses between his home and the Boone's. There were woods in each backyard running for fifty to one hundred yards, keeping Todd well hidden from the main road. He heard cars honking and frustrated drivers screaming, panicked and impatient people stuck in traffic.

It was oppressively hot, as North Carolina is every July. Todd was dripping by the time he arrived at the Boone's sliding glass backdoor. He cupped his hands and peaked through the glass, spying a dark kitchen and apparently empty house. His sweaty hands and nose left an odd print on the clean glass, like a comma inside of parenthesis. He wondered if the symbol represented something, if teens used it on their phones to signify a sweaty burglar or peeping tom.

Todd tried to slide the door. It was locked.

"So much for easy." He mumbled. Todd walked off the deck and around the house to a side door leading into the garage. It was also locked. He paused, took a deep breath and walked as casually as he could to the front door. He turned the handle and went inside. The hazmat people had left the door unlocked after removing the bodies.

Todd shut the door quickly. Instinctively he called out, "hello?" He waited a second, but there was no response. "Hello?" He yelled again loudly.

The house was empty. Todd moved down a hallway to the kitchen and went to work. He had been in the Boone's house for a few parties over the years, but he was not completely familiar with their layout. He was going to have to search for the food stores.

Like most houses built in the neighborhood, the Boone's kitchen included a walk-in pantry. Todd stacked the food next to the sliding glass back door. He would use one of his kid's wagons to retrieve the supplies after the sun went down, moving them under the cover of darkness.

Todd paused again. "Hello?" He called out. He could not shake the feeling that someone else was in the house. It was just a feeling. He was alone. The Boones were dead. No one was on their street. Everyone was gone. He ignored the eerie feelings and began to search through the kitchen for food not kept in the pantry. He opened the fridge. "Let's see what we have here..."

3

A white van pulled into the cul-de-sac and parked. Four people in yellow Hazmat suits got out of the vehicle. They split up and worked in pairs, two people approaching each house. One of the people carried a clipboard, the other an automatic weapon.

The rifleman stood guard as the clipboard person knocked on the front door. If no one answered, the case in all four of the other houses on the street, the clipboard person walked to the top of the house's driveway touching the street and spray painted a black symbol before moving to the next residence.

Todd watched the van from his upstairs bedroom window. He saw the four people split into pairs and begin their door to door search on the other side of the street. He nodded to Emily, and she took Brian, their oldest son, to the attic. Jay was asleep in his bedroom. Todd followed his wife and son.

The attic was unfinished and sweltering hot, the temperature increased as Todd trudged up the stairs. He walked to the lone window overlooking the driveway where he could watch the front doors of the two houses next to him. After a few minutes he saw the yellow puffy suits approaching the front of each home.

"They look like teletubbies. You remember teletubbies?" Todd asked Emily.

"Not the time." She said, trying to entertain Brian and keep his mind off the uncomfortable room. "And why are we up here again?"

The four yellow suited people met at Todd's house, the fifth on the street. One of them walked up the steps and rang the doorbell. Todd opened the front door. He was red faced and sweating from his time in

the attic. The yellow suit stepped back quickly, shocked to find a person at home and answering the door. The two armed people gripped their rifles in a ready position.

"Sir, are you aware there is a mandatory evacuation of Raleigh? You need to leave." Todd was unable to determine the sex of the people until now. An elderly woman spoke to him through a clear plastic face shield. She looked hot and uncomfortable, her face was flushed and her forehead glistened.

"My son is sick." Todd told them solemnly. "He has..."

The woman cut him off, raising her arm into the air and showing her palm. "We need to see him."

"Please, come in, help us if you can." Todd pleaded.

The woman took another step away, backing down the stairs. "Just bring your son to the door, and put this in his mouth." She tossed him a white box with a thermometer. "Is there anyone else home?" The woman looked at her clipboard. Todd guessed it was a census description. "Your wife and other child?"

"Do you need to see them too?" Todd tried to act lethargic and groggy.

"We need to see everyone." The woman was not polite.

Todd shut the glass storm door and went inside to get his family. He walked slowly and deliberately to the top of the stairs, knowing the woman and the three other people were watching him. He turned left and opened the attic door. "Emily, you need to come down and stand in the doorway."

"I'm dripping from head to toe. It's a sauna up here." She came down the attic stairs with their seven year old. Mother and child were sweating and red faced.

"I'll get Jay." Todd went into Jay's room and lifted his son. Jay was suffering through an actual bought of the flu, one Todd hoped was a benign version rather than the one that killed the Boones. Jay continued to sleep. He was flushed, and soaking from night sweats. Todd put the thermometer in his mouth, and carried him down the stairs. Sweaty Brian and Emily followed.

The Hazmat woman stood in the doorway, observing everything through the glass storm door. When she saw Todd and the three seemingly ill people, she backed down the front steps and into the yard.

Todd turned the handle and pushed the front door open with Jay's feet. "Please, what should I do? Our neighbors died a few days ago. Does he have it?" Todd was a horrible actor, but the situation was so real the four yellow suits did not realize the ruse.

The clipboard people spoke to each as they wrote. "This area is supposed to be cleared. I'm not a doctor, I don't get paid to deal with this stuff." The other hazmat person was upset to find the Dixons home.

"Have you had any contact with the Boone family in the last month?" The woman asked Todd.

"Yes, a lot, Jay played with them almost every day. Why? Is that bad? Does he have it?" Todd took a step forward. The men with rifles pointed the guns toward him.

"Why didn't you call the mandatory medical hotline?" The other person asked. Part of the television scroll below the videos of Raleigh was a phone number to self report fevers and other flu like symptoms.

"I don't know what you're..." Todd continued his lie.

"Sir, stay on your porch. You are officially quarantined. I am going to mark your house as such. Do not leave your residence or attempt to leave Raleigh. Do you understand?"

"I, I do. Can't you help us? Can't you help my son?" Todd took a step back towards his house.

"A medical team will be through soon." The woman pointed to the van, motioning the guards and her associate to go back to it.

"Don't you want the thermometer?" Todd asked, begging her for help.

"Please stay in your house. Your actions may save the rest of us." She started towards the van before stopping and walking back to Todd. "Mr. Dixon? God bless you and your family. Good luck." Her voice was kind and full of sympathy.

Behind her, the other clipboard person was arguing with the riflemen. "I don't have orange paint, I'm not a doctor. They only gave me black paint. What the hell am I supposed to do? They aren't dead or gone."

The woman approached the end of the driveway, and Todd saw her head shake back and forth.

The four people got in their van and drove to the next cul-de-sac. Todd stood on the front porch holding Jay until the van left his street. He looked at the four other driveways in his cul-de-sac. Three of the driveways had black "V's", probably indicating "vacant." The new paint ran down the slopes. The Boone's driveway had two symbols, the first was an orange circle with a line, given to them after a visit from government health officials. Painted over that symbol two days ago, when their bodies were removed, was a black circle with a line.

Todd went inside. He carried Jay to his bedroom, and kissed him on the forehead, "feel better buddy." Car horns continued in the distance as the last residents of Raleigh sat on nearby roads, waiting to join the slow moving river of fleeing cars on the highway.

Todd came downstairs and into the kitchen to speak with Emily and Brian. "Well," he told them. "It looks like they bought it."

The Boone's, warehouse shoppers and a family of six, tripled Todd and Emily's food inventory. Cases sat on the floor as Emily decided how and

where to store the excess.

Todd's phone rang. His brother Hank's picture flashed on the screen.

"What the hell is happening down there?" Todd heard screaming from the cell before he could bring the phone to his ear.

"Hey." Todd said. "I don't know. Jay is sick."

Hank was silent.

"I know," Todd acknowledged the gravity of the situation, "but I think it's just the flu, not the bad flu, the real flu. Maybe I'm delusional. I gotta believe, right?"

"Jesus." Was all Hank could muster.

"Seriously, I think he's going to be fine." Todd replayed the government interaction from the morning. "I don't know why, I just don't trust the disease people right now. This thing killed my neighbors in a week, and there is still a message to be calm. Calm is not an option."

"What are you going to do?" Hank was a world away in Dayton, Ohio. There were no confirmed cases in the U.S. outside of Raleigh. The government was praising itself for containing the disease.

"I'm going to spray paint our driveway with a symbol that says we're dead. We are loading up on food, and laying low. This is going to go one of two ways for me. Either Jay is fine, or the four of us will be dead very soon."

"Jesus." Hank muttered again. "What do you mean spray paint your driveway? The girls want to stay home from school, and I'm telling them it's okay."

"Hank, do me a favor. Emily and I are turning off our phones. We are going to play possum for a few weeks. Please relay our status to the family. I am leaning towards paranoia right now."

"Sure, Jesus, anything."

"And Hank?" Todd said before turning off his phone.

"Yeah?"

"Keep your girls home from school."

4

Five days later Todd left his home before dawn. The car horns had stopped days ago. He walked through his subdivision in hopes of finding other people, friends who could help him through the crisis.

He was back at his house by 7am. Emily stood in the kitchen drinking coffee. Jay and Brian were still asleep. Jay was fully recovered from his fever.

"How many people are still here?" She asked anxiously. Neither of them had left the cul de sac since the yellow hazmat encounter.

"You don't want to know. I went through ours and three other subdivisions." He went to the coffee.

"I'll walk around myself." She threatened.

Todd poured a cup. He turned around and faced his wife. He dropped his eyes and stared at the floor as he responded. "Every house is vacant or dead." He raised his eyes from the floor and looked at his wife. "We're alone."

Emily put her hand over her mouth in shock. "Do you know who is dead as opposed to gone?"

"Most of the people are gone, two thirds of the houses have a "V" in the driveway. About twenty-five have a black circle. The Mitchells are dead, so are the Vogels and the Taylors." Todd's voice was flat, emotionless as he relayed the deaths of their friends.

Emily bent over. She was almost sick. "All those kids, oh my god." She started crying and stood upright for a hug and comfort from Todd. "This has to be a nightmare. Tell me this is a nightmare."

"We're going to be okay. Let's stick to our plan, stay in the house, maybe the backyard or the pool next door. We don't go in the front yard or cul-de-sac until we know it's safe. I will retrieve as much food as I can." He held her tightly. "We're going to be okay. The rest of the world is screwed, but we're going to be okay."

Emily sobbed uncontrollably in her husband's arms.

5

Todd rode his bike a few miles from his house. Sweat dripped off his forehead from the stifling heat and humidity. He used a paved bike path system called the Greenway that ran through woods and public parks throughout Raleigh. The Greenway kept him off the main streets.

When Todd was far enough away from his house, he pulled off the path and into a subdivision. He did not find a charged cell phone until the third house. He only went into homes with what he now call 'the black circle of death.'

The power was still working in Raleigh. The front door opened into an air-conditioned home. Todd welcomed the cool air as he searched.

He dialed his brother, John Dixon, in Charleston, South Carolina.

"John, it's Todd."

"What the hell is going on up there? Are you okay? Is your family okay?" John had not heard from his brother since the start of the epidemic. All he had was second hand news from Hank.

"We're all fine. I'm going to explain everything. Let me conference Hank and Paul into the call."

John heard the phone click and go dead. One minute later the four brothers were on the line together.

"We all on?" Todd asked the group. He received three "yeses."

"Seriously, what the hell is happening? Raleigh is a dead spot on the map. There is no communication. Whose cell phone is this?" John was desperate to know what was happening. The flu had taken its first victim in Charleston yesterday.

Hank and Paul were equally excited and curious to hear the happenings in the "dead city" as it was referred to on the news.

"About two weeks ago my neighbor died, followed days later by his wife and four children. Jay and Brian played with those kids every day since we moved here." He went on to talk about the Hazmat suited people, Jay's flu, and the markings on the driveway.

"No one has been back since. I haven't seen any trucks or people for about a week. I think everyone is either dead or gone. It's crazy. We really are a dead city." Todd waited for questions. When none were asked, he continued.

"So far we are fine. Jay's flu came and went. It helped us fool the government people. We heard army trucks rolling up and down the main streets all the time, but since the pandemic has moved to other cities, the military bugged out. If there are people alive in Raleigh other than us, I haven't seen them."

"What are you going to do?" Now that the basics were answered, Paul was curious about the future. He and his wife Rachel were in Cincinnati, Ohio.

"We are holding tight for now. The power is still on. I plan on stealing a generator if it goes off. Of course, then I have to figure out how to work the damn thing. I've been collecting food from other houses, food and water, and rain barrels."

"We had our first case yesterday, first death I should say. It's here in Charleston. You've all seen it, it's everywhere along the east coast." There was panic in John's voice. "Greg is up at Hightower for baseball camp. I don't know what we're going to do. The travel restrictions and checkpoints mean I can't get to him and he can't get back here." Greg was John's fourteen year old son, stuck at his prep school in Massachusetts.

Todd did not have an answer. "I don't know if I'm out of the woods yet.

A lot of people left Raleigh healthy. They might still be healthy like me. Maybe my time hasn't come yet."

"Rachel hasn't been eating. She's been picking her food for months." Paul was talking about his wife, his voice was soft.

"My girls are losing weight too, but Paul, they're women, none of them ever eat. Don't panic yet. There is hope for a cure or a vaccine, just hold tight." Hank was upbeat.

"I don't want to stay on the phone too long. The government may be monitoring, and I don't want them coming back to my house and finding healthy people. I'm not calling from my house, but if they trace who I called, it won't be hard for them to figure out I'm Todd Dixon and not the dead owner of this phone. We should plan on speaking again, developing a plan. Assume you will survive and figure out what our next steps are. I won't have access to a phone for another few days. I'll try you again when I do."

"The whole world dies and you think the four of us will make it?" Paul asked him.

"Yes." Todd lied. "And let's make some plans for when that happens."

Todd left the cell phone on the counter and checked the house for any food or supplies he could fit in his backpack. Scavenging was a habit now, but it was not necessary. Todd and Emily had more food than they could eat in ten years. He put three un-opened boxes of cereal and two bottles of water in his pack, opening a third water to drink before walking to his bike.

He clicked the button on his walkie-talkie. "All good. Heading home."

"You didn't say 'over'." His son Jay crackled from the other device.

"Be back in thirty. Love you, over." Beads of sweat returned to Todd's forehead as he rode home.

6

The Dixon brothers spoke weekly, updating each other on the status of their towns. Media outlets were useless, spewing propaganda and false information about a cure and hope against the unrelenting death.

They were two months into the pandemic. John, Todd, Hank, and Paul remained healthy.

"Rachel died today." Paul said solemnly. "Why I'm not dead, I don't know. We did everything together. It's been in Cincinnati for weeks. I should be sick."

"I'm so sorry, Paul. I wish we could be there for you." Todd offered.

"I buried her behind our house, under the lilac trees she loved." The last word was lost as Paul sobbed.

"My girls were sick too. They're all gone now." Hank's voice was empty. His family died two phone calls ago, but the memory was fresh and painful enough that he continued to tell his brothers.

Paul answered loudly through his tears. "Hank, we need to turn ourselves in. We can help. There is still time here in Ohio. They can use our blood to test for a cure. We're the answer. It's what Rachel wanted me to do, to save people."

"No." John said firmly. "You're a fool if you do it. If you believe those yellow suited assholes are going to take a pint of your blood and thank you for your service, you're insane. If you don't end up locked in a room after everyone else is dead, you'll be carved up with your liver in a bowl inside of a week."

"You selfish jackass." Paul yelled. "I'm talking about saving the rest of humanity, and you're scared they might detain me for longer than I want? You've seen the news. No one has a clue what to do. Maybe we have antibodies in our blood. I've contacted people at the university here, doctors I can trust. We can help."

"Everyone calm down." Todd found himself breaking up the same arguments during every call. "Paul, we voted, you need to stay hidden. Hank, you have to get it together and keep yourself alive. Focus."

There was a pause before John spoke. "My kids are still fine. I don't think we are going to get sick. We need a place to meet. All of us." John did not talk about his wife, Sharon. It was understood non-Dixons would succumb to the disease nicknamed "the rapture."

"You could be saving her." Paul interjected.

"You son of a bitch, you think if I believed that for a second I wouldn't turn myself in? If I thought the idiots left in the world could figure out how to save my wife with my blood?"

Todd cut him off. "I want to meet in Hanover. I know it's cold, like, all the time, but it's remote. I don't believe any bad people or things will find us up there. If we pick a good house, like the house we grew up in, well, it was built a long time ago, before modern conveniences. It has fire places, wood stoves, a wood room connected to the house. It's almost colonial. It's right next to a pond for water and fishing. We could keep the land around the pond cleared for crops." He paused to the let the idea sink in.

Hanover was in New Hampshire. It was their hometown.

"Greg is still at Hightower. He's not sick. He can get to Hanover on his own. I don't know when I can get there. My family would have to avoid DC and New York and Philly and Boston. It might take a long time without cars." John's brain worked through the idea, but he was sold. Todd could tell from the response.

"Hank, Paul, think about it. I'm going to ride out the winter here in North Carolina. When it starts to get warm, I am going to make a move. That's about six or eight months from now. Frankly, everything should be over by then. Either we have a cure and we are rebuilding our world, or we don't have a cure and avoiding people won't be much of a problem. Either way, setting up camp in New Hampshire isn't a bad idea."

Paul continued to weep.

Hank responded. "Things are still crazy here. We're probably in the middle of the cycle, so I don't know if I can leave by spring or if I'll even be alive. The government has stepped up the raids and collections. If I make it through, I'll get to New Hampshire by May or June." There was life back in Hank's voice. "I'll be there."

"Hank, what do you mean by collections?" John suspected the government was kidnapping healthy citizens, but he had not witnessed it.

"Just keep to yourselves and don't trust anyone. Paul, believe us when we tell you to stay home. Don't turn yourself in." Hank's tone was firm. "Don't trust anyone."

"Paul? Take care of yourself, think about our plan." Todd brought the conversation back on track.

Paul cleared his throat. "Hank, I'll come up in the spring and we'll make the trip together. It's too dangerous for me to try and get up there now. I'll be there in the spring. Please don't leave without me." Hank lived one hour north of Paul.

"I wouldn't dream of it brother. I'll see the rest of you in Hanover." Hank issued another warning. "I'm going to say it again, because it's important. Don't trust anyone."

They said their goodbyes and condolences to Paul before the brothers hung up for the last time.

John held the phone in his palm. "Matt, Craig, come in here for a minute." He called his sons into the room. They were around a corner listening to the conversation.

"Aunt Rachel died." John told them quietly. "We're meeting your uncles in Hanover next year. I need to call Greg and tell him what to do."

John put his hand on his youngest son's shoulder as he dialed Greg's phone number in Massachusetts.

7

John hung up the phone, closed his eyes, and bowed his head. His sons, Matt and Craig, stood in the living room with him, listening to every word their father said to their brother.

John's request for Greg to stay alive hung in the air.

"What do we do now, Dad?" Matt asked. "Do we start to make our way up to Hanover? We might make it before the first snow." Matt, 17, was a few years older than Greg. He was doing well at a local private school, and had hopes of going north for college next fall.

"But Mom is upstairs, and she's still alive. We can't leave her." 10 year old Craig yelled at his older brother. The young boy was crying.

John opened his eyes and looked at his sons. He was the father, but there was nothing that prepared him to lead a family through this type of situation. The world was in chaos, his partner was days from dying, and one of his sons was 700 miles away. John's head was swimming.

"Your mother isn't dead. We would be killing her if we leave and a cure is found. We don't leave, we stay with her. Do you understand?" John looked at Craig as he said the last sentence, reaching out and wiping the tears from the boy's face. His sons nodded. Craig cracked a small smile.

"When your mother gets better, and we think we can make it up to Hanover? We leave, and we decide if Craig stops at Uncle Todd's. He can ride out the first winter in Raleigh. Todd and Emily will need a lot of help with your cousins."

"I don't want to split up." Craig said quickly.

"I know, that's why I said we will decide later. Hey, maybe the government will come through with a cure, and this whole thing will be over." John gave them a weak smile, a knowing smile that told his boys none of that was going to happen.

"Has Mom had anything to eat?" Matt asked.

"No, but she's a fighter." John was the only one who had been in Sharon's room in the last two days. Once the end symptoms of the rapture began, she asked her sons not to see her again. She gave a teary goodbye three days ago.

It was not a bad thing for her kids to see her. During the final phase of the rapture a person was delirious with joy. A rapture victim was more creepy than scary. The high fever or bacteria or virus, whatever it was, boiled the brain to the point where people felt happy, peaceful, and full of joy. The name was coined by the rapturous like emotions exhibited at the end of the disease.

John was devastated. He knew there was no cure coming, and his wife would be dead in 24 to 48 hours. He continued to lie to Craig, though he assumed even the boy knew the truth.

While the last three days for a rapture victim were peaceful, the world's last few months were chaotic and violent. Countries were filled with looting and rioting. Governments were unfriendly to survivors, seeking healthy people who did not exhibit symptoms. Distrust and paranoia reigned.

The crazy time was winding down. It had been two months since Raleigh went dark. Everyone in North America was sick or dead. There was still mild panic, but "it" was over. Humanity was finished. The world slowly accepted its fate.

Even as the population dwindled, and the military's power disappeared, John believed there were roadblocks on every route headed north. Information was sparse. All he had to work off of were looped television images of yellow suited people with guns and thermometers checking cars and separating families. John would not make a move north until he was positive everyone was dead, and by the time he could be sure, winter would block the way to his son.

For now, at least for another day or two, John would care for Sharon. How his wife had lasted this long he did not know. Every other person from their circle of friends had been dead for weeks.

8

Greg's eyes opened with the sun. He looked at his watch out of habit. It read 7:37am. He had been asleep for 2 hours, taking the first nap of a schedule he devised and implemented one week ago. Greg was reversing his sleeping habits, sleeping in the day and staying awake at night. His plan was to leave his school and travel under the cover of darkness.

His first thought was always, "I'm late for breakfast!" His stomach ached with hunger pains. Reality quickly set in. As much as Greg wanted to forget his current situation, the fact that it was freezing in his dorm room, and he was a smart and grounded 14 year old, made it impossible. He was alone at his prep school, Hightower Academy, outside of Boston, Massachusetts. His friends, teachers, and everyone else at the school were dead, rotting in a building just yards away.

Three months earlier the pandemic struck New York City, Boston, Washington D.C., Philadelphia, and all the cities up and down the coast. Panic ensued and roads shut. Greg was 700 miles from his home in South Carolina, attending baseball training camp in Massachusetts. With at least ten major cities closed between him and his family, Greg was stuck.

The last phone call he had with his father was over a month ago. It came with news that his mother was sick, which meant she was now dead.

Greg replayed that conversation in his head every morning. His father was strong in the face of the disease. "Look, I don't know if you are going to get sick. I don't know if I am going to make it either, but right now we aren't sick, and that's weird. Your Uncles are healthy too. We have a plan. It starts with us heading north, away from people. We are going to Hanover, up to the lake house to figure out a life. Do you think you can get there?"

"I guess, I mean, I know how to read a map, it's kind of far, I can't drive." Greg was terrified.

"Don't try to drive, the highways are shut. You'll get picked up. Locked up. Studied. You have to go at night, in the woods, or on back roads. When you see the military, you have to hide."

"You really think everyone is going to die?"

"Greg, you are about to grow very fast. Yes, everyone is either dead or in bed with the rapture. The phones are going to stop working, maybe even today. The power is going to stop working, maybe today. Here is what you need to do. Stay low at school for another few weeks, hiding like we talked about. Wait until you don't see anyone for three or four days. As soon as you are clear, head to Hanover. Get up there, find a house, maybe the one where I grew up. Find food, make fires to keep warm, boil water. I'll come for you when I can. Use the lake house if you want, but get up there. If I live, I'll get there. Your Uncles will get there. Remember, people are scared, they're desperate, don't trust anyone you aren't related to. The police, the government, they are trying to find a cure. If you aren't sick, they'll take you and do whatever they can to try and save others. Don't get caught. "

"Dad, I'm scared."

"I know. I'm scared too. I'm sad, I'm scared, but I know you can do this. I love you, know that I love you." There was a pause. "Greg, tell me you understand what you need to do. Stay at Hightower, hiding, and then get to Hanover when you know everyone is dead."

"I can do it. I love you too, Dad. Tell Mom I love her. Tell Matt and Craig I love them. I'll see you soon. Whenever you get there, I'll be in Hanover waiting." Greg was crying.

"Greg, I love you, your mother loves you, your brothers need you to stay alive. I don't know how long it will be, but we'll see you again. Don't lose faith. Stay alive, just stay alive. I love you."

Cell phones signals ceased a day later. Greg did not tell his dad about his food situation, or how the radiators were out and the cold was keeping him awake. He could not talk about the smell, which grew stronger and more rancid every day. Greg kept all of the windows and doors shut in his dorm to escape the odor.

Greg was cold, and he was almost out of food.

Late October in New England is beautiful, but it can be unpredictable. Greg looked at the thermometer suction cupped to his window, 42 degrees inside his dorm room. "I have to leave today. It will be freezing over night in the next few weeks." He talked to himself. It helped him deal with the new world's silence, and almost made him feel as if there were other people around. He was not having conversations with himself. He was not losing his mind. At least he hoped he was not losing his mind.

He looked at the other bed in his room. His roommate, Darrin, died months ago when the rapture spread through his dorm and the rest of the school. School had not started. Greg and Darrin were attending a baseball camp. Half of Hightower Academy's students were back on campus attending academic or athletic clinics. Darrin left to go to the quarantine dorms the first week. Of the six dorms at the school, four were converted into hospitals, servicing the students, faculty, and residents of the town. Two of the dorms were converted into morgues soon after. Travel restrictions meant parents could not claim bodies. Most of the parents were sick or dead. Even without the travel issues, the kids and their bodies, were orphans.

Darrin and Greg were best friends since the first day freshman year. They played baseball together in the fall and spring. When roommate signups came out the previous year, they knew immediately they would room together, share baseball stories from the summer, help each other out on homework. It was a friendship that lasted a lifetime, Darrin's lifetime.

Greg kept Darrin's bed made and left his side of the room alone after they took Darrin away in August. Darrin did not like his property touched, not that anyone did, but he was particularly protective. Greg kept to his side of the room for the first month, even after he knew Darrin and all the other kids were dead. Greg did not so much as sit on Darrin's bed or touch his books, desk, or clothes.

Soon after the last phone call with his father, Greg went through Darrin's things. He looked for anything he could find that would help him survive; better clothes, knives, maps, anything. Greg searched the entire dorm. He knew he had to travel light to Hanover. He treated his mission like a scavenger hunt. One day he looked for the best pair of pants. He would find a pair and put them in his shoulder bag until he scavenged better pants with more pockets or warmer fabric. The scavenger hunt list included essential items he needed for the long trek north.

Greg began sleeping under his bed after they took Darrin away. He set up soft blankets on the floor, and went under at night. Anyone looking for students or scavenging for food and supplies would not see him through the small door window. Greg found a master key on one of the dead counselors in the morgue dorm. He randomly locked rooms in the dorm so it would seem natural that his room was locked. He also messed up his room, giving it the appearance of having been picked over. He found food in the cafeteria and moved it to his room so he would not have to leave the dorm. He stopped using light at night.

Greg was used to being monitored. He was 14 and at prep school. It was hard for him to understand that no one was looking for him. Even after the phone call with this father, when it was explained that everyone was dead or dying, Greg was certain there were other people around. He treated finding food, staying out of sight, beefing up his supplies, like it was a game. How quickly could he get in and out of a building, how slowly and stealthily could he move through campus?

Greg was too young to realize Hightower Academy's campus shut down weeks earlier. Doctors worked in the dorms, people in yellow hazmat suits moved bodies from the quarantine to the morgue, but all activity stopped long ago. The power was off. The phones did not work. No one came to campus. Greg managed to slip through the cracks. He was the only person alive at Hightower, and had been for close to a month.

Greg stayed in his room and hid, but no one was looking for him.

The world was dead.

After the doctors and yellow plastic people left campus, Greg continued to hear airplanes, helicopters, and loud diesel military vehicles. When Greg spoke to his father on the phone, the helicopters and jets were a constant in the air, moving from air force bases in New Hampshire and Boston. Each week the number of aircraft lessened until there was one plane a day or every other day. One week ago Greg saw a jet heading out to the Atlantic, straight East. Since that last plane, all manmade noise ceased.

Greg was in New England in late fall, needing to travel 100+ miles by foot or bike to Hanover, New Hampshire. He studied maps, and knew the two highways he needed to take. Despite his father's warnings, Greg planned on using major highways to Hanover. Today he decided to leave campus and walk to his English teacher's house in the town near the highway. He packed his bag during the morning hours, thought about his route, and went to sleep at 10am.

Greg awoke in the dark. He got dressed, brushed his teeth, and grabbed his gear. He was used to working in the pitch black after four weeks with no power. The moon was half full, and provided enough light when he left the dorm.

The smell hit Greg as soon as he opened the door. He put the crook of his arm over his mouth and nose, and hoped the odor would subside as he moved away from campus and the morgue dorms. It was cold, crisp and dry outside. Leaves covered the ground. No one was around to rake them and keep the campus its typical immaculate condition. The dry refuse crunched under Greg's feet as he walked out of the school's gates.

Hightower Academy was a mile from Greg's destination house. He wanted a test run on this first night, staying close to campus. If he ran into people, Greg could return to the safety and security of his dorm room. Campus was deserted, and he believed he could tough it out for another 8 months, if he could find food and stop the horrific smell.

Greg picked his English teacher's house because he saw her in the morgue dorm when he lifted the master key off his dorm counselor. Ms. Berry was a single woman just three years out of college. She lived alone. Her house should be empty. It might be ransacked, but there would not be any bodies in the house. Greg was brave, and growing braver everyday of his independence, but he was still 14, and decided he would rather not sleep in a house with a dead body.

Greg remembered being dropped off three months ago by his mother. They turned off the highway and drove three blocks when Greg pointed to the small yellow house.

"That's where Ms. Berry lives. She had our English class over for a cookout last year. "

The car ride was the last time Greg saw his mother. She insisted on driving him to school, spending the time with him. He wanted to fly, despite his secret fear of flying, land at Logan Airport in Boston, and take the shuttle to Hightower. His mom would not let him. It was like she knew their time was fleeting. She forced him to take the long car ride with her.

He missed his mother. He missed his family, but he could not let his grief stop him from moving forward.

Greg made the two turns onto the town's main street, and began the long walk towards Ms. Berry's. Every house was dark. It was 8:30 pm. The smell of fire and smoke should have flowed out of chimneys all over town. Other than an occasional bird or squirrel, and the crunch of Greg's feet in the leaves, there was no sound or indication of life.

Clouds drifted in front of the moon, blocking Greg's source of light, and he stopped to listen for noises. He did not hear any. He walked for 10 minutes, and as far as he could tell, he was the only animal on two feet out this evening.

Greg moved painfully slow, and he was soon frustrated with having to watch his step in the dark. He came to the crest of a small hill. Normally, while he could not see the city of Boston, there was an orange glow over the horizon. Tonight, on this late October evening, there was no light. A town of several million was dark. Greg expected fire, carnage, something to show such a large concentration of people once existed, hopefully still existed. Nothing. No sound from the highway. No light from the city. He might as well have been walking through a secluded rain forest or national park.

Greg decided not to talk to himself while on his trek, but he could not stifle the "wow," as he let the realization sink in that he was probably alone in New England. How many people had the disease killed? Were the survivors friendly? Were there even any survivors? For the last month he followed his father's advice, hid from people, moved around at night. He was more or less playing a game rather than living in fear. Now he did not know how to feel.

Greg looked around. He had a creepy feeling that he was being watched. He did not hear or see anyone. He shook off his fear and continued towards his destination. After twenty minutes he stood in front of Ms. Berry's. The house was dark and quiet. He tried the front door. It was locked. He walked around the house to find a backdoor he remembered from the cookout. That door was also locked.

"Darn it." Greg muttered. He noticed a window was open a crack. He reached over and pushed it up. The window was at chest level, and Greg struggled to pull himself up from the ground. He looked around in the moonlight and noticed a lawn chair. He pulled it under the window, and a moment later he was inside Ms. Berry's house.

It was cold and dark inside. Greg timed his journey with a rising half moon. He had two weeks of half to full and then back to half moon again. It provided light for his hike. Inside the house his only source of light was gone. Greg stood in the kitchen just inside the window, as if he were a burglar, keeping quiet and still. He considered using a flashlight, but he did not want to draw attention to the house.

The home was empty. It was a perfect place for him to spend his first night, but Greg was wide awake. The short trip had taken more time than he expected, but there was plenty of night left for him to walk.

He considered his options. He could go back to campus, and settle into The Founder's Library at Hightower. It was a small brick building with comfortable furniture and a giant fire place. He could live there through the winter. He thought the cold might mask the smell of the rotting corpses.

Hightower was the safe and easy choice, except there was no food. Greg scoured the dining hall kitchen for non-perishable food, but it was all gone, eaten by healthcare workers and government officials during their occupation of the school. He scavenged a few cans of franks and beans, and one large can of green beans, but his food options were reduced to sifting through dorm rooms for candy bars and snack foods. Yesterday he ate his last bowl of beans.

Greg had not spoken to anyone for a month, and he desperately wanted to see another person. Hightower was deserted. If making the trip to Hanover gave him the opportunity to find his father and brothers or one of his uncles, and he could talk to someone? That reward alone was worth the journey. Greg needed companionship.

He made the decision to move forward towards New Hampshire. The practice run to Ms. Berry's was over.

Greg's eyes adjusted to the darkness as he felt around the kitchen cabinets. He opened several in hopes of finding food. He was rewarded with a pantry of soup. He pulled the top off a can and used two fingers like a spoon to taste the contents. He could not read the label in the dark, but was so ravenous he did not care what flavor he scooped. He brought the can closer and continued to finger the thick, cold split pea soup into his mouth. Despite the temperature and unappealing consistency, Greg devoured the can quickly.

He washed his fingers in the kitchen sink before cupping water into his mouth to drink.

Greg placed the two additional cans of soup from the cabinet into his backpack. His former teacher was a single woman who hated to cook. The only other food he could find was a box of raisin bran. Greg pulled the plastic bag from the box and placed the cereal in his pack before zipping the top compartment and slinging it.

He unlocked the door to the backyard, walked outside, and made his way to Highway 93 North.

His stride was longer and his pace quicker as he began the journey to meet his family in Hanover, New Hampshire.

"Rock and roll." He said aloud. His white teeth reflected the moonlight as he grinned.

9

When the Dixon brothers hung up the phone on what would be their last call, Paul was in mourning. His house was in a small subdivision setback from the road and away from busy streets. His location provided the advantage of being in a populous area, Cincinnati, while remote enough that it would be overlooked. He was in essence hiding in plain sight, and faced no danger of being found or captured.

Cincinnati, Ohio's population was just over one million people. Like many Midwestern cities, it did not have a natural border such as a large lake or ocean. It sprawled in all directions. Some might argue the Ohio river presented a boundary as it ran along the southern border of the city, but in reality, the river posed only a state change to Kentucky. People who worked in Cincinnati commuted across state lines. The million plus population of Cincinnati lived over hundreds of square miles, multiple counties, and dozens upon dozens of towns. Without a centralized population to patrol or contain, the government was helpless with regards to looting, rioting, and unrest, and was toothless implementing any plan to capture the population. As Cincinnati burned, Paul lived safely in the house he and Rachel shared for the last ten years.

He ate, listened to the radio, and read books while he waited for everyone to die. If Cincinnati's timeline was consistent with other major cities on the coasts, Paul would be safe and alone by the end of October. He would begin looking for survivors in November or December.

Paul was a packrat. Rachel kept him honest, making him part with broken items, but Paul's basement held things from his graduate school and bachelor years. He found his old hotplate and an electric tea kettle, both of which would work off his solar panel back-up generator. His inability to dispose of bachelor days provided a way to boil water and cook food.

He owned an additional handheld solar charger for small electronics, and a solar shower if he needed to get clean. Paul and Rachel enjoyed hiking, and utilized solar technology when possible. They were not environmentalists per se, rather outdoor enthusiasts who wanted fully charged cell phones while on the trail.

Paul's life was boring, safe, and offered a few conveniences when the sun shined.

He and Rachel, though a household of two, shopped at warehouse clubs. They typically had a few months' of food stored around the house. He had a 25lb bag of rice and a 10lb bag of dried beans. He had pasta in all shapes and sizes, and he had 30 or more cans of tuna fish. He and Rachel were athletic, power bars and gels were abundant. Without scavenging at other homes, which he intended to do, Paul had several months of food, perhaps half a year, if he rationed.

The first month of Paul's solitude was stressful. Paul listened to the radio as newscasters relayed panic and hysteria, the death tolls in the East, the devastation on the other continents, and the 100% contagion and mortality rate of the rapture. Scientists and doctors spoke about not having enough time to figure out the disease. After the first month, the radio broadcasters were gone, replaced by a government loop message "Survivors should come to government shelters. If you are not sick, seek help immediately. Food and water will be provided."

Each day Paul sat on his deck and debated going to a shelter. Some days he would get into his car or jump on his bike, but he never made the trip. Paul was not sure if the shelters were a trick to round up healthy people and use them as guinea pigs, or if the invitation was sincere. The swiftness of the rapture made Paul's decision for him. Everyone died before he could turn himself into the authorities.

Paul stayed in his house, bored, whittling away the time reading or staying in shape on his bike trainer. During his third month of solitude the government messages stopped broadcasting. The lights from Cincinnati were out. Paul waited two weeks after the radio went dead before he set out to find other people.

It was the beginning of December.

An avid cyclist, Paul pulled down one of his bikes to take a ride. The sun was shining, it was a warm late fall day, and Paul needed to see if there were any survivors. He packed a light backpack with two power bars and two bottles of water. He included a handgun he found in a neighbors house, and pedaled towards the city.

His house was east of Cincinnati in a town called Anderson. Decades before, it was a rural area, but urban sprawl turned it into malls, banks, and subdivisions. Before the plague, Paul commuted 10 miles into the city for work, and with all the people in Anderson doing the same, it could take up to 30 minutes to go those 10 miles.

As Paul rode towards the city that morning, he made several detours through popular subdivisions. Trash was everywhere. Not the kind of trash he expected to find. Not burned out cars and destruction, but rather regular trash that accumulated over the last months of civilization. When everyone became sick, people stopped working or going outside. Garbage was not picked up. There were mountains of trash as if there was a garbage strike. Birds and other scavengers ripped and picked at the black plastic bags, spreading waste and debris across the lawns. Grass, unmowed for the last four months, grew out of control and went to seed, once manicured lawns were overrun with weeds.

Every neighborhood Paul visited was the same, no people, mild damage, lots of trash. There were a few houses where the front doors were open, maybe a few windows were broken, but nothing was on fire or showed signs of malice. Paul was sure the open doors and broken windows were from people scavenging for food when the stores went empty.

After leaving the last subdivision, Paul stopped at a grocery store. He did not expect to find any usable food, and he did not need any, but curiosity made him hop off his bike to take a look.

Outward appearances told Paul his peek was a lost cause. Several of the large glass bay windows, typical for grocery stores, were broken. Even though it was dark inside, he could see most of the racks were knocked over and empty. There were paper products scattered about, but most, if not all of the food was gone.

He took a flashlight out of his pack, walked through the broken front window, and strolled through the store. When the disease began late in the summer, and roads were closed, the trucking industry failed. With no one to move or deliver food around the country, stores could only offer their remaining inventories. The food shortage meant groceries were ransacked and vandalized.

This market was no different. Paul waved a beam up and down the aisles, but he saw no food, no spoiled meat, not even a box of lentils, nothing. Paul grabbed a few packs of batteries from a revolving display toppled on its side, a box of strike anywhere matches, and left.

He stopped, turned around, and called "Hello?"

He waited a few seconds, "Is there anyone in there?" Why a person would hide in a ravaged grocery store instead of one of the thousands of abandoned houses, Paul did not know, but he thought he should at least try and find other people. "Hello?" He called out one more time. There was no answer.

He slung his pack, jumped on his bike, and continued downtown. He passed the baseball and football stadiums, the financial district, the urban neighborhoods, the university area, and ended his ride through a high end area close to the city named Hyde Park. He pedaled slowly, calling out for people with his "hello?" Paul received no response.

He rode down Observatory, his favorite street in Hyde Park. It was a beautiful road ending at Ault Park, a wonderful public space that he and Rachel visited regularly. Paul rode through one of the 25 most populated cities in the U.S. and did not see a soul. He did not see any signs of life, a light, a fire, or smoke from a chimney. He did not hear a sound, a horn, a gunshot, a car, or a bike bell. He was alone.

He sat on a stone bench in the park for over an hour. His head was in his hands for much of the time. Why did he not help? He might have prevented all of this, or most of it, if he had just volunteered to have his blood tested for a cure.

Paul rode back to his house. He took a shower on his deck using his solar shower, a black rubber bag that warmed five gallons of water in the sun and used gravity to dispense the warm water out of a small shower head onto a cold Paul. He decided to pack his things and ride to Hank's house in Dayton. There was no reason to stay in Cincinnati, and there was no reason to stay locked in his house. The world was over. He had to find a place to survive the winter, and surviving with his brother was going to be easier than surviving alone. He hoped Hank was still alive.

The next morning he woke up and hitched a baby stroller attachment, scavenged from a neighbor, to his bike. It was like a two wheeled crib with an orange tent over the top, and zipped a child in for rides. Paul loaded it with memorabilia, food, extra clothes, water, etc... He did not know how the roads would be up to Dayton, and decided to travel light and on two wheels. The roads around Cincinnati were clear, but that did not mean he could get a car to Dayton. There could be parked car jams, accidents, road blocks, and bridge destruction. A bike afforded Paul options and the ability to travel between and around obstructions.

The ride to Hank's house was about 80 miles. Paul was not sure he could make it in one day. The days were getting shorter, and he was towing a stroller, which would weigh him down. He hoped to be up there by early evening, but picked a few points south of Hank's as contingency stops.

Paul took weather forecasts for granted his entire life. What is it going to be like today? Is it going to rain tomorrow? Will a storm blow in? Paul was riding blind to Dayton. For all he knew it could be sunny in the morning before dropping 40 degrees and snowing by the end of the day. It was December in Ohio. When the current warm front would end was a guess for Paul. He hoped the answer was a few days from this morning.

Paul went into the back yard to say goodbye to Rachel. He cried, made his peace, and stood at the end of his driveway by 9am.

Paul gave his home of 10 years one last look. He and Rachel had been happy here, blissfully happy. They carved a wonderful life with each other.

That life was gone. It died with Rachel. He turned and pedaled towards his new life. There was little chance he would ever be as happy again, but whatever lay ahead for him in Hanover was better than living in the shadow of his former life.

Paul picked up highway 75 North towards Dayton. Unlike the day before, he did not call out in search of others. He put his head down and rode.

10

The rapture began in the U.S. on the east coast, ravaging the large cities up and down the sea board before leapfrogging the center of the country to devastate the west coast. Dayton, Ohio did not have a confirmed rapture death until over a month after Raleigh went dark.

Hank Dixon survived the rapture. His wife and children did not. He married late in life, and his children were adopted from his wife's previous marriage. None of them carried the cure, or resistance, or what saved Hank and his brothers. Losing his wife was devastating. The death of his four children was soul crushing. Physically Hank was alive. Emotionally he was dead.

Hank's neighborhood was relentlessly combed and monitored for rapture resistant survivors. Many of his neighbors were picked up. Visibly sick or not, they were bused to who knows where for who knows what. Hank's family died early. They were five of the first confirmed cases. As soon as he had a plan with his brothers, Hank burned his house to give it the appearance that it was destroyed during looting.

He set the southern side of his house on fire, charred the east and west, and scorched the north side. He control burned the inside, taking out the top floor, and marring the walls, floors, and staircase. He kept the basement free from harm, the first floor structurally sound, and the roof weather proof.

Hank moved into his basement, hiding under his apparently destroyed house. He collected water from a hose he ran from his downspout into two rain barrels, and scavenged enough food for the two months he planned to live underground.

He knew everyone would die. He just needed to wait them out, or not.

Hank held a revolver in his hand the first month. He had it to his head or in his mouth most evenings. He alternated between the revolver and a shotgun as he debated joining his family in heaven or his brothers in New Hampshire.

He stopped eating. The pounds he accumulated through decades of bad food melted off his body.

Hank was not a drinker. He did not seek solace in a bottle or through drugs. He was not a man of faith, and could not pray his pain away. He lived with his anguish. He stared at the grave markers twenty feet from the basement dormer window, and he held a gun to his head while he tried to think of reasons not to kill himself.

Hank could think of only one.

Hank believed his lost teenage nephew, Greg Dixon, was alive and in peril. Without knowing and through no action of his own, Greg Dixon saved his uncle's life.

Hank emerged from his basement when his crank radio remained silent for weeks. He was pale, filthy, smelled like a dirty sock, and wanted desperately to talk to someone. Despite the time of year and the insanity of his plan, Hank prepared for his rescue trip to New Hampshire.

Hank exited the basement with his first stroke of luck since the rapture began.

"Hank?" A voice called out to the disgusting man. "Holy crap are you thin. You must be down 100 pounds."

Paul stood over a bike having pedaled the 80 miles from Cincinnati. He was soaked with sweat, and panted as he spoke.

The men walked towards each other and embraced in a strong hug, weeping with joy.

"Okay," Paul said through tears as he stepped away from Hank. "I'm prepared to stay here, but only if we find you a shower. You really, really smell."

"We're not staying here." Hank told his brother. "I have to get to New Hampshire to help Greg."

Paul replied with a laugh. "Are you crazy? It's the middle of December. We won't make it through Pennsylvania. No, we find a house here. We stay safe here, and move in the spring. We're no good to anyone dead. For all we know, John and his boys are already in Hanover with Greg."

Hank spoke in a firm and even tone, leaving no room for argument. "You can do what you want. I'm taking a shower, and I'm going to find Greg."

11

Todd spoke to his brother John by phone one last time in September. They connected an hour after the brothers' agreement to meet in Hanover. Todd no longer travelled away from his home to use a dead stranger's cell phone. He called from his living room. Todd assumed and hoped the government and military were too busy to care about a single survivor in Raleigh.

"What's your plan?" Todd asked his brother bluntly. "You have to find Greg, right? Do you want to leave Matt and Craig, or maybe just Craig with me? "

"If I leave one or two of my sons with you, I'm in the same situation I'm in now. Greg is heading to Hanover as soon as he can. I can't risk all of our lives to get up there. If I leave now, we'd get caught and experimented on. If I wait the 2-3 months I assume it will take for everyone to die, it will be winter and I risk dying on the trip. I have to wait." John was resolute in his decision, even though it meant leaving Greg on his own for a harsh New England winter.

"Then what is your plan for coming here from Charleston? Do you want to make the trip to Hanover together? I have young kids. I could use your help and the help of your boys." Todd could make it on his own, he and Emily were strong. He had two good kids, but the trip north would be easier with three additional people.

"I'll be there in April, maybe March if it's warm, but let's count on April. Things have started to calm down around here. I'm going to keep the boys in the house and lay low for the next few months." John's voice was tense, worried, scared.

Todd tried to assure him. "I don't hear planes unless they are very high in the sky. I'll hold on until April. I won't think about leaving until May. We'll go up together. I'm only 30 minutes out of your way." Todd added a laugh to the last comment. He heard John chuckle in response, but it was hollow. There was no humor in the situation for John and his boys.

"If the phones go dead before we can talk again, I'll see you in April. Leave a note at your house if you leave earlier." John cleared his throat. "Love you, brother."

"Love you too, John."

Todd hung up the phone and turned to Emily. "We have six or seven months."

"Let's wait another two weeks and start exploring. I know we've talked about staying in the attic and living bunker style, but I don't think that will be necessary. Do you? It will start to get cold at night. We'll need the fireplace in the living room for warmth." Emily was bored. She kept the kids home since the outbreak started in July. There had not been another sound in Raleigh since the beginning of August.

Her children were tired of their yard and watching DVD's. The neighbor's pool was too cold to use, dropping to the low 70's as the nights grew longer. Emily and her kids needed to get out.

"I think it will be over everywhere soon, it just happened here first, so it ended here first." Todd patted her knee. They embraced, holding each other for several minutes.

"Let's get some sleep, and we'll see what tomorrow brings." He whispered into her ear. They went up to their bedroom hand in hand, checked on their children, and went to sleep.

Brazil was the first country to have the disease, experiencing a mini-outbreak with 100 people dying within one week of each other. It was thought to be the flu, a deadly strain of the flu, but nothing beyond extra hand washing and "don't touch your eyes and nose" advice was issued by governments.

When similar cases occurred in three Asian countries, Nigeria, and Ireland, the alarm bells went off globally. The first person died in Raleigh two weeks after the first person died in Sao Paulo. The rapture was worldwide, and more importantly, it was stateside.

For the next two weeks, while the world panicked and struggled to contain a rapidly spreading pandemic, Raleigh, North Carolina was the only U.S. city with confirmed cases.

Scientists retrofitted ideas to explain the symptoms and outcomes, trying to calm the public. The Raleigh outbreak occurred one week after the State Fair. All of the confirmed cases attended or could be connected to a person who attended the fair. Some 'concluded' the rapture was an animal transmitted flu, similar to swine or mad cow. Another theory believed it was a mutated canine or feline illness, possibly an airborne version of rabies, explaining why domestic dogs and cats perished during the epidemic.

Others believed companies operating out the Raleigh's Research Triangle Park made trips to Brazil, were exposed to "the rapture" as it was being called, and brought it back to Raleigh. This theory in particular allowed the U.S. government to believe the disease could be contained.

Few people knew the truth. The Research Triangle companies brought the rapture back from Brazil 12-18 months prior to the actual outbreak. Containment was not possible, every person in the U.S. had already been exposed, and the incubation period was over.

Panic did not begin with the first confirmed case in Raleigh, but after one week and more 1, 500 dead North Carolinians, panic was too mild a word. Throughout the country, daycares, schools, restaurants, and stores closed. Public events were cancelled. Downtown streets, typically filled with people, were empty. It was not the 1,500 people dead in Raleigh, it was the 100,000 dead around the world and the millions suffering from symptoms, that caused hysteria.

The entire population of Raleigh was mandated to leave. Similar to a hurricane evacuation, people were ordered to go somewhere else, anywhere safe. All of the roads heading out of town were jammed with cars for three days. If a person's temperature was 1 degree above 98.6, Center for Disease Control officials, as well as U.S. military officials stationed on every road, directed the car to a containment area.

Todd stayed in Raleigh because he was afraid of the containment areas. He grew up watching pandemic and outbreak movies in which the government was typically a villain. Todd feared Jay would be taken from them, sequestered, hidden, and lost. If his son was going to die, he would die with his parents and brother, not in some cold quarantine room.

No healthy citizens remained within 100 miles of Raleigh. The residents fled without shopping or looting the stores, packing only clothes in expectation they would soon return home. Food and bottled water sat in pantries and kitchens across the area. Supermarket, big box stores, and warehouse clubs were abandoned, still fully stocked.

Todd and Emily made smart choices during the weeks of panic. They stayed home, stopped using lights, and powered down their cell phones. They stocked food, used rain barrels to collect water, and prepared for at least two months of solitude. Jay's benign summer flu, which made them stay in Raleigh when everyone else fled, was a stroke of luck.

When the rapture struck outside of Raleigh, the government did not have the means to handle an epidemic in every state, city, and town. Just a few months into the pandemic, world governments and militaries collapsed.

While the globe exploded into hysteria, violence, and looting, the Dixons lived comfortably in their house, safely hidden in the empty city of Raleigh, North Carolina.

12

Greg walked for what felt like hours after he left Ms. Berry's house. He quickly made it to US 495 and then to US 93 North. He was cold and scared in the half-moon light. Despite what he thought was a quick pace, he was moving slowly and looking around too often. The adrenaline rush of starting his journey wore off, and he was exhausted by midnight.

He was on an overpass when he came upon a large sports utility vehicle abandoned on the side of the road. A white towel dangled from the driver's side window. Moonlight showed the car was empty. Greg tried all the doors, and as luck would have it, one was unlocked. Exhausted from just two hours of travelling, he decided to take a quick nap inside. He folded the back seats down, crawled inside, unfurled his sleeping bag, and fell asleep instantly.

Greg woke to sunlight streaming through the windows of the SUV. It took him a few moments to get his bearings, and he soon realized he was trapped and exposed on the highway, half a mile from the nearest woods. Unless he broke his own protocol and walked in the daylight, he was stuck.

He felt a tinge of panic, like a dog when the owner shuts the door and leaves the pet in the car. He looked at his watch, 7:30am. He had two choices, stay in the car for the next 10 hours using all of his water, or take a risk and walk in the daylight for the next 10 hours. Maybe it was that part of him that was 14 and considered himself immortal, or maybe it was the part of him that had grown up in the last two months and realized he was the only person alive within 700 miles, but Greg left the car.

"Play time is over. I have to get up to Hanover, and daytime is the best time to travel." He spoke aloud, like he did back in the dorms. "I can do this. I can see people coming in the day. I can see animals in the day. I can avoid rocks and things that will twist my ankles in the day. Let's go, Greg, time to move."

Greg pulled out his map, saw an exit about 20-25 miles up the highway, and started walking. He stopped and ate a can of cold soup at noon. At 4:30 he stumbled off the highway and onto a rural road along 93N. He covered just ten miles of his route.

He found a combination general store and gas station, pulled out his sleeping bag, and slept on the floor. The next morning he filled his water, grabbed what little food was available, and hoped to make it at least fifteen miles by sunset.

The highways of Northern Massachusetts and New Hampshire are cut through mountains and valleys. The roads move up and down, winding around rivers and streams. What a crow flies in ten miles can take a New England highway twenty miles to connect the same two points. When Greg planned his trip, he did not realize how hard it was to walk long distances in New England. He assumed he could log 35-45 miles a day and would be in Hanover by the end of his third day. The late fall season meant exposure to wind and cold, and Greg was not prepared for the up and down aspect of the journey. After two days of hard walking, he reset his daily goal to 15 miles, but he never reached the goal. He spent each morning mapping how far he needed or wanted to go. If he saw a house that was close to the mark, he would stop for the night. At the end of his third day he was just 28 miles away from Ms. Berry's house, and still over 70 miles from Hanover.

Greg found the trip to be slow and hard going, and his number one challenge was staying hydrated. He kept two water bottles in the slots on his backpack. When he finished the first bottle, he stopped at the next exit to find a way to refill. Sometimes he could get water right away at a gas station or general store, but exits were further apart as he went north, and stores were not immediately off the exit ramps.

Keeping hydrated added time and effort and extra miles to his trek, but if he stopped drinking water he felt weak and his head ached. Greg might walk twenty miles during the day, but only eight of those miles were towards his destination.

Greg also needed food, and was faced with the decision of carrying weight or relying on scavenging. He opted for scavenging.

The rapture was a devastating disease, but it was custom built for survivors. The earliest symptom was loss of appetite. Supermarkets were looted and emptied, but all the looting did was transfer the food to houses where it sat uneaten. Greg had early success scavenging, but as he entered more rural areas, food was scarce to non-existent.

Despite the viscous, cold, unappealing soup he found in cans at the homes where he squatted, Greg was so ravenous he did not care what he ate. One night he considered eating cat food when it was the first and only thing he found in that evening's home. He stayed in the 'cat house' and slept on a couch, but ventured next door and found stale granola cereal. The next morning he held the small can of cat food, weighing it in his palm. It was light, and would provide a quick meal when he needed it. Greg put the can on the table. "I'm not there yet." He told himself.

The weather turned on Greg's third day. Gray clouds rolled in and the temperature dropped to the mid 40's as he walked. Rain fell on him in a steady mist. If the rain down poured, he would stop, but it teased him by keeping him soaked to the bone while never coming down hard enough to halt his progress. It was colder at night. Greg cut his walking time short each afternoon to find an empty home with a working fireplace. His sleeping bag was soaked and heavy. He abandoned it after the first day of rain. Greg relied on sheets and blankets he found in homes along the highway.

Seven days after leaving the broken SUV on the overpass, Greg walked through the toll booths at the end of US 93. He was sixty miles into his journey. He rummaged through the State liquor store at the N.H. state line for water and food. Greg was half way to Hanover. A trip he anticipated taking three, maybe four days, was going to stretch for at least two weeks. Greg was down five pounds in the last week, and over twenty pounds from when his mother dropped him off at Hightower. He was dirty, cold, slowly losing his sanity, and more importantly losing his will to continue.

The pocket of his backpack held two cans of cat food. Unlike the first time he found the light weight meal, Greg did not leave the cans behind when he discovered them at a house the previous night. He had one power bar left before he was out of human food, one step away from eating Super Cat Feast.

It was close to 5pm. He had an hour of light left. Dark clouds remained as rain continued in a steady drizzle. There would be no moon to help him after sunset.

Greg left the liquor store with two bottles of water and ate a snack size bag of nuts he found near a register. He quickened his pace towards the junction of US 89/93. He considered staying at the liquor store, but it had no fireplace, no food other than the measly bag of nuts, and no blankets. Greg was wet and needed a fire to dry his clothes.

He approached the intersection of the two highways at 5:30pm. He noticed a town off to his right, and went to find a place to spend the night. He walked down the South Street exit of 93 North, passing the highway motels, and continuing towards town.

There were several homes close to the exit, but Greg learned to venture further into towns to find nicer homes away from the highway. He was losing daylight, and his legs were tired, but the reward of a higher end residence was worth the extra few minutes of walking. A nicer home meant a better chance of food. Low income families did not keep large pantries. Their homes were bare after the food shortages caused by the rapture. Rural communities, like the ones he found on his trip from

Hightower, were also devastated from the food delivery issues. Tonight he was in an upper middle class suburb of Concord, N.H, and had high hopes of locating food other than the feline variety in his pack.

Greg strode into the first subdivision and stopped dead in his tracks. He smelled smoke. He smelled smoke and food. He definitely smelled food. It had been months since he smelled food being cooked. It was a welcome aroma. He lost himself in the moment as he breathed it in, standing in the same spot for several minutes, dreaming of a warm dinner. He snapped out of his daze with the realization there was someone else alive, a survivor, another person.

It was past dusk, and the sun was almost gone. Greg determined the direction of the smell, and noticed light coming from a window in one of the houses just off of the street. Before he realized what he was doing, Greg ran towards the smell. He was cold, wet, and hungry, and did not want to stay outside much longer. He needed to get out of the elements and into shelter.

His heart raced in anticipation of finding a fellow survivor. His mouth drooled as the smell of food grew stronger.

"What should I do?" he whispered to himself. He went over his choices. He could avoid the survivor, like his father advised, and keep going to Hanover, or he go to the house and meet the person. The risks and rewards of another survivor were equally great. Two people could survive the winter more easily than he could alone, but meeting an evil person could be fatal.

Greg wanted to catch a glimpse of the person before deciding. He made his way to an adjacent house, found the front door unlocked, and went to the second floor for the best vantage point. The light coming from the other house was from a fire. Greg was hungry before but famished after smelling the cooking food. He pulled his last power bar from his backpack, and ate his now unappealing dinner. He was still hungry, but out of food. Greg held a can of cat food in his palm. "I'm still not there yet, but I'm a lot closer than ever I thought I'd be." He zipped the can back in his pack.

Drawn curtains blocked the windows of the other house, but Greg made out a silhouette of at least one person. Unfortunately, because it was a distorted shadow, he could not tell the gender, age, or size of the person.

He went downstairs to the kitchen to scavenge for food. There was furniture in the house, but the cupboards were bare. He pulled a drawer open and felt for utensils. It was empty. "Just my luck." He muttered. Greg was in a house that was for sale before the rapture.

It was cat food or no food for now.

Greg went back upstairs and sat in the window for an hour watching the shadow move around the room. If it was an older person or a woman, someone he could escape, Greg would knock on the door. If the survivor was a man, Greg would leave and return with his father and brothers next spring.

The house with the fire looked new, built to mimic old New England. It was brick on the sides with a large wooden front porch. The roof and shutters were black. The fire was burning in what Greg assumed was the living room. There was little space between homes, standard for modern subdivisions. Greg could easily sit in his cold house and look down upon the warm fire and food house.

He was in an upstairs study on the corner of the second floor. A wall faced the fire house, and another faced the street. Occasionally Greg walked to the front window to look out. He wondered if any other survivors were coming home. He could only make out one shadow in the fire house. Greg decided, because it was dark and cold, no logical person would be out on a night with no moon to guide them back home.

Greg noticed a dozen trash cans lined up on the street in front of the fire house. Large bins that trash trucks grabbed with their mechanical claw. While Greg was staring at the trash cans, wondering why they were there, light appeared on the front lawn. The warm fire and food house's front door was open. Greg ducked down in the window, peering over the sill. A figure walked from the porch to one of the trash cans with a small plastic bag. The figure opened the can, threw out the bag, and skipped back into the house.

Skipped? It was a girl, a young girl. Greg was not a good judge of girl ages, but since she was alive and working with fire, he bet she was at least 12 or 13.

Greg knew instantly he was going to approach the survivor. His next decision was how and when to approach her. Did he want to wait a day, come up in the daylight so she was not scared? Did he want to go over tonight so he could be warm next to the fire and eat the food he smelled cooking? He was so excited to find another person, and to find another person close to his age, he decided not to wait.

He grabbed his pack, walked down the stairs, walked out the door, and slowly approached the front of the other house. He did not want to scare the girl, and being direct was his best approach. She was probably just as alone and desperate for company as he was.

"Should I knock?" he asked himself. "Should I just open the door and say "hello?" The front door was wood framed with a large glass upper half. There was a storm door with a sign reading *Model House – Rutledge*.

"This isn't even the girl's house, she's squatting." Greg noticed. He wondered where she lived before moving into this house.

"Here we go." Greg muttered to himself. He raised his hand and knocked politely but firmly.

The girl was on a couch reading a book next to the fire. Her head popped over the back of the couch and looked at the door. Greg wore a big grin, waving slowly. He spoke in a loud voice, making sure she could hear him through the glass doors "My name is Greg. Can I come in? I'm 14 and alone. I just want to say hello and warm up by your fire."

The girl jumped up and ran to the door with a huge smile on her face. "Oh my god! A cute boy's here to rescue me!" She screamed through the other side of the door.

"A cute boy?" Greg thought to himself. The first person I run into in months is a teeny bopper?

The girl hesitated for a second. "You're alone, right? You're not with the army or anyone else?"

Greg shook his head. "At least she is a smart teeny bopper." He thought.

The girl turned the deadbolt and let Greg inside the house. She threw her arms around him and hugged him for a few seconds. "Oh my god! Oh my god! You're real, and you're another person! And," She paused. "You're all wet." She stopped hugging him, pulled back and hit him with a barrage of questions.

"What's your name? Where did you come from? I can't believe you found me. I haven't seen anyone for 7 weeks, since the army truck with like four people in yellow suits drove through town really fast. Have you seen anyone? Is there anyone else alive? Is the world going on somewhere? Oh my god, my name is Rebecca. What's your name? I already asked you that, and you already told me your name is Greg, sorry. Okay, I'll be quiet now." Rebecca was a out of breath from the excitement and asking so many questions.

Greg stood in the doorway and felt the warmth of the house in front of him. The cold air was still on his back. He let the questions come. "Hi Rebecca, my name is Greg, Greg Dixon. May I come in and sit by the fire. Maybe heat some of my food?" Greg lied about having food in hopes of eating some of hers, or because he was too tired to remember he did not have any. "I'll tell you everything I know, I swear. I am just as excited to meet you. I haven't seen anyone, and I mean anyone, in months."

"I'm sorry! I'm sorry!" She replied excitedly. "I can make you some soup. That's pretty much what I have, lots of cans of soup. My parents ran the local grocery store, and they held the last two shipments of soup in the basement. I have just about any kind of soup you want."

"Do you have the one with little hamburgers in it?" Greg loved that soup, but would eat anything she had. She could warm a bowl of water, and he would drink it just to heat his insides.

"I do. Let me get it." She moved aside to let Greg into the house. "Come in. Put your stuff anywhere you want, and sit by the fire." Rebecca bounded through the living room ahead of him. She opened a cupboard next to the fireplace and pulled out a can with a red label. She pulled the tab off of the top and poured the soup into a metal pot, more a cauldron, with a wire handle. She hung the pot on a metal rod with a hook and swung it over the fire. "I looked at a house with a woodstove, but there were people upstairs, you know, not alive, so I decided I could work with a fireplace instead. My dad loved the store that sells all this fireplace cooking stuff. I make it work. Oh my god I'm so lonely. I'm sorry I'm talking so much."

Greg warmed his hands, letting heat flow through his freezing body. He sat down and took off his coat and boots. Rebecca continued with questions. She rambled about herself. She even started crying at one point. Greg waited for the soup and listened. He gave yes or no responses when prompted. He knew the girl wanted to talk to someone more than she cared about his answers.

Greg was almost in shock. He was hungry, dehydrated, and exhausted. He was not capable of giving more than the one word responses he offered.

When the soup was hot, Rebecca used an oven mitt to grab the pot handle and pour it into a paper bowl. She gave Greg a plastic spoon, and sat quietly, waiting for Greg to eat, and more importantly, to answer her questions.

"I walked from Boston, well Hightower." He began. "I'm headed further north to Hanover. My family is meeting me there, probably not until the spring, but maybe this fall. I don't know which, but I know I have to get up there." Greg explained as his warm, full belly brought energy back into his body.

"You walked here from Boston? Wow, that's pretty far. Even if we had a car it would take you over an hour to get to Hanover, and you want to walk? I went to volleyball camp in Hanover last summer." Rebecca stopped talking. "Wait, you think your family is up there? Your family is alive?"

Greg nodded. He explained the phone call with his father. He told her that his father, brothers, uncles, and cousins were not getting sick, and they decided to meet in Hanover. He told her one of his uncles was in Raleigh when everything began, and was still alive after a few months.

"My parents died about two months ago, just like everyone else in town. Concord and Manchester died early for New England. My parents said it was because half the town worked at the airport and caught it early, but I don't know. I think the whole country died at about the same time." Rebecca was not as frenetic in her conversation. She was serious and sad when she spoke of her parents.

"How did you end up here? How did you survive on your own for so long?" Greg was curious because Rebecca was young.

"I'm 13 years old. I'm not a baby. Once I realized I was going to survive, I made some rules, made some decisions, stuck to a plan my parents wrote for me. You know, most of the kids died first, I think because we're younger and still growing, or because we're smaller, but whatever. It was weird that I didn't get sick like everyone else at my school. My parents kept me home, told people I was sick, and held back canned food for me. Right at the beginning, when Raleigh happened, they started hoarding the food, mostly for the town and survivors, and then specifically for me. You know, people could tell they were sick. They weren't hungry, had to force themselves to eat. They just got wiped out. My parents knew, probably a week before they caught fevers." She paused, wiping away a tear. "It feels good to talk about it, you know, to talk to someone."

Greg nodded. He knew they would have a lot of time to talk about what he had seen. He wanted to ask more questions about the rapture. He was locked in his dorm when the sick were moved to the infirmary. He did not know much about the disease. Greg knew his mother was dead, and wanted to know how she died. How she was at the end.

"Anyway, I wasn't sick, and my parents kept all this food, and we wrote down some rules: Don't trust the military or the government. Don't trust adults. Don't go outside or be seen or have fires until you know everyone is dead. Don't share your food. I stuck to those until about four weeks ago. I haven't seen or heard anything for weeks. At first the airport was crazy busy, and I could see military planes and big jets coming and going all the time. I would sneak up there and watch. Guards were posted, but they weren't paying attention. The military was moving people and equipment and supplies. I have no idea where. After the first week, there were less and less soldiers, less planes. Then there weren't many planes landing. I hid in our house. My parents went to the neighbor's house to die. They wanted to make sure I had a clean place, no dead bodies to deal with. I stayed there until the gas ran out in the fireplace. Oops, great planning, huh? Gas fireplace?" Rebecca laughed. Greg smiled. He loved hearing her story. He enjoyed the sound of another voice.

"I knew they built this subdivision pretty close to us, and there was a model home with a fireplace, a wood burning one, not gas like ours. I moved supplies over here, took wood from other houses, and I moved. I kept waiting for someone to show up, even a bad person or the government, I didn't care at this point. You know? I just wanted to see and talk to someone."

Greg continued to nod. "Yeah, I know. I walked off the highway and smelled the fire, and thought the same thing. I had to see another person, even with the risks. I didn't want to be alone anymore." He felt light headed, weak from his journey, and he swayed slightly from side to side as if he was about to blackout.

Rebecca sat on the couch while Greg was on the hearth warming his bones and finishing the soup. She got up and sat next to him, giving him another hug. She began to cry again. Greg was not an emotional person, but this time, unlike the first time she hugged him, he hugged her back tightly.

Rebecca felt Greg's ribs under his thick fleece pullover. He was a skeleton. His clothes were filthy, and he was soaking wet. She could feel him shivering. She saw the color drained from his face.

"You have to get out of these clothes." She announced. "I don't know how you aren't sick as a dog. How long have you been walking in the cold and rain?"

Greg had to think about his trip before answering. He was a zombie. "A week, I think. I can't remember." He began to cry. "I don't know. Oh my god, I don't know. A week? I can't get there. I keep walking, and I can't get anywhere. I have cat food in my backpack. I almost ate cat food." Greg's composure was gone.

Rebecca stood. "Take off your clothes. You need a bath, and some clean, dry pajamas. I don't think you have a fever, but you need to rest. I'll drag another couch in from the other room." She picked up the soup pot and poured water into it from a nearby bottle.

"Get out of those clothes." She said to him again. "Don't be bashful. Stay by the fire. I'm going to get some dry pj's for you." She hung the water pot over the fire before heading upstairs.

Greg pulled off his fleece, folding it neatly on the hearth just behind where he sat. His fingers were clumsy, nearly useless. He was more exhausted and feeble than he realized.

Rebecca came back downstairs holding an armful of linen, pajamas, a robe, and a set of slippers. She dropped them in front of Greg. A towel sat on top of the pile.

"I'm going into the other room. Call me when you are changed." She looked at the water over the fire. It was forming bubbles, but not at a boil. "Try and hurry. I'm making you more food. You feel like a skeleton. Also, it's cold in the other room. I don't want to be in there long."

The young woman went around the corner into the dark. "I'm waiting." She called, as if she knew Greg was still sitting on the hearth and not getting dressed.

He shook his head to clear some of the cobwebs that were forming, took off his clothes, and dried himself with the plush towel. He pulled on the clean pajamas, wrapped up in the robe, and slipped the fuzzy shoes onto his feet. "Okay." He called to her.

Greg looked like a little old man. Matching light blue plaid adorned his body. The clothes were flannel and warm, but they were slightly too big for him, particularly in his current malnourished form.

Rebecca bounced around the corner and clapped her hands. "There. You are starting to look healthier already. I can wash these clothes tomorrow if you want to keep them. I think they should just go in the trash, but it's up to you." She picked up the folded wet outfit Greg wore just minutes earlier and placed them on the bottom step of a staircase. "I don't know if you will be able to keep it down, but I'm making you some ramen. I know it's salty, but it's calories, it's fast, and it's warm." She opened a cupboard next to the fireplace. Greg saw rows of soup, pasta, and ramen. He saw canned vegetables, fruits, soda, and bottled water.

Rebecca grabbed a package of chicken ramen noodles, placed it into the now boiling water, and stirred the noodles with a metal fork.

"One more thing." She jumped up anc ran through a swinging door. She returned with an egg, and a cold soda she offered to Greg.

"An egg? Where did she get an egg? How old is that egg?" Greg's mind asked questions while his mouth remained silent. He opened the bottle of soda and began to drink. Despite his attempts to find water during the trek, he was always on the edge of dehydration. The clear, sugary liquid felt fantastic against his dry throat.

Rebecca cracked the egg into the ramen, stirring the noodles rapidly to scramble the concoction. She used her mitt to pull the pot off the rack, and poured the mixture into a large plastic bowl.

"Eat what you can. I mean, when it's cool enough to eat." She placed the bowl of steaming food next to Greg. The metal fork she used to stir rested across the top.

"I know you're dead tired, but I've been so lonely. Do you mind if I just talk to you? You don't have to respond. I just want to talk to another person." Rebecca looked at him eagerly.

"You have someone to talk to now." He said quietly. "We each just made a new best friend." Greg reached passed the food and wrapped his arms around the young girl.

They stayed by the fire for a few minutes, hugging. Rebecca let go. "One of my house rules, trash goes outside in the containers. No trash in the house."

Just like that, with the listing of a house rules, the tender moment was over.

Greg did as he was told, walking out to the trash can in his newly acquired outfit to throw away the egg shell and ramen wrapper. It was cold, and sleet drizzled down on him. He was happy to be in a house with a fire, and not trudging towards Hanover, or curled up on the floor of a random house, hungry and cold. He came back onto the porch and noticed firewood stacked on half of the covered porch, conveniently placed next to the door. Rebecca was a smart girl.

Greg grabbed an arm full of wood to load into the basket by the fire.

"There is another sofa in the other room. We can pull it into here. Do you think you can help? I know you're tired. You can call it a night if you need to rest." Rebecca hoped for his help, but would manage without him if necessary.

"Sure. I have one more burst of energy left, especially after the egg ramen." Greg replied. He ate all of the food. His stomach ached from overeating. Six months ago he could eat an entire pizza by himself. Today his stomach was so small a bowl of soup made him feel full.

He followed her into the other room, and helped her move the piece of furniture.

When the sofa was in place, Rebecca ran upstairs and came back down with a blanket. "You can take a bath tomorrow. We still have water pressure. I heat water on the fire and fill half from the tub faucet. It's where I wash clothes too. Anyway, you smell really bad." She paused. "Let's get some sleep."

"Okay." He said with a smile. Rebecca was getting smarter by the minute.

Greg grabbed the blanket from the back of his couch and laid down facing the fire. He was the most comfortable he had ever been in his life. Exhausted physically and mentally, his eyes fluttered momentarily as he drifted to sleep. The last words he heard were additional instructions from his new friend.

"Good night Greg Dixon from Hightower. " Rebecca said as she threw a log on the fire. "If you wake up in the night, please put wood on the fire. You can use the bathroom. As I said, we have water pressure. Please flush, we're not savages."

"Good night Rebecca. I'll see you in the morning." Greg mumbled.

Rebecca sat on her couch watching him sleep. Tears streamed down her cheeks as she enjoyed her good fortune. She smiled at her sudden companion. Tomorrow she would begin to act like herself, not the young girl she pretended to be.

And she would show him everything.

13

"Craig's gone again." Matt stood over his father.

John opened his eyes, rubbing the corners to clear the sleep. "How long?"

"I don't know. He's getting better at sneaking out, could be hours." Matt sat down on the side of the bed and tied his shoes.

"I swear I am going to strap that kid down tonight. Like I don't have enough to deal with." John's anger was short lived. In a matter of weeks Craig lost everything in his world, school, soccer, friends, his mother. If John could run away right now, he would too.

"You think he's at the soccer fields again?" Matt was done tying his shoes. He stood and looked vacantly out of the bedroom window.

"Part of me wants to put out a saucer of milk and wait for him to come home on his own. I know he's running away so we'll have to find him, well, at least part of his running away is so we'll come find him." John swung his feet off the side of the bed, taking the spot left by his son. John was fully dressed except for socks and shoes. Searching for Craig was an almost every morning event. He was prepared.

"Is that what you want to do? It's not like it's cold or raining outside. We could let him run around on his own for a day. I doubt he's swimming in the river or skateboarding off roofs." Matt was as exasperated as his father.

John paused. "We can't. If he gets hurt, well, we've lost enough. He wants to get rescued. It's the least we can do. It's the least I can do."

Craig ran away for different reasons each time. If he slipped out daily,

John really would tie him down or dead bolt his windows and door, but Craig might go a week without leaving, or just a day.

Matt and John were caught off guard this morning. They spent the previous day hunting him down. That usually meant a few days reprieve.

"He never goes to the same place right away. I have an idea." John slipped on his second shoe and stood next to his son.

In the few months since Sharon's death the line between father and oldest son had blurred.

"Let's take a car and head over to Highway 17. I have a feeling yesterday was a smoke screen. He's off to find Greg again, and wanted us to spend the day looking in town spinning our wheels." John walked out of the room. Matt followed, shaking his head.

"I wish I could figure him out, help him out." Matt replied.

"In a way, I appreciate the diversion. If I'm thinking about him, looking for him, I'm not thinking about the shit storm our lives have become." John grabbed a granola bar and bottle of water from the counter as he walked out the door to their garage.

"I hope he's on the road. I'm tired of walking into homes with dead people." Matt's body gave a shiver.

They drove in silence, eating their breakfasts. Their taste in music was so drastic, each preferred silence to the other's CD choices.

"We need a purpose." John finally said. "A ten year old has to be kept busy, be given a reason not to ride his bike off into the night."

Matt did not respond. He chewed his breakfast.

"We need a new house, and we need to get him fishing. He needs to be able to walk down to a pier and throw a line into the water, or maybe have one of us take him out into the bay." John already contemplated a move to the bay as the days shortened. "We can pick any house we want. Let's find one that doesn't hold all of our memories. Let's find a new neighborhood that won't remind us of your mother or our friends." John drove slowly through the empty streets of Mount Pleasant, South Carolina.

"So it's done. This is it." Matt replied flatly. "We're all that's left. You think the city is dead."

John let the truck slow to a stop before turning to look at his son. "Let's find your little brother and start a new life. I'm not saying it's the life either of us wants, but it's the one we get until we leave for New Hampshire. This is it, Matt. The world lost. I'm sorry to have to tell you, but yes, it's over."

He took his foot off the brake and the car ambled north on Highway 17. John and Matt searched for a young boy riding a bike.

14

Greg woke when he heard a log tossed on the fire. The sun was not up, but he could tell it was morning.

She was real. He met a girl the night before, and ate hot food, and was on a couch in front of a fire, and he could talk to someone. Well, if he could get a word in edgewise he could talk to someone. Greg lay motionless to make sure Rebecca was still friendly and okay with the idea of him being there.

He looked around the room. His excitement and exhaustion the previous night prevented him from noticing how neat and organized the living room was. Rebecca had a brown leather couch of her own that faced the fire. On each end of her sofa were tables with lanterns. A small table and chairs rested against the wall next to the fire. A placemat led him to believe she ate her meals at the table. A silverware caddy filled with plastic forks, spoons, knives, and paper napkins sat in the middle of the table along with salt and pepper. A stack of paper bowls and plates were on a built in cabinet next to the fire. "This is orderly and precise for a young girl." Greg thought. "I would swear there is an adult living with her." He lifted his head and looked for signs of a second person, but there was only the one placemat on the table.

"Good morning." He said, as he stretched and sat up. "It wasn't a dream. I'm really in a house with another person" Greg was positive Rebecca was happy he was there, but he still felt out the situation to make sure. "That couch was a little more comfortable than sleeping under my dorm bed at Hightower, or bunking on the floor of a general store. Thank you for everything, the soup, the couch."

"You're not leaving, are you?" Rebecca asked. "You are thanking me as if you are going to leave in a minute. Can you stay for a little while? I have a few more surprises, a few secrets I didn't tell you last night. You fell asleep quickly. I was so excited for another person I didn't sleep at all. Plus, all I do is sleep. It's boring being alone. I do my chores, get firewood, keep things clean, then sleep away as much time as I can."

Greg smiled. He liked Rebecca. She was like the girls at Hightower, excited about life, excited about talking, and excited to tell you everything about themselves. She was a little bit different too. He could not put his finger on it yet, but she was special.

He missed people, and he particularly missed people like Rebecca, girls who liked to talk. Greg was shy. He kept his feelings and motives to himself. Finding a Yin to his Yang was perfect. If he had stumbled upon a person similar to himself, neither one of them would have spoken.

"I want to get up to Hanover, but I'm not leaving now. Besides," he pointed to the window out the front door, "it's raining. I'm not going to start off in the rain on a two week hike."

"Oh, yeah, no, I guess not. Well, let me show you one of the lucky things I have." She pointed to the flannel robe she gave Greg the night before. "And maybe we can get you a bath later, cause, well, you know, you still smell."

Greg did know. He was excited to get the grime off of his body, and do it using hot water.

He stood up, slipped on the scuffs Rebecca set out for him, and followed her through an archway to a kitchen. They went out a backdoor into a yard where a large chicken coop sat with live chickens strutting about. Rebecca opened the back of the coop and pulled out 7 eggs.

Greg did not count, but guessed she had at least a dozen chickens.

"Urban farmers, can you believe it? One of our neighbors had this coop and three chickens. Once I knew I was going to live here, I moved it. It took me two days to dismantle and put back together, but so much easier than walking all the way over to the neighbors every morning for eggs. Then I found another house with chickens. Let's just say, I eat a lot of eggs. Did you know they lay one every day?"

Greg realized he had to use the bathroom. "Just a second, let me use the restroom..." Eggs! He thought to himself. That's not out of a can or a wrapper. He used the bathroom, flushed a toilet for the first time in a week, and walked back into the cold kitchen.

"The rest of the house gets really cold, colder every morning. I don't know what I can do. The living room is getting more difficult to keep warm. It is losing too much heat, and it's too large to warm from the single fireplace. I'm thinking of hanging up plastic strips, like you see in a meat locker, or maybe just two blankets in each entry. We could walk through the slit in the middle. We would keep most of the warmth where we need it. I know a barn a little ways from here. We could get some heavy wool horse blankets."

Rebecca cracked the eggs into a non-stick pan. "I hope scrambled is okay. I crack right into the pan, saves me a bowl to clean. I use a plastic fork to scramble them." She threw some salt and pepper in the eggs and whisked as she walked into the other room. She set the pan down and moved a wire cooking rack over the fire. It was cast-iron and allowed her to put the egg pan right over the flame. "Another one of my Dad's fireplace cooking toys," she said with a smile.

"I would eat them raw. I've been living on franks and beans, power bars, and green beans for two months. Actual food is going to taste fantastic."

"You said you were eating cat food." Rebecca frowned.

"I said I almost ate cat food. That's different. I never ate the cat food. It's in my backpack."

"Can you get two paper plates and forks from over there? These cook quickly. I can't leave them even for a second. I usually just eat out of the pan, saves room in the trash cans, but that's gross with two of us."

Greg retrieved the plates. Rebecca spooned the eggs out equally. They sat at her small table and ate breakfast. Greg noticed she put a second placemat out for him while he was in the bathroom. Rebecca smiled and stared at Greg.

She finally spoke. "Did you get as lonely as I did? I was starting to go a little insane."

"I talked to myself, not in a crazy way, like it was a conversation, but just to hear a voice. That helped, but in the end, yes, I was lonely." Greg ate his eggs in less than a minute. "Do you mind if I cook something else? I'm still hungry. I'm sure I can find a house with food in this subdivision."

She smiled. "I don't think you realize how much food I have."

Greg was intrigued by her comment and sly expression, but he was hungrier than interested.

"How about this," she told him. "I'll make you some soup, and you take a bath so I can focus on the conversation instead of your smell. I will warn you, the bathroom is cold, so while the water will be warm, you are basically taking a bath in cold air." She went to her cupboard.

"Fair enough, I'll get clean." Greg could tell Rebecca enjoyed a plan. She kept her house spotless so rats and bugs did not come in. She kept her clothes and sheets clean to keep her humanity. He had a feeling she would go to Hanover, if he could show her it was the correct strategy. He had to convince her that leaving a food supply and a safe warm house made sense.

Greg ate the soup while four pots of water warmed over the fire. He filled half the tub with the cold water from the tap, and enjoyed his first hot cleaning in two months. If he closed his eyes, it was almost as if the rapture had not happened. He had a full belly, a warm bath, a friend...

He opened his eyes, looked at the disgusting gray water around him, and pulled the plug. He wrapped in a towel and bathrobe before putting on clean clothes placed neatly outside the door.

Greg was ready for the day.

"You're even cuter when you're clean!" Rebecca told him, blushing as she said it.

"Okay, what do we need to do for the day. Do we need firewood? Do we need to feed the chickens? What chores do you normally do alone that I can help out with? Do you want to walk to that barn and get those blankets?" Helping her was the best way to steer the conversation away from being called cute.

"It stopped raining. I have two bikes, let's go over to the barn and get the blankets. I can show you some other stuff too. I have a few winter coats, one should fit you. They have hoods and will keep any rain off if it starts up again. I washed your clothes, including your jacket. I was bored after you went to sleep. They are hanging up to dry. I have a bike helmet, if you want it."

Greg found a black jacket in the coat closet that cost $500 before the rapture. The tags were still attached to the sleeve. He slipped it on and followed her back into the kitchen and through a door that led to the garage. There were eight bikes in the garage, four mountain and four road bikes. High end bikes in different sizes. "I collected things in case people showed up," Rebecca explained. "It cut through the boredom, gave me something to do, and gave me hope."

It was a two car garage. In the far bay was an SUV hybrid which looked new. In the closer bay, next to the bikes, was just about everything Greg could imagine; snow shovels, clothes, jackets, gloves, tents, sleeping bags, sleeping pads, propane tanks, kettle grills, coolers, and camping gear upon camping gear. There were rain barrels and seed racks taken right from the stores. She had stacks of food; soups, noodles, flour, sugar, bottled water, energy drinks, enough to keep herself alive for years.

Greg grabbed an expensive mountain bike and helmet. He followed Rebecca to the side door of the garage. The rain stopped, but it was cold and damp outside. They saw their breath as they road down the street. Greg stayed next to Rebecca.

"Where did you get all that stuff?" He asked her.

"The Concord Mall is about 10 miles away. I used to drive my dad's delivery truck sometimes, just a few blocks, back when there was a world. I know how to drive. I took the delivery van and 'shopped' for things. The government was not focused on a single truck driving around Concord, N.H. I went through people's houses, mainly their basements and garages." She turned and gave him the look that meant she stayed away from bedrooms with dead bodies.

"I have a lot of stuff in the house, mostly in the garage and on the second floor. I keep additional canned goods in the basement. I don't like clutter. I space supplies out to make them accessible but also so I won't be climbing over things." She rode at a leisurely pace, making it easy to talk during their ride. "I know what you're thinking. I don't act like I'm 13 years old."

That was exactly what Greg was thinking.

"It was just me and my parents. They owned the grocery store. They used me for a lot of errands, stocking shelves, running the register, cleaning. I did just about everything to help them out. I like to work and learn. It's hard for me to stay still. They made me do volleyball at school so I would interact with kids, rather than come straight home and work at the store. When the world ended, well, I focused on getting stuff I might need, as well as what people who found me might need too."

She turned left onto a country road. "Here's the barn up ahead. "

Greg listened, "I didn't think you were too young to do all this stuff. We've both probably grown up a lot in the last few months. I lost my mother, some of my cousins, my aunts, my grandparents. You don't go through that kind of loss without getting stronger. I'm 14, a sophomore in high school, I should be going to football games and dances. Instead I'm in Concord, N.H. riding a bike in the rain getting horse blankets to keep one room in a model home warm enough to stay alive." He shook his head. "We've both grown up. I think you figured it out a lot faster than I did, which is why I asked. I would still be in my dorm room eating beans, playing spy, sleeping under my bunk, if I didn't have a purpose. If I didn't want to find other people and my family."

They were in front of the barn. Greg began to cry again. He did not realize how lonely and sad he was, how much he missed his mother, how much the idea of never seeing any of his friends weighed on him. He did not realize how much he missed his old life. He was living in the moment every second since the phone call with his father, since the world became sick. He was too busy staying alive to grieve.

"Why did this happen?" Greg said through his tears. "Why did I live? Why am I alone so far from my family?" He sobbed like a child, sucking in his breath, sniffing his nose. His shoulders bounced as he wept.

Rebecca stood over her bike, watching him cry. She laid it down on the ground, went over to him, and gave him a hug. He hugged her back. The night before, when she hugged him, he put his arms around her, but he had not been hugging her, it was a polite response. Now he hugged her, held her tightly, like a lifeline or life jacket that was keeping him afloat.

"I miss my Mom so much." He said to her. "I miss my whole family."

"I miss my parents too." She replied, gripping him tightly, "but no matter what, it looks like we have each other now. Two has to be easier than one, Greg Dixon from Hightower." She paused, "Our new name is officially Greg and Rebecca. We are going to get through this together."

She pulled back from their hug and smiled, giving a little bit of a giggle.

"I'm not saying this isn't going to be hard, but it has to be easier together. It has to." She took tissues from her pocket and gave him a few.

"Seriously," he said, still sobbing, "why do you have all this stuff? Tissues? The world ends and you keep tissues in your pocket?" He laughed. Rebecca was a girl with a plan.

"I always keep tissues in my pocket. You'll see. I'll start to rub off on you, and you'll be more prepared." She flashed a smile, and walked towards the barn. The teeny bopper girl from last night was gone. Greg realized the frenetic questioning and apparent helplessness was an act. The real Rebecca, the girl who kept a spotless house and tissues in her pocket, was no teeny bopper. This new girl acted like an adult trapped in a teen's body.

Rebecca approached a side door with a slide bolt lock at the bottom. A latch door handle, a long piece of metal slipped into a notch, kept the door shut. Rebecca undid the bottom bolts, opened the door, and went inside. A second later her head popped back out the door. "Are you coming or what?"

It smelled like rotting hay inside. Greg did not like it, but he followed Rebecca over to a set of lockers next to the horse stalls.

"I let the horses go two weeks after the town got sick. No one could feed or tend to them. I thought they might be better out in the wild. I don't know if that's true, but if they stayed here, well, they were going to starve." She opened one of the locker doors. It was empty. She continued opening lockers until she found blankets. "Here we go." She grabbed an armful, "well, come on, let's get back before it starts to rain again. These smell fine now, but wet wool blankets? I won't hang those in the house."

"So if you can drive," Greg started "why didn't we bring the truck over here? Why did I have to ride a bike in the cold and now balance blankets on my handle bars?" Greg questioned some of the girl's story.

"I have no idea how long gas stays viable, and as far as I can tell, we have a finite amount of it. I am not wasting gas when we can ride to get blankets. Keeping yourself fit, making sure you don't just lay around the house, getting out into the fresh air? It's important.   Plus" she looked at him as they got back on their bikes "I wanted to go on a bike ride with a cute boy. It's been a long time since I have done that." She started back to the house, quicker than she rode over.

'Greg and Rebecca' he thought to himself. 'I like it.' She was getting ahead of him. Greg jumped on his bike and pedaled hard to catch up.

15

Paul and Hank Dixon left Dayton, Ohio the day after Paul arrived. They headed East, travelling as far as possible during the freakishly warm December. Hank's neighbor had two Honda Goldwing motorcycles with large saddle compartments. The brothers, despite their questionable motorcycle capabilities, rode the bikes out of town early that next morning. They knew motorcycle riding was more dangerous and colder than using a car, but taking two bikes meant one could breakdown without stranding them. Motorcycles were easier to navigate through potential road blocks, accidents, and traffic jams.

They stayed on large four lane highways, riding along US 70 the first day. The roads were clear, and they kept their speed at a constant 75 miles per hour. Paul did not have the confidence to ride faster. They stopped briefly for lunch and to siphon gas from abandoned cars. They finished their day on the north side of Harrisburg, PA. The first four houses they searched had the odor of death. The fifth smelled clear. Exhausted, they ate cold beef and noodle soup from cans before climbing into their sleeping bags just after the sun went down. Paul and Hank exchanged no more than 100 words the entire day.

The next morning they turned north towards Albany, NY. The clouds rolled in and a light snow began to fall before noon. They avoided New York City, and moved into the snow belt of New England. They adjusted their speed to safely navigate the dusting of powder and rolled into Rutland, Vt, in the afternoon. They were only an hour or so away from Hanover, but on the wrong side of several large mountains.

It was the shortest day of the year, the sun was almost gone, and it was snowing.

The snow melted as it hit the ground in New York, but Vermont's streets disappeared under a blanket of white. Riding motorcycles, dangerous before because of their novice abilities, was quickly becoming too great a risk.

Hank slowed his bike to a stop. Paul pulled next to him. "Let's stop here, I can't ride anymore. It's dark. I'm tired and hungry." Hank was exhausted.

"We're an hour away, I think we can push through and make it." Paul was equally tired, but wanted to get to Hanover.

"Paul" Hank yelled through the increasing loud and blowing wind. "It's snowing. We're in the mountains on motorcycles. It's pitch black. Best case we get to Hanover in the complete dark. Let's find a place to bunk here, stay out of this mini storm, get up there tomorrow. I'm beat, and we may only be 50 miles away, but in this weather, on bikes, it's going to take us two hours, maybe more."

Paul conceded the night. They stood over their bikes at the intersection of rural routes 4 and 7. The roads met at a 'T,' with 4 merging into 7 with a left turn. In front of them was a concrete wall with a small hill continuing behind it. Paul looked down the street, Main Street conveniently enough. To their right and slightly up the hill was a large white house with an enormous wraparound porch. A sign hung on metal eyelets off a white wooden sign post. Paul could not make out the wording through the falling snow.

"That has some chimneys." He pointed at the house. "Maybe it's a B&B or an old hotel. We can get a fire going."

"Sounds good." Hank nodded and turned his bike towards the white home. The snow was accumulating quickly. They half rode, half walked their bikes to the bottom of the hill and up the steep driveway. Their tires spun in the new snow. Hank read the sign as he walked passed, The Rutland Inn.

Paul and Hank pulled their bikes against the hotel in hopes the overhang would offer some protection from the snow. They walked up three steps onto the porch and tried the front door. It was unlocked.

"Hello?" Paul said loudly into the pitch black lobby. He could tell the hotel was empty. The inside temperature matched the outdoor temperature. There was no smell of decaying bodies. The white house on the hill appeared to be uninhabited and clean.

"Wow, it's really coming down now." Hank pointed two flashlights towards the outside. He pulled out a box of tea candles and a lighter from his backpack, and began lighting the main room of the hotel. "I saw wood under a cover in back. You want to grab some? I'll light the room and find a fireplace."

"Got it." Paul replied. They had been on the road for just two days, and seldom spoke, but found they worked well together. He went back outside. It was colder than it had been just an hour ago. The snow was falling much harder. "Hank made a good call stopping." He mumbled to himself. Paul found the wood, grabbed an armful, and went back inside.

Paul kicked open the door and the gust of wind that followed him blew out half of Hank's tea candles. The few that remained lit cast enough light to show Hank kneeling inside a large fire place with one arm stuck up the chimney. "I think this is our best bet tonight. I opened the flue. We can get it going with a quick light log and your first armful of wood."

Hank and Paul packed synthetic logs in their motorcycles to start fires quickly and easily. The quick starting logs meant not worrying about kindling or paper, and gave them an hour of steady light and fire to gather additional wood.

The snow came down harder. The wind began to howl through the open front door, pushing through a cloud of frozen powder.

Paul pushed the door shut. "You know I don't like to feed your ego, but it was the right decision to stop. You may have saved us. Can you imagine getting stuck on Mount Kilington in this crap? Who knows how long we would have lasted up there." Paul unzipped his backpack and pulled out soup, a bag of instant rice, and a liter of bottled water.

"I wish I could claim intelligence, but I'm just tired. There wasn't thought put into it other than me not being able to go any further. Don't forget, I'm old."

"We should move the bikes behind the hotel. They are getting pelted next to the building." The structure behind the hotel where Paul found the wood was a four bay carport.

"Good idea. They might get snowed in where they are. Of course, they will get snowed in over there too, but at least they will be dry." Hank agreed, sitting on the hearth and rubbing off the black ash from the flue now covering his hands.

Paul went back outside. He wheeled his bike towards a bay in the carport. Firewood was stacked to the ceiling in one of the bays. The wood was dry and ready to burn. "Look at that, nice New England people ready for the winter." Paul said to his brother, walking behind him and pushing his motorcycle.

"Let's hope we don't need much of it." Hank replied as he parked his bike against the back wall.

Tonight was not about settling down for the long haul. Tonight was about eating, getting warm, and sleeping with as much comfort as possible before they made the final push to Hanover.

It was their third night together. They worked as a well practiced team. Paul grabbed the quick starting log from Hank's saddlebag and went back to the house. Hank spied a log carrier with wheels and pulled it over to the stacks of wood. He filled the roller with as many logs as he could and pulled it into the house. Paul lit the synthetic log and placed three wood logs on top of it to start their fire. When the fire caught, Paul searched for a kitchen to locate a pot to warm their rice and soup.

The front room was bright with light from the fire and tea light candles. Hank snapped on a head lamp before he moved his bike and gathered wood. He clicked it to off when he walked into the hotel lobby with the log carrier.

Paul came back into the room through a swinging door that led to the kitchen.

"Are you ready for another piece of Hank Dixon luck?" Paul was grinning. "There is a woodstove back there, a working woodstove. I don't want to fire it up tonight, I'm too tired, but tomorrow morning? I bet the stove will make the kitchen warm and cozy."

"Now I am starting to think I'm a genius for stopping." Hank said back. He stood by the fire with his hands on his hips to take stock of the lobby. The hotel was a converted Victorian Mansion. Hank and Paul stood in the combination lobby and breakfast eating area. The good news was the room had a fireplace. The bad news was the room was large and would be difficult to heat from a single fire source. Hank eyed two full length couches facing each other in front of the fireplace.

"Hey, Paul, let's move these right next to the fire and facing the heat. I bet it will be just as cozy tonight as your kitchen will be tomorrow morning." He grabbed one end of a couch. Paul grabbed the other. They faced the first couch towards the fire two feet from the fire screen. They moved the other couch in a similar diagonal position. The top of each couch touched in the middle four feet away from the fireplace, creating a 'V' shaped wall to trap heat.

Paul pulled the tops off of two cans of soup, poured the contents into the pot, dumped the instant rice into the mixture, and placed the pot next to the roaring fire. "The wood is dry, it's burning well."

Hank unpacked the rolling cart, stacking the wood on the hearth. "I'm going to grab another cart of wood so we have some more inside. I want to make sure you have some to make my breakfast tomorrow morning. Do you think you can find some blankets and sheets upstairs, or do you want to use our sleeping bags?"

"I'm on it." Paul said, jumping up from next to the fire. "I want to take my coat and boots off once, let's get all our stuff together right now. I'll get some bowls and spoons too." Paul wore a headlamp similar to Hank's. He turned the headlamp on and grabbed a flashlight from his backpack. He walked to a set of stairs on the wall opposite the front door and followed them to the second floor. He did not feel like entering any rooms for fear the rooms were still 'occupied.' He stood at the top of the stairs, pointing his flashlight down a long hallway. Brass numbers hung on several doors running down the length of the hall. Paul noticed two of the doors did not have numbers, and guessed correctly the doors were closets. The first closet held cleaning supplies and paper products. The second closet housed sheets and several thick polyester blankets encountered in modestly priced hotels.

"Jackpot" Paul said to himself.

He walked back downstairs, dropped the linen on one of the sofas, and went into the kitchen to retrieve spoons and bowls. As he opened cupboards he found a well organized kitchen and an extremely well stocked pantry. His hunger prevented him from spending too much time admiring. He grabbed a large stirring spoon, two bowls, two soup spoons, paper towels, and headed back into the living room. As he came through the swinging door he noticed a distinct difference in the temperature. It was cold in the kitchen, but it was close to tolerable in the living room. The fire took the chill and dampness out of the air.

He put the bowls and spoons on the floor, stirred the soup in the pot, and moved the pot to the other side of the fireplace so the cooler side faced the heat. He noticed a coffee table and pulled it next to the hearth, between the couches and the fire. They could use it as a dinner table, allowing the brothers to sit on the large hearth or on the couches while they enjoyed hot soup and soaked in the warmth of the fire. Paul unzipped his jacket, untied his boots, and settled in for the night.

Hank opened the front door and came in with a third cart of wood. His shoulders and hair were white with snow from the 25 yard walk to the carport.

"I bet there's an inch down already, and it's snowing harder." Hank did not look happy. "You think they have early plow service? If not, we might be here until June."

"There's nothing we can do about it now. Let's eat, sleep, and come up with a plan, if needed, tomorrow." Paul poured potato and bacon soup into each bowl. The mixture was think and lumpy with rice.

Hank unzipped his coat, took off his boots, and walked over to the hearth. "Wow, I'm almost 'not cold' for the first time today. That has to count for something." He looked at his bowl. "No tiny stars in my soup tonight?" He still teased his brother for serving him children's style chicken noodle soup the first night.

The two men ate in silence, letting the fire and food warm their bodies. Hank, utterly exhausted, found the bathroom, threw two more logs on the fire, and lay down on one of the couches. He pulled two of the fuzzy blankets Paul draped over the back of the couch on top of him. "If you wake up, throw another log on the fire." Hank yawned as he said fire. He was asleep before he finished his yawn.

"Sleep well old man." Paul responded in a whisper.

Before he went to bed Paul proactively built a fire in the woodstove for the next morning. He was not far behind Hank in the exhausted department. He blew out the few tea lights that remained lit, and curled up under the blankets on his couch. Paul's head was inches from Hank's, separated by the arms of their couches at the top of the 'V' formation. Paul ignored Hank's light snoring, and soon fell fast asleep.

Hank awoke in the dark. Embers from the fire cast flickers of light onto the ceiling and the room. Paul was asleep next to him. All was quiet and safe. He got up, threw three logs on the fire, went to the bathroom, and fell back into a deep sleep. Paul awoke and had a similar experience later in the morning. Aside from the single wake, both men slept soundly throughout the night.

Hank awoke to a bright room. The sun was out, shining through a bank of windows on the dining side of the lobby. He sat up and stretched his arms. The fire was still burning. Red embers kicked off enough heat to keep the hearth area warm. The couches, faced towards the fire, collected heat throughout the night. Hank slept warmly for the first time in months. He stood to put a fresh log on the fire.

"Do we care what time it is?" Paul said from his couch. He lay on his back and stretched his arms in front of his head, letting out a slight groan. "I have to get up too. I'm starving and I have to go to the bathroom."

"I haven't slept that well in a long, long time. I was warm. I felt safe. I knew I couldn't go anywhere, and I wasn't in a hurry to get to the next place. That was my best night's sleep in probably five months, since I read about the flu in Brazil." Hank sat on the hearth in navy long johns and a red waffle shirt.

"Yeah, I know. Even two nights ago in Harrisburg, I was antsy to get to Hanover. I didn't sleep well. And, well, it wasn't comfortable. This fireplace is awesome." Paul sat up on his couch. "I'll brave the kitchen and light the woodstove. I made it after you went to bed, should just take a match." He stood and went into the other room.

Hank walked to the front of the house. He looked out the bank of windows. "Holy shit." He said to himself. The sun was shining, but everything outside was white. There was at least a foot of snow on the ground, probably more. He and Paul were not going to Hanover today, not on motorcycles.

Paul came back through the door. "Fire is on. The kitchen will be warm soon, and we'll be eating something good."

"I hope we have a lot of food here, because unless we find a snowcat, or wrecker with a plow, we might be here a while. I know I was joking when I said June, but, well, it might be June."

Paul was used to Hank exaggerating and being too serious, "Okay, calm down. I'm sure we'll be able to get going..." Paul walked across the room to look out the window. He let out a small gasp. "Well, we do have a lot of food in the kitchen, and I mean a lot of food." He picked up a digital thermometer on one of the window sills in the dining area. It read 11 degrees. "Look at the temp. It dropped 40 degrees from lunch yesterday." Paul let out a small chuckle. "Hey, no school."

Hank was not amused.

"Where the hell are we anyway? Rutland? There has to be a tourist map or info sheet in this place. It's a hotel. I'm going to investigate while you make breakfast. I'm sure we can find a truck to get us over the mountains to Hanover. Worst case is we're stuck here for a while. It's 11 outside, but I bet it's 60 in here, warmer on the couches. As long as we have wood, we are going to be warm and dry." The feeling of calm and happiness Hank felt when he woke were gone, replaced by panic. He felt trapped.

"Let me give you the good news then." Paul placed his hand on Hank's shoulder. "Grab your headlamp. You have to see this kitchen."

Hank grabbed his headlamp and a flashlight and followed his brother into the kitchen. Hank had not been in the room yet. He was impressed with how nice a kitchen it was, outfitted in high-end, restaurant grade appliances. It was immaculate, and noticeably warmer than the front room. The woodstove kept in the corner as a novelty heated the backroom quickly and efficiently.

"This place is fantastic." Hank said as he looked around. Hank was an avid cook before the rapture. "I could do some damage here."

Paul's voice could be heard from behind a large open door. "That's not what I want you to see. Check out the pantry I found last night." Hank saw a metal door with a large silver handle. It looked like a walk in freezer, but was instead a pantry large enough for a mini cooper or punch buggy. Hank walked to the other side of the door to inspect the storage room. Paul stood in the middle, his arms outstretched to either side to emphasize the amazing find.

There was more food in the pantry than either of them could imagine, good canned food in perfect condition. There were vegetables, fruits, canned meats, canned fish, broths, and coffees. The pantry went from floor to ceiling with shelves eight feet high and two feet deep. There appeared to be six to twelve months of food.

"What do you think? Were these people preppers? Did they plan for the apocalypse?" Paul picked up a can of salmon.

"I bet they stocked up for the high season, made sure they had plenty of food for the winter months, maybe used their cash at the end of the previous year to stock up on things for next year. If they bought throughout the summer and kept things in here, they wouldn't have to worry about food prices or their winter cash flow as much. I don't know." Hank picked up a light blue can, turning the label to show Paul. "Do you really think preppers would stock high end organic broth? People prepping for the end of the world are about utility, not gourmet." Hank was impressed with the quality of the ingredients. He was also excited to see meat and fruit. He had eaten enough soup and instant rice for a while.

"Look at the pastry section; flour, yeast, sugar. I am making bread tonight, oh man, I haven't had a piece of bread in three months." Hank pointed at the dry goods shelves with excitement. He grabbed a box of pancake mix. "Hey, how about pancakes? Let's do pancakes!" He was as giddy as a little kid. It was a wild Maine blueberry pancake mix. "We don't have eggs, but we can do without eggs. Oh man, real syrup, pancakes. Being stranded with you might not be so bad." Hank's mood changed again. He was no longer scared and trapped. He had warmth, shelter, food, and companionship.

"Ummm, okay, you're scaring me a little. Are you really that fired up about blueberry pancakes?" Paul was excited to find the food, but Hank's enthusiasm bordered on maniacal. "You're acting like you haven't eaten real food in months."

"I haven't!" Hank shouted back. He left the pantry in search of a bowl to mix his pancakes. "Pull out that mini solar radio thing. Let's get some music going. I want a full belly before I think about being stuck in Rutland, Vermont for the next four months." Hank, having found a bowl, opened drawers looking for measuring cups.

Paul tried the door next to the pantry and found steps that led to a wine cellar and additional food, including cured meats and cheeses imported from Italy and France. The Rutland Inn was a jackpot.

Hank was right about the owners. Their names were Steve and Nicole. Running the B&B was their second career. They left lives in academia at the ages of 50. The Inn catered to skiers in the winter and leaf peepers in the fall. Each spring they used their cash to purchase food throughout the summer months, whenever high end items were on sale. The couple took in a few boarders in the spring and summer months, but mostly prepared for the high season of October through April. Every July and August Steve and Nicole closed the Inn and travelled to Europe. They did not make it back to the U.S. this trip, dying in a Venice hotel from the rapture one day apart. No one thought to loot a three star bed and breakfast on a busy street in Rutland. The Inn remained untouched until Paul and Hank stumbled into the front door that December, a door left unlocked by the friend who was collecting packages, fliers, and newspapers. Rutland was a safe town. People seldom locked their doors anyway.

The blueberry pancakes were Nicole's favorite brand. Hank and Paul would never know the story of the people who saved their lives in Rutland that winter. They would never know that Nicole taught psychology at Indiana University, while Steve taught English Literature at the local community college. No one was alive to remember how Steve declined repeated offers to teach at several Universities, believing community colleges filled an educational void when state colleges decided to compete with private universities for money and rankings. Nicole was a trained pastry chef. Steve was a triathlete. Their story was gone, like billions of other stories taken from the world in just five short months by a disease no one saw coming or had time to understand. Steve's favorite picture of the couple hung in the lobby, taken as they stood on the steps of a random old building in Italy.

Hank and Paul sat at one of the tables in the dining area. The fire was going strong. They were comfortable in pants and long-sleeved shirts. Their empty pancake plates in front of them as they looked outside at the snow.

"We're not going anywhere today." Paul said, breaking their silence. "I'm tired. Let's enjoy the day at the hotel. We have food. We're 50 miles from Hanover. I say we take a break. I'd like a break. I've been stressed out and planning crap for months. I want a day off."

"You know what? I agree. I might research the area with the maps and guide books from the lobby desk, but you're right. Let's enjoy the day." Hank sipped his coffee. "When was the last time you had coffee? It's been three months for me. Man, I miss coffee."

"Seriously? It's only been three days for me. I had coffee the morning I rode up to see you. Not all of us lived in a hole in the ground for two months. Actually, I lived quite nicely. I had food and music. I read books. I was lonely and bored, but I had coffee and some of the finer things in life to keep me comfortable."

"Asshole. I didn't have coffee. I drank dirty water most of the time. It was purified, but it had dirt in it."

Paul stared at his brother, "I'm sorry about your family, Hank. I'm sorry I wasn't there to help."

"You lost too, Paul. We both lost everything. I won't forget, but I have to move on." He took another sip of coffee. "I cried a lot. I still hurt, but I have to fight forward."

"Yeah, I know. " Paul nodded and looked down at his feet. "So," he said, looking back up. "Why, exactly, were you living in a hole for two months? What the hell were you thinking?" Paul was dying to ask Hank the question for the last three days, but they never had the time to talk. Riding motorcycles tandem across the country was not conducive to long conversations.

"I was trying to lose weight. If I had stayed in my house, like you did, I would have continued to live my unhealthy lifestyle. Think of my hole as a self imposed eating intervention." Hank's wry smile emphasized his sarcasm.

"I'm all for the new trimmer Hank, but seriously, were there government roundups in Dayton or something? Was the military patrolling? What's up?" Paul did not have issues in Cincinnati. His house was off the beaten path. Hank's house was two blocks from a hospital, next to a school, near a highway, near stores. Hank was not downtown Washington DC, but his house was more conspicuous than most.

"You know the golf course was my social network, right?" Hank started.

"Yeah, and a few work people." Paul replied.

"Yeah, but work was pretty far away. When all the crap hit the fan, I was in Dayton. There were five of us that weren't getting sick. Panic was pretty much everywhere. Cell phones still worked. The five of us would keep in touch." He paused. "The girls were sick. I spent my time caring for them, although as you know, there wasn't much to do. They didn't eat anything, or hardly anything, and they weren't uncomfortable. I was more or less just spending time with them, trying to nurse them back to health, keep them alive for a cure. Enjoying my last days with them." Hank sighed.

"Anyway, I would keep tabs on my friends, who was sick, who was already dead, what people planned to do. Like I said, there were five of us that were healthy, or at least five of us that weren't sick yet. We were conferencing in with each other, three of the guys hadn't eaten in a day or so, but they didn't have fevers. They were telling us they were okay, just not hungry from all the excitement and worry. I knew they were dead, I'm sure they knew too, but you tell yourself whatever you need to tell yourself to get up the next morning." He took another sip of coffee.

"So Fritzie is one of these five people, and we're all on the phone together. He is talking about how he is eating, he's not sick, he's been out and about recently, went to one of the government meetings going on every night. He asked me to go, but I stayed home with the girls. He said they had scanners you walked through when you came into the hall, checking body temps, seeing if anyone was contagious. He is literally the only person that pops a 98.6, everyone else is 100 degrees or more. He was laughing about it to us, how funny it was." Hank set his cup down.

"He's on the phone and his doorbell rings. He slips his phone into his pocket. The rest of us can hear what's happening. We hear him answering the door. I'm screaming, don't answer the door, hide, run, don't get the door, but he ignores my screams. All we hear is him saying 'yes officers' and then we hear a scuffle and the phone is dead. He was gone."

Paul looked at his brother. "You're kidding."

"I waited for the girls to die. I buried them. I burned the house. I was nervous about talking on the phone with all of you after Fritzie was taken, but I had to know the plan. I had to know where to go."

"I can't believe the government, as desperate as it was, would snatch people up like you describe. It had to be something else."

"I went to his house a day later, late at night, like some fat ninja dressed in black sweats. His front door was still open and his cell phone was on the ground, smashed. You believe what you want to believe, but I know what happened. I crawled into a hole I made for myself and drank muddy water for two months. It was a better alternative to being grabbed by the Feds."

"Did you hear the stats on how many they thought would live?" Paul asked. "You had a radio, right? Something to stay connected?"

"I monitored the broadcasts a little. I tried to make my batteries last. I didn't have the radio on all the time."

"They theorized that one out of every million people was immune. Some of the immunologists thought maybe no one, but finally estimated 300 people might survive in the US. If the government was able to find a few of these people, I wonder if those unlucky people survived the government. How crappy would it be if your buddy was immune to the rapture, but died locked up in a government facility?"

"You don't have to ask me. You know my answer. I holed up, I listened to the radio every once in a while for an hour or so. When I found dead air for a few weeks in a row, I came out of my hole. I didn't bury my family in the dead of night behind my house, like some criminal, to end up getting prodded and poked by government doctors." He picked up his coffee and cradled the warm mug in his hands.

"You know why I think they had those meetings? Those handouts or information sessions?" Hank continued. "I've had two months to think about this stuff, so if I sound crazy, well, maybe I am a little crazy. Anyway, I think the government lost so many smart people, and the technology companies shut down so fast, the Feds didn't have the capability to monitor cell phones or regular phones or email or anything. They were so short staffed, and the people left were probably so dumb, the Feds had to trick people like Fritzie into outing themselves. The community meetings were a ruse concocted to find healthy people." Hank shook his head. "Poor bastard, who knows if

Fritzie was really immune. There weren't a million people in Dayton. If I lived, the odds both of us played golf together and were immune? Whatever. Damn Feds. I didn't like them before the whole thing happened, I certainly don't like them now."

Hank finished his coffee and stood up. "Look who lived and look who died. I win. Let's focus on the future, not the screwed up past. What does this town have to offer? I think we need to find snow shoes and warmer jackets. Not today, but after our day off." Hank walked over to the front desk and looked for pamphlets or a town guide. He opened the desk drawers and pulled out a Rutland yellow pages. "Look at this!" Hank held up the floppy book for Paul to see. "Internet my ass, right?"

Paul laughed. "Internet my ass."

"Do you think we can find a couple of snowmobiles in this town? How far can a snowmobile go on a tank of gas? Can it get to Hanover?" Hank had the yellow pages opened to 'S.'

Paul could tell this was Hank's first coffee in two months. His brother was wired.

"If we find a dealer, I'm sure it's on the specs." It appeared their day off was fast becoming less of a day off than Paul wanted.

16

Todd and Emily played catch with their sons in the cul de sac on October 1st. A football was thrown between kids and parents. They had not heard or seen another living person for months.

Raleigh was dead. The government pulled out when the pandemic spread to other cities and towns. Scientists needed survivors. Raleigh did not have any that they were aware. Healthy people evacuated in July, and the residents who stayed were dead the same month. The power went off in September.

Todd went on regular patrols, usually at night, sometimes during the day. He had not seen a sign of life in the last eight weeks. He went in homes, took food, water, soft drinks, and supplies. He never saw a living soul. He did not see smoke from fires. He did not hear machinery or cars. Todd was positive he and his family were the only people alive in Raleigh. He knew for weeks, but he kept Emily and the kids safely confined to their house.

The looting and rioting that plagued the rest of the U.S. was not present in Raleigh. People fled or died before panic began. Todd found provisions and helpful items at malls, supermarkets, and warehouse stores. He acquired a solar generator and solar powered lights. He had gas generators for cloudy days and cold evenings. He had boxes of batteries, a dozen propane tanks, and more fire wood than he could use in two years. He had ten rain barrels running along the side of his house, and another ten on his neighbor's house to catch water. Todd and his family were outfitted for the upcoming winter. There was not a single item he or Emily could imagine they would need that he had not already found and brought back to the house, except, of course, other people and something to occupy their time.

Todd could not alleviate the boredom. Emily was becoming a caged animal in the house, wild from not being able to go about her normal routines or leave her neighborhood. She was a social person, much more than Todd. Emily craved friendship, companionship, and excitement. Before the rapture she was in two book clubs, had regular lunches with three of her friends, and was a fixture at her kids' school as a board member of the PTA. She also worked full time as a senior partner for a risk management firm.

Todd was happy seeing only his family and remaining at home. Emily needed to be on the move. Her type-A personality was stifled by the lack of stimulus.

"I want to go today." Emily did not whine, she stated her argument. "You promised if we did not seen anyone by today, and it was sunny, you'd take me." Emily had ideas about how she could become 'unbored.'

She threw the ball to Jay, and continued to plead her case. "Let's all go downtown and we'll just try the front door. If you want to stay here, fine, the kids and I will go, or maybe I will go alone, and you and the kids can stay here." She was determined. Todd knew he could not contain her, not after two months of sequestration in their house and yard with only a few trips around the neighborhood and surrounding areas.

"Fine, fine, I give." Todd held his hands above his head in an expression of surrender.

"Yea!" Emily cheered and high-fived her children. "We'll pack some snacks, drinks, and go in a little while."

Brian, 7, was supposed to be attending 2nd grade. Jay, 6, should have been in 1st. Emily used her energy to home school the kids, splitting lessons between reading, writing, math, and survival training. The kids learned how to read, and they learned how long to boil water before they could drink it. They learned how to use fire without getting burned, while also learning how to add two digit numbers. Emily alternated between one day of school and one day of fun. She did not have to comply with a traditional calendar. She did what worked for her and the kids. Todd brought a whiteboard home from the nearby office supply store along with several hundred boxes of markers in a multitude of colors.

Today was a day off from school. Emily was tired of staying in the neighborhood. Raleigh was known for its wonderful parks, one of which, Pullen Park, was downtown and had a gas powered train ride, paddle boats, and playground equipment. She wanted to take the kids on an outing. She wanted the kids to see the governor's mansion, both inside and out, and visit the local library for more books. Todd kept her at bay for a few months, but today was her day to break free.

Todd gave Emily a small pistol to keep in her pack. He slipped a large caliber pistol in his and off they went. They drove a hybrid SUV before the rapture, and saw no reason to upgrade.

One of Emily's favorite things to do before the world ended was touring homes. She loved to attend open houses or go on home and neighborhood tours. It fulfilled her curiosity into how other people lived, and gave her ideas about how to decorate and coordinate her own home. Suddenly every home in the country was open for a tour. She walked through as many as she could in her neighborhood, and most of the surrounding neighborhoods, only venturing into homes that had a "V" painted on the driveway.

Emily was not weird about touring homes. She understood the horror that preceded her opportunity, but she was bored. She rationalized her sojourns by assuming the identity of an anthropologist. Raleigh was a snapshot in time. The hasty evacuations and lack of looting left homes in pristine condition. Emily walked through houses and enjoyed how people really lived in them. She did not steal from the homes, and she was not looking for decorating ideas. Emily approached the homes as shrines or museums to a dead world.

She wanted to tour the governor's mansion for years, having seen pictures of it in a North Carolina magazine. She had a few other places she wanted to check out too, homes that always caught her eye when she drove by, or homes featured in local magazines and newspaper articles.

Todd suspected they would be taking "side stops" on their trip to and from the park. They had plenty of food and water for the day out. The weather was clear and warm for October, and he felt like the family might enjoy a normal day, or at least a day outside of the neighborhood.

Pullen Park was twenty minutes away. One habit that Todd could not shake, even after months of driving on empty streets, was observing the speed limit. He might drive a few miles per hour faster, but if the posted signs read 45 m.p.h., he stayed within that range. He wasn't sure if the habit stayed with him because he had been driving for so long, or because he trusted that the signs were the proper safety speeds. He assumed he would not be driving much past this winter, unless they found an oil well and a person who could refine oil into gasoline.

Their hybrid SUV used batteries at lower speeds. Fuel was abundant, but Todd still conserved when possible. The process to siphon gas from other tanks was time consuming and dirty. He drove slowly down the road towards the park. The windows were down. His arm rested on the open frame.

Jay and Brian were ecstatic to get out of the neighborhood. While Emily ventured on house tours, and Todd explored the town for safety and scavenged for food, the two boys had not left the cul de sac or backyard for three months. A television show played on the car entertainment system, but the kids ignored the media and opted for the view outside of the car window.

"Where is everyone?" Jay asked. "Is it Sunday morning or something? Why are there no other cars?"

Todd and Emily looked at each other. Three months of telling the boys that people were "gone" and their friends were "not around anymore" was obviously not specific enough. The 6 year old could not grasp the idea that everyone was dead. It was difficult enough for Todd and Emily to comprehend.

"Honey," Emily started. "We talked about this. Everyone is gone. Remember watching all of the cars leave that day you were sick? Remember watching the television and hearing about how everyone was getting sick?"

"Yeah, but everyone?" Brian responded with amazement. "I just thought maybe they all left for a while, and were coming back. You mean everyone is dead? You think Charlie is dead too?" Charlie was Brian's best friend at school.

Todd stopped the car and placed it in park. He turned around to look at his sons. "Guys, I don't know if everyone is dead, but they probably are. I'm sorry if Mom and I were not clear about this, but it's one of those times that parents try to protect their kids from bad stuff. I know two months ago your cousins and Uncles were alive. If we are alive, and they are alive, maybe other people survived too, but no one here in Raleigh did. I've been around the city for the last month, up and down streets, blasting music, yelling for people, there isn't anyone alive that I can find."

There was a quiet moment as the boys processed the information. They were sad, but they seemed to understand and process the information.

"So the power is never coming back? We're never going to have TV again?" That was the response of a 6 year old.

"No, probably not. It depends on who survived and if anyone who survived knows how to fix things and get electricity going again. As for TV, well, we can use it sometimes, we have power for that, and Mom and I have all the DVD's for all the shows we could find, so we have like 50 years of TV to watch."

"Can we just go to the park? I want to feed the ducks." Jay was not a patient child, particularly when the discussion was topics about death and not having TV.

Todd turned around and started downtown. He spoke over his shoulder to the boys.

"Mom wants to go on a house tour, do you want to go before or after the park?"

"Seriously? We get out of the house for the first time in like 10 years and we have to do a house tour? Really?" Brian was 7 going on 13. His cheeks were wet with tears, but his sadness was quickly replaced with outrage.

"We can drop Mom off at the house and go to the park ourselves. She could call us when she's done, and we will come back and get her, or she can walk over." Todd was not interested in the house tour either.

"Now it's my turn to say 'seriously'?" Emily looked at Todd, who stared at the road instead of making eye contact. "You want to leave your wife alone in a dead city? That's how you want to play this?"

"Do you want time to enjoy the mansion, or do you want the 15 minutes you will get if we all come? I can drop you off, use the long range walkie-talkies, let me know if there is a problem, everyone has a fun afternoon. There's a bike shop downtown, just grab one of the bikes from the store and pedal over. It's like three miles. You have protection in your bag, the mace or the other thing."

"Oh, I can do this, I know that, but I am letting it sink in that you would rather drop me off, abandon me, alone in the city, than do a house tour with me." Despite her complaining, Emily knew Todd was proposing the best solution. She was not worried or scared, she milked the situation as much as possible.

"Looks like we are dropping Mom off!" Todd said excitedly to the boys.

"Yay!" They both yelled.

"I just want to make sure you do one thing for me." Emily said to Todd as he drove.

"What's that?" Todd asked, looking over at her.

"I want duck for dinner, so after you feed them, they feed us."

"I am way ahead of you." Todd said with a smile.

The kids settled into a TV show in the back seat and did not pay attention to the last exchange. Todd and Emily grinned as they drove the rest of the way downtown in silence. They pulled up to the governor's mansion within ten minutes.

"Okay, it's 10am, do you want us to meet you back here at noon? We can go to Marbles Kids' Museum as long as we're down here." Todd wanted a plan to get him away from the outdoor park in a reasonable amount of time.

"Let's do this. I will meet you in front of Marbles on the square at noon. I'll call you on the walkie-talkie if I need to get picked up sooner, but plan on being there for lunch. The kids can play in Marbles after lunch." Marbles Kids' Museum was a large indoor amusement area. Emily was not sure how much light would be present without electricity, but they would give it a try.

Emily opened her door and got out. She walked to the back of the SUV to get her backpack. Todd met her at the trunk.

"There isn't anyone here, but be careful. You have a gun. As long as it isn't me or the kids, I don't care if you shoot anyone. Seriously, kill them if you have to. I want to make sure you are safe when I come around the corner at noon." Todd helped Emily put on her pack, before giving her a hug and a kiss.

"There is no one left to kill. I'll be okay. Don't let the kids get hurt. We don't have an emergency room to take them too. I'll see you in two hours." She spun around and walked towards the mansion's gate. It was closed but not locked. The iron hinges creaked when she swung the doors apart.

Todd got in the car, clicked on his walkie talkie and pressed the button. "Testing."

Emily's voice crackled two seconds later. "Works fine. Love you."

"Love you too." He put the car in drive and pulled away. The kids watched their video, oblivious their mother was gone from their sight for the first time in three months.

Emily watched Todd and the boys pull away from the curb. "Okay," she said to herself. "You're on your own now." She walked up to the door of the mansion. There was a large knocker and a doorbell. She lifted the knocker several times, letting it fall heavily onto the door with a loud thump. She yelled "hello, is anyone home?" She ignored the doorbell. There was no electricity. After five drops of the knocker she tried the door. It was locked.

Emily knew the mansion was vacant. The Governor fled Raleigh at the onset of the epidemic, moving to her western residence in Ashville, announcing she would govern the state from there until a cure was found and she and her family could safely return to the capitol. The staff evacuated as well.

Emily walked around the mansion to try other entrances before she broke a window. She went back down the fronts steps and turned to her left. She noticed a carport on the left side of the building, and thought the service door might be unlocked. Emily looked at the grounds as she made her way to the second entrance. What was once beautiful and manicured was now overgrown with weeds and out of control. Vegetation grows quickly in North Carolina. Without weekly weed control and pruning the mansion gardens and grounds were ruined.

She arrived at the carport and turned the knob. "Success!" she said aloud as the door pulled open. She stepped into the mansion's mudroom. She peered through the door on the other side of the small vestibule. She could see a sitting room on the right and a dining room to her left. The house was dim, but not dark enough to need a flashlight. Built in the late 1800's, before electric light, its windows were large and illuminating.

Emily opened the door on the other side of the mud room and was met by a funk so powerful she questioned whether she could continue. Not only was the stench repugnant, she was not keen on the prospect of stumbling into rotting corpses. She stood in the doorway for a moment. The smell was different than decomposition. She smelled bodies in her travels during the last month. Rotting corpse was an easy smell for her to recognize. The mansion smell was more a combination of rotting food and poop. Emily imagined a huge diaper pail left overflowing during the evacuation.

A refrigerator left open or food left out would account for half of the smell. While hard to believe rotting food would continue to smell for the three months since the mansion was abandoned, Emily guessed it was possible.

The poop smell was a mystery. "A sewer backup?" She asked herself.

"I'm here. I can't let a little odor stop me. If nothing else, I'll open a few windows as I go." She pressed onward, walking into the sitting room on her right. It was decorated in uncomfortable Victorian furniture, leaning heavily on style over substance. "I wouldn't want to sit in this room too long, or try to enjoy a movie or television on the furniture." She mumbled. It was beautiful furniture, but the straight backs and high arms were unwelcoming. The first floor was designed for State dinners and receptions not comfort. If the first family of North Carolina wanted to host a Super Bowl party, they would have a room full of sectionals rather than ottomans and ornate sofas.

Emily spent several minutes touching the furniture, sitting on the couches and chairs, examining the lamps and artwork, but her tour was rushed. She could not ignore the stench. She walked to a window, pulled the pane open, and stuck her head outside for fresh air.

"Maybe I can get a crosswind." She thought. She pulled her head back inside and walked towards the dining room on the other side of the hall. She was between the sitting room and the dining room when she heard the scratch.

She froze, standing motionless in the hall for what felt like an hour before she heard it again, another scratch. The sound was nearby.

It came again from the left side of the house, and appeared to emanate from the dining room. Emily unslung her pack and took out her mace. She looked at the gun sitting at the bottom of the open cavity next to a bottle of water, as if it were natural to carry water, mace, and a gun for a tour of a governor's mansion. She was staring at the gun when she heard the scratch again. She pulled the pistol out and held it in her left hand. The mace was in her outstretched right hand for immediate use.

She took a step into the dining room. It was magnificent. A gorgeous chandelier hung from the ceiling over the most beautiful table and chairs Emily had ever seen. The dining set was probably made by one of the many furniture artisans of North Carolina. There was an enormous fireplace on the left wall. Emily imagined heating the room on cold winter nights in 1895 with a roaring fire. Between the portico Emily was standing under and the fireplace in the far corner was a door. It was a swinging door. Emily could tell from the hinges. Emily heard the scratch again and saw the bottom of the door move towards her ever so slightly. The smell was stronger as she stepped in the room and towards the door. She looked at the top of the door and saw a bolt locking it shut from her side. Whatever was making the scratching sound was prevented from getting through the door by the bolt.

"Okay, what should I do?" She thought to herself. "It can't be a person.

A person would break a window or get out some other way. If it's a raccoon or squirrel or whatever, well, I don't feel like getting rabies and dying myself. The best thing to do is probably leave the house." Her right hand remained straight in front of her with the pepper spray pointed at the door.

She heard a whimper and another scratch. It was not the hiss of a raccoon or opossum. It was the whimper of an animal that needed help and knew the sound of human feet.

Emily hesitated. She placed the pepper spray on the table, took her pack off, and returned the gun. She picked the spray up as another scratch hit the door. "Whatever it is, the pepper spray will work." She told herself. "I'll slide the door open and see what's back there. Bad animal? Pepper spray. Nice animal? Well, I'll figure it out."

Emily pulled a chair from the table, positioning it for a quick jump up. If the mace did not work, she would leap onto the chair and then the table.

She put her hand on the bolt at the top of the door and slid it down.

A final scratch pushed the door open slightly. Emily grabbed the edge and pulled the swinging door towards her.

The smell was incredible. Feces and rancid food flooded her nose. She was almost knocked back, but she kept her eyes open and the pepper spray at the ready. Lying on the ground was a dog. It was almost dead, its ribs showing as it breathed shallowly. It lay on its side inches from the swinging door. Emily knelt down and looked at the poor creature. It was a white bulldog. She guessed it was a beautiful specimen before being locked in a room for months. She looked into the kitchen and saw a once majestic room completely destroyed. Animal excrement covered everything. The dog managed to pry open a pantry door left slightly ajar. It pawed cupboards and ate all the food it could find.

Emily stepped over the dog to find a bowl. The kitchen's cabinets were glass front. "How can people keep their shelves this orderly?" She mused as she found a pasta bowl. She walked back to the poor animal and stroked its head. "It's okay," She paused and looked between the dogs legs "boy. Here is some water. You're okay now. You're okay." She went to her pack for a bottle of water and poured some on the dog's mouth. It licked the air. She moved the dish towards the licking tongue. The dog caught on quickly. It was too weak to sit up, but it lifted its head slightly to drink.

"That's right, drink the water. I'll find you some food." She looked for canned food fit for a dog. The smell was beginning to get to her, and she frantically opened doors looking for the pantry. She found two cans of salmon, and after flipping open three drawers she found a can opener. Emily grabbed several bowls from the cabinet before walking out the dining room. The bulldog stopped drinking and lay on its side.

Emily went outside. She breathed in deeply. The fresh fall air cleared her nose and rid her mouth of the horrendous taste associated with the kitchen. She regained her senses, opened the can of salmon, and dumped it into a bowl. She filled a second bowl with water.

She took a deep breath of the fresh air before walking back into the mansion to the dog. Its eyes were closed and it panted slowly. "You're okay big fella, don't worry, you're okay." She stroked its head. Emily had to pick up the dog and take him to the food. It needed to be out of the foul air and in the sunshine and fresh fall day. The problem was the dog was covered in crap. It was literally covered in its own feces and rotten food. Emily was not a priss, nor did she want to pick up a poop covered dog, soiling her clothes and hands in the process.

She looked for a tablecloth or towels, something that she could wrap the poor dog in and shield her hands from the gook that covered him. Nothing was in sight.

She walked back to the Victorian sitting room and spied a throw. She grabbed what was probably a priceless cashmere blanket and returned to the dog. His eyes were still closed. She gently put the edge of the blanket against its back, grabbed its legs, and rolled him on the blanket. Emily pulled the blanket across the hardwood, sliding the dog gently out of the kitchen and into the dining room. She shut the swinging door to block the smell. She leaned over and picked up the blanket wrapped dog, taking him to the food and water bowls. The dog opened his eyes and did not struggle.

She gently placed the dog on a mat by the backdoor. She pulled the bowl of salmon next to his face, pinching a piece of fish in her fingers and placing it next to the dog's mouth. The dog opened his mouth and chewed weakly. Once the fish was in his mouth his eyes opened wide. He put his face in the bowl of food and ate quickly. The fish was gone in a few seconds. Emily was afraid another can would make the dog sick, particularly on his empty stomach. She pushed the water bowl into the salmon bowls place and the dog drank. He finished the bowl of water before looking up at Emily.

"That's enough for now buddy. Let's get you over to the museum, see if they have water pressure and maybe we can get you another drink. You are definitely taking a bath to get that funkiness off of you." The dog tried to get up, but he was too weak. It lay back down. His legs wobbled as he tried to stand again before collapsing a second time.

"I got you big guy, don't worry, I got you." Emily reached down and picked up the dog. It should have weighed fifty pounds or more, but he was at most twenty five. The fish gave the dog some energy, not enough strength to walk, but the salmon put a light in his eyes. Bulldogs do not have tails. This dog had a little nub that Emily could see moving back and forth. The dog was happy.

She slipped the water bowl into her pack, put the pack on her back, and leaned over to pick up the dog. She kept the throw between herself and the nastiness.

"It's not far, I can carry you." Emily said to the dog's face, "and even if that water is cold, you are getting a bath. Marbles has water stations where kids play. They are perfect for washing a little doggie like you." Emily spent a lot of time at the Marbles Kids Museum with her two boys. She knew the layout inside and out. She hoped she could find soap.

She made her way down the four blocks to the kids' museum, talking to her new pet along the way. She went to the corner of the museum that faced the park and the arranged meeting place with Todd and the boys. Emily put the dog on the sidewalk and turned to face the museum. She had little hope of finding an open door. The museum was locked up tightly. Emily contemplated which door to break and how to break it. The museum had glass doorways on three of its sides. The door in front of her, the main entrance, passed through a gift shop.   Emily remembered the gift shop had a chain link door separating it from the rest of the museum.   She and Todd attended a fundraiser at the museum, the gift shop was sealed off. She walked to the door, cupping her hands against the glass to peer into the shop. She saw the chain mesh on the other side. "I can't get through that." She said over her shoulder to the dog.

She decided to try a door on the side of the building next to the museum's garden. Not only was the door near the water stations and kitchen Emily needed to wash the dog, but there was a slight chance the door might be unlocked.

"Okay, I'm going to pick you up again, lil' buddy. One more time before your bath." Even in the fresh air the dog smelled. She bent down and picked him up, walking quickly around the building to the garden area. She held the dog away from her face, and walked through the dead garden to the side door. Emily saw the giant wooden pirate ship and submarine on the other side of the glass. She tried the door. It was locked.

Emily's other reason for selecting this door was the large rocks the garden staff used as decorative bordering. Emily put the dog down several feet from the door, "it's going to be loud, but it's okay."

She picked up a rock and threw it at the door. It did not go through the safety enforced glass, but it made a small hole and spider webbed the door. She picked the rock up and threw it again. This time the rock went through. Emily kicked the glass away from the frame.

"I'll find a broom and sweep that away from the pirate ship, don't worry." She said to the dog. She went through the door by ducking under the handle bar that went across the middle. She kicked the large pieces of safety glass out of her way and walked to the water stations she hoped to use for a dog bath. She could not find a knob or valve to turn on the water. "Damn it," she muttered. After a few minutes of futility, she opted for plan B, a kitchen sink. The kitchen was next to the pirate ship. It was an interior room, windowless, and pitch black.

She opened the kitchen door, and tested her flashlight to see if it gave her enough light to work. "Well, it's not ideal, but it will have to do." She was pleased to see the sink was a large enough for the dog. The sink's faucet sputtered, coughed built up air, and flowed.

"I win." She said softly. Emily looked in the cabinet under the sink and found dish soap. "And it's lemon." She put a stopper in the bottom of the sink, squirted soap, and walked outside to her new friend. She examined the glass door for a knob to open the lock, but it required a key on both sides. She ducked under the handle.

"Okay buddy." The dog had not moved. He was asleep and snoring. "This is going to be a harsh wake up." She picked him up, maneuvered through the door and under the handle, walked into the kitchen, and put the dog, blanket and all, into the sink of cold water. Emily rolled up her sleeves to minimize how dirty she would get, and rubbed the soapy water all over the dog. The dog was too weak to fight. He stayed in the sink and took the abuse.

There was a collar around his neck Emily refused to touch until now. It slid over the dog's head easily, a testament to how much weight the poor animal lost during his imprisonment.

Emily washed him three times, draining the sink with each bath. After the third bath she was happy with the condition of the dog. He was clean and almost fit to be in their car. He just needed to get dry.

She picked the wet and disgusting cashmere blanket off the floor and threw it into the trash. She sighed. "Your last use was a noble one, expensive cashmere blanket." Emily moved the flashlight around the kitchen and saw a metal storage closet in the corner.

"Bingo" she said as she opened the locker and found stacks of towels. She grabbed an armful and went back to the sink. The dog was asleep in the bottom. "You don't let a little adventure get in the way of your nap time, do you?" Emily whispered to him. She used two towels to dry him off in the sink. She spread other towels on the ground, gently picked the dog up from the sink and setting him on the ground. He slept as she rubbed him dry.

Emily let him sleep on the pile of towels. "Grab it while you can," she told him. "You're about to meet two young boys who will not leave you alone for the rest of your life." She looked back at the sink and picked up the dog's collar. She did not touch it directly. She used a towel to avoid the grime. The tag read: "Hubba; First Dog of North Carolina."

"I would have thought Georgia's first dog would be a bulldog, not North Carolina's. Shouldn't ours be a hound of some kind? Whatever, Hubba it is." She looked down at the snoring beast. "So, Hubba, my name is Emily, welcome to our family." Hubba continued to nap.

"That seems about right." Emily responded. "While you get some well deserved rest, I am going to see if there is some sort of stroller or cart I can use to move you around until we get home. You are a little heavy and damp to carry. Stay here." She chuckled at the idea of him moving. "I'll be back."

Emily took the flashlight and headed off to the rest of the museum. She needed options for transporting Hubba. There were toys in a big play area of the museum, a canvas postal bin her kids used for toy packages in a mailroom area, or toy shopping carts used in the supermarket area. Neither option was ideal, but both could work.

Emily hoped to find a better solution. She bypassed the play area for the front desk. She looked for strollers, but she could not remember if the museum rented umbrella strollers to parents. She was out of luck.

Emily peered through the metal door of the gift shop for anything that might be useful. There were a lot of toys, some snack foods and drinks, but nothing that would help her transport an enfeebled dog.

She went to the play area, resigned to the idea of the postal cart. The toy shopping carts were too low to the ground. Emily did not want to bend over as she pushed.

The first floor play space was enclosed by a four foot high wall used to keep children from wandering away. The entry door had a clasp at the top accessible to 'tall' people. Next to the entry gate was a short school bus. The bus was complete with a steering wheel and three rows of seats. The back was open and a slide flowed into the play space. Kids entered the bus door on one side of the wall, and slid into the play area.

"What the hell." Emily said. She walked onto the bus and slid into the large fun room. The walled area was enormous. There was a fire truck, a flat bottomed boat, a kitchen, a dress up area with a stage. Her two boys loved playing in the space for hours. The postal station was in the far corner from her. Emily walked through, stopping briefly to examine the once beautiful fish tank littered with algae and fish bones.

The mock postal room had a conveyor belt with rollers and fake packages. Children could fill a canvas bin with boxes by sliding the packages along the conveyor. Emily looked at the cart. It was deep and the bottom looked uncomfortable, but if she put blankets or towels in the bottom, it would work to transport Hubba. She grabbed the cart and rolled it towards one of the play space exits. She passed a puppet station. She stopped and put all the puppets into the bottom of the cart. She found stuffed animals from the story room and put them in the bottom. She ripped down the thick velvet curtains used on a small stage to lay across the top. The cart looked like a rolling royal purple pillow.

"A bed fit for the First Dog of North Carolina." Emily said as she approached the kitchen. Hubba was out of the kitchen and sleeping on the blue "ocean" carpet of the pirate ship. He snored in the sunlight.

"You seem to be doing okay for a dog that I found half dead an hour ago." Hubba opened one eye and lifted his head. He looked like he was happy. He put his head back down and started snoring again. Emily rolled the royal bed over to him, picked him up, and placed him onto the purple velvet. He didn't have the strength to stand up on the pillows. He stayed on his side, looking at Emily with his big brown eyes.

She checked her watch. It was 11:55. She walked to the kitchen to get her backpack. When she got back to the cart Hubba was laying on his stomach, arms stretched out in a Sphinx pose. He looked ready for the ride.

"Here we go, Hubba." She pushed the cart over the broken glass, under the metal arm, and out the door. She pushed him all the way down to the street, across the road, and to the park to meet Todd.

It was noon. The always punctual Todd pulled around the corner. Emily whispered into Hubba's ear. "Your life is about to change for the better."

Her husband rolled the window down. He raised an eyebrow at the dog sitting on a purple pillow in a canvas mail cart. Hubba looked like a large Chihuahua with a Bulldog face. His skin showed every rib. Screams came from the backseat "A dog, a dog, Mom got us a dog!"

Todd deadpanned. "We are both supposed to have input before purchasing a family pet."

"He came free with the mansion tour. You've always wanted a dog, and you know it. Let's make a stop at a pet store and get some food. Marbles will have to wait for another day. I want to get him home. He's pretty frail. "

"Did you give him a bath? He looks wet. Where did you find him? You know how crazy it is that you found a dog?" Todd was full of questions. Emily was not answering.

"Does he have a name, Mom? Can I name him? Can I?" Brian spoke excitedly.

"He does have a name. It's Hubba, and he is the First Dog of North Carolina."

"Hubba!" The kids yelled.

Hubba was scared by the screams. He backed towards the corner of the postal bin furthest from the screaming children.

"Okay, let's calm down. I'll tell you all about my adventure on the way home. The dog is scared, and weak, so you have to be quiet. I am going to hold Hubba on the way home so feels safe."

"Oh my god" Todd muttered, rolling his eyes. "A royal pillow cart and now you hold him on the way home? I just met the dog and he's already spoiled."

"That's enough out of you. Could you please get a towel out of the back that I can use to hold him?"

Todd retrieved a towel and gave it to Emily. He opened her door as she gently picked up Hubba and got into the seat with the dog on her lap. Todd closed the door for her. He walked back around and got into the car.

"I am excited to hear the story of how you were dropped off for a mansion tour two hours ago and end up with a clean, wet bulldog named Hubba."

"Before I start, did you all have a nice time?" Emily turned to face the boys.

"Dad killed three ducks, gutted them right in front of us. It was nasty." Jay said, scrunching up his face to show his disgust.

"There were a bunch of cars, so he was able to fill our tank with their gas, and fill the spare can on the back." Brian liked to talk about stealing gas, even though Todd and Emily explained that it was not stealing anymore. "He got the train to work too." The best part of their trip was relegated to an afterthought.

"The train works! That sounds like fun we can have many more times." Emily patted Todd's shoulder. He wore a smile of pride and accomplishment.

Emily paused before she began. She used her best story telling voice. "My adventure begins when I open the door to the governor's mansion. I was hit by a smell so bad I could barely breathe."

The car was riveted by her story, everyone but Hubba, who was asleep and snoring in Emily's arms the entire ride home. He did not wake up when Todd stopped at a pet store and loaded five 40 pound bags of food into the truck. The dog did not wake up when they pulled into the driveway of his new house. Hubba snored against Emily, his savior and new master, and dreamed happily about his new family.

17

Rebecca was exceptionally smart. She was thirteen years old and a senior in high school. Her genius was a gift and a burden. She did not attend school with children her own age. She studied at the local high school. Girls and boys her age were still in 7th or 8th grade.

She had eaten lunch by herself since she was five years old and identified as "gifted.' She did not mind not having friends in school. School was for learning, but not having friends after school and on the weekends was hard. Her parents convinced the school board to allow her to play 8th grade volleyball despite her high school status. Volleyball only got her close to girls her own age, not boys. She started to like boys when she was twelve, but she had a hard time meeting ones her age.

She had one semester of high school to complete, and was accepted to several universities with full academic scholarships for the winter semester. She was deciding on location more than institution. Did she want to be in Northern California? Did she want to stay close to home in Boston? Did she want to stay on the east coast in Baltimore?

Despite the big life decisions she had to make, Rebecca's mind was consumed with meeting boys her age.

She was a cute thirteen year old with dark red hair and pretty greenish/hazel eyes. She did not go through an awkward phase like many girls. She was average height with an athletic body, and developing into a woman in all the right places. She had confidence which showed through in her actions and personality. She sat alone at lunch, not because she was an outcast, but because she wanted to read, study, or think about her next steps. Rebecca had plans. She always had plans, and she made them happen for herself.

The one puzzle she could not solve was how to meet boys, cute boys her age, and it frustrated her. She had aspects of her life she could not control. She controlled her grades and her classes, but she could not control where she took the classes. High school was for older boys. She was young. She had no solution. After Christmas the problem would get worse. College boys were even older. Rebecca spent most lunches staring off into space, thinking about her boy problem rather than focusing on her studies.

When the plague struck Sao Paolo, Brazil in June, Rebecca knew it was trouble. She brought it up at dinner with her parents.

"Did you see all those people are sick in Brazil? It looks weird, like some sort of flu." Despite owning a local grocery store open until 10pm, Rebecca and her parents had family dinner together at least four nights a week.

"It's winter in Brazil, isn't it? Isn't that a different hemisphere? I'm sure it's just some winter flu epidemic." Her mother was a great 'mom' who always tried to calm her daughter's fears.

"That's pretty far away from here too, squirt. I'd be more worried about making the v-ball team this fall than a flu in Brazil." Her father was volleyball crazy.

"Dad, I bet this gets more press. Why don't we order some extra canned goods and bottled water, extra dry goods, dried fruit, jerky, those kinds of things. I bet people will want to buy survival stuff if the flu gets worse. We can always keep it in the storage basement if it doesn't sell right away."

"You have an opportunistic business mind, Rebecca. I'll put the order in after dinner." Her dad beamed at her with pride. He loved that his daughter thought about his business. He did not realize her ulterior motives.

Rebecca followed medical blogs and chats every night. She knew Sao

Paulo was not normal. Doctors could not connect the people who died. Their symptoms were odd. Panic alarms were going off in the private medical blogosphere.

Three weeks later Raleigh, North Carolina went through an outbreak. South America was a giant hot zone on the news station maps, Africa was a hot zone. Europe was painted with red circles. Asia had red circles. Rebecca stayed calm and followed the blogs and chat rooms. She wrote down the identified symptoms. She tried to figure out a pattern, a way to avoid the flu, or "the rapture" as it was being called. The news spoke of an impending cure. The internet said otherwise.

One night in July, just before the epidemic spread outside of Raleigh, Rebecca hacked into her favorite private medical chat room. It was populated with MD's researching the disease. Rebecca loved contributing when possible. She was reading the conversation when a virologist posted.

"Testing theory of 6-9 month dormancy, possibly year. If true, we're all dead." - S.P. Brazil

"Concluding same. need cure, not vaccine, all infected" – P. France

"Agreed. We are screwed." B. China

Rebecca knew one of two things would happen. Either she would die, or she would live while everyone else got sick. She had been different all her life, exceptional. She continued to make plans to survive.

The first symptom of the rapture was lack of appetite. It was the only indication of infection before the major symptoms of fever, lethargy, and euphoria began two weeks before or as little as five days before death. People focused on the fever because it was easy to diagnose. Rebecca wondered when a person lost their appetite. Was it when they contracted the disease? Was it a late stage symptom?

She had access to data, her family's grocery store sales. Sales could indicate a decline in food purchasing for the area and the onset of the disease. Her father did not share the store's sales volumes with her, but he did not password protect his computer either. She snuck into his office the day after she read the disturbing chat room posts. She pulled the last three months of sales. June was 10% lower than May. July was 15% lower than June. Not only did the sales figures explain her father's somber mood for the last two months, the numbers indicated most of the people in the area had the rapture.

Rebecca pulled up the last year of sales. July of last year the store had double the sales of this July. She studied the past twenty-four months. Two summers ago the store's sales grew each month from July through January, peaking in December. Holiday sales drove the increase over the last six months of each year.

Last July to August showed a small increase month over month until October. Sales were flat in November and December, and declined steadily each month after the new year. February showed a modest dip of 4%. March dropped 7%. April dropped 7.5%. May dropped 8%.

Rebecca attended advanced classes during the summer. It was technically 'summer school.' Most kids who attended had to attend. Rebecca did not daydream about boys during lunch anymore. She watched the other kids eat, except they did not actually eat. They talked and acted normally. Kids ate pudding or apple sauce. A bag of chips might be opened, but no one ate anything of substance.

Rebecca observed the same at dinner. Her mother made spaghetti and meatballs, but neither of her parents finished their plates. Rebecca ate all of her dinner. Her parents threw most of theirs away. Rebecca found Tupperware upon Tupperware in the fridge. Most of the previous week's meals were in plastic containers, untouched. Her parents, like the kids at school, ate enough to survive but not much more.

"Hey, Dad?" Rebecca said to her father, walking into his study later that night. He stared at the computer, most likely fretting over the grocery's sales numbers. He looked frail in the computer monitor light. Rebecca suddenly noticed how much weight he had lost.

He perked up when she came in the room. "What's up, squirt?" Her dad loved her. She could tell every time they spoke.

"Well, I was thinking about inventory at the store. I know I talked you into ordering more stuff, and I've noticed that you haven't needed me to restock too much lately."

He interrupted her. "Yeah, I think this flu thing has people scared to shop, but it will turn. I mean, people have to eat, right?"

She gave a laugh, which was fake, but the appropriate response to her dad's comment. "Yeah, that's what I mean. I know people have to come back in full force eventually. While it's a little slow, do you mind if I work through the expiration dates on the food, put the stuff that is closest to expiring upstairs, and move some of the further from expiring in the lock room downstairs? People are going to need food, a lot of food soon. I bet we can make this lull work to our advantage, move older inventory. I was thinking of raising the price a nickel on each item, something really small, but will help our bottom line."

The pride in her father's face was noticeable, and his smile was ear to ear. "If you want to do that, I think it's a great idea." He opened his arms, the universal sign for 'gimme a hug.' Rebecca ran over and jumped into his arms. She hugged him tightly.

"I love you, Daddy." She cried softly.

"I love you too, honey. I love you too."

Rebecca spent Saturday and Sunday moving inventory to the locked room in the basement of their store. She convinced her father to leave the upstairs shelves a little bare, a marketing technique to make people believe the store was running out of food. He loved the idea, and Rebecca moved more food to the basement.

One week later, the disease spread outside of Raleigh, and the store shelves were sold out. The first cases of the rapture hit Concord, N.H. on a Wednesday. Panic ensued and people flocked to the store for provisions. Rebecca and her father did not have time to restock their shelves. The market's staff did not show for work that day or ever again.

Rebecca's mother was at home, weak and feverish. Her father did not look much better. He hid his symptoms well.

Friday he was too weak to get out of bed.

Most of the people in Rebecca's subdivision fled. Where they went, she did not know. The houses on either side of her were empty.

Rebecca's parents were too sick to travel.

"We have an idea, squirt." Her father said as she brought soup to their bedside.

"Your mother and I want you to help us move to the Johnson's house. You can take care of us over there. They are gone, and have a much bigger television in the bedroom."

"Why don't I just bring the television over here?" Rebecca did not like the idea. She knew what her parents were doing.

"We can't steal their television, honey. Just move us over there. We're afraid you're going to get sick." Her mother smiled weakly.

Rebecca was usually good at separating emotions from practical decisions. She understood her parents did not want to die in the house and leave Rebecca to deal with two dead bodies. She got it, but Rebecca did not want to admit her parents were dying.

She also knew she would move out of their house once her parents died. The fireplace was gas. She could not depend on a gas fireplace.

"This is your house. You've lived here for fifteen years. You should stay here. I can go to the Johnson's, but only if I need to go there. You know what I mean. I don't think I'll need to go, but if I do, well, I'll move over there." Rebecca reached out to hold their hands. "Like you said, they have bigger TV's and I think they have lots of video games."

"What, you suddenly play video games?" Her father joked. Rebecca played word games or read on her handheld. She never played video games.

"With school closed, I might have to start, or I can just read. You know I like to read." Rebecca sat on the bed with her parents. They talked all afternoon, laughing, and enjoying each other's company.

The television broadcast awful stories from all over the world about military crackdowns and government roundups. The promises of a cure were quickly fading.

One week later Rebecca was still healthy.

"I have a feeling you knew all of this was coming, Squirt." Her father said softly. "I know you well enough to know you have a plan too, but let me say what I want to say anyway."

"I'll be okay, Dad. Don't worry." Rebecca held her father's hand. Her mother slept beside him.

"You put food in the store's basement weeks ago. You had me order the survival food. You are on top of this disease. You were more than a month ahead of everyone, like you always are, I know, but let me speak." He sat up in bed. Rebecca helped him place pillows under his back and neck. "Not many people are going to survive. I'm sure you know."

"I do, Dad. The number of survivors will be in the dozens, not hundreds or thousands. I won't have to worry about food or shelter." She sat with her parents every day, treasuring the last conversations.

"No, no, you don't understand, or maybe you do. Food and water will be abundant. Intelligence will be scarce. Genius will be coveted. You can't trust anyone. No one, do you hear me?" Her father tried to sound forceful, but he was too weak. "When you meet other survivors, and you will meet them, you cannot let them know what you are."

Rebecca giggled. "Dad, I'm not a robot. I'm smart, but whatever."

He squeezed her hand. "Promise me you will act like a thirteen year old and not what you really are. Survive, thrive, but keep your secret. You are the most valuable asset left in the world."

Rebecca's face grew serious. She dropped the fake persona she maintained to fit into society and not intimidate people.

"Dad, I know. Don't worry. I promise." Her green eyes fixed on him with a combination of pure intelligence and unwavering confidence.

He loosened his grip and continued to hold her hand. "I'm sorry we are leaving you alone." He reached out with his other hand and stroked her hair. "I love you, Squirt."

Rebecca's parents died one day before their 20th anniversary. They passed within an hour of each other. Rebecca moved into the Johnson's house before settling in the model home. The genius girl anticipated and planned for every aspect of the rapture except for one small thing.

The disease that killed her parents, destroyed the world, and took away everything in Rebecca's life delivered a cute boy her own age.

18

Greg and Rebecca were on their third day together.

Most of what Rebecca told Greg was true, she just framed all of her planning and ingenuity as her parents' ideas. By day three Greg realized there was far more to Rebecca than her being a bright or even very bright 13 year old.

"What grade were you in, you know, before all of this happened? I was a Sophomore, well, I was about to be a sophomore. I came up to school early to take some prep classes and attend baseball camp. Anything to get out of the South Carolina heat."

"I was a senior." She replied. Rebecca had a new rule. Never lie to Greg.

"What? You're only 13. Are you some sort of genius? Well, I can tell you are a genius, but are you one of those Doogie Howser type kids?" Greg was shocked she had not told him she was a senior.

"I guess, I mean, I was going to college after Christmas. Wow, it's weird to say 'was.' Even after all that's happened. I still think of college as a future thing."

"Where were you going?"

"I had yet to decide. I got in everywhere I applied. I think it's because I am a bit of a Doogie Howser, but I'm old enough to not be a freak. It's not like I'm 8, and colleges don't want me on campus because my parents have to stay with me. At 13 I can navigate college on my own. At least that's what I thought."

"Where were you leaning?" Greg had not thought about college or where he wanted to go. He had ideas, but his opinion changed monthly.

"Maybe you can help me decide. That could be a fun game for us."

"Well, right now I want to talk about you going to Dartmouth College with me." Dartmouth was in Hanover, New Hampshire, and Greg was anxious to get moving. Rebecca was resistant to leaving Concord. They would not split up the team. One of them had to give.

Rebecca folded the sheets on their couches. She folded every morning. Keeping her living area clean was important. She stopped folding and frowned. She wanted to stay with Greg at this house or possibly travel further south. She did not want to drive north in New England in November.

"We have to figure this out, don't we? You and I have to make a decision about what our next step is, whether we stay here for the winter or move, and if we decide to leave, where are we going?" She liked to lay out equations, if then statements when possible.

"My family is alive. They are coming for me. It was too crazy when I spoke to my dad, but when spring hits, he's going to come up to New Hampshire, my entire family is coming. I have three uncles and two cousins. If things calmed down sooner, they might be in Hanover now." Greg said this to her a dozen times in the last three days.

"Greg, I know this is hard to understand, but do you know how crazy you sound? You have to face reality. It's you and me and maybe a few other survivors somewhere else, but your family is dead. I'm sorry. I don't want to be mean, but you can't keep making decisions based on an idea that has no basis in reality."

"They weren't sick. I'm not sick. They lived, I know it. They are coming for me. They may be waiting for me up there. Either way, I have to get to Hanover."

"My parents died and I'm still alive. Surviving doesn't mean anything. Greg, they're gone. You said it yourself. Your mother was sick. You know that means the rapture was in your house. Think about part of what you just said. Do you really think they would stay in Hanover and not come to get you at school? That they would just wait for you up there? Come on, even you have to realize how crazy that sounds."

Rebecca was stuck. Greg was going to Hanover. She knew it. She was not attached to her current setup, but it made more sense than moving north to a small town in the middle of nowhere. She had food, water, wood, a fireplace. She knew the area. She could hunt or trap in the woods by the barn. She was comfortable, at least in the short term. Hanover was an unknown. Could they find appropriate shelter? How bad was the looting? Were supplies available?

She worked through the pros and cons of leaving her house, her safety net. If Greg was going to commit to a new life, he had to be convinced that his family was dead. The only way to convince him was to have them not show up in Hanover next year. Greg was now the most important thing in Rebecca's life. Staying with Greg superseded everything.

"Look, Rebecca…" he started.

"Shush, I'm thinking." She put her hand up to stop him from talking. She knew the facts. She was formulating an opinion.

"Did you just shush me and give me the hand? Are you serious?" He grinned. He had gotten to know her in the last three days, and he liked her, a lot. He was not in love with her romantically, but as a person, she was one of the best he had ever met. Rebecca was funny, practical, whip smart, and compassionate. When she held him by the barn during his meltdown, she had true empathy for him. Greg was weak when he arrived at her doorstep. Rebecca opened her doors to him. Gave him food. Shared her supplies. After three days together he trusted her implicitly. He would walk through fire for and with his new friend.

The shushing was new. She was forward with her decisions, Greg noticed, but she was never as domineering as she had just been.

"If we go, we have to go in the next two days. It's November. I don't know how there is not snow on the ground already. There might be ice on the roads to Hanover. Snow means we are stuck here until spring. We have to decide how we are going, which car we take, and what items we take. If we go, you and I have to realize, we're up there until May. Do you even know where in Hanover we are supposed to go?"

Greg could not believe she was agreeing to go. He was struck dumb.

"Are you kidding me? You don't even know where we are supposed to meet? Just 'Hanover'? It's a good thing you are cute, Greg Dixon, because you are not impressing me in the smarts department. Let's have some breakfast and start making lists. I guess we can just find a house when we get up there. I'm glad we aren't meeting your family in 'Boston' or 'New York City.'" She teased.

"What's with the one eighty on going?" He was finally able speak.

"If you say your family is going to be in Hanover in the spring, well, we have to be there. Now is the last chance we have to travel." She was lying, something she vowed never to do to him.

"I don't believe you, but I understand. We're not separating, and you know I have to go. It's okay if you don't believe my family is alive. I'll believe enough for the both of us. You get me up there and keep me alive until spring. That's your job. Don't let me do anything else stupid, like uprooting two people who are safe with ample food and shelter and move them to an unknown place based on an idea that is most likely insane."

"Let's make some lists." She said, looking at him and putting her hand on his shoulder. "I hope I'm wrong about your family. I'll keep you alive until the spring, and I'll try to keep myself alive too."

They smiled. In three short days they were best friends. Like two kids transferred to a new school at the same time, stuck in a place with no other friends, they bonded. They knew how lucky they were to find and like each other. Greg considered finding Rebecca to be the luckiest thing that had ever happened to him.

Greg moved the barn blanket hanging above the portico and stepped into the cold kitchen. It was his turn to collect eggs for breakfast. Their house had an six foot privacy fence around the backyard, but Greg was able to see a wild turkey two yards over. It was walking in the grass looking for food.

"Rebecca!" He yelled.

She came through the blanket door quickly. "What's wrong?" She was scared he saw other people, bad people.

"Look at that! It's a turkey. Do you think we can get it? I'd love to have fresh turkey."

"I do not think we can catch that turkey. First of all, despite what you probably think, that is a bird with wings that can fly away if we try to grab it. If you want to look very dumb, you can try to catch that bird. I'll make breakfast while you do."

"I specialize in looking dumb, particularly around you, smarty pants. I bet the breakfast dishes I catch it." He did not like being told he could not do something. He also felt dumb for thinking turkeys could not fly, though he did not admit it to Rebecca.

"Deal, and good luck. I am going to enjoy this." Rebecca went back through the blanket door to put on a sweatshirt. She wanted a front row seat for Greg's hunt.

Greg turned and went into the garage. He looked around for a hoe or scythe or something he could use to whack the bird. He settled on a hoe, but it was one that was hollow in the blade area. It looked like a metal trapezoid on the end of a long stick. Rebecca's father loved the tool. It broke up topsoil in his garden. Rebecca brought it over from her house to start a garden with in the spring.

Greg believed he could get the metal trapezoid around the turkey's neck and yank quickly to snap it. He might behead the bird altogether. Worst cast he would try to hit the turkey with the hoe. He was a baseball player and would use blunt force.

He thought about using a gun, the pistol from his pack. Rebecca had several guns too, but they were nervous about attracting other people with the sound. He considered throwing something heavy at the bird, a baseball bat or an axe, but he did not see such a tool available. Rebecca did not have an axe in the garage. She found all of her firewood already chopped. Greg wished he had a baseball or a lacrosse ball, but neither were available.

Greg needed to hurry. He held the hoe, practiced the snare and jerk, and decided it was his best option. The side door of the garage creaked open and he walked outside. It was cold. Rebecca was right. They had to leave this week or winter was going to make their decision for them. The garage door opened outside the backyard privacy fence. He walked towards the turkey, blocked by the fence until he got to the end of his yard where he could see the bird. It had not moved. It was pecking the ground, oblivious to him.

Greg took the obvious approach. He walked towards the bird slowly and steadily. When he was close enough, he would bring the hoe down on the bird's head. The turkey was about 25 yards away from him. It was big from the kitchen window, but even larger up close. Greg guessed it weighed at least 35 pounds.

He was five yards closer, walking slowly, nice even movements, five yards closer. The bird looked up., flapped its wings, and flew away.

Greg did not want to turn around. When he did, Rebecca was doubled over laughing at him through the window. She opened the kitchen door to get the eggs. "Now that, that was funny."

"Yeah, yeah, I'm a clown. At least I'm trying." He knew he looked foolish. He deserved the ridicule.

"That promise to keep you alive? It's going to be tougher than I thought." She laughed harder.

Greg laughed at himself as he waved her off. He walked back with his head down and his shoulders slumped. "Now we know there are turkeys near here. Maybe we can catch one." He thought to himself.

"I will clean up breakfast. Big man hunter no catch food." He joked loudly as he came through the kitchen door.

"I took it easy on you. We're doing soft boiled eggs for breakfast, no pan to clean. I sliced some of your bread from last night. I did not realize how much I missed bread, and I am still in awe of your bread making skills."

A pot hung over the fire. Greg saw six medium eggs cooking in the water. There were slices of bread waiting to be toasted. "I wish my turkey catching skills were half as good."

Rebecca made breakfast while Greg thought about catching a turkey.

"When did you know you were a genius?" Greg asked.

"I don't know, I mean, school has always been easy for me. I'm not a nerd. I'm a regular kid. I like the same things kids our age like. I just do well at school, and puzzles, and planning. If you want to know when everyone else realized, I guess it's when I was in kindergarten and I was reading Harry Potter, all of the Harry Potters in a week. There are a lot of kids that read books in kindergarten, but I was tested, and I skipped to third grade."

"I completed grades in about half the time. I couldn't skip the work. My parents were very adamant about making sure I read and did all the same work as other kids. I had to read the required books, and take the required exams. It created a time constraint to moving up in grades, but I was about to finish high school. This was my last semester. I was going to be done before Christmas, but I couldn't start college until a new term began." She looked at the pot as she spoke.

"I get the work wasn't hard. Was it hard being 13 and a senior? Has it been 7 years since you took classes with kids your own age? It must have been tough." Greg thought he understood. He felt out of the loop when he came back to Charleston after his first year at Hightower. He hung out with his brothers and family because his social structure was gone. It was one of the reasons he went to baseball camp early and returned to where he belonged.

"It's all I've known. I don't know if it was more difficult or not. School is hard socially, whether you are me going through what I had to deal with or you dealing with whatever you had to deal with. There are bullies and mean people all over. I might have been insulated more, adults paying special attention to me because I was younger. I don't know, I never had it different. You know what I mean?"

"Yeah, I know, school is rough no matter how you do it, same age group or advanced."

They sat in silence for a few moments before Greg asked another question.

"So why did you really decide to come up to Hanover? What was your thought process?" Greg liked the way Rebecca thought, systematically and logically. He was curious why she changed her mind about leaving their current location.

"You're right. I don't think your family is alive. I'm sorry, but it doesn't make sense. I hope they are, but I don't think they are." She stopped, the timer dinged to take the eggs out of the water. She used a slotted spoon to pull each egg out and put them in paper bowls. She would use the hot water to wash clothes later.

She placed the bread to toast on the wired rack sitting above the fire.

"Make sure I don't burn the toast while I'm talking, okay?" Rebecca asked. Greg nodded in response, though he knew she could multitask.

"I like our current digs." She continued. "But there are flaws in the location. This house is new. It's not colonial. We already modified it to trap warmth with the blankets. It isn't that cold yet. When the temps drop low, I have no idea how cold this house will get. It might get too cold for us to use. The homes in Hanover? There is as strong possibility we can find one much older, brick, set up for the extremities. We might find a woodstove, bigger fireplaces, bedrooms with fireplaces. We might improve our situation."

She flipped the bread and continued.

"I'd also like to find a place near water. We don't have water here. We were going to have to move in the spring. Why not make a move now? We can re-assess in the spring in Hanover. Eventually I think we'll end up somewhere other than New England, but if we are going to find out the truth about your family, we are going to stay in the north for at least the next 9 months, right?"

Greg nodded in response.

"I know you won't ditch me, but I won't make you suffer. If I know we are going to leave this house anyway and I have questions about its viability, well, it makes sense to leave this house now. Hanover seems to be a decent place. We'll have a river, lakes to fish, mountains to hunt. There are stores we can use to find things we might need. As long as we can get up there safely and we take all my food, I decided it was not only a viable option, it's probably the right option." She used metal tongs to take the bread off the toasting rack.

"Wow." Greg said. "I'll be honest. I thought you were going to say you agreed because I'm cute." He took his piece of toast from her outstretched hand.

Rebecca blushed. She did not expect his response.

"You keep your ego in check, Greg Dixon. We have a lot of planning to do, and being cute is not going to help you through a long Hanover winter."

He laughed, and cracked the eggs onto his toast. They sat across from each other. She was on the fireplace hearth while he sat on one of the couches. There was a coffee table between them. She mixed orange juice concentrate for them during his turkey hunt.

"Do we have a large truck? Did your store have a delivery van or anything like that?" Greg was not going to let Rebecca do all the heavy lifting with regards to the planning, although he knew she probably had their trip planned in her head. He was hoping to be more than just the "labor" part of the equation.

"That's not a bad idea. I left our van at the store. We can take all the food, and fit the chickens in the back along with of our blankets, bikes, that kind of stuff. The less we have to scavenge, the better, particularly in the short term. We want to be able to get our bearings for a few days before we have to start looking for supplies."

"My father told me to go to the house he grew up in, an old brick house. I know where it is. It has a wood stove and like four fireplaces. There is a pond right down the street." Greg took a bite of toast. "My family has a small cottage on another lake, but it's remote, way outside of town. We would be stuck if it snowed. It's winterized, sits on a lake. It has a woodstove that heats the entire place. If we had our food with us, it would work, but I'd rather stay in town." Greg was contributing for the first time. It made him feel good. He relied on Rebecca's work since arriving.

"Let's walk over to my old store, figure out what we want to take, and start packing up the van. It takes diesel, but the tank is full. Hanover is not far away. We will have enough fuel to get there and back here if something bad happens. Worst cast, we scavenge a vehicle up there.

I'm sure there are plenty of cars."

Rebecca pulled out a legal pad and started making a list of items she wanted to take.

"Could you put 'Greg' and 'Greg's backpack' on there? That has my contributions covered."

Rebecca smiled, but she was not amused. Serious things were serious. Joking while working was not her thing. She focused and got her jobs done. She knew Greg would get his work done, but probably not as quickly or as efficiently as she got her work done. Part of Rebecca's wiring made her serious.

Greg was focused and determined, but he was 14. He acted like a sophomore in high school. He made jokes, goofed around, procrastinated every once in a while. Greg was considered the serious one of his friends, his family, pretty much everyone he knew until he met Rebecca.

"You clean up. I'll keep working on the list. We know what we need. I'm making this so we can check things off when we put them in the truck."

Greg let her do her thing. He put the paper plates and plastic forks into a bag and walked out to the trash. It was a cold and gloomy day, classic weather for New England in November. It was well past the first frost. All the leaves were off the trees. Their newer sub-division had no trees and no leaves to rake. As Greg's eye moved towards the older neighborhoods he saw the yards and streets covered in browns, yellows, reds, and oranges that should have been raked, bagged, and picked up long ago. Tall grass poked through the leaves, evidence that the lawns were unkept before the leaves fell.

Greg turned to go back inside. He neglected to wear a coat, and the short walk outside gave him a chill. Rebecca was on the porch in her coat holding car keys.

"Now that I don't have to conserve fuel, let's take the car. It's not far to the store, but it's cold and I don't want to walk." She jiggled the keys. "I also need to practice my driving if I'm going to make it all the way to Hanover."

"Practice?" Greg replied in a tone that relayed question as well as concern.

"Just get your coat and let's go. We're burning daylight."

Greg did as he was told. He grabbed a coat, jumped in the SUV, and buckled his seatbelt. The garage door was closed. Rebecca sat in the driver's seat.

"Well?" She asked.

"Well what? I'm here, ready to go." Greg told her.

"I can press the garage door opener as many times as you'd like. It's not going to work. Could you please pull the garage open so we can leave? I mean, is chivalry dead?" She looked at him impatiently.

"Oh, yeah, hey, let me get it." He unbuckled and jumped out of the truck to open the door. When he was back in his seat he apologized. "Okay, sorry, now we're good."

Rebecca turned the key and put the small SUV into reverse. She slowly took her foot off the brake and the vehicle backed out of the garage. There was a small down slope to the driveway and the SUV picked up speed. Rebecca did not panic, but she did not respond quickly enough. She spun the wheel to turn the speeding car towards the store. She and Greg rocked to their side, out of control as the SUV spun. Rebecca slammed on the breaks and the teens whipped forward. Greg almost hit his head on the dash.

"Whoa." Greg blurted.

Rebecca maintained her composure. "Sorry about that. I'm a little rusty. To be honest, I'm also not that great a driver. Now you know the real reason we rode the bikes to the barn." She gave Greg a shoulder shrug before sliding the gearshift into drive and pulling her foot off the brake.

They jerked forward and backwards as Rebecca practiced her driving. The store was a mile away from their house. It was a good sized grocery, but not the size of the large box stores. Greg was reminded of the family owned marts that served island and beach communities up and down the southern coast, stores with six aisles, a meat counter, and basic items.

"I already took everything out of the store, we just need the van. It's pretty dark in there, or I would show you around. I used to work in it with my parents almost every day after school or volleyball practice. It's nothing fancy, but it made a living. My father loved feeding the community, talking to people about the local happenings. It was a great store." Greg looked for sadness in her voice, but Rebecca was happy when she spoke of her old life with her parents.

She parked the SUV next to the van, and walked over to the delivery truck. The keys were on the seat where Rebecca left them. A sofa cushion was propped against the back of the driver's seat.

"The seat doesn't move and I can't reach the pedals. Don't worry, I can drive it. I'm actually better at this truck than I am that SUV. It has less power. I don't jerk forward and back as much." She cranked up the van, told Greg to jump in, and they were on their way back to the house.

Rebecca was right. She was better at driving the van than she was the SUV. The progress was slow but smooth.

She backed the van against the garage, and they spent the rest of the day loading food, water, and a spare chicken coop into the back. A metal ramp extended from the bottom of the truck. Greg was strong enough to pull large dollies of goods into the back.

Greg convinced Rebecca there was a bike store and five or more camping/outfitter stores in the Hanover area. Food, animals, clothes, blankets and a few days of firewood were the only necessities. They worked quickly and had the van loaded by late afternoon.

They sat down on the hearth to enjoy dinner, Rebecca with her back to the fire, Greg on the couch opposite her. It was 6:30pm. The sun was down. They were ready to leave tomorrow, ahead of Rebecca's schedule.

"I'll miss my hometown, but I'm glad to be leaving. There are too many memories here. I need a new start." It was another reason she agreed to move to Hanover. Concord reminded her of her parents and how their bodies were in a house just a few blocks away.

"I don't think this is a mistake for team Greg and Rebecca, I really don't. If it doesn't work this winter, we'll figure something out before next season."

"You don't have to keep convincing me." Rebecca replied. "Let's eat our fried rice, get some sleep, and hit the trail tomorrow."

Greg improved the food quality substantially since his arrival. He made bread from the pantry ingredients to accompany their soup most nights. He made spaghetti with flat bread his second dinner. Tonight he used eggs for 'fancied up' packaged fried rice. He loved to cook. Now that he had ingredients and a frying pan, he could work his magic.

Rebecca was a utility eater. She took the path of least resistance to calories. Soup and cereal were staples in her diet. She enjoyed more involved meals. She just did not want to cook them.

It was hardly gourmet fried rice in front of them. Greg made a packaged fried rice mix, let it cool, and cooked eggs and dried chorizo sausage. He re-introduced the previously cooked rice into the proteins, stirred, and voila. It had good flavor and maybe too much heat. He was happy with himself. Rebecca was happy to not eat soup.

"Look, if you want to pass on the gin tonight, I totally understand." Greg said in reply to Rebecca's idea of going to bed after dinner. "I mean, you're down, well, a lot, and I wouldn't want to keep losing. Losing isn't a lot of fun. I've lost before, not to you, but in the past, and..."

"You're hilarious. Look, it's a card game, based on the cards I'm dealt, and the guessing of which cards to keep and throw. The skill level is very low. It's mostly luck, probably why you are so good at it." Rebecca did not like to lose, and she rarely did. Greg's teasing stung.

"Oh, okay, well, we can try luck some other night then. I didn't mean to get you upset or anything." He smiled. "It's not all the much fun to win all the time. Maybe a break would be best."

"You clean up your rice pan, I'll shuffle the cards. We are going to play until I win a hand."

"Wait, we have to get to Hanover before the first snow. How about we play until you don't lose so badly?"

That was the last straw.

"Just wash the pan before you become team Greg again, all by yourself, walking to Hanover in the dark with a backpack and cold cans of beans and franks. Actually, I still have that cat food."

Rebecca did not win until the seventh game. She still did not like to lose, but she enjoyed playing cards with Greg. His company was a fair trade for losing. Her worm would turn, and she would be the lucky one. At least she hoped her worm would turn. They clicked off their lanterns at 8:30, exhausted and excited for a new adventure.

19

The chickens were not excited to leave their coop. They had no choice, but they did not go quietly or nicely. Greg wore oven mitts to corral them into cages for the trip. He kept the mitts on to transport the cage to the van as the chickens pecked at him furiously.

The teens ate their eggs, cleaned up the living room, and left a simple and informative note on the door;

Two people, alive on November 19, heading to Hanover, N.H.

Highway 89 North is breathtaking with rolling hills, scenic valley overlooks, rivers, and mountains. Everything one would expect and want of a New England drive.

Rebecca was not a confident highway driver. The 60 mile journey took over three hours. She hunched over the steering wheel the entire trip, focusing on the road and her speed.

Greg encouraged her when possible, but kept quiet for most of the ride so she could concentrate. He had not spoken in over an hour when he noticed the exit for West Lebanon, New Hampshire, a town bordering Hanover.

"Stop here, on the overpass." He asked.

"What's up?"

"This is Lebanon, the town next to Hanover. It has shopping malls, an LL Bean, Home Depot, all the box stores and specialty shops we need. I want to see if the stores are okay."

The van rolled to a stop on a bridge. Greg looked out both windows. "It looks good, doesn't it?" He did not wait for a response. "We're close.

One or two more exits and we'll be there."

"I know I'm driving slowly, but I feel like I've got the hang of this. Don't you?" Rebecca held the large steering wheel, turning it back and forth slightly. Her small thirteen year old hands barely wrapped around the black plastic. She put a second seat cushion behind her that morning. She was sitting on eight inches of truck seat.

"You are driving great." Greg replied absently, still looking at the shopping malls. He did not want to hurt her feelings. She was a terrible driver.

Rebecca patted the wheel before slipping the van into drive. They rumbled up and down several hills before exiting the highway, crossing the Connecticut River and driving up a steep hill on Wheelock Street into Hanover, N.H.

The sun was shining as they reached the center of town. They stopped at the top of a hill where Wheelock Street intersected with Main Street. Downtown Hanover stretched towards their right. Dartmouth College began to their left and front. The Dartmouth College Green sat off their left front bumper. The Green was a large open area slightly larger than a football field and in the middle of the campus. The normally trimmed grass grew out of control. Deep drifts of leaves covered the open field and much of the campus. Aside from the landscaping, the college and town were intact. There did not appear to be looting or destruction. Hanover was pristine and preserved.

They idled at the corner of Wheelock and Main Street for a few minutes until Rebecca spoke. "It looks like people fled or died in their homes. I don't see any looting or damage. It just looks empty."

"There aren't that many people up here. If the tourists didn't come, and the college students weren't here, it would just be the people of the town, and, again, there aren't that many of them." Greg visited his grandparents in the summer between terms at the college. The town was not crowded when the college was out of session.

"It's only noon. We have a lot of time to find your father's house, and most importantly find more firewood. We need to stock up immediately. We can live off the food in the truck all winter, but we have to find firewood to survive." Rebecca turned to Greg while she spoke. He was staring straight ahead, down Wheelock Street.

Greg's face was long. He was silent as he looked through the van's windshield.

"What's wrong?" Rebecca asked.

"I'm trying to get my bearings. I think we take a left here, or the next street, I mean, this is a one way. Not that we have to worry about going the wrong way. So, yes, take a left here." Greg stumbled through his words as he fought back emotions.

"Seriously, what's wrong?" Rebecca asked again.

Greg blinked his eyes before turning to look at her. A tear rolled down his face. His other eye was glassy.

"I thought someone would be here. I didn't think I'd be the first one. I thought my Dad would be up here with my brothers. I thought there would be a sign at the top of this hill or smoke visible from a house. I don't know why, I just thought, you know, if he was alive, he'd be up here." Greg's eyes dropped tears down his face. "They're dead, aren't they? I'm the only one alive. Everyone is dead." He sat expressionless, tracks showing on his dirty face. Greg realized for the first time he may be the lone survivor of his family.

"I don't know. Your dad said he'd be here in the spring. It's only November. Maybe it didn't kill everyone in South Carolina right away and he couldn't leave. Maybe he got caught by the police. We don't write them off until summer. Remember our deal? You believe for the both of us. I keep you alive." She put her hand on his leg. "We can do this. We need to find the house and set up. It's going to be cold tonight. We need fire. We need to get ready for winter. It could snow tonight or this afternoon."

She squeezed his knee gently. "Greg, I need you."

He sniffed his nose loudly. Rebecca reached into her pocket and gave him a tissue. "Okay." He sniffed again. "Okay. Drive up to the next road on the other side of this field and take a left." Rebecca followed his directions. Greg recognized the Medical school as a landmark. "Take another left, then take that catty corner."

"What's a catty corner?" Rebecca asked. Her face scrunched up like he was talking gibberish.

"What do you mean? It's a hitch in the road. You see it up ahead. This road stops and then continues but five feet to the right. That's a catty corner." Greg was stunned she had never heard the expression. It was so common to him.

"I think you're making that up, but okay."

They drove a short way down the road. A pond was on the right. Tall tan field grass surrounded the water. The pond was still free of ice. Greg instructed her to take a left at the bottom of the hill. Two houses up the road was his father's childhood home.

"I can't believe I found it so quickly. I mean, it's not a big town, and I've been here a bunch of times, but I thought I might get lost."

"So this is it, huh? Wow, it certainly is big."

The house was enormous, a giant red brick home on a corner lot. It looked old. There were two chimneys visible.

"My grandfather worked at the college. This was the house they gave him. It's old, old enough to have lots of New England winter essentials. I mean, I guess, that's what my dad told me. I've never actually been in the house."

Rebecca turned to him. "What? You've never been in this house? You brought me up here and you have no idea if the fireplaces are gas? You don't know if it's been remodeled inside, and not suitable for a non-electric winter? Are you crazy?"

"Calm down, it's like you said, there are other houses we can find if this one doesn't work. I know our family cottage will work if this one doesn't. The cottage is small, heats well with the wood stove, is on a lake in the woods. I have a back up."

Rebecca could not hide her anger.

"I'm sorry." He conceded. "I wasn't trying to hide it from you. I didn't think about it. I am following my father's instructions, I just blindly assumed he would lead me to a good house."

"Greg, we are all we have. It's you and me. We have to make decisions together with all the available information. This is life and death. We're in serious stuff." Rebecca, all of thirteen, understood the gravity of the situation. Playtime was over. Greg had to realize chasing turkeys and not telling her everything about a new location was unacceptable. It was life threatening.

"Got it. Lesson learned. Let's move on and check out the house." Greg understood. Before he became a team he could make mistakes like falling asleep in the SUV during his hike from Andover. He was only hurting himself. Future mistakes put Rebecca at risk.

They backed the van into the driveway, put on coats and gloves, and got out to investigate. Greg opened the back of the van to let the chickens breathe fresh air and see sunlight.

They clucked angrily from their cage. One chicken lay motionless in the cage.

"Damn." Greg muttered. "One of the chickens died."

"It was going to happen in the move. If we only lose one, I'll be happy."

Rebecca looked at the other birds for indications of stress or illness. "I factored in the risk when we moved. I assume we'll lose all of the chickens. They are finicky animals, prone to illness, stress, whatever. I knew taking them from their home would do this."

"You didn't tell me the chickens would die." Greg was surprised. "Why did you agree to move?"

"Like I said, I was moving anyway. They would have died anyway. Maybe they die sooner because we came to Hanover, I don't know, but you were coming here with or without me." She shrugged her shoulders and moved passed him towards the backyard.

The house's lot was sloped showing three stories from the front, and four stories from the back. The basement was built into the hill. The center of the house encompassed the four stories. Two story sections flanked the main house.

An attached garage on the right had a sunroom above it. A railing on the roof of the sunroom suggested a deck.

The left flank was brick with a turret of stairs to the second floor.

The basement was a walkout spanning the entire bottom floor of the four story main house. A roof covered a back patio area.

"It looks dark in the basement. Let's grab some flashlights." Greg went back to the truck and got headlamps and floodlights. Rebecca tried the back door. It was locked.

Rebecca tried a second door on the back of the house towards the left side. The door did not have a window. It was also locked.

"What do you want to do? Break the door? We can't do that if we want to live here. Break a window? I'm not sure that is a good idea either." She looked for potential ways into the house.

"Let's try all the doors and windows before we jump to conclusions about how to get into the house." Greg walked towards the left side to try the door at the top of the brick turret of steps.

"Duh, yeah, that makes sense, sorry." Rebecca followed him around the house. The grass was long and leaves covered the ground. "We have to rake the leaves. That's going to take time." She looked at the yard.

"I don't know why we'd clean up the yard, but if we do, I'm using a leaf blower." Greg could tell Rebecca did not do yard work.

"I don't care about appearances, if that is what you are implying. We have to clear space for the chickens to scratch. We should have a clean yard for planting in the spring, to keep animals out of the yard, to make sure we don't slip and fall on the wet leaves. This is where we live. The outside and the inside are going to be clean, livable spaces."

As they rounded the corner to go up the stairs they saw a bank of windows. Greg and Rebecca beamed their flashlights into the darkness.

"It's a kitchen. Weird, why would it be in the basement?" Greg shook his head in confusion.

They walked up the steps to the side door. There was a storm door which opened, but the knob on the inside door was locked.

They went back down the stairs and looked into the basement again. The windows were above a counter. Greg tried to slide each of the windows open.

"Are you sure you don't want to try the front door first?" Rebecca asked.

"We're here." Greg responded with a grunt as he pushed up on the second window. It slid open with a creak. "So why not try?"

Hanover was a safe town with almost no crime. The window was left unlocked in perpetuity as a way for the occupants to get into the house when locked out.

"Do you want to go in first?" Greg offered.

"I'm good. You go ahead." Rebecca wanted Greg to go in first.

He slid onto the counter, jumped down, and helped her do the same. Greg opened a door next to the counter and saw a half bathroom. The long kitchen stretched out before them. A swinging door at the end of the room was open and they could see the dark rooms on the other side. A windowless door, similar to the one on the outside of the house, was in the middle of the right wall.

"Is this the windowless door on the outside that was locked?" Rebecca asked. She walked over and turned the knob. The door exposed a dark room.

"Jackpot!" She said happily. "It's a firewood room, and it's stocked. How sweet is this? You can load it from the door on the other side, and wood stays dry in here. We won't have to go outside in the snow to get wood. I bet we have enough for a long time, not all winter, but if we get snowed in, it's enough for a month, maybe more." Rebecca did not realize it was an old coal storage room with separate access for the coal truck and the homeowner. The room was converted into wood storage to service the multiple fireplaces and woodstove.

"I guess we know they have at least one wood burning fireplace." Rebecca concluded from the storage room.

"Hey yeah, that's right." Greg replied.

They walked out of the kitchen and into a large room in the center of the basement. There was a second room straight ahead, and a corridor to the right that led to the backdoor. Rebecca walked down the corridor and unlocked the door before joining Greg in main room. The floor was tiled and did not contain furniture. The only light came from the kitchen behind them and windows on the back of the house. The wall on the front of the house had no windows. There were two doors leading off the room. Greg and Rebecca opened both and shined their lights. Each room was filled with boilers, hot water heaters, furnaces, and other mechanical devices. The rooms and equipment were worthless.

The far room was carpeted and had several sectional couches. There was a large television mounted on a wall. The sectionals faced the television in a "U" formation.

"I bet this is an entertaining floor, and that is not the main kitchen. They must have parties on the back porch and in the yard, and they use this entire basement as indoor party prep and hosting." Rebecca concluded. "Other than the wood room, this floor is useless to us. No fireplaces, no way to heat it. It will be nice and cool in the summer, but impossible to work with in the winter."

"Okay, let's move upstairs." Greg responded. He agreed with her assessment. This floor was not suitable for their needs. He wondered if the entire house was too big for them. It would take too much wood to heat, and appeared to be built for entertaining more than living through a tough winter without electricity and gas.

A set of stairs led to the main level. A window at the top led their way up and around a corner. There was a door at the top the stairs allowing the basement to be closed off from the rest of the house. On the other side of the door was a small landing with a half bath. Another four stairs led to the main foyer. It was a large room at the center of the house, similar to the large empty room in the basement. The entry room was designed for entertaining more than living. Straight in front of them was the front door. Rebecca unlocked the door as Greg opened a door to a small room on the right. It was a study or den. The small room had a fireplace.

An open arch to the right led into a formal living room. A similar archway on the left displayed the dining room with table and chairs. An open swinging door showed the main kitchen.

Greg pointed down the formal living room, "there is a fireplace, but it's not useful. The room is too big." The first floor was bright from windows. "The windows probably lose a lot of heat. This house is old, but I don't think it was pre-coal furnace. They obviously didn't rely on fireplaces to keep warm."

Rebecca nodded in agreement. She walked through the living room to a door she noticed in the far corner. It led to the sunroom visible from the back hard. Rebecca did not open the door, but noticed a woodstove.

"It's like this house has elements of what we need, but its size disqualifies it. There's a woodstove, but it's outside, or basically outside. We can't waste wood to cook on it."

She looked at the sun through a large bay window in the living room. "We don't have much daylight. This is our house for now. We make it work until we find something better. We can put the chickens in the garage, leave the cages for them to sleep in with hay, water, whatever. Let's get a fire going in the little room, plan on sleeping in there tonight. We will use the fireplace cooking tools."

"There has to be something better." Greg told her.

"Well it's after one thirty, Greg. We have a couple of hours of work no matter what house we find, and I don't want to work in the dark. We have to get the chickens settled, a fire started, food cooked, beds made. One night or a week here won't kill us." She stood at the doorway to the study.

"Let's move the furniture out, the study furniture anyway, the desk, cabinets, etc... We can leave the chairs. I'm going upstairs to find twin mattresses we can pull in for the evening. I don't mind sleeping on the rug for one night, but I'd prefer a mattress or a couch. I doubt two couches will fit in here. We can lean the mattresses against the wall during the day."

Rebecca worked the equation in her mind. They could make the house and room livable. They had to for at least one night.

"I vote to keep looking for a different house. We should stay near the pond. We'll give the chickens air while we walk around to see if we can find a smaller home."

Rebecca moved books and papers off the desk into a chair, placing a desk lamp on top. She rolled the desk chair passed him.

"I know you're disappointed. I know you want to look, but today is done. I'm exhausted from driving. We've already lost a chicken. We can't risk getting caught in the dark without a fire, beds, and food. This will be fine if we move things out and find mattresses." She left the chair in the dining room across the foyer. "Can you check the garage? Maybe grab some wood from the basement? I want this room toasty, and I want the chickens out of the cages."

Greg did not move.

Rebecca walked through the foyer to a large set of stairs leading to the second floor.

"Hey, let's move." She clapped her hands. "Grab me a power bar or pop tart or something too. I'm starved. We have plenty of time to get our work done, but not if you are going to stand there." She went up the stairs.

Greg nodded absently. "This house sucks." He said under his breath. "I brought Rebecca up here for nothing. My family is dead. We are further north. Damn it."

He heard a commotion before a mattress appeared out of nowhere and landed at the bottom of the stairs. Rebecca threw a twin mattress over the top railing of the stairs.

"Grab that, will you?" She yelled from the second floor. She paused. "Greg?"

"Yeah, I got it. And then I'll be outside with the chickens."

Greg pulled the mattress off the stairs and into the study. He moped out the front door towards the van and chickens. This was not how he envisioned his arrival in Hanover. He expected to find his family. He expected the house to be perfect for surviving a New England winter. None of his hopes were becoming a reality. "And I brought Rebecca up here." He kept muttering.

Greg focused on his work. He broke into the locked garage by kicking the flimsy door. It made him feel better to kick and break something. A sedan was parked in one side of the garage, but the other side was an open bay and gave the chickens plenty of space. He donned his oven mitts and carried the chickens to their temporary home. He spread feed on the ground, filled their water dish, gave them freshly shredded paper, and shut the broken door.

Rebecca packed several 'day bags' as she called them. She had a grocery bag with three days of food and essential items like a pot, paper plates, plastic ware, soups, crackers, and tea bags. She did not want to waste precious time searching for things they needed the first night. She packed a quick bag of clothes, sleeping essentials, and additional snacks. Greg grabbed the overnight supplies, fatwood kindling to start a fire, and walked back towards the front door.

Rebecca pulled the desk a few inches at a time out of the study and towards the dining room. There was a second mattress at the bottom of the stairs.

"Did you get the wood?" She asked.

"Geesh, give me a minute. I've done everything else." He set the bags on the ground and helped her with the desk.

At 4:30 the sun was behind the mountains surrounding Hanover, and daylight was fading. The temporary study was set up. The fire cast warmth and light throughout the small room. Unlike the Concord house, where the living room was too large to adequately heat with a single fireplace, the small study was toasty.

"I like it in here." Rebecca said. "It's not perfect, but it's cozy." She sat in one of the lounge chairs they placed next to the fire. A warm mug of soup rested between her hands. She sipped the broth before eating the noodles, chicken, and vegetables.

"I'm sorry I brought you up here." Greg told her. "This was a mistake. I don't know why I thought they were alive. You're right, I'm being stupid, and I'm taking risks with both of our lives."

"Alive or not, I did not expect your family to be here. Your younger brother?"

"Craig."

"This may sound harsh, but your father can't risk his own life, your older brother's life, and the life of a young boy. Coming up here for the winter? Getting stuck in a snow storm in New York or Boston? It's too risky. He told you he'd be up in the spring because it's the safest time to travel. Sit tight, Greg Dixon. We'll figure out where to live. Keep believing in your family, and I'll keep us alive."

"I believe you." Greg said softly.

"You believe they're alive?" She asked.

"No. I believe you can keep me alive." He reached out and touched her hand. "Thank you."

Rebecca felt her face grow hot as she held Greg's hand. She hoped her palm was not too sweaty. They sat by the fire silently until she let go of his hand and went to her mattress to go to sleep.

20

"What's a coach house?" Rebecca asked. "Is that another made up Greg expression like catty corner?"

"No, Ms. 'I grew up in a subdivision.' A coach house is a small house behind a larger residence, used for servants or guests. I bet we can find one around here that has a fireplace or even a woodstove. Coach houses are one room with maybe a separate bedroom. It would be tiny. We could heat it with fire."

"Lead the way." Rebecca said.

"Should we call this day one or day two in Hanover? I feel like this is day two, but we started in Concord yesterday." Greg made idle chatter as they walked down Choate road towards the pond at the end of the street.

"Day two, definitely day two." She told him. "I hope our chickens make it to day three." She found two more dead chickens when she tried to collect eggs that morning. Her coop of ten was down to seven. She consoled Greg by telling him she expected the chickens to die during the winter anyway. It was a white lie. Greg was depressed enough about not finding his family and the failed house. He did not need to feel responsible for dead chickens.

They stood at the end of the street and looked towards both sides of the water. There were houses on the right side of the pond but none on the left. Houses on the left side were across a street and up a hill. It was a large pond, probably 300 or 400 yards from top to bottom and 150 yards across.

"I want to live on the water if possible, not across the street." Greg pointed right and they walked towards the homes with direct pond access.

They arrived at the previously discussed catty corner. Town was to the right, the medical school was in front of them, and a road named "Rope Ferry," stretched off to their left. Greg and Rebecca turned left and walked towards the first house.

The first two homes they entered were remodeled with large rooms, high ceilings, and open concepts. The houses were not designed for life without central heating or electricity.

"I doubt any of these houses are going to work. That last one had gas fireplaces." Rebecca was not worried, but three houses into their search, she was frustrated.

Each house took them a little over a half hour to search. They had to find a way into the house, check for a corpse smell, walk around and talk about the positives and negatives. Rebecca searched the kitchens for food, placing supplies in boxes or bags at the now unlocked doors for retrieval later in the week or month.

The experience might have been enjoyable were it not a search for life and death accommodations.

"We have to keep looking. Are you warm enough? Do you want to stop and rest?" Greg pulled a cereal bar from his pocket. One of many they found in the last home.

"I'm fine." She told him. "Let's push forward."

At 3:00pm they were back in the Choate road study holding their hands by the fire trying to gain feeling back in their fingers and toes.

"Maybe we should take a break tomorrow. Check out the town for supplies. See if there is food." Rebecca did not want to discuss their failed day.

"I need to focus on the positives." Greg told her. "We are safe and warm. We found another few months of food. You found that couch."

"That couch is awesome." Rebecca agreed.

"We can survive in here, store food in the living room, thaw snow for water. If we need it to, this study will keep us alive. I'm not sure what I was expecting, but I'll admit it was more than this tiny room."

"I wasn't." She told him. "Did you see where I was living in Concord? This is a step up, not because it is nicer, but because it is smaller and will heat from the single fireplace. It's going to get cold in here, but we can keep it above freezing, maybe keep it in the 60's with the fire. You're right, the rest of the house is useless for living, but it's great storage. We can put wood in the dining room or downstairs, out of the snow and wind. We can live through the winter here, but," she smiled. "That doesn't mean I don't want to upgrade."

"I feel like I should keep apologizing to you. The chickens are dying. We are further north and a few degrees colder. I really screwed up."

"Stop it. Just stop it, Greg." Rebecca's voice was stern. "Let's get one thing straight. I don't do anything I don't want to do. I made the decision to leave Concord and come to Hanover. I know we will make it through the winter. We will see if your family is alive, and we'll make decisions based on that information. You did not bring me up here against my will. We are a team. Do not apologize to me again."

"It's just, you had..."

"I had what? A house I couldn't heat? I was alone? I ate soup and cereal? We're fine, and we'll make whatever we need to work. I'm done talking about coming to Hanover as a mistake. Stop apologizing and stop whining."

Greg cracked a smile. "I didn't think I was whining."

"Well you are. Whining does us no good. If there is one thing I hate more than anything, it's whining. Tomorrow we walk into town, we go to the local real estate offices and look for a house that will work for us. We look for listing with woodstoves. We look for green homes with solar power. We take control." She finished her soup with a slurp. "I'm tired. I'm going to bed. When you wake up tomorrow, I want you ready to work and with a better attitude, Greg Dixon."

"Yes, ma'am." Greg replied. "I'm," he stopped himself and lowered his head, still smiling. "Rebecca, it's three in the afternoon." Greg began to laugh. "It's a little early to call it a night."

Greg's eyes opened when the study door shut. Rebecca returned from feeding the chickens.

"Something tried to get into the garage and eat our chickens." She told him. "Maybe a fox or a fisher cat."

"What's a fisher cat?" He asked.

"A marten."

"Like a bird? A bird tried to eat our chickens?"

"That's a martin with an i, this is a marten with an e. It's like a badger or weasel, and it's after our egg source." She removed her coat. "It didn't get in, but there were scratches on the door and concrete floor."

"Can we catch and eat them, these martens?" Greg asked. "We could use some meat."

"I guess. We can read about them in the library. I would assume, since they are coming after our chickens, we can set a trap for whatever it is." She stood by the fire. "I like your new attitude."

"Let's eat and walk into town." He said as he sat up on his mattress.

The real estate office was a useless exercise and took up the entire morning. They accepted defeat and walked slowly to their house for lunch.

"I thought we'd find someplace." She told him.

They were at the top of Choate road and about to make a left towards their home when Greg stopped.

"Wait, I have an idea." He suddenly blurted.

"I'm not moving. What do you mean 'wait'?" Rebecca enjoyed using

Greg's sarcasm.

"Funny." He said, acknowledging her attempt. "During one of my summer visits I had to go to this museum. My mom never let us just hang out, she always wanted to do something, you know, give us culture, whatever. Anyway, there is a cottage, Daniel Webster's House or something like that. It's a museum, kept in the old style, fireplaces, woodstove. I think it all still works too."

"Are you serious? Why didn't we start there?"

Greg looked at her. "Because I didn't think of it until now, that's why. I assumed my father was sending me to the best place."

"So where is this museum?"

Greg turned and pointed to a white sign twenty feet away. "It's right there."

Rebecca smiled and held up her hand for a high five before turning and walking to the front of the tiny museum.

"It's a two story house, but it's small. You can tell it doesn't have ten foot, or probably even eight foot ceilings. This house was built to heat from a fireplace or woodstove, and to keep heat in the rooms. Look how small the windows are." Rebecca made initial observations.

"Don't forget, we can move and use our own furniture. We're just looking for heat and cooking sources. We can move rain barrels to collect water, and if you don't think I'm going back to that house and getting that awesome couch? You are wrong. Did you sit on that green one? OMG, it was so comfortable. Incredible. liked that small dining table they had in the sunroom too. It was perfect for two or four chairs." Rebecca continued to talk about furniture as they made their way to the front door.

The door was unlocked. "That's a good sign." Greg said to her as he pushed it open.

The front opened into a small mudroom with benches on either side. It was set up for guests or owners to sit and remove their muddy boots before entering the house. It kept warm air in the house and cold air outside.

"This is kind of like a space ship airlock. You have to close the outside door before you get into the main ship." Greg said as they entered the house.

"What are you talking about?" Rebecca responded. "Are you telling me that you're actually a SciFi geek. You were able to keep it a secret, but now it's out there. You're a geek. The whole world dies and I get stuck with a 14 year old Trekkie."

"Whatever." Greg smiled back. "I'm not a geek, and I refuse to be called a geek by a 13 year old college freshman. If you want to step up and get measured on the nerd-o-scale, be my guest."

The second door opened into a short hall. To the left was a living room furnished with old style chairs and a couch. To the right was an open door leading into a bedroom with an old fashioned four poster bed. A fireplace was visible on the far wall of the bedroom.

The ceilings were low. The two rooms were small. It was dim in the house, partly because of the small rooms and low ceilings, but also because the windows in each room were tiny with deep window boxes.

"The bedroom has a fireplace. We could put twin beds in there, and it will be perfect." Rebecca sounded hopeful.

A staircase led to a second floor. It was a steep staircase that was shorter than a modern set needed accommodate ten foot ceilings and duct work between floors.

Greg ignored the stairs, turning to his left and into the living room. A fireplace with a wood storage cut-out sat in the center of the wall. Three small windows let in light, trapped heat, and kept cold air out.

The windows were old with wrought iron panes separating imperfect glass. The walls were thick. The glass was set on the far side of eight or ten inch window frames.

"This is another great room. These windows could use some help. Have you ever seen the plastic stuff at the hardware store you can put up on windows to keep drafts out? We need a hair dryer to finish the job. I bet we can figure something out." Greg used the plastic insulation in his dorm room last winter, preventing the draft in the old dorm window from blowing on him at night.

"I'm getting that couch from the other house. This stuff is all hitting the curb." Rebecca shook her head. Greg got the sense she had already decided on the house. Instead of inspecting each room for viability, she was re-decorating.

"So you think this is a fit?" Greg asked her.

"If the kitchen has a woodstove, you've struck gold. This house is perfect, literally perfect for living through a no electricity Hanover winter. Did you notice the house next door has about a cord of firewood stacked against the outside of the house? It looks like a dorm or something. Whatever it is, that starts our wood collection."

"I haven't seen a woodstove. Let's hold off on declaring this our new house. It does seem pretty perfect though. If we hang one of our wool blankets to block off the second floor, we can keep even more heat on the first floor."

At the far end of the living room there was an archway into a dining room. The opening between the rooms was the size of a door, not like a modern home with the entire wall removed for an open concept. Another door on the far wall looked into a study. It was a small room with a desk and bookshelves. They would shut the door and leave that room closed in the winter, use it for wood storage if necessary.

The dining room was a good size with its own fireplace. On the other side of the dining room was an open door that led into a kitchen. Greg saw a woodstove and a large farm sink.

"I think we've found our new home, check out the stove. It has an oven on the side, four burners on the top. We are in business. We should try to start fires in each fireplace, make sure these are all working heat sources, then walk back and get the van. Starting fires means we come back to a warm house. It's a little chilly and damp in here." Greg walked around the dining room table and into the kitchen as he spoke. There was a pantry to the side of the kitchen, and a back door that led to a large sunroom they could use to store wood.

Rebecca looked down at her watch. It was 1pm. There would not be time to get the additional furniture today. They needed to make fires, get the van, unpack food, boil water, and get settled for their first night. "I don't think we'll be able to get the single beds and the couch today. Let's focus on the basics. We'll start the fires and unload the van supplies into the pantry. We'll do a full house set up tomorrow."

"Hey Greg," she said to him as they walked back to the front room to check the flue and light the pre-made fire left by the museum staff.

"Yes?"

"This was a great find, and a better situation than we left at my house in Concord. You probably saved us for the winter." There was no sarcasm in her voice. She wanted him to know that he was the hero.

"Thanks, I think this house will work out. I mean, it already has fires made in every fireplace. It's destiny or fate or whatever you want to call it." He moved cobwebs and heard a creak from the hinges as he pushed opened the flue of the fireplace in the living room.

The fireplaces and woodstove worked. Greg and Rebecca spent the rest of the day unloading supplies and moving wood from the house next door onto a covered side porch of the Webster Cottage. They constructed the chicken coop next to the back door of the kitchen. The birds were happy to be free from their small cages, clucking and scratching around their new home.

The sun set at 6:00pm. Greg made dinner while Rebecca made camp in the living room. They fell asleep in sleeping bags on top of a woven rug next to a roaring fire, exhausted from the stress and work of the day.

21

Greg's eyes opened to a dimly lit room. The sun rose on the kitchen side of Webster Cottage. The living room was bright in the afternoon and dark in the morning. He could hear Rebecca in the kitchen. He rolled over and got out of his sleeping bag. The fire kept the room warm through the night. He checked the outdoor thermometer they set up the night before, 28 degrees. Not too bad an indoor temperature for a freezing outside temperature. He walked towards the kitchen rubbing his eyes.

He swung open the door to find Rebecca boiling water. The kitchen temperature was above 70 degrees.

"We only have two eggs. The gals are upset after the move. I suspected as much. Ramen noodles with scrambled egg for protein. That should get us going." She spoke while concentrating on the stove before looking over her shoulder at Greg. "And you need to make some bread for dinner. I want my morning toast tomorrow."

"You're in a good mood. We have a lot of work to do today. Why so chipper?" Greg enjoyed the light hearted Rebecca, and wondered why she was cooking.

"We are in Hanover. We found a great house. Your family is going to show up in a few months. This is the best scenario we could have hoped for when you ran into me a week ago. It might be our best scenario possible when the world ended, period. Sure, there are challenges ahead, but team Rebecca/Greg stumbled into a great find. If we fix the furniture situation, we'll be good until spring."

She was right. Things were looking up from when Greg slept under his cot at Hightower.

"I was thinking, you know, before I passed out from exhaustion last night," he paused, deciding whether to mention his idea. "Do you think we should light some kind of signal fire? Maybe when we are all set up? If there are other survivors in the area, we might be able to help them and they might be able to help us."

Rebecca's rules were clear, and her number one rule was to trust no one.

"I don't know, Greg. I just don't know if that is a good idea. It's easy to think that everyone will be like us, friendly and helpful. What if they're not? What if we bring a desperate person, cold and hungry, and they see our house, and our food, and, well, they haven't been around a woman in a long time. I have more to worry about than you." Greg could see fear in her eyes as she spoke. Rebecca did not appear to be afraid of anything, but rape was not just 'anything.'

"Okay, I get it. It was just an idea. Let's work over the next few days, get our living situation finished, scout out the town, and then we can talk about it again. I would never do anything unless we both agreed." Greg left the door open for further discussion. He believed adding people could help them survive. He also understood the risks involved with engaging strangers.

"First things first, we get our beds. We can use the van. I don't want to sleep on the floor for one more night."

"Agreed" Greg's back agreed too. He was stiff after two days of loading and unloading supplies, driving, and sleeping on the floor.

They ate breakfast and drove the van down Rope Ferry Road. They struggled mightily to load a green couch and two single bed frames into the van. They nabbed an additional leather couch when Greg declared he wanted his own napping spot for snowy afternoons. After the furniture was secured, they systematically grabbed the food neatly boxed by each front door.

At the end of day five their house was set up with couches, beds, and enough fire wood to last several weeks. They had a half of a tank of gas left in the van.

Greg lit the fire in their bedroom and walked back into the warm living room. Rebecca sat on her green couch, contently watching the fire in the living room.

"I hope it doesn't get too hot in there, I like to sleep cold. Not 30 degrees cold, but not hot either." Greg began.

"I doubt being cold will be an issue in a few weeks, particularly if the fire goes out while we are asleep." Rebecca said back to him. "Man is this couch comfortable. This is the nicest piece of furniture I have ever sat on, seriously, hands down the nicest."

"I'm excited to sleep in a bed with sheets. It's been a while." Greg sat on his brown leather couch running parallel to Rebecca's and perpendicular to the fire. "Couches are comfortable, but those beds we picked up this morning? They looked really comfortable."

Thirty minutes later they were tucked into their new comfortable beds. The bedroom did not get too hot. Rebecca and Greg had been together for two weeks. It felt like summer camp, sleeping in twin beds next to a fire in a log cabin type structure. They talked into the evening, facing each other, elbows bent, heads in hands.

"What do you miss most about the old world, aside from family and friends, of course?" Greg wanted to know more about Rebecca's life.

"Well, I miss school, the structure of my life. I'm all about routine." She started.

"No, no, not that kind of stuff. I mean, what kind of frivolous thing do you miss? I miss take-out food. I know that at private school I didn't have to cook, but the best nights were when a few buddies would order pizza, and we'd get it delivered to the front entrance of the school. It would be hot and smell so good. We'd eat the pizza, and tell other kids they couldn't have any, and laugh and joke for hours. Ordering take-out with friends was one of my favorite things. That's what I'm asking, what do you miss that we are never going to be able to do again?"

"I miss going to the movies. I loved the movies. I had a subscription to Entertainment Weekly, and I was up to date on all the new releases, when the sequels were coming, who was starring in what. I loved Hollywood and movies. I would go on Sunday afternoons, always hitting the 2pm showing of the latest release. I'd sneak in a box of candy, because my parents owned a store, and just soak them in. I don't like to think about never seeing them again, because maybe we can get a projector working. It makes me sad. It's been twenty-one Sundays since I went to a movie."

"That's a good one. I didn't think about movies. See, you probably didn't think about take-out food as something to miss. It's funny how we have grown up the same, but miss different things." Greg smiled at her. Rebecca was doing a long stare, looking through Greg.

"I don't know how similar we grew up. I'm an only child, and my father ran our store most nights. He'd come home for dinner, that was a rule, but my mom and I spent a lot of time together. The three of us were close, a tight unit. At the end, when they knew they were going to die, and worse, that I was going to live, I think that was hardest on them. Can you imagine? Dying, and knowing your 13 year old daughter is going to be alone in this harsh world." She spoke n a distant voice, not necessarily to Greg.

"Well," Greg said in response, "My dad had to tell me to survive until he got here. I'm not comparing our two situations, because your parents are dead. I still believe my father is coming, but I think we have a similar story. Your parents knew you were going to live, and mine knows I'm alive and he can't get to me for another five months. Both are agonizing situations. Both affect us, meaning you and me."

Rebecca came back from her stare and looked into Greg's eyes. She nodded. She thought about his father, on the phone, telling his son to stay safe, stay alive, how horrible that must have been. Her parents are at peace. His father was alive somewhere, thinking about Greg constantly.

"I'm a middle child. We get ignored. I am sort of the opposite of you. I talk loudly to be heard, I speak my mind. I went away to school because I didn't want to follow my brother through high school, always living up to his accomplishments." Greg yawned.

"Okay chatty Cathy, let's call it a night." Rebecca replied. "Geesh, you do prattle on." She said it with a smile. She spoke non-stop since he found her. She was surprised Greg's ears had not fallen off from her constant yammering.

"I apologize for rambling." He said in a deadpan voice before yawning again.

"Goodnight, Greg."

"Night, Rebecca. See you in the morning."

And just like that, they fell asleep in their new lives together.

The room was warm when Rebecca woke up the next morning. Greg silently placed a log on the smoldering embers when he woke an hour earlier, and the fire came back to life, heating the room after he left. He was in the kitchen making breakfast. The back side of the house was warm from the woodstove. Rebecca walked in wearing a robe.

"In our weeks together, you've never gotten up before me."

"I thought I'd shake things up a little." Greg said back. "I have French toast cooking in the oven, and warm tea if you would like some. It's colder today, but you can see, the oven heats this room nicely." He handed her a mug of warm tea.

"Um, thank you. Wow, get you a bed and you become a whole new person."

"I'm excited to explore town today. I want to see what the condition of the area is. I need some new pants, and I want to see what supplies we can find. I bet there are some great lanterns at the hardware store we can use, and there are three or four sporting goods stores over in West Lebanon, about five miles away. There's even an LL Bean. There have to be solar power options for lights, and other stuff to make our lives more convenient." Greg was eager to get moving.

Greg wanted to find an animal trap. Thanksgiving was in a few days, and he wanted to catch a turkey. He could keep it in the cage they used to transfer the chickens. He found some sweet potato vines growing in pots at a couple of the houses they passed, and he had bread for stuffing. He knew he could make a great feast for the two of them. Getting a turkey would be a great way to celebrate their new life.

"Um, okay" It was the second time Rebecca said 'um,' conveying her confusion at the new Greg she encountered that morning.

"You know what I want to find?" She said after a few sips of her tea.

"I want to see if we can catch some fish. I bet there are fish in that pond. Fresh fish? That would be great right now. That pond is going to freeze over in a little while if it hasn't over the last two nights. We need to find a fish and tackle shop."

"My grandfather belonged to a fishing club over the bridge in Vermont. I don't think I could find it, but if we got a map there is a chance. It was some private lake stocked with rainbow trout. They almost jumped in the boat when we went. You can fish from the pier and catch some whoppers. I'm not a big trout guy, but fresh fish does sound good. I have this fish stew recipe that will knock your socks off."

"Alright, you know I like a plan. Let's eat and head over to LL Bean. I get to go shopping again! Let's think about getting a smaller car or SUV too. The van is good for this trip in case we want a canoe for the pond. I might grab a bike as long as we have the trunk available."

"Don't we have to pay for things for it to be shopping? I mean, technically speaking? Aren't we just going to a place to pick stuff up more than shopping?"

"You call it what you want, I'll call it what I want." She smiled at him as she poured syrup on her French toast.

The house was coming together nicely. They had a table in the kitchen to enjoy meals in the warmth of the woodstove. There was no running water but the kitchen had a large sink with a drain running to the outside. Rebecca set a small rain barrel on the counter next to the sink basin. As long as the barrel was more than a quarter filled with water, there was decent pressure out of the spigot to wash dishes and hands.

They dressed warmly for the brisk 26 degree temperature outside. Rebecca drove the van towards town so they could take an inventory of the specific stores and supplies available within walking distance. They also wanted to see if initial appearances were true, and the town was intact, as their first view of the pristine town might have been inaccurate.

Greg knew there was a back road to the shopping malls in West Lebanon, but he was not positive he could remember it. He wanted to drive through town before turning around and taking the highway they knew to the malls.

"Let's drive down Main Street before we jump on the highway." Greg asked. "I want to see how the town looks, maybe head over to the grocery store to see if they have any food."

They drove through the center of town. It was abandoned and peaceful. All the store windows were intact, and some of the window displays were still up. "This joke might be lost on you, but this is the first time I've been in Hanover when I could get a parking spot." Greg laughed to himself, thinking of the endless circles his grandfather made in search of a parking spot in town.

"It was usually busy? It seems like such a sleepy little town."

"You have no idea. In the summer? You had all these college students, tourists, locals, all crowding the streets. There were kids our age, there were retired people. It was just people upon people. Then, the funny thing, there would be these random smelly hikers. The Appalachian trail is right around here. These smelly people with beards and nasty clothes would be sitting around talking to each other, right in the middle of town." Greg's thoughts of Hanover were fond, and driving down Main reminded him of his Grandparents. They both passed two years ago. "It was a great place to visit."

Greg kept talking as they drove. "We would come up for a week or two, spend it at my grandparents lake cottage, fish, boat, and swim the entire time. We'd come into town and go to lunch or dinner, and sometimes we'd come during town events, like the Fourth of July. There would be a parade and activities on that square field. The one we passed before hitting town, it's called 'The Green.'"

"That sounds fun." Rebecca said, acknowledging Greg as he continued.

"I was always bored when my mom would make us go on her cultural tours. We spent a day at this cow farm over in Vermont, it was like 100 years old or something like that. They had milking cows, chickens, lots of animals. It was fun for a little while, but you know, when you're a kid, that stuff gets boring pretty fast." He looked up towards the sky. "Who knew that my mom would save my life with her boring tours. Finding Webster Cottage is all thanks to her, like she was looking out for me." He continued looking up. "Thanks, Mom." He smiled as he said it, thinking of her, how much he missed her, and how much he loved her when they were together.

Greg was not paying attention, he was too caught up in his thoughts. He did not tell Rebecca to turn around before leaving town. They were five minutes outside of Hanover when Greg realized his mistake.

"Oh wow, I'm sorry. We were supposed to turn, like, way back there." He looked around and saw they were entering the town of West Lebanon.

"Well, where are we? This is your area, Greg." Rebecca did not mind an adventure, and they could hardly get lost if they stayed on the same road.

"You know what? This is Lebanon or West Lebanon, I'm not really sure of the difference. We are going to come to a Dunkin' Donuts at a fork in the road. Take the right fork and we'll run right into LL Bean and West Lebanon. This is the back way I didn't think I knew."

They drove down Main Street in West Lebanon, a straight road with businesses on either side. The town was looted, most of the shop windows were broken. One of the stores, "The Paint Barn," was burned out. Black smoke stains clung to the side of the building around the front doors and broken windows.

"What the heck? I haven't seen this anywhere else. I don't have a lot to compare it to, but I did walk by a few towns between Hightower and Concord. The State Liquor Store was looted for booze, but it wasn't ruined." Greg worried about the stores in West Lebanon.

"This was vandalism, not looting. Look at the spray painting on the Paint Barn. It's punks who did it, not looters. Who loots a paint store during an epidemic?" Rebecca pointed to the black words scarring the side of the building.

The Lebanon library was on their left, it too was covered in symbols and words. Its front doors were broken.

"I heard about towns like this on the radio." Rebecca continued. "If the police got sick, and no one was there to stand in for authority? The bad influences took control. There was some bad stuff going on all around

New England. People realized there were no repercussions for their behavior. It got ugly, quickly. Not a lot of places, but some. This part of Lebanon went to the mobs."

They did not see a sign of life. Despite the destruction, they could tell no one had been around for months. Leaves covered the ground, unmoved except for animal tracks.

They arrived at the Dunkin Donuts and a fork in the road. The donut shop was untouched by the violence. "I guess even mobs have their rules. Don't mess with the donuts." Rebecca said, surprised that one store would survive above all the others.

"Should we make a joke about how all the police were probably at the donut shop, and that's why it survived?" Greg laughed at this own joke with a loud chuckle.

"Nice." Rebecca complimented. "Nice."

The turned right and headed towards the big box stores. Greg wanted to visit the high end indoor mall.

"Up there, on the left, that's the LL Bean and sporting goods store." He turned his head to examine this area of West Lebanon. "Everything looks fine here. I bet the police drew a line in the sand at the Dunkin' Donuts. Maybe they decided these stores were more valuable. There are two groceries over here. Food must have been a priority." Greg was pleased to see this part of town was not burned to the ground.

Rebecca became more animated when she pulled into the indoor mall. "I love LL Bean. There was an outlet in Concord. You could buy monogrammed stuff that people sent back, so if you didn't mind having someone else's initials on your luggage or backpack, you got a sweet deal. It was the best store."

They parked by the mall and got out of the van. Greg walked up and tried the entrance door. It was unlocked. He held it open for Rebecca, and followed her inside. LL Bean was the first store, anchoring the mall on one end. Eastern Mountain Sports anchored the other. The roof of the mall was glass, sunlight shone brightly throughout the mall.

"Brrr" Rebecca said as she rubbed her hands on her arms. ""I bet it's five degrees colder inside than out. I'm not sure how long I'll last shopping in here."

"I agree. Let's make quick work of this place." They tried the doors at the LL Bean store. They were locked. Greg went outside and picked up a large rock from the stream that ran next to the mall. He came back inside and threw the 15 pound stone through the glass door. "Don't call the police." He said to Rebecca as he kicked the jagged glass away from the frame.

"Don't worry, one of my uncles was a cop. I can get us leniency." She stepped through the gap left by the rock. "We have a very large van. Whatever you want, take. I'm getting several sets of flannel sheets, and a whole bunch of snow pants. I'm not saying this is our last trip to West Lebanon, but if it snows later today or tonight, this might be our last trip to West Lebanon."

Greg went to the clothing section to find pants and shirts. He carried a large black plastic trash bag and began stuffing underwear, shorts for next season, hats, gloves, anything and everything he could think of for winter into the bag as he walked by the circular racks. He made two trips to the van with four bags full of clothes before he found the camping section.

Greg stopped dead in his tracks. Set up as a display was the most beautiful thing he had seen in months, a portable camping bathtub. The red canvas frame folded out like a baby crib with strong aluminum cross bar supports. The tub was six feet long, three feet wide and three feet deep. A plastic drain opened at the bottom, perfect for their house with no running water. He could set it up in the dining room, kitchen, or their bedroom next to a fire.

Greg checked to see if Rebecca had seen the bathtub. She was busy on the second floor of the store walking through the women's clothes. He folded the tub and ran it out to the van. He put his clothes and new sleeping bag over the tub. He wanted to surprise Rebecca later that day.

He jogged back inside, passing Rebecca on her way out with an armload of clothes. "I love this store, I really do. It's awesome."

Greg went back to the camping area, grabbing four pair of snow shoes and walking poles. On his fourth trip into the store he found another key item, a shotgun, a one hundredth year L.L. Bean anniversary shotgun on display in a wood and glass case. He broke the display case with one of the snow axes nearby and picked up the gun. It was heavy, but perfect for hunting or defense. He went back to the van with the shotgun, the snow axe, and used his free arm to grab a handful of lanterns.

"I'm going to drop this stuff in the van and head down to the other sporting goods store. You staying here, or do you want to come?" Greg called to Rebecca.

She poked her head over the railing. "Did you get boots? We need good snow footwear. We should get all the available sizes."

"Yes, ma'am, I did. I also put several pair of snowshoes in the van. We'll need them along with the boots."

"Okay, let's see if the other store has a better bike selection, and I want to find a smaller canoe, one I can handle on my own."

"You are a picky shopper, aren't you?" He said back to her. She scrunched up her face with a smile that told him "whatever."

They walked down the center of the empty mall looking at the shops. They stopped at a novelty store and loaded up on board games. The candy shop provided a quick snack of pre-packaged Belgium chocolate.

"Look at these stores, handbags, jewelry. None of this has value anymore. And look how cute that purse is! " Rebecca sighed as she walked to the store window. "I can finally get one of those expensive bags, and they aren't worth anything now. "

Greg looked at her. "Yeah, life can be cruel, you survive a plague, only to be cursed with unnecessary accessories. What a world."

She scrunched her face at him again.

Eastern Mountain Sports had a better bike selection and a smaller canoe. It also had better sunglasses, which Greg took full advantage. "I love sunglasses. I could never afford them, or more than one pair, but I coveted all these sunglasses. Unlike your purse, these still have value. I win again!" He smiled as he put a pair on his face, the tag hanging down his nose.

They spent almost two hours shopping in the stores. They wanted to get home to eat lunch and unpack their haul before it got dark. Greg looked at the sky as they loaded the canoe into the truck. "It's going to rain or snow, look at the black clouds coming over the mountains. Let's go through a few more stores and call it a day."

"We have to go to Home Depot or the hardware store to find the window sealers. I'm glad we have all these lanterns, because Home Depot and Walmart typically do not have windows. You want to go to those two stores and leave?"

"Sure." Greg replied. "There's a hunting store up here too. I want to see if I can get some shotgun shells for the shotgun I found."

"You got a gun? For what?"

"Thanksgiving is coming. I owe you a turkey."

"Okay, whatever, like you are going to be able to bag a turkey. I don't like guns. You're more likely to shoot your foot off." Rebecca frowned.

"I'll be fine." He rolled his eyes. "I'll just run into the store and grab what I need." He pulled down the backdoor of the van before walking to the passenger's side. Before he did, he walked to the sidewalk and picked up a large stone from the river, similar to the one he used to break the LL Bean entrance. He put the rock next to him on the bench seat. "I can't forget the key to these stores."

Rebecca drove down the road and turned into a strip mall, one of many that filled West Lebanon. A hunting and fishing warehouse sat at the end of the parking lot.

"I'm coming in with you. I forgot my fishing stuff. " Rebecca told him.

"Works for me." Greg said back, picking up his rock and walking to the front door. He threw the rock through the glass and cleared the shards with his foot.

Rebecca tried the door. It was unlocked. "Men." She said as she went passed him.

She shuffled off to the fishing section. Greg made his way to the hunting area. It was dark inside. Greg turned lanterns on as he walked passed a display. He soon located his shotgun shells. He grabbed a case of them. As he walked towards the exit he found a trap display. He put down the shells and examined the cage. A "critter" entered one end, tripping a door that closed behind it, trapping the animal. It was used to humanely trap and transport pest animals. Greg would use it to trap food. He brought the shells out to the van, and returned for a dozen of the traps.

Rebecca sat in the warm van waiting for Greg.

"There is an Orvis store in Hanover if we need more fishing stuff, and the hardware store carries fishing rods and tackle too. I took fly fishing lessons at Orvis one summer. My grandfather loved to fish. You should see my little brother, Craig. It's all he'd do if we let him."

"You only talk about Craig. What's your other brother's name?"

"Matt. You'll get to meet both of them. Matt is a bit of a character, not serious like me."

"Wait, you're the serious one? You?" She feigned shock in her voice.

"Yeah, me. I'm the serious one. Really."

"What do you say to skipping Walmart, grabbing the window stuff at Home Depot, and going back to town? Heck, let's skip Home Depot and get the window insulators at the hardware store in town tomorrow. It's getting late. We have to unload. I don't know why we would run ourselves ragged when we are staring down the barrel of endless time." Greg was tired and sore from moving the furniture yesterday. He wanted to setup the bathtub and soak for a while.

Rebecca shook her head. "Let's get the window stuff. I don't want to risk a storm blowing in and dumping a foot of snow and suddenly we can't get back over here. If hardware store doesn't have the plastic we face a problem we don't need to face. You just run in and grab the stuff."

"Perfect." Greg replied.

She turned the engine over and drove to Home Depot. The cab of the van was hot. They enjoyed the warmth during the short drive.

Greg smashed the glass door with his rock, turned on the floodlight he held in his left hand, and braved the dark warehouse by himself. There was no light inside the windowless box store. He flashed the flood beam to read the aisle markers and quickly found the window insulating sheets. He picked up an entire case. "No reason to only take one package." He mumbled as he walked back through the store. His eye caught the fireplace section. He already had plenty of tools for their fireplaces, but he inspected a carton of easy light logs. He moved the flashlight around before spotting a shopping cart. He placed four cases of the starter logs in the cart, putting the window insulation on top.

He rolled the cart over the broken glass and out of the store. The van was running, but Rebecca was not in the driver's seat.

"Rebecca?" Greg called out. He was nervous not seeing her.

"Rebecca?" He yelled again.

"Over here!" He heard her reply. "You have to see what I found."

Greg rolled the cart to the back of the van and walked to where he heard Rebecca's voice. She was standing next to two large blue port-a-johns, leaning a hand against the one closest to her. She smiled from ear to ear.

"They're both empty. Can you believe that? They are both 100% empty! Let's get them into the van. This is the biggest score of the trip!" She was excited and proud of herself. Greg knew the bathtub was going to trump her find, but he let her have her moment.

"No more walking into the next house. It's still going to be cold, but we can set one up next to the kitchen door, or off the side door of the house." Greg replied.

The one flaw with their current house, something neither of them noticed when they decided upon living there, homes built in 1790 did not have indoor plumbing. Greg and Rebecca did not have an indoor bathroom, an oversight they remedied by using the bathroom in the sorority next door. When the weather turned colder, the pipes would freeze and the bathroom would be useless. The port-a-john meant they could use facilities close to their home and remove their waste to another location. A nasty job, but better than letting their poop pile up.

They opened the back of the van, pushed all their supplies towards the far wall, and made room for the large blue toilets. The blue plastic boxes were heavy, but by using the edge of the truck as a fulcrum, they managed to get them into the truck bed.

"That's enough work for today. Did you get the window stuff?"

"Yep" Greg replied, panting a bit. "I have an entire case. I also found boxes of those ready start logs in case we ever have an emergency and need to start a fire quickly." He pulled the van door down, and walked around to the warm cab.

"Ah, that feels good." Greg slumped down into the seat. He pulled salmon jerky out of his pocket acquired from LL Bean, opened the bag and offered Rebecca a piece.

"Thanks," she said.

"I got a case of this too."

"Isn't shopping fun?" Rebecca said as she slipped the van into drive.

"Once again, this wasn't shopping. We didn't pay for anything."

"Well, it sure felt like shopping."

They chatted and ate salmon jerky during the ride back to Hanover. They backed the van onto the yard and around the house, getting as close to where they wanted a bathroom as possible. The port-o-johns were big, heavy pieces, and it took a lot of muscle to get them next to their back door.

There was a small back porch extending off the back door of the cottage. Four steps led onto a concrete slab. They decided to put one of the bathrooms just off of the slab. It was going to be cold, but as convenient as an outhouse could be.

"It's an improvement, that's for sure. We'll figure something else out in the spring, but for the winter? I think we're good." Rebecca stood with her arms crossed and a smile on her face, admiring her find.

"Okay, that's enough posing. You did well. Let's move the van and get the rest of our stuff inside." Greg was excited to surprise her later with the offer of a hot bath.

It took them an hour to unpack the van. Greg snuck the bathtub in while Rebecca pre-built a fire in the woodstove.

"I propose we continue to use the bathroom next door until the pipes freeze or the water pressure fails. Let's use the port-o-potty when absolutely necessary." Rebecca disliked the idea of an outhouse, and wanted to delay its use as long as she could.

"I totally agree. I'll shovel the path to next door as long as we need to." They sat on their couches, sifting through their items. It was 3:30. Greg was exhausted.

"We have two hours of daylight. Let's catch some fish for dinner. Walk down to the pond with me. We'll use jerky for bait. Come on, fresh fish for dinner!" Rebecca had an endless supply of energy.

"Seriously? No way, I'm done. You go ahead." Greg was too tired. He wanted to organize his new stuff and sit on the couch, keeping warm next to the fire. "It's cold, it's cloudy, it's gloomy, and I think it's spitting rain out there. We can fish tomorrow."

"I want fish for dinner. I don't want to go alone. You're my only option. Get off your butt, put on a coat, and let's go. You're 14 not 40. Pick yourself up and let's catch some dinner."

That was that, Greg was going. "Okay." He grumbled. Fish did sound good. He took the fishing pole she extended to him, put on his coat and gloves, and walked out the door with her.

Rebecca loved to fish. She did not know why. Fishing was outside of her other passions. For some reason floating a line in water brought her joy.

They turned left on Choate Road and walked the quarter of a mile to Occom Pond. The grass was tall as they left the road and entered the field surrounding the water. They found a nice spot to stand and cast their lines close to the water's edge. Rebecca carried an old fashioned wicker creel from the hunting store, and she dropped it from her shoulder to the ground next to her.

"Let's fill this thing up." She threaded a piece of jerky on her hook and cast it out into the water. The red and white bobber bobbed for a few seconds, then became still.

"Are we here to catch dinner or are we here because you like to fish?" Greg watched Rebecca's stride down to the pond. She had an extra skip. He saw her expertly bait her hook and adjust her bobber. He marveled at her perfect cast and the extra distance she obtained with a practiced wrist flick. She was an angler.

"I wanted to fish this afternoon, get some fresh air, catch some fresh dinner in the process. I love to fish, is that a crime? " Her line pulled. The tip of her rod was pointed towards the water. She waited for a sustained tug on the line or a second strike. She felt both and jerked her line into the air to set the hook.

"Got one before you even have your line in the water!" She reeled her line. The fish fought, bending her rod over. "It's not a big one, but it will have some meat on it."

She held the fish up for Greg to see. "That's a nice sized perch." She commented.

"So it is." Greg said. He was enthused by her success, and put jerky on his line.

She stood looking at Greg, the fish dangling from her line. He cast his jerky out into the water.

"Greg?"

"Yes, you have a nice fish, I already said that. How many times do you want to say it? You caught the first fish, okay."

"No, um, well, I've never kept a fish before. My dad and I would always catch and release. What do I do with it? Just put it in the creel?"

"Well, well, well, the young woman and the pond doesn't know how to finish the job." Greg's line went tight and he set his hook in the fish's mouth by pulling his rod tip skyward. "I guess you'll just have to watch me." He reeled in a fish, similar in size to Rebecca's, a bass instead of a perch.

"We can do two things, put the creel in shallow water and let the fish swim until we leave, or we can crack them on the head with a rock and use the creel for storage. It's cold out. We don't have to worry about the fish spoiling, and I doubt we're going to be here much longer. I'm cold, and they're biting. If we get four or five fish, we'll be good for dinner, right?"

Rebecca listened to Greg's advice. She was not excited about hitting the fish with a rock or stick. "Can you do my fish at the same time you do yours? Please? I'll be able to get a line in the water faster."

"Sure, and I'll even wave the Dixon family rule 'he, or she in this case, who catches, cleans.'"

"I don't mind cleaning them, but I don't know how. If you teach me, I'll clean the fish next time. I'm not that girly. If the fish are already dead, I'm fine with cleaning them."

"You keep catching. I'll kill and clean them as you reel them in." Greg pulled out a boning knife he took from a store that morning, and began to clean the fish. He would finish cleaning one as she would catch another. They had four nice sized and one very large fish for dinner. She hooked three smaller fish that she threw back.

Rebecca pulled a bottle of soap from her pocket. "Let's wash our hands here, save our water back home. It's lemon scented soap, should help the fish smell."

Greg was accustomed to Rebecca having exactly what they needed. He was not surprised by the lemon scented soap. He washed his hands in the water, cleaning off his knife as well. He picked up the creel and they headed to their house.

They walked ten paces when they heard a gunshot. It was distant but distinct. A rifle discharged. Rebecca and Greg froze. A second shot fired.

She looked around nervously.

"That shot was very far away, three miles, maybe more. If it rang up a valley, and with absolutely no other noise to mask it, it had to be miles away, maybe five." Greg tried to calm Rebecca.

"Could it have been thunder? There is a storm coming." She asked hopefully.

"You and I know it was a gun, a rifle I think. I don't hunt, but growing up in the south, I know the sound of a gun. There is definitely someone else alive up here, somewhere." He was looking around too, trying to figure out the direction of the shot. "Wow, what are the odds?"

Rebecca stared at Greg. "What should we do?" She was rattled. She was smart, level headed, and brave, but she was also a 13 year old girl, vulnerable to almost any attack from any adult. She knew her weaknesses.

"We go home and decide if we have any next steps." He looked at her and saw the fear in her eyes. "Hey, come on, it's no big deal. If two is better than one, then three has to be better than two, right? It's the first noise we've heard since we've been here. There can't be a lot of people, it might even be someone driving through who stopped to kill dinner. Let's go home, make our own dinner, and figure out if we want to do anything. For all we know right now, the person could be loading a deer onto the hood of their car and be 10 miles south on Highway 91 by the time we get to the house. Remember, Canada is getting colder, as is Maine. People might be moving south for the winter. Who in their right mind would stay in New Hampshire for the winter? Only crazy people, right?"

He put his arm around her. "We're team Greg and Rebecca, don't sweat it."

She gave him a weak smile.

Greg was a big fourteen year old. He was close to 5' 10" tall, and while thin, his broad shoulders were intimidating to approach without concern. His face betrayed his youth, but his stature relayed a strong male figure. A stranger spying the teen from afar might mistake Greg as a medium sized adult.

No one would mistake Rebecca's age.

When he put his arm around Rebecca, she felt better. She was an average sized 13 year old girl. She was maturing into a young woman, but without Greg she was a target.

They walked to the house as the sun moved over the mountains to the west. The temperature dropped quickly in the afternoons. Greg spoke as Rebecca's tongue disappeared for the first time in two weeks. He talked about fishing with his family in South Carolina, saltwater versus fresh water, and his brother Craig's passion for fishing. Greg tried to take Rebecca's mind off the unknown rifle shot.

"I have a surprise for you. I wanted to wait until I could really surprise you, but I think you need a happy surprise right now. Can you go in the kitchen and light the woodstove? I'll put it together in here. Don't peak until I call you, okay?" Greg was giddy.

"What is it?" Rebecca asked, suddenly excited.

"It's a surprise. I can't tell you. Go in the kitchen for a few minutes. Okay?"

She giggled and went through the door. "Don't take too long. I want to get out of these clothes and into my pajamas."

"Don't worry." Greg said as he opened the dining room closet and pulled out the canvas bathtub. He lit the fire in the dining room and placed the bathtub four feet in front of it. The large dining table was in the back left corner with the chairs resting on its top. They were tired of walking around a table and saved it for emergency firewood.

"Okay, come on out." He called.

Rebecca walked through the door with her hands over her eyes. "I have my eyes covered for affect. Should I open them?"

"Wait, let me walk you over to the surprise." He grabbed her elbow and led her next to the bathtub. "Okay, now."

She opened her eyes and looked down. Her mouth dropped open.

"Is this what I think it is?"

"I found it at LL Bean and snuck it out to the van. It's a bathtub. You solved the potty issue, I solved the bathing issue. We can take baths right next to the fire. How awesome is that? The drain unscrews on the bottom. We'll figure out how to pump the water out through a window."

"Oh my god! Can I go first? Can I go first right now? I feel so dirty. Please? Please?" She jumped up and down.

"Of course, I'll make dinner while you take a bath. I'll stay in the kitchen. Take your time, enjoy it. I'll go when you are cleaning the kitchen after dinner. Deal?"

"Anything you want, just let me take a bath. I'll clean the dishes forever! I promise!"

They ran a hose from the house next door through a window and into the tub. They filled it half way with the icy water while four pots boiled on the woodstove burners.

Greg tapped her on the shoulder as she watched the pots warm. "One more surprise." He handed her a bottle of lilac scented bath gel. "There was a shop in the mall. I thought you might like this."

She looked at the bottle and then up at him. She was touched and began to cry. Rebecca rarely showed emotion. She looked back down at the bottle, and after a pause she thanked him.

"Through all the death and horror came a person as genuine and thoughtful as you." She said quietly. "Thank you, Greg. You're the best friend I've ever had." Rebecca lifted her head to look him in the eyes. She stood onto her tippy toes and kissed him gently on the cheek. She closed her eyes as she kissed him. It was the first time Rebecca kissed a boy.

"Don't let it go to my head. You've saved my life. I'm glad I can make you smile. Let's get that water warm so you can take a bath."

Rebecca stayed in the tub for almost a half hour. Greg made his fish, waiting to bake hers until she was out of the tub. At the 20 minute mark she asked him to boil another pot of water so she could warm the bath.

She washed her hair and soaked in front of the fire.

When she was done, dried off, and in her pajamas, she walked into the kitchen. "Sorry I missed dinner. Wait until you get in there. It's incredible. It makes you feel like you're normal again. Really, you feel normal."

"Well, the rice is kind of warm instead of hot. I cooked your fish in the oven when you called out that you were getting out of the tub. Watch out for bones. There are a million of them." He put a plate in front of her with rice, fish, and warmed canned peas.

"Veggies? You're making me eat veggies?"

"We've got to keep up our strength. Peas are good for you." He spun around to leave the kitchen. "I'm out! Don't bother me for at least 20 minutes. I'm going to smell like a beautiful lilac when I'm done!" He ran out of the kitchen, coming back a minute later in his new flannel robe. He grabbed a boiling pot off the stove and went into the bathing room to warm the water.

Rebecca heard him slip into the tub. She picked up her food and walked into the other room. Greg pulled his knees to his chest to cover himself.

"Hey! What are you doing?"

"Don't worry, I'm not looking, much. I'm going to eat at the table with my back to you. Let's talk about the gunshot."

"I didn't bother you." He whined.

"Oh come on, you're a guy. You can lean back and enjoy yourself while talking to me, can't you?" She pulled a chair off the table and sat with her back to him.

She began. "I believe we have three options. Ignore it like it never happened, actively seek the person or people, or passively seek them with a signal fire."

"I like the last option." She said after a pause. "Being proactive is our best approach, but trying to find them is a waste of gas and time." Rebecca was serious in her tone.

"If a giant, mean looking person comes out of the woods and up to our fire with guns and knives, we make a decision. If a child comes out, we make a different decision, but lighting a fire and luring the person here gives us options. We control the encounter." Greg had a feeling his input was not necessary.

"Let's light it tomorrow morning." She concluded before turning to lighter conversation. Rebecca talked about how fun it was the fish again, how her dad had taken her on weekends when he could get away from the store. When she was finished with her dinner, she got up and averted her eyes for her walk back into the kitchen.

Greg enjoyed his soak. He stepped on the towel Rebecca left for him next to the tub. He dried off and slipped his robe back on. He looked down at the dark gray water filled with dirt and grime. "Man did I need that for both my body and soul."

He put his pajamas on and pulled out one of the board games they found at the mall. When Rebecca came out of the kitchen, she sat down. They spent the rest of the evening trash talking, laughing, and having fun. It was a rewarding end to a long day of work. They fell asleep in their twin beds within seconds of hitting the pillow.

The morning sun brought a new day of challenges. As planned, they built a fired in the middle of the college Green. Greg used wet leaves to create smoke, a trick he saw on a survival show. The fire sent thick black smoke high into the air.

They watched from the corner office of a nearby college administration buildings. The office had a fireplace they used to keep warm while the waited.

Greg and Rebecca lit a signal fire for three consecutive days.

22

Paul and Hank were socked in for days. The sun shined briefly the first morning they spent at the Rutland hotel, but the clouds rolled in later in the day and snow began to fall. It snowed for two more days. Three feet fell before the storm was over. The front steps were gone as the snow drifted above the porch landing.

They stomped a path to the wood pile, stayed in the hotel, and debated their next steps.

The winds blew drifts and the temperature outside settled into the low twenties during the day and single digits at night. Hank studied the phone book and the local area maps. Paul discovered a hotel cribbage board, a backgammon board, and dozens of puzzles. The Inn had a mystery library in the lobby with a small sign that read "free for guests, please return before departure."

Paul and Hank were stuck. They did not know for how long, but they assumed they would be in the Rutland Inn for a while. Despite the situation, they considered themselves lucky to have provisions to last them through the entire winter, water (thanks to the snow), fuel, and companionship.

The Inn's Honeymoon Suite was a large room on the second floor with a fireplace and a hot tub. Paul and Hank heated the room at least once a week to bathe. Paul unpacked his solar shower which they filled with warm water in the kitchen before hanging it above the Suite's tub.

They found clothes in the Inn's lost and found and the owner's quarters, and made themselves as comfortable as possible.

The snow was so high that even if they found snowmobiles, they could not find the road. Neither Paul nor Hank knew the area well enough to risk going over a mountain in deep snow and sub-freezing temperatures.

Their second week at the hotel brought Christmas. They did not exchange gifts, but they did make a feast from the gourmet pantry. Despite the uneven and high cooking temps of their woodstove, Paul was able to bake a small chocolate Buche de Noel.

The brother's retired after their holiday feast to a fire in the main room and a vintage port from the wine cellar.

"To us, brother, to us." Hank said, drunk, but lucid enough to toast their luck.

"We can ring in the new year next week, but I am glad to put this one in the rearview. Despite a pleasant holiday with you, this has been the worst year of my life." Paul, also drunk, tipped his glass and took a sip.

Hank tipped his glass, paused, and responded. "I have never known pain like I did this year, but you know what? I've never had to stop my life like I have this year either." He poured himself more port. "You and Megan, you lived your lives differently than I did. You travelled. You spent your weekends working on the house or at shows, movies. You lived."

"We didn't have kids." Paul replied.

"I know, I know, and I loved the girls, but that's not what I mean. These last days, sitting in this house, not working or worrying, decompressing about the last months, about my last 50 years, it's been incredible and cathartic. I cannot do anything right now. Literally, I can't do work, there is no way for me to get to Hanover. I have enough food, water, and fuel. I don't need to gather anything. I can't get to the mall. I can't call anyone." He sipped his port. "I don't have work tomorrow. There isn't a college football game on TV. I have been forced to stop. I have to sit back and enjoy my time with you."

"And" Paul asked.

Hank sipped his port. "I don't know. I still have an urge to 'do.' I feel like we need to prep for something, but I don't know what. We can't plant. We can't build. I am socked in by a storm, perfectly comfortable and with months of provisions. It's made me slow down. I'm not taking stock of my life, or saying I have regret in how I lived my life, but this pandemic, it's brought a new kind of order to my mind. It's simplified everything." Hank continued to drink.

"I'm rambling, because I'm a little drunk. What I think I'm trying to say, what I think I've realized is, the rapture has created a world where I can enjoy a game of cribbage with my brother. Before all of this destruction, my mind was always half somewhere else. I was thinking about work, or mowing the lawn, or whatever. I'm free of that now." He paused, took another sip of port.

"The price was too high, but I had to pay it, you know? I feel like I should make the best of the bargain, make the best of the situation. Yes, this is the worst Christmas I've ever had. My life's partner, my four girls, they are all dead, but there's nothing I can do about that. To honor them, I will take the gift I earned from their deaths and savor it. I'll enjoy my life."

Hank smiled. "This is great port." He raised his glass to the sky. "Thank you Steve and Nicole for your fantastic taste and hospitality." Hank and Paul, having found the hotel's ownership information, frequently thanked their presumed dead benefactors.

Hank started again. "Do you know how many people I fired during my time at work? I didn't keep track, but it was north of thirty. That's how I lived, climbing on the backs of others. It's how it used to be. Life isn't like that anymore. Life is pretty simple for us now. Eat, keep warm and dry, protect each other, go to sleep. Do I get to play golf? No. Will I miss a lot of things? Absolutely. But there is a purity to my life today."

Hank leaned forward, rolling the port around in his glass as he spoke.

He watched the maroon liquid swirl. "You know why I burned my house and crawled in a hole for two months?" Hank did not look up from the glass.

"You told me, to avoid the government." Paul put his hand on Hank's knee. He patted it, smiling at his drunk brother.

Hank looked up to meet Paul's eyes. "I wanted to die. I burned my old life to the ground and crawled into a grave next to my family. I never expected to come out of my tomb. I'm not sure I wanted to come out of my tomb. I debated killing myself, kept a gun in my hand, in my mouth, to my head almost every day." Tears rolled down Hank's face. He sat back, arms stretched out to either side. He and Paul sat by the fire on the highest holiday of the year, warm, dry, and fed. They had much to be angry about, but much to give thanks and praise for as well.

Hank sniffed in his nose loudly. He used his sleeve to wipe tears from his face as others streamed down. "As I said, I paid all I had for this new life. I don't want it, but it's mine now, and I am going to accept it, enjoy it, and savor it while I can." Hank gulped the last of his port.

"You think anyone else is alive? You think Greg is making it through the winter, wherever the hell he is?" Paul thought of his nephew every day.

"I know they are, Paul. I know they are, and just like us, they are sitting around a fire cursing and giving blessings for the year." Hank placed his empty glass on the table before leaning onto his side and putting his feet on the couch. A loud drunken snore erupted almost instantly.

"Merry Christmas, Hank." Paul whispered. He stood, steadied himself, and put two logs on the fire. He went back to his couch, still fully dressed like his brother, rested his head on his pillow, and fell asleep.

Book Two

23

John, Matt, and Craig sat in the Charleston harbor fishing. It was brisk out, but their desire for fresh fish outweighed their discomfort. They also felt the need to get out of the house after three days of rain. They used a boat for inlet fishing, one of many left along the harbor. It was early, 10:30am, and they already had two good sized sea bass. John wanted one or two more fish before he called it a day. The cold weather made him lean towards going in with his current haul.

"I got one." Craig said excitedly. "Big one too."

"You're going to feed us all today little brother." Matt smiled and looked over at his father. If Craig landed the one on his line, he was responsible for two of the three fish.

Craig reeled in his catch, another sea bass. It was almost double the size of the first two. He quickly baited his hook to recast his line.

"I think that's enough for one winter's morning," John said to his son.

Matt reeled his empty line in ten minutes earlier in hopes of heading home to a warm fire. "I think you'd sit here all day fishing if we didn't stop you, Craig." He told his younger brother.

"Just one more?" Craig asked.

Matt and John looked at each other. Matt shrugged his shoulders with a 'what else do we have to do' expression.

"Okay, but hurry up and get another one. I'm cold." John smiled. He reached over to a bag and pulled out a bottle of water. In the few months the harbor was free of boat traffic, the fish made a tremendous jump in population. John knew it would not take long for Craig to catch another fish.

They found Craig pedaling towards Myrtle Beach all those months ago. He was thirty miles from their house, a valiant effort for a young boy on a bike with only six gears. John hugged his son as Matt put the bike in the back of their SUV. Craig cried. He kicked. He screamed. He hit his father.

"You're letting Greg die like you let Mom die." Craig yelled. John hugged him tightly. "I hate you, and I'm running away again tomorrow, and the next day, until I save my brother."

But Craig did not run away again. Matt spent an hour with his younger brother that evening. They spoke behind a closed door, away from their father. When Matt came downstairs he assured John the days of Craig fleeing were over.

"You've had a rough few months, Matt. I have too, but you've had it worse than me. You lost your best friends, your football team, you girlfriend, of what? Two years?"

"Almost two, it would have two years at New Year's" Matt replied. He sat on the couch next to his father. Craig was asleep upstairs, exhausted from his long day.

"Greg is lost in Massachusetts or New Hampshire, your other brother keeps running away, and to top it all off, your mother died." John paused. "I'm your father, and I will always be your father, but I need a friend as much as you do. I need a second in command, a partner to raise your brother, a partner to get us to Uncle Todd's, a friend to confide in when I don't know the answer. This isn't a great thing to ask of my 17 year old son, barely old enough to drive, but it's something I have to ask of you. You've had a bad few months, and I can't promise things are going to get better, but consider today the day you become a man. "

Matt was serious since his girlfriend's death. His sense of humor was gone, and he seemed to be muddling through life. Before the rapture Matt was a happy person, willing to laugh and joke through any situation. The end of the world snuffed out his spark. John needed to light it again.

"You need to snap out of your haze, your depression, whatever is bothering you. I need you to start helping around the house, food gathering, cooking, wood gathering. You have to be a better influence and role model to Craig." John looked directly into Matt's eyes.

"And above all else I need you to be my friend." John stopped and let his words sink in.

Matt stared at his father. He nodded slowly. "Okay, I get it. Okay." John could tell when Matt was lying, telling him what he wanted to hear. Matt had been lying for weeks. Tonight was not one of those times. In the last two minutes, John broke through the wall building between father and son since the beginning of the pandemic.

"I can still call you Dad, though, right?" Matt knew the answer, and asked with a partial smile. It was his first joke in weeks.

"I'll always be your dad, but we have to fast forward our relationship about ten years, where I realize you are too old for me to boss around, and we become friends."

They stayed up late into the evening, talking about plans for the winter. Every day was a 'long day' after the rapture. Matt was tired. He yawned, stood up, and said he was going to bed. He picked up his solar lantern and went to his room.

Matt sat on the edge of his mattress for a few minutes. He pulled a backpack from under his bed and started to unpack his things. It was a large hiking pack he scavenged from a neighbor's house. Matt planned to leave Charleston to find Greg, abandoning his father and younger brother. After the conversation with John, Matt realized he was not leaving to save Greg. He was leaving to run away from himself. He was running away from his dead friends, girlfriend, and mother. He finished unpacking and shoved the empty bag back out of sight.

Matt fell asleep the instant his head hit the pillow. Unlike previous nights, when he lay awake and planned his escape, Matt's life had a new purpose. His spirit was renewed, and his conscience cleared. He slept soundly for the first time in months.

John found Matt's backpack earlier that week. He knew his son was planning to leave. John could not stop Matt. He could stop Craig, but Matt could drive, all he needed was a car. Matt had to want to stay. Matt had to want to help. John knew Matt had convinced Craig not to runaway by telling him he was leaving to find Greg.

When John found the empty pack under Matt's bed the next day, he knew their talk had worked. Every word of their conversation was real, and John held up his end of the bargain.

Months later, as they sat in a boat in Charleston Harbor, John continued to treat Matt as an equal. Craig caught two more fish, a fourth sea bass and a flounder. Matt turned the key on the whaler and powered the boat towards the pier. "Great fishing Craig. You know the rule. He who catches, cleans..."

"Man, I hate cleaning the fish when it's this cold out," he lied. Craig loved everything about fishing, the bait, the actual fishing, the cleaning. He even enjoyed eating fish.

They pulled up to the dock, and Craig grabbed one of the fish, jumped onto the pier, and walked toward the end to clean his catch. He was a skilled angler, and cleaned the first fish quickly. Matt tied up the boat, and John put the other fish on the pier for Craig to clean.

"I like the flounder. You don't have to clean them. Just filet and eat." Craig smiled at his father. He was becoming a resourceful young man. John feared Craig would lose his childhood to the plague, but in spite of everything, Craig still had the wonder of a 10 year old. He flicked the fish guts off the dock and watched the sea birds and small sharks fight for the meal in the water below.

The water was eight feet below them and deep. When a larger shark, 8 feet long, lunged through the surface for the fish guts, Craig laughed in excitement. "Dad, Matt, there is a huge shark right at the end of the pier. You have to see this!" The two men rushed over to watch the giant fish. It was a fitting end to a fun morning.

They stood on the pier until John broke the silence. "We'll eat the flounder as soon as we get home, smoke the smaller bass, and ice the big bass for dinner. Sound like a plan?" John was excited for fresh fish. They had not fished for a week due to rain and cold mornings.

The Dixons grabbed their gear and walked to a truck parked next to the dock. John found the small Toyota in town. It was perfect for hauling to and from the harbor. The Dixons moved out of their family home to escape their memories. They scouted Mount Pleasant, the town north of Charleston, landing in one of the island communities near the ocean. The family settled into a house with five fireplaces built in the style of an old southern mansion. It was convenient to the fishing piers, and away from any main roads.

John was not concerned about rapture survivors finding and threatening his family. During the outbreak, when scientists were studying the disease, the rapture was determined to be 99.99999% communicable. The chances of surviving were one in a million. South Carolina's population was around four million. There 'might' be one or two others in the state.

Probability suggested there were only 300 to 350 people in the entire country who 'might' have survived the disease. Had all of these people been healthy otherwise? Had all of these people been old enough to survive on their own? Had any of these people needed medication to stay alive? Medication that was now gone? Had any of these people been old enough to pass away naturally since the disease began? John estimated there were at most 200 people alive in the United States. He guessed half of that 200, maybe more, travelled to California, Texas, or southern coastal areas to stay warm through the winter.

John felt secure in Mount Pleasant, squatting for the winter months in a mammoth house near the ocean. His family was fifty miles from Interstate 95, the main artery of the east coast. If there were large bands of roving survivors, they would skip the mild climate of Charleston for the warm temperatures of central and southern Florida.

The truck was loaded and the fish were cleaned. Matt drove back to the 'mansion,' as they called it. He parked and immediately walked around to the house's deck to start the grill. He was hungry, and lighting the fire meant he was closer to a flounder lunch. They would transfer the coals from the grill into the smoker after lunch, smoking and preserving the meat of the smaller sea bass.

John and Craig made sure the rods and fishing gear were clean before they exited the garage and walked into house. John was washing his hands in the sink when Matt came in from off of the deck.

"Fire is going, we should be ready to cook in a few." Matt said. "I'll put a pot of water on so we can have rice or noodles."

"Craig is putting the fish on ice." John looked out the window as he rubbed his hands together. They kept lemon scented liquid soap at the sink to rid their hands of the fish smell. Their house was several rows away from the water, but he could see the harbor from the kitchen window. "Let's do rice. It goes better with fish. Don't you think?"

They considered several locations and homes. All of the homes had some kind of generator or back-up energy system. This particular house had two, a gas generator they used occasionally and solar panels that powered a few items during the daylight hours, including a water pump and water heater.

Initially, after moving into the solar house, John and the boys lived like they did before the rapture. They kept multiple lights on, played video games, plugged appliances in all the time, and used the garage door opener. They learned quickly that plugged in appliances use power, and their solar power cells were consistently drained each evening. Their gas generator would turn on and burn precious fuel.

The only appliance plugged into a wall socket was the refrigerator. When they needed light, they used one lamp or they lit candles. They set a limit to television, movies, and video games. As the days grew colder and shorter, energy was conserved for electric heaters.

The solar panels allowed them to keep parts of their old life during the day, and kept them attached to their old humanity. Learning to conserve energy taught them the new life of finite heat and light.

Four five gallon coolers of water sat on the counter next to the stove, boiled and purified the day before. The kitchen looked like a sporting event, as the yellow and red coolers were mainstays at soccer, baseball, and football games. Matt pressed the white spigot at the bottom of the cooler by placing his thumb on the button. He measured four cups into a pot and walked outside to boil the water on the grill. He rarely used the indoor stove. With the water started, he went back inside to select a packet of 'just add water' rice from the hundreds stored in the kitchen pantry.

"I feel Caribbean today." He mumbled to himself, pulling a green box from the shelf.

Matt typically cooked fish on aluminum foil. It was an easy clean up. He poured olive oil on the foil, put the filleted and skinned flounder down, and generously applied seasoning. He waited for the water to boil and the rice to cook before he started the fish. Flounder cooked in just a few minutes.

It was Monday. Matt and Craig had school. John established a school schedule once their lodging and food were secured. Craig could not continue through life with a fifth grade education. Craig did not need to learn much more, but he did need basic math, physics, and better reading and writing skills.

Matt was a senior in high school. He had a firm base of education to get him through the rest of his life. One of his new roles was to tutor Craig. John was too far removed from school to be an effective educator. One day a week all three of the Dixons learned and practiced basic survival skills like starting a fire without matches and making snare traps.

Monday meant a visit to the local library, located just three blocks from their house. Matt found books on math, engineering, physics, survival, and most importantly, farming. He was obsessed with planting crops and setting up irrigation systems once he travelled to Hanover. New Hampshire had a short growing season. He studied which vegetables he could grow, how to harvest the seeds after the season, rotating the crops, watering the crops, pest control. He studied canning, and how much food they would be need for a group of ten or more.

Matt and John studied livestock, how to milk a cow, how to pasteurize milk, how to slaughter animals, how to mate and grow a heard. There were endless topics to learn if they hoped to survive in the new world. Before the pandemic they did not know which berries were edible. They spent Monday through Thursday learning what they could eat.

As he waited for the rice to cook on the grill, Matt looked at math worksheets for Craig. He also paged through an edible plants book for his younger brother to read and write a one page book report on by Friday.

John and Craig stood in the kitchen chatting about fishing and laughing about John not catching anything for the third outing in a row. "Maybe Matt will share some of his farming books with you, Dad, you don't seem to be able to catch anything lately. Growing might be your thing."

"Okay, so I'm a little cold. I'll get my lucky touch back. Wait until we get to New Hampshire and I can fish with worms. I'll be much better there." He smiled as Craig continued to rib him. The sun poked through the clouds, and the temperature warmed ten degrees.

Craig walked to the sink to wash his hands. John went out on the deck and let the breeze blow in his face. It was still cool, 55 degrees, but a warm breeze blew from the south.

"The wind is up from the south again today." He looked over his shoulder at Matt, standing by the grill and watching the rice pot. "That's two weeks. It's time to go."

"It's still cold in the morning. Think how bad it will be in New Hampshire. It's only February." Matt was comfortable where he was. He did not want to leave.

"I like this house too, I like the ocean, I like how safe we are, and having electricity, and heat, and food, but we need to get up to Hanover and start a life with our entire family. Don't forget for one minute that you have a brother up there, alone, probably not living in a solar house eating fresh flounder and rice." John did not speak with anger or admonishment. He used a matter of fact tone. "We cannot let our comfort cloud Greg's situation, which is probably dire."

Matt knew his father was right. It took him a second to reply, but when he did, his voice acknowledged he was ready.

"When do we go?" Matt asked.

"We make a list of things we should take, we pick a vehicle we can load with extra gas and operates off road if necessary, we pack up, and leave this week. " John stated the obvious. "And we frame this as nothing but positive to Craig. You should work with him today on school, maybe mention he will be the teacher when we hook up with his cousins."

"Okay, I'll start to prep him, and I'll get the books we might need for the trip. The extended cab suburban is going to be the best option. We can fill it with food and water, convert the third row into a bed. The fuel economy stinks, but getting fuel is not a problem right now. It's also a beast off-road in the grass and mud. I'll start to pack."

"Can we have some lunch first? I'm starving." John said with a smile. "You're always so serious, lighten up a little bit." John's smile widened.

Matt was seldom serious. John enjoyed teasing him.

"Someone has to be the adult in the house. Another reason the Suburban is a good call? I was never taught how to drive stick, leaving army vehicles out of my capability." Matt walked away from his still smiling father in a mock huff.

Craig listened to the conversation from the other side of the sliding glass door.

"So I guess you heard all of that." John said in a loud voice so Craig knew he was talking to him. John pushed the door open and walked inside.

"Yeah." Craig replied in a sheepish voice that said he knew he should not have been listening.

"What do you think?" John asked. Craig proved himself to be a valuable member of the group. John spoke to him with the respect he deserved. While not a decision maker, Craig was always allowed input.

"I miss Greg. I want to leave. I don't care about this house or any of this stuff. I want to find my brother." Craig stood tall he spoke to his father. "I also like the idea of bossing around two kids younger than me. You tell me what I need to do. I'll pack up and leave whenever you tell me. Heck, I tried to leave months ago." Craig smiled at his joke.

"We'll leave as soon as we can, but not before I eat the fish you caught. Let's set the table and enjoy." John walked over to Craig and roughed up his son's mop of a hairdo. Both of his sons had grown up in the last few months, more than John realized.

John, Matt, and Craig sat at a round table in the kitchen's breakfast nook next to a bank of windows. The clouds were gone and the sun beamed welcome rays and warmth through the panes. They laughed and ate, enjoying lunch a little longer than usual. It was their last fresh meal at 'the mansion.'

Matt did not give Craig the math worksheets or edible plants book. Their afternoon was spent packing and preparing for the departure to Raleigh, NC.

24

Hubba sat on his bed in the corner of the kitchen watching the people run around. He was used to excitement and commotion. He stretched out his front legs, closed his eyes and waited for his call to the study later in the day. The kitchen was his favorite haunt. The nice men in white jackets always flipped him food.

The people running around the mansion were not nice today. They were frenzied. Hubba did not understand what was happening, but again, he was used to commotion. He happily drifted off to sleep in the sunny corner of the kitchen. Maybe the white coats would show up later, giving him a few snacks before his evening meal of kibble.

"What about the dog?" One of the men asked.

"Forget the dog, they are supposed to be carriers. Did you see the reports from Brazil? He'll be dead soon anyway. My dog died last week. He was old. I thought it was age. Now I know better."

"So we just leave him here? He'll starve. That's cruel."

"You want to bring a terminal disease carrying dog with us to Asheville? You'll never get through the security checkpoints. That dog stays here. Take it outside and shoot it, or open a bag of food and leave it on the ground if you want, but it ain't coming with us. The governor left on the plane this morning. Her kid has a fever. I doubt she's worried about the dog."

The first man shrugged his shoulders. He went to the cupboard and pulled out a bag of Hubba's food. He set the bag on the floor and tore the top open all the way. He placed two large roasting pans full of water on the floor next to the food.

"Good luck buddy." He said to the sleeping dog. He ran out of the kitchen, letting the door swing closed behind him and shutting the bolt at the top.

Hubba woke up later in the day. All the people were gone. He knew it would be calm at some point, but did not expect to be alone. It was unusual for no one to be in the kitchen. He walked over to his automatic water bowl and slurped, splashing water over the back and both sides of his dish. The bowl had two gallons of water, inverted in a jug, and would refill the bowl if the water fell below a certain level. Hubba watched the air bubble glug in the plastic jug, signaling more water filling his bowl.

He had to go to the bathroom. He always did after he drank. He walked to the back door and hit it with his paw. No one came. He hit the door again.

He waddled to the swinging door that led to the rest of the house. He hit it with his paw. No one came. He barked.

He waddled to the back door, lifted his leg, and peed on the floor. He went back to his bed and fell asleep.

Hubba was an evolutionary wonder. Typically the strongest and most adapted of a species moves along the evolutionary ladder. Hubba was a standard bulldog, a breed that is almost exclusively delivered caesarian, typically cannot breed without In vitro fertilization, and has no ability to hunt. Yet Hubba was the last of his kind. Canines fell victim to the rapture, or a mutated form of the rapture. Unlike apocalyptic movies with packs of wild dogs roaming the landscape, the post rapture world was void of wolves, coyotes, dogs, and dingos.

Despite being abandoned by the governor of North Carolina, Hubba survived seventy-five days in filth with little food and water. Today he slept happily on the front porch of his new owner's house. It was warm outside, but the red brick landing was cool from the night's low temperature. Hubba had the best of both worlds, a hot sun baking his back, and cool rocks on his belly.

It was good to be Hubba again. Winter was over, spring had sprung, and he had a new family that loved him.

His ears perked up as a large black truck pulled into his cul de sac. He lifted his head off the brick, stood up, and barked wildly.

Todd looked out the front window to see why his dog was barking. He saw the black SUV with red fuel canisters strapped to the roof and back. He grabbed a shotgun off the top shelf of his coat closet and went to the second floor. He wanted the element of surprise and the advantage of position over the strangers in the truck.

The black vehicle pulled into the driveway. Todd heard doors open and shut as he made his way up the back stairs.

"Todd? Anyone home?" It was John's voice. Todd was halfway up the staircase when he froze, ran back down and opened the back door to the garage.

"John! You're a month early! I was about to shoot you!" Todd ran over and threw his arms around his brother.

"It got warm. We decided to drive up. Man is it good to see you. Are your boys alive? Are they here?" John asked with apprehension. Tears of joy ran down his face, but worry clouded his questions.

"Yes, yes, they are in the woods." Todd looked over at Matt and Craig. "Oh my gosh, look how tall you are! I haven't seen you guys in a year or more. You're huge. Get over here, let me give you a hug." Todd pulled Matt in. His nephew was significantly taller than him.

Todd began to cry. He was the emotional brother. He held Matt tightly. "Get over here too, Craig. Give me a hug." He reached his hand out and grabbed his nephew by his shirt, pulling him in for a hug. Todd felt John's big arms wrap around the three of them.

"God damn I missed you guys." Todd sobbed as he hugged his brother and nephews.

John felt an animal nudging his calf. "Where in the world did you find a dog? Didn't all the dogs die? What the hell is this beast doing alive?" He bent down and gave Hubba a scratch. The dog panted, losing his breath during the short run from the front porch.

"That's a long story. His name is 'Hubba.'"

"Matt! Craig!" Brian and Jay were screaming and running across the backyard after spotting their cousins. When they got to the edge of the driveway, they slowed in an attempt to act cool.

"Hey." Brian said to Matt, flipping his head up casually.

"Hey? You come here little dude." He picked Brian up and flipped him over. Brian's feet were next to Matt's face. "It's been a while since I played the Brian guitar." Matt proceeded to strum tickles on Brian's tummy in mock guitar play. Brian was screaming with laughter, begging his cousin to stop.

Craig looked over at a smiling Jay. "I think this is a dueling guitar number." Jay bolted towards the back yard and the play equipment.

Matt put Brian down, "You have three seconds before I play my second number."

Brian screamed and ran. Matt turned to his Uncle, "the game's afoot!"

Todd turned to John and gave him another hug, tight and full of love. "I knew you'd be here, I knew it. I hung up the phone four, maybe five months ago and thought, he's still alive, he's coming, but then everyone died. Everyone, and I questioned if I was sane to believe my entire family would survive." Todd cried again.

"I know, Todd, I know." They broke their hug, stepping back.

"Do you need anything?" Todd asked. "Food, water, anything?"

"No, no, I'm good. We had a huge breakfast, lots of food and drink on the way up. I'm good." John bent down to pet the dog again.

"How was your winter?" John got down to business. "Has it been tough? Are the boys okay? They are young to lose their mother and all their friends."

"To steal from Mark Twain, 'the reports of my death have been greatly exaggerated.'" John heard a woman's voice respond from behind him.

He spun around. "What? You're alive?" He walked to Emily slowly. He placed his hands on the outside of her arms, holding her as if she were a mannequin. "How? How did you live? How is it possible?" He pulled her into his body and wrapped his arms around her.

"Um, I don't know, the same way you did, I guess?" She could tell John was shaken by her survival, like he was hugging a ghost.

"Dude, you going to stop hugging my wife? I know we're brothers, but I think I have to fight you if you don't stop soon. Plus, I think it's been a while since you've seen a woman."

John did not let go. He hugged Emily as if he was hugging his own wife. "I just assumed you were dead. My god it's good to see you. Megan and Jenny both died, I just, I'm sorry." He pulled away and looked at her again. "It's unbelievable, like a miracle."

"I think our boys have taken yours into the woods to show them the big fort they've been working on all winter. It's pretty cool back there. I'm sure you'll get a chance to check it out." Emily knelt down to pet Hubba. "Hey, did you meet our dog? I picked him up downtown last fall."

John was in shock. Tears streamed down his face. He expected to find his brother and nephews, but seeing Emily was too much for him to handle.

"Can I walk around a little? I drove the entire way." John continued to keep a hand on his sister in law.

"Absolutely. Do you want to walk around the neighborhood?" Todd could tell John was rattled.

"How about you let me go and I take you into into the woods to see the fort?" Emily said.

John released her, wiping his tears and nose on his long sleeved shirt. He walked to his truck and reached through the open driver's window for his bottle of water.

"How were the highways and roads? Did you take 95 the whole way?" Todd had not ventured beyond Raleigh.

"I made it in two and a half hours. We drove 100+ the entire way. Insane. No cars. Literally open highway. There was one roadblock we had to drive around, some kind of barricade or something at the state line, but it was minor, I hesitate to call it a road block." John took another swig as he walked into the backyard. "I did notice that some of the exits into towns were blocked off, like people didn't want visitors coming off the highway, but the highway itself was clear."

They could hear the kids yelling, laughing, and playing,. "I've tried so hard to give Craig a childhood since this all started. I guess it was easier with two young ones. We've," John paused, "had more setbacks than you."

"What is the word on Greg? He's obviously not with you." Emily asked curiously.

"The last time I spoke to him he was up at school, safe in the dorm. I told him to wait until he thought everyone was dead before making a break to Hanover for the winter. It's why we came up a month early. If it's warm down here, maybe it's warm up there." John stopped. "I'm so glad you're alive. It's a bright spot in the horrible nightmare we're all living." John cleared his throat. "Can you do me a favor and not talk about Greg too much with Craig and Matt? I don't know how long it will take us to get up there, if the roads are blocked around New York, if we have to go through the mountains. Who the hell knows? Let's keep it as casual as we can."

"Sure, John, sure." Todd looked at Emily. She nodded. John turned back towards the gate in the fence that led to the woods behind the house. Todd reached out and grabbed Emily's hand, squeezing it. He smiled at her. It felt great to have other people around.

"Matt, Craig, come over here and say hello to Aunt Emily." The boys looked up from behind a wall of sticks and leaves. They ran over for the reunion. Emily cried. Craig was bashful. Matt acted mature, but also cried.

The Dixon reunion party lasted for the rest of the day. Todd thawed hamburgers, an exciting treat for John, Todd, and Craig. Emily made orzo salad, and they opened a few cans of corn. Everyone laughed and played while enjoying an old fashioned cookout. Hubba made sure there were no leftover burgers.

At 7:30 the young kids were asleep. Craig was on the upper bunk in Jay's room. Brian made his upper bunk up for Matt, but did not stay up for his bunkmate to come to bed. The youngest Dixons were exhausted after the long and exciting day.

Emily, Matt, John, and Todd sat at the kitchen table. Solar lamps illuminated the room. John enjoyed a beer. His shoulders relaxed as tension left his body. Finding Todd and Emily shifted burden from him to other members of his family.

"So you haven't seen anyone else alive? No one? " Matt asked. He played with his brother and cousins all afternoon. This was his first chance to speak with the adults.

"Just Hubba." Emily answered. "We kept low for several months before actively seeking others. We gave up in October. As far as we can tell, there is no one else alive in Raleigh. If there were survivors, they left during the initial outbreak and they haven't come back."

"How are you on supplies? I mean, if you served us burgers tonight, I guess you're doing pretty well." John could tell that his brother was well stocked. He wanted to know exactly how well stocked.

"We are doing well on supplies. Raleigh was unique. Everyone left. The stores were abandoned, and left full of food. Hell, I have a warehouse store down the road with enough canned food to feed a hundred people for a year." Todd paused. "I'm worried about two or even three years out more than I am two months out. When all this pre-made stuff is gone or rotten, when we can't find canned tuna or pasta, when all the flour goes bad, if we don't know how to do it ourselves, we're screwed."

"I know, but at least we have two, maybe three years to figure out how to make and find our own food." John looked at his beer.

"We have a long time to talk about this stuff. Let's focus on what's been happening. I have to hear the story of that guy." He tipped his beer glass towards the snoring dog in the corner.

"That, my dear brother in law," Emily paused for affect, "Is the first dog of North Carolina." She told the tale of finding the dog on her mansion tour. John and Matt laughed so hard they cried at some of her stories. Todd sat back and smiled as his wife entertained them. It was a great night, the best any of them had since the rapture.

Todd and Emily's house was cold in the mornings, not as cold as it had been in the winter, when the entire family moved mattresses down to the living room to sleep next to the fire, but cold enough that all of them wore heavy shirts or light jackets inside.

"The standing house rules," Todd began. "The first person awake puts a fire bundle in the fireplace along with two logs, let's Hubba out, and presses the coffee maker button. The coffee maker runs on batteries, it was by far my greatest find. Emily can endure a lot of hardship, but not having coffee is not one of them."

Todd made the fire bundles in advance, forming small sticks, dry leaves, and old newspapers into a loose mass of tinder. There were typically a few coals left from the night before, the fire bundle, when put on the hot ashes, would catch after a few minutes, and was a safe way for his young boys to start the fire each morning. Emily did not like her six and seven year olds playing with fire, but realized that her new reality meant the boys had to learn how to make and sustain fire safely.

The adults said their goodnights and were asleep before 10pm.

Todd was usually the first one up, or he would wake when he heard Jay or Brian go downstairs. If Todd was up first, he would make the fire from scratch, conserving the fire bundles. If he came down with one of the boys, he would walk them through making the fire. This morning was different. Todd heard Jay come out of his room talking to his cousin, Craig.

"We have to start the fire to heat up the living room, then let Hubba out, and then press the coffee button. You do not want to see my mom if she doesn't get coffee. Seriously, she's like a bear. We call her mommy bear if she doesn't get coffee." Their voices trailed off as they went downstairs. Todd rolled over and looked at Emily. She was smiling. Her eyes were still closed.

"He's right about that." Todd said to her.

She opened her eyes. "Are you going to talk to John about Hanover?"

"He has to go. His son is up there. There is no option for him. If he and the boys go, you know I believe we should all go."

"I know, but we can't live up there. It doesn't make any sense. It's too harsh. We can't grow anything, and there's no reason to put ourselves through those conditions. My boys are too young. Hanover was fine when we thought other people might be alive, when we were concerned about lawlessness or chaos. Everyone is dead. We can live anywhere. We can live here."

"Emily, you and I have talked about this. We are going. We don't have a choice. Greg is up there. Hank and Paul are up there. If we end up back here, or down in Florida or somewhere like that, okay, but I think you have to resign yourself that we are staying together, and that means going to Hanover."

"You need to talk to John before we go, so he understands it will be an up and back excursion. Maybe float the idea that you two go alone. I can stay here with Matt and the kids."

"Okay, okay. Let's feel out the situation."

Halfway through the short but cold North Carolina winter, Todd reconsidered a move to New Hampshire. As he and Emily discussed their options, it made sense to live in a place like North Carolina or Virginia, where the winters are mild and the growing seasons are long.

A place like Florida created the opposite problem to New Hampshire. The summers are too hot and oppressive. Todd and Emily discussed the topic endlessly, deciding the mid-Atlantic states were their best option. They wanted to settle and get seeds in the ground as soon as possible.

On one of their many family days out, they visited a family farm amusement park. Emily picked the park because it had big slides and fun buildings, rather than mechanical rides requiring power. Similar to Pullen Park, the farm had a diesel train Todd was able to get working. The train went around a large oval, and was considered "lame" by Jay and Brian. Todd agreed about the ride, but what he noticed during their trip around the track was the antique farming equipment on display. The owner had an incredible collection of old-time tillers and seed row makers, things that Todd thought would be useful in their new life.

He went back to the farm the next day and unbolted several pieces of equipment, loading as much of it as he could into a U-Haul van. The equipment was in a neighbor's driveway, ready for use this spring.

The farm amusement park also had livestock, which Todd and Emily adopted. Goats, chickens, roosters, and rabbits lived in their neighbor's backyard in hutches and coops built last fall. Goats were a source of milk and easier to manage than cows, and they ate just about anything given to them. The chickens were a source of eggs and meat. The rabbits were delicious.

Todd and Emily were not eager to leave their safe and sustainable family compound to brave a northern New England winter.

Todd got out of bed and went downstairs. Jay took Craig next door to gather the morning's eggs. Their hen population was growing thanks to Emily's incubator. There were more than enough eggs for the three additional mouths.

The coffee was done. Todd placed sugar in a cup and poured himself a steaming mug of morning energy. He moved from the kitchen to the living room, where the fire was warming the cold morning air.

John came down the stairs and sat in a chair across from his brother and near the fire. "We had a solar powered house in Charleston, right next to the bay. It was fantastic. We fished for our meals, kept the house warm with electric heat, ran lights at night. I believe we could have lived down there for quite a while."

"Until a hurricane slammed into you without warning." Todd replied.

"Well, yes, until a hurricane came." John pointed to the coffee. "Do you mind?"

"John, you are not a guest, everything we have is yours. We have to think as a single family or unit, not two families that are visiting each other. Yes, take some coffee."

"You don't have to freak out because I politely asked for coffee in your house." John was not used to Todd being the serious one. Todd was the youngest, the funny one, the sarcastic brother who was seldom if ever serious.

"You know what? Now you can't have any coffee."

"Good luck with that. I'm taking the coffee."

The men watched through the back windows as Jay and Craig walked towards the house with a basket of eggs. Jay was non-stop talking to Craig, telling him about everything he could. Craig smiled and nodded. He was a great older cousin, and understood his role. They opened the back door and walked in.

"So you have to be really careful with the goats, because they are mean sometimes, and hiss at you, but we still milk them. You put their heads in this wood thing that my dad made, and then you can milk them. "

"So where's my goat's milk for my coffee?" John asked Jay.

"I don't milk the goats alone. I was just explaining that to Craig. It's a two person job, and we usually do it in the afternoon, when it's warmer." Jay was a fountain of knowledge.

"There is milk in the fridge in the garage. The food stays cold in there right now." Todd offered to John. "It's on the shelf below where you got the beer."

"Oh, okay, I was just kidding, but I'll take it. Great." John got up and walked into the garage to get the milk.

Todd went onto the back porch, still in his slippers and robe, to light his pizza oven. Designed by a famous American cook, the oven was large enough for several items, but small enough to light every day without burning too much wood. Todd made bread, pizza, and roasted meats. This morning he was going to bake bread from dough he made before going to bed. He placed a large cast iron pan on one side of the oven to pre-heat for an herb frittata.

He came back inside to knead the dough into shape.

"I will repeat my accolades from last night. That is one sweet pizza oven." John was in awe.

"It's portable, and is coming with us wherever we go."

"We're going to Hanover though, right?" John looked at his brother after the "wherever we go" statement.

"Of course, but if we pick a place after Hanover, it goes with us." Todd did not avert his eyes, he answered firmly, directly.

"Okay." John replied slowly.

Craig and Jay did not pay attention to the exchange, they continued to talk about "stuff."

"We usually have toast and eggs, or maybe pancakes and eggs for breakfast. I guess we're having fresh bread, which can take a while, 'cause my dad needs to heat the oven. He usually lets us have a granola bar or a cereal bar or something like that until the big breakfast is ready. Do you want one?" There was no one more excited to talk to other people than Jay. He was a chatterbox. The previous options of Mom, Dad, and brother knew all his stories, introducing new people gave him a new audience.

"I'm good." Craig replied. "You want to go kick the soccer ball around until breakfast is ready?" Craig was equally excited to meet up with younger people who would play.

"Yes!" Jay did a gesture with his arm, making a fist and pulling it down so his arm was bent.

"I'll call you when breakfast is ready. Have fun." Todd said as Jay and Craig pulled on heavier coats.

"Okay," they both replied, running out the door.

"We have a good life here, the growing season is longer, the winters are mild. The summers are hot, but not horrible. It's a nice place, John, a great place to consider."

"Wait a second," John started. "Wasn't Hanover your idea? Aren't we heading up there because you suggested it six months ago? Now you don't want to go?"

"A lot has changed, John. Look at the animals I've gathered. Look at the weather here in February. You know there are still snow storms headed towards Hanover. Six months ago I didn't know how this would all shake out. Now we do know. There aren't roving bands of marauders that we have to avoid. There hasn't been a military crackdown. Six months later we're it. Emily and I need support to raise our kids. You need support to raise your kids. I can't make this decision alone, but I can tell you, Hanover is not the best option for survival."

John nodded. He agreed. "We screw up in New Hampshire, we have no options, we're dead. We screw up here, miss the harvest, bugs eat our food, we can get to the coast and eat fish. I know. Up there, we freeze and starve."

"Let's forget about long term for now. We have to go. Your son is up there. Our brothers are meeting us there. I'm not saying my house is the best option, maybe your solar house on the coast is better, but we have to discuss our future. Emily and I are not going to move to Hanover just because we said we would during the chaos of a pandemic."

"So today's discussion is not where to live, it's when we leave." John said as he drank his coffee.

"Yep, right now we talk about getting up there. We'll talk about where we live later, as long as you agree it isn't Hanover."

Brian came downstairs asking where Jay and Craig were. Todd and John pointed outside and said one word, "soccer." Craig pulled his shoes on as fast as he could, screaming "thanks!" as he ran out the door.

Emily was next into the kitchen. She walked straight to the coffee pot. "Who has been drinking my coffee?" She stared at John. "You brought your own pot and coffee, right?"

"Nope." John said, taking a long, dramatic sip from his cup.

"It's only the second day, but I'm not sure this is going to work." Emily said to Todd. "He's your brother, so please talk to him about the rules. Rule one, don't touch my coffee. Rule number two is to follow rule one, and you'll do fine."

Todd turned to John, "Don't drink all the coffee. We need Emily to drink her coffee."

"Apparently." John replied.

Emily smiled as she poured herself a cup. "So what's on the agenda today?" She asked bluntly.

"I say we enjoy ourselves for a few days while we try to plan our next steps. Is that what you are thinking?" John answered.

"That sounds like a great idea. We have a lot to talk about, and a lot of decisions to make." Emily knew her husband broached the subject of Hanover and where they should settle. "But first, let's figure out how we are going to feed our kids, and what sort of fun we want to have." She took a sip from her mug. "There is a lot of fun stuff we can take Craig to today. We have working trains, slides, paddle boats, fishing."

"I think he'll be happy to play in the street with his cousins all day. It has been a while since he's had other kids his age to kick or throw a ball with." John looked out the front windows. He smiled at his son playing with his cousins. "He's had a hard time. I love that he can finally play."

Todd spread olive oil and salt over the top of his bread, getting ready to put it in the oven outside. He poked his fingers into the top and sprinkled sliced shallots and rosemary onto the focaccia. "Well, you're here now. We'll let the kids enjoy a few days before we talk about next steps." He continued to work, cracking a dozen of the eggs into a large bowl with a fair amount of goat's milk. He began to whisk the bowl, stopping to add salt and pepper before whisking again.

Todd had the dough in a pan on a large pizza paddle. He picked it up to walk out to the pizza oven and start baking his morning bread. It would not take long to cook. He had enough dough to make four pans of bread, two for this meal and two for lunch or supper. In the new world of finite fuel and materials, he always utilized a hot oven for multiple baking.

Emily went to the cabinet and pulled out a box. "I'm going to make some brownies, as long as the oven is on and we have eggs."

"Homemade brownies? Now I understand why you don't want to leave this place." John was excited for the food. He had electricity and fish in Charleston, but he had not eaten fresh eggs or bread in months. His family survived on rice, pasta, and fish. He was also excited about the fresh goat's milk, relegated to non-dairy powder for his coffee since the pandemic.

When Matt stumbled down the stairs there was a bounty on the table of eggs, fresh bread, milk, and coffee. He was happy to enjoy the feast, but less enthusiastic when he learned one of the house rules, "last one up does the dishes." Brian, on the other hand, was excited Matt was in the house, as he was consistently on breakfast dishes duty.

The day went according to plan, lots of playing, catching up on stories from the winter, and decompressing from the previous six months.

Matt returned to the role of 'kid,' enjoying games with his younger brother and cousins.

The Dixons ate a late dinner. Jay, Brian, Craig yawned before finishing their brownies. Fifteen minutes after the brownies, they were in their beds fast asleep. Emily tucked the children into bed and came down the stairs in comfortable pajamas and a robe.

"We have three very tired boys upstairs." She reported to the group.

"That was a great day Aunt Emily, thank you." Matt put a log onto the fire in the living room and sat down next to it. "You were talking about planting crops at the local Y?" Matt restarted a conversation from earlier in the day.

"Yes, there is a fence around this huge open space at the Y just down the road. There are two levels, probably four or five acres. We could use a tractor to plow this spring, get crops into the ground, and it is close to the house." Todd sat down in a chair in the living room with Matt.

"Where is the water source? Is there a natural lake or something nearby? We can't rely on rain." Matt asked questions based on his months of farm studies.

"There is a reservoir pond that is pretty close, maybe 100 or 200 yards away, but it's down a hill. I don't know of a river or stream that is close." Todd leaned towards Matt as he spoke.

"A reservoir is nice, but it will dry up just as quickly as our crops if there is a drought. We need a natural body of water that will withstand drought, otherwise we risk losing all or our food in a matter of weeks. If it doesn't rain during the month of July or August, and we don't water our crops, we're done. If we do use a reservoir, well, it needs to be above the crops so we can use aqueducts to move the water to the fields as needed. We can't use watering cans and walk 200 hundred yards up a hill."

Todd nodded. "You're right." He said. "You're right. That field would work if we could guarantee rain all year, but if we get three weeks of no rain? Done."

"If we don't have a natural water source near here, I'm not sure we can live here, meaning this house. We can't risk losing water. Rain barrels won't keep us going if we have to use them for ourselves, crops we have at the house, and the animals."

"Okay, I got it. You're right. If we have a drought like we had a few years ago, when it didn't rain for about three months, 100 rain barrels won't keep us alive, let alone our crops and animals."

Emily entered the room with a glass of wine. She sat on the couch and listened.

"We could get closer to Falls Lake or the Neuse River, those are both large water sources to sustain our crops and livestock." Emily interjected.

John walked into the room, having cleaned the dishes after dinner. "We want a body of water nearby so we can drink it, hunt the animals that use the water, fish, and use the water for crops. Water is life."

Todd hunched forward in his chair to think. "If we are going to move from this location, which is a certainty after Matt's points." He smiled at his nephew, "We should open our prospects to anywhere. Moving what we have a few miles is just as difficult as moving it 100 miles or even 1,000 miles."

"It should be an established farm. There is no reason for us to dig up grass and prep soil. I understand that we'll have to clean up last year's crops, probably left un-reaped, but that is easier than burrowing under grass." John considered locations in and around Hanover that would work. "Matt, you know that farm your mother used to drag us to each year? The one with the cows? It was owned by some wealthy family or something like that? That spot would fit the bill for this year."

"John," Todd started. "The gasoline is going to be bad by the end of the summer. We have to be where we want to live, permanently, by the end of the year. If we set up crops at that farm in New Hampshire, it's with the long range plans of living up there, forever. If we want to move after this summer, it's probably by horse and buggy, or by foot."

There was silence in the room, only the crackling fire's pops cut through the air. Hubba, enjoying a post dinner nap in the corner, rolled over and farted. The adults laughed at the dog.

"This isn't something we are going to solve tonight or need to solve tonight. It's probably not a decision we are going to make without Paul and Hank." Todd stood and stretched. "I don't know if tonight is the night we want to discuss our departure date for Hanover either. If it is, I'm okay, but if it isn't, we should discuss some short term goals." Todd sat back down.

"We, and when I say 'we' I mean Emily, have been home schooling the kids. We don't teach them every day, we alternate lesson days."

John cut him off before he could continue. "We do the same with Craig. Matt is an excellent teacher."

"They can be a little rambunctious, but as long as they are learning to read and write, well, I'm not worried about history and literature as much." Emily turned to speak directly to Matt.

"I work on reading and writing with Craig, but he's got both of those down well. I need him to learn math so he can help with farming and cooking. He doesn't need calculus as much as he needs basic survival math skills." Matt explained his teaching strategies to Emily.

"Good," Todd said. "We can continue their education for the short term. John and I will figure out and acquire our necessary supplies. To be honest, we might leave here in two weeks and find that we cannot get to Hanover by road for another three months."

Emily, sensing a turn to the serious topics, steered the conversation back to the day. "What a fantastic day this was. Matt, you and Craig are a welcome breath of fresh air for our kids. Craig particularly, being the right age to play. Thank you for being so patient and kind to your cousins."

Matt grinned. "They are fun kids. A little energetic, but that's okay. It's not like I have texts to return or posts to make to all my friends. The last six months have been weird, focusing on the people in front of me, rather than making sure people who aren't with me get messages. Weird, huh?"

"Not weird at all." Emily replied, "Not weird at all."

The families merged effortlessly, settling into routines over the next weeks. Craig, Jay, and Brian studied in the mornings and played until dinner. Matt and Emily traded off teaching and entertaining. John and Todd tended to the animals, hunted, and fished for fresh meals.

Despite their comfortable lifestyle in Raleigh, there was constant discussion and preparation for their departure.

"I know we've been over this a hundred times, but let's walk through our trip one more time." Todd and John ate peanut butter and jelly sandwiches in their newly acquired SUV. It was cool and raining outside, the temperature dropped to 53. A steady downpour of rain added dampness to the cold air.

"Let's take two vehicles, a motor home and a truck towing an animal trailer. We can use the truck to store fuel and food. We can stock the motor home with food. We have to assume we can scavenge the rest of our needs along the way and when we get up to Hanover." It was almost as if John was reading off a script he replied so quickly.

"We tow a flatbed behind the motor home with a small SUV in case we run into trouble with the other vehicles. We can get 400-500 miles on its fuel tank alone, which is a nice safety net. We would set the animals free. And hopefully, albeit a bit cramped, get somewhere safe or to another vehicle in 400 miles of driving."

"We'll take turns driving the RV and the truck." John took a bite of sandwich.

"When do we leave?" Todd and John knew what to take to New Hampshire. They struggled with when to leave.

"I say we leave on April 1st. We may catch an early spring thaw and get through on the roads. We have to decide which way to go. Do we hit the major cities, or do we use a rural path and risk going through the New York and Pennsylvania mountains?"

The men debated their route over and over, never settling on a decision. The mountains could bring snow and potentially strand the vehicles or cause them to crash. Washington DC and New York had potential bridge outages and confrontation with survivors. Do they take the rural route and avoid survivors, or do they embrace the idea of engaging other people by driving through major metropolitan areas?

Emily wanted to find people and other 'tribes' as she called them. She pointed out severe weaknesses of their current tribe. They had no doctor. If any injuries, something as minor as appendicitis, befell the group, they did not have the skill set to survive. Their group was missing women. Emily was spoken for and Todd had a vasectomy. Perpetuating the species was not going to happen in their current make up. They needed children and laborers to help sustain their families. She cried at night while talking to Todd, "will the world end up being Jay and Brian, and then the one of them left? Wandering the earth as the sole human survivor? How pathetic and sad a fate we could be leaving our two children. We have to find all the other people in the world and start a village. We need to maximize what's left of the human potential to create a better place to live and a better future for our boys."

Emily wanted grandchildren, and hope for a future. She talked about finding engineers and inventors that could create a village with electricity, lights, and technology.

John and Todd were wary of finding other people, particularly an evil person who might kill or hurt a member of the family. They were afraid of picking up a lazy freeloader who would not carry their weight, yet use resources. What could they do after a person was part of their village? Kick the person out in the cold to die? They had few options once they found people, so it was best not find people at all. Who would be in control of a village? Would there be a person who suddenly had control over the water? The food? Could the Dixons be subjugated to workers? John and Todd's outcomes were negative and bleak, but they were not unrealistic. Having a doctor would be nice, and finding women and children would be great, but at what risk?

The adults, including Matt, debated until late into the evenings. What future did they hope to bring to the world? What future did they hope to bring to themselves? Matt sided with Emily, and was vocal about finding other people. He wanted people his own age, if possible, or at least within a decade of his own age. He wanted people with different skills, and different abilities, and he knew he needed more hands to work. As his father, aunt, and uncles grew older, providing for the family would fall on him and the younger kids.

John was steadfast. He did not want outsiders in their group. He did not want to cede power to anyone. He wanted to live his life his own way. If he had to yield to a vote by his brothers and Emily, he could live with that decision, but yielding to a group of outsiders was not part of his plan. Outsiders meant the creation of laws, and laws had to be enforced. John raged endlessly against this new 'tribe' Emily wanted, and ranted about the perils of creating a new society.

Todd was the deciding vote. He understood Emily's logic about wanting a physician in the group. A healer was a necessary function in any working society. If they could find a doctor, the doctor could train one of the kids, handing down knowledge for the future. Todd understood Matt's argument about his future, his society. He could empathize with John's fears, but Todd felt the fears were overridden by the needs of the group. The benefits outweighed the risks.

Todd and John sat in the truck, rain streaming down the windshield.

"I vote for going up through Washington D.C. and New York. We'll bring the Suburban to tow the animals, not a flatbed truck. If we find people, we'll let them ride in the RV." This was the first time Todd voiced his new opinion to John. "There are probably 30-40 million people between us and New Hampshire. I bet we find, at most, ten survivors, maybe less. If we find 50, well, we find 50. They can join us or stay where they are, but we need to grow our group, John. I know you are against it, and I get your reasons, but I'm voting with Emily and Matt. I'm voting for Jay, Craig, and Brian's future, for wives for them, for lives for them past our deaths, for grandchildren for you and me. I'm voting with hope" Todd was overly dramatic in his speech, and he knew it, but he wanted to make John comfortable with the decision, a decision which was now final.

"I get it. I understand, and I support the group." John cleared his throat. He understood the decision, and wanted to make it himself, but he was afraid of who they were going to find on their travels. "If we find 50 people, and even 40 of them are like us, we're making the right call. I want this new society we are creating, this new tribe." He cleared his throat again, turned and looked at Todd. "I will say this to you, and I'll say it to Paul and Hank. If we take on new people and they're good, hard working, decent people, I will be the happiest man left on earth. If my boys can find partners for their lives, and have children of their own, well, it's worth it." John looked down at his feet, and then back up at Todd. "If any of the people we hook up with are bad, and they do anything bad, I'll kill them." John let it sink in. "I'll kill them if they even have the smell of doing something wrong to my family. Play time ended when the world died. Anyone who enters our group earns their keep. If they don't, I take care of it."

"Jesus, John, you don't have to go crazy on me here." Todd was taken aback.

"No, don't get squeamish on me. Know the decision you have made. I think it's the right decision, but understand   have your back, and Emily's back, and Matt's, Jay's, Craig's, Hank's, Greg's, and Paul's backs. I will take out any problem we have, and I will co it without hesitation. We don't live in a world of hesitation any longer. We hesitate on where we should live? We die. We hesitate on when to plant? When to harvest? What to plant? We die. I won't hesitate on eliminating threats."

They sat in the truck, listening to the rain coming down on the roof. They stared at the lot of RV's, deciding which one they wanted to take, waiting for the rain to stop so they could see which ones had fuel and would get back to the house.

"If we find any New Yorkers, they better god damn not be Jets fans. This is a New England tribe, and I'll be goddamned if I will hear stories about the Jets. If someone stands up and has a green football jersey on? We keep rolling, doctor or not." John used the same tone, but was obviously joking, at least Todd thought he was joking.

"John, it's a good idea, stopping for people. I know you focus on the negative scenarios, but think of the upside. If we find a mechanical engineer, an electrical engineer, a person who can get some of the power working? A doctor who can save the kids, set a broken leg, I think there is tremendous upside."

John held up his hand to stop his brother. "Todd, I know, it's the right call. You're making the right decision. I agree with you 100%. I just want you to know, you don't have to worry about the negative aspects of this decision. I will take care of it. I hope I don't, but I will, and I won't lose sleep and I won't bat and eye."

They sat for another half hour, eating their sandwiches and talking about where to live. Neither of them brougt up the conversation again. When the rain did not stop, they decided to find an RV regardless of how wet they got. They tried four different 'homes on wheels' before settling on a giant $400,000 diesel with every bell and whistle available. It boasted the most horsepower, and could tow a small SUV without a problem or additional loss of miles per gallon.

They attached a car platform and John drove the behemoth back to the house. Todd followed in their SUV.

Emily was ecstatic about the new RV. It was beautiful, and provided all the comforts they needed for a potentially long trip north. She also agreed with the April 1st departure. She began to move supplies into the RV immediately, taking stock of its storage capacity.

The RV was incredible. There was a bedroom in the back with a king bed, perfect for sleeping three to four at once, as long as two of the people were Jay and Brian. There was a sleeper sofa and another full sofa in the living room area. If they brought blow up mattresses, they could sleep seven comfortably in the giant rolling house. There was a kitchen with burners for purifying water and cooking meals, and an oven for baking. There was a large television with a DVD player. The RV had the potential of being more comfortable and entertaining with more utilities than their current house.

"We should have moved into one of these months ago." Emily said after inspecting the vehicle from top to bottom. "I've got a month's worth of food in there already, and we still have tons of storage. Jay and Brian are filling the water tanks with bottled water, and Matt is taking care of the non-potable tanks with the water from the rain barrels. We'll be ready to go by March 15th, and definitely ready on April 1st."

"Aye, aye captain." Todd replied in a sailor voice.

Emily gave him a look, "You might find yourself sleeping out here sooner than April 1st if you keep that attitude."

"I'll just keep the current home humming along, you get the rolling house prepped." He gave her a wink and a smile.

At the end of another long day Craig, Jay, and Brian were in bed, Matt, Emily, Todd, and John sat in the living room next to a fire. The days were warmer, but the nights still had a chill. The fire was necessary and created a nice ambiance.

"I have a few requests, which might alter our timetable a bit." Emily started, catching the three men off guard. "I'd like to make a few stops on the way up to New Hampshire, sight-seeing if you will. I think it's important for the kids, Craig included, to see some of our nation's history. This might be our last opportunity."

The men were silent before John spoke. "What did you have in mind?" John looked over at Todd with a, 'really? You couldn't have brought this up sooner?' look.

"Don't blame Todd, he had nothing to do with this. You two are concerned about routes and snow, I think about the kids. I want to tour the White House. I want to see the Lincoln Memorial and a few other highlights. We can even sleep in the White House. That would be pretty neat, don't you think?"

"You realize we are bringing the chickens and goats, right? You want to spend a few days in D.C. with livestock in tow?" John told her.

"Yes, to both questions." Emily did not back down. She seldom did. "This is it, our last time in Washington D.C. You want to take the Declaration of Independence? The Constitution? Keep them as souvenirs? We can. We can grab any art you want when we get to New York, drop by the Metropolitan and take Monets and Van Goghs, line our walls with them, but after this trip, we're done. We have no way to show our kids the Washington Memorial except through pictures. No way to show them New York City except in movies. This is not a joke from the crazy lady who likes to tour homes, this is a request from a mother who isn't going to have another opportunity to give her kids memories." Emily's tone was serious.

"I'd like to see that stuff again. I haven't been since I was like 7." Matt chimed in.

"I haven't been since I was 21. I'm in too." Todd said in support. "Hey, John, we can stop at the Meadowlands, pick up some Jet's paraphernalia, whatever you want."

"You're hilarious, Todd, just hilarious." John waited a second before responding. "I have to admit, you make a great point. I doubt we can get up to Hanover this early anyway. Making some stops, grabbing some memorabilia is an interesting idea. We want to find survivors, and driving into the heart of D.C. and New York is part of the plan anyway. We might as well take the kids to the sailboat pond in Central Park."

"Now you're getting into the spirit. I mean, let's not go crazy, make this a three week tour of the east coast, but let's not pass up the opportunities we have during the trip." Emily was excited by the acceptance of her plan. She thought about it months before, but was afraid to bring it up. Now that they had a house on wheels, stopping a few times on the way to New Hampshire was not a problem.

"Are we going through Philly?" She asked. Their route was fluid at the moment, changing with each conversation.

"Let me guess, you want to see the Liberty Bell?" Matt joked.

They all laughed. John put it back to the group. "If we want to hit cities, our current route takes us through Richmond, D.C., Baltimore, Philly, New York City, and going a little out of our way to hit Boston and specifically Hightower to see if Greg is there. That is just about every major city on the east coast north of Charleston."

Todd nodded, "I don't feel like we need to go out of our way to engage any more metro areas. My question is no longer how we are getting to Hanover, but rather how long are we staying in each city? Are we buzzing through Baltimore? Are we slowing down and blasting music or something? What efforts are we making to find other people?"

They thought about the question. Matt answered, "I say we leave a week earlier than planned and we make strategic camps in each city. I don't know how big Richmond is, maybe we spend one night there, but we get up there, we light a fire, a big fire, we blast some air horns, maybe every hour, then we pack up and leave the next day. Maybe D.C. is three days instead of one, and we move the camper each night to a different part of the city. Obviously we could spend weeks doing this up and down the coast, but we don't want to delay getting to Greg, Uncle Paul, and Uncle Hank. We make sure we can get to Hanover by mid to late April, and we make a strong effort to find people."

"You're a lot smarter than most 17 year olds, you know that Matt?" Emily smiled at him.

"I might be the only 17 year old in the world, but thanks." He smiled back. "I feel like I have ownership of the plan to round up people, and I've been thinking about it for a while. You gave me the courage to bring up stopping in each city. As long as we are sight-seeing, let's find people too."

"Is there anything keeping us here?" Todd asked. When no one had a good response, he suggested a new departure date. "Let's plan on leaving in a week."

Jay, Brian, and Craig were the most excited about the proposed adventure. They envisioned two days of boring drive time to New Hampshire. Now they had high hopes of meeting other people and seeing interesting things.

Matt created a lesson plan for the kids. They made a trip to the library to check out books about New York and Washington D.C. He talked to them about Camden Yard and Yankee stadium. He showed them pictures of the monuments they were going to see. He had so many books about New York City, he began to get excited about the trip too.

"There is one big rule the three of you have to follow. It's the number one rule." Matt and the parents had a lot of rules for the kids.

"Seriously, I have to follow this one too, okay?"

Craig, Jay, and Brian nodded.

"We are going to meet new people on this trip." Matt paused. "Well, we hope we are going to meet new people."

"Yeah, we know that." Craig responded. He was less in awe of Matt than the two younger kids.

"Yeah, okay. Well, the one rule you need to follow, no matter what, you should never be alone with any of the new people. Ever. Don't let them get you alone. I'm not allowed to be alone with them either. We are always in pairs and one of the pairs is always an adult. No exceptions. Do you understand?"

"What if the new person is a kid, like us, are we allowed to play with kids by ourselves?" Brian asked. Surely a kid was not off limits.

"No, you always have one of us there. If you are ever caught alone, you're in big trouble. This is a dangerous trip, you need to stay with us, never get alone with anyone other than your family. Never."

The kids nodded again.

"We're going to have a great time, don't sweat the rule too much, we just want to make sure we all have fun, and we all stay together. These cities are big places. We don't want to get lost. Stay with one of us, and you won't."

It was the first conversation of many Matt and the parents had with the three younger Dixons. Taking on new people meant preparing for potential issues.

John continued to have fantasies about encountering evil hoards of survivors. "If we come across hostile gangs, people who are starving and want our vehicles and food, I am just going to drive. We hop in the RV and the truck and we just drive, fast."

Todd acted sincere when he listened, but he did not share his brother's bleak world view. If his family, with a six and a seven year old, could survive comfortably, it meant other families or people probably did the same. He wondered if entire families survived like his and John's, or if people were one off survivors like Paul and Hank.

After one more week of preparation and planning, Todd was about to find out if there were any survivors. He, Emily, and the three young kids piled into the RV with Hubba. They pulled out of the cul de sac early in the morning. The kids watched a movie. Emily sat shotgun.

Todd and Emily said goodbye to their house and neighborhood the night before. She turned to him as they pulled away. "This was a great place to raise our family. I'm sad that we won't ever see it again." She doubted Raleigh would be their final location choice. It was too far from the Ocean.

"I liked it here. We had great friends, and a great community, but it died last year. We'll build our life in a different spot."

John and Matt drove the SUV, pulling a livestock trailer filled with chickens and goats.

It was only a three hour drive to Richmond. Emily made the commute several times a year for business. She recommended the Museum District off the highway as their first campsite.

The highway was empty. Todd feared bridges and overpasses would be destroyed, but they made an uneventful drive north on US 1, merging onto US 85 North, and again merging onto US 95 North, the road that would take them all the way into Boston.

Emily pointed to their exit, and Todd pulled the behemoth house on wheels off the highway. He drove a few blocks into the suburb, and came to a full stop in a town square. He laid on the car horn for a full minute. Hubba barked loudly. The kids held their ears and screamed.

John and Matt were out of their car pulling a metal trash barrel to the center of the street and filling it with debris. There were dead leaves covering the ground. The town was unkept and abandoned.

"I don't hold out much hope. There are only 300,000 people in this metro area. The idea that we could attract the one or two survivors, well, it's a speck on a needle in a haystack." John continued his role as group pessimist. Statistically he was correct, there should not be a survivor in Richmond. "Besides, if I lived here, I'd bolt for the Chesapeake as soon as I could. That is a much better resource for food than anything around here."

"There's nothing that says we have to stay here an entire day. Let's light the signal fire, have a picnic lunch in this square, see if there are any supplies we can take, and move along this afternoon. We'll leave the fire burning and hang a sign with instructions to our next stop." Todd knew they had time to burn, but having idle time did not mean he wanted to burn it sitting around the empty city of Richmond, VA.

"I'll make some sandwiches, and we'll hang out for a few hours." Emily announced after listening to John and Todd's exchange. "Why don't one of you blow an air horn a few times, maybe two or three bursts in each direction, throw some wet leaves on the fire?" She ducked into the RV to make lunch. Hubba stuck his head out, jumping down the steps. He waddled over to the center of town and used the facilities.

Todd turned to John. "One good thing about the end of the world, no leash laws, and I don't have to pick up dog poop in public places."

John nodded, but did not acknowledge the weak attempt at humor. He walked a few paces and blew the air horn, holding the button for a three count. Hubba went crazy, barking loudly and bee-lining it back to the RV, up the steps, and out of sight.

John blew the horn three more times. Thick black smoke rose from the trashcan fire. Survivors had three hours before the caravan pulled out of town.

Two hours and two horn blasts later the boys were playing soccer in the square, and the adults were peering into a few of the local shops. A car engine hummed in the distance. John yelled for the kids to get into the RV, and he pulled a gun from his waist. He ducked into one of the stores.

Emily and Todd walked towards the RV and saw a small red car driving towards them. They started waving in a friendly fashion, wearing big smiles on their faces. "Is your crazy brother really hiding with his gun pulled out, waiting to pounce on this person?" Emily said through her smile.

"I guess. It's not a horrible idea, but it's not the most welcoming approach either."

"Matt's got the kids in the RV. I think we are a go." Emily was nervous. Finding and engaging new people was her idea. She hoped it went well. The red car drove cautiously down the road towards them. Emily could make out one figure in the driver's seat of the small luxury coup. The car pulled up short of the waving Todd and Emily. A young woman rolled down the driver's window and stuck her head out.

"Oh my god you are actual people, real people. I thought I was alone, but you are real people. Are you broken down? Do you need help?" The woman had a slight accent, Latino, Italian, or Spanish. Emily could not be sure. The girl had a dark complexion, jet black hair, brown eyes, and was attractive.

Emily and Todd decided if they met a woman or a child, Emily would engage. If the new person was a man, Todd would lead.

Emily stepped forward. "No, we're doing well. My name is Emily Dixon and this is my husband Todd. There are seven of us and we are headed north to find family members. We are trying to find other survivors to join us."

"It has been months since I have spoken to someone or heard another voice." The girl did not cry, but tears welled in her eyes. She gripped the steering wheel to maintain her composure.

Emily continued. "We're nice, normal people. We even have a dog. Are you hungry? Would you like something to eat or drink? Again, my name is Emily, this is my husband Todd. What is your name?"

The woman turned off the car and opened the door. She stood and fell into Emily's arms. "I am so lonely. At first I was scared, but now I am lonely and bored. I cannot believe you found me." She cried. Emily held her, patting her back, and telling her, "It's okay, it's okay."

Todd waved to the small faces looking through the windows of the RV. The door opened and the boys spilled out with a barking Hubba. The dog trotted to the new girl and sniffed her feet and legs.

"You really have a dog? I thought all the dogs were dead?" The girl was calm. She backed out of Emily's arms to bend down and pet the dog. Hubba was indiscriminant about scratches. He sat and enjoyed new person. He was panting from the short burst of energy displayed jumping from the RV and jogging to the new person.

"That's Hubba." Jay the chatterbox told her. "He's the first dog of North Carolina. My mom rescued him from a mansion. My name is Jay." The six year old walked to the girl and stuck out his hand.

The young woman stood and took Jay's hand. "My name is Solange, but my friends call me Sol." She sniffed in her tears. "Because you are now my friend, you may call me Sol. Very nice to meet you, Jay."

Solange was young, 28 or 30 was Emily's guess. She was thin with an athletic build, and normal height for a woman, maybe a little taller. Now that Solange stood in front of her, Emily realized the woman was not just attractive, she was drop dead gorgeous.

Solange turned to Emily. "Nice to meet you Emily, I am sorry I lost control for a moment. I have been alone for a long time." She leaned in to give Emily another hug, and a formal greeting.

Jay decided, since he was Solange's first friend, to introduce her to the group. "Sol, this is my brother Brian. He's seven." Jay held Solange's hand and walked her to the other children.

Brian was shy when he met new people. He stared down at his feet and mumbled a soft "hello."

"He's kind of shy when he meets new people, but he'll warm up to you. This is Craig, my cousin, he's ten." Craig shook hands and said hello. Craig tapped Brian on the shoulder, said "tag," and ran off to play soccer. Jay decided soccer was a better option. He dropped Solange's hand, and ran off, yelling over his shoulder, "and that is my cousin Matt, he's like 17 or something like that!"

"Hello Matt, very nice to meet you." Solange shook his hand and walked back to Todd and Emily. "And very nice to meet you, Todd." She leaned forward and hugged a surprised Todd. "What a nice young boy you have, young boys I should say." The introductions sent the group into a pre-rapture paradigm. Solange stood silent, waiting for the adults to speak.

"My brother in law, John, is somewhere over there, waiting to see if you are friend or foe. He is Matt and Craig's father, and should be out at some point." Emily was embarrassed, but believed candor was the best policy.

"I understand. In this new world, it does not make sense to be too trusting." Solange spoke controlled and proper English. "My full name is Solange Wright. I am an exchange student from Ecuador studying at VCU. I was enjoying my summer semester when the sickness began. I had no way to get home to my family. Travel to other countries was halted after Brazil. I have been living near the VCU campus. I had nowhere to go."

Solange shrugged her shoulders. "I stayed in the dorm until it became cold. I hid from the police. When everyone was gone, I found a house and have been living by myself. I have plenty of food, and I am excited to talk to you, to meet all of you. As I have said several times, I am lonely." She wore jeans that were loose on her waist and legs, a gray t-shirt with gold VCU written across the front, and a long sleeve flannel shirt, unbuttoned and hanging loosely like a jacket.

"Do you know if your family survived? Do you know anything about Ecuador?" Matt stepped forward.

"The internet stayed up longer than the phones, and I followed my family until they were taken by the rapture, or el encantado as we called it. My family, my parents, my two brothers and one sister, all died. It is just me. It is why I stayed here. I really do not have a place to go. I waited to see if the government would arrive. It appears you have come in its place." She smiled.

"Have you seen any other survivors?" A voice said loudly from across a street. John emerged from the store. He walked up to the new woman and held out his hand. "Hello, I'm John Dixon."

"Solange Wright, very nice to meet you, sir. As you can see, I am not a threat, just a young woman who has not seen a single survivor in months. I have driven around Richmond trying to find another person. I have not seen anyone."

Todd extended an invitation to Solange. "Sol, if I can call you Sol, my family has been living in Raleigh, North Carolina for the last seven years. John's been in Charleston, South Carolina for the last ten years. We have two brothers that are meeting us in Hanover, New Hampshire this spring. John has a son who is trapped at a boarding school, much like you were trapped at VCU. We kept in touch with them until late September. We are positive they survived el encantado. We are driving to New Hampshire, seeking out survivors and inviting them to join our group. We aren't sure we are going to settle in New Hampshire, but wherever we do settle, we'd be happy to have you join us. We have some livestock, and plenty of food. We can stay in Richmond for a few days if you need time to consider coming with us, but we welcome you with open arms."

"New Hampshire is cold, right? Very cold?" She replied.

"Yes, which is why we probably won't settle there. John and I grew up in Hanover. When we had to pick a meeting spot during the chaos, our families decided on a place we all knew."

"I do not have to think about it. I would like to join your group, if you will have me. I will work hard to become a strong member. I do not have many belongings, but I would like to get my clothes and my family pictures. If you will give me some time, I do not live far from here. May I come back in a few minutes?"

"Absolutely, take your time, we will wait. Welcome to the family, Solange." Todd said with a smile.

"Do you need any help?" Matt offered. "I could come and help you pack and carry."

"No thank you, Matt, I can pack quickly on my own. I will be back shortly." She turned and jumped into her beautiful two-door, cherry red, Mercedes Benz. She slipped it into drive and sped away, much more quickly than she pulled up to the Dixons a few minutes earlier.

"Matt." John said to his son. "What's the first rule? Were you about to get in a car with a stranger? I know you haven't seen a girl in six months, but let's keep your head on, okay?" He rustled Matt's hair. "I'm also counting that as a 'denied.' So, ouch."

Matt hung his head with a smile. "That was not a play to meet her, I swear. I was just trying to make her feel welcome to the group."

"Uh, huh, like you helped me pack, or anyone else pack for this trip." Emily razzed. "You just got sacked, player QB. Take a seat on the bench." The adults had a good laugh at Matt's expense.

Jay ran over from playing soccer. "Where's Sol? Is she gone already?"

"She'll be back. She's going to come with us." Emily told Jay.

"Sweet! Hey guys! Sol is coming with us! I call her on my team!" He ran back to Craig and Brian.

"What do you think?" John asked Todd and Emily. "I know my son's opinion." He looked at Matt with a smile.

"Best case outside of a person with needed skills, although we did not ask her about engineering. Maybe she is an electrical or mechanical engineer, and can help us get things running again." Todd said back.

"She has great taste in cars." Emily said. "That's a good sign."

John looked down the empty street. "I don't think anyone is that good an actress, but just in case, Matt and I will hide until she gets back. If she was a scouting party, we may be sitting ducks. She got all of our intel."

"Intel?" Emily repeated. "Seriously?"

John ignored the comments. "Matt, grab a rifle and find a building on the other side of the square, just until she comes back alone." Matt nodded to his father before walking towards the Suburban to find a rifle. John made his way to a new hiding spot on the square.

Todd and Emily clasped hands and went to supervise the soccer match.

Solange drove back to her house a half mile from where she had met the Dixons. When she arrived at her cape cod just off campus, she sat in the car and cried.

She wiped her tears and ran into the house to pack. She stuffed her tablet into a brown leather purse, threw her clothes into a Louis Voutton rolling bag, and jogged back to her car. Solange kept family pictures and videos on her tablet, charging it through the car's cigarette lighter. It was all she had of her family and country aside from memories.

Surviving a plague alone in a foreign country, unable to be with her family as they died, earned her this new start with the Dixons. They did not need to know about her past.

"Adios." She said to the house, speaking in her native tongue when she was alone. Solange turned her music on shuffle and put on her ear buds. Kelly Clarkson sang "Stronger." She sped back to her new friends, returning in under twenty minutes to her new life.

Solange parked the car across the street from the RV. She slung the shoulder bag, pulled the roller from the passenger's seat and announced, "I'm ready."

"You travel light." Emily smiled. "I like that."

"I have all of my personal items on these." She held up the technology. "And I do not have many winter clothes. I have found that I can acquire new clothes where ever I go. I only bring essentials. I buy or take what I need when I travel." Emily assumed Solange was referring to a post rapture lifestyle, but Solange used the same strategy before the rapture. She brought only the one suitcase and purse with her from Ecuador ten months ago.

"We believe the same. It's nice to see you have a head on your shoulders." John emerged from his sniper spot. He was impressed with the young woman. High praise, considering he was holding a gun on her just a half hour earlier.

"I'll get the kids and we can head to D.C." Todd announced. He walked over to the park. "Kids, let's go."

"Is Sol back?" Jay asked excitedly.

"She is. I don't know if she is riding in the Suburban or in the RV, but she's decided to come with us."

Jay and Brian ran towards the RV. Craig collected the ball and walked towards his uncle. "She seems nice. Is she American? She talks funny."

"She's from Ecuador, that's in South America." Todd told him.

"Like Mexico?" Craig asked.

"Kind of, but not really. You know Mexico is in North America, right?. It sounds like you need a geography lesson. Maybe she can help you learn more about Ecuador and South America." Todd took a step towards the RV and felt something soft under his foot.

"Nasty." Craig said. He saw dog poop ooze from the sides of Todd's shoe.

"You have got to be kidding me." Todd muttered. He held his profanity in front of Craig. Todd dragged the bottom of his shoe through the grass, attempting to get the crap off. The poop was imbedded into the treads of his sneaker.

John watched. "You know, people picked up dog poop so they wouldn't step in it themselves. It wasn't just a societal rule."

"Asshole." Todd said back.

Emily stood at the door of the RV. "You're not coming in here with those shoes. Find a hose and clean them off or throw them away, but that poo is not stinking up our home."

"These are my favorite shoes. You know they don't make them anymore." He pleaded, looking around for a hose.

"No one makes anything anymore, Todd, and maybe you'll clean up after Hubba next time." She said.

"He's your dog." Todd muttered.

"Clean them or chuck them." Emily shut the door on her husband. He heard a click as she locked the door.

Todd walked towards a street of homes, hoping to find a working hose. These really were his favorite shoes.

"Where would you like me to ride?" Solange asked John. "In the house or in the truck?"

"You pick. I'm driving the truck. We have music and conversation. If you ride in the house, you can watch a movie or play video games with the kids."

"I would like to ride in the truck with you and Matt, if you do not mind." She asked politely. "I have been without adult conversation for six months. I like children, but I would like to talk, at least during the first part of our trip." Solange walked towards the SUV with her suitcase.

"How long is the trip to New Hampshire?" She asked.

"We can get there in a day, if there isn't any snow, and if we didn't have plans to stop in Washington D.C., Baltimore, Philadelphia, New York City, and Boston." John said back, opening the door. "Would you like to say goodbye to your car?" He nodded towards the Mercedes.

"It is a car, a very nice car, but a car. I will not miss it. I enjoy people more than things." Solange replied.

"Sol is with us." John yelled.

Todd waved back. He walked towards the RV in socks, holding wet but clean shoes.

The tribe was one member stronger as it headed towards Washington, D.C

25

It was February, and Hanover was cold. The snow had been on the ground for three months. It continued to snow each week, piling and drifting above the window sills. Greg commented that it provided nice insulation against the wind, which howled most days. Rebecca was warm, dry, and well fed, but she was stir-crazy.

The weather turned on the two teenagers in December, becoming bitterly cold at night, and not much warmer during the day. Greg and Rebecca quickly realized they needed to get serious about winter preparations. They gathered large amounts of firewood, and stored it just about anywhere they could. They filled the side porch at the front of the house as well as the upstairs bedrooms with wood. They filled the back of their van with wood, and parked it next to the house for easy access. They knew the van would be useless once the snow flew. More wood filled the halls and rooms of the sorority next door, seasoned and dry when needed.

Their chickens lived in a butlers shed at the back of the cottage. Rebecca created a coop by shredding newspapers, books, and computer paper in place of hay. The coop was warm despite the outside temps. It smelled bad, and Rebecca vowed to change the paper once a week, but the chickens did not mind the smell, and they continued to lay eggs. Rebecca and Greg found five other chickens during their first weeks in Hanover and were back up to eleven.

They had more than enough food to get them through the winter, but Greg was obsessed with hunting fresh meat. He bundled up in as many clothes as he could, and headed out with his shotgun a few times each week. He set traps in hopes of snagging smaller animals, and to his credit, he captured dozens of squirrels and other small game, giving welcome meat to stews and rice dishes.

Greg could hunt for about an hour before his fingers and toes began to freeze. The snow was so deep he found it impossible to go far without suffering complete exhaustion. His typical hunt involved walking the half mile to the Hanover golf course and setting traps in the woods and running trails.

Rebecca suggested he use a snow blower to clear the trail to the course. The trick worked perfectly. Greg blazed the path to his hunting area, leaving the blower under a tarp at the course. When it snowed, he trudged over in his snow shoes and used the blower to clear the path on his return trip.

Greg was off on a hunting trip to the golf course, and Rebecca was washing clothes in the bathtub when a high pitched noise, like the whine of a dirt bike, hummed through the walls of the cottage. She rushed to the window and watched two people on snowmobiles move in front of her house before making a left turn down Choate road. The snow mobiles dragged sleds with large packages.

Rebecca was alone, and quickly considered her options.

"What should I do?" She said out loud. "Get in clothes and make a break for a dorm, waiting for Greg to get back? Hide in here? Do I think they saw or smelled the smoke from our fires? Of course they did, or they will eventually. They are going to come back. I know they are going to come back. What should I do? Think Rebecca." She was trapped. If she fled, her fresh footprints in the snow would lead anyone to her new location. Her best bet was to hide, and hope it bought her enough time for Greg to return with his gun. If she stayed in the house, the only tracks out the door were Greg's. The snowmobilers might not search the house at all, believing the sole inhabitant was outside.

She heard the whine again. It got louder as the snow mobiles came back in her direction. She did not look out the window. She grabbed her heavy coat and ran upstairs to one of the wood storage rooms.

While loading the upstairs bedroom, Rebecca made a hiding place large enough for two people. She put a four person dining room table against the wall at the start of the second row of wood. She stacked wood on top of the table, and blended a panic spot into the five rows filling the room. She left a gap at the end of the rows on the far wall that was large enough for her small frame to squeeze through. If someone looked in the room, even peered over the top of the wood stacks, the rows appeared solid, concealing her hideout. She kept two bottles of water, unfortunately now frozen, and several protein bars in the hiding spot. She had a lantern, but did not turn it on. Half a dozen fleece blankets were folded neatly under the table.

She huddled in her hiding spot. Her breath was visible in the cold upstairs. She was panting, nervous. "Calm down, Rebecca. No one will find you. If you control your breathing, stop making noise, you are safe until Greg comes back." She gained her composure.

There was a loud knock on the door. She squeezed her eyes shut, hoping it would make the people go away. She knew the smoke coming out of the chimney meant they were coming inside the house.

The outer door opened and Rebecca heard feet stomping in the mud room. The inside door opened and a voice called out. "Greg? Greg, are you in here? It's Uncle Hank and Uncle Paul. "

Rebecca opened her eyes and began to yell. "Oh my god, you're alive! I didn't believe him when he said you'd be alive, and you're really alive!" She shimmied out from under the table and around the wood stacks to run down the stairs.

Paul and Hank stood in the vestibule, stopping when they heard a female voice. "Uh, who are you?" Paul asked. He was covered in snow. He wore a neoprene face mask, large ski gloves, and a black ski suit. He pulled goggles off his eyes to display a bearded and pink wind burned face.

"My name is Rebecca. I'm a friend of Greg's. He's out hunting, but should be back soon. Oh my god, you're both alive. Come in! Come in! Shut the door, get warm by the fire."

"Wait, who are you again? Greg is hunting?" Paul was dumbfounded.

Hank pushed passed his brother and into the house. He was cold and did not care about Paul's questions.

"My name is Rebecca. I met Greg in Concord on his trip from Hightower to here. We came to Hanover in November."

The men were stone faced. They did not expect to find someone other than Greg, let alone a young girl. They stood by the front door, now shut, unsure of what to do next.

"I don't have cooties, you can come in and warm yourselves by the fire. I have some water boiling. Would you like tea or hot chocolate? I can make soup too." Rebecca switched into her no-nonsense get things done mode. These were Greg's Uncles, they were family. She needed to get them inside by the fire to warm up. "Where did you come from?"

Paul relaxed and embraced the situation. "Hi Rebecca, my name is Paul. This is my brother Hank. We are Greg's uncles. Anything warm sounds great, but if you have chicken noodle soup, I'll take you up on that." He started taking off his snow gear; gloves, hat, and suit. "Is there a place I should put this stuff to dry? I hate to get the living room floor wet."

"I'll take them and put them in the kitchen. The woodstove will dry your clothes quickly. Please take off your boots and leave them in the mud room shoe bin." Rebecca held her arms out to receive the snow covered clothes.

"I can do it, just show me the way." Paul elbowed Hank, who was still standing near the door in shock.

"Nice to meet you, Rebecca. My name is Hank. Soup sounds fantastic. Lead us to the kitchen."

The men took off their boots before following the young girl.

Paul and Hank looked around the living room. It was immaculate and tastefully decorated. Two sofas ran perpendicular to a warm fire along with two comfortable chairs at the top of the formation facing the blaze. A coffee table sat between the sofas. A game of Monopoly appeared to be in progress. Hank looked right and saw the two beds, neatly made, in the bedroom next to the front door.

Rebecca turned and said, "this way to the kitchen." The men followed her, going through the dining room, or the bathing room as Greg and Rebecca now called it.

"Is that a bathtub?" Hank asked her.

"It is. We use it as a washing tub too, clothes not dishes. We set it up next to the fire so we could be warm when we took baths."

The door to the kitchen was open and the woodstove assisted in heating the rest of the house. The open door also kept the kitchen from getting too hot. Rebecca went to a cupboard and pulled down two cans of chicken noodle soup. She casually grabbed a pot, poured the soup, and set the pot on the stove to warm.

The kitchen was as clean and orderly as the rest of the house. Paul pointed to the rain barrel on the counter next to the tub sink. "That's a great idea, using a rain barrel for running water."

"Thanks! It was one of my first fixes to the 'no running water' problem. This house is great for the winter, but no water is kind of a pain. I doubt we would have running water if we were in a normal house. It's been so cold, the pipes would have frozen at some point along the way." She paused. "Oh, if you have to use the restroom, we have an outhouse right next to the back door. It's cold, but not as bad during the day when the sun heats it. It's right next to the house." She pointed towards the back door. "Not too far a walk."

"Rebecca, how old are you?" Paul was the only one talking. Hank was too confused and flabbergasted to engage.

"I'm 13, but have a birthday in April, so I'm practically 14."

"And you and Greg live here by yourselves? No one else is here?" Paul asked.

"I know, I look young, but I'm pretty driven. Yes, we came here in November, as I said, and were able to set up this house before it got too cold. We tried the other house, the one you all grew up in, but it wasn't practical. There was no way we could heat the rooms, it was too big. Greg remembered this cottage, his mom made him take a tour one summer. It's perfect." She stirred the soup, which boiled quickly over the already hot woodstove. "There is the rack we put up for drying clothes." She pointed towards a wooden dowel with several plastic hangers. "See the hangers? You can put your wet clothes up there. Things dry quickly in the kitchen with the woodstove."

Paul walked over to hang his winter clothes on the line. Hank stood in his full gear, unsure about what to do.

"May I ask a favor?" Rebecca said, looking at both of them.

Paul, focusing on hanging his clothes, answered "Sure."

"Can I give you hugs? I'm so happy to see you. Greg talks about you endlessly. I didn't believe you could be alive. It's been so hard doing all this by ourselves." Her composure was gone. Despite her high I.Q., the 13 year old girl came through. She started crying as she stirred the soup.

Hank, a father to four, knew what to do for the first time since he walked through the front door. He walked over and put his arms around her. "As glad as you are to see us, we're even more excited to meet you. It's okay. You don't have to do this alone anymore. Paul and I are here." Rebecca held him tightly, wiping tears and her running nose against his jacket.

"I'm so sorry." She said, jumping back. "I snotted up your coat."

"Rebecca, I had four daughters. You just made my year. I miss moments like this. You can snot up my shirt, coat, or sweater anytime you want. You're part of the family now." He held his arms open for her to give him another hug. Rebecca was sobbing uncontrollably. She stepped into his arms to continue their hug.

Rebecca savored the hug for several moments. She backed away, taking a tissue from her pocket to wipe her face. Hank unzipped the jacket and hung it on the drying rack.

Rebecca poured the soup into two bowls and handed each of the men a spoon. "Do you want to eat in here or in the living room?"

"Paul? What do you think? I'd rather stand in here and eat. I've been hunched over that snowmobile for over two hours." Hank stripped down to his base-layer of khakis and a long sleeved silk shirt he found in a Rutland sporting goods store.

"Yeah, stretching out a little sounds great." Paul took the soup off the counter. "Thank you." He said genuinely. "And to answer your question, we came from Rutland this morning. We've been stuck there since mid-December, trapped on the other side of the mountains after the first big snow. We decided to pack up and make a try at coming over on snowmobiles, and well, it worked." He took a sip of soup, and his insides warmed instantly. "I'll be honest, it was kind of fun too, at least until my face was so cold it felt like it was going to fall off, then, not so much fun."

"You've been over at Kilington this whole time? That's amazing. We heard a gunshot back in November. Was that you?" Rebecca hoped to solve the mystery of the lone gunshot.

"Not us, but that gives us hope there are other people alive. I mean, not more hope that meeting you, since you are a non-Dixon survivor." Hank took big slurps of soup between replies.

"I didn't realize you were so hungry, would you like some bread? We have half a loaf from last night. I can toss it in the oven to warm up." Rebecca noticed the speed with which Hank was eating.

"I'll take it room temp, I'm starved. Is there any jam or jelly?" He asked.

Rebecca retrieved both from a cabinet.

"Fortnum and Mason strawberry preserves! Where did you get this?" Hank held the English preserves in his hand.

"There was a William Sonoma at the Concord mall. I cleaned them out after the rapture. I have a bunch of their pancake and waffle mixes too." She smiled at his excitement.

"You're a keeper. You can stay. Well, I guess this is your house, so of course you can stay, but I mean as part of the family." They laughed as Hank ripped off a piece of bread. He stared at the chunk for a second, stunned by the realization it was made by either a 13 or 14 year old.

Paul continued to tell Rebecca about how they connected in Dayton, rode almost the entire way to Hanover, were trapped in a B&B in Rutland, and spent the last two months gorging on gourmet food and playing cribbage. When the storms appeared to break for a few days, and they practiced riding the snowmobiles enough, they made their attempt to Hanover.

"How did you get here? How did you meet Greg?" Paul asked between bites of bread. "I know we are going to have a lot of time together, but I have to hear all the stories of meeting, getting up here, selecting the house. This is all amazing, and for two teenagers to accomplish it? Unreal."

She started from the beginning, as the men stood and listened in awe of what they heard. Rebecca was a talker. She was more than happy to tell her story. Every once in a while Hank or Paul would interject with a question, "How did you think to do that?" or "Why did you make that decision?" It was a fun story, one that, of course, had a happy ending.

"The bathtub was a wonderful surprise. We both loved taking that first bath, but then the water sat in the tub for four days, gray and nasty, before Greg finally said, 'I'm drilling a hole in the floor, we'll just drain it right into the bottom of the house. ' It worked perfectly. We attached a piece of hose to the tub drain and threaded it through the floor."

After 45 minutes of stories, the three cleaned up the kitchen. Paul and Hank asked where they could store all of the supplies they brought on the sleds attached to the snowmobiles.

"Well, this is your house now too. You don't have to ask permission. We can unpack your supplies into the dining room. I want to take an inventory before we put it in storage. We need to have a conversation about where everyone is going to sleep. The downstairs bedroom is the best option, but there are only two beds in there. We should consider finding bunk beds in one of the other houses so the four of us can sleep in there. It makes more sense to have one fire going at night, rather than double our wood consumption heating two bedrooms. At least, as long as neither one of you snores." She flashed a smile.

Paul was amazed at Rebecca's planning. Her intelligence was far beyond that of a regular 13 year old. She actually asked to inventory their supplies. "Let's get unpacked, wait for Greg to get back, and we can decide on where to go for beds. You're right. We have another three months of fires, and while there is plenty of wood, there is no reason to waste it."

Paul and Hank grabbed their gloves and caps, opened the front door, and walked outside to unhook the supplies from the back of their sleds. Greg was next to the snowmobiles, his shotgun pointed towards the door. He was crouched behind one of the machines, resting the gun on the seat. The barrels were aimed at the men.

"Hold it right there." Greg yelled.

"Greg, it's your uncles. They made it!." Rebecca poked her head between the two men.

Greg dropped the shotgun and ran towards them. He put an arm around each uncle and hugged tightly. They stood in the cold, embracing. No one spoke. Greg wept.

"I knew you were alive. I knew it." He finally said. "And if you're alive, that means the rest of the family is alive." He hugged tightly, refusing to let go. Hank and Paul were confirmation that Greg's father and brothers were alive.

"Greg, I don't have a coat on, and it's really cold out here. Can we go inside?" Hank broke the hug.

"Oh, god, yeah, I'm sorry." His eyes were red and his face was wet from crying. "You met Rebecca? She saved my life."

Paul smiled. "We've met. She filled us in, gave us a great meal, very nice girl."

"Wait a second." Greg walked back down the two front steps and to the sidewalk cleared by the snow blower. He bent over and picked up a string with three animals tied to it. "Three squirrels today! That's the most I've gotten in one outing. I should have known there were be more people arriving. How crazy is that?"

He walked into the house and looked at Rebecca. "I told you they were alive. I believed enough for the both of us, and you kept me alive."

Greg cleaned the squirrels out on the trail. It was the reason he was gone for more than his typical one hour.

Greg strode passed his uncles. He put the squirrels into a pan, drizzled them with olive oil, salt and pepper, and put the pan in the oven. His boots were in the shoe bin by the front door, per Rebecca's house rules, but he was still in his coat. He washed his hands in the sink before turning back to his uncles.

Paul and Hank were stunned. Their 14 year old nephew took care of his business before moving forward with pleasantries. Greg had transformed into a survival expert during the last five months. Managing the food was more important than conversation.

"Okay, so what's going on? How did you get here? Where were you? Have you spoken to my father or heard anything else?"

Paul and Hank brought Greg up to speed on their last three months. "We can talk about the rest of the world, the rest of the country later." Hank said in conclusion. "Rebecca caught us up on your lives. When was the last time you spoke to your father?"

"I spoke to him right after your call, the one about coming up to Hanover. He said my mom was sick, but no one else, so I think my brothers are okay. He just said to stay alive, get to Hanover, and he would be coming for me." Greg looked at Rebecca. "With her help I've kept my end of the bargain."

"Well, we've got three or four more months to go, but we'll make sure we keep your promise." Hank said to him. "Not that it appears you need much help from us. We might actually pull you down a bit with two more mouths to feed."

They sat on the sofas in front of the fire. "By the way," Paul cut in. "This is the most comfortable sofa I've ever sat on. "

"I know, right? We found it in a house on Occom Pond. It almost killed us getting it into the van and over here, but it was so worth it." Rebecca nodded.

"Let me get a sit." Hank was on the other sofa with Greg. "Is it really that nice?"

"Hank, you'll be stunned, it's like sitting on a slice of heaven. It's firm, but comfortable. Whatever happens, I think we need to take this couch with us."

Hank sat down on the couch. "Damn, I mean darn. This is nice. I could get used to this."

Rebecca stood so Hank could swing his feet up and lay down. He put his head on one of the throw pillows and was asleep in seconds.

"It was kind of a long ride up here. I think it took it out of my brother." Paul said. "Let's go in the kitchen so he can grab a snooze. He has this new philosophy of taking life easy, no stress, no apologies for napping."

Rebecca scrunched up her face at Greg with her a 'what the heck? Did that just happen?' look as she followed Paul into the kitchen.

The roasted squirrel was out of the oven and was resting on the counter. The light faded as the sun dipped. It was 4:30pm. Paul, Greg, and Rebecca talked for hours. "Hank and I will sleep on the couches tonight. We'll have to keep two fires going for one night. We can find and secure bunk beds tomorrow."

"Is he going to be able to fall asleep tonight if we let him take a nap now?" Rebecca looked towards the living room.

"Don't worry, it will be my problem, you two can go to sleep in the bedroom." Paul assured her.

Greg pulled canned peas and carrots from the pantry along with chicken stock, instant potatoes, and stuffing. "Let's have a feast. This is a true celebration day. Maybe the food will wake Uncle Hank."

They enjoyed a homecoming supper that evening. Paul told the story of the filthy caveman Hank emerging from his hole in the ground. Rebecca had the uncles rolling as she talked about Greg trying to bag a turkey with a garden hoe. Their stories lasted late into the night.

"Thank you." Greg said to Rebecca quietly. His head was propped up on his hand. He looked at her as she faced him in the same pose. He stretched out his hand, and she grabbed it. They squeezed hands together.

"You are welcome, Greg Dixon from Hightower."

He squeezed her hand again. "Don't think we aren't still team Greg and Rebecca. We're a group of four now, but I have your back. I'll always have your back, just like I know you have mine." He did not drop his eyes. "Don't ever think I won't have your back."

She smiled. "I know." She closed her eyes, still holding his hand. "I know."

Greg opened his eyes and rolled over the next morning to find Rebecca staring at him. Their fire was out and the room was cold.

"It's about time you got up. Put on a robe and start the fire in the kitchen. I'm freezing, and I don't want to get out of bed until I know it's warm in there."

"Okay, okay. Just keep the covers over your head and I'll call you when it's warm." Greg got out of bed and put on a thick fleece LL Bean robe, slipped his feet into his fleece slippers, and opened the bedroom door. He was met with a blast of warm air. His uncles were up, and the main house was warm.

"Looks like they beat us up, the house is warm. What a nice treat." Greg did not wait for Rebecca. He walked through the house to use the bathroom outside the kitchen. He said good morning to his uncles as he hurried to use the facilities.

When he came back through he saw them cooking sausage from the food their brought on their sleds. "Weren't there any eggs?" Greg asked.

"Eggs, from the Easter Bunny? Where are we going to get eggs?" Hank asked as he ate sausage off his plate.

"From the chickens we have in back. Did we not show you the coop attached to the house?" Greg went to the door leading to the coop. He was followed by Paul and Hank. Greg grabbed a basket off a hook next to the door. He opened the roost, gathered the ten eggs available that morning, thanked the chickens, and told them he would be back to feed them in a minute.

"You hunt squirrels and you have chickens?" Paul said flatly.

Rebecca came into the kitchen and saw the lone plate of sausage.

"No eggs this morning?" She asked.

26

Todd typed 1600 Pennsylvania Avenue, Washington D.C. into the GPS on the RV dashboard. The satellites circling the earth were still functioning, and the GPS was based on a pre-loaded hard drive. The directions to the White House were flawless.

Dusk was settling onto the capital city when they pulled up to the building. A tall iron gate blocked the entrance.

Todd picked up a walkie talkie and called John. "You think I should just put the front bumper against the gate and floor it slowly? We should have enough horsepower to get me through, right?"

"Nothing to lose but the bumper, maybe the front tires if spikes pop up or something."

"Spikes?" Todd said to Emily. The boys rushed to the front window to see the action.

"Are we going to ram it?" Brian asked. "Let's ram it."

"Ram it, ram it!" The boys started chanting.

"I'm not going to ram it. I'm going to gently push it open." He paused. "If I can." He edged the front of the RV passed the empty guard shack and against the gate. "Ready? Everyone hold onto something." He pressed the gas. Nothing happened, the engine revved. He pressed down and the gate suddenly broke open. The RV jolted forward as the iron gate swung violently to the side. Todd took his foot off the gas and the vehicle coasted to a stop.

Todd looked towards Emily. The RV and all of its passengers were fine. Only a few items had fallen off the counter.

"Welcome to the White House, kids." He announced with a smile.

"Nice work." John called through the walkie talkie.

Todd moved the RV up the driveway to the White House, parking next to a overhang with a wide set of stairs. A red carpet led into the house. The rug was badly stained from the winter weather.

"This must be where the president and first lady got in and out, covered to keep rain and snow off. See the red carpet with the big seal on it kids?"

"Are we going to eat? I'm starving." The word starving was emphasized by a dragging of its pronunciation. Jay was not fun when he was hungry.

"We're having spaghetti and meatballs. Let's do it!" Todd developed a recipe for meatballs from cans of beef chili. He made a batch while they were in Richmond, and left them simmering in the pasta sauce. He was lucky the sauce had not fallen on the ground when they breached the gate. Todd poured water into a pot and turned on the burner. "Fifteen minutes until dinner. Why don't you three go out and play soccer on the White House Lawn? Maybe walk the dog?"

Hubba was thrown out of his bed during the gate opening. He sat by the RV door waiting. "And make sure you pick up his poop this time." Todd said to Craig.

There was enough daylight left to kick a ball around the lawn. Brian grabbed the glow in the dark soccer ball they had for just such occasions and ran out the door. With the water on the stove, and the meatballs and sauce bubbling, Todd walked out of the RV with Emily to talk to John, Matt, and their newest tribe member.

Todd was too late to speak to Solange. Jay co-opted her to play soccer, and she was off with the boys kicking the ball around.

"That was an easy trip." John said. "I've never gotten to D.C. so quickly.

This no traffic thing has its benefits."

"How's the new girl?" Todd asked.

"She's sharp. She has a great idea of shooting fireworks off both here and in New York. She said they would be more effective than the horn and smoke. She earned her dinner tonight. Where we get fireworks? I have no idea, but it's a good plan. I think even a flare gun would work. Maybe we can use the GPS to find a boating supply store."

Emily nodded, "Matt seems to like her addition."

John smiled, "Yeah, he does, but I don't think she's seeing it back. She may be only 27'ish, but she's mature. It takes guts to leave your family and come to the States. And to endure what she's had to? I'm not saying she's out of his league, but I think she sees herself as more our peer than his. Anyway, that's the vibe I got during the last two hours." He looked towards her kicking the ball with his son. "I trust her. She's open about herself, and she is a keen observer. She knows the shit storm we are all in, and she knows we have a long road ahead. This isn't some sort of picnic."

"High praise coming from Mr. Trust No One." Emily gave John's arm a soft punch.

"Spaghetti and meatballs tonight, I'm about to drop the pasta. Let's plan on 6 to 7 minutes." Todd went inside to finish dinner. He made three boxes of thin spaghetti, more than necessary in case anyone showed up for dinner. Todd was wary of cooking extra and unneeded food, but knew he could serve pasta as leftovers the next day.

Eight minutes later he rang the dinner bell. The food, a large bowl of meatballs next to a larger bowl of pasta with red sauce, was presented on the RV eat-in kitchen table. They used plastic plates, cups, and utensils to minimize the dishes and water use.

Todd handed Solange a plate. "Please, go through the line first. I don't know how well you've eaten, but I hope you enjoy your first meal with us. Do us the honor."

Jay stepped forward. "I'll show her how to do it." He grabbed a plate from his father. "It's a buff-end. You walk through and grab what you want as you go."

"That's buffet, dear." Emily corrected her youngest, who had a tendency to make up words that were 'almost' correct.

"Buffet, yeah, come on, I'll show you. He touched Solange's hand. She let him lead her to the table of food.

Solange smiled at Jay. "Thank you, sir. Thank you too." She said to Todd over her shoulder.

They sat in the RV, Emily and Solange shared the loveseat, and the four boys used the dining table. Todd and John sat on the sofa. The evening's darkness dropped the outside temperature into the 50's, preventing them from eating outside.

"This is delicious." Matt said to his uncle. "How did you make these meatballs? Where did you get the meat?"

"You have to get creative when your sources of protein are limited. I take canned chili, the mildest I can find, and mix it with bread crumbs from yesterday's bread, break a few eggs, Italian spices. They firm up nicely and resemble meatballs. It stretches a few cans of meat into a meal for all of us."

"I swear I taste cheese. Where did you get cheese?" Matt was the cook in his group, and was eager to learn.

"Oh, yeah, I added some goat's milk ricotta. I made that the other day for a lasagna, and I had a little left over. Thought it would go well. I found a cheese making book, and started using the goat's milk to make ricotta and mozzarella. When we get settled, I can show you how to make the fresh cheeses that don't need aging. It's pretty easy, though it does take quite a bit of milk."

Solange sat next to Emily. She barely touched her food.

"Are you okay, Sol?" Emily asked.

"I am overwhelmed. You are all so nice, and you have accepted me so easily. I have not spoken to anyone in six months. I am grateful. Please forgive me if I cry. It is hard to describe. I am relieved and happy to have found you, or be found by you."

Emily put her arm around the young woman. "Take all the time you need. We understand."

"She calls soccer football." Brian said loudly. "She said soccer is called football in aqua-door. That's weird. What do they call football then?"

"It's Ecuador, and they don't have football in Ecuador, they play soccer and baseball and other sports, but not football. Football is just an American sport, well, and Canadian I guess." Todd told him. "Soccer is called football in every other country but ours. We are the weird ones."

"Oh." Brian tried to process the information. He had a confused look on his face. "Are there even other countries anymore?"

The adults looked at each other. Emily responded after an awkward pause. "I don't know, I guess not. We are probably all in this together."

A voice called from outside. "Hello? Is anyone in there? Hello? My name is Peter Reinhart. I saw your lights."

The people in the RV froze. John's hand went to the gun on his hip.

"Really John?" Emily said. "It sounds like an older man." She stood and went to the door. She walked over a sleeping Hubba and quipped, "again, great watch dog you've become."

"Emily, hold on." Todd said.

She looked over her shoulder and shook her head. "Do you not understand either? We are all in this together, everyone."

She opened the door. "Hello!" She wore the same smile she did when Solange drove towards them in Richmond. "My name is Emily Dixon. Welcome." The door of the RV was on a spring. It closed behind Emily as she walked outside. The last thing the inside group heard was, "hello to all of you."

Todd jumped up and leapt the few steps to the door. He opened it to find Emily shaking the hand of an elderly man, probably in his late sixties or early seventies. He was accompanied by four people, three children and a woman. None of the people looked to be related. The woman was Asian, the older man was Caucasian, two of the children were African American, and the last child, a younger girl of approximately three or four, sported beautiful red hair and freckles.

The Dixon group lined up behind Todd.

"Todd, come meet the people." Emily said to her husband as he stepped out of the RV. "Everyone, come out, it's okay." The Dixons and Solange stood by the RV, an awkward silence fell over the two groups.

"Hello, I'm Todd Dixon, Emily's husband, very nice to meet you. This is our family." Todd made introductions and included Solange as part of his family, though she was just five hours into her tenure with the tribe.

Peter was 68 years old.

Melanie, or Mel as she preferred, was 37.

Jacob and Jaclyn Jones were 8 year old twins.

Casey Frank just turned 4 years old. She was shy and clung to Peter's leg, peaking out from behind the tall man. Jay, the child ambassador of the group, walked over to her and said simply, "My name is Jay Dixon. Want to be my friend?" The little girl nodded and shook Jay's hand. "We have spaghetti and meatballs inside. Would you like some? How about you guys?" He offered food to Casey and the Jones twins.

Casey nodded and looked up to Peter.

"It's okay, Casey, you can trust them." Peter gave the little girls head a pat. "Go ahead. You all can."

"I made enough pasta for everyone." Todd went back in the RV to assist the children.

"It's cold out here. You are welcome in our RV. It will be a little cramped, but it's warm and there are lights. We offer you anything we have that you might need." Emily opened the door.

"I'd love to come inside. It's freezing out here. I don't like the cold." Melanie said quickly. Emily followed to help manage the six young children inside waiting to eat dinner.

"John is it?" Peter asked. "Where did you come from, and where are you going?"

John appreciated the blunt questions. "We drove from Raleigh. I am originally from Charleston, joining my brother a month ago. We are headed to New Hampshire to meet my third son and my two brothers. We are stopping in cities along the way to meet survivors, invite them to join our group. We hope to gain strength through additional numbers and increased skill sets." If Peter was going to ask straightforward questions, John would give no-nonsense answers.

"Well, John, as far as I can tell, having searched for the last two months, you are meeting all the Washington D.C., Annapolis, and Baltimore survivors. We are glad to meet you and your clan. I can't speak for the group, but I'd like to hear more. I'm too old to keep caring for the twins and that little cutie." Peter looked tired. He was clean shaven. His complexion and waistline were healthy, but his eyes wore dark circles from stress and lack of sleep.

"I was an airline pilot for 30 years after serving as a Navy pilot. I retired eight years ago with my wife. She taught at Georgetown. She passed this fall from the rapture. We returned from a trip to Virgin Gorda before all hell broke loose. I was almost trapped down there. I guess that wouldn't have been so bad, although I don't think they have much fresh water." He paused as he thought about the Caribbean and his last vacation with his wife. "Anyway, I am a hard worker, I just can't work that long anymore."

"Peter, it is great to meet you. My son, Matt, and I have been living in Charleston for the last 10 years. His mother passed from the rapture. I don't know how or why, but my three boys and I are immune. I owned a small company in South Carolina that paid our bills. Matt is a smart young man. He contributes more to the group than I do most days." John put his hand out and patted Matt on the shoulder, the pride John had for his son was obvious.

"My youngest brother, Todd, and his wife are both immune, as are their kids."

"I'll be a son of a gun, a married couple who both survived?" Peter could not believe it.

"I know, insane that Todd and his kids survived, but his wife Emily too? It makes no sense, but we are thankful for it. I have two other brothers, both from Ohio, meeting us in Hanover, N.H. They were still alive and healthy when we spoke to them last fall. We grew up in New Hampshire, and it was the last place we mentioned before the phones went out. Our long range plans do not involve Hanover, but our short term plans are firm. My middle son, Greg, was at prep school when this all happened. He was alive when I spoke to him last September. I have to get up there to find him. After Hanover we are open to other locations, and would enjoy input. We have ideas on where we want to settle, but no concrete plans."

Peter nodded as John filled him in on finding Solange, on their dog, on their plans for New York City and Boston. "Those three kids need to come with you. I don't know how excited they will be to leave me and Mel, we've been taking care of them for five months, but I can't do it anymore. I'm too old, and they need kids their own age. I guess I should talk to Mel before I speak, she's more their mother than I am their father, but that's my opinion."

"How did you find each other?" Matt asked, curious to hear why he was sure the group of five were all that was left of the D.C., Baltimore, and Annapolis area.

"You know the story, what happened to the big cities, the curfews, the round-ups, particularly here." Peter started. "I was in the Navy. I knew what it meant to get rounded up. I saw it in Vietnam. Screw that. I stayed with my wife, stayed with her until she passed. I mourned her, then I hid for a few weeks. That damn disease was like a brushfire. It killed places in days, maybe a week, it didn't take long for the city to dwindle down to nothing." He looked towards the White House.

"When the President died, well, that was it. He lasted longer than his cabinet, two weeks longer than his wife and daughters. That man was a fighter. When the radio broadcasts announced he was gone and said the military was in charge? That was September, and I was like, what military? Are there ten of you in a bunker somewhere broadcasting? I hadn't seen a tank or jeep or motorcycle in days."

"I stayed in my apartment eating dry cereal and canned fruit. The electricity didn't go off until mid-October. I could cook things, and keep some food cold in my fridge. I scavenged in my neighborhood, but didn't venture farther than a few houses. I don't eat much. It was easy to stay alive. The streets were empty. The trash smelled horrible, the stench of death and rotting bodies was almost unbearable, but I stayed in my row house in Georgetown. The radio broadcasts went out, I waited another week, and then I got in my car and started driving around. I found the Jones twins breaking into homes and eating out of trash cans. I took them in, gave them a hot meal, set them up in my guest room. They're great kids, a little energetic, but they are smart and respectful. The three of us drove around for another week, and I suggested we take a trip to the ocean, go over to Annapolis, try to find other people, maybe catch some crabs or fish."

"We get over there, we're downtown, I wanted to go to the harbor and find a boat, maybe take the kids fishing, and we run into Casey and a woman named Barbara Stevens. She wasn't Casey's mother, but a survivor who found the little girl wandering the streets. Barbara is late stage breast cancer, lost her chemo when everything went FUBAR from the rapture. She grimaced with pain at every step, every time she moved, but she'd cared for that little 3 year old girl with everything she had." He looked at the ground, he choked up for a minute before clearing his throat.

"Anyway, we meet, I tell her I can help take care of Casey. Barbara comes back to Georgetown with us, lives for another week, making sure I'm not some sort of pedophile or horrible person, that I really will take care of this sweet little girl. I came into the kitchen on the morning of the eighth day, and she was sitting at the table. She asks me to forgive her. I nodded, I knew what she meant. She weighed 80 pounds by then, she could barely move. She took a bottle of pills and died quietly in a house down the street. Can you imagine? You survive the rapture, but you've got cancer and die anyway?"

Peter stopped for a moment, pulling a handkerchief from his back pocket to wipe his eyes and blow his nose.

"Jake and Jackie knew the situation, just 8 years old each of them, but they understood. I'm old, I can't take care of Casey all the time. The twins took on most of the responsibility of caring for her. I still cooked, but the twins kept the house clean, they kept Casey entertained, they read to her. They suggest I move a third bed into their room so she can sleep with them." He looked over to the RV. "I hope they can play with your kids, get some of their childhood back, whatever they can reclaim after this, this horror."

John put his hand on Peter's upper arm. "My son, Craig, is young. I worry about the same things. He ran away for weeks after the rapture, after his mother died. He plays with his two younger cousins like it's a long weekend from school. He gets his work done, he knows the score, what the world is right now, but he also plays. The twins will be okay, you did a great job with them, keeping them alive."

"I did what I could." Peter responded, choked up again. "I did what needed to be done." Peter cleared his throat and continued. "A week after Barbara left us, we decided to look for other people. We headed over to Baltimore, and I am driving around in my car. I installed a car seat for Casey. We have movies going for the kids. I turn a corner and we almost run over Melanie. She's walking in the middle of the road, crossing the street. I almost mow her down. It was a fine way to introduce myself, driving like a maniac. She's coming back from Johns Hopkins, where she's been trying to keep a baby alive in the NICU. She's a doctor. The baby boy was immune, and in the old world, would have made it, but didn't have the lungs to keep himself alive. Mel is walking around like a zombie, having hand pumped the babies' lungs for 14 hours before she collapsed from exhaustion. The power was out, the generators at the hospital finally failed, and she had to move the little boy from the electric ventilator to a hand ventilator. She couldn't do it alone. She woke up in a chair with the little boy dead in her arms. She was pretty rattled up by it." Peter shook his head.

"I stop the car and she gets in. We introduce ourselves, talk about plans, and she comes back to D.C. to help me with the kids, and see what the winter brings. Casey sat on her lap, and I saw a tear roll down Mel's face."

"We made additional swings through Baltimore and Annapolis, but we haven't found anyone else. If there are other people in D.C., we can't find them. We burned signal fires, we blew horns, no one until you drove up."

"Mel had the great idea to move to here, near the White House, as these building were cleared by the military during the rapture siege. There isn't rotting corpse smell, you don't run into bodies when you look for food. It is a clean zone. It's also how we saw you pull up to the White House."

He rubbed his hands and blew into them to warm them up. His ears were getting red as the temperature dropped.

"So that's it, that's our story, the abbreviated version. We've had our ups and downs. We've struggled in some areas, but we've kept those kids alive, we've kept them fed, and Mel has done a nice job trying to get them to read and write."

"You're cold." John said, "and I hate for you to miss out on my brother's meatballs, if there are any left. Let's go into the RV and get you some food."

Matt put his arm on the old man's shoulder and led him into the RV. "Again, welcome to the group. Where did you grow up? Are you a native of Washington D.C?" Matt opened the door for Peter. The spring shut the door behind them.

John turned and saw Solange standing firm by his side during the conversation. "He is a nice man." She said. "He reminds me of my grandfather."

"I didn't realize you were still out here. Aren't you cold? You said you hated the cold." John was surprised she stayed outside instead of going in with Emily, Todd, and the new people.

"I wanted to hear his story, and I wanted to make sure you were not left alone outside. It is okay to trust people, but I do not trust people 100%. Four people standing outside is less of a target than three. If he was part of a larger group, a scout sent to see our weaknesses, having three of us with him was a sign that he or his group could not get us into situations where we might be vulnerable, when there would only be one of us."

"Thank you." He said, glad another person was thinking of security and weary of survivors.

"You are welcome." She said, flashing a smile, the first John had seen her make. She looked down at the ground for a second, almost as if embarrassed to smile at him. "I hope there is still some food. I did not eat very much, and I am hungry."

John opened the door for her. "Let's find out." He put his hand on her back, an instinctive gesture to help her into the RV. She turned and smiled at him again before going inside.

John could hear children's laughter from the RV. The group was talking loudly. The two tribes were merging into one.

Sleeping arrangements were complicated. Jackie and Jake wanted to sleep with their new friends on the floor of the RV. Casey was scared to sleep without Melanie. Melanie did not want to sleep on the floor or on a couch. Jay said he would go back to Melanie and Peter's apartment and sleepover with Casey, but Todd and Emily would not let him go alone.

Peter described their three bedroom apartment, and there appeared to be more than enough room for a few children and at least two adults.

Todd and Emily went with Jay, Casey, Melanie, and Peter to sleep at the apartment. Jake, Jackie, Brian, and Craig slept in sleeping bags on the floor of the RV. Matt slept on the couch. Solange slept in the large bed in the bedroom of the RV. John slept on the pullout.

Before they split up for the evening, Peter and Melanie agreed to travel to Hanover. Peter was a man who made decisions quickly, and after eating his meal and seeing how well the children played together, he took Melanie aside and asked her if she was willing to join the new group.

"I don't like being cold, Peter. You know that, but you're right, this is the best scenario for us and the children. I want to bring our own vehicle so we have options, but staying with this family seems like a good idea. I like them, and I trust them after just one meal."

Peter announced his decision to join the Dixon tribe, and suggested they leave for New York as soon as the next day.

Emily protested immediately. "If you think I am leaving before I tour the White House and show my kids Washington D.C., well you are mistaken. Part of this trip is creating memories."

"You know what?" Peter admitted. "I've never toured the White House. I'd like to do that before I leave. It's also been a few years since I walked the Wall. I would like to say goodbye." Peter typically avoided the Vietnam Memorial as he knew too many names etched into the black stone.

"Part of our plan is to take the Declaration of Independence and the Constitution with us, if we can. We are also open to art, so if you see anything or remember anything from the National Gallery, or during your White House tour, grab it."

Melanie had not considered taking art with her. She loved art, and was a patron at most of the museums in town. "We should take these things, preserve as much of the world as we can." She turned to Peter. "With new people come new ideas."

The tribe agreed on at least one week of site seeing and playing before departing for the next city, Philadelphia.

John spoke with Emily and Todd before splitting up for the night. "What do you think?"

"What do I think about what? The people? They are smart, hard working, honest people who want to join us. There is no downside to this scenario." Emily told him bluntly. She had no time for conspiracy theories or distrust.

"I agree, I'm very comfortable with all of them, but I don't want Craig, Jay, or Brian left alone with anyone." John replied.

"John, that's just parenting etiquette. Do you really think I am going to ask Peter to look after my young kids?" Todd was annoyed with his brother. "Look, I appreciate that you are looking after us, but I don't think there is anything sinister happening here. If there is, I trust that you have it under control."

"Okay, okay, I'll lighten up, but please try to elevate your senses a little. We're not in Raleigh, a place you combed for survivors. We're in a huge metro area, there could be a bad person or people."

"You're right, and that is a reasonable statement. I don't think the new people are bad, but there could be another person out there. I'll keep a gun with me, and I will have my walkie talkie turned on all the time." Todd conceded John's fears as he and Emily prepared for their evening away.

"We'll see you back here tomorrow morning. Make sure you have eggs and milk ready for us when we get back." Emily patted John on the back.

"If we are here for a week, we are setting the pizza oven up first thing tomorrow morning. It's only been two days, but I'm already jones'ing for some fresh bread." John gave Todd a hug.

"I will make fresh dough in the morning. You, Matt, and I will get it set up after breakfast."

The parties split up for the night. Solange was the only person who protested her sleeping arrangements. "I am new to the group. Why do I deserve the big bed?"

John calmed her protests. "Sol, there will be plenty of time for you to sleep uncomfortably. Take the high points when you can get them." She relented and went to sleep, happy in her big bed. She was ecstatic to sleep with people for the first time in 6 months.

The morning was chaotic. The Jones twins woke up early, very early, waking the rest of the RV in the process. It was only 6am, and still dark outside. John would not let the kids play on the White House lawn. He put a movie on the television, and made himself coffee.

Matt, kicked off his couch by the kids watching television, moved to the converted third row bed in the Suburban. He mumbled something about needing more rest, put on a winter cap, and stormed out of the RV.

John sat, sipping his second mug of coffee, reprimanding the constant screaming and fart, butt, and poop comments from the four kids. The bedroom door opened at 6:30. Solange emerged, fully dressed and put together for the day. She sat down with John at the small dining room table.

"Tonight I suggest the kids go to the apartment or we get a turn in the apartment." She smiled at him. "Is there enough coffee for me to have a cup?"

"I would never deny another person coffee. I am not a savage, yet. Please, help yourself, now and always."

She poured herself a cup and spoke to John as if there were no kids screaming at the top of their lungs at the cartoon movie.

"So few people left, we do not have much to build a new world." She took a sip of her black coffee. John pointed to the sugar and a small bottle of milk on the table. She shook her head. "On our trip here, you said we might grow to twenty by the time we arrived in New York. I believe we will be lucky to have twenty after New York."

"I know. We will be pressed to find better people than the five we just met, but it would be nice to find stronger hands. A doctor is a fantastic edition, but taking on three more children and an older man? The tribe is going backwards."

"Less alpha males means less threats, but you are right, we also sacrifice strength. Peter is a leader, but he is also wise and silent. He will not cause trouble."

John looked at her after the alpha male comment. "You are an interesting person, Solange. I know why I am paranoid, but why are you so distrusting of others?"

Solange took a sip of her coffee. "I was not the only survivor in Richmond. There was another person, a man, young, my age. He was a local man, and did not go to college. He drove around trying to find survivors in a big black pickup truck. It was November, late November, and I had not seen anyone for months. The first time I saw his truck, I let it drive by. I am a young woman, and I cannot defend myself, but after months of solitude, I decided to trust the driver." She paused and looked at John with vacant distant eyes. "It was a decision based on my selfish needs, not safety. I will not make a mistake like that again. The boy, his name was Fred, just Fred, he never told me his full name, let me in his truck, told me his survival story, something about being a kindergarten teacher, living with his parents to help them with money. I think the story was a lie, I do not know for sure. He asked me to tell him my story. I stupidly told him about how I was alone, how I was not from the area. He drove while I tell him things. I did not realize, but he drove in circles and zig zags." She sipped her coffee. "After 30 minutes I have no idea where I am, where he has taken me. It is not close to the highway, it is not near town. Even though I later found my way back to Richmond, I could not take you to where I was." She glanced at the children to make sure they are not listening. "It is best they do not hear my story. I did not want Matt to hear it either. He is too young to know such evil."

John gave a polite nod of acceptance.

"We stop at a house on a small farm. It looks run down, but there are many nice things, things Fred stole or took after the rapture. I was driving a nice car, we all have things now. I was not concerned about the nice things. I was scared that I was alone with him, and we were in a place I did not know, and I had no way to leave the place, but I am young, and I was more trusting five months ago. I told myself I was being silly."

"There was a pond next to the house. He said there were fish in the pond, great for eating. He told me to take a fishing pole, catch him fish for dinner. I was confused, and I asked him what he was talking about. He raised his voice to me and said, 'you see all this stuff? It's mine. The rapture has given it to me and made me a king. I am in charge, and you will do what I say or things will go badly for you. Take a pole, dig for some worms, catch me a damn fish before I beat you.'" She did not raise her own voice while retelling the story. She kept a natural tone, as if the events happened to a different person.

John stared at her. She maintained a distant look in her eyes. "I am so sorry." He said, putting his hand on her hand resting on the table.

"If the children start to listen, I will stop. I will not let them hear my story." She nodded her head in their direction. "So Mr. Fred sits down on his porch, and stares at me. He has a small refrigerator on the porch plugged into a generator, and he pulls out a beer and starts to drink. I say to myself, 'Sol, this is bad, you cannot run or walk away right now. You need to smile and do what he says.' So I take one of the fishing poles leaning against the shack, I pull up a few of the flagstones on the dirt walkway, find a worm, hook the worm, and throw it into the pond. I fished with my father in Ecuador. I know where to find worms, how to catch fish. I catch a fish. I reel it in. I hold it up to show it to him"

"This Fred, he walks over to me. He looks at the fish, and he punches me in the stomach, very hard. I drop on the ground in pain, coughing. I have tears in my eyes, but I do not cry. He yells at me, 'you think a fish that tiny is going to feed me? Try again. I will not punch you in the face. You are too pretty to look at, but I will punch you in the gut until you get it right.'"

"I am dirty and thirsty, and tell him I will try again. I ask for a glass of water. 'You want something from me when you cannot even catch me a big enough fish to eat? You can drink the water from the pond.' I tell him that I have water in my pack, my water, not his. He walks over to his truck, takes my pack out and throws it into the pond. 'I own everything. I own you. You will drink and eat when I say. You will earn your food and water. You catch me a fish, and I will tell you how you can earn food.'"

"I drank the water from the pond, and I did not eat for three days. You can guess how he wanted me to earn my food. He said he did not want to rape me, that he was not interested in that. He wanted me to 'want' to be with him. He thought making me be with him for food was different than raping me."

"Fred was a strong man. He worked with his hands before the rapture. He was a little heavy, and his arm muscles were very big. When he punched me in the stomach, it hurt me. I decided to die on my feet. I went to him the third night, I caught him three fish and held them up for his approval. He stood in front of me. I could smell the beer on his breath. He nodded at me. I lifted my knee to his groin with as much strength as I had. He was not expecting the move, and he went down coughing. I jumped on him, putting my hands around his throat, squeezing as hard as I could."

"This Fred, he was strong, but he lacked determination. I do not. He swung his arms wildly, hitting me all over. I clung to his throat, staring into his eyes. When he tried to get up, I kneed him in the groin as hard as I could, over and over, holding his throat, keeping my grip as tightly as I could. His eyes were filled with terror. His head and face turned red, then purple. His punches became weak. I clung to his throat long after he stopped moving. I kneed him in the groin even when his eyes were shut and he no longer flinched. I held onto his throat until my hands ached." She took a sip of coffee, looking at John calmly. "As I said, I possess determination and strength of will."

"Fred was a weak minded, stupid beta dog. The rapture set him free for a little while and made him think he could act like an alpha dog. When I was killing him, he became the beta again. He submitted to me, like weak people do. He pretended to be something he was not." Solange looked at the children again, making sure they were not listening. "An alpha would have taken me, not played some game to make me earn my food. This new world does not accept weakness or stupidity. I was stupid to get into that truck, but my strength set me free." She took a final sip, calmly setting the mug on the table.

"I fished my pack out of the pond. I dragged his body off the porch and put it into the pond. I cooked the fish I caught for him. I ate his food. I drank his beer, wincing as it burned on my bloody lips. I woke up early the next day and used Fred's truck, following the sunrise east to the highway. When I got back to campus, I moved into a nicer house, lived there for five more months, and now you have found me."

John's coffee was gone. He did not refill his cup. Solange got up, walked to the pot and brought it back to the table. She filled his mug and set the pot back on the coffee maker. She sat down, put a spoonful of sugar and milk in his coffee, and stirred it with a spoon to mix. "El encantado did not rid the world of evil. I learned that lesson the hard way."

John did not respond. He sat at the table with her. After a sip of the coffee she poured for him he spoke. "If you put the sugar in before the coffee, it melts and tastes better."

"I will know for next time." Solange put her hand on top of his hand, similar to his earlier gesture. "Thank you for listening to me, John Dixon, and thank you for being a good man."

John smiled at her, but it was his turn to look down quickly, uncomfortable with the exchange. He even blushed. A young woman, almost half his age, whom he had just met the afternoon before, was touching his hand. He could sense a connection, but he did not believe she could have feelings for a man his age, particularly after only one day. John chalked up the touch and exchange of smiles as innocent.

At 7:30 the door to the RV flew open and Jay jumped inside. "Their apartment is awesome! They have a fireplace, and tons of blankets, and books, and games and stuff. It's so much fun!" He looked around the RV. "Is there any breakfast?"

"I can make some." John replied with a smile. "No one else has asked, they are glued to the movie." The kids were watching cartoons. John and Solange finished their coffee, and were planning their day. "I'll go see if we have any eggs. There is always cereal or instant oatmeal."

"Okay." Jay replied distantly. He watched the television, and barely paid attention.

Emily and Todd came in the RV. Melanie followed, carrying Casey. They were chatting about the day, laughing about Casey doing something funny.

"Good morning." Todd said enthusiastically. "How did we sleep over here?"

"The RV was up at 6am. Solange and I decided it will be your turn with the kids tonight, or more importantly tomorrow morning."

"Someone is grumpy." Emily replied. "Are you sure you've had enough coffee, John?" She rubbed him on the back, the way a sister in-law can.

"Don't get me started. My other helper huffed off and is sleeping in the SUV." John made a gesture towards the kids. "I've resorted to the electric sitter."

"Well, let's have some breakfast and figure out what we are doing." Emily looked at the TV. "Okay guys and gals. Five minutes and it goes off. Go play outside. It's cold. Put on sweatshirts."

The kids screamed and ran around for a second. They put on shoes, pants, coats, grabbed soccer, kick, and footballs and ran outside.

"Hey, make sure Matt is awake in the car. Pound on the sides and get his lazy bones up." John grinned. He turned to Melanie, "We have cereal and fresh milk. It's goat's milk, but pretty tasty. I haven't checked for eggs yet. We might be able to offer you some fresh eggs. I think you, Peter, and Solange get first dibs. It's probably been a while since you've had fresh food."

"You have no idea. That would be wonderful." Melanie replied, excitement in her voice.

"Let me make sure there are eggs. Hate to make false promises." Todd replied.

"May I see the chickens? I love farming and gardening. If I wasn't a surgeon, I would be a farmer. I want to see what kinds you have." Melanie was genuinely excited to look at chickens and goats.

"Absolutely. You can take over the coop if you'd like. We have no any idea what we are doing. We just make sure they have water and food, and eggs magically appear the next morning." Todd smiled. He opened the door for her and they went outside.

Todd and Melanie bumped into a disheveled Matt, standing in pajama pants, slippers, a fleece winter cap, and a blanket over his shoulders. He looked as though he woke abruptly.

"Morning, Matt!" Todd said as they walked by.

"Morning." He grumbled.

Solange handed Emily a cup of coffee. "John said you like to walk through houses, and that you are excited to see the White House."

"I do, and I am." Emily said back.

"Would you mind if I joined you? I also like to see houses and rooms. I would enjoy touring the White House with you."

"Sol? May I call you Sol?" Emily ask.

"Please."

"May I give you a hug?" Emily did not wait for a response. She put her arms around Solange. The young woman returned the hug uncomfortably. "You just gave me one of the best surprises I have had in a long time. Of course you can join me, and I'm excited to find another person who likes to walk through houses. These other people think I'm weird." Emily pointed around the room. "I toured homes in Raleigh for the last three months. It's how I found Hubba." She gestured with a tip of her coffee cup to the still sleeping dog. "Seriously, how is he still asleep?"

She looked back at Solange. "Thank you for the coffee. Did you sleep well last night? I hope the kids weren't too much of a bother."

"I did sleep well. I have a large family, or I should say I had a large family, and I miss a full house. It was nice to be around people, and wake up with screaming children. I had many nieces and nephews, and during family get togethers, they woke me up early to play. It was a nice memory. I do not know if it will be nice tomorrow, but it was nice today." She smiled.

The morning proceeded with breakfast. None of the children under 10 wanted to tour the city. Emily and Todd decided to give the kids a pass. The previous day was a long drive, filled with excitement and meeting new people. If the kids wanted one day of playing on the White House lawn or watching television, that was okay.

Emily and Solange spent the morning touring the White House, while the men put together the pizza oven. Melanie and Matt set up a short term coop and pen for the animals.

Melanie and Matt also checked the White House garden for salvageable vegetables. Mel minored in botany at Yale, and Matt, mildly obsessed with farming, tried to learn as much as he could from her.

Peter had yet to make an appearance. He hinted at spending a morning alone, a well earned day of rest after months of looking after children.

The sun was shining, and it was warm by 10am. Late March weather was unpredictable, and the day was on the 'great' end of the spectrum. By 10:30 Jake, Jackie, and Casey walked back to their apartment to retrieve shorts and t-shirts.

Lunch was served outside the RV. Emily and Solange located tables and chairs during their tour of the White House press room, and pulled them outside for a picnic. The pizza oven was assembled, and had a fire burning. Todd made pizzas with dough and fresh goat's milk mozzarella. Peter arrived in time to eat pizza with real cheese.

"Who wants to drive around and haul up fresh Maryland crab for an old fashioned crab boil tonight?" Peter asked. Craig's hand flew up at the hint of fishing. Matt and John joined him. Todd assumed kid watching duty for the afternoon. Melanie came with Solange and Emily on the second half of their tour.

The women walked to the second floor of the White House to tour the bedrooms.

"Casey has really taken to you, Melanie. You have done an incredible job as her mother. I see you still have a ring on your finger. Did your husband die during the rapture?" Emily felt comfortable being candid under their current situation. In the old world, she never would have asked such a personal question.

"No, he was killed by a drunk driver last May. I don't know if that saved him from the rapture, or if he might have been immune. I was still in shock when the pandemic hit. I wasn't back to work at the hospital yet. I saw the insanity unfold from the television in my apartment."

"I'm sorry. We've all lost so much from the rapture, we don't think about all the tragedy before. How long had you been married?" Emily felt bad for prying, but now that the door was open, it would have been impolite to stop talking. "Unless you don't want to talk about it."

"No, no, it's okay. I've had a long time to think about him. Peter is wonderful, and has been incredible with the Jones twins and with Casey, but he's not someone I talk to about personal thoughts. We are a team, and I trust him without reservations, but he's not a girlfriend kind of talk person." She smiled at the women as they examined the Lincoln bedroom.

"My husband, David, and I were together for over 10 years. He was in finance, and I was driven by my surgical career. We decided to start a family at this late age, and were glowing with my pregnancy. When he was taken away, well, it was hard."

"Pregnancy? You were pregnant? You lost your baby and your husband so close together?" Emily asked with confusion.

"Well, I lost David, and my family helped me through the rough time, and then I gave birth to our son, David junior, prematurely, in September. He was six months along, and had a hard road ahead, but he was doing well. The rapture took him before he had a chance." Melanie sat on the bed. "I still hurt from the loss, and it's why I have bonded so well with Casey, Jackie, and Jake. I needed children, and they needed a mother. I'm glad for the help now. I'm so tired. I will always love them for helping me through my own loss." She looked down at her feet before picking her head up. "I almost felt selfish, caring for the children. They were in need of a mom, a parent, an adult, and they thought they were taking from me, but the whole time I was using them to fill up the holes in my heart. I needed them so much more than they needed me." Melanie's eyes grew glassy.

"After a few months, you know, Christmas, I realized, this is hard damn work. I'd earn their love. I deserved their love." She laughed. "It may have been selfish at the beginning, but by the end, wow, I had no idea how much time and energy it takes to raise three kids. I was only prepared for one!"

Emily sat down next to her on the bed, putting her arm around her. "I know it doesn't help, but if your son died from the rapture, your husband most likely would have passed too."

Melanie looked at her. "My baby didn't die from the rapture, he died because of it. He died in my arms. I spent every day with him at Johns Hopkins, and he was close to being able to breathe. All the chaos, all the craziness, and he fought, and I took care of him by myself. The nurses died. The doctors died. The other babies were long since gone. He and I made it through, until the damn power went out." Melanie's eyes dropped large tears onto her shirt. "The god damn power went out. I could have taken care of him until he was ready if the damn power had stayed on, or I had been able to move a generator into the room, or if one other person had been there to help me, but it was only me, and I didn't know what to do."

She was sobbing now, her shoulders heaving up and down.

"So the power went out, and I pulled him out of the respirator cube, and he couldn't breathe. His little lungs weren't strong enough yet, they needed more time. I pumped the hand respirator for him, I breathed for him. I pumped for almost a day and a half before I collapsed and passed out." Melanie looked at Solange. "And when I woke up? I woke up in the glider chair in the ICU. It was dark, and the moon streamed in from a skylight. My precious baby, my son, the only thing I had left from my husband and marriage? He lay motionless in my arms." Melanie put her hands up to her face and covered her eyes.

Solange sat down on the bed, and pulled Melanie towards her. "It is alright. You are okay. You were as strong as you could be, there was nothing you could do." Solange rocked the woman gently.

Melanie cried in the young stranger's arms for several minutes before withdrawing. She went into the bathroom and cleaned herself up. "Wow, I look horrible. My eyes are red and puffy from crying."

Emily wiped tears from her own cheeks. "Mel, I am so sorry, I had no idea. Peter told us you were caring for a baby in the NICU. He never said it was your own son."

Melanie sniffed in her nose. "He doesn't know. He is a sweet man. He doesn't need my baggage. He needed my help. I told him why I was upset, but didn't tell him the whole truth." Melanie started to chuckle as if something was funny.

"So I bet when you agreed to let the new girl on your White House tour, you didn't expect such high drama in the first room. Huh? I'm sure you're both like 'who let this one come with us?' I swear, I'm not this emotional, you're the first women I've spoken to in six months."

"And you've known us all of 15 hours, so of course you open up and bear your soul, that only makes sense." Emily laughed. "I expected this. Didn't you Sol?"

"I thought we would be braiding hair and talking about boys by now. Maybe in the next room?" Solange's joke shocked the older women.

Melanie and Emily stopped laughing and looked at her with their mouths agape. "You're funny too? You're beautiful, resourceful, hardworking, and now you're funny? This is not going to work at all." Emily shook her head.

They laughed at their jokes. Melanie laughed so hard she started crying again and had to return to the bathroom to wipe her face.

The White House visit was more fun than the women expected. They laughed, they picked up mementos, they saw rooms not on the official tour. It was an afternoon of female bonding. They emerged as the sun sank in the western sky.

The kids were exhausted. Casey's thumb was in her mouth as she sat under a blanket on Todd's lap.

Todd was in a folding chair on the lawn, enjoying the warm weather. He found a large pot in the White House kitchen, and constructed a brick stove above a fire. He stacked the bricks, allowing for vents on all sides, so that the pot was just above the flames. He left one side open to feed the fire wood. He saw the technique on a cooking show by a famous American chef who made paella over an open flame. The large pot was filled with water, waiting for the crabs. A box of bay seasoning rested on the ground near the brick tower.

He looked at the smiling women as they laughed and joked with each other. "That must have been some White House tour."

Emily walked to her husband. She leaned over and gave him a kiss. "We have found wonderful people. Thank you for letting me spend the afternoon with them."

"I'd claim the kids were trouble, but really, they have been playing nicely and independently all afternoon. I swear, it's like we have new kids. They played tag, soccer, tag again, hide and seek."

"The other men are not back?" Solange looked for Peter, John, and Matt.

"I bet they couldn't get Craig to stop fishing. It's why I started the fire. He said they were coming back by five. I want this pot boiling so we can drop the crabs right into the water. I have the pizza oven going to roast the fish. It should be a tasty meal tonight." Todd's mouth watered at the thought of fresh seafood.

"Did Matt tell you we found garlic, onions, and herbs in the garden?" Melanie asked.

"He did, and along with the dried chorizo we scavenged, I am planning a big paella party tomorrow night. Now that I know we can catch fish, it should be fun to make. I'll have bread to sop up the sauce. Tonight?

Crab boil."

"Where did you find this one? I loved my husband, but he didn't cook. Are there any more around like him?" Melanie asked.

"Stay away from him, he's mine. Besides, he's fixed, he can't help repopulate. I figure that keeps him tied to me." Emily put her arms around Todd's shoulders as he sat in the chair.

"Fixed? Did you drink on that tour? I feel like a piece of meat." Todd feigned indignation.

"What does fixed mean?" Casey asked Melanie. She listened intently from her spot on Todd's lap.

Brian ran up, "Can we watch a show? We've been outside all day. Please?" Todd refused the request all afternoon.

"If you wash your hands, and get ready for dinner, you may put a show on. No movie, just shows." Todd replied.

"Yes! Hey guys! We can watch a show! We need to get ready for dinner first!" Brian ran into the RV to wash his hands.

Solange looked at the tables they used at lunch. Todd set them with disposable plastic tablecloths, napkins, and plastic flatware. "You made the tables?" She said to him before looking at Melanie. "He is a keeper. He cooks. He sets up the table."

"Okay, that's enough from the two of you. He is going to get a big head." Emily was smiling, her arms still around Todd. She liked hearing how great a catch she had.

Todd saw the SUV turn a corner in the distance and head towards the entrance gate. "Dinner has arrived." He said, jumping up from his chair and walking towards the RV. "And just as the pot has started to boil, now that is timing." He entered the RV to drop boxes of New Orleans style dirty rice into water he was boiling on the stove inside.

As the sun set and the night temperature dropped out of the 70's, the day of playing caught up with the children. Jake, Jackie, Brian, Jay, and Casey were exhausted, and whined to go to bed. They were told they could sleep in the RV using sleeping bags or extra blankets. Casey jumped on the couch, and the other kids gladly slept on camping pads. Melanie promised her children she would stay at the White House location for the night.

John turned to the rest of the adults, "Solange, Matt, and I have done our time. We are going with Peter to the apartment. Todd? You and Emily get the early shift tomorrow morning. Craig and Matt can come with me."

"Are you leaving now?" Todd asked. "It's still early."

"If Peter will take us over there, I wouldn't mind. Craig is tired, I'm tired."

"I'm tired. I never got back to sleep." Matt whined like the younger children. "I'm a growing boy. I need my 12 hours a night."

Peter was out of his chair. "Okay with me. I can sleep all the time if you let me. Mel, this is our first night apart in a long time. I hope you will be okay."

Melanie smiled at the kind man. "I'll try to make it through, Pete. I'll see you in the morning. We'll have breakfast going for you tomorrow, if you can make it over before noon this time." She gave him a wink.

"I'm going to take advantage of my second retirement. You'll see me when you see me." He waved to the group.

Emily turned to her new friend. "Is he as nice as he seems to be?"

Melanie nodded, watching the elderly man walk towards the apartment with the three others. "He is. These three kids, they owe him. He could easily have turned the other cheek. He's not 80, but he's not 45 either. It's been hard work keeping them alive. Keeping them educated.

Keeping them warm. He made decisions for us, stepped forward to say what was right and wrong." She turned to Emily and Todd. "I wouldn't be alive if it weren't for him. I probably would have killed myself. He gave me hope, showed me compassion."

"As much time as we spent together, he never opened up to me, he never gave me the full story on his life. I know he lost his family. I know he was a pilot, but both of you know that from spending five minutes with him." She took a sip of her instant decaf coffee. "I never pushed him to talk. We all have secrets to keep. We all can choose how we go forward in this new world. Maybe Pete wants to start again, be different than he was. I don't know how a 68 year old man changes who he is, but maybe he wants to try."

"What would you be?" Todd asked her.

"What?" Melanie replied, snapping out of the philosophical haze she entered while talking about Peter.

"What are you going to be now? I can tell you, you're never going to operate on a person's head again. What do you want to be?" Todd was curious what her clean slate would become.

"I have always wanted to grow things, to provide for people with my hands. It's not so different than being a surgeon. I was at a fork in the road in college, and I let my responsible side win, or maybe my greedy side. I have a talent for medicine. I have a passion for it too, helping people, but most of all I have a passion to be the best. You don't get much higher on the ladder than a neurosurgeon at Johns Hopkins. If someone said they were better than me, it would be hair splitting. I would be lying if I didn't tell you that is why I did what I did, surgery. I may have taken the first step into medicine for the good reasons, but for the last 15 years I've been in it for competitive reasons. I'd like to get back to working with my hands for altruistic purposes."

"I bet the people you saved didn't care about ego driving your career." Emily consoled Melanie's harsh indictment of her past.

"I care that I was like that. Look where it got me? My family is dead. All the capital I earned; human, career, monetary, it's all worthless."

"Mel?" Todd interrupted her. "You need to look at the positive. You are going to help with your botany, your farming, and you're going to help with your medical skills. I hope you can pass along your knowledge to one of the kids. Whatever drove you a year ago, whatever got you to the pinnacle of your profession, the results are even more valuable now. Finding a doctor was a driving force in our decision to seek others. Think of your new practice. If we find more survivors, you will be the doctor to friends and family. You'll know your patients, will look them in the eye." He paused. "Of course none of us can pay you."

"You joke, but I guarantee you within a year I will have the most chickens or livestock, or whatever works as currency." She had a smile on her face. "One year, Todd."

Melanie took a sip before asking Todd the same question. "What are you going to do? What missed opportunity or passion will you follow?"

"I am offended that you would imply software sales and consulting was not, and does not continue to be my passion. I am going to keep on moving in my career. Sure, it's been a bad couple of quarters, but that only means I can bounce back." He laughed.

"I love to cook and feed people I care about. You can tell from my last few meals, I think I have a talent in the kitchen. I did not explore a career because I never wanted cooking to be a burden. If I had to go to a restaurant day in and out, cooking the same meals for hundreds of strangers, I might have tired of cooking. If we stay together as the tribe I envision, I hope to cook meals for the family we create."

"Tribe?" Melanie asked. "You think we're a tribe?"

"Um, that's my fault." Emily confessed. "It's a term I used to describe what we want to be, or what we have become. I said we needed to leave Raleigh to find other surviving tribes, see if we can merge and add skills."

"I like the idea that I have joined a new tribe. It's certainly accurate when you think of my last five months."

"Anyway," Todd said in an effort to continue. "I enjoy planning and making these big meals. I know that eventually, when we settle in one location, we'll naturally find our own homes, and cook our own meals, but I like the role of cook. I envision our tribe, or village, or colony, whatever semantic we use, coming together once a week for a large meal or celebration. I want to be able to pass along skills to younger kids. Teach them what tastes go together, how to best cook things, be it boiled, fried, or sautéed."

"I've never seen a brick tower built over a fire pit used to boil water, and I'm excited to eat paella tomorrow night. You're doing a nice job so far. And the bread? Oh my, I have never had bread as good as yours, before the rapture included."

"If you don't get some wheat grown and flour made, the bread train will come to a stop quickly."

"Is no one going to ask me what I want to be when I grow up?" Emily asked.

"This is an organic conversation. I didn't realize we had to prompt you." Todd joked.

"No way, you asked Melanie first, then she asked you, and then you both started talking about bread, and wheat, and now I'm just sitting here wondering if you are going to ask me about my new life goals." She feigned anger.

"Emily, I'm curious what you would like to do, now that your options are open." Melanie asked, rolling her eyes at Todd.

"I saw that, but I'll ignore it." She sneered at both of them. "And you know what? I have no idea. I've been in the rat race for so long, grinding at my career, pressing to make the next sale. It's been what? Seven, eight months since I worked, and I still find myself thinking about hedge funds, and i-banks. Isn't that sad? Those things don't exist anymore, but they crowd my thoughts."

Emily pulled her blanket tight around her shoulders. The evening air was chilly, even next to the fire.

"Todd will tell you, I am not one who can sit around. I keep busy, cleaning, teaching the kids, touring homes, but I don't know what my long term prospects are. I know I will stay partners with Todd."

"Thanks!" Todd said energetically.

"Well, at least in the short term." Emily added after his comment. "And we'll raise our children, and help raise yours, and John's, but I don't know where I fit into all of this madness. I'm not a doctor, or engineer, or hunter, or farmer. I don't know, I guess I'll try to fill in whenever I can." Emily looked up at the stars and moon.

"It's almost scary, knowing how I fit in life for so long, matching my talents to the correct career for 20 years, and now, I don't know what I am going to do. I enjoy teaching. I always volunteered at my kids' school, just an hour here or there in the mornings. I like helping kids move forward, but whether I can do that day in and day out? I think I need to take life as it comes."

Melanie nodded. "It's funny, isn't it? We have so much to do, grow our food, find a home, teach our kids, yet we still sit around and try and define our careers. Your approach is more realistic. I want to be a farmer, but that may only be a small part of my new life. Maybe we will all become dynamic in our skills. The old world rewarded specialized talents, making sure people contributed in a unique way. Companies, hospitals, they did not want redundancies, people had to make their skills special."

She leaned forward, as if she was coming to a realization, "I can't get fired from being Casey's, Jake's, and Jackie's mother. I can't get fired from the tribe unless I break a horrible rule. I don't need to make sure I am indispensible, because we are all indispensible. There are only a handful of us. Each of us will need to know how to hunt and clean animals, sow and reap crops, build and repair homes." She sat back. "Wow, what a burden and yet what a relief. Each day is about surviving, not about maximizing my time. My day is no longer about seeing enough patients to make sure my practice is profitable, my life is about helping my tribe survive."

Todd agreed. "It's so basic, if you think about it. Tomorrow we need to get food to make meals. We need to take the kids on tours, go to bed. Done. There is nothing on the horizon. There is no deadline or sales' goal."

They sat in their chairs quietly for a few moments reflecting on the conversation.

"Were any of you against looking for other survivors?" Melanie asked.

Todd nodded. "John is still against it. I was on the fence. Emily and Matt pushed for engaging other people."

"I'm glad you found me, found us. I'll go wherever you go, do whatever you do, if you'll have me. I see how well you are raising your kids. I want that culture for my three. I understand what you are trying to create with the tribe." She stopped. "But I understand where John is coming from. We need firm ideas and rules when we get to New York. If there are people up there, and they are in a group, they will have leaders, and ideas of their own. "

"We know, but it's important to get everyone together." Emily started.

"I understand. We have to go, don't get me wrong. What I am saying is, we need to have a solid idea on where we are going after New Hampshire, and how we are going to get there. If we run into a tribe, a term I will adopt because I like it, when we run into the tribe, we are probably going to have to convince people to leave their tribe and join our tribe. We might not get everyone. They might try to convince me to stay, knowing I am a doctor. We should consider hiding the fact I am a doctor, unless we believe it will incent people to join our tribe. They might want Peter because he is a man, Matt because he is a young man, or Solange because she is a woman. I don't know if I want you to show your pizza oven to a large group. If things become violent, it might not continue with us."

Emily shook her head. "That is the same paranoid mindset I had to fight John about. This isn't the Road Warrior, we aren't savages."

"No, Emily, we aren't savages, but who knows what a larger group might be by now. Imagine 10 mouths to feed instead of 4. Imagine New York City, which was looted and burned, bridges destroyed, tunnels blocked. Imagine the desperation some of those people feel or at least felt during the rapture. I'm not saying they will take the pizza oven because they are evil. I'm saying they take the pizza oven because they are trying to survive. If you had to steal an oven to feed your children, you'd do it, right?"

"I wouldn't think twice." Emily conceded.

"Now imagine that you meet the only doctor left on the east coast. Imagine you meet a woman who can bear children, and you are a group of men. Imagine you have no other way to make food other than a fireplace in an old building, and now you see a portable pizza oven. There are going to be choices made, decisions about joining our tribe or staying with another tribe. We need strong selling points, but not key strengths. Not 'we have a doctor,' but rather, we have good, honest men, women, and children, and we are going to this place to start a society."

"So you don't think we can just drive up there and say 'hey, we're the Dixon's from Raleigh, North Carolina. Want to come with us to New Hampshire to pick up our nephew, and then figure out where to live?'"

Todd joked.

"No, I don't. I think you got lucky with Solange, Peter, and me. We need to have a better plan for meeting a larger group." Melanie looked up at the sky. "I've lived in a city my entire life. I knew there were stars in the sky, but who knew there were so many?" She stretched her feet out and put her hands behind her head. The sky was clear save for a few light puffy clouds drifting across the brilliant stars and a three quarter moon.

"We have a few days to hone our pitch. I don't know where Peter is on all of this. I will speak with him tomorrow. I'm with you, and Solange is with John, so worst case, we have all of us."

"What do you mean Solange is with John?" Todd asked.

Melanie and Emily exchanged glances. "You haven't noticed how she looks at him? She's usually not more than a few feet away from him. Trust me, she's with him." Melanie wore a smile on her face.

"Are you crazy? She's half his age. You two have no idea what you're talking about." Todd shook his head. "Solange and John, he wishes." He mumbled.

"Let me guess, you had to ask him out first?" Melanie said to Emily.

"Yep." Emily replied.

27

March roared into Hanover like a lion, and did not become a lamb until the final days of the month. A warm sun was slowly melting the snow. The daily temperatures crept into the high 30's and low 40's.

The residents of Webster Cottage were ready for spring, and even more ready for summer. Winter was harsh in Hanover, particularly without power or water.

"We can't spend another winter here." Paul declared. "We won't survive another winter here. We need crops, animals, there is no way we'll have enough of each to make it through."

He and Hank had been with Greg and Rebecca for five weeks. Frozen cottage living was taking its toll. They melted snow for their water, but it took a large volume of snow to generate a small amount of water. The daily gathering was a grind. Canned food was plentiful, but fresh food was scarce. Hank and Greg spent endless hours trapping for small rewards. They cut holes in the local ponds for minimal fishing gain. The group was surviving, but it was not thriving.

Today's project was emptying the full port-a-john. Greg decided on a path to a sewer opening on a street near their cottage. The drain was far enough to keep the smell away from the cottage. The melting snow would wash the sewage away in a day or two.

Greg, Hank and Paul rocked the full bathroom back and forth until it was on a large plastic dumpster hood they were using as a sled for Greg and Hank to tow to the sewer. The blue bathroom was pulled away using the snowmobiles.

Paul moved the second, empty, bathroom onto the concrete slab before going into the house and sitting down on the couch opposite Rebecca.

Using barometric pressure readings, wind direction, and temperature charts Rebecca found she could accurately forecast the weather over the next few days. She predicted when storms were going to hit, and when they needed to batten down the hatches. She sat near the fire in the midst of one of her weather calculations.

"Are you the Rebecca that won the Westinghouse science competition last year?" Paul ran admissions for a medical school, back when there were medical schools. He was responsible for an undergraduate medical school fast start program. He knew about talented high school students, particularly talented science students that applied to his school.

"Yes. You know they don't call it that anymore, right?" Rebecca said, keeping her face down as she wrote figures in her book.

"I have been wondering for over a month now. I knew you were from Concord, and it was big news that a 12 year old girl from New Hampshire won. After seeing you work with the weather calculations, well, it makes sense it was you."

"My mother went to your school. That's why I applied. I'm sorry I was never seriously considering it, but thank you for accepting me." She looked up and smiled.

"I don't want to make you uncomfortable, I was just curious." Paul paused. "Wait, you know I ran admission at Cincinnati Medical and admitted you?"

Rebecca continued to smile. "I remembered your name from the admission's letters. When Greg told me his uncle Paul worked at the University of Cincinnati Medical School, I put the two together."

"Wow." Paul replied, amazed, "you are smart." He stared at her. "Have you told Greg about all of your honors and awards?"

Rebecca put her pencil down. "I told him the truth, I was a senior, I was looking at top colleges. He knows I'm smart, or whatever smart meant before all of this. I'm not ashamed of how intelligent I am, and I think it's an asset to us, but no, I did not go into detail about Westinghouse or how well I did on kids' Jeopardy or the debate awards, or anything like that. I haven't had a serious friend my own age since I was five. Greg likes me for who I am, and I'm being who I am, so I don't want to bring up a lot of baggage from my previous life. You can, I don't mind, I just don't think it's relevant. I mean, Greg was good at baseball. He hasn't told me about specific games he's won, just that he played baseball."

"Rebecca, I get it. I won't say your secret is safe, because you're right, it's not a secret. I was just curious and wanted to know. I thought you were the same Rebecca, and you are. No biggie. Does it mean I am going to treat you differently? Probably. I might rely on your opinion more, or ask for your advice more, if that's okay."

"That works." Rebecca picked up her pencil and started working again.

"One more thing." Paul said.

Rebecca looked back up. "We can't stay here. Here in Hanover I mean, for the long term. It's too harsh. When my brothers arrive, we are going to tell them as much. Maybe you could work up a formula, a system that would give us best locations? I leave it up to you to decide on the final variables, but let's look at climate, water, food sources, farmland, and proximity. We can't get to Australia, so even if it tops our list, we need to discount or exclude locations based on availability."

"You have letters after your name. Are you going to help me with the project?" Rebecca knew Paul was a PhD. Her photographic memory displayed his printed signature as she spoke.

"Yes, but based on our skills and abilities, I'll be the research assistant. You tell me what you need from the library, I will fetch and deliver."

Rebecca looked up, not at Paul, but towards the ceiling in the stereotypical way scientists look up when they are thinking. "I do like a project, and we certainly have time. We have to start with variables, like you said, but I bet we can come up with more. Predators, poisonous insects and reptiles, rainfall, natural disasters, there are hundreds of things to consider. I'll get a laptop from the computer store, something I haven't turned on in a long time, and we can run some models. Let's hope Hanover doesn't come up number 1."

She looked down from the ceiling and focused on Paul. "I've never had an RA before. I am demanding, but it's for the work. Don't take it personally." She giggled.

"Rebecca, this is the most important project you've ever worked on, be as demanding as necessary." Paul did not giggle back, he stood and left her to work on her weather charts.

As he was leaving the room he turned around. "And just for the record, Greg wasn't that good at baseball. I hope he hasn't been telling you otherwise." This time it was Paul's turn to chuckle.

28

The Dixon tribe rumbled north after a week spent collecting memories, art, and artifacts in Washington D.C.

Peter was on board with anything Melanie decided. He wanted to stay with the group. Peter liked to fish. He and Craig were fast friends, fishing together their last four days in D.C., while the rest of the group took in the sites. Matt had to tag along and sit in the boat for the first two days, maintaining the rule of never being alone with new people. John took pity on him and switched places with him for the last two days.

The Dixon tribe acquired a second RV from a Virginia dealership, doubling their sleeping quarters, and providing guaranteed shelter from the harsh New England spring. They refilled the propane tanks prior to departure, securing warmth and cooking abilities for the next few weeks.

Their stop in Philadelphia produced no new people and plenty of anxiety. The city appeared abandoned. Philadelphia was looted and ravaged. It was the worst case scenario for a large metropolitan area. There were entire sections of the city burned to the ground. No one in the tribe was familiar with the town. They drove aimlessly through neighborhoods, all of which showed some level of destruction. The University of Pennsylvania was in piles of ashes.

They parked RV's and SUV next to the charred remains of the once prestigious campus.

"The devastation is incredible. Didn't people know it was pointless?" Emily was shaken by the condition of the city.

"If you are desperate, you do not think like a person. You think like whatever did this." Solange witnessed similar behavior in Richmond. Peter and Melanie saw the same in D.C.

Melanie continued for Solange. "You were in Raleigh. Your city was evacuated. Baltimore was a war zone for weeks. People didn't know what to do. It was crazy, and then it just stopped. Everyone was gone, dead. I'm sure these fires were started and just never got put out. They might have burned for weeks."

They set off fireworks their first night, played music and blew air horns the next day, and left Philadelphia within thirty six hours.

John believed all of the cold weather cities had been abandoned for warmer weather.

"Would you stay in Philly if you were able to go somewhere warm? If I had a car, I'd hightail it for California or Florida, or someplace with food and heat. I'm not staying through a winter by myself." John had little hope they would find people in New York. He spoke as they pulled off the road at the first "Fireworks" warehouse sign in New Jersey. Per Solange's plan, they were ready to light up the New York City sky to find people.

The RV tires found snow and ice fifteen miles outside of New York City. Drifts piled against buildings and road signs. The three vehicle caravan rolled over the crusty remains of winter and pulled to a stop at 5th Avenue and 59th Street. They parked next to the Plaza Hotel at the southeast corner of Central Park.

"It's cold here." Todd buzzed over the walkie talkie. "I miss the South already."

They drove around Manhattan, opting for the GW Bridge rather than taking the Lincoln or Holland tunnels. No one was sure where the best area was to find people in a city of such size. They decided Central Park was as good a place as any to start. They would move to the other four burrows if Manhattan was vacant.

It was noon. The sun was shining, but there was a chill to the air.

They piled out of the vehicles, and knew immediately they had crossed from the south into the northeast. The kids screamed "snowball fight" and ran off to play. Casey stayed close to Melanie. She liked playing with the older kids, but the words "snowball" and "fight" did not bode well for a 4 year old against 6, 7, 8, 8, and 10 year olds.

"It looks better than Philly. There are some rough areas, but where we drove was intact. The stores aren't looted. The shop windows aren't broken. New York seems to have come through pretty well." John looked around with surprise in his voice.

"David and I used to come here a lot. He worked for a firm downtown. I'd tag along when I could. We really loved this city." Melanie was holding Casey's mitten encased hand. The little girl's head was covered by a fur rimmed hood.

"If it's this cold now, I bet it will drop into the 30's tonight. We're eating inside until June." Todd made plans for their stay. He looked around. "There are plenty of cars. Refueling won't be a problem. I know a parking garage close to here too, one of those year round places. It should be loaded with cars if we need additional gas." He continued to scan the horizon in all directions. He listened for sounds of life. "Nothing, not a sound or sign anyone was here recently."

Emily stood next to Todd, watching the kids play in the snow. "Would you stay here? I don't know. Maybe I'd head for Long Island. John maybe right, people may have left for warmer climates in October and November, when the disease was gone and before the snow flew."

"We'll set off the fireworks for a few nights, see if anyone comes. If not, we'll try to make it up to Boston." John had an atlas on the hood of the SUV. "You know what Emily? I bet you're right. I'd head somewhere else if I were here. It's not like I want to fish out of the East River or the Hudson. I would lay low in the city, if possible, before I made a beeline for Long Island or somewhere south. There is almost nothing that would keep me here. There is no game to hunt, no fish to catch, no food to scavenge. This was the most populated place in the country, but only because it was a city. It's not the optimal habitat for anyone post-pandemic."

"People like to stay where they live." Peter said unexpectedly. "They get attached to homes. Let's give it a go with the sparklers and if we strike out, we move further north." If the survival statistics held, there would be 15-20 survivors in the general area of Manhattan. Peter believed most of them would still be in their homes.

Todd found a trashcan on the street corner. It was on its side, knocked over months ago. The can was partly submerged in snow and ice. He picked it up, dumped out the snow, and filled it with trash from the area. He searched the newspaper boxes and singles ads dispensers for old paper. He asked the kids to find sticks and branches from the park, dry wood if possible. Todd went into the RV and returned with a bottle of grain alcohol he scavenged from a liquor store in D.C. He poured some of the bottle into the can, struck a match from the pack in his pocket, and lit the signal fire. The can roared to life. If Todd had not stepped back, the initial explosion would have taken his eyebrows.

"One signal fire lit." A few minutes later he picked up a handful of wet leaves, abundant near the park, and threw them on the fire. Thick black smoke floated into the sky.

"Do we want to get some tires, light them on fire? It would be the most effective, as long as we stayed away from the smell and fumes." The tribe employed a similar strategy in Philadelphia. When they pulled out of the city, the black ribbons of smoke continued to billow into the clear cityscape. If survivors located the tire fires, directions to Hanover lay in plastic bags near the blazes.

"You know what? Yeah, let's see if we can find a few tires, get them going. We have to keep the kids away, maybe start it down on 57th or 56th and over on Madison." John liked any idea that conserved their fuel. Burning tires meant not having to gather firewood. It also meant not having to man and feed the signal fire.

Todd turned to his wife. "Hey Em? What's the Met from here? Like 20 blocks north? I watched the kids for you in D.C., any chance you'll take a turn and let me go up and look at some art?"

"Absolutely. I want to take the kids over to the Natural History Museum straight across from there." She pointed northwest across the park.

Melanie listened to the exchange. "I'm in on the Natural History Museum. I love that place, and now that I can bring Casey? Done deal. We should drive the Suburban." She walked over to Jake and Jackie to get them ready.

John turned to Matt. "Can you go with your brother and cousins? I would feel more comfortable if one of the men went."

"Sure, I can dig on some dinos." Matt walked to the suburban and pulled a shotgun from the back. The newest addition to the groups supplies, acquired in D.C., was a gun locker in the back of the suburban. It was stocked with several shotguns. There were better guns for defense, but shotguns were visible, easy to use, and loud. None of the adults, save Peter, were comfortable with guns, but firearms were deemed necessary in the larger cities. The tribe hoped the sight of big shotguns would deter an attack. If a small group was attacked, a shotgun blast would signal the rest of the tribe.

Matt checked to make sure the gun was loaded and the safety was on. He handed the weapon to his father. Matt was driving the SUV to the museum, and could leave his weapon in the back until they arrived.

"May I go with you to the art?" Solange asked Todd. "I believe there are some Matisse's and Picasso's. I would like to keep some."

"I would enjoy the company, Sol. Thank you." Todd put on his winter cap and gloves. He grabbed a headlamp, two flashlights and some snacks, all of which he stuffed in a day pack slung on his back. He grabbed one of the shotguns from the Suburban. Todd walked to Emily and the kids, giving each of them a hug and a kiss.

"I'll see you in a few. I love you." He told them.

"I love you too. Pick out some nice art." Emily smiled and hugged him.

"Peter and I will hold down the fort, start the tire signal fire, maybe have dinner ready." John announced as the groups departed. He held the shotgun in his hands while wearing his pistol on his belt. "Be safe." He said to Emily.

Todd and Solange headed north on Fifth Avenue. They were offered a ride, but opted for the cold spring stroll to the museum.

The sidewalks of New York were filthy with old leaves and trash. The snow was black with dirt and grime. The ground was half melted ice and half snow. It was slippery as they stepped gingerly and made their way. The once majestic park was on their left and large expensive apartment buildings towered over their right.

"What were you studying at VCU? You know, before all this happened?" Todd had not spent time with Solange. He wanted to get to know her.

"I was an engineering student. I loved electrical engineering and mechanical engineering, playing with things until they worked." She smiled as she thought about a time when she studied with joy.

"I was never that put together. I've always been someone who studied English Literature. I didn't focus on college as a means to a career, which was a mistake. I looked at college as a time to have fun and learn some things, maybe take a trip to Italy or something. I should have taken it more seriously." Todd regretted his approached to education.

"I like to tinker with things, so my choice is similar to yours. I picked electrical engineering because it is what I enjoy. If you like to read books, then it makes sense that you would study literature. It is the same thing, is it not?"

"It is, I agree, and I have enjoyed my life. Regretting decisions that brought me here, well, it's silly, but still. I look at how I could have approached college, how I could have been more serious in my studies, and if I'd done things differently I could help get the power going when we find a place to settle. Maybe I could help keep a car running. Right now I can read the owner's manual, tell you how well it's written." He laughed at the thought of how useless he was.

"Unless we can refine oil, I do not see us using cars for very much longer. I will be interested to see if we can generate electricity when we choose where to live." Solange stopped and pointed towards a building. The windows were broken and streaked with black smoke burns. "It seems New York might be a little bit like Philadelphia after all."

The aroma hit them at 71st street. It smelled like rotting animals or decomposition. They could see birds, carrion, crows, vultures, eagles, circling one section of the park. The smell grew stronger as they walked closer to the museum.

A buzz came over the walkie talkie.

"Todd, is there a horrible stench near you?" It was Emily. She was at the Natural History Museum. "There are flocks of birds, circling something like they would a dump. It smells horrible, I don't think we can see the museum, the kids don't want to get out of the car."

Todd pressed the button on his walkie talkie. "We smell it, and we see the birds. Do you have any idea what it is?"

"We don't want to know. We're leaving. It can't be good, and I don't want the kids to see it." The walkie talkie popped off, then back on. "See you back at the camp. Let me know if you want to get picked up."

"Okay, will do. See you soon." Todd clipped the walkie talkie back to his belt and turned to Solange. "Do you want to head back?"

"I would like to see the museum. It might not smell inside. If it gets too bad, we can turn around."

Todd nodded. "The scary thing is, the wind is coming from the south. It smells this bad and the wind is at our backs." They continued to walk north on 5th Avenue.

The destruction they noticed on the first apartment buildings escalated as they moved further north in the posh upper east side neighborhood. The city looked abandoned and untouched at 59th. By 68th street there was fire damage on every building. There was evidence of looting. Trash cluttered the opposite side of the street from the park. Black car skeletons littered parking spaces, obviously left burning so many months before. Some of the cars were crashed into the lobbies or against the sides of the large buildings.

Above 75th street New York City looked like a post-apocalyptic war zone, and the stench was almost unbearable. Todd and Solange were too curious to turn back. They wrapped scarves around their noses and mouths for relief from the horrible smell.

When they arrived at the museum they had little hope of recovering art. There were four large green army trucks parked in a semi-circle on the front steps. Dead bodies littered both sides of the vehicles. Rotted corpses of men in fatigues lay between the museum entrance and the trucks. Bodies of men and women in normal clothes were scattered on the opposite side of the street. There were guns on the ground around the dead. The bodies rotted, froze under the snow, and beginning to thaw and rot again.

Solange pointed to a large white sign with black block letters that read 'Food, Water, Provisions.' "I think the people wanted the provisions, but did not want to wait."

"This is unbelievable." Both of their voices were muffled behind their scarves. Todd was impressed that Solange could look at the violence without shock and horror, or at least not express her shock and horror. He was rattled, and used her strength to keep moving.

The doors to the museum were open. There was a body hanging half in and half outside. The man's top have was busting through a pane of glass in the swinging doors. All of the museum's glass doors were shattered, riddled with bullet holes and shotgun blasts.

"What happened? How did this devolve into a gun fight?" Todd said, half to Solange and half aloud. He watched as birds flew around the bodies on the other side of the street.

"Do you want to go inside?" Solange asked through her scarf. "Do you think it will be worse inside?"

"I do not want to go inside, and yes, I think it will smell worse and be worse inside." Todd looked at her. "We have to go inside though, don't we?"

"I think we have to go inside." Solange acknowledged. "If it makes you feel any better, I do not want to go inside either." He could see the edges of her eyes crinkle with a smile.

"I can smell some of the bodies, but that isn't the big smell. There is something else, not in the museum, but somewhere around here. It's bad. It must be where all those birds are." He pointed over the museum where hundreds, if not thousands, of birds circled in and out of the area.

"If this is what happened in New York, I do not think we will meet many people. I would not have stayed if there was this much violence and destruction. I would have left for a suburb or small town." Solange spoke as she and Todd walked around the trucks and fallen soldiers. They climbed the steps to the entrance of the building. The ice and snow made it treacherous, and Todd instinctively grabbed Solange's arm to help her.

The large arched windows on the second story were shot out, and the building was marred with bullet damage. "I visited East Berlin when I was a child. I remember this is what the buildings looked like. They hadn't made repairs since World War II, and all the buildings had bullet holes and chunks taken out of them." Todd's head was moving in circles as he surveyed the damage. Even the stone steps they walked up had pieces missing.

"It is sad that such a beautiful building is ruined. I fear all of the art is destroyed or gone." Solange pointed to the damage as she walked.

At the top of the steps two glass doors flanked a revolving door entrance to the lobby. A dead soldier's body hung out of the door on their left. His face was down, touching the stone entrance. A helmet was still strapped to his head. He held a large rifle. Todd did not know guns. He assumed it was an M-16. That was the only 'army type' assault rifle he knew.

"He was shot from behind." Todd said, pointing to the tears in the back of the man's shirt. "There was a fight inside too." They walked through the broken glass door on the right side of the revolving door. It was dark and cool inside, cooler than it was outside. The stone walls and floor of the museum held the winter cold like ice blocks in an old refrigerator.

Todd put his shotgun down and unslung his backpack. He took out two headlamps, handing one to Solange while slipping the other on his head. He pulled out two flashlights, giving one to Solange. He slung the backpack, stood up and asked "where to?"

Solange looked around the room. "It looks like there are temperature stations there." She pointed to a bank of tables near the entrance. "The people were moved into two areas for provisions." Her flashlight highlighted signs posted over two doorways. One sign read 'healthy' and the other 'sick.'

"I suggest we ignore this and head to the European Exhibits." Todd was more interested in locating art than solving the mystery of the gun fight.

"I do not need to see more death. I would like to see a Picasso." Solange focused her flashlight beam on the stairs to the second floor.

"Let's grab a museum map and try to steal some art. I hope we can salvage something out of this mayhem. What a waste. They all would have died anyway, but they would have died at peace. What could they have been thinking?" Todd shook his head as bent down to pick up one of the hundreds of museum maps scattered around the lobby. His headlamp provided reading light. "Looks like we need to go up the stairs and to the left. European art, here we come."

The cold museum interior acted like a morgue freezer, and protected the bodies from decomposition. Todd and Solange stepped over a solider whose body blocked the top of the stairs. There were bullet holes and marks all along the staircase. The dead soldier was shooting down at the front doors. He had bloody spots on his back where he was shot from behind. His body fell to the top of the landing.

"Poor bastard." Todd said as he stepped over him. "He thought he was holding the line, and whoever was attacking came in another door and hit him from behind." They continued to the top of the stairs, his flashlight leading the way. They entered the first gallery and their hearts sank.

"It is destroyed." Solange said sadly. Bullet holes filled the walls and pictures. Frames lay on the ground, smashed and ruined. "The fight took everything with it."

"Europe is pretty far from the center of the museum, maybe the wings did not see as much fighting." Todd said hopefully.

The destruction to the art and building decreased as they moved away from the stairs and main hallways. Bodies, however, were scattered throughout the museum. Blood, long since dried, left black circles on the floors and smears against the walls.

Solange and Todd entered the first room of European art.

There were knife cuts through most of the paintings. "My god, these are Monets. Who would do this? Why? Why would you do this?" Todd lost his composure. "It seems like they were fighting for food and water. Fighting for their lives, but then to come in and cut up the art? This shows contempt for humanity."

They walked around the first two rooms. Todd stopped in front of a Monet haystack. His eyes dropped and he shook his head. There were crude rips through the painting made with the nose of a rifle or gun. Several spots on the wall were vacant. Art thieves had beaten Solange and Todd. Todd wondered if the paintings were taken before, during, or after the attack.

"Let's keep going and think positively." Todd encouraged. He moved towards the room on his right. He and Solange relied entirely on their flashlights and headlamps to make their way through the pitch black and windowless gallery. Todd pointed his flashlight beam on a picture as soon as he walked through the doorway. A Monet, Water Lilies, hung without damage. Pristine as it was before the rapture.

"This is going to sound pretentious, but I'm not a Monet person. I get why people love his work, but I am not a fan, and if I have limited ability to carry, I'll stick to other works." Todd felt funny passing on a Monet.

"If one of the others would like it, they can come back through and pick it up." Solange said. "Still..." She walked to the painting, studying the work. "I like it. I will start with it. I will see if something else is in good condition. Maybe this Monet is all we will be able to save."

"Good point, we can always leave it if we find something else." They continued through a door to the next room, not hesitating to enjoy the gallery. They came for Picasso's and Van Gogh's. The violent deaths robbed them of any desire to gallery stroll, as did the smell of rotting death. The odor was weaker in the building, but still present in the air.

Todd's light beam pointed at the first painting in the room. It was the Van Gogh Todd wanted. The one he dreamed about since seeing it 10 years earlier during his first visit to the Metropolitan. Todd rushed ahead, almost tripping over the large wooden benches bolted to the floor. The art label read: Wheat Field with Cypresses, Vincent Van Gogh, 1889.

Todd never enjoyed or paid attention to art. 10 years earlier he visited New York with Emily while she was on a business trip. Stuck by himself while she was in meetings for the day, he went into the Metropolitan to kill time. He strolled through the galleries, nodding at some pieces, walking briskly passed most. When he saw the Van Gogh he was floored. The colors and textures, always muted by photographs in books, were incredible. They were alive and unlike anything Todd had seen before. He sat on the bench in front of the picture, Wheat Field with Cypresses, for fifteen or twenty minutes. He could not get enough of the painting. He yearned for other Van Gogh's, visiting exhibits in any major city he knew had works by the artist.

Todd reached out and touched the frame. It was flush against the wall, not hanging from a wire or nail in the wall. Todd put the flashlight and shotgun on the bench facing the picture. He grabbed the frame on each side and pushed up. The picture began to move, kept on the wall by a tongue and groove system.

"That is the one we came for?" Solange asked.

"Yes." Todd said, looking at the large picture with the light of his headlamp.

"I am going into the next room. If we do not find a Picasso, I would like to leave. The stench is too much for me. It is getting stronger in these rooms." Before she turned to go through the archway to the left she held up the Monet she was carrying. "May I leave this here?" She asked.

Todd was lost in his new treasure, but snapped out of it to answer her.

"Oh, yeah, of course, sorry. I'll bring it." She set the painting down next to him, leaning it against the bench as she left for the new room.

Todd prepared for the walk back to the RV. Solange was correct, the smell was unbearable. They found and collected some art, it was time to call it a day. He was eager to report to the group about the fire fight and destruction.

Todd set his painting down, leaning it against the Monet. He turned off his flashlight, deciding to use his headlamp the rest of the way, freeing his hands to carry paintings. He put the flashlight into this day pack, and put the pack on his back. He used the shoulder strap on the shotgun, and slung it behind him. He tightened the scarf around his mouth in an attempt to block out the smell before joining Solange into the next room.

Her flashlight beam was focused on a painting, a man at a table feeling for a pitcher. The imagery was powerful.

"It is beautiful. It is more than I expected. I would like to take this one and the Matisse I already pulled off the wall." She moved her flashlight beam to a picture of flowers. "My father loved Matisse. It will remind me of him." She turned the beam back to the Picasso. "This will remind me of what the world was like, when we were able to enjoy art. Maybe it will inspire a survivor to become an artist, if we reach a time when we can be idle again, and the world can create artists."

"You are one serious young woman, Solange. We'll have idle time again. It might not be in the next few years, but when we've found a place to live, when we've found other people, when the engineers of our new world, people like you, help to rebuild some of the mechanics of society, people will paint again." They admired the Picasso. "Until there are painters, these pictures will get us through."

"I agree." She nodded and her headlamp beam bounced up and down on the wall. "Let us follow my bouncing ball and get away from this horrible place. I cannot stand the smell any longer."

Todd laughed at the bouncing ball joke. Maybe Solange was not as serious as she let on. She carried the Matisse, and Todd managed with the other three frames.

According to the map, they were near a back emergency exit of the museum. They walked through several archways until they saw daylight peaking through the bottom of a door. A sign above the door read 'Exit.'

Todd turned the handle and walked into the stairwell. The powerful smell almost knocked him back. "Oh my god." He said, as he held the door open for Solange.

"We might have to go back through the front." Her eyes squinted from the smell, as she came through the door sideways with the large painting.

The window at the top of the stairs was shot out. Glass lay on the ground. The smell came through the hole. Solange walked to the gap and looked towards the park behind the museum. Leafless trees should have displayed softball fields and open spaces. Instead, Solange saw a large hole in the ground. Flocks of carrion swirled around and on top of the pile.

Solange turned her face away from the image. Tears formed in her eyes.

"What is it?" Todd asked. He saw the torment on her face. He was holding his three paintings and did not look through the broken glass.

"Go back, we have to go out the front. We cannot go out this way." She was crying, and scooted around Todd as he held the door open.

Todd put his paintings on the floor and walked to the glass. The door shut behind him. Rancid air blew through the broken window's opening. He saw what affected Solange. There were tens of thousands of bodies, maybe hundreds of thousands. They filled a hole the size of a football field, and were piled as high as a three or four story building. Birds feasted on the remains.

"Good lord." Todd muttered. He saw more evidence of the gunfight. Men in fatigues lay dead outside the back door. Bodies in street clothes poked from behind trees and a nearby dumpster.

Todd shut his eyes, took stock of the scene, and turned to leave. The door was locked from the inside. He knocked for Solange. He saw the door handle turn. A composed Solange held the door for him.

"May we go now?" She asked solemnly.

"I cannot go fast or far enough." Todd picked up the paintings and they made their way out of the Metropolitan Museum of Art.

They pulled the scarves from their faces when they were close to 71st street.

"That was the worst thing I have ever seen." Todd said to her.

"I will never see anything as horrible again. Those birds eating the rotting flesh? How can a place that held all the beauty of humanity become such a nightmare? What happened? Why was the army there? I did not hear anything about a gunfight in New York City. I listened to the news every day." Solange maintained a quick pace towards their camp despite the poor conditions in the ice and snow.

"I don't think we'll ever know." Todd paused, stopping to look at her. "And you know what? I don't think I want to know."

29

The U.S. government's initial takeover of the media was not nefarious. Television networks were devastated by the pandemic. Broadcast journalists fell to the rapture immediately, exposed to it sooner than the general population by foreign correspondents returning from assignments.

The President needed information distributed. He appointed an Office of Information, and used the military to control television and radio networks.

There was no cure for the rapture. The population was dying at in increasing rate, and the major cities were crumbling.

As the pandemic worsened, the Office of Information became a tool for control. The country was in critical shape. The new edict from the Secretary of Information was to broadcast positive stories and non-specific information. The Secretary assumed control of the internet and social media outlets in an attempt to positively spin all rapture messaging.

The Battle at the Met, as it was called by the few survivors of the fight, occurred after the government media takeover. The event did not qualify as 'positive,' and was kept out of the news, and off the internet.

The CDC theorized it could derive and synthesize a cure from healthy, immune citizens, and it used the military to locate and detain those citizens. The military lured people to community meetings with the promise of food, water, and information. Body temperature scanners identified healthy people. Healthy citizens, typically pulled aside from the main meeting, could volunteer to assist in testing or be forcibly 'volunteered.'

The program yielded no results. Those captured either contracted the rapture within days, or died from the disease without developing a high fever.

As the military continued to take custody of individuals, the population became suspicious.

'Information' events were held at libraries or other public spaces. New York City suffered a food and water shortage almost immediately, and the promise of supplies brought large crowds. The military events held at the Metropolitan were popular. The attendees, many of whom went regularly, began to notice people with low temperatures were disappearing.

The military, pressured to find as many healthy people as possible, became sloppy in their kidnappings. The government believed the end, a cure, would justify any means. When an eight year old girl was taken from her family, New Yorkers organized to end the kidnappings at the Metropolitan.

The initial attempt at halting the government was an old world response. People arrived at the Metropolitan with protest signs, blocking entry to the museum and scanners. The military arrested all of the protesters, locking them in a containment facility.

"We have rights, you can't do this to us." A detained lawyer argued.

"Do you want to die here, or do you want to die in your home with friends and family? That is your choice. I am releasing you in one hour, but we have your names and photos. If you try to stop our programs again, you won't be released. No one will ever see you again." The cold certainty in the sergeant's voice told the captives it was not an idle threat.

The people in the containment area exchanged names and set up a meeting. They organized a different kind of protest, one which would end the public roundups immediately.

The military doubled their presence at the Metropolitan, but they were not prepared for the assault. Twenty military personnel fought hundreds of armed citizens. Despite their superior weaponry, the sheer number of attackers doomed the soldiers. The Battle at the Met was bloody and shocking. Bodies of citizens and soldiers lined the steps and corridors of the museum.

Riots erupted on the upper east side of Manhattan. Buildings were set on fire, military vehicles were attacked. The army had no response and no ability to stop the uprising.

The neighborhood around the museum burned for days.

30

Solange and Todd saw the black smoke of the signal fires as they approached the camp. The kids were watching a movie in one of the RV's, while Melanie and Emily supervised.

"Looks like you made out." John said to his brother, walking towards them with a smile on his face. "You're back sooner than I thought. Did you see everything you wanted to see?"

"Did Emily tell you about the smell that chased her from the science musem?" Todd's face was serious.

"You let a little smell scare you away? Come on br..."

"It was a mass grave. There were tens of thousands of bodies." Todd turned to Solange. "Maybe more?" He asked her.

"I did not look at it for more than a second, but yes, there were hundreds of thousands of bodies, and birds." She shook her head. "The birds were horrifying."

Todd continued. "We shouldn't go north of here again, maybe three or four blocks, but nothing more. I say we check out the statue of liberty tomorrow, the Empire State building, and leave. There's no one here."

John was confused. "I get why no one would live up there, but there might be people in lower Manhattan. We need to give this a shot."

"Let me put this art away, and we will tell you what else we saw." Todd went into the RV to say hello to Emily. He asked her and Melanie to step outside. The kids cheered when they saw Todd, but quickly returned to their movie. Todd could not compete with Jim Carey.

Todd and Solange recounted their experience at the Metropolitan to the circle of adults.

Peter was the first to respond.

"I read about that whole thing towards the end of the rapture. I guess I forgot about it, or maybe thought it was a hoax. We didn't have anything like that in D.C. I assumed it was fiction. I'm sorry guys, sorry I sent you up there without even thinking about it."

The group stared at Peter.

"Wait, what? You knew about the gunfight and you didn't say anything?" Todd was not upset, he was stunned.

"Well, kind of, but not really. I was very into the computer in my last few years. I read everything I could, had some deep blog contacts. There was an email that circulated, the government shut down the actual internet. Hell, you couldn't even use the text part of an email, you had to write what you wanted in an attachment, cover it with innocuous things in the body. Anyway, I was getting a newsletter, happenings around the country. Some of it was crap, I mean, I lived in Washington, and the newsletter would say 'the White House is in flames.' When I read there was a firefight at the Metropolitan Museum of Art, well, it made no sense. I put it in the fiction category."

"Did the letter say why it happened? Did it talk about the mass grave in the park?" Todd was interested in these newsletters, as was the rest of the group. The letters might hold a key to survivor's locations.

"The newsletters always talked about healthy people being snatched up, about how no one should attend the government information sessions or food giveaways, that everything was a ruse to identify and take healthy people." Peter could tell he was losing the group. "I told you some of the information was hard to believe."

"Your newsletters claimed the government was rounding up healthy people? Why?" John believed the newsletters, and he could sense

Peter was uncomfortable talking about the conspiracies.

"There was one post from a woman who lived in Dallas. She attended a government wellness meeting because she needed water and food. She had a normal temp. They asked her to come into the next room, and she met with a younger man in fatigues who asked her to 'volunteer' to come with him. He was asking anyone who was healthy to volunteer to be tested in the hopes of finding a cure. He told her that his orders were to take people by force, but he didn't want to follow orders. She told him that she had two children at home that were sick, and still needed her and the food and water she was bringing back. The man told her to never attend another wellness clinic, to take the food and water from her neighbors or anywhere else but never trust the government. The army man pulled a digital thermometer out of his pocket, stuck it in his mouth, waited for the beep and handed it to her. He said to show the people at the desk the new reading, and tell them she failed his follow up exam. The temperature read 102. She thanked him, told him 'god bless,' and she finished the seminar to get her food and water." Peter stopped.

After a long pause he continued. "Well, the army people in New York City were not as moral as the young man in Dallas. They were taking people, and were not smooth about it. After a group of protesters were arrested, the city went crazy. There was a post about the upper east side being engulfed in flames, and riots occurring around all of the military armories and stations. It was an unbelievable story, like the ones about D.C. I assumed they were false. There were several posts about a gunfight at the Metropolitan Museum of Art between the army and a group of attackers rushing the guards, shooting people, taking the museum, trashing art, burning buildings, stealing the food. None of it made sense."

Everyone was quiet. Matt asked the obvious question. "Do you still have these emails? Did you bring your laptop or tablet? I'd like to read them."

Peter nodded. "They are all on my computer. We just need to charge it."

Melanie looked at Peter. "You are full of surprises. Why didn't you ever share with me? Four months together and you never mentioned any of this."

"Some of the past needed to stay in the past. What did it matter? I didn't want you to think I was some conspiracy loon, which I probably am. I saw too much in the military to not be suspicious." He turned to Todd and Solange. "I'm sorry I didn't warn you. It honestly slipped my mind. I hope it wasn't too horrible."

Solange put her hand on his shoulder. "It was horrific, but I am okay. You are right, the past is the past. I wanted the Matisse, and I feel like I earned the painting."

"Did the writings say anything about the mass grave?" Todd wanted a peak at those emails too.

"Every city had mass graves." Peter said solemnly. "I saw the one in D.C. The sheer volume of corpses was staggering. I would think New York would pick a better spot than Central Park, but I guess not. No, I didn't know it was there, but I knew there would be one somewhere."

John moved to more practical questions. "Do you think any of the people on your email string stayed alive? Do you know where anyone is?"

"I don't know if anyone is alive, but probably not. No one mentioned a specific location. We assumed the email was being monitored. If you are looking for a post that says 'we are leaving Manhattan for Montauk', you're not going to find it. No one would give up that kind of specific information for fear it was being tracked."

John nodded. "Do we have a new plan? Do we think we are wasting our time in New York City? We can drive down to the statue, take a look, and drive up to Boston. Not a problem for me."

Peter was the first to speak. "I would like to give it at least one full day. I want to walk down to St. Patrick's and light a candle for my wife and children, and one for the world. I will come back and man the fire and blow the horns tomorrow. I vote to give New York City two days."

"We can go to Ellis Island tomorrow." Emily said excitedly. "I bet we can find a boat or something to get us over there."

"Are you crazy?" John responded. "It's freezing. It's windy. How the hell are we going to find a boat to take us to Ellis Island?"

"Don't try and talk her out of it. She is crazy." Todd said to John. Todd received a punch on the shoulder along with a laugh from his wife.

Five minutes after the adult meeting, the kids emerged from the RV. A full tribe soccer match began in the park. Todd bowed out to make chili and corn bread, while the rest of the group chose sides. The temperature was brisk. Laughter and screaming echoed off the buildings around the park. New York City, silent for too long, welcomed the raucous match.

The air filled with the aroma of dinner as Todd opened the door of the RV to place the chili on a picnic table. He set the pot down and watched the soccer.

"Excuse me." Todd heard a meek female voice. "My name is Kelly. I'm so hungry. May I have some of your soup?"

Todd spun around to face a woman in her mid twenties. Her face was dirty, and she was thin. Her legs and arms were sticks in her jeans and top. Her cheeks were sunken and sallow. Tears ran down her face and made tracks in the grime. Todd could not help but notice she wore beautiful designer clothes.

"Of course, my god, please sit down. My name is Todd, Todd Dixon." He ladled a large portion of chili into a paper bowl and offered her a seat with the food. "Sit down, eat, you're with friends now. Anything we have, just ask." He handed her a paper cup of hot chocolate. "Would you like to eat inside, out of the cold?"

The woman said nothing. She ate ravenously. When she was done, she looked at Todd with thankful eyes.

"Would you like more? There is plenty." He could tell she was still hungry but was afraid to ask.

"Please." Her eyes streamed tears of joy and relief.

The rest of the group stopped their soccer game and stared at Todd and the stranger. John kept the crowd away to give the starving woman space.

Jay broke from the group and ran over to the woman.

"Hello," he said extending his hand. "My name is Jay Dixon. I'm six. What is your name."

"Hello Jay Dixon." She said, taking his hand. "My name is Kelly Maddox. I am 28."

"This is my dad, Todd." Jay said, flipping his thumb over his shoulder in Todd's direction.

"Your father makes excellent chili, and is a very generous man." Kelly said. She stood and offered her hand to Todd. "Thank you for your kindness."

The rest of the group walked over to meet her. "Before I introduce myself, I am on a scavenging mission for a group of survivors living in a seminary near Chelsea. There are eleven of us, and we need food desperately."

"Okay." Todd started. "What is the age range of the group?"

"We have three children, three teens, five adults. One of the adults is in her late sixties." Kelly drank a cup of hot chocolate as she answered the questions. Todd made her a double mug as she ate the chili.

"Should we move down there or send a party to pick them up while I make food?"

Kelly paused, "I think you should have us come up here. I can go down with a few of you to pick up the group. We have a van. We don't use it because of the snow."

John cut in on their conversation. "Is there anyone we should be worried about bringing to our camp?"

The question hung in the air.

"Look, I will help anyone. None of us asked for this situation, but you didn't hand pick the 10 people you survived the rapture with. I have two sons and two nephews, and three other children I have grown fond of in the last week. We have young women. I would like to know if you think there is anyone in your group I should be keeping an eye on."

Emily was annoyed John asked the question in front of the children, but she was glad he asked the question. She could sense Kelly was intimidated by John's forward manner. She added to his question. "We are going to give you food, don't even think not getting food as an option. I am a mother. You met my son, Jay. Please let us know if you think there is someone we should be worried about."

Kelly dropped her head. "I don't trust Sal. He's stoned most of the time. He's a big guy, worked construction, his hands are scarred from years of hard labor. He's a pill popper. I'd keep an eye on him. I think he wants to steal things and run away, which would be fine with me. He's not around much, but you'll be able to tell right away if he is at the seminary. He must have been a scam artist or grifter before all of this. I swear he's still looking for an angle. The rest of us have figured out, there are no angles anymore." She looked back up at the group. "The rest of us, me and the other 9, we're good people. Well, one of the teens is a punk, but he has a good heart." She pleaded with Emily. "Please help us. We need water as much as we need food. We drink dirty snow and rain puddles." Kelly dropped her face.

The eight days together honed the new tribe into a well oiled machine. The Dixon family and the Washington D.C. family sprung into action. Melanie, Todd, Matt, and Emily elected to stay with the children. John, Solange, Peter, and Craig would take Kelly to Chelsea, meet her clan, and invite them back to the park for dinner. The decisions were made quickly, and the greeting party prepared for a drive down Fifth Avenue.

Craig was excited to meet the new people. His father pulled him aside. "Craig," John started, "you're an important part of this group. We want the kids to feel safe and excited to come with us. Make sure you are friendly. Let's get you a bag of candy, maybe some lollipops or something that you can hand out." Craig nodded, keeping focused as his insides danced with excitement.

"You won't need candy." Kelly overheard. "Bottles of water are needed more than lollipops or candy bars."

Craig was handed a box of juice pouches.

Peter walked to his fishing buddy, Craig. "You and I are the two friendly faces in our group. Your dad and Solange are serious enough for the four of us." The old man laughed, rubbing Craig's hair like old men like to do.

"I can be nice. I just have not found people I would like to be nice to yet." Solange said to Peter, smiling at the tall white haired gentleman. The young woman and old man continued to trade one liners as Craig opened the door to the truck and moved into the third row.

Craig examined the new woman sitting in the second row. She did not say anything. She sat in the Suburban and stared. The SUV was on and warm inside. The woman leaned her head back, enjoying relief from her hunger and cold for the first time in months. Craig liked her even though he had not spoken to her yet. She had a kind face, and long pretty blond hair. Her hair was filthy but beautiful. It stuck through the back of a Minnesota Twins baseball cap, dangling into the third row area.

Kelly turned around to look at Craig. "Hello, my name is Kelly. What's yours?" She smiled at him.

"My name is Craig Dixon."

"Another Dixon? Did your entire family survive?" She continued to smile as she asked.

"My mom died, and so did two of my aunts. My brother and uncles are alive in New Hampshire. We have to go find them when the snow thaws. Until the snow melts, we are looking for people like you." Craig explained.

"I'm sorry about your mother." Kelly frowned, as if she said something wrong. "I'm glad you found me. There are three young kids, two girls and a boy, who will be very excited to meet you."

"Awesome." Craig said back.

"It is awesome." Kelly agreed, nodding. Her eyes moved from looking at Craig to something over his shoulder. Craig turned around to follow her eyes. She was staring at Hubba as the bulldog hopped down the steps of the RV.

"That's our dog, Hubba. My Aunt Emily rescued him. He probably smelled the chili. He doesn't do much, sleeps most of the time."

Kelly had her hand cupped over her mouth. She moved out of her seat in the SUV and opened the door, running passed Peter, Solange, and John as they moved toward the Suburban to leave. Kelly's hand was still over her mouth. Hubba's nose was high in the air sniffing the chili.

Kelly crouched down onto the tips of her toes and hugged the dog.

Emily watched. "Um, that's our dog, Hubba." She paused. "Are you okay?"

Kelly was crying, rocking and hugging the dog. Hubba licked her tears, finding something tasty in the young woman's dirty face.

"I'm a veterinarian. I haven't seen a dog in half a year." She turned and faced Hubba. The dog still licked her face. "You're a good boy, what a good boy."

"Hubba's my miracle dog. For obvious reasons, but also because I found him on a house tour, half dead, locked in the governor's mansion. He's made a full recovery, as you can see." Hubba enjoyed the attention and the salty tear face. If he had a tail, it would have been wagging.

"I didn't think I'd get to see a dog again." Kelly smiled and backed away. "I can't believe you found a dog." She rubbed Hubba behind the ears.

"Kelly? We should get going." John said from the driver's side of the Suburban. "Hubba will be here when you get back. Trust me, he doesn't go anywhere."

Kelly stood and looked at Emily. "Thank you. Thank you for coming for us. Thank you for feeding me. Thank you for having a dog." She stepped forward and hugged Emily.

"You're welcome." Emily replied, surprised by the emotion, and embracing the stranger.

Kelly let go. "Okay, I'm off." She looked down at Hubba, sitting at the feet of his new friend. "A dog. An entire family and a dog. Unbelievable." She shook her head as she went back to the Suburban.

"So, you really like dogs, huh?" John said, smiling.

"I am, or was, a vet, large animals mainly, horses really. I worked at the Aqueduct racetrack and at Belmont racetrack, and I volunteered for the NYSPCA a lot too."

"Sounds like an exciting job." Peter chimed in.

Kelly was suddenly at ease with the group, less reserved than she was before she met Hubba. "Well, most of the horse owners and trainers had their own vets. I was just on call. It's how I got the job at such a young age. I didn't get to do much. I've only been a vet for a year. I was the assistant vet, doing a large animal residency at the racetracks."

"Well, we are glad to meet you. As I said, my name is John Dixon. My son, Craig, is behind you. Before we take off down Fifth Avenue, can you tell me where I am going? I'm not from Manhattan. When you say 'Chelsea' I have no idea what you are talking about, other than knowing I can hit golf balls there."

"Okay," Kelly laughed. "You are going to stay on Fifth Ave until you get to Madison Square Garden. Take a right onto 21st just past the Garden. 21st goes right to the seminary."

"And we're off." John said as he put the Suburban into gear.

31

"Eleven more people." Todd said to Emily and Melanie, shaking his head as he watched the SUV drive away. "This is going to cut into our food in a serious way. We can feast tonight, maybe for a few days, but we will need to stop in some towns and scavenge for food stores on our way to Boston."

"We'll do what we need to do. I knew taking on more people was a risk, but think about the upside of having twenty four people heading to Hanover rather than seven. We have fifteen adults now. Let's get through the next few meals. We can figure out what to do." Emily was not worried. They had enough food in the RV's to feed the group for a month. She also believed they would find food as soon as they left New York City.

"And you picked up a doctor." Melanie smiled, hinting she was part of the described upside.

"I know, I know, I just worry about the food. We have enough." He stared at the pot of chili. "We'll let the kids eat this chili now, and I'll get started on something else. How long do you think I have? An hour?"

Emily and Melanie shrugged their shoulders and held up their hands in the universal "we don't know," gesture.

Matt was busy directing the younger kids in preparation for the arrival of the new group. He was tasked with setting up chairs, getting the other tables out from under the RV's, getting paper plates and flatware ready. They had two fire pits that needed to be set up and set ablaze.

Matt pulled the kids into a tight circle around himself.

"Okay guys and gals, let's go eat and then be ready to help when the new people come to camp. Eat until you are full so you aren't thinking about food later. Great job on setting up the tables and making the camp inviting."

"Do we know if they like soccer?" Brian asked excitedly about the kids coming to the camp.

"No, we don't. I don't know their ages either." Matt answered questions, as off the wall as they were.

"So there might be another little girl?" Casey asked hopefully.

"Um, I'm a girl." Jaclyn said quickly.

"You're not little though, and you like sports." Casey clarified.

Matt jumped in to avoid a problem. "I don't know the ages or whether they are boys or girls. I don't know if they like soccer either, but we will find out soon." He handed bowls of chili out as the kids walked up to him.

"Are they going to come with us to Hanover like Jaclyn, Jacob, and Casey?" Jay asked between large spoonfuls of chili. Soccer made him hungry, and he was afraid he would have to share his food with the new people.

"We don't know." Emily said as Matt struggled to answer. "All we can do is be nice, and ask them to come with us. They will decide on their own." She patted Matt on the back, and left him to run the group.

Todd and Melanie were inside the RV preparing food. They ate bites of chili as they worked. Emily came inside to join them.

Todd made spaghetti with meat sauce. It was kid friendly and easy to prepare. The meal also saved well, allowing him to make more than he thought necessary and put leftovers in the fridge. He was not sure how much the new people would eat, and he prepared enough for an army.

"I wonder why they stayed in New York City if they didn't have enough food." Melanie said as she opened cans of green beans and poured them into a pot. She always insisted on serving a vegetable.

"That's a great question. I don't know. Maybe they were trapped by snow until recently. Maybe they thought they had enough food to get through the winter and miscalculated. We'll have to ask them. " Todd placed two pots of water on the stove to boil.

"Kelly seemed nice for the five minutes we got to speak with her." Emily looked out the window at the kids, who laughed as they ate. "I just realized I haven't had dinner." She opened the door and walked out to the chili, filling a bowl and grabbing two cornbread muffins.

"Who's ready to meet some new people?" She asked the table.

"Us!" the group replied enthusiastically.

Emily winked at Matt. "I am too." She said. "I am too."

32

Rebecca turned the cottage's dining room into a project center. The bathtub was still next to the fireplace because of the hole they cut into the floor, but chairs were no longer stacked on the large table. A computer, books, maps, and charts were spread out in their place. Print outs and models adorned the alcove's walls.

Inputting information was the new favorite pastime of the house. They had eight laptop computers. Four were plugged into solar chargers and placed near a window, while the other four were used to input data. Rebecca selected a topic for the day. She would simply say "rainfall" and the group would input rainfall statistics from the past 25 years by month for North America. The days of copying and pasting large datasets from the internet were gone. Inputting the information by hand was the new reality. Their use of the computers was limited. They would charge batteries on the solar chargers during the day, and input for the two or so hours the battery life allowed. It was a frustratingly slow system, but it was working. They had climate, animal, insect, reptile, amphibian, and crop information inputted. They used thumb drives to move the data from each of their laptops onto Rebecca's master computer.

Rebecca, Paul, Hank, and Greg discussed relevant statistics endlessly. The most subjective factor was "availability." What did that mean? Could they realistically get to Australia if they needed to get to Australia? Was Okinawa a realistic destination? Was the Mediterranean? Days were spent debating their ability to move to California as opposed to Virginia. Should travel be incorporated into the model? Did moving 500 miles require the same effort and difficulty as moving 2,000 miles?

The cottage did not spend all of their time working on the model. They had to survive. Greg had become a skilled trapper in the last few months. The shotguns and rifles were considered a finite resource, and the group relied more on trapping or bow hunting rather than bullets. They did not know how to fill shotgun shells or make gun powder. The guns would soon be as obsolete as cars.

As the weather turned warmer, they were able to fish. Soft spots opened on Occom Pond and the surrounding lakes. They cut holes in the ice and dropped lines. Hank and Greg spent hours trying to catch fish and game for dinner, while Paul and Rebecca stayed in the cottage working on the "destination model."

Hank and John were brothers, and they loved each other, but they were not close friends. They did not see each other outside of family events like weddings or anniversaries. The brothers drifted apart over the last 30 years, as did their families. As a result, Hank did not know his nephew well. They spent much of their time getting to know each other.

Greg enjoyed his Uncle Hank. They had a mutual love of baseball, and talked endlessly about statistics and players. Hank had seen most of the players Greg idolized.

The snow was melting at the beginning of April. Hank and Greg enjoyed their first 45 degree sunny day, and joked about how it felt like 80 degrees after the long cold winter. They drove a Jeep Wrangler to a trout club on the other side of the Connecticut River. A pier was left in the frozen lake, extending out into deep water. Using heavy rocks and long sticks, Hank and Greg made holes in the thinning ice at the end of the pier. They caught five rainbow trout using bait and hooks. Hank commented at how aghast his father would be if he were alive to see bobbers and bait at the esteemed dry fly club.

The lake was owned by a trout fishing club, tucked away in Norwich, Vermont, across the Connecticut River from Hanover. Heavy snow had prevented access to the lake except by snowmobile, and upon arrival they would have to dig a path onto the lake, and use a chainsaw to cut through the thick ice. It was an arduous method for fish, and took the entire day to yield a few if any trout. As the snow melted and the ice thinned, the journey became easier, and the fishing more rewarding. Now that Hank and Greg had better access, they fished the well stocked lake often.

Hank parked the Jeep, tricked out with large tires and giant treads, at the bottom of Wheelock Street. The street's intimidating hill was still covered in snow and ice. It was an invitation to wrecking the Jeep, and injuring the drivers. They opted to walk the half mile to and from the cottage each time they fished for trout.

Today was their third outing to the trout club in the last week.

Hank used the trip to the club to teach Greg how to drive. They practiced going to and from Norwich, sometimes two or three times each trip.

"Don't get too used to driving. We're going to run out of gas, or the gas we have is going to go bad soon. Unless we find a person who knows how to refine oil, we'll be riding bikes and horses from here out." Hank teased.

"I'm glad I learned to drive before cars become useless. I'll always be able to say 'back when we drove cars...'" Greg bragged.

They finished the steep walk up Wheelock hill and turned left on Main Street heading to the cottage. The five large fish swung from the chain creel hanging from Greg's hip. They were friends more than uncle and nephew, and talked about baseball as they made their way home.

"I saw Randy Johnson pitch in Cincinnati. He was with the Diamondbacks, and was incredible. First of all he's like eight feet tall, and he's only 60 feet away from you and standing on a mound, then he's throwing heat that breaks, then he's throwing a pitch with the same arm motion that is like 80 m.p.h. I don't know how the Reds' batters put wood on the ball." Hank enjoyed talking about his baseball experiences. Greg soaked it up.

"That's crazy. So he's the best you've ever seen?" Greg could listen to stories about baseball all day. Growing up in South Carolina meant he did not have access to the major leagues. Even though he spent the last year near Boston, he did not see any Red Sox games.

"He was up there. I saw a lot of guys though. Maddux would give up hits, but he never gave up runs, so he was totally different. He'd throw 80 pitches and be done in 2 hours. Such a rare pitcher, he didn't waste pitches." Hank finished his comments as they reached the cottage. It was noon, and he was hungry.

Hank swung the interior mudroom door open and felt the warm dry air blow out of the cottage. "The wood stove is definitely on." He said to Greg.

"Hey!" Rebecca waved to them excitedly from her seat at the computer. "We've narrowed our move to a few places. I think we'll end up near the ocean in Virginia or make the long trek out to Northern California. I can't decide if earthquakes are worse than hurricanes. Both are about as likely. It depends on how long we want it to take to get to our final spot, and if we want to incorporate finding other survivors into our model."

"My dream of living in Hawaii is gone?" Greg lamented.

"It's too far. We don't have boats or planes. I mean, I guess we have boats, but we don't have anyone to captain the boat to get us there." She explained systematically. "So yes, it's over Greg, sorry."

"I was so close. So close." He laughed.

"Hey, Rebecca, how is the morning going?" Hank asked. The angry, sad, paranoid man who arrived at the cottage two months ago was melting away, replaced by a happy and relaxed father figure. Rebecca's optimistic and infectious view of life was the leading cause of Hank's rebirth.

"I don't know. Am I eating trout for lunch?" She asked.

Hank held up the five large fish. "Lunch and dinner."

"Then I am having a great day." She said with a smile. "Paul and I can tweak the model more, but I don't think the results will change. Greg is right, Hawaii would be our number one choice if we could get there, but given the travel limitations, California or Virginia are our next best options. Also, Hawaii probably means not finding new people."

"But if we can get to Hawaii?" Greg asked.

"Well, if we can get there, then we should go. Kauai has chickens, wild boar, fish, few insects, no snakes, no predators, it is always the same temperature. It always rains on one part of the island. It's always sunny on the other part. The growing season is 12 months. If we bring seeds and livestock, we could create a sustainable colony. Other than sunburn, it will be the best place to move. I can't see how we can get there without modern equipment, but if we can get there, pack your bags." Rebecca spoke with authority and confidence.

Hank undressed from the morning expedition. "Well then, let's switch our efforts from where to go to how to get there." He hung his fleece lined flannel shirt on a hook next to the door. "If you say Kauai is where we need to go, let's figure out how we can get there. If you tell me we can't get there after research, I'll believe you and we'll focus on California or Virginia. Let's give the Hawaii plan a good try."

"Another project?" Rebecca asked.

"Another project." Hank agreed. "Let's have some lunch first. Greg has exciting news."

Paul walked in the room from the kitchen. He looked at Greg with anticipation. Greg sat on the floor pulling off his socks. Despite his waterproof and insulated boots, his socks always seemed to get wet. "Oh man does that feel good. I can't wait to not wear two pair of socks."

"Well?" Paul asked. "What's the news?"

Greg smiled and looked at Hank, then back at Paul and Rebecca. "We saw the highway through the snow. We saw road down the valley. The snow is clearing. We can leave if we need to." He paused. "More importantly, people can come here if they try."

Smiles crept across the four faces. They beamed in silence, reveling in the news for a few moments.

"I say it's business as usual, but we prepare for other people to arrive during our spare time." Hank suggested.

The comment elicited a chuckle from Paul. "Yeah, all of our free time."

Hank brought the fish into the kitchen. He used olive oil, herbs, and seasoning on three of the trout before placing them in the oven for lunch. He packed the largest two in snow on the porch for dinner.

Hank found several indoor herb kits at the hardware store when he first arrived, and grew dill, basil, thyme, cilantro, and parsley on a kitchen window sill. He used the herbs sparingly. They added a great dimension to fish and other foods. He typically used the abundance of dried herbs, but some things, like trout, called for fresh. Hank opened two cans of mixed vegetables and placed them in a pot on the stove.

Fifteen minutes later the fish and vegetables were ready. The extreme heat of the wood stove oven and burners meant food was finished quickly. The group sat around the kitchen table. They tore bread from a large loaf baked that morning, ate their fish and vegetables, and drank water.

"We have at least a couple of weeks before John and Todd arrive." Paul began. "We've had a great few months, living as a little family here, but it's time to plan for our next phase." He put some of the fish in his mouth and let out an audible 'mmm.' "You've outdone yourself, Hank. The flavoring and preparation of the fish is getting better every day."

"Thank you, sir." Hank replied. "And I agree. We should clear the upstairs bedrooms of wood, sweep them, get them ready for occupants."

"We've used all of the wood upstairs. Paul and I have been filling the wood bins from the van supply for a few days. We do need to clean the upstairs. We have clothes and boots for newcomers. Let's focus on acquiring all the food we can find. Dried food, canned food, boxed food, anything we can move." Rebecca added.

Greg ate his fish, bread, and vegetables in silence as the other three made plans. It was too much for him to hope. He was a few weeks from seeing his father and brothers. It had been seven months since he heard his father's voice. Eight months since he joked with his brothers, or threw a baseball to Matt. Eight months since he sat around a table with his family and shared a meal. If he thought about it too much, he was overwhelmed. 'Focus on the day to day.' He often told himself.

Greg felt a hand bump his leg under the table. It was Rebecca's. She squeezed his knee, and he looked up from his food to smile at her. She gave him a knowing look. They talked about his family all the time. She knew how excited he was to see his father and brothers. Greg slipped his hand under the table and placed it over hers.

Hank and Paul laughed about some old story from their childhood in Hanover while the teens held hands under the table.

33

Kelly was shy and reserved at their camp, but a few minutes into the drive to Chelsea, she would not stop talking. All John, Craig, Solange, and Peter could do was nod and said "okay" and "sure."

"Obviously the racetracks were closed right after Raleigh, and I wasn't needed there, so I went to the SPCA to see if I could help, but all those animals died. One after another, they just got sick and died, faster than people did. And I'm sitting there saying, 'what am I going to do with my life? Horse racing is gone, domestic animals are dead, great career you've picked.' But then, everyone started to die."

Kelly stopped to drink a swig of water from a bottle given to her by John. "Thank you for the water. You have no idea. We started rationing water four months ago, unless you wanted to boil water from the river, and I am not drinking water from the Hudson or East River, no matter how long you boil it." She drank another swig. "Anyway, I was living on the upper West side with a girlfriend from college. We had this TINY one bedroom, but we were never there, except now we were always there, because neither of us had jobs to go to, and it's not like you wanted to go out into crowds or anything, so there we were in this tiny room together. My family was in Kentucky, which is why I love horses, and her family was out in Colorado, and neither one of us had a car, because we live in New York City, so we had no way to get home, not that we wanted to go home, because everyone was sick anyway. Then Sarah, my roommate, gets sick, and I have to try and keep it together, and I stay with her, and we cry and she dies, and I'm like 'what do I do now?.' So I call the morgue, and they actually picked up her body, like, the next day, it was amazing, nothing is running in New York, not the subways or the cabs, but the morgue service comes in 24 hrs? Insane, right? I'd heard the stories, about people who aren't sick, you know, disappearing, so before the morgue people come, I run up and down the stairs of our apartment building a bunch of times, get a good sweat going, get all flushed, and then I cough a few times. There was a woman with them, she was in fatigues, and she had a pocket thermometer, and I guess she's supposes to take my temp. She takes one look at me and decides I'm sick already." Kelly took another swig of water. "And the woman says to me, 'If you have the faculties, and can call us when you get close to the end, we'll come by to see what we can do. God bless.' See what they can do? She meant she'd pick up my body. Then she puts a big red sharpie marker 'X' on my door, and I look up and down the hall and see that all the doors have a red X and a black X too. I hadn't left the apartment in over a week, since Sarah got sick, so I had heard doors open and shut, but had not paid attention. Sarah was Korean, or half Korean and half American. She was a Ramen noodle and pasta nut, and she had cases of the stuff laying around, literally, this high end Ramen Noodle she ate, that you couldn't find in the bodegas, and if you did it cost like $2 a pack, she would buy a case of it at warehouse stores and live off the stuff. Well, I lived off that during the week she was sick. So the lady is walking down the hall, and I cough and ask her, 'I get the red X, but what is the black X?' and she looks back and says, 'The black X means we've made a second visit. Those apartments are empty.' Then she steps in the elevator and is gone. That's when I realized I was the only one left alive in my building. I go up and down each floor, it's a ten floor building, 65 apartments, every single door has a black 'X' on it. Well, the good news was, there weren't any bodies left in my building, the bad news was, I was alone in a big scary building."

"Oh my gosh, what did you do?" Craig sat behind Kelly, enthralled by her story. At 10 years old, he was following it like it was fiction. He hoped there would be a ghost or vampire responsible for the deaths.

Kelly turned around to speak directly to Craig. She seemed to speak a thousand words a second. "Well, I went to my apartment and thought for a while. I was a little tired of eating ramen noodles, but I didn't have any other food, so I went to the basement apartment, where my super lived. Sure enough, there was a black 'X' on her door. She was this sweet, hardworking, wonder woman named Sylvana, who took care of everyone in the building like we were her children. Anyway, Sylvana kept a hidden key to her apartment in a magnet box in the laundry room down the hall. Only a few tenants knew about it. She kept UPS and FedEx deliveries in the apartment for everyone, and she trusted a few of us to have the key to help out if she was not around and people wanted their packages. So I knock on the door for a while, then I get the key and open the apartment. Everything is there, but no Sylvana. I was looking for her master key, so I could scavenge for food in the rest of the building. I scour her place and find some great dried sausages, tuna fish, and a big ring of keys."

Craig couldn't help himself. "Did you find any bodies?"

"No. The black 'X's' were accurate. My building was empty. Bizarre that I would luck out and get an empty building. Anyway, I found as much food as I could. I moved into the top floor penthouse, and I waited."

It was John's turn to ask. "Waited for what, Kelly?"

"For it to end." Kelly said quietly.

Peter, Solange, and John knew what she was talking about. Craig looked at her curiously and asked. "For what to end?"

Kelly looked out the window at the passing buildings. "The world."

Craig looked at Solange. The story was not over, and he wanted answers. He opened his mouth to ask another question, but Solange held up her hand and shook her head.

Several seconds passed. Kelly snapped out of her trance. "There used to be people in all of these buildings. Now there are just red and black 'X's' on the apartment doors. It's so sad." She paused again, looked at Craig, took a quick drink of water, and started. "Seriously, this water is so delicious." She screwed the cap back on and turned to Solange. "I'm sorry that I ramble on, but I don't talk much within our group. It felt good to get it all out. I'm okay now, I can't promise I won't slip into more ranting, but I hope to keep it together."

They drove slowly down the avenue. The ice and snow made it hard to control the SUV. John pointed to Madison Square Garden as they turned onto 21st Street.

"That's was where the Knicks and the Rangers played. A lot of the big bands played." John said to his uninterested son. Craig wanted to hear more of Kelly's story.

"How did you meet the other people in New York?" Craig asked Kelly. The boy ignored Solange's head shaking.

"We'll have plenty of time to talk about that." Kelly told him "I don't know for sure, but from what I could see in the few minutes I was with ya'll," Kelly's Kentucky accent came through strongly as she said 'ya'll.' "You have a cohesive unit, working together and making good decisions. My group is not as unified. We want to stay alive, but we don't work well together. It's one of the reasons we didn't leave New York when we should have. I work best with Bernie and Jamie. We take care of the younger kids. There are three of them. I would include Meredith, an eleven year old girl, but she usually stays close to Avery, a 17 year old girl, and they are pretty much self sufficient. The teens do some chores, but not too much. They'll help if we ask. Anyway, Ahmed was a hot shot banker, and while he and Bernie are close, he keeps coming up with 'plans.' He works hard, but I can tell he wants to be somewhere else and with other people. He isn't happy, but he does his work. I'm okay with him, we're just not close. We have two people who are useless. Sal is a big man who could be a great asset, but he's addicted to pills. He sleeps and drinks most of the time. He scares me more than a little, and we try to keep the kids away from him, not get him angry. He shows up to eat, talks about doing a bunch of stuff, starts a project, then gets high and leaves us alone for a few days. The last person is

Antonio. He was in a gang in the Bronx, and he can't let it go. He wears his colors, keeps a gun and knife with him all the time, calls me 'bitch' a lot." Kelly stopped and looked at Craig and then at John. "I'm sorry."

Craig replied quickly, "It's okay, I know what bitch means. I don't say it, but I know what it means." Everyone had a quick chuckle.

"Anyway, he tries to hang out with Avery, the older teen girl, but she won't have anything to do with him. Antonio takes food, walks around muttering Spanish about all of us, and doesn't help."

John looked over at Peter. Peter nodded back at him. They paid close attention to Kelly's descriptions. John looked in his rearview mirror at Solange. She was looking back at him and nodded. Solange turned to Kelly and said, "I joined this group a week or so ago. They welcome everyone."

"Craig told me you are headed to New Hampshire to meet his uncles and brother?" Kelly asked innocently. "Did your entire family survive?"

John nodded. "That's the plan. We met Solange and Peter in Washington. We have to go to New Hampshire. It's not an option for most of us. We are inviting anyone who wants to come. We can't stay in New York. I have a 14 year old son who is alone in New Hampshire."

"Greg is 15 now, Dad. His birthday was in January." Craig chimed in.

John shook his head. "You're right, damn, I missed his birthday. I have a 15 year old son in New Hampshire. Wow. Anyway, after New Hampshire we are open to suggestions about places to settle, but we have to go to New Hampshire first."

"I'll talk to my people, which doesn't include the entire 11, and see what they think. The fact that you have so many young kids is inviting." Kelly sat back in her seat, taking one last sip of her water. "That's the seminary up there on your right. The red brick building. See the smoke coming out of the chimney?"

"Is there a place to pull in, or should I just park on the street?" John asked. "I don't want to freak anyone out by showing up unannounced."

"Just park by the hydrant. I doubt anyone is looking. The car noise will be strange, but we're not as with it as your group. Sal is probably sleeping one off or has disappeared. If the kids are screaming, no one will hear us." She wore a smile as wide as a child at Christmas. "This is going to be exciting. I went out to find food, and I find food AND people. Heck, if you show the bottled water, most of us will follow you to Canada."

John pulled up next to a red brick complex of buildings with a black iron fence running along the street. A gate led to a large grassy common area in the middle of the buildings. John turned around to face the rest of his group. "Everyone ready to make some friends?"

They opened their car doors and stepped out. It was cold. The sun was sinking off to the west, and the large skyscrapers of Manhattan blocked the sunlight that remained. John looked north to see if his signal fire was visible, but the skyscrapers blocked the black smoke. If Kelly had not stumbled upon the group, John doubted the tribes would have met.

Kelly walked to the gate.

"I'll call everyone. As I said, half of us will be friendly, the teens will be indifferent, and I don't know if Sal and Antonio will come out or are even around."

She walked into the center of four buildings. It was a beautiful arboretum with stone benches and walkways connecting the buildings. The paths were shoveled and the courtyard was maintained. As John stood in the common area of the buildings, he could almost imagine nothing was wrong with the world.

They entered one of the buildings through a coat room. Kelly held the door to the main area, which was warm but not comfortable in temperature. The veterinarian walked across the room to a door. She opened it and yelled. "Jamie! Bernie! Kids! Everyone! I found survivors! Come out and meet them!" Kelly yelled for her groups. "Come on out, they are great people. They have food for us, food and water."

John held Craig by the shoulders. The boy stood in front of him. Solange and Peter flanked John on either side. They smiled warmly. John pointed Craig towards the door where Kelly yelled. Three small faces appeared in a window next to the door. A little girl waved to Craig. Craig waved back to her. All of the kids smiled and began to talk to each other. A woman in her late 30's or early 40's appeared in the window above the kids. She was shocked to see other people, and she moved the kids behind her.

Kelly saw the woman and waved. "Bernie, it's okay. I met these people up on 59th. They are from North Carolina. It's a group of survivors." The woman waved to Kelly, and made a gesture as if she was wiping sweat from her brow and mouthed 'whew.'

The door opened and the woman entered. She wore a hooded sweatshirt with the hood pulled up to cover her head. "It's still cold in here." She said as she walked across the room to greet the new people. "The kids will be here in a second, I told them they needed shoes and jackets." She finished zipping her jacket.

"You brought visitors. That's great. It's wonderful to meet new people." She hugged Kelly, and walked towards John. "My name is Bernadette Evans, but everyone calls me Bernie." She held out her hand to Craig.

Bernie was an attractive African American woman. She was 5 foot 8 inches with a kind face and trusting brown eyes. She did not have gray hair yet, and her curly locks grew out of control and stuck out of the front of her hood. She was noticeably thin. Gaunt was the best description. She was thinner than Kelly.

"My name is Craig Dixon. I'm from South Carolina." Craig shook her hand. He looked down as he spoke. He was not as bold as his younger cousin, Jay, and shied away from new people.

Bernie gave Craig her attention until the introduction was done. She moved to John, Solange, and Peter. "Hello." She said enthusiastically and genuinely. "You are a sight for sore eyes. Please, come inside by the fire. We don't have much food, but what we have we will share."

"John Dixon, Craig's father." John said, shaking Bernie's outstretched hand. "Great to meet you too."

"Solange Wright." Solange said, ignoring the handshake and instead giving Bernie an informal hug.

"Peter Reinhart." The last of the new group said. "Very pleased to meet you."

"Bernie." John started. "We are a group of 13 people camped at 59th and Fifth Avenue. We have plenty of food, and are cooking a hot dinner for anyone in your group that would like to join us. Kelly told us you were light on food, so if you would like to invite any and all of your group, please, follow us back up." He paused to let the invitation sink in. "If that is too forward, we completely understand. We brought supplies to give to you as well. No pressure, no cost, just hospitality. Honestly, we are survivors just like you. We offer any assistance, and can leave some of our supplies with you when we leave New York."

It was a blunt start to their relationship, but John did not want to tip toe around the facts. Come eat with them, or do not eat with them. Accept their supplies, or do not accept the supplies. It was all done with an open and honest heart. His cards were on the table.

"Have you and your group eaten?" Bernie asked. She looked at Craig for an answer.

"No, ma'am. We met Ms. Kelly and heard you were hungry, so we jumped into our truck and came down here to invite you back."

"Let me get our people together and see what they want to do. I will gladly bring the children up to the Plaza for dinner. I'm sure a few of the other's would love to come. One member of our group has disappeared for the day, but there are 10 of us here. I hope that's not too many."

Peter stepped forward. "We have plenty of food, please do not feel like you have to make choices on eating or staying. There is more than enough for all of us and for you." Peter reached into a bag he was holding and pulled out a bottled water. "Kelly hinted that you might enjoy some fresh water. We have a case in the car that is all yours. I brought some to share immediately."

Bernie looked at the water, at Kelly, and back to Peter. Tears formed in her eyes. "Thank you Peter, thank you for your generosity." She gratefully took the water, then bowed her head and said a quick prayer. After saying "amen," she opened the water and took a long taste. Her eyes remained closed for a second after taking the swig. "I'll remember that taste of water for as long as I live."

Bernie looked at John. "Please have a seat, meet our group, and we'll get ready to follow you up to the park." She waved them towards a hearth surrounding a central fireplace. "It's the warmest place in Chelsea. We have some heat in the rooms, but nothing beats sitting next to the fireplace, when we have wood to keep the fire going that is."

She gestured towards the hearth a second time. "Please warm yourselves by our fire. I'll get the kids ready." She turned to Kelly. "Kelly, could you wake Jamie? She went to her room for a nap. I think the other two are playing cards upstairs or listening to music with their headphones."

John gave Craig a friendly shove towards the door, and he turned to Solange and Peter. "Not the most cohesive group of people, huh? Either of you need help with the waters?"

"I think we can get them." Peter replied. He patted the bag of bottled waters. "This will make Solange and me the favorites. We'll keep the water." He nodded to Solange.

"Okay, I was just trying to help." John said back.

"You were trying to take our thunder." Solange told him. "Peter and I get to win their hearts through water."

John shook his head in defeat and went towards the fireplace with Craig. A fire was ablaze. A pile of broken chairs and other furniture sat in a pile next to the hearth waiting to become fuel.

John looked down the hall and saw the three young children standing in their jackets while Bernie spoke to them. She waited for nods before she led them through the door.

"I apologize for not bringing the children in earlier. I wanted to make sure you were good people before I let you meet them. I hope you understand."

John nodded. "Bernie, if you had brought the children out before sizing us up, I would have thought less of you." The kids were young, below the age of 6. There were two little girls and a young boy.

Casey was going to be excited to have playmates.

Craig walked to them. "Hi. I'm Craig, I'm 10." Children liked to establish ages in their greetings. "This is my dad, John." Craig pointed to John, "and my friends Solange and Peter."

The children looked at Bernie. She nodded and smiled. "It's okay, they are good people, you can say hello." The kids were scared despite the 'okay' from Bernie. They were gaunt, dirty, and their hair was tangled and messy.

Solange stepped forward. She was the least intimidating of the three new adults. She pulled juice boxes from her satchel. "Would any of you like some juice or water?"

The little girl with red hair raised her hand meekly.

"My name is Solange." She handed a juice to the girl. The girl took a small sip and handed the box to one of the other children. "No." Solange said gently. "You each get your own. You do not have to share." The other two children suddenly put their hands in the air. "Good, here are the juices." Solange pulled the straw off the side and poked it into the hole for the youngest boy.

"I know how to do it." He said, smiling when he took a sip of the juice. "Thank you."

She handed an extra juice to each child.

John could tell the kids were weak and malnourished. They had no energy. He turned to Bernie. "Do you have a car? Maybe Kelly could take the kids with Peter or Solange back to our camp and get them dinner right away. Craig and I can stay with you."

Kelly shook her head. "I already ate. You go, Bernie. Take the children, get some food. I can wait for the rest of the group. Jamie should only be a second, she can go with you."

Bernie nodded. "You're right. Let's get them some food." She turned them. "Okay kids, let's take a car ride. Who wants some hot food?"

The children nodded excitedly without removing the juice box straws from their lips.

An older woman with long white hair pulled into a tight ponytail walked into the room. She was shorter than Bernie and frighteningly thin. She had tired green eyes. She managed a weak smile. "Hello everyone, my name is Jamie, Jamie Norse." She paused and held on to the back of a couch for support. "I am very glad to meet you. I'm just not feeling all that strong today. Please forgive me if I don't seem more excited."

Peter stepped forward and put his arm around the woman. She was as thin as a piece of paper when he gripped her. He noticed she wore at least four layers to keep warm. "Us old people have to stick together, let me help you. My name is Peter Reinhart. This is Solange, John, and young Craig." He handed her the water he had in his hand, the cap already twisted off. "Have a swig of water, and let's get you in the car we are taking to dinner."

The older woman looked over at Bernie and Kelly. Bernie nodded, "We've been invited up to the Plaza for a nice dinner with their group. They have supplies and hot food."

Jamie looked up at Peter. "Bless you sir. I will take your arm to get to the car, if you don't mind, though I don't know who you are calling old." Jamie let out a small chuckle.

A man stepped into the hallway from the stairway door at the end of the hall. He walked with authority towards John. He was dressed well in khaki pants and a flannel shirt. He wore expensive walking shoes that were dark brown to match his belt. His hair was combed, and he did not have the dirty appearance of the rest of the group. He wiped his face before coming down to meet the new people. Despite his put together look, his cheeks were sunken, and his pants hung off his hips. The flannel shirt gave the appearance of weight, but the man was a bag of bones.

He strode up to John with his hand out. "Ahmed Cook." He shook John's hand firmly. "I was an M.D. at Morgan before all this started. Very nice to meet you."

John did not drop his gaze from the man's eyes. He shook Ahmed's hand firmly and said one of the funniest things Peter Reinhart had ever heard. "John Dixon, I'm the guy with an RV, food, and supplies AFTER all this started. Very nice to meet you, Ahmed."

Ahmed's mouth opened a bit in an "oh" gesture. He was stunned by John's reply, but accepted the bluntness. John did not care about Ahmed's former life.

John continued. "We invite everyone up to our camp at 59ᵗʰ and 5ᵗʰ. We open our kitchen to you. Bernie, Jamie, and the kids are headed up to eat. "

Ahmed turned to Bernie, "Bernie, are you comfortable going up there? Maybe I should come with you."

Bernie knew how hungry Ahmed was, how many meals he skipped so the children could eat. He used the offer of protection as an excuse to salvage his pride in front of John. Ahmed was not a man who typically accepted handouts. "I'd appreciate that Ahmed. It would be great if you could help with the children."

"Don't even ask twice, I'm always here to help." He nodded to her and back at John. "Thank you for your generosity."

No one noticed the two girls standing the other side of the room. "May we come to dinner too? We're starved." The girls looked like sisters with long hair combed neatly and flowing over their shoulders. They wore clean coordinated clothes. "We can share the dinner if we need to."

Craig stood by the fire. He was overwhelmed by all of the new people. He watched as Solange moved from the young children to the two older girls. She introduced herself and said they would not need to share. The girls nodded, walking around to meet John and Peter before stopping in front of Craig. He was nervous, and the exchange was painful. The girls were attractive, and one was close to his age. Craig managed a weak, 'hi,' never picking his head up to look them in the eyes.

"Do you have a vehicle to get everyone up there?" John asked. Bernie nodded and mentioned a church van. "We'll unload the supplies we brought for you. Craig can go with Peter and the rest of you to our camp. Solange and I will stay here with Kelly to meet the last people."

"I don't know when Sal will be back. He sometimes goes away for a few days, and he walked out at lunch." Bernie turned to Kelly. "Did you see Antonio? He was upstairs the last time I checked."

The older girl near Solange, Avery, responded. "He's up there. He said he was busy." She rolled her eyes.

Ahmed stood next to Bernie. "Are you sure you don't want me to stay? I don't have to go up with the group."

Bernie turned to him, pinching his waist. "Ahmed, you need food more than most of us. Come, I need your help with the kids."

John stepped in. "Ahmed, Bernie is right, go with her. I can wait, as long as Kelly doesn't need more food." He turned to her.

"I'm good for a day after that chili and cornbread." She gave Jamie a look and nodded. "Real food Jamie. I swear one of them is a chef."

Jamie turned to Peter. "Well let's get me up there. I haven't eaten in two days." Peter nodded and they made their way to the coat room exit. Peter was practically carrying the thin woman.

"My dear, if you had not told me your name was Jamie, I would have guessed it was Flat Stanley." They went through the door, and he helped her put on a coat. The two continued outside and made their way to a green van.

John turned to the children and the two girls. "You can get in when you're ready." He motioned for everyone to get going.

Ahmed stepped forward and took the two little girls' hands. "Come on kids, let's get some food!" The little boy grabbed Ahmed's shirttail, and they made an airplane noise. It was a formation he used before. John smiled and reformed his opinion of the 'Managing Director.'

John turned to the older girl. "Avery is it?" He asked her.

"Yes." She said.

"Can you help us unload some supplies from the back of the SUV? Solange and I will carry them in here, but your help to get them onto the curb would be appreciated." He handed her a bottled water as he asked.

"Sure. I can stay to help if you need me, but please let Meredith get some dinner." The girl took the water and began to drink it. After two gulps she offered it to the younger girl.

"Here, please take your own." John handed the younger girl a bottle before responding to Avery. "You know what? Forget about helping, it was wrong of me to ask. You need to eat too. I just wanted some help with the supplies right now." He turned to Solange. "I'm going to go see about this Antonio. Why don't you get the truck unloaded on the sidewalk."

"Okay." Solange replied. She turned to the girls. "I love your hair." She said to both of them. "I have tried to grow mine that long, but it never looks good." The girls instantly started talking about hair techniques as they followed Solange towards the coat room.

John motioned to Kelly. "Maybe I can convince Antonio to have dinner with us. If not, I will leave him the supplies."

"That's not a great idea." She said. "I'll put the supplies in Bernie's room before we go. Please do not mention them to Antonio."

John gave her an odd look.

"You'll understand when you meet him." Kelly told him over her shoulder.

Kelly led John towards a door marked "stairs." They went up one flight and opened a door into a hallway. Glow in the dark stickers of big stars, little stars, planets, moons, and alphabet letters covered the walls. The stickers gave off a faint green glow that illuminated the dark hall.

"I like the stickers." John said looking around. "What a great idea. Did it keep the hall lit all night?"

"Can you believe it was Meredith's idea? She is the young girl with Avery. She had these stickers when she was growing up, used them as night lights in her bottom bunk bed. We went up to FAO Schwartz and found these things. Yes, it worked pretty well." Kelly walked down the hall and pointed towards the doors. "This is the bedroom area. The fireplace was set up to heat most of the room. Some sort of green heating option, using a central fireplace to heat the rest of the building. It is a radiator system. Water tanks sit on either side of the chimney, they heat up, the water flows through the pipes, heats up the rooms. It did an okay job, but the rooms were still pretty cold during the winter. Now that the coldest nights are behind us, the rooms are tolerable. Antonio stays in his room most of the time, comes down for meals when he runs out of food."

"He has his own food?" John asked. "It seems like everyone shares."

"Not Antonio, not with us anyway. He takes, but doesn't give to the group, unless it benefits him." She pointed to a room. "He's a good kid, but he can't get out of his old mindset. I've seen him care for the little ones. He sneaks them food, not the adults, but the three little kids and Meredith? They always end up with a cereal bar during the day. I saw the little boy, Cameron, fall on the ice. Antonio was the first one to him. Came out of nowhere. He was gentle and talked him through the tears. As soon as Bernie showed up? Tough guy came back. Anyway, I don't know if he'll come up to your camp."

"Well, the only way to find out is to ask, right?" John knocked on the door.

"You the guy from the Suburban?" He heard someone yell from the other side.

"Yes." John replied loudly.

"Where did you take everyone?"

"Up to dinner. We have hot food and supplies. We invited everyone, no strings, no questions, just come and eat."

The door opened. A boy stood in the frame. He wore jeans, a white t-shirt, an unbuttoned flannel shirt, and black high-tops. He had a black bandana on his head. He was trying to grow facial hair. The hair was not cooperating. John stared at the perfect stereo-type of an inner-city gang member.

"How come you didn't wait for me?" The boy said defiantly when there was no cause for defiance.

"You were told we were downstairs, you didn't come, and you missed the first boat up to 59th and Fifth. I'm here now. If you would like to come up with us, we are taking a separate car."

The boy laughed. "You people, New York is dead and you still want to stay at the Plaza. Unbelievable. Suckers then, suckers now."

"Let me get off on the right foot. My name is John Dixon. I have my family with me and 10 other people. I came up from South Carolina, met my brother and his family in North Carolina, met the woman downstairs in Richmond, and met five more people in D.C. We are here to meet more survivors. What is your name?" John stuck his hand out.

Antonio looked at his hand but did not take it. "My name is Antonio Pais. I grew up in the Bronx. I can take care of myself, but thank you for the dinner offer. If you leave me alone, I'll leave you alone. I want my cut of whatever came out of that truck and is sitting on the curb." He looked at Kelly. "You can give it to me now, or I'll take it when you are gone. I might do both." He kept his eyes on Kelly. "If you give me my share now, I won't tell Sal about the food."

Solange walked down the hallway. Antonio scanned her with his eyes, his head moving up and down. He let out a whistle. "Now that's what I am talking about." He said something in Spanish to Solange. She stopped, squinted her eyes at him, and smiled.

"I am only interested in men, not little boys. I would be more likely to change your diaper than kiss you." She stood by John and Kelly. "I speak English. It is not polite to speak another language when they do not understand."

Antonio spoke in Spanish, looking at John and Kelly as he said something. Solange did not acknowledge him.

"Okay then." John said. "Antonio, if you would like to join us for dinner, we're leaving. If you want to stay here, that works too. From your comments, I guess we'll put the supplies back in my car. The group can bring them when they return from dinner." He walked down the hall. He stopped and turned around. "It was nice to meet you Antonio. We'll be loading the car. You have five minutes before we leave. I will tell you, my brother is a very good cook. You will regret your decision not to come. There really are no strings. Come up, eat the food, don't talk to us, I don't care. We are sharing food. No agenda." John walked away.

Solange reached into her backpack and took out a bottle of water. She flipped it to Antonio before turning and following John.

Kelly looked at the young man. "I hope you come with us Tony. I know you have food, but a hot meal? None of us have had that in a while. I had two bowls of chili and a few corn muffins. Think about it. We'll be outside." She followed the other two down the hall.

Antonio stood in his doorway waiting for them to get to the stairs. When the door closed behind Kelly, he turned to his room and shut the door. He went to his single bed, lifting the sheet that blocked the underneath. He had several boxes of food, energy bars, breakfast bars, breakfast drinks. Most of the boxes were empty or almost empty. His supplies were low. Empty cereal boxes were pushed behind his dwindling food.

He sat on his bed and thought about his options. If he stayed, Sal might come back. Antonio did not like being alone with Sal. If he went, he would get a hot meal. He looked out the window, the people were almost done loading. Antonio jumped off his bed and ran downstairs. He made it to the SUV as the last door shut. He held up his hands for them to wait.

Kelly opened the back door.

"I'll take that dinner, but you better not try anything funny." Antonio said, using his best tough voice.

"Not even a knock knock joke." John said in reply. Kelly shut the door and they pulled away towards dinner.

They were a few blocks east on 22nd when Kelly began to talk again. "You have to tell me the story of the dog. Hubba is it? I haven't seen a canine or feline in half a year. How is it you have a dog?"

Antonio sat in his own row behind Kelly and looked out the window in an obvious effort to appear disinterested. When Kelly mentioned a dog, he looked towards John and Solange. "You have a dog?" He asked. Antonio loved dogs. He had three dogs in his apartment in the Bronx. While his friends bought Rottweilers and Dobermans, Antonio picked up strays from the SPCA. His gang nickname was 'Mutt.'

Solange saw the first spark of interest from Antonio. "We do have a dog. John's sister in law rescued it from a house in Raleigh. It was left behind, and lived in its own filth with no food or water for months. Like all of us, the dog is a survivor."

"He looks great now." Kelly replied. "I can't wait to check him over."

Antonio gave a simple, "that's cool," and went back to staring out the window. Instead of a sneer, he had a faint smile on his face. Solange could see his mood brighten as she continued to talk about Hubba.

"He smells up the RV. Something about the breed, he has horrible gas, but he is a good dog. He is very friendly with the kids, sleeps most of the time. He loves to have his belly rubbed." Solange crinkled up her nose when she talked about Hubba's gas.

"Bulldogs know how to make it funky, that's for sure." Kelly spread her arms across the back of her bench seat.

"How long did you stay in your building? You know, waiting for the world to end?" John asked Kelly.

"I had enough food for five weeks. God, if I knew how horrible this winter would be, that food would have stretched for twenty weeks." She wore a wry grin and shook her head.

"I filled bathtubs in every apartment, assuming the water was going to run out at some point. I saw this movie about zombies taking over London, and this father and daughter had plenty of food, but they ran out of water, and it didn't rain, so they had to leave their safe apartment."

"28 Days" John replied. "I love that movie."

"Yeah, well, I learned from that one, make sure you have water. I filled all the bathtubs. I watched the smoke rise from the other side of the park. I heard the gunfights at the Metropolitan. I stayed low in my penthouse, but no one ever came. Two weeks after the fires and firefight, I didn't see anyone on the streets. There were no cars. There were no sounds. I would hear an occasional airplane, but that was maybe once every other day. I decided to go outside, walk around. I went down the stairs and out the front door. There was a big black 'X' painted right on my building's door. My building was marked as dead. No one was going to bother me if I stayed there, but my food would not hold out." Kelly looked out the window at the buildings.

"You see all these buildings? They probably have food in them, but the food is behind these dead bolted steel reinforced apartment doors, and you can't even get into the buildings without smashing some triple pane wire sewn glass. Then you get into the apartments and there really isn't much food. A box of pasta or some cans of soup or my favorite is a box of cake mix. That's all I could find when I finally got into places. New Yorkers weren't big on pantries or stockpiles. The bodegas were everyone's pantries, and they sold out in the second week of the panic. Food is not easy to come by. I'm not the strongest person, but even someone who has strength, like Antonio," Kelly motioned with a flick of her head towards the boy. "He expends more energy getting into places to look for food than what he gains in the food he can find."

Antonio looked forward and nodded. "Manhattan was a horrible place to stay. I kept telling everyone, we need to go to Queens and go to neighborhoods. We need to find places we can get into by breaking windows, not smashing through metal doors, but then it snowed, and we got stuck. I kept telling you, didn't I Kelly?"

Kelly nodded. "He did, and we should have listened, but we were scared, and we had the kids by then. Bernie had this great place with a fireplace, radiant heat, and she had some food stored, and we thought we had enough, but we didn't have close to enough, so here we are."

They were almost to the park. Antonio looked out the front window. He could see the tables and fire pits. He saw the kids, girls, Ahmed, Bernie, and Jamie eating off plates. He saw cups and pitchers of something white.

"Holy shit." He said. "You have milk? How the hell do you have milk?"

"My brother has goats." John was excited to hear Antonio warming to the dog and milk aspects of his group.

"Damn, I told you we should have left Manhattan, Kelly. I told you." He leaned forward in his row, his head sticking over Kelly's seat. He licked his lips, almost visibly drooling. "Damn, we should have left Manhattan. Milk? I'd drink monkey milk right now."

They exited the van. Todd walked towards John and Solange. "Everyone is eating well, that's for sure." He turned to Antonio, his hand outstretched. "Hi, Todd Dixon."

Antonio looked at Todd's hand and did not take it. "I'm here for the food, fool. I'm not here to make friends. Where's my plate, and I want some milk." The boy's chest was puffed out. He stood as tall as he could.

"Everything is over there." Todd replied, pointing to the buffet style table of food.

"Wow, everyone else in the group has been so friendly." Todd told John and Solange.

Antonio stopped and turned back around. "What did you say?"

Todd turned to Antonio. "I said the rest of your group is friendly. You are not. Am I wrong in that statement?" There was a pause in the table conversation as Antonio looked at Todd, moving his eyes up and down. He looked at John, standing behind Todd, then over at Peter and Matt at the table. Antonio realized his situation, his weak position. He backed off.

"Whatever, fool, just give me my damn food." Antonio turned back to the table and piled pasta on a plate. He poured himself a glass of milk, drank it, and poured another glass. He found an end seat at the table next to a fire, and sat to eat.

Everyone was silent, nervous Antonio spoiled their dinner invitation. John dismissed the tension and walked to the table. "I'm glad you came to meet us. Everyone enjoying the food? Thank you for coming."

The first person to speak was Avery, the young woman who John judged to be between 17 and 21 years in age. She was so thin it was hard for John to be accurate with her age. "I've used up most of my faith and hope over the last six months, but I can honestly say this is the best meal I have ever had in my life. You have come into our lives when we needed it most. Thank you. Thanks to all of you. Meredith and I will come to New Hampshire with you. We can't stay here anymore. We won't." She turned to Bernie. "I'm sorry, Bernie, but faith hasn't fed us.

Hope hasn't fed us. I need to go with these people."

Bernie nodded to her. "It's okay, Avery. You're right. We can't stay here. My faith kept us here, and it brought us salvation through meeting these people. I understand I'm the only one that might believe that." Her plate had bread and corn bread, but no meat sauce covered pasta or chili. Emily opened a can of tuna fish for her. Bernie explained that it was a Friday during Lent, and she could not eat meat. "It is Friday. Would you consider letting me have one last Sunday in my chapel? We can leave after service on Sunday morning."

Antonio muttered something in Spanish under his breath, then looked at John with anger in his eyes. "No agenda, huh? You bring us up here, give us food, lure our people into your group? You want us to go to New Hampshire? " He looked down the table. "Are you people crazy? Do you know anything about this guy? These people are nice to you for 30 minutes and now you're leaving your family because he makes a box of pasta and some jarred red sauce?"

Antonio said additional things in Spanish. "I'm not going anywhere." He sat at the end seat at the table, his left arm was firmly blocking the girl beside him, Meredith, from getting near his food. The boy was territorial and selfish.

Peter ignored him. "Jamie, these people, I only met them a week ago, but they are good. I considered staying behind, living out my days alone, but we're not that old. We can make contributions and help."

The woman looked at him. "Why are you talking to me like I'm 80? I'm only 68. Of course I'll come. I have years left, and I hope to spend them with people. I'm weak because we don't have any food. Once I get my strength back, you'll see who I really am. I'm actually a hell of a lot of fun."

Kelly was not at the table, she sat on the ground petting Hubba. Emily sat next to them, and was in conversation with the young veterinarian. Kelly locked eyes with Bernie, nodding to let her know she was going with Jamie and the new people.

Jamie looked down the table at Antonio. "Things happen fast now, kid. You see a good opportunity, you better grab it. You were right when you said we needed to leave the seminary, none of us listened to you, and we almost paid the price. You need to listen to us now. There is strength in numbers. People are scarce, let alone good people. They aren't staying, so we need to be going. Don't let your pride or machismo get in the way of your life."

"You've got some moxie in you." Peter laughed. "I like that."

"Life's too damn short to hold it in." Jamie told him. "We learned that the hard way."

John turned to Bernie. "What do we do if Sal isn't back by service on Sunday? We can't leave without him. Can we?"

The adults of the New York group looked at each other, some of their eyes fell. The young children were asleep. They ate and curled up in their chairs.

"I can leave that man, and do it with a clean conscience. He would leave me in a second." Jamie answered. "It may not be the Christian thing to do, but it's the world we live in. Besides, if you don't have Duane Reade's where we are going for him to search for his pills, I doubt he'll leave New York."

Antonio let out a laugh. "You're alright, Jamie. You're alright." He told the older woman.

"We can't leave him." Bernie said quietly. "but I don't want to wait a week and deplete our resources or keep you from your family. We can worry about Sal if he doesn't come back by Sunday."

Ahmed sat next to Jamie, silent during the conversation. He looked at Todd and John. "If we come with you, what standing will we have, what voice? I hope we'll have some sort of agreement that gives us rights to food, that we will distribute work fairly."

Todd answered quickly. "I understand your question, and your concern, but both are founded in an old paradigm. There is no 'society' anymore. We are a group, a tribe. 75% of it happens to be my family, but we are a group that has decided to work and live together. We share food and labor. I am not prepared to give you any promise other than, right now, you will receive an equal share of everything. When we have food, we all eat. When there is work, we all work."

"That isn't very democratic. Your family should get one vote, not multiple votes." Ahmed negotiated.

"There is no voting." Todd said flatly. "Don't you get it? We just do. Did we discuss coming to New York City? Yes, but instead of putting stones in a bag, we discussed and did it. You'll have a voice and a decision to make every day. Do you want to stay with the group or leave." Todd was blunt. Life was different now. He sensed Ahmed did not want to let his old life and status go.

Bernie stood and motioned to the three children. "We should go home, or at least get these three, and maybe Meredith a bed."

Meredith's eyes were half closed. She perked up at the mention of her name. "I'm okay, just a little tired. I'll go home with Avery. I'm okay."

"Let's all go home." Jamie said. "I'm sure we have a lot to talk about separately." She turned to Peter. "Thank you for your hospitality sir. I hope to see you tomorrow. "

"We'll be here." Peter replied to his new friend. "Don't worry. We'll be here."

"Good bye Hubba." Kelly said to the dog, rubbing his ears. Hubba snored loudly as she rubbed him. Kelly walked over and picked up Cameron, carrying him to the church van. She placed him on the seat against the window. He did not wake up. She walked around the van, got into the driver's side, and started the engine.

"Can we help clean up?" Bernie asked.

"No worries." Todd told her. "We're going to fold the plastic tablecloths up and throw everything in the trash. I'll clean the pots tomorrow." He gave her a quick hug. Todd put his hand out to Ahmed. "Get a good night's sleep. Think about our offer. We don't need a decision tonight or even tomorrow." Before John and Solange arrived with Antonio, Todd and Emily briefed Ahmed, Bernie, Jamie and the rest of the group on the master plan of traveling to New Hampshire.

"We'll see you tomorrow." Ahmed said to him.

"We have eggs and pancakes planned. Just as Antonio said, we're luring you with food." Todd gave Ahmed a pat on the back and a smile. The former banker picked up one of the little girls and took her to the van.

Avery thanked her hosts before grabbing the last sleeping child. "They are tired from hunger. It makes you so weak." She told them. "Thank you." She and Meredith climbed in the van together, placing the sleeping girl in between them.

Antonio finished his last bite of pasta, walked over to Hubba, bent down and gave the dog a quick pat on the head. He looked at Emily, "cool dog," was all he said. He opened the passenger door to the van and jumped in.

Bernie shut the sliding side door, and the New York tribe headed down 5th Avenue.

"Well, that was a quick strike." Emily commented. "Matt, did you even say anything?"

Matt shook his head. "I set up the kids in the RV watching some cartoon movie and came back out, but everyone was stuffing their faces. They seem nice. Obviously Antonio is a little rough, but he likes Hubba, so he can't be all bad."

"He is not so tough. He is scared. He, Ahmed, and this Sal guy are the only men in his group. Now he is entering a group of almost all men. He needs to find his place." Solange was a keen observer.

"I'm interested to meet Sal. I mean," Todd chuckled, "Jamie wanted to pack up and leave from here tonight. What kind of person must he be?"

"Did you catch the little girls' names? I heard Cameron for the boy, and Meredith and Avery, but what about the youngest girls?" John was at a loss.

"Wendy and Bridget." Craig spoke up. "I talked to them on the ride up. They are 5 and 6. They went to kindergarten together. How weird is that? They told me, every day, Wendy and Bridget would show up, and another person would be gone, until it was just us and the teacher, then the teacher didn't show up. Wendy's parents died, and Bridget's parents were still alive, so they took her in, and they knew Cameron's parents, and when they died they took Cameron in too. So the three little kids were together until Bridget's parents died. The kids went outside, started walking around the upper East side." Craig paused. "I don't know what that means, but anyway, they are walking around and were told to head to the seminary. Bernie had the word out that she was accepting people and orphans. The kids walked from 89th and 3rd to the seminary, I don't know how far that is, but Bernie said it still amazes her when she thinks about it."

"It's a long way, let's just say that." Todd told his nephew.

It was 7:30 and dark. Todd stretched out his arms after the long day. "I'm exhausted. I'm going to clean up and go to bed." He walked over to the trailer where the kids were watching television and opened the door. He slipped inside to say goodnight to his sons, and make sure they were ready for bed. Melanie was in the RV, hiding from the New York group.

"I almost forgot you were in here." Todd said to her. "I didn't realize you weren't going to come out and meet everyone."

Melanie gave Todd a bashful look. "I fell asleep. Honestly, I was going to come out, but Matt set the kids up with a cartoon, I put my head down on the pillow, told them to wake me up in five minutes. Yeah, I just woke up."

Melanie slipped out the door and sat down at a table. Solange and John were eating cold pasta and bread. "Did you miss the party too?" She asked.

"We never got to eat." Solange filled Melanie in on the new people.

John gave his opinion. "I didn't meet anyone that wouldn't be a great addition to the tribe." He twirled his fork to get another bite of dinner. "Ahmed and Antonio are good people, they just live in the past. Once they step into the new reality, they are going to be great contributors. If you saw Ahmed with the little kids, he's a natural."

Todd came out of the RV. "The kids are all down." He whispered. "Where am I sleeping?"

Emily looked at the group seated at the table. "He doesn't know it yet, but I booked us a room at the Plaza." While Todd and Solange were on their adventure at the Metropolitan, Emily and John scouted out rooms in the hotel. Peter, Melanie, Craig, Todd, and Emily would stay in the hotel while Solange, Matt, and John took a night in the RV's. Matt pulled the kids' trailer duty for the evening.

The adults cleaned the camp area, balling up the tablecloths as promised, and throwing them in a trash can down the street. It made little sense to use a trash can no one would ever empty, but old habits die hard.

The Dixon tribe was enthusiastic about their new friends, and fell asleep with hopes of a stronger tribe when they left New York City.

The New York group went to bed with full bellies for the first time in months, each putting a bottle of water on their nightstands before drifting off to sleep.

34

Todd woke up early the next morning, sunlight streamed through the window of his second floor room. He was in a king bed with Emily on sheets he hoped were fresh. The air was cold in his room. He rolled over and quickly jumped into his clothes. He snuck outside and into the adult's RV parked in front of the hotel. John sat at the small dining table with a paper cup of coffee. He did not look like he had slept.

"Well older brother," Todd asked as he poured himself a cup of coffee. "What's the plan?"

He doctored his coffee with sugar and milk, and sat down across from John.

"I'd like to leave today, but I respect the priest's request. I can wait. Besides, aren't you and Emily headed down to Ellis Island today?" John had a smartass smile on his face, mocking his brother for having to follow his wife's wishes. Despite the teasing, he envied Todd for still having a wife.

"Today I am going to play it casual. I'll make breakfast, if the New York people come, they come. They know we're here. Emily, Melanie, the kids, and I will leave for our trip at around ten. Anyone who would like to come can join us. We'll do a big stir-fry or something easy for dinner tonight. It will be an open ended invitation." He sipped his coffee. "No pressure."

"We can leave on Sunday and still be in Hanover by 4 or 5pm. It's getting warmer. I bet the roads are clearing." John looked exhausted. "I'm worried about what I will find up there. I'm losing my mind, knowing Greg is there alone. I worry more that he isn't there at all." He lowered his head. "I don't sleep much anymore. I'm having trouble keeping it together."

Todd looked at his brother, unraveling with each passing day. "Wake your sons, take the Suburban, and leave. There's no reason for you to wait on Bernie. Put chains on the tires, drive slowly. Go, find my nephew. We'll meet you up there."

A woman spoke from behind John. "You should go, John. We can handle everything from here." Solange stood in the doorway of the bedroom. "We will see you in a few days." She smiled at him. She did not want him to leave, but she knew it was the best thing for him.

"I'm leaving you a little light on the muscle if both Matt and I go. Even Craig has been a big help."

"I made it through a few months in Raleigh without you. Emily is strong, Solange is strong. Peter and Melanie can help. Take some food and get out of here."

"I'll get Matt and Craig." John stood up and put on his coat. "Should we come back here if we find him? Should we meet in Boston?"

"We'll come to Hanover on Sunday. I know we aren't going to stay there, but maybe it will be a nice break for us. We've been on the road for almost two weeks. Let's get up there, take over a few houses, figure out what our future holds. We can always swing through Boston after Hanover." Todd stood and gave John a hug. "Go find Greg. I'll see you in two days."

Solange stepped forward and gave John a hug as well. "Be safe." She said, kissing his cheek gently.

He nodded to both of them, a tear fell down his cheek before he opened the trailer, and went to get Matt and Craig.

"So, it is up to us." Solange said to Todd.

"Yep." He replied, sitting down to finish his coffee. Todd jumped back up. "You know what? Let's give him the animals or the U-Haul. Well, I guess the animals." Todd ran out of the trailer as Matt, John, and Craig walked towards the SUV.

"Take the animals." Todd said to them. He held out his hand to shake Matt's. "I'll see you in a day, Matt, you too Craig. Help me hitch the chickens and goats to the SUV."

"Are you doing this so the New Yorkers can't take them?" John asked. "Or to lighten your load?"

"A little of both. It will be one less thing I need to take. Solange is grabbing this morning's eggs. If they don't want to come, we might give the New Yorkers the second RV. The rest of us can squeeze into one and tow the U-Haul. I like the option of going in one vehicle." Todd was babbling, trying to ease his brother's conscience as well as talking himself into the intelligence of his plan.

Solange emerged from the animal trailer with a basket full of eggs. She came over and hugged Matt and Craig. "Take care of your father, and say hello to your brother from me."

"Will do." Matt said. "You're going to like him. He's the serious one."

Solange laughed.

John backed the Suburban to the animal trailer hitch, locked the ball down, and pulled away towards the George Washington Bridge.

Solange turned to Todd. "Your wife is going to be upset he left without saying goodbye."

"She'll get over it." He turned to go back into the trailer, then paused and looked over his shoulder "At least I hope she will." There was concern in his voice. "I need more coffee. You?"

"Always." She said.

They sat at the dining table, drinking coffee, and thinking about their day.

"What made you trust us that first day in Richmond? Why did you get out of the car? It was just me and Emily standing next to the RV. What was it that worked?" Todd was trying to figure out what he could do to make the last few people in the NYC group trust him.

"I did not trust you. I had three guns in the car, a pistol on my lap and two shotguns on the other seat. That is why I did not let you come with me in the car. Once I met you, spoke to you, I knew I was safe. You give off, I believe you call it, a good vibe."

"You had guns?"

Solange nodded. "Would you like to know my other secret?" Solange sipped her coffee. "That was my car. I drove the Mercedes at school. I came from a very wealthy family. When I took the Matisse and said it would remind me of my father, it is because he had a Matisse hanging in his home study."

Todd's mouth dropped open a bit. "No way." he muttered as an impulse.

"I was a princess, not literally, but I was a spoiled princess from Ecuador. My father's favorite. I lost a lot during El Encantado. My family, my country, my money is all gone." She sipped and looked at Todd. "I have found a new family, and I will do whatever it takes to make sure I do not lose it. We are leaving tomorrow after services. If Sal is not here, that is Sal's problem." She put her paper cup down on the table. "You are a good person, Todd." She reached across the table and put her hand on top of his. "You have a good heart. I will make sure we use our head tomorrow. These people know the plan, they know where we are going, it is up to them to decide what to do. I will make the hard choices if we need to make them. I know you could, but it is not your nature to make the evil decision."

Todd nodded because she was right. Todd was too 'nice' to make a hard decision like leaving people. He appreciated her honesty and her strength. "Today we will check out the sites, and tomorrow we leave at noon." He replied.

"Bien." She said, patting his hand before standing up.

"I am going to wake the children. They have been watching too much television. It is time they learned how real futbol is played."

Solange opened the door to the other RV, and found the kids watching a DVD. "No more television today. Put on your clothes, we are playing soccer before breakfast. We are playing soccer after breakfast, and then you are going to see the Statue of Liberty."

"Ahhh, no, come on." They whined in unison. "Just one more show. Please?"

"No, come outside. You have been watching too much television. Today is an outside day. I will give one dollar to anyone who can score a goal against me."

Brian was on to her. "We don't use money anymore."

"Don't be so sure." Solange lied.

The kids reluctantly put on their outside clothes. Casey and Jackie wanted to be on Solange's team, girls against guys.

"That's not fair without Craig and Matt." Jacob complained.

"We can take them. Don't worry about it." Jay was always the optimist and perhaps a bit overconfident in his skills.

Todd watched from the RV window as Solange brought the kids into the street. There was soon screaming, yelling, and laughter. A warm wind brought spring weather, and while it was chilly, it was not as bitter as the previous day. The sun shone down 59th street from the east.

Todd made French toast from the leftover dinner bread. He liked the combination of carbs, protein, and sugar to give the kids energy for the long day of sightseeing. It also allowed him to conserve most of the eggs for the new people.

The RV door opened, and Emily walked in. "Where is the Suburban? Did John drive down to pick up the other people?"

"He left."

"I know, where did he go, and why did he take the animals?" She poured herself a cup of coffee, walking up behind him and giving him a one armed hug with a kiss on his cheek. "It was nice to sleep in a king bed with you again. Last night was almost like a vacation."

He turned around and hugged her face to face. "I know." He kissed her on the mouth, and they enjoyed a husband and wife moment. "John, Matt, and Craig left for New Hampshire. They took the animals, and we're meeting them up there tomorrow." He told her quickly, like he was ripping off a bandage.

There was a stunned silence. "That seems to me it should have been a group decision, not a Todd and John decision." Emily stepped back from their hug with an angry look on her face.

"He took his truck, I asked him to take the animals. I don't want to get into an argument. Would you ask someone's permission if Jay or Brian were alone in Hanover, and you wanted to go after them? John leaving to rescue his child is not a 'group' decision. He woke up, and decided being five hours away from Greg for another day because some woman wants to have a church service was not in the cards. He offered to stay, I told him to go. He deserves to be selfish about this one."

Emily's shoulders sagged, and she dropped her head, closing her eyes. She let out a sigh. "You're right, I'm just upset he's gone, that we're separated again." She looked up at him. "I heard Craig's door open and shut this morning, but I didn't' want to get out of bed. I wish they had waited to say goodbye, that's all." She sipped more of her coffee and sat at the table. "It's only one day, we'll be fine."

Todd's cinnamon-sugar French toast made the RV smell delicious, despite Hubba's attempts to make it otherwise.

"Let's stick to our schedule. We go down to the Statue of Liberty. We try to get over to Ellis Island, we have a fun day in New York City. Solange wants to run the kids around. She says they have been watching too much TV."

"Well, she's right there, but we've been kind of busy." Emily was preoccupied thinking about John. "I'll go out and cheer them on. How long before breakfast?" She clipped a leash on Hubba, not because he would run away, but because it was the only way she could get the dog to come outside in the morning.

"Ten minutes? I want to get a crust on the French toast. I have two pans baking." He walked over to pull on his coat. "I can watch the kids too."

The couple exited the RV with their dog, walking to the soccer game. Brian ran over, red faced and panting. "Solange owes me three dollars." He ran off again.

Melanie was awake and watching the game. She ambled towards Todd and Emily. "I was lazily watching from my bed. Did John take the animals and go somewhere?"

"He went to New Hampshire to find his son. He couldn't wait another day. Todd asked him to take the animals to help us out." Emily watched the game while she told Melanie, hoping her nonchalant attitude would play down the magnitude of the comments.

"I'm surprised he lasted the full week in D.C., let alone another day here. I would have left the group a week ago. Good for him." She walked towards the RV. "I need some of that coffee."

35

Craig slept in the third row bed. Matt and John drove quickly towards Hartford, Connecticut. Once they got onto a highway, they drove as fast as the conditions allowed. The snow was dangerous, but the chains on the tires gave enough traction for a safe 60 miles per hour.

"We have a decision to make when we get to Hartford." John told Matt. "We can drive towards Boston and check to see if Greg stayed at Hightower, maybe consider looking for survivors, or we can skip Boston and drive directly to Hanover, doubling back to Boston from Hanover if we don't find Greg up there."

"I'm still not sure what's going on. Why did we suddenly jump in the car and drive to Hanover? I thought we were waiting until Sunday." Matt envied his youngest brother, sleeping in the back seat bed.

John could not take his eyes off the road, he was driving too quickly over the ice and snow, but he wanted to look at his son and let Matt see the sadness in his father's face. "I couldn't wait, I'm sorry. I miss my son. I can't take not knowing if he is alive. If the snow was that low in New York, there is a good chance it's melted up in New Hampshire. Maybe we can get through. It's a sunny day, the snow will be slushy, easier to manage."

"You just woke up and couldn't take it? I mean, I'm excited we are finally going to find Greg, but I don't get it." Matt looked out the window at the scenery racing by.

"I'm sorry if I'm scaring you or causing confusion. I was at a breaking point. I can't sleep, I'm not eating as much as I should. I had to go." He paused. "What do you think? Hanover or Boston?"

"Hanover" Matt said with confidence.

"Agreed." John replied. "He's in Hanover, you and I know it."

Matt looked at his watch, double checking the time he read on the dashboard clock. "It's only 7:30?"

"Yeah."

"Well, I didn't get breakfast, Craig didn't eat, we just hooked up and left. I'm not even sure I have clothes."

"Don't be such a wimp. We'll find you some clothes up there. Grab some of the cereal from the box in the seat behind you. All Todd's home cooking as made you soft. Time to toughen up, enjoy the adventure." John teased his son.

"I'll be okay." Matt whined. "It's just, I could have gotten some breakfast." He reached behind his seat and pulled out a box of corn cereal. He looked for something else, anything else, and found only a bottle of water.

"Are we out of the breakfast shakes? I get dry corn cereal and water? Come on!"

"Soft, this new life has made you soft. Unbelievable."

"I can tell this is going to be a fun ride. I hope there is food up there. Food that hasn't gone rotten in the last 6 months, or burst from being frozen."

"Soft." John repeated. "Marshmallow soft."

They reached Hartford in 90 minutes. After Philadelphia and New York, John believed there was little chance survivors stayed in the northern cities. Finding the New York survivors was a fluke, a mistake made by people who did not leave when they should have. As John drove further north, to colder cities, he assumed they were empty. What could keep a person in Hartford? The ocean was 200 miles east. "I'd have gone to Providence, if I stayed up north at all." John thought to himself. "Being near water is a must."

"Are we stopping?" Matt asked. It was the first thing he said since their breakfast debate. "You think anyone is here?"

"If we come through, honk our horns, maybe survivors will be ready for the caravan tomorrow. No, I don't want to stop. We have a tough drive left, lots of turns and probably snow covered roads. I don't want to wait and talk to any survivors. It will take too long."

"So unless someone flags us down or runs in front of the car..." Matt said jokingly.

"I'll slow down and yell where we're going, how's that?" John said back.

"What's going on?" Craig sat up, waking from the conversation. "Did you carry me from bed and put me in the Suburban? Where are we?" He was confused.

Matt turned around in his seat. "We left to find Greg. The rest will follow us tomorrow. We decided, as a family, that we waited long enough. It is time to get our brother. What do you think?"

"Awesome!" Craig yelled. "But what's for breakfast?" He leaned over to look in the trunk area of the SUV. "Oh, never mind, I found a box of breakfast shakes."

Matt glared at his father.

"Yeah, that's where I put the breakfast stuff. Sorry about that. I knew we had it somewhere."

Craig flipped Matt a milkshake.

John turned on the CD player. He respected Craig's sleep time, but Craig was awake now so the music came on.

Two hours after Hartford the road became tricky with lingering snow. John was forced to reduce his speed. They hit patches of ice on overpasses and perpetually shady spots on the highway. Most of the time there was a single strip of clear road. John kept his right tires in the strip for traction. The snow, while a hazard, was soft and slushy. John was confident he could make it to New Hampshire, but it was going to take time. Towing a heavy trailer full of animals did not help his situation.

"We'll make it, I just didn't realize it would take us all day." He explained as they passed a sign that read, 'Lebanon – 21 miles.'

Matt slapped Craig on the back. "That's where we're going. 21 miles!" He rolled down his window and yelled. "We're coming for you Greg!"

John slowed the Suburban to 35 miles per hour. "Probably an hour unless we hit a clear patch, or a bad patch." John checked the fuel gauge. They still had over half a tank. He looked at Matt. "Give him another yell. Tell him it will be an hour."

Matt rolled his window down again and repeated his father's statement. Eight months of heart ache were coming to an end. John felt like he could run the last miles if needed.

50 minutes later they were looking down at West Lebanon's shopping centers as they drove slowly over the frozen bridges. The SUV was silent, hoping Greg was alright, praying they would find him in Hanover at John's childhood home. The drive was slow, but thankfully uneventful. John kept his speed low, and the truck with trailer under control.

They approached the exit ramp to Norwich, Vermont and stopped at the top. John inspected the exit's condition. "Just snow, it doesn't look like the ice is too bad. I'm going to take it slowly." He let up on the break and inched the truck down the ramp. The chained tires gripped the snow, and they had no issues. John continued his slow pace down the small hill towards the bridge spanning the Connecticut River and separating Norwich from Hanover. Matt pointed across the bridge.

"Is that a jeep? It doesn't have any snow on it. It's parked in the road. Wait, does Greg know how to drive?"

"Maybe he learned." Craig replied.

"It's possible, or there could be another person here. Maybe Greg found someone. Look at the worn tire marks from the bridge into Norwich. Whatever the situation, it tells me that Wheelock Street is too icy to go up. We'll have to walk from here. It's not far, don't worry." John pulled the Suburban next to the Jeep and turned it off. "I hope you brought your snow boots."

"I'm not sure I brought a jacket." Craig said, looking around the backseat.

"It's 48. I think you'll live in your sweatshirt." Matt rubbed his brother's hair. "Have the last few weeks made you soft or something? Unbelievable." Matt's wry smile was pointed at John.

"We'll come back for the animals, figure out a different way into Hanover. It might require us to drive back through Lebanon where the hills aren't as bad." John pulled a backpack out of the Suburban and stuffed water and power bars into it. He did not know if he would find Greg thirsty and hungry like the people in New York or healthy like the people in D.C. He prepared for both.

The Dixon men walked up the hill, following the footprints left by Hank and Greg that morning. "There is at least one person here, and they've used this hill a bunch of times. I'm not a tracker, but I swear there are two sets of footprints. There is fishing tackle in the jeep. There must be a good fishing spot for the person to drive to. Maybe in Norwich?" Matt enjoyed a good mystery. He knew his brother did not know how to drive, and self teaching was an interesting theory, but not probable.

"Dad's fishing club." John said to himself. "There's a fully stocked trout pond, you both remember, right? How would he remember that? How could he even find it?"

"Greg must have remembered." Craig was getting excited.

At the top of the hill they looked into the town and at the buildings surrounding the Dartmouth Green. The leaves from autumn poked through melted patches of snow. It was just after 3pm.

"It's so peaceful, just like everywhere else we've been." Matt spun around. "It's nice after New York. I thought that place was creepy. All those buildings and windows? I felt like people were watching us."

"Me too! That's so funny. I stayed in the trailer because I didn't like looking up at the buildings." Craig laughed, happy someone else was scared of New York.

"Come on." John turned left on Main Street. "We can come back and check out the town later. Let's get to the house and see if anyone is there." They walked briskly, a purpose to their steps.

The snow was a few inches deep on the street. The men were not prepared. Even though they stayed in a well worn path from town, their sneakers were soaked. They walked about 200 yards down Main when they noticed a port-a-john one road over from them. It was sitting on its side next to a storm drain. There was a patch of road shoveled out around the blue plastic rectangle. A dumpster top sat next to the bathroom.

"That was recent. Someone shoveled the snow." John looked around. "How did he haul a heavy bathroom over to a storm drain? Why did he haul a heavy bathroom over to a storm drain?" They walked between two administration buildings and inspected the plastic box. There was a snowmobile track behind the bathroom. "Let's follow this. It must lead somewhere." They stepped into the path made by the sled used to haul the bathroom. "Two snowmobile treads. I know your brother doesn't know how to ride a snowmobile, and even if he could, I doubt he could ride two at the same time. There is someone up here with him, or two people with him."

They walked down the road, following the trail. The tracks passed a large white building used to raise money for Dartmouth College and turned left on Main Street.

Matt continued to inspect the area. "The town looks intact. No looting or fires or crazy damage. It looks peaceful and empty."

John turned to his sons. "This is leading us to my old house. He must have found a port-o-john to use when the pipes froze or the water gave out. Smart thinking. We're going to take a left at the top of Choate road, walk right down my old street." John's heart beat quickly. No one else would move into that house except Greg. He was alive. "I used to drive down this road every day in an old Ford stat on wagon. The high school is on the other side of town."

"We know, Dad, we've heard the stories." Craig rolled his eyes, and turned to Matt. "Do you know how bad it is going to be when Uncle Paul shows up? The two of them together in Hanover? I'll be going to bed at 7 just to get away from it all."

Matt laughed at his younger brother. "I'll probably join you. It's going to get bad."

"That's enough from you two. I do not tell that many stories." Did he? John started thinking, maybe he did tell too many stories when he and Paul got together.

"My feet are soaked." Matt looked down at his wet shoes. "I really should have packed some boots." Matt bumped into his father. "Whoa." He said. "Sorry."

John was stopped at a white house near the corner of Main street and Choate road. Smoke billowed out of the chimney. The front path was cleared using a snow blower. There was a clean trail from the front door heading towards the golf course. The sign in front of the house read "Webster Cottage."

Matt looked at his father, then back at the house. "Mom made us take a tour here. Daniel Webster lived in there, or slept there, or something, I couldn't figure out what he did, but it's some historic cottage built in the late 1700's. It has a woodstove and fireplaces in every room. It's a smart place to live." He looked at Craig. "Do you remember that tour? It was like 85 in Hanover, and Mom made us go in that tiny house that did not have air conditioning, and walk around while some lady talked about colonial times. Brutal."

"Well." John announced. "Let's see who's home." They walked up to the front door.

John knocked.

There was a pause before the door opened. "Hey, John! Glad you could make it." Hank looked at his brother and nephews. "Did you guys walk here?" Hank wondered why he did not hear a vehicle. He looked around for a car or truck on the road.

"Hank? You're here? How did you get here? When?" John was confused.

"Greg?" Hank yelled into the house. "It's for you." He stepped down and gave John a hug, but he could tell his brother was not interested in him. "Go ahead, John, he's in there." Hank looked at Matt and Craig. "You guys are huge." He stepped out of the cottage. "You're brother is inside. He's fine. We're all fine. We just finished cleaning up after lunch."

John walked into the house, scanning the surroundings. The bedroom to the right had four beds, neatly made, and the living room to the left was clean and uncluttered. John felt like he was dreaming. Not only had he found Greg, but it looked like his son was living a perfectly normal life.

Hank held his nephews at the door. "Give your dad a minute, even 30 seconds alone with your brother. Okay?" Matt and Craig nodded, they understood.

Hank had to know. "Where is your car? How did you get here? We were just talking about how the road is clear, and someone might be coming soon. Unbelievable, literally, and hour ago at lunch we told Paul and Rebecca the roads were clear."

"Uncle Paul is here too?" Matt asked.

"Who's Rebecca?" Craig asked at the same time

John was in the living room when Greg came around the corner from the kitchen with a wide grin.

"You made it." He said to his father.

John lost his composure immediately, dropping to his knees and weeping, his face in his hands. He shoulders heaved under his coat. Greg got on the floor with his father, hugging him. "We made it Dad. We made it. It's okay. We're all okay."

"You're all I've thought about for 8 months. I had to keep your brothers safe, or I would have walked here to find you."

"I know, Dad, I know. I'm okay."

"Please forgive me for leaving you, please, please understand." John hugged his son tightly. "I love you so much, I'm so sorry, I'm so sorry. Forgive me, I'm sorry."

Paul and Rebecca watched from the dining room. Rebecca was crying. Paul put his arm around her, pulling her close.

Hank let Matt and Craig into the house after a minute. He could not hold them back any longer. John and Greg rocked on the floor, kneeling together in a hug. Matt tapped his brother on the shoulder. "Hey, how are things?" Greg stood up and grabbed him. He opened one side of the hug and pulled Craig in.

"We all made it, can you believe it?" Greg was overwhelmed his brothers were alive. "We all made it." Greg broke his hug. "You guys have to meet Rebecca. She's my best friend. I met her on my way up here, back in October. She saved my life, I wouldn't have made it through another week without her." He looked into the dining room. "Rebecca, come meet my family." He waved her over.

Rebecca stepped into the room. Paul followed her and went to his twin brother.

"How are you?" Paul asked as they embraced. "Have you heard from Todd?"

Hank stepped behind the two men and patted John on the shoulder.

John composed himself. "There is a lot to talk about." He sniffed loudly, wiping his hand on his sleeve. Rebecca extended a tissue, which John took while giving the girl a bewildered look. "Todd and his family are in New York City, and planning to come up tomorrow afternoon. He has seventeen other people with him, survivors we've met on the way up here."

"Huh?" Hank said. "Did you say seventeen people plus Todd and his two kids?"

"Don't forget Aunt Emily." Matt said, not realizing Hank and Paul did not know she was alive.

"Wait, Emily is alive? That's impossible." Paul's mouth was half open in amazement.

"Like I said," John gave Paul a pat on the back. "We have a lot to talk about."

"So you saved my son's life." John looked at Rebecca. "Thank you." He said. "Thank you with all of my heart, but how did you two kids make it up here and survive through winter?"

"Pretty easily actually." Rebecca told him, "but we don't want to do it again." She smiled at Greg. "Not if we don't have to."

"Okay, first things first," John began. "We have a Suburban parked at the bottom of Wheelock next to your jeep."

"I can drive now!" Greg blurted out. "Uncle Hank taught me."

John paused, giving his son a smile. "Okay, that's great, but what I need to say is, we have chickens and a few goats in a trailer that we need to bring up. Do you have a different route to get into Hanover?"

"Goats?" Hank asked. "Where are we going to keep goats?" He turned to Paul. "Did he seriously say he brought goats? This is where the world is? People show up with goats and expect to stay in your house? I had a problem when people wanted to bring dogs to my house, now I have to accommodate goats?"

"Four goats, 15 chickens." John replied dryly.

Rebecca thought about it before speaking. "We have a coop set up, but I don't know if it can handle 15 more chickens. Maybe if we put a ramp or something out that back door. It's not cold anymore. We can house the goats in the wood room off the porch, you know, clear some space for them there? Put some of our shredded paper in there?"

"You already have chickens?" John asked.

"Yes, I brought them from Concord. I had some neighbors who were urban farmers. I took their chickens." Rebecca explained.

Matt looked at Greg, and gave him and elbow, winking about Rebecca. Greg blushed. "Dad?" Matt said. "Why don't we walk the goats up here, maybe carry the chickens? It might take a few trips, but faster and easier than handling the roads and hills."

"Sounds like a plan, we can talk while we walk." Paul moved to the coat rack in the corner of the living room near the door. He pulled on his coat and went for his boots. He looked down at the new arrivals' feet. "Do you three want to borrow some boots and dry socks?"

"That would be great." John said, taking his backpack off and setting it on the floor. "The goats can wait. Do you have any food?"

Paul hung his coat back up. "Yeah, I think we can feed you. I'll put the last two trout in the oven and put some water on the stove." Paul left the living room.

"Dad's trout club, I knew that's why the jeep was down there full of tackle. Have you been using baited hooks at Dad's club? Are you insane?"

Hank smiled. "If we are here when the ice melts, I'll use a bobber and worms. The fish are giant at that place."

Matt walked into the dining room and looked at the computers, data, and maps adorning the walls. "What's this?"

"Rebecca is running some models to show the optimal place to live, to settle. We've been inputting data about climates, crop yields, that sort of stuff. We have some things to talk about too."

They gathered in the kitchen, letting the new Dixons eat at the table, while the others talked about their adventures. There were endless stories, and the conversation continued until dusk and the walk to the bottom of the hill to get livestock.

Everyone laughed and cried countless times that afternoon.

Practical questions arose. Where were the three new people going to sleep? "It's 6pm." John said to the group. "Let's walk down to the old house and see if Hank, Paul, and I can get three beds into the study or upstairs master. Both have a fireplace. We can make it one night there, right? We have more than 20 people showing up tomorrow. We have to figure out where everyone is going to sleep."

"There are two twin mattresses in the study, and it can fit at least one more. Greg and I spent our first few nights in Hanover there." Rebecca told them. "It's a cozy little room. We almost lived there."

"Let's grab an armload of firewood and walk down." Hank announced. "We might as well open up the old house. It's where someone will be sleeping tomorrow night."

By 7pm the goats were on the porch, the chickens were making friends in the coop, a fire was pre-made in the old house with three mattresses on the ground, and Hank was cooking cassoulet in the kitchen. The rest of the group sat on the couches and chairs in the living room.

"What if I told you we have a pilot. Would that put Hawaii back in the mix? If we can find a plane that works and has fue , do we think we can make it to Hawaii?" John asked Rebecca, updating her on the skill set of the arriving tribe.

"I don't know enough about planes to say, but absolutely. If we can get to Hawaii, it is our best option, hands down."

John nodded. "I'll talk to Peter when he gets here. He's a retired military and commercial pilot. He'll be able to answer those questions."

"What happens if we fly to Kauai or Honolulu and the airport runway is jammed with planes? Do we crash land in the ocean? Do we try to land on the beach? It's not just taking off and having fuel, it's what the heck do we do to get back on the ground." Paul ran the scenarios through his head a few times.

"Who else do you have in the group other than a pilot?" Rebecca was curious about the talent pool John described.

"A surgeon and a veterinarian, but the neurosurgeon has dreams of being a farmer. She was a botany minor in college." John, who vehemently opposed meeting new people, now c aimed credit for the success.

"We'll probably need a farmer more often than we'll need a neurosurgeon." Paul noted.

"Solange is a great soccer player, but she calls if futbol." Craig added.

"I didn't get to meet the New York group for more than a few minutes. They appeared to be like us, muscle and labor rather than trained skills. There was a priest, an i-banker, a few teens, and some younger kids."

"If your pilot, our pilot I should say, does think we can make it to Hawaii, we can drive down to Logan to look into planes. I doubt Lebanon Regional has a plane that can make it to Honolulu." Paul sat back after a long afternoon of excitement.

They ate in the living room. The kitchen table was not large enough, and the dining room table was occupied with Rebecca's work.

Hank's cassoulet was delicious.

"We are about to share a very small room together, and you serve me beans and sausage for dinner? You're a brave, brave man Hank." John joked.

"Is this a fancy frank and beans?" Craig enjoyed the meal but was confused about the name.

"Something like that." Hank assured him.

The men made their way to their old home soon after dinner. "I'm beat." John confessed. "It was a long and tough drive up here. I'm about to fall asleep on my feet." They said their good nights. John gave Greg an extended hug.

"I expect breakfast on the table when I arrive." Paul said as he walked out the door. "I'm sleeping on a floor tonight. I deserve a hot meal."

"We'll give you a call when it's ready. Sit by the phone." Rebecca replied wryly and dripping with sarcasm.

As they walked down the road John asked his brothers. "So, Rebecca, what's her story?"

"I'm pretty sure she's your new daughter in law." Paul smiled. "It was basically blue lagoon in Hanover when Hank and I arrived."

Hank agreed, and gave an endorsement. "Greg says she saved his life. She's about to save all of our lives with her intelligence and abilities. She's a great kid, just fantastic. You're lucky Greg bumped into her. We're all lucky."

"Being thirteen and having the burden of her intelligence, she had it pretty rough before the rapture. I'm not saying this was a good thing that happened to her, losing her parents was not a good thing, but her new start on life, meeting Greg, finding someone her age that likes her, being able to fit in for the first time in a long time. She's incredible." Paul opened the door to the house. It was pitch black except for their flashlights and lantern beams.

"Her intelligence?" John asked. "Just how smart is she?"

"Pretty damn smart." Paul assured him.

The house was freezing. Hank lit the fire, and their tiny bedroom warmed.

"You said there is a priest in New York? A person of faith who still has faith?" Hank asked.

"The reason I left? She wants one last service in her chapel. She is a strong believer. I'm as surprised as you are, but I respect it."

Paul stared at the ceiling. "21 people, that's a lot of mouths, children or not. We have to get near the ocean quickly. Our current supplies and anything we can scavenge will last a few years, but we can't build a future roaming from town to town for rotten canned food. We have to get somewhere and build a colony. We have to learn to plant, hunt, and fish." He sat up. "Son of a bitch, this all just got very real to me."

"It just got real to you?" John asked him. "Seriously? Everyone in the world died seven months ago, and you're just feeling it getting real?"

"Well, yeah. You know, it's been a whirlwind. I got food and stayed in my house, I biked to Hank's, we rode to Rutland, took snowmobiles to here, lived with Greg. It's been a fluid timeline. I've never had to worry about food. I am very worried about food now. 21 people can burn through food quickly. We won't even see it coming, and poof, we'll be out of food. Damn, we have to get somewhere other than the frozen tundra of Hanover, and we have to get there this summer." Paul rolled onto his side. "It's great to see you, John. It really is. I'm going to get some sleep. We have a long day and a long week ahead of us."

"It's great to be up here, finally." John turned to Hank. "So, Hank, how much weight have you lost? Were you this thin before?"

Hank and Paul laughed, "Wait until you hear the story of caveman Hank, living in a hole for two months. It's a classic." Paul started, "when I rolled up on him in Dayton? Oh man, it was like finding Tom Hanks in Castaway. He was filthy. He smelled. Wow."

"I can laugh a little now, but this is what really happened." They told stories well into the night, sometimes laughing, sometimes quiet as they absorbed the impact of the last eight months. They cried when the talked about their wives' last days, and the decisions each of them had to make. They were only asleep for a few hours when the sun came up over Balch Hill the next morning.

Hank was the last to wake, his eyes opening to the noise of Paul and John getting dressed. "So let me get this straight. It was Todd's idea to meet up here, and to live in our old house, and he's the only one who's not here. We're stuck sleeping on mattresses in a tiny room, and he's at the Plaza?"

36

The kids were inside eating breakfast when the church van rolled to a stop next to the RV. Todd, Emily, Melanie, Peter, and Solange stood at the front door of the RV, drinking coffee and eating French toast out of a pan. The van door slid open, and the three youngest jumped out with Avery and Meredith.

"Good morning!" Emily said enthusiastically, over emphasizing her excitement to see the group of kids. "How is everyone this morning?"

Kelly slipped out of the passenger side with a smile. "We are well. I hope we're not intruding."

"Not at all," Emily continued. "Kids, take the rest of this French toast, and you can join our crew in the RV. It's warmer inside." She handed Meredith the tray filled with Todd's cinnamon goodness.

Peter stepped forward to assist Bernie and Jamie out of the van. He was already talking to Jamie, taking advantage of meeting someone his own age.

"Is it a dumb question to ask if you already ate?" Todd asked Kelly.

"We have not." She replied, hanging her head, knowing she was asking for a handout.

"Alright, but no freeloading this morning. Kelly, you come with me to help make the eggs, and the rest of you are on cleanup duty after breakfast. We share the food, and we share the work. Sound good?"

"I'd love to help make breakfast." Ahmed said, stepping out of the van after the two women. "I put myself through college as a short order cook. I can fry a mean egg."

Todd turned to Kelly, "I guess that means you're on cleanup. Grab some coffee, and we'll be out in a few. Em'? Can you take orders? We have twenty eggs left. I can do two any style or we can scramble them all. Let me know if there is a consensus. Ahmed and I will go to work on the hash browns and sausage." Todd motioned his new co-chef into the RV. "So, you were a cook, that's great. Funny, that's a better skill than anything else you learned in college, huh?"

Emily assumed hostess duties, pouring cups of coffee and offering people their selection of eggs. To make sure everyone ate expediently, the order for 'all scrambled' was sent into the kitchen. Avery came outside to talk to the adults.

"Did Matt leave? I don't see him here." Avery turned to Melanie. "I'm sorry, I don't think I met you last night. My name is Avery."

Melanie shook her hand, "Matt left this morning with his father and younger brother. They went ahead to New Hampshire to find Matt's other brother. My name is Melanie. I joined the group in D.C. via Baltimore. Very nice to meet you, Avery." She went on to explain that Casey, Jaclyn, and Jacob were under her care. Melanie turned to meet Bernie and Jamie.

"Is there someone still in the van?" Melanie asked. She saw a solitary figure in the back row, knit cap on, leaning against the window.

"That is Antonio. He wanted to come, but has decided to stay in the van. I think he is afraid of being alone if Sal returns to the seminary, but he doesn't want to mingle either." Jamie liked Antonio. She defended him often. "He's a good kid. He has a good heart, he's just a little mixed up. I don't know how he grew up, but it wasn't good. I know his family was nice, but his neighborhood was not. He'll work it out." Jamie smiled politely. "So you're from Baltimore? I used to date an old Baltimore Orioles pitcher back in the day. He grew up outside of New York, and we went to high school together. He and I stayed a couple for a little while, but the distance was too much. Back then you had to take the train to and from New York, and it was just too much."

Emily walked to the church van and opened the sliding door. "Antonio, would you like some coffee?" He did not reply. "We'll have breakfast ready in a minute. Are you going to join us?" She heard music coming from the headphones dangling from his ears. "Well, if you would like some food, it's here, fresh eggs, hash browns and sausage. It's not real sausage. It's these little Vienna sausages from a can, but they still taste great with eggs. Anyway, it's out here." She slid the door shut and left him alone.

Emily made her way through the people, talking and getting acquainted. The kids were eating and socializing at the table in the RV. Todd placed warm sausages in front of them. Casey was in a deep discussion with the three young newcomers about her role in the group. Meredith was joking with Jackie and Jacob. Everyone appeared to be getting along as they drank Tang and told stories.

Ahmed and Todd discussed New York restaurants. Emily put her hand on Todd's back. "About how long?"

"We're good. Ahmed knows how to sling the hash. Do we want to set up on plates and have you walk it out to people?" He turned to his cooking partner. "Ahmed, please, grab a plate and eat. I had some toast before you came."

The thin man accepted happily. "I was hoping you'd say that. Standing over fresh eggs? I'm starved. I'll take a plate out with me when I go." He spooned eggs, potatoes, and sausage on two plates, and headed towards the door. "Jamie? Come and grab this plate and eat the eggs fast, before they get cold."

Todd served the food, and Emily walked two at a time out to the adults. There was a mountain of eggs, and once the adults were eating, Todd offered seconds to the children. The new kids raised their hands.

"Don't be shy, come over, we have plenty." He handed them new plates with the fresh food. Todd made a small plate for himself and went to talk to the group. He saw the adults standing in a circle, eating and talking. Antonio sat in the open van door with his feet on the ground. He ate his food in silence. Todd walked over and asked if he could sit down.

"Whatever." The young man replied, not moving to give him space. Antonio muttered something under his breath in Spanish.

Solange walked over to the van.

She stared at Antonio before turning to Todd. "Bernie is having second thoughts about leaving tomorrow. She would like to stay until Easter Sunday next week."

"That crazy bitch won't learn." Antonio muttered.

"Excuse me?" Todd asked, annoyed at his tone and word choice.

"You know why we got stuck in New York City? You know why we almost starved? She won't leave her seminary. I said to all of them, we have to leave, we have to go to Queens or Connecticut or someplace with houses, find another church, we can't stay. Crazy reverend Bernie wouldn't leave, came up with every excuse to stay in her chapel. 'We have heat here' or 'we know the area' or 'someone will be coming for us in New York.' Always the same shit." Antonio did not lower his voice, he spoke loud enough for everyone to hear. The adults were quiet, looking at Antonio or the ground uncomfortably. Bernie hung her head.

"I think she's waiting for Jesus to come riding through on a horse and take her to Candyland or something." Antonio laughed.

"That's enough." Todd said quietly to him. "We get the point."

The young man stood and faced Todd. "Did you just tell me to shut up?"

"No, I asked you to stop talking about Bernie. We understand, you made your point, saying any more would be mean, and I know you aren't trying to be mean." Todd stood his ground, though he was not comfortable with the confrontation.

Antonio muttered something in Spanish under his breath, smiling to himself as he did it. Solange stepped between the two men. She slapped Antonio hard across the face.

"What the hell, bitch?" The boy screamed, rubbing his cheek.

Solange slapped him again. "If you are a man, say what you said to his face in English." Antonio looked at Todd and then to the other adults. He lowered his face in shame.

"The breakfast that we made for you is still on your breath, it is still hot in your belly, and you disrespect him and us like that?" She was inches from his face.

"If you are a man, do what you said. Walk. Survive on your own. We do not need another mouth to feed, and we will not feed a disrespectful child like you. If I ever hear you speaking Spanish again, you will wish all I do is slap you across the face." Solange reached out and put her hand under his chin. She lifted his face to meet hers.

"Whatever you did before el encantado, it's over. You are not a punk anymore. Be a man. Step up and help us. Do not disrespect people by speaking insults in another language. Be a role model to the kids we know you love. Grow up." She squinted her eyes to look deep into Antonio's face, trying to read his thoughts. A tear rolled down his cheek.

"Do not be a boy. If you do not want to come with us, walk away. That is a choice, but acting like you are is not an option."

Antonio sniffed as more tears rolled down his face. He nodded. He pulled the blue banana off his head.

"I am sorry, sir. It will not happen again." He said to Todd. "Thank you for the food."

Solange put her arm around him and whispered Spanish in his ear. Antonio chuckled.

Todd was interested in what she said, but Solange let him know it was her secret. "I can speak Spanish as much as I want. I have earned it." She patted Antonio on the head, and walked back to the breakfast table.

"Well, that was exciting." Jamie blurted out. "You grew up more in those 30 seconds than you have your entire life kid." The older woman said encouragingly to Antonio. "And Bernie?" She turned to her friend. "The kid's right. We have to leave, and we have to leave tomorrow. I love you, and I hope you make the right decision for yourself, but I'm leaving with these people. Your selfishness, your need to stay in that chapel, has already separated three of them from the big group. If anything happens to them while they are alone, I hope your conscience can handle it. Take your last service, pray on what you want to do, but I'm out."

Jamie walked to Antonio and put her hand on his shoulder. He sat back down on the van's floor, wiping his tears away. "You spoke the truth, Antonio, as mean as it sounds to the new people, you spoke the truth. Now, I have a little surprise for you all. Antonio?" He picked his head up to look at her when she said his name, "his father was a ferry boat operator. He knows how to pilot and more importantly fix most of the boats down in the harbor. He's your ticket to Ellis Island."

"Huh?" Antonio said, confused by the request.

Emily clapped her hands and jumped up and down in excitement. "Incredible, I knew we could find someone to get us over there." She walked to the van and sat next to Antonio, explaining their plans for the day, the Statue of Liberty tour and the Ellis Island visit.

"Yeah, uh, I can do that, if we can find a boat that I can get to work.

They've been sitting in water for a long time." Antonio looked at Emily as if she was crazy. "I guess we can try."

"Great!" Emily said back, rubbing his shoulders. "Thank you!"

Antonio scrunched his shoulders, twisting uncomfortably at her touch. He was not used to so much physical contact or gestures of kindness. "Yeah, uh, can I ask a favor too?"

A stunned Emily managed to reply. "What may I do for you?"

"Can I pet your dog? I really love dogs, and I miss mine. Do you mind?" Antonio stood in hopes she would say yes, and he could find and pet Hubba.

"You don't have to ask again, please, pet away. Take him for a walk if you can. Please, Antonio, consider him your dog too. I'd love the help taking care of him, if you decide to stay with us."

"Cool." He said back, in a somewhat return to his stoic and distant mannerisms. He thought about his reply for a second and continued. "Thank you, that's real cool of you, I'd like that a lot." He strode past the group, stopping to give Jamie a high five. "You got fire, Jamie. You got fire." Antonio slipped inside the RV to find the dog.

Kelly stood next to Bernie. The reverend looked sad and distant. Kelly turned to her. "I'm going too. Avery, Meredith, and the kids will come with me. We can't stay here, Bernie. It's over. This place is dead, and if we stay, we'll all die too. The kids need you as their mother, but not if you want to stay in New York. I won't let you do that to them."

"I know." Bernie replied, her voice hollow. "I know. I'll decide tomorrow." Her head dropped. "I'll know what to do tomorrow."

"Did everyone get enough?" Ahmed, uncomfortable with the conversation, changed the subject and mood of the group. "Is there anything left, Todd?"

"Absolutely, please don't let it go to waste. Everyone should eat more if they can." Todd turned to go into the RV. "I'll bring the rest out so people can take what they would like." He went inside and saw the kids playing nicely. Jackie and Jacob had Legos out for the little kids. Meredith and the twins were helping them make things. Antonio sat on the floor next to Hubba's bed. Jay sat on the opposite side of the bed, talking nonstop to the older boy. Antonio looked at Jay, nodding and maintaining respectful eye contact. Antonio looked at Todd when he walked into the trailer, flipping his head up with a 'hey' gesture.

"We're going to the Statue of Liberty in about an hour. If you want anymore breakfast, now is the time to get it."

Cameron stood. He held an airplane made from a multitude of red, blue, yellow, white, and black legos. "May I have some more potatoes and sausage, please?" He was a cute kid, thin and tiny from a winter with no food. Todd got him a new plate and spooned more breakfast for him.

"Here you go, champ."

Before he could ask, Todd put more food on a plate and gave it to Antonio. "Jay will talk to you all day. Let me know if you need a break."

"He's cool." Antonio nodded. "I had a little brother. He was six. He didn't make it. It's why I like the little kids. They remind me of him." He gestured at the plate. "Thanks, we're all good in here. I'll be ready to help with the boat in an hour."

"Thank you." Todd put his hand on Antonio's shoulder. "Welcome to the group." Todd did not want to make a big deal out of it. He turned and left the RV with the remaining food to pass out to the adults.

"I'll take cleanup duty." Jamie stepped forward. "Show me where I can clean the pots and pans, and if you have a trash bag." Peter and Kelly assisted.

Todd and Emily went to the other RV to get ready for their day. The door opened and Melanie came through with Solange. "What's the deal with Bernie? Is she seriously considering staying here? Why would she do that?" Melanie questioned.

"There is not logic to her thinking." Solange commented. "She has gone crazy. I am surprised more of us did not lose our minds with all of the death."

"Well, she seems nice enough, and we can always use another pair of hands. I agree, she's popped a gasket. I hope she snaps out of it." Emily paused. "Has anyone figured out the deal with this Sal character? Are we leaving him? Is he dangerous? Is he even going to show?"

They looked at each other. Melanie shrugged her shoulders. "Hey, I just met all these people. Now there's someone else?"

"You just take another nap, we will wake you up if anything happens." Solange teased.

"You're funny, Ms. Tough Girl. You going to slap me in the face too?"

"If you need to be put in your place." Solange gave Melanie a steely eyed stare.

"Okay, that's enough from you two comedians." Todd stood between them. "You know what? I'm going to enjoy the day. Tomorrow is tomorrow, let's round up the group and see some landmarks."

He stepped out of the RV into the sunlight. It was shaping up to be a beautiful day. The air was warming to the mid-fifties. Avery had the kids outside playing games, kicking the soccer ball or playing hopscotch on grids she drew with sidewalk chalk. "I volunteered at the elementary school as my junior volunteer credit. I know how to entertain this age group." She explained to Todd. "Brian said you are going to see the city, may I join you? I'd love to see New York one last time. I haven't been to the Statue in like five years, and I don't remember Ellis Island. I went there once on a field trip in fourth grade."

"I went last year. It's pretty fun. I can show people around." Meredith volunteered. "If I get to go too."

Kelly listened, "you girls can make your own decisions, especially you, Avery. This is your life. If you want to stay in New York with Bernie, speak up, if you want to go to New Hampshire and join the new group, it's up to you."

"I just wanted to go to Ellis Island today." Meredith responded, "I didn't know it was part of a bigger choice."

"It's not, honey, I'm just saying, you two are old enough to start making some of your own decisions, or decide as a team. I'm going today and I'm leaving tomorrow. I'm taking Bridget, Wendy, and Cameron with me, today and tomorrow." Kelly turned to Todd, who watched the conversation with interest. "We might need to take some breaks, my kids are not as strong as yours. They haven't been eating as regularly."

"Absolutely. I'm bringing plenty of snacks, as well as bread, peanut butter, and jelly. I might even bring along a jar of fluff for fluffer nutters."

"What's a fluffer nutter?" Meredith asked.

"Peanut butter and marshmallow fluff mixed together in sugary brown goodness." Todd offered. "If you grew up in New England, it was a regular in your lunch."

"Sounds kind of sugary and caloric." Avery told her friend, "I'd stick with the pb&j's."

"I'll be honest with you, Avery. Our new life? Don't worry about calories too much. You want to take in calories, as many as possible. Video games, television, sedentary activities? Those are a thing of the past. If you don't like fluffer nutters, well, that's another story, but don't worry about what you eat. We are going to run out of processed food and be eating fish, fruits, and vegetables for the rest of our lives." Todd smiled. "So if you see a jar of fluff? Take two fingers and swipe a big mouthful!"

Meredith laughed. "Okay, I'll try it."

"Let's have some fun today, okay? It's probably been a while since anyone in your group had a fun day, a good old day of not worrying about food or work. Just kick back, enjoy this beautiful spring day in New York, and see it one more time." Todd clapped his hands. "Okay kids!" He called to the younger ones. "We are going to get together for a day out, how does that sound?"

Todd turned to Kelly, "We are short of convenient vehicles, any chance we can use the van?"

"Let's put the little ones on our laps and head out. Antonio?" She turned to the teen who was out of the RV. "What's our best shot at finding a boat that is big enough for all of us and in working condition?"

"If we start at Chelsea we can work our way down until we find a good boat, but there is probably one at the piers. We have to find keys to the boats, maybe hope the dock master's office keeps a set." He walked towards the van. "If we get to a good boat, I can get it started, probably without the keys." He smiled at her as he said the last line.

"Peter? Jamie? Bernie? Would you like to join us?" Emily stood at the van, moving the line of kids in by touching their shoulders.

"Peter has challenged me to a day of cards and walking around the park. I've seen Lady Liberty enough, and said my goodbyes to the City. One day I'll tell you my story, but I haven't lived in New York for over thirty years, left when I was in my twenties. I was on a trip and got stuck. I'll be glad to depart tomorrow morning. Enjoy yourselves." Jamie sat in a folding chair Peter set outside of the RV. He plunked down in a second chair next to her. He gave Emily a 'thumbs up.'

"We'll hold down the fort, Emily, you show the kids a good time."

Todd was packing a second backpack, "Ahmed, you can stay here or get dropped off at your home. We can handle this. Enjoy a day of rest. If you stay here, have dinner ready when we get back." Todd smiled at the investment banker turned fry cook.

"Are you kidding me? I've never been to Ellis Island. I worked 80 hours a week, minimum. I never got to see the sites. If I wasn't at work, I was playing big shot at Yankee Stadium or the Meadowlands. This will be a real treat." He waited for Todd to zip up the backpack before grabbing the handle to sling on his back. "I had a three year old son. I talked about taking days like this, showing him New York. Now I'll do that for these kids, and dream I'm with him." He gave Todd a pat on the back. "I didn't live the way I should have, always working so that someday I could take my family places. Someday was stolen from me. I'm going to enjoy today."

"I'm sorry about your family." Todd replied solemnly.

"I've cried for seven months. I am ready to start living again. I think it's what held a lot of us back, the memories of our families here in New York. I will never forget, but I have to move forward. I have to learn from my mistakes." Ahmed paused, "This day is about fun. Let's have some fun. I want my last memories of New York to be happy."

Bernie sat in the passenger's seat. Todd and Ahmed were the last to get into the van. The rows were packed with people and kids. Kelly put the van into gear and headed down 5th Ave towards Chelsea. There was still snow on the ground, but the tire tracks from the multiple trips exposed black pavement.

The van was abuzz with conversation. What were people's favorite cartoon characters, the last great sandwich they ate, the last vacation they took. Everyone wanted to get to know each other. They made a quick stop by the Empire State Building and St. Patrick's. Todd lit a candle for Peter's wife and for the world.

Bernie engaged a little, talking about St. Patrick's as she went inside to say a prayer, but she was withdrawn from the group as she sat quietly in the front seat.

Kelly turned down 21st and towards the piers. They were still talking and laughing when the van pulled up to the seminary. Bernie asked Kelly to drop her off. "I want to collect some things, get prepared for tomorrow."

Antonio pointed to the chimney. "There's a fire going. Sal's back. I bet he's freaked out right now."

"I'll talk to Sal. We'll get up to your camp on our own. Enjoy your day. Peace be with you all." Bernie opened the door and got out.

"Shotgun!" Antonio called from the back row. "I got shotgun, gimme that seat!" He struggled past Avery and Jacob to move up in the van. Once he sat down he turned to Kelly, "Let's go, before that dude comes out and ruins the day."

"To the piers!" Kelly yelled.

"To the piers!" The van shouted back. Even Antonio was excited and involved. He wanted to get on a boat, and be reminded of his father.

Bernie waved as they pulled away from the curb.

37

The smile fell from Bernie's face as she watched the van pull away towards the Hudson River. She was deeply troubled and conflicted. She did not want to leave her seminary. It was her sanctuary, her place of solitude, the center of her spiritual universe. She prayed for understanding in the chapel too many times to walk away. Her daughter was baptized in the chapel. Her husband held her child's head as Bernie administered the rite. She had fond memories that she did not want to lose.

Bernie had bad memories too. She delivered her daughter's last rites in the chapel followed by her husband's five days later. She gave last rites to hundreds of people, maybe thousands of people who stood in line outside the chapel to receive their dying peace. She worked tirelessly to give solace to the sick as she remained healthy. She believed that her purpose was to carry on the word of God, to be His lone soldier left on earth. Like many times in the Bible, she was being tested. Her family was taken from her so she could focus on the Word.

But where was the rainbow? Where was the dove? If the rapture was the great flood, washing away humanity, where was her sign that it was time to start anew? Was she supposed to go with these new people? Was she supposed to find a new place to spread the Word? Had her chapel been painted in so much innocent blood, the blood of her own daughter and husband, as a sign to walk away and find a new sanctuary?

Bernie did not know, and her prayers went unanswered. She had one night to decide.

It was cold on 21st street. The sun had not climbed over the buildings, and the night air hung over the shaded street. Bernie shivered and walked through the courtyard into the seminary looby. She saw a large figure hunched by the fireplace sitting on the hearth. She opened the door to the cloak room, hung up her coat and removed her boots. Before she could finish unlacing her second boot the door to the main room opened. After five months of people telling him not to hold the door open to let the warm air out, Sal still did what he wanted.

"Hey Bernie, where is everyone?" Sal wore dirty khaki pants and a large flannel shirt. His clothes no longer fit, draping off his large frame. His drug addiction ravaged his once hulking frame. He was still an intimidating man, but he was withering away.

"Sal, where have you been?" Bernie tried to push passed him into the warmer room. "I'm cold. May I warm up by the fire?"

Sal moved from the door as Bernie walked through. He followed her, answering her question and repeating his. "You know, I was out looking for food for the group." He seldom if ever returned from his sojourns with food. "Where is everyone? Did we move?"

Bernie sat on the large brick hearth. She did not like being in the small cloak room with Sal. She needed space to handle him. He smelled, and could be erratic in his moods. She looked at him, his pupils were dilated, and his hands were calm and not shaking. Sal was medicated.

"There is a lot of news to share." Bernie waited for Sal to sit down. "Did you find any food?"

He shook his head.

Bernie smelled peanut butter on his breath. She looked at the fire. Sal used almost the entire pile of wood. No matter how many times they asked him to keep the fire small, to conserve their fuel when he was home, Sal made a large fire with all of their wood, and left without replacing the pile. Bernie grew more annoyed, but swallowed her feelings.

"A group of people pulled into town yesterday, survivors from up and down the east coast. They have food and supplies."

"Are you serious? That's fantastic." Sal recognized an opportunity to freeload.

"Yes, they are wonderful people, with children and adults and teens. It is a perfect match for our group." Bernie paused, "but they are leaving tomorrow morning after my services. There is a second group up north, there is a plan to meet and form one big tribe."

"North? They want to leave the City?" Sal calculated his options. He might find a few drugstores scattered outside of New York, but unless they were in a larger city, his supplies would run out quickly. "Are we voting on this? I don't know if I like that plan, Bernie. I think we need to talk about it."

"It's done, Sal. Everyone has decided to go. I am the only one who is not sure what to do. I don't know if I can leave the seminary. I have to pray and hope for guidance." She bowed her head, not to pray, but to think. "You can go. These are good people. They know a hard life awaits, but starting a colony outside of New York is the best option for all of us. I know you aren't afraid of hard work, and they can use a strong man like you, Sal."

Sal hated hard work. His whole life had been work, building things for other people and getting paid barely enough to cover his bills, not even enough to pay his bills. The rapture took his wife and children, but it set him free. He could sleep until noon, he could nap every day, he could take food from other people. He could enjoy the buzz and calm his pills brought to him. New York provided an endless supply of pills. 'North' would not provide pills and it would bring work back into Sal's life.

Sal became agitated as the gears of his mind turned. "We should have voted on this, I didn't get to vote or say nuthin'. This ain't fair. I know what's fair, this ain't fair."

"We didn't vote, Sal. Everyone just decided to go. The new people have young kids, they have food. How could we vote and stop people from going? This isn't a prison. If Kelly wants to leave, Kelly is going to leave."

"This ain't right." Sal stood up. His world was changing, just when he had found a huge supply of pills, and was getting ready for summer and warmer temperatures, and sending all the people out to find him food, it was all ending. In the current group, Sal was the biggest, the strongest, no one had the courage to stand up to him. He could dominate and take what he needed. That's the way it should always have been. He was always strong, but the old life did not work that way. In the old life he was on the bottom. Now he was on top, and he was not going to be taken down because of new people.

"Sal, calm down. Can't you see the shape we're all in? We're starving. We've been given a chance to live and be with other people. This is a good thing." Bernie listened to her own advice, and she realized it was a good thing the new people arrived. She was starving. She was dying. Now she had a chance to live.

"We're all going." Bernie put her hand on Sal's arm. "We have to go."

He looked down at her, towering over the diminutive chaplain like she was a child. Sal was a lot of things, drug addict, con artist, thief, but he was not stupid. If the winds of change had already blown through his group, he needed to conform and create the best situation for himself.

He was still stoned, and he let the calm spread over his body. "Tomorrow?" He asked, feigning a bit of anger.

"After I enjoy one last service."

"You wanna stick around here, or you wanna head to their camp for the day?" Sal ate a jar of peanut butter with crackers for breakfast, but if there was more food, particularly if someone else had already found it for him, Sal would eat.

"Well, almost everyone has gone to Ellis Island for the day, but we could go up and meet Jamie and her new friend Peter."

Sal was confused. Ellis Island? Why would they go to Ellis Island? Was this a tourist stop for these people? If he was dealing with a group of southerners who decided to sightsee on their way to the frozen northeast, Sal's position in the group was looking better.

"What do they have up there?" Sal wanted to look around their camp while they were gone.

"They have two RV's, a U-Haul trailer full of tables, fire pits, that kind of thing. They are stocked with food, staples like flour and sugar. I didn't see anything out of the ordinary, just food, clothes, things like that." Bernie was thinking about what she would pack. She was not paying attention to Sal's questions, and answered them absently.

"Sure, let's go and meet Jamie and her new friend, but I betta' pack some things first, ya know, get ready to leave tomorrow."

"Okay, Sal, that works. Let's meet back here in a half hour or so? We can use one of the little cars. The snow is melting on the streets where the sun hits, and there are thawed tire tracks on 5th Ave."

"Where are they anyway?" He still did not know where 'there' was.

"They're at 59th and 5th Ave. At the bottom of the park."

"The Plaza? Are you kiddin' me?" Sal was now certain he could dominate the new group. He walked down the hall and went to the second floor. Sal had taken the last room down the hall from the stairs to keep his privacy. The room had the last radiator before the warm water went back down the side of the chimney to re-heat, and Sal received the least amount of heat, but he preferred the solitude to warmth. He also believed it made him look magnanimous to the group.

Sal did not keep much in the seminary. He had an apartment on the upper west side, a pre-war building with fireplaces in each room. It was a tiny studio where the fireplace heated the entire space. Sal had food, water, and drugs stashed in his real home. He would go there for days. It was much more comfortable than living in squalor at the seminary. Every few days he would get lonely and wander back down to Chelsea. If he cared, he would have told them about the building. It was easier to heat, and closer to places where he could find food, but he did not care about these people.

Sal's problem was that all of his drugs were at the other apartment. He had cases of pills there and only a small bottle in his pocket. He had to get up to the other apartment before they left.

Sal's bigger problem, and one he did not know about, Antonio was aware of Sal's other place, and was at that very moment telling the adults about Sal's lies, and how he hoarded food and stole from the group.

Sal sat down on his cot, ran his hands through his dirty thick hair. "Think, Sal, think. You either gotta sneak out tonight, or run up there first thing in the mornin', when Bernie's doin' the church thing. That'll work, first thing, just say you gotta go somewhere's, say goodbye to Shea Stadium or something like that. No one will care, they'll be busy packing." He would sneak out, take a car, a duffel, pack up his stuff, and meet them back at the Plaza.

Sal stuffed a few of the useless things he kept in the room into a small backpack. He slung the pack and went downstairs by the fire. Bernie was waiting. Sal had been in his room for an hour. His drug induced haze made it almost impossible for him to judge time.

"I put some pictures, some clothes in this pack. I'll leave it here for tomorrow." Sal made a big deal. "I want to take a car up to my old neighborhood in the morning, say goodbye, ya know, the right way. Just like you are doin' your last service. I gotta say goodbye."

Bernie nodded. "I know it's tough, Sal, but we have to say goodbye to our old lives. We have to move on." She put her hand on his shoulder affectionately, empathizing with his grief.

"She bought it." Sal thought to himself. "She bought it hook, line, and sinka'."

They continued small talk as they left the seminary. Bernie's thoughts were elsewhere as she sat in the passenger's seat of the car Sal kept for his runs around the city. There was a hint of cigarette smell, a residue from the only bad habit Sal was forced to quit after the rapture. He detested stale cigarettes, and went cold turkey rather than use stale packs. He relied on his pills to get him through the nicotine detox.

"So, these people, they seem nice?" Sal drove too fast across 22nd street.

"Yes." Bernie was furious with herself for not driving. Sal was probably a bad driver when he was sober, but she had never seen him sober, so she could not be sure. Bernie was sure that he was a horrible driver while stoned. She grasped the handle by the window tightly, digging her left hand into the seat leather.

"They seem like they wanna take care of the three little ones?" Sal believed asking about the kids was his best way to win Bernie. He could never remember the children's names, and she knew it. His question had the opposite effect.

"Wendy, Bridget, and Cameron? Yes, they have young children the same age, it's a perfect fit."

Sal took a hard left turn up 5th Ave faster than needed. They were not in a hurry. Bernie heard the tires squeal and the car fishtailed out of control.

"Yeah, the kids, I know their names, the kids." He pushed down on the accelerator. Sal loved driving fast in the city. He loved being able to do what he wanted to do. He did not have to listen to anyone anymore. Sal was in charge of Sal. He never had freedom. His father was a tough bastard who made Sal follow rules, slapping him around to keep him in line. When Sal moved out after high school, believing it was his time to shine, he ended up working construction to pay his bills. Do this, nail that, work this Saturday, stay until 10pm, don't talk back or I'll fire you. He started his own business, but then it was the customers that bossed him around, or the banks that held liens on his house, car, and business.

Sal's business failed two years before the rapture. He owed money to everyone under the sun. His oldest daughter's braces had not been adjusted in five months because he was six months late on the bill. He could not get the damn orthodontist to take them off of her. His car, a ten year old piece of crap, was repossessed. His son, a little too much like him, was suspended from public school. Sal was paying to have him in private school so he would not miss a grade, except Sal could not pay the tuition bill. His son sat at home playing video games all day. Sal was facing his third driving under the influence and possession charge, which meant lawyer fees, fines and court costs. Sal's wife was an alcoholic who enjoyed shopping and opening store credit cards. Sal, a drug addict himself, did not know how to stop her.

Like a fire that burns down a forest so new trees can grow, the rapture destroyed all the good and the bad from Sal's life. It took his family, but it took away his yoke. It took away civilization, but it took away the burdens that shackled him. Sal was free. He drove too fast through the streets of New York City because that is what Sal wanted to do, and no one told Sal what he could and could not do anymore.

The BMW screeched to a stop short of the RV's at 59th and 5th. Jamie and Peter sat in their chairs eating soup for lunch. A small fire burned in a pit at their feet. Hubba was on a bed in between them. He sat up and barked.

"That's Sal." Jamie told Peter. "He must have come back." There was no joy in the woman's voice. Jamie was disappointed. She wanted to leave Sal behind.

"Well, let's meet this young man." Peter put his hands on each armrest and pushed himself up. He was tall, taller than Sal and the other men in the group. As he aged, his knees and hips tended to get sore quickly. Despite his fantastic physical shape, he needed leverage to stand.

Peter towered over most people. Sal was big, but not tall. Peter had at least four inches on the dirty drug addict. As the men shook hands for the first time, Peter did so from a position of strength. Sal was immediately irritated. Peter looked like the banker that told Sal he was in pre-foreclosure.

Sal had many faces, and today's face was one of friendliness and thanks.

"Very nice to meet ya, Peter. Sal Torvale," Sal gripped the man's hand tightly. "Bernie told me a little bit about ya." Sal grinned, almost purred to the older man.

"Jamie, how are ya? It must be great to have found someone yer own age." He went in for a hug with the woman, but she sat back down as he leaned towards her. Sal was high. The pills he popped in his room at the Seminary were kicking in. He was clueless to the fact that bringing attention to Jamie's age was rude.

"I'm afraid it's just us here, Sal. The rest of our group went to see the sights." Peter pointed to the RV. "There is some soup on the stove if either of you are hungry. I hope you do not mind, I'm going to eat mine while it is still hot. I know it's 50 out today, but that will cool ham and potato pretty quickly." Peter sat down next to Jamie and picked up his soup.

"Soup sounds wonderful. I'm a bottomless pit when I come up here. I need to fill up from all those months of being empty." Bernie pointed towards the other trailer. "Over there?"

"Right in there hon, there are bowls in a sleeve next to the pot with spoons in a box." Jamie looked at Sal. "Sal, there are chairs in the trailer, be a dear and grab a couple. You two can join us."

Sal squinted his eyes. He did not take orders from the old woman, but he was in a peculiar spot. He needed to keep a friendly façade with Peter. Jamie had not asked him for favors in months, knowing he would ignore her. Sal, high and irrational, believed she was trying to get him to show his true spots, or worse, was taking advantage of the situation.

"I'm not very hungry right now. I think I'll take a walk around the camp. It's been a while since I've been to the park, and this will be my last time. If Bernie is hungry, she should have all the soup." Sal turned his not getting the chairs into a magnanimous gesture. "I'm going to stretch my legs a bit."

"I'll get Bernie a chair." Peter pushed himself up again. "She can use mine. I'll grab another."

Sal turned angry. The tall man who looked like the asshole banker who took Sal's house, was now showing him up. And who the hell was Jamie to give Sal orders anyway? This was really her fault. He hated that old woman. She was bossy and had a mouth on her. She needed to learn some respect.

Sal stormed off without saying another word. He flipped up the hood to his sweatshirt to hide this face, twisted in anger. "Just keep it cool, Sal, just be cool." He thought to himself. Sal wore work boots, the same boots he wore for three years. He loved the boots, the leather was broken in and comfortable. He had jeans, a maroon t-shirt with a faded, stretched out collar, and a dark tan sweatshirt. Unlike the others in the New York group, Sal kept the same clothes he had before the rapture. He had a new car, but the same comfortable clothes, the same drug habit, and the same angry attitude.

Sal did not want to wander in the park. It was early, and walking the ten or fifteen blocks to his apartment was his idea all along. He would take a nap, pack up his things for the next day, and return to the RV's later. He did not like Peter, and had never liked Jamie. Spending four hours talking to those two, or listening to them talk was not high on Sal's list of things to do. By the time Bernie came out of the RV with a bowl of soup and glass of punch, Sal was a few hundred yards away, walking towards the upper west side.

"Where is Sal going?" Bernie asked, confused as to why he was leaving.

"I bet he's going to his apartment. That son of a bitch, I hope he gets high and passes out, and we leave him here. He's worthless, worse than that, he's a drag on the group." Jamie spat venom.

"Apartment, what are you talking about?" Bernie sat down, soup in hand.

"Antonio, he's a good kid, he and I talk sometimes when everyone else is asleep. He puts up a tough front, but he's lonely, he misses his family, his friends, anyway, he opens up to me, and he followed Sal a few months ago." Jamie took a sip of water. "And that bastard has an apartment on the upper west side, some old brownstone. He has fire, and food, and that's where he's been going. We thought he was scavenging for drugs, but he has drugs. He goes off to be comfortable while we are starving. While those little angels are starving, while he saw Ahmed dropping down to weighing nothing, and probably damaging his kidneys from giving his food to the rest of us, that son of a bitch, Sal." Jamie let out a cry as tears rolled down her face. "That son of a bitch was letting us all die. Have you noticed he hasn't lost much weight? He's still a big strong guy. The rest of us are withering away, and he stays fat and burly. I say we call him out on it and leave him to fend for himself. He doesn't want to help us in our hours of need? He can try to survive on his own forever."

"He had an apartment? That can't be true. He didn't do that, Jamie, he didn't. No one could do that." Bernie put her hand on Jamie's leg. "Antonio made that up. Sal isn't a bad person. He's just mixed up. The drugs have control of him, but he's not bad. Antonio is playing with your emotions, trying to turn you against..."

Jamie cut her off, "My god, Bernie, do you even hear yourself? Who feeds the kids when he can? Who stayed with us even when he begged us to move to Queens. Who always stayed between Avery and Sal? Antonio is the good one. He tries to act tough, but he's just a kid. You think Sal showing up for one of your services every other month and saying 'amen' to you means he's a good person? That he's seeking redemption? He's a conman, Bernie. He's a lousy, stinking, conman, and his time is up."

Peter remained quiet. When Peter was young his father described a loud and obnoxious man by saying, "What's on his mind is on his tongue." The comment so affected Peter he became the opposite, seldom giving his opinion without first considering the consequences. Peter led by example as a pilot, father, and husband. The new world was different. It required him to be vocal. He was one of 25 people left in the world, and an important member of the group. It was time to step forward.

"Bernie," he said calmly. "I know you are having a hard time believing Jamie or I guess really, Antonio. Let me ask you this, what if it's true? What if Sal has been keeping a life with heat, food, water, and drugs, and he's been keeping it separate from the group? What would you suggest?" He looked at her as a friend.

"I can't believe it." Bernie replied. "I can't believe anyone would do that to others. If it's true, well, it means he's betrayed us, betrayed us every second of everyday." She lowered her head. "I don't know what it means if it's true. I hate to think what the group would want to do to him." She lifted her head and looked towards Jam e. "My god, all those nights the girls cried themselves to sleep in hunger pains? All those tears Cameron cried? All the times I averted my eyes as Avery was getting dressed, her body like an extreme anorexic's, and I was ashamed I couldn't feed her? All that time, Sal had food? What kind of person is he? It can't be true, because if it is, that man is a monster."

Bernie set down the soup, disgusted. Peter picked the bowl up and offered it to her. "Eat. You don't look much like a sumo wrestler yourself. You need to finish this soup and get another bowl. I'm afraid you are going to blow away."

Bernie blushed, her chocolate brown cheeks turning a light shade of red. "You're right." She took the bowl from Peter and continued to eat. "You are a quiet man, Peter, but when you do speak? You know what to say."

"I would enjoy attending your service tomorrow morning. I have missed my faith, and appreciate your leadership in my search to reconnect with it." Peter smiled at the woman. "There are decisions that we must make about Sal, and we'll make them as a group. It will not be one person's burden. You are taking too much on yourself. Please realize, there are more of us to carry the water." Peter grabbed Jamie's hand after he said it. "Both of you, understand, we're a family now, or a tribe as Emily likes to call us. We have individual decisions to make, but we can also grow stronger as a group."

"You sound like a televangelist." Jamie told him, lightening the mood. "If you try to talk both me and Bernie into marrying you right now, the answer is no." Jamie gave a loud laugh at her own joke.

Bernie let a warm smile creep across her face, she loved the old woman. Jamie made everything seem better. She found humor all around her. "I am going to say no, too."

Peter blushed. "For the record, I did not ask either one of you, let alone both of you. When you tell this story to the other women, I never asked."

"You were about to. I could tell." Jamie snickered.

"You are welcome at my service tomorrow morning, Peter. I would enjoy your attendance." Bernie continued to eat as she spoke. "We can reconnect to our faith together." She took a last spoonful of soup and stood, "but right now I am going to continue my reconnection with food. May I get anyone else more soup? I put another can on the stove. It should be warm."

"Just bring out the pot, we'll all take more." Jamie was trying to put weight back on after the long winter of starvation.

When Bernie went into the trailer, Jamie turned to Peter. "I'm an old woman, I've seen a lot in my life. I'll tell you this, whether Sal comes with us or not, his time with this group is limited. He can't keep himself under control long enough to function. He'll run out of drugs, or walk off during chores, and we'll have to make a hard decision. Feed a man that won't do anything, or make it so we don't have to feed him anymore." She looked at Peter with all the seriousness of a heart attack. "It would be best if he passed out and we left him. If there is still a God in heaven, Sal Torvale is on a drug binge right now. Better we leave him, knowing he has food and will live and die by his own hand, than having to kill him down the road."

"Jamie, we're not going to kill anyone." Peter tried to console her. "You're exaggerating,"

Peter hoped she was wrong, but he knew hard decisions were on the horizon.

With the Sal conversation behind them, Peter, Jamie, and Bernie enjoyed the afternoon. They had no responsibilities. They ate, sat, and talked for hours. Jamie asked her friend, "Bernie, you've been walking around like a ghost for half a year, and now you are happy and fun. Are you drunk?"

Bernie shook her head. "I have been living in the past, living with my grief for too long. You are right, Peter and his friends arriving was a sign, a sign that life must gone on. Sitting in my chapel praying that my daughter and husband are still alive is selfish and dumb."

"You had a daughter?" Peter asked her. "What was her name?"

"We named her Sarah. We loved her above all other children. That was our religious family joke." Bernie beamed when she spoke about Sarah, her soccer team, her choir recitals, her math and science grades. She had pride and love in the memories.

"My oldest daughter was named Sarah." Peter told them. "She had five children, bless her heart. I managed to have two, and I thought that was tough. Two kids of my own, and we ended up with eight grandchildren. Can you believe that?" Peter chuckled. "You'd think I raised my kids Catholic or Mormon, not Episcopalian."

"I had 13 grandchildren. My daughter was also named Sarah, my second child, the only girl among three brothers. She was the strongest. I spoke to each one of them before they died. I could not visit them, spread across the country like they were, but we spoke on the phone. Each one of them would ask me, 'Mom, are you sick yet? You're going to beat it, Mom.' And I would tell them they were crazy."

"I didn't know you had a daughter named Sarah." Bernie said to Jamie. "Funny we had daughters with the same name. We should start a club. It's going to be a pretty small club." She chuckled.

The church van rolled up at 4:30pm. Sal had not returned.

Bernie could hear singing from the van "and we're too busy singing, to put anybody down..."

Antonio was in the front seat. He was smiling, but his hand was on his forehead. He wore a baseball cap, and shook his head back and forth. Kelly was laughing in the driver's seat, as was the second row of Ahmed, Todd, and Emily.

The door slid open and Avery jumped out. "I have to get out of here before they start singing again. They are making up songs, ridiculous songs, and claiming they are real." She pleaded to Bernie to make the singing stop.

"That's not made up, that's the Monkees' theme song." Bernie tried to explain.

"Oh my god, you're in on it too. Oh my god." Avery walked away to find solace with Jamie and Peter.

The younger kids were laughing and talking. Wendy, Bridget, and Casey sang their new song "Hey, hey we're monkeys, and people say we're monkeys so long, but we're too busy singing, to be monkeys." They laughed.

"Avery!" The children yelled after singing. "Can you play hopscotch?" The girls ran to the chalk drawn grid and started looking for rocks to use on the squares.

Jay walked to Peter and told him about "the island where all the new Americans had to go, and how there was luggage stacked up, and shoes all around, and signatures, and hospital rooms." Peter nodded as the young boy told him of the day's adventures.

Before Jay could finish, Brian, Jaclyn, Jacob, and Meredith pulled a soccer ball out of the RV and headed to the grass for a quick game. When Jay saw them he explained to Peter. "Sorry Mr. Peter, I, I, I gotta go!" He stuttered in excitement, not wanting to be rude to his older friend, but not wanting to be left out of the soccer fun either.

"You can tell me all about it on our way up to New Hampshire tomorrow. How's that?" Peter asked the boy.

"Okay!" Jay screamed over his shoulder, running towards his brother and friends.

Brian paused as the group kept walking. He turned and yelled to Antonio. "Hey, Tony! Would you like to play? I know we're little kids, but we're good at soccer."

Antonio, or Tony as the group discovered he preferred, looked at the adults, shrugged his shoulders, and walked towards the kids. "Sure, little man, I'll kick the ball around for a few." He trotted towards the grassy area that was their soccer field.

Jamie, still sitting in her chair, looked at Solange. "If I had known a slap in the face was all that kid needed to engage, I would have done it five months ago."

Solange nodded, "I believe the five months with your group had more to do with his new found life than my slap in the face. Your group has been sleep walking, and our arrival has woken you. He understands what life has in store for him." She paused. "He is a good person, but from what I can tell, he is not a good soccer player." She laughed as she watched him try to dribble away from the little kids. His size and speed allowed him to score. His skills were horrible.

Melanie walked up to Peter. "No Sal?"

"Oh, he was here." Peter stood to give Melanie a quick hug. It was the most they had been apart for seven months. "I had the pleasure of meeting the man, but he was not interested in talking to me or Jamie. He wandered off to take a walk in the park. That was three, maybe four hours ago."

The adults formed a circle around Jamie, who stayed seated. The good feelings from the fun day were gone. Tension settled over the group.

"Did Jamie tell you about the apartment?" Emily began. She was upset, furious that a person would let young children starve while they stayed fat.

"Yes, yes she did." Peter replied. "I can say, after meeting the man, I'm not all that shocked. He seemed angry from the second he got out of the car with Bernie. He said two words, and stormed off for his walk."

Ahmed looked around the circle, "I know it would be natural for you to think the New York people are going to circle the wagons for one of our own, but that bastard is not with me. We took on whoever needed shelter, whoever wanted to be part of our group, whoever would help us. He fits none of those categories. Maybe he did in the beginning, maybe he will down the road, but for the last six months he's been nothing but a drag and scourge to me and the rest of us. If this were a job? I'd have fired him long ago. If he was living with us before the rapture, I would have kicked him out. Unfortunately, I don't know what to do, but know this, I'm not going to defend him or go against the will of the group just because he was living in the same building as me for six months. I'm done." He took a sip from his water bottle. "I hope I can be a good member of our group, and please consider me part of whatever you call yourselves. I'm not a member of the New York clan any longer."

There was a pause before Solange broke the silence. "That is the most you have said in two days. Where did that come from?"

Laughter erupted. Ahmed was reserved and quiet for the last two days, speaking here and there, but not opening up. During the outing today, he stayed with Cameron and the two young girls, making sure they felt comfortable and had fun. He answered questions when asked, but did not offer long opinions like the one he just gave about Sal.

"Well, I just..." Ahmed began.

"I get it." Todd cut him off. "We get it. You want to make sure we don't put Sal in a category with the rest of you."

Emily was fuming, despite the joke by Solange. "It's time we decide. We know where he is. He's getting high in his apartment. Tony can show us which one. Do we go there now, talk to him about his options? Do we see if he comes back before we leave, talk to him then? Do we leave if he isn't here tomorrow?"

She left the questions in the air.

"That would be killing him." Bernie said quietly. "I'm not sure I can kill him, despite his bad behavior. He's still a person, a human being."

"How is it killing him?" Melanie asked her. "He knows our plan, he knows we're here. If he wants to brave the world on his own, or wait for the next group of survivors to arrive to see if he likes them better, those are his choices."

"I don't know, Mel, I don't know if I can leave him. Have we really come to a place where we make decisions like that? It's like Ahmed said, if this were work or before the rapture there would be options. Now? I don't know what our options are." Emily stood next to her husband. She reached for his hand. "I'm enraged right now, but I don't want to be a savage just because the world is up for grabs. As my husband has said for months now, this isn't The Road Warrior. We don't have to act like it."

Melanie replied directly to Emily. "What are you going to do when he steals food from your children in six months? What happens when he decides he does not want to take his turn in the fields, and we do not get part of our crops in the ground, or some of our crops die because he refuses to help, yet we have to feed him? If he becomes a drag on the group and is taking food from the mouths of the children, what will your options be then, Emily? He has shown he has no regard for other people. He has shown he does not want to be part of the group. If he wants to stay alone is New York, I do not think we should go knock on his door and bring him with us. He is making his bed."

"So we let him kill himself when we know that is what he is doing? We offer no help? If he was drowning, even though he went into deep water not knowing how to swim, you'd rescue him, wouldn't you? How is this different?" Bernie interjected.

Melanie answered easily. "If the water he went into had sharks and alligators and endangered my life? I'd let him drown. There are bad people, Bernie, and it is not my job to help them at the expense of my own well being and the well being of all the other people in my group. A year ago, I would have helped Sal, but his behavior would not have directly affected me or my children. Now, his bad behavior has a direct negative impact on my ability to survive." Melanie looked around the group. "Leaving him is not a popular or easy decision, I know, but it is the easiest way to fix the problem. If we make an effort to bring him with us, I am convinced we will have to make a much more difficult decision down the road."

"You mean kill him ourselves." Todd said. "You are saying we can walk away, never knowing how he ends up, or take him with us and probably have to kill him ourselves in a year. That's what you think? That we would do some sort of public execution or something? That we would hang him in the village square as a message?"

Solange answered. "We would not use him as an example, or scare our children, but yes, I am sure we will have to kill him. We might try to throw him out of the tribe, make him leave, but a man like Sal? He will not leave without hurting our chances for survival down the road, and/or stealing food and necessary tools. Granted, I have not met him, but I know the type of person they have described. He cannot change who he is, and we cannot change who he is either."

"You nailed him. Don't worry about not having met him, you've nailed his personality, and you're probably right." Ahmed backed Solange's assessment. "I say we leave him. If he shows up, wants to come, fine, but I'm not groveling over to 71st to beg him to join us. No way. And you know what? If he wants to come? He walks onto the RV with empty pockets and no bags. He leaves his drugs here. No more drugs."

"I'm with Ahmed and Solange." Kelly nodded.

Jamie stood up from her chair. "I'm with them too. If he shows up, we bring him along, naked as a jay bird, but we don't go after him, and we don't let him follow us with a car full of drugs. Solange, I wish I was as strong as you, but I can't leave a man behind if he wants to come. I think that's where you're headed, leaving Sal no matter what. Okay, I get it, but I have too much of the old way left in me. He's a son of a bitch, that's for sure, but as Bernie said, he's a person. If he comes, put him in the RV, away from the children. No pills, no booze, just Sal on his own to detox. That's my opinion. If we bring him and it goes wrong? I'll take him out back and kill him. I'm old. I won't have to carry the burden as long as the rest of you would." She looked at Solange, "will that satisfy you?"

"It is not a matter of me being satisfied," Solange began before Jamie cut her off.

"I know, dear, I know. You are thinking like we all should. What I'm asking is, do you believe this is a good compromise? If Sal wants to come, we give him parameters, let him make his choice. If it goes bad down the road, I'll take care of him."

"No, we have a decision to make now, and then one we'll address if needed later. You are not going to assume responsibility for Sal." Emily shook her head. "This conversation is about whether we pick him up or we leave without him. I don't want to talk about the future. We can't control the future."

"I agree." Melanie said. "But I also agree that we should consider the future. Regardless, we have to make a decision for right now. Do we pick him up, do we wait for him, or do we leave him."

"I never said anything about waiting for him." Emily replied. "We either get him or we leave him, we aren't delaying our trip to Hanover. We leave tomorrow. The third option is, do we leave a note for Sal telling him where we are going? That would put the ball entirely in his court. He would be making his own decision to stay alone or join our group."

"But won't that invite a drug addict to follow us with a car full of pills and the same bad attitude?" Ahmed did not like Sal, and wanted him left behind.

"Again, I can't control the future. Sal will eventually run out of drugs, even if he brings a car full of them. Whether he detox's here or six months from now, if we can gain strength from him, I say it's worth the risk." Emily's mind was set.

"You know my position." Solange said firmly, "but I accept the decision of the group. I will state my case in simple terms. I do not see us gaining strength from Sal. I see us becoming weaker because of him. I believe the odds are in favor of him hurting the group down the road. If he shows up, I will not throw him out in the cold. I vote for leaving him with his fate in his own hands and decided by his own actions."

"Okay." Todd said after Solange finished. "Let's decide on the first thing. Does anyone believe we should go get Sal if he doesn't show up tomorrow?"

Bernie raised her hand. She looked around the group. "My life is about rescuing people, about redemption. I cannot stop because the world died."

"Are you okay with us not getting Sal? You can leave with us?" Todd asked her.

"I may be in the judgment business, but I am not judging any of you today. This is the right decision for the group. I know that. Sometimes, even though you understand it is the best thing to do, you cannot vote the way you should. I cannot vote to leave Sal behind. I hope you do not judge me as a coward, unwilling to make the hard decision. I am certainly not judging you. You are kind and generous people. These are hard times, unusual times, don't be ashamed of what we are doing." She waited for a second. "I do, however, plead with you to leave the man a note."

"Well." Todd continued. "That is our second decision. We are pulling out of here tomorrow. If Sal is not here at 12, he's going to be left behind, that is decided." Todd looked around the group for any expressions of dissent. There were none.

Kelly nodded. She gave a weak smile towards Bernie. Kelly often thought back on that day, the day she voted to leave Sal behind. She wondered if her personal hatred and opinion that Sal was "creepy" influenced her vote. Kelly was young, in her twenties, and not used to making grand decisions like the one they made that day. What she would later come to realize, no one, except Solange, was comfortable with the decisions they were making.

"The decision in front of us is whether or not to leave Sal a note about meeting us in Hanover." Todd looked around the circle of people again. "I want to leave a note. A simple note that reads, 'We went to Hanover, N.H. Highways 95N to 91N to Norwich, VT exit.' No ultimatums about leaving his drugs behind, no language that asks him to come, just simple words left here, maybe on his car."

"I agree." Melanie said quickly.

"I do too." Emily echoed.

Kelly, Peter, and Bernie agreed. Solange, Ahmed, and Jamie dissented.

Sal was thrown a life line.

Bernie addressed the circle. "Thank you for doing this. I don't know if my words swayed anyone, but I believe this is the right thing to do."

Solange nodded, "I voted against the note, but if people believe we should leave one, I agree." Solange walked over to Todd and Emily, putting her arms around the two of them. Her head was between theirs, and she whispered in their ears, "I hope you do not think I voted against you. I voted my beliefs. I am not against you, ever." She pulled back and kissed each of them on the cheek. "Let us get ready to leave tomorrow. I do not like this city."

She turned and walked towards the soccer game. "Antonio!" She said loudly. "Have you never played futbol? I cannot believe your foot skills! Come over here, and give me that ball!" Solange wore tight jeans with a tight sports hoodie that accented her figure. Her hair was pulled back into a ponytail, and it bounced back and forth as she strode towards the soccer game. She was a gorgeous, confident woman, and even Emily watched her as she walked away.

Emily turned and punched her husband in the shoulder. "Don't get any ideas about that girl. You're still mine."

"Me? What are you talking about? You were looking at her more than I was. She kissed you too." They hugged each other and gave a quick kiss.

"Really? Come on, get a room." Melanie groaned.

"Wow. I mean, all we did was hug and kiss." Emily said back.

"Don't listen to her, honey." Todd gave Melanie a sneer. "I have to think about food anyway. It's almost five. We need dinner, and get the camp packed for tomorrow." He stuck out his tongue at Melanie before walking towards the U-Haul trailer. Todd had a fun idea for dinner, and pulled a kettle grill onto the street. He went over to the kids. "Okay, break in the game for a few minutes. I need firewood for the grill. Everyone grab a few pieces of dry wood from the park. Not huge pieces, just a few each, and bring them back to me. We're having a cookout tonight!"

A cheer arose from the kids. They scattered to get branches. Solange looked at Todd and asked the obvious question, "Cookout? What do we have to cookout?"

"Grilled ham, baked beans, and macaroni and cheese." He grinned at her. "And we have graham crackers, chocolate, and marshmallows, so there will be s'mores for dessert."

"I look forward to the day when we hunt for meat." Solange frowned. "Canned ham does not sound like something I want to eat. I did not eat canned meat in Ecuador."

"Trust me, you'll like it. It's good." Todd walked back to the grill whistling. He had a five pound bag of charcoal he pulled from the trailer and placed in the bottom of the grill. It was a light the bag brand. The coals were presoaked with lighter fluid. He needed the extra firewood to heat the large grill, but the small bag was perfect to get the fire started.

One by one the kids brought armfuls of sticks, twigs, and a few logs, until there was a pile of usable wood stacked next to the grill. Todd selected smaller twigs and medium branches, laying them across the bag of coals. He looked at Cameron, whose nose barely came to the top edge of the metal cauldron. "Would you like to start the fire, Cameron?"

The boy's eyes lit up and his mouth opened in an "oh my" expression.

"Sure." He said excitedly. "But I'm not tall enough."

Antonio offered a hand. "I'll hold you up, little dude. You light the bag." Antonio flipped his baseball cap around so the bill pointed backwards, picked up the little boy, and hung him over the kettle grill. Todd lit a long twig and handed it to Cameron.

"Put the flame at the edge of the paper bag. Once it's on fire, you can drop the branch on the pile." Cameron held the flaming stick with both hands as he hung in the air. The rest of the kids were standing close, watching Cameron light his first campfire. He stuck his tongue out as he concentrated on touching the flame to the red and black bag.

"It's not going to burn me is it?" He asked, pulling the flame away from the bag.

"No, dude, you're good. Just light the fire, we're all hungry." Antonio encouraged him.

Cameron re-focused on the flame to bag task, and after a few seconds, saw that the bag was on fire. He let out an "I did it! I did it!" and dropped the stick onto the pile. Antonio made an airplane noise and zoomed Cameron around the grill, landing him next to Jay and Brian.

"Did you guys see that? I lit the fire!"

"That was awesome." Jay told him. "Let's go get some more wood for your fire!" Before Todd could tell them he had enough for the night, the kids ran off to gather more wood.

"I can always put it in the grill for next time we use it." He said to Antonio.

Antonio's transformation from cold and angry street kid to warm and helping teenager was nothing short of miraculous. Ten hours earlier he was a punk who was only interested in helping himself. Tonight he spun a four year old around like an airplane. Todd was astounded at the change.

"Tony?" He asked, still a bit intimidated by the tough kid from the Bronx.

"Yeah."

"So what made you change so fast? What switch clicked? Why were you angry at 7am and now you are playing soccer with the kids?" Todd had to know.

"Well, getting beat up by a girl in front of you helped." He chuckled, "but it's choices, you know? My life has always been about choices and roles. When I lived at home, I had good parents. father and mother, two little brothers and a little sister. We were poor. I made some bad choices, hung out with the wrong kids. I could never bring that home. When I was in the house, I had to respect my parents, and I loved my little brothers and sister. When I was at school, well, I had to be the guy you met. When my family died, I didn't have the family role anymore, I didn't need to show respect, and I fell into the bad group I had from school. They lived longer, they helped me steal food, they helped me stay alive." Antonio looked at the tray of food Todd readied for the grill.

"Dude, are we eating canned ham?"

"Um, yeah, is that okay?"

"If that's what we have, that's what we eat." He stated. "Anyway, I'm with this bad group of kids, stealing and doing bad stuff while all hell is breaking loose around the Bronx. I guess I just stayed in that mode. I thought being a badass was what kept me alive. When Sol slapped me in the face she told me in Spanish, 'this is your family, you don't disrespect your family, you know that.' And she was right, I did know. Family kept me alive this winter, not being a badass."

"Jamie told me you were always good to the kids."

"Well, yeah, I mean, what kind of dick is mean to little kids? I'm gonna watch them starve while I have food? Ahmed? He's a grown man. He needs to find food, but Cameron and the girls? They can't get food. I'm not going to let them starve. That's just evil, dude. There's a difference between badass and evil."

Todd nodded. "So what do you think we should do about Sal?"

Antonio's face, which up to this point was cheerful, became serious. "That dude is evil. I'm sorry, but he's mean. I'm not saying you haven't known mean people before, but you probably haven't. I have. There was this one guy in my gang? He liked to torture shit, animals, fish, anything that he could see suffer. It's like, if he could make something else's life suck more than his, he was making his own life better. I don't know, that's probably giving this dude too much credit, like he knew why he was being evil and shit. Anyway, he was evil. You wanted something really bad done? You go to Edgar. Dude sent shivers down my spine. I avoided Edgar." Antonio noticed the cans of baked beans and picked one up. "Dude, I love baked beans, sweet. You pour them over the ham. The sweet with the salty, that's a great meal." He put the can down.

"Sal is a little like Edgar. Sal's snapped, he doesn't give a shit about anyone. He's at his apartment right now, probably high as a kite, not giving a crap about us. That dude is stone cold evil. He hasn't dropped a damn pound since I met him. He's been eating food and keeping his weight up, watching that little girl Bridget go from a fat little obese girl to skin and bones." Antonio saw the look on Todd's face. "Yeah, you didn't know? She was a fat little girl, one of those kids you would look at and be like 'why is a five year old so heavy?' Look at her now? She's what? 35 pounds? Sal? He didn't care a bit. He would stroll into the seminary, high, full of food, talk about doing this, helping out with that. Bernie would get excited about how Sal is finally coming through, and then poof, Sal would be gone again. He doesn't want to work. He doesn't want to be around other people. He is trouble."

"So what do you think we should do?" Ahmed, who walked up to the fire, listened to Antonio's assessment of Sal.

"Me? I'd leave his ass. I'd put sugar in his gas tank, put him at the back of our caravan, and watch his car sputter and die while we keep on driving. Ain't no room for a guy like that in our group. He don't want to be in the group anyway, so why pretend? Cut him loose."

Ahmed patted the kid on the back. "Can you help me get some pots for the beans?"

Antonio nodded, and they walked towards one of the RVs.

"Ahmed, Tony, wait a second." Todd walked to them. "You two are in charge of the Mac and Cheese. We have oil instead of butter, and you have to use the goat's milk, but please make five boxes. People are hungry. Let me know when you put the noodles in the boiling water and I'll start grilling the SPAM. I can heat the beans in a pot on the grill."

"You got it." Ahmed replied. "We're on it." He turned to Antonio and started talking about the Ellis Island trip. The boy nodded and engaged. It was their first conversation in all of their months together.

Jamie and Peter were back in their chairs as Melanie, Kelly, and Bernie set the tables for dinner. Solange, Avery, and Emily talked as the younger kids played soccer.

Todd lit the second fire pit. Peter and Jamie still had the first one blazing near their chairs.

"I see where you are going with this, Todd. I like your idea. May I borrow some of your wood pile?" Peter stood from his chair to help.

"Absolutely. The sun is going down and the temp is going to drop a bit, let's have both fires going, and we can eat around them and my kettle grill."

Jamie stood. "Well, I guess it's time for me to do something today." She followed Peter to the back of the trailer.

Todd opened the ham using the flat key on the side, working it around the tin container. He cut thick burgers from the loaves. He set a pot of beans on the fire to warm. The beans boiled and sputtered within minutes, sending a sweet smell of brown sugar and bacon into the air. Ten minutes later the tribe enjoyed an old fashioned cookout, sitting on blankets or chairs next to fire pits. It was fantastic evening, capping a fun and memory filled day.

Solange tried the SPAM, and after smothering it in beans, agreed it was a fine meal. The s'mores were the highlight of the night.

Everyone opted to sleep at the camp. It was late, and the seminary would be cold. There were more than enough beds around. Kids and adults scattered between the two king beds, pullouts, and couches in the RV's, as well as the four rooms in the Plaza.

Todd sat next to Emily by the fire after everyone was gone.

"And just like that, we're alone." Emily said to her husband, holding his hand next to the dwindling fire. "Are you ready to start our new adventure tomorrow?"

"I'd like to think we've been on an adventure for a few months." He chuckled back.

"Yes, but tomorrow we are getting to Hanover, at least I hope we get there tomorrow. Anyway, that was your plan, get to Hanover and start a life. Tomorrow we'll be there." She pulled their clasped hands towards her mouth and kissed the back of his.

"I know. Tomorrow is the start of a new life." They sat by the fire, talking, and enjoying the quiet of each other's company before walking into an RV and the last remaining bed.

38

Sal left his meeting with Peter and walked to his apartment across the park. He swallowed his favorite mixture of pills and vodka, and he passed out. He awoke from his stupor as the sun was going down. The reds, oranges, and yellows were a beautiful scene outside of his west facing window. There was a small balcony at the front of the apartment, more of an awning than a balcony. Sal opened the window, unzipped his pants, and urinated. It was one of his favorite things to do, pee straight onto the New York City street. He felt the warm temperature outside, and left the window open to let fresh air into the tiny room.

He looked at his stash of food and grabbed a can of beef stew. The can had a pull top, and Sal ripped the ring to expose his dinner. He enjoyed eating cold stew from a can. It reminded him of his early days in construction, when he kept cans of stew in his truck on job sites. It was a time before he met his wife, before his kids, when he earned cash bonuses for putting up the most drywall or framing out the most rooms. Cold soup reminded Sal of the days when his wallet was fat.

He sat in his chair and stared at the sinking sun. Sal picked an apartment looking straight down 71st street, unblocked by high rises. He liked to watch the sunsets each night, when he was coherent enough to see them. The west facing apartment also minimized the stench from Central Park.

After the sun went down Sal decided to go back to the camp and meet the new people. He put on his coat and shoes, and walked towards 59th, crossing the park on one of the old pedestrian sidewalks. As he approached the east corner of Central Park South he saw the campfires, smelled the food, and heard the laughter. He paused, assessing the situation before he made his entrance. There were a lot of people. Sal felt uneasy. He could intimidate Ahmed and the women, but there was that tall older man, Sal could not remember his name, and there appeared to be at least one other guy. There were a lot of kids and women too.

It looked like a party, fire pits blazing, people laughing and talking. Sal was reminded of how his life used to be and the parties he had at the shore. He stood in the dark and watched. Sal was aware of his current reputation. In a bizarre act of kindness he decided not to spoil the party. "Let them have their fun." He mumbled. "I'll come back tomorrow for some breakfast, meet the new neighbors." He chuckled to himself, "meet the new neighbors." He liked that line.

Sal stayed for another ten minutes, enjoying the scene as the little kids toasted their marshmallows in the fires. The last time he saw them, they were frail and weak. The New York group had four good meals in their bellies and renewed energy. "It looks like the gravy train has pulled in tah' tha station." Sal thought to himself. "I won't have to hide food. I can just eat all of theirs. People will bring things to the table for me, instead of me havin' to find it myself." He turned and walked back to his apartment. "Enjoy your last night of solitude, Sallie, tomorrow you join the group." He whistled as he made his way back to his studio.

When Sal got to the apartment, he was bored. When he was bored, he drank and took pills. He used to smoke things, but he ran out of those types of drugs long ago. Sal mixed different combinations of pills with Vodka, Goldslager, or whatever he could find. An hour after he walked through his door, he was looped and laughing at nothing. He sat back in his recliner giggling. His laughter filled the studio and echoed out of the open window for 20 minutes before Sal Torvale passed out for the night.

Sal picked the west facing apartment because he enjoyed sunsets, and because he did not like morning sun through his window. He slept late, another benefit of his new life. Today his eyes opened at 6am because the window he left open had his room temperature in the 40's. Sal stood up, peed out the window, shut the window, and curled on his large leather sofa under several blankets. He popped a quick pill to stave off the headache he felt forming, and drifted back asleep.

His eyes opened again at noon. It was still cold in his apartment, and he did not have wood for a fire. Sal sat up on the sofa, letting the covers fall onto the floor. He was fully dressed. He rubbed his forehead and eyes and looked at his watch. "Let's go see if the new neighbors have a decent cup of coffee." He chuckled again at his new neighbors line. Sal stood, steadying himself by placing his hand against the wall. When the room finished spinning, he made his way towards the apartment door.

It was a solid fifteen minute walk to the campsite from Sal's apartment. He used the time to shake out the cobwebs lingering in his brain. Whatever pills he mixed, he could never remember the next day, had been a brutal cocktail. They knocked him out. He was still groggy. He was looking at the ground when he walked right off the curb onto Fifth Avenue. Sal stopped. The RV's were gone. The trailer was gone. There was a small SUV on a car flatbed sitting where the RV's used to be.

"Holy smokes, Sallie, what have you gotten yourself into now?" He panicked. He looked around frantically for the RV's, thinking that if he looked back and forth a few times, they might appear. Piles of trash, neatly stuffed into old cans, were all that remained. Ashes lay in the spots where the fire pits burned brightly the night before.

Sal walked around the empty campsite. He looked to the spot where he and Bernie parked his car. It was still there. He ran over and noticed a piece of paper stuck under the windshield wiper.

He pulled the paper from under the wiper and looked at it: "Hanover, N.H. Highways 95N to 91N to Norwich, VT Exit"

"What the hell is this supposed to mean?" He roared angrily.

"I helped those people survive for six months and they leave me a cryptic damn note? Are they out of their goddamn heads?" Sal dropped the paper on the ground while he thought. "Okay, Sallie, let's get things under control." He walked over and sat down on the steps of the Plaza Hotel. He put his head in his hands and rocked. He burst into tears, crying uncontrollably. "You really did it this time, Sal. You really screwed up. This is like losing the house all over again. You messed up bigger this time." He began to scream. "God dammit, why did this happen? Why can't you do things right?" He rocked back and forth crying and screaming. Suddenly he stopped and lifted his head.

"Stay calm, you can figure this out." His head was fuzzy, still fighting through the drug haze. "They left, but they gave me a note with directions. I can just follow them when I want to go." He looked around the campsite again, hoping there might be something else. Sal was alone. The RV's and people were still gone.

He became enraged again.

"I was bored with these people anyway." Sal said to himself. "I didn't need them, they needed me. I can do better without extra mouths to feed and that stupid seminary. Find the silvah lining." He thought. Sal stood and used his sleeve to wipe the tears from his face and the snot from his nose. He walked down the steps to his car. He turned the key and the engine zoomed to life. He peeled out of the parking spot next to the plaza, leaving thick black tire marks as he headed back to his apartment and his sanctuary.

The piece of paper Sal pulled from his windshield blew down Fifth Avenue.

Three weeks later Sal was in a parking garage to siphon fuel into his car. He tried to open his gas flap, repeatedly pushing a button on the dash to pop the latch. When it would not open, he walked to the back of his car to inspect the flap. As he wiped dirt and grime from the car, he noticed a smiley face along with an A and P etched into the paint. As much as he tried, Sal could not pry it open. Antonio had glued that tank flap shut the night of the cookout, sealing the threads of the gas cap below for good measure. The teen left his initials to let Sal know who had done the deed, a final insult from the people who left Sal behind.

39

Bernie gave her last service in her beloved, New York, seminary at 10:00am. She did not expect people to attend, but the entire tribe was there. She was touched by their gesture, giving a brief homily about Noah and the great flood, comparing the RV's to her personal rainbow. God's sign for her to leave the old world behind for the new one He created. The adults cried. The kids were restless.

The tribe divided between the RV's by 10:45. Ahmed volunteered to drive the RV without a trailer, and Todd sat behind the wheel of the RV pulling the storage locker. Todd honked his horn twice, and there was a loud cheer from the cabin. The vehicles pulled away from the seminary and were across the GW bridge towards their new life before Sal's eyes fluttered open at noon.

Todd was awarded the "girls only" RV with Bridget, Wendy, Casey, Meredith, Avery, Solange, Kelly, and Emily. It was a peaceful vehicle filled with coloring, crafting, and a princess movie. Ahmed's RV was the "boys rule mobile." Loud music, wrestling and video games were promised. Jamie and Peter loved the action of the boys' RV. Melanie lost the coin flip with Solange, as did Bernie with Kelly. They sat on a sofa in the boys' car. Antonio sat next to them. He was tired, and not ready to join in the fun.

"Let me know if you need to stop, otherwise, Hanover or bust." Todd's voice crackled through a walkie talkie.

"The boys are already screaming. I might need a cold compress on my forehead in about a half hour." Ahmed shot back.

"We should think about stopping in a few hours, maybe on the other side of Hartford, Connecticut. We'll grab lunch and walk around. Talk to you then." Todd accelerated out of New York.

"Good riddance." Solange proclaimed as they left Manhattan.

Book Three

Brad Manuel

40

The Dixon brothers walked from their childhood home on Choate Road to Webster Cottage. It was in the low 40's. The road, thawed to the pavement in several spots, did not re-freeze over night. The sun was up, and the sky was clear.

It was a beautiful late winter day in Hanover, New Hampshire.

They stomped their feet on the mat outside the cottage, and opened the mudroom door to a house busy with activity and conversation. Rebecca was showing Craig how to make the beds, and explaining to him that it was "required" at the cottage. Craig nodded, but the look on his face said "really? Every day?"

Matt and Greg were in the kitchen laughing. John waved good morning to Craig and Rebecca, hung his coat on the coat rack, put his shoes in the boot bin, and walked back to see what the laughter was about.

"What's going on back here?" John gave Greg a hug. "I still can't believe we found you safe and sound. I bet you're in better shape than when we dropped you at Hightower this summer."

"Good morning, Dad. Coffee is hot in the pot. Squirrel hash is in the oven." Greg's cheeks were red from laughter. "Matt was telling me about all the things you fed him. You know, before Matt kind of took over the cooking."

"You mean the month of tuna mac? Is that what you're laughing about? Me keeping you alive?" He scoffed in mock anger towards Matt.

"Month? Really, Dad? You think it was just a month of tuna mac? If I see another can of tuna mixed into macaroni and smothered in Italian dressing..." Matt could not contain his smile.

"Well, it's what we had, and I changed up the pasta when I could. There was tuna spaghetti, and tuna rotini, and tuna penne. There were a lot of tuna pasta's. That's how I kept it fresh." He shook his head as he poured his coffee. "And you make fun of tuna mac but say nothing about squirrel hash? That's not fair."

"Squirrel hash? Oh man, I was hoping it was going to be squirrel hash! Did you crack the eggs on top?" Paul walked into the kitchen and poured a cup of coffee.

"I did. Should be ready in a minute. I have the bread sliced to put in the oven." Greg replied. The kitchen smelled delicious. It was warm from the heat of the stove. "So what's on tap for today? I assume we need to get ready for visitors. How many did you say exactly?"

"Twenty, twenty people, ten kids, ten adults." John said through a sip of coffee. "We are going to need a lot of trout and squirrel."

"That won't be a problem." Hank said as he walked into the room. He smelled the air, "Squirrel hash, nice." He gave a nod to Greg.

"Does everyone know about squirrel hash? Am I really that out of touch with the new world?" John held his arms out on either side in confusion, a paper cup of coffee in his hand.

"We should block off the road at the Lebanon exit, put signs up so the RV's go through Lebanon. We need the supplies and RV's here, not at the bottom of Wheelock. It will be tough to turn those big vehicles around if they make it to Norwich and across the bridge. I will follow you with the jeep, and we can park the suburban across the road, put an arrow on the side to show them the way, leave a note." Matt watched Greg open the oven and pull out a lasagna pan to rest on a wood chopping block. The pan contained potatoes and squirrel meat mixed with vegetables. Eight sunny side-up eggs sat on top of the mixture. Greg popped the bread into the oven.

John's mouth watered. "Todd and I have two way radios. They should have a range of 25 miles or more, but with these mountains, who knows." He stopped. "I'm done talking until I eat some of that hash."

"Squirrel hash," Greg corrected.

The addition of John, Craig, and Matt made eating in the kitchen cramped, but the new Dixons were a welcome presence. Perhaps it was because Greg spoke so often of his family, but the change from Greg and Rebecca just a few months earlier, to a kitchen full of people seemed natural.

"We need to split up and attack the chores separately. Should we just volunteer? Are we going to follow a leader here? How does this dynamic work? " John was used to being in control. He did not want to step on toes. Hank was older, Paul was his twin.

Hank understood John's dilemma. "I have heard a lot about Craig's fishing. Too much about Craig's fishing." He looked at Greg. "I wouldn't mind taking him over to the trout club and seeing if we can catch a few fish for dinner tonight." There was a pause while Hank waited for Craig and John to respond.

"Craig, you up for a morning of fishing with your Uncle Hank?" John asked his youngest. "You have to provide for the entire group. It might take a while."

"Not the way we're going to fish. We'll be back by lunch with twenty fish, easy." Craig threw up a hand for Hank to high five.

"Paul?" Hank asked. "Do we need to get a giant Weber grill from the hardware store?"

"We have one of those, don't worry about it." John cut in before Paul could respond. "A few bags of charcoal would be great if we can get them."

Paul looked at Rebecca. She kept meticulous account of their food, fuel, and supplies.

"We have charcoal in the dorm next door. Greg and I hit the Home Depot and Walmart in Lebanon, and I brought some from Concord. There are 27 bags of forty pound regular and 31 bags of the self starting five pound bags." Rebecca rattled off the stats between bites.

Paul turned back to John. "We're good."

John stared at Rebecca for a second.

"My parents owned a grocery store. I'm used to keeping inventories in my head. It's just a thing I do." She explained.

Paul continued. "Why don't the rest of us figure out the sleeping arrangements. It's still cold at night. We need rooms with fireplaces. We have two bedrooms upstairs, and we can use the study and bedroom at our old house. How many singles do we need?"

"We have to find other houses, close houses with fireplaces that are free of bodies. The RV's use propane for heat, and I'm not sure we should rely on them as an option."

Matt looked at his brother. "This squirrel hash is crazy good. When did you learn to cook?"

"We've been working with him." Hank replied. "He's a great student, and since he's the one who is catching almost all of the game, he wanted to start cooking it too. You should have tasted the roasted squirrel he made the day we arrived. He is a fantastic prairie chef."

"They taught me about herbs, pairing things together, and well, using wine. Rebecca and I didn't use wine in our cooking. The squirrel hash was my invention. I mixed potatoes and squirrel one night, added vegetables the next morning, and voila, squirrel hash."

"Well it kicks ass." Matt told him.

"He's a natural, that's for sure." Hank forked the last bite into his mouth. "Craig and I will head out in a few. Greg has to check his traps.

Rebecca has to tell us about the weather for the next few days."

"Sunny and 50's during the day, mid thirties at night. I don't see any storms for the next three days." She said quickly.

"Okay," Hank continued. "One of you can come with me and Craig. We'll follow you to the Lebanon exit so you can leave the suburban there, and we'll drive you back to the bottom of the hill. The rest of you can find bunk beds to put upstairs, and locate more homes to use for sleeping. I would suggest checking the houses on this street that haven't been renovated. We aren't looking for a place to live, just to send people to sleep each night." Hank looked around the table. "Sound like a plan?"

There was consensus around the room. "How was that for planning a day without naming a leader?" He asked John. "I hope the rest of the people you've rounded up are as reasonable as we are."

"You know what? I think they are. There is one guy that might be a problem. A drug addict. I did not get to meet him. The rest? Nice, hardworking, honest people who understand the situation we are in and want to move ahead and build a life, at least for the most part."

"I have a question." Craig chimed in unexpectedly. "Can Greg come with me and Uncle Hank? I haven't seen him in a long time, and want to spend some time with him."

"You got it little brother. You and I can drive in the Jeep together behind Uncle Hank. I was going to ask the same thing." Greg told the white lie to make his younger brother happy. "I can show off my driving to you."

The day was set into motion. Hank, Greg, and Craig put on boots and warm weather gear for the walk down to the cars. While they got dressed, Rebecca made a few signs and arrows on white paper to direct the RV's towards the correct exit.

As the fishing party said goodbye, Greg gave a nod to Rebecca. They exchanged smiles. She was sitting at the table with her computer print outs, double checking her weather calculations. "See you when we get back. Don't let my brother push you around." He said to her before the door shut.

"Greg Dixon, in all the time you've known me, have I ever given you the impression I am a person who can be pushed around?"

"No, ma'am." He said with a smile. "I guess I should say, please go easy on my brother and father."

"I will, and I'll see you when you get back. We have a busy day." She looked down at her work.

Greg shut the door, grinning as he always did after talking to Rebecca.

"Okay, Craig, here's the deal. You can't show Uncle Hank up too much. Try to let him get a few before you really pour it on." Greg put his arm around his younger brother.

"Hey, now. Let's not forget who caught the first fish up at the trout club. It wasn't you, Greg." Hank said defensively.

"I understand." Craig looked at his older brother and nodded with a smile. They walked towards Wheelock Street and the steep hill down to their vehicles.

Rebecca sat at her table focusing on her weather charts. She had a few projects going, but did not like to divide her concentration.

Matt moved from the kitchen to the dining room to talk to her. He looked at the charts and calculations taped to the walls and realized he was out of his depth.

"Is all of this yours or is some of it Uncle Paul's?" Matt asked Rebecca. He was not yet aware of her advanced intelligence.

"We work on some of it together." She said, turring around in her chair. Rebecca made a vow, never put work ahead of conversation with friends. She used to sit in the library at school and be upset when a person interrupted her, annoyed that she was being pulled away from her figures. She did not regret her past behavior, but decided to change going forward.

"That's a lie. I don't understand half the stuff she's doing." Paul yelled from the kitchen.

Rebecca blushed. "Well, I guess it is mostly mine, but Paul helps with some of it."

"Lie." He yelled again.

"So what is all this? I heard about where we should live, is that what all of this is about? Calculations about deciding where we should live?"

"Some of it. I figured out the best places to live pretty quickly. We are refining which place is best based on how easy it will be to get there, and what things will already be at the location. f we decide to move to Iowa, which we aren't, but let's say we are moving to Waverly, Iowa, you'd expect to find seeds, crop seeds, fields cleared for planting, irrigation systems, etc…. What is something like that worth to us? How does that factor into our calculations? Should we accept twenty extra days of winter in exchange for cleared fields? Should we move to a lower January average temperature if it means we don't have to find and haul corn and wheat seed? I've been trying to assign weight to those types of variables."

"Uh huh." He said, nodding his head, but not understanding the formulas. He grasped the concepts, but not the math behind her work. "How old are you?"

"I'm 13." She kept her chair turned around and attention on him.

"And you're in what grade?" Matt pulled his eyes away from the graphs to look at her.

"I'm not in any grade anymore, but I would be a freshman in college right now. I don't know where I would be, but I was starting last Christmas."

"She was coming to UC to be in my medical program." Paul yelled from the kitchen.

"No, I wasn't, but I did get accepted early at Cincinnati." She turned towards the kitchen. "Thank you, Paul." She yelled to him.

"Okay, none of this makes sense to me. Not the charts, and not that you are only 13 and were already in college, but in the grand scheme of the last year? I guess nothing surprises me anymore." Matt pulled out the chair next to her. "Can you teach me some of this? I'm not saying right now, but down the road? Just the weather." He stuttered while pointing to the weather charts. "I mean, if it's not too much trouble. I don't want to hold you up or anything."

"You couldn't if you tried." Paul said from the doorway. He came into the room to get ready for the day. "If I didn't hold her up, you won't either." He went passed them into the living room.

Rebecca laughed at Paul. "Of course I can. It's a good idea to have two people who can predict the weather. I'm not using many variables, just barometric pressure and temperature. Anyway, yes, it would be great to work with you."

Matt continued to look at some of the paper on the table. "What's all of this?"

"Well, depending on where we decide to go, I have recommended items we will need to take. The length of the list is a factor in the location we choose. I know, it's kind of a chicken and the egg thing, but that's what you're looking at right now. If we go to Key West we need a lot of things, which actually hurts our chances of picking Key West as a location."

"Let's start with the weather." He said to her. "I understand the weather."

John walked into the room drying his hands with a towel. "Okay, are we ready for a fun day of house and bed hunting?"

"If we decide to put the kids upstairs, I say we use mattresses. Hanover is not our long term destination. I'm not busting my back, literally, to move bunk beds upstairs when four year olds can sleep on mattresses." Paul stated.

"There are single beds up there already, one in each room. We never moved the wood frames, just stacked around and on top of them. All we need are mattresses. An adult can sleep in a single. We'll put mattresses on the floor for their kids."

"Done." John agreed. "Where can we get mattresses?"

"The building next door was a sorority. There are at least twenty mattresses ready to be brought over here." Rebecca told him.

"I guess that leaves house hunting." John said, relieved he would not be moving bunk bed frames.

"Why don't you and Rebecca find houses while Matt and I check the traps. Matt can relieve Greg of some of the burden if he knows where the traps are. We might check them twice a day when the new people get here. We'll need a lot of food."

"I'm up for that." Matt said enthusiastically.

"We can throw a few lines in Occom Pond on our way back, see if we can grab a few fish and help out the fishing party." Paul told him. "I doubt the holes have frozen over."

Matt gave a thumbs up as he put on his new boots. Rebecca gave him a pair out of her stash. Craig and John wore the same style.

"Looks like you're stuck with me." John told Rebecca.

"We'll be done and back in the warm cozy house first. We win." She said, getting up from her chair to prepare for a walk around the neighborhood. "We broke into all of the homes for food. We looked in kitchens and avoided bedrooms for obvious reasons. Every house on Choate and around Occum is unlocked. Do we have a plan for previous occupants?" Rebecca could do a lot of things, but disposing of a dead and decaying body was not one of them.

"Let's cross that bridge when we come to it. Maybe we will get lucky and find an empty house with five bedrooms with fireplaces. We can use the first floor dens with fireplaces in houses that have bodies. We aren't staying in Hanover for the long haul. We just need a few rooms we can heat with wood and have space for a mattress."

John looked at the ceiling, a habit he had when he thought. "Let me see, how many bedrooms do we need? Melanie can sleep with her three kids in a room upstairs. Todd and Emily can sleep at our old house in the bedroom with their kids. Bernie or Kelly can sleep upstairs with the three kids from New York." John paused and was about to suggest that Rebecca take notes, but when he looked down, she was back in her chair, writing what he was saying.

"How many people are there?" She asked him.

"We have Avery and Meredith, two teenage girls who can share a room. Paul, Hank, and I can stick to the study." John paced while he thought. "The rest of the people are singles; Ahmed, Kelly, Solange, Peter, Jamie, and Sal." He stopped pacing. "Wow, that means we need seven more bedrooms."

"We might not be the first back to the house." Rebecca joked with him, standing next to the coat rack and slipping her arm in the sleeve of her coat. "Let's confirm the houses on Choate Road, but from your head count and the rooms I know are available, we should be fine."

"What do you mean confirm? Don't we need to check?" John asked.

"I don't know what you think Greg and I did this fall, but it wasn't all fun and games. I know the streets and homes around this cottage like the back of my hand. We arrived in Hanover and tried your suggestion. I don't know what is up with your old house. It's cavernous in every room except the bedroom and den. We couldn't live in that house if we tried."

"Now that you mention it, we did wear a lot of sweaters growing up." John went to the coat rack, slipped on his coat, put on his new boots, courtesy of Rebecca, and walked out the door. John kept the two way radio turned on and strapped to his belt in case Todd arrived early.

"So Rebecca, tell me about yourself." John said as they walked the few feet to Choate Road. "How did a nice girl like you get mixed up with my son?"

Rebecca had been around adults her entire life, teachers, tutors, professors, people who came into her life because of her talents. She was confident around older people, and comfortable speaking with them on their level. It did not occur to her to view John in any other way but as an equal. She told him the whole story, everything, her life, her parents, meeting Greg, coming to Hanover.

John barely said a word. He understood why his son was so taken with this girl. She was extraordinary in the truest meaning of the word.

John also noticed that Paul and Hank already deferred to her for advice and information. She rattled off charcoal inventories, weather predictions, and models about their new colony site with ease and surety. Despite his desire to lead the new tribe, this young girl seemed to be the natural choice.

"I'm sorry about your parents." John snuck in during a break in her story. "Greg lost his mother, my wife, at about the same time. I lost my parents a few years ago, but it's not the same as losing them at the age of 13, and losing both parents at the same time none the less. I'm sorry."

"I loved them, and they will always be with me. I was sad, but I understand, this is how it is. They are gone, I can't change it, I have to move on, so I do." They were two houses down from the family house on Choate road confirming one last bedroom. Two of the houses on the street were vacant and provided a master bedroom and a den with fireplaces. Two other houses had dens with fireplaces, and occupants on the second floor. "Greg was devastated about his mother. I know he's still sad he didn't get to say goodbye, that he wasn't there." She paused. "You know she is the reason we made it through the winter, right?"

"How do you mean?" John asked.

"If she hadn't dragged Greg on that tour of Webster Cottage, hadn't insisted that he receive culture while he was on vacation up here, instead of letting him just rot his brain, well, he would not have known or remembered about the cottage, and we would have struggled in some other house. We were living in the den of your old house. We checked all the homes on Occom Pond, and were coming back from a failed visit to a real estate office, when he suddenly remembered Webster. He thanked her right then, looked up at the sky and thanked her."

They stood in the vestibule of the last house as Rebecca told John the story. His eyes filled with tears.

"Anyway, it's a nice story, and I thought you would like it. Your wife helped save our lives. A lot of people did. My parents, you, your wife, all the influences we've ever had helped two young kids live through a Hanover winter alone and without power. Your wife, she put the roof over our heads."

John was moved. "Thank you, you're right, it is a nice story, and one I doubt I would have heard otherwise."

She leaned forward and hugged him, partly because she could tell he needed a hug, and partly to thank him for being Greg's father. He hugged her back, tightly. John said through tears and with all the sincerity in the world, "thank you, Rebecca, for keeping my son alive. Thank you for keeping him alive for me."

"We saved each other, we really did." Rebecca confessed. "How was a 13 year old girl going to survive a winter by herself? I had as much of a chance as a 14 year old boy. Together, we thrived, alone, we probably barely survive. Greg saved me as much as I saved him." She released her hug. "Whatever or whoever is up there looking out for me, they sent Greg to my house last fall. The odds of him picking that exit? But he did, and we made it."

"Yes you did." John told her, "yes you did." He wiped his nose and eyes on the sleeve of his coat until he saw a tissue dangling from Rebecca's hand. She pulled it out of her pocket and handed it to him. He looked at her with confusion, and accepted the tissue "where did you? Um, thank you."

"I like to be prepared." Rebecca smiled.

John blew his nose and wiped his tears. "I guess you do." He gave her a quick squeeze on the shoulders and kissed her head. "Let's finish finding a room for our new clan, and figure out where we go from here."

They went into the last house and where Rebecca said there was a den on the first floor with a fireplace. Even she was surprised when it had a couch with a pull out queen bed. To give themselves options, they confirmed the final bedroom with a fireplace upstairs. The last house on the block was also vacant, providing an extra bedroom and den.

"Let's cross off the two houses with bodies, and stick to the four houses that are empty. People can double up in a house as long as they have their own rooms." They stood on Choate Road in front of John's childhood home. "We'll park the RV's out here so people can use the water and bathrooms. I think Choate road is going to work."

"It will take a lot of firewood to keep these houses warm at night." Rebecca thought about their current supply. "We're fine for tonight, but as the stay extends, we are going to have to gather firewood from all the houses around town. There is plenty of fuel, we just have to find it and get it to these houses."

"Hard work is not a problem. People will gather the wood tomorrow." He looked at her. "That's what our life is now, hunting and fishing for food, gathering fuel to cook and keep warm."

"At least we know where we can find all of it, that's more than half the battle." They turned and walked to the Cottage. Greg stood at the top of the street and waved to them.

"How'd we do? Are we all going to be crammed into the cottage?" He shouted curiously.

"Only if wood becomes scarce, otherwise, we should be good on rooms." John yelled back to his son.

"Either of you want to walk to the golf course with me?" Greg thought he still had traps to check.

"Paul and Matt are taking care of it. You are off duty." John lowered his voice as they drew close enough to Greg to speak normally.

"I had Uncle Hank drop me off at the bottom of the hill so I could check for animals. As long as I'm here, let's walk to the pond and throw lines in the water. I have the bait in my pocket. Come on, Dad, let's show Uncle Hank and Craig how it's done."

"I'm game." Rebecca told him. "Come on John, when was the last time you got to fish with your son?"

"It's been what, 10 months since we've gone, Greg?" They turned around and walked down Choate Road toward Occom Pond. They followed the path Greg blew clean of snow and ice. As the pond came in view, they saw two figures already standing next to ice holes.

They made their way to the water and said hello to Matt and Paul. Uncle and nephew had two rabbits and three squirrels from the traps, along with five white perch and bass from the pond. Today was a good day for food.

"We cleaned the animals next to the fishing hole and used the guts to chum the water and for bait." Matt explained to his father. "It's a great system, and one I find hard to believe my brother developed."

Greg punched him on the shoulder. "Necessity is the mother of invention." Greg told him.

"What are we going to do with all the excess fish?" Matt asked. "Do you have a smoker?"

"We do, but we can pack it in snow, put the animals and the fish we don't need in ice in the fridge on the back porch. The low temperatures, the fact that we keep it out of the sun, means we can store meats in there for two days if needed." Paul explained. "Smoking the meat limits our cooking options. Unless we need it to travel, we hunt, ice, eat."

They stayed at the ice holes talking and fishing for another half hour, pulling a dozen fish from the pond. They decided they had enough for lunches and dinners for the next two days. They packed the meat and fish in snow, and headed back to the cottage.

It was warm out, hitting the upper 40's before lunch. Streams of melting snow passed by them and under their feet as they walked up the incline of Choate Road. "We may not have snow to use for packing in a few weeks." Matt said to his uncle. "Smoking or curing will be the way within a month."

"Or we eat what we kill immediately." Paul replied.

They fed the dwindling fire in the woodstove and prepared for lunch. The Webster Cottage was filled with happiness and enthusiasm about the future, a welcome change for the last people alive in the northeast.

"If we decide to stay here, or stay for a year, we need to stop fishing in Occom." Greg announced. "We've been pulling fish out of there since fall, and I bet the population is shrinking. Our population is about to grow 4X, and that means we would need four times the fish. There is no way such a little pond can sustain our group with continuous fishing." He spoke expressively with his hand, something he did when he addressed a group. "It's our closest option in the winter, and one I believe should be a last resort. In the summer we'll have to use cars or bikes to get to other places, other lakes. We could even figure out how to properly fish the Connecticut. I bet there are some whoppers in that river."

"We have to leave. It's too cold up here." John told him. "It's just too cold, and we can move to Virginia, gain twenty degrees in average temp, gain a month on either end of the growing cycle, be on the ocean. It makes a lot more sense. Sure, we'll still have winter, but our food and farming options grow exponentially."

"I know, but if everyone gets here and the decision changes, if we decide to stay for a year, grow strong as a group, then make a move, well, I'm saying we need to conserve that one resource and not fish it all summer."

The front door was thrown open. Hank stood in the doorway.

"There is a moose on the green." He panted. "I ran here as soon as I saw it. Craig is behind me with the fish." He caught his breath for a second. "Seriously, there is a big moose walking across the green right now. What do we want to do?"

"That's enough meat to feed the group for a week, longer if we can store it." Paul was already pulling on his boots. "Get the rifles."

"You really want to kill a moose?" Rebecca asked. "They are so beautiful."

"Rebecca," Greg looked at her. "I've been killing five or more rabbits and squirrels every day. You haven't complained once. What's the difference?"

"Size, I guess." She thought about it. "I had a stuffed animal moose when I was younger, and I've always loved moose. I don't care about rabbits and squirrels."

"I like moose too, and if we can get this one, he's going to sacrifice his life for all of us." Hank came back from upstairs carrying two rifles. "Can you imagine the look on Todd's face when he pulls up and we're grilling giant steaks? 'Oh, hey Todd. What's up? You don't have steaks where you are?' This would be huge!" The men ran out the front door.

"You had rifles this whole time? Why weren't you hunting?" John asked his son. "Why are you trapping when you can just shoot things?"

"This is going to sound like I'm a hippie, particularly after the Occom Pond comments, but hunting isn't sustainable." Greg made his way to one of the front windows. He watched his uncles run down Main Street. "I have a finite number of bullets. Learning to shoot a rifle isn't going to help me in three or four years. Learning how to trap, that's sustainable. I can do that forever. We have the guns for times like this, but honestly, we've never had a time like this. I've seen like four or five moose all year, and always from a distance, across the river."

"We had no way to get a moose back to camp if we shot it in the woods." Rebecca chimed in. "Plus, as I have established, I'm opposed to hunting moose."

The door opened. Craig was holding a rope which pulled a purple plastic sled with a large cooler set inside of it. Craig was sweaty and out of breath. "I had to pull," he panted, "this thing," pant, "all the way from the top of Wheelock. There are," He doubled over and put his hands on his knees.

A loud shot was followed by a second report. Everyone ran to their boots and pushed Craig aside. He stood in the doorway trying to catch his breath.

"Hey, there are 13 good sized trout in here!" He yelled as the four people hurried out the door and down Main Street. Craig sat down on the front step, watching his family jog towards the gunshots. "Fine." he muttered to himself. When a third shot was fired, Craig stood and jogged after them.

Craig rounded the corner of the library and saw a circle of people standing around a large animal. Hank and Paul had their arms around each other's shoulders sporting grins. Craig made his way to the circle and asked the obvious question. "What do we do now? How are we going to get this thing back to the cottage? It's bigger than a car."

His question wiped the smiles from his Uncle's faces.

"Let's get the snowmobiles, try to pull this thing somewhere so we can string it up and clean it. We have to move quickly, I don't want the meat to spoil." Hank spoke to Paul and Greg. They were his hunting partners for the last several months. "We need a lot of plastic tubs filled with snow or ice. We should pack the excess meat and freeze it immediately."

"Rebecca," Hank pointed to his other teammate. "Can you find a book about butchering a moose? Maybe we can use it as a guide, get all the meat we can off of him."

"John, Matt, and Craig, you take care of the fish, make lunch, and help us when you're done. I think this is going to be an all afternoon exercise, but worth the effort when we get the meat stripped." He slapped Paul on the back. "Oh, man, look what we got brother. Look what we got."

"Obviously this comes at a great time. The group arrives later today. We did not need this much meat for the four of us. I swear, someone is watching out for us." Paul looked up as he said the last line. He checked the wristwatch he still wore. "It's 12:15. Let's try to have this done and some steaks cooking by 5pm."

"You know what it is? It's Todd, that lucky son of a bitch. He's supposed to be here today. His luck brought a moose. He's going to eat steak, and through no work of his own. I swear, it's like our grandmother used to say, you can throw him down a well and he'll come up with an arm full of roses." John feigned bitterness as he reminded his brothers of the old family joke.

"Todd's luck, divine intervention, it's all the same right now. Let's get the moose moved and cleaned." Hank clapped his hands, and the group went into motion. Rebecca leaned down next to the moose's head and whispered in its ear. After a pause, she stood and caught up to Greg.

"What did you say to it?" Greg asked her.

"I said I was sorry, and thanked him for his sacrifice. I know I've never done that for your rabbits and squirrels, but, you know, I like moose." She broke away towards the library to find a book about slaughtering large game.

She found a field guide relatively quickly in the stacks of the Dartmouth College Library. She referred to a section on hunting in New England several times over the months to help Greg learn more about trapping, and was familiar with the topic's location. She grabbed a "Big Game in New England" book and headed out to the moose, book open, reading as she went. She bumped into Paul and Hank as she exited the library.

"Okay, you need a big sharp hunting knife, or butcher's knife, or maybe a cleaver." Paul and Hank held up knives. "And a bone saw, some trash bags, and a bunch of rope." They stopped in their tracks.

"I bet we can use a hacksaw, I'll run back. I'll grab a pack of the blades with the biggest teeth we have and pick up the other supplies." Paul turned around and ran home.

"Don't run with the knife!" Rebecca yelled after him.

"It seems pretty straight-forward." She continued with Hank as they walked in lock-step towards the moose. "We should clean it here. We won't worry about a mess, it's far enough away from camp. Anyway, we are going to clean and quarter it." She held up the book and showed Hank the picture. The finished product was two back legs separated, and two front legs separated.

Rebecca was a speed reader. She skimmed the "field techniques" synopsis while they waited for Paul to return with a saw. "We need to find a place to age the meat, preferably a freezer that is around 40 degrees. That's why we are quartering the animal, so we can more easily transport and hang the meat for aging. We need to age it for a week for the best results, but at least 3-4 days to let the meat get tender. Regardless of aging, we have to get it cleaned and out of the open field asap."

Paul came around the corner of the library in a slow trot accompanied by Matt. They arrived at the body quickly, holding up two saws, one big knife, and a giant cleaver. "What's the plan?" He said, panting. "Can we do this?"

"Yes, check out the picture." Hank pointed to Rebecca's book. "It might take an hour, but we can get this done. I'm going to tie the rope to the front leg. Matt, you run it around that tree." Hank pointed to a tree about twenty yards away. "We'll follow the directions."

Rebecca continued to read the procedures, but as Hank had said, the pictures were straightforward. She supervised, and 45 minutes later, the men were bloody and finished cleaning and quartering.

Greg walked up with rabbit sandwiches for lunch. The workers ate ravenously despite the ghastly job they just completed.

"Moose steaks for dinner? You did an incredible job." Greg handed out compliments.

"Not really." Rebecca told him. "We have to transport the legs to the basement of the old house and hang them from the rafters. We get moose steaks in a week." She looked at the men, covered in blood, sitting in the snow eating sandwiches. "You know we still have to skin the quarters, right? We can do that after we hang them up."

"We didn't know that, but we do now. Let's get it to the house and strung up. I bet each of these legs weighs a couple of hundred pounds." Matt responded for the butchers.

"Is there anything we can eat tonight or tomorrow?" Greg asked, hoping they could start eating the meat soon. Even with the large group of twenty five people, it was going to take them a long time to utilize this much animal.

"We can make moose burgers whenever we want. The reason we are aging the meat is to make it tender. If we run it through the hand grinder a few times, it will be fine to eat." Rebecca pointed to a heading *What To Eat First*.

"We have fish for tonight." Hank reminded them. "Let's get this over to the house. We'll chop off pieces as we need, and grill steaks starting next week." He finished his sandwich and stood. He looked down at his clothes. His shirt and pants were covered in blood "Wow, so much for this outfit. Paul, let's walk back and get our snowmobiles and the sled trailers. I bet we can get two legs on each one." He trudged towards the cottage. Paul stood up and followed behind. Both moved slowly, trying to keep their cold, wet, blood soaked clothes from bouncing against their skin.

Greg walked back with his Uncles, telling them about the progress he, Craig, and his father were making with the beds and sleeping arrangements. They had starter logs and pre-made fires along with stacks of wood in each bedroom.

Matt was done with his sandwich. He remained seated in the snow. He turned to Rebecca, "Can I skin it here? I peel it back with my fingers and cut it with a knife, right?"

"That's what the book says. It's easier to do when it's hung up, but yes, you can skin it now"

Matt picked up his knife began to skin one of the legs. It was easy work, and he had the first leg skinned in less than five minutes. He was working on the second leg when the hum of snowmobiles was heard in the distance.

Hank and Paul came around the corner towing large wooden sleds. "Wow, you've already skinned one of the legs? You do nice work." Paul said to Matt.

"I decided we should finish all of the dirty work here." Matt pulled the hide off the second leg.

"Hank, I'll start skinning the other ones, you and Matt can work on getting these monsters onto the sleds when he's done skinning that leg." Paul got off the snowmobile, picked up a knife, and followed Matt's lead.

Hank dismounted and picked up the sharp cleaver. He kneeled in the snow and worked on skinning the last leg.

Rebecca stood a few feet away in the sunlight, reading other sections of the book and learning about moose meat. "Okay, the last thing we need to do is cover the meat in cheese cloth or something like that, I think it's supposed to be a breathable fabric that will keep dirt and insects away." She thought about it for a moment. "I bet a sheet would work just as well, as long as it's cotton. I'll go back, warm up a little, and meet you at the basement." She turned and walked before stopping to face the men again. "And just so you know, I don't think we have the skill, time, or need to keep the hide. I know it seems like we are wasting it, but seriously, it's pretty detailed what we would have to do. Also, John said a dog is coming. I don't believe him, but save the heart and liver for the dog tonight."

The men paused, looked at each other and at her. Hank replied, "I had not thought about it, but thank you. I'm sure Paul would have tried to save the hide."

"Why am I getting picked on?" Paul asked. "What have I done?"

"You know you'd try to save it. You save everything. When was the last time you threw something away?" Hank ribbed his brother.

"Walking away from all of my possessions and my house in Cincinnati counts."

Rebecca left the bickering brothers. She could hear them arguing until she was out of earshot. She rounded the library corner and walked down Main Street towards the cottage. Rebecca found it difficult to judge the passage of time, particularly during a large project like the moose cleaning. Paul said it was 12:15 when they started. She assumed it was around 2pm, maybe later. She was cold, and her feet were wet from standing in the snow. Rebecca hoped there was a pot of hot water for tea.

She arrived at the cottage to find Craig and John hauling a mattress in the door and up the stairs. "This is our last one." They puffed as they struggled up the tight stairwell. "The moose almost done?" John asked her as he moved up the stairs and away.

"I'm meeting them in the basement of the other house with sheets. The meat is ready for transport. I'm sure we'll have to hit the hardware store for hanging supplies." She left them to their work and went into the kitchen. She felt warm air coming from the door as she approached. Greg stood by four large pots of water waiting for them to boil.

"I assume they will want to take baths or clean up a little when they are done." He said as she walked into the kitchen. "No one thinks about the cleanup until they need to."

"We're done. We have to transport and hang the meat for aging. Do you happen to have four pulley's laying round I could attach to the ceiling of your father's childhood basement?"

"Let me see." Greg pretended to look around the kitchen. "No." He smiled at their exchange. "You know, if it were me, I would figure out a way to use a metal pole, move that old fridge and freezer together, place the pole on the tops, and hang the meat that way. You don't want to put pulleys and eyelets in the ceiling. This isn't a long term project. You just need a temporary place to hang the one moose we are going to kill."

"Greg Dixon, you are as smart as you are cute." She gave him a kiss on the cheek. "Can you make me a cup of tea or chicken soup? I am frozen."

"I'll get anything for someone who calls me cute." Greg responded.

"I don't think you're cute, but I'll take some tea too." John walked into the kitchen with a broad smile on his face. His son blushed, and Rebecca made a quick exit.

She went to the building behind the cottage where they stored their dry goods. She quickly found two sets of t-shirt sheets.

"Ah, water for baths." John nodded. "You might just be as smart as you are cute." John patted Greg's shoulders, moving next to him to sit down at one of the tables. "Seriously, I'd love some tea if you are making it." John glanced at the shortwave radio. "It's 2:15. I bet they arrive at around four, maybe later if they drive as slowly as I did."

"Anything left to do?" Greg grabbed three insulated cups and placed decaf teabags in each one. He used oven mitts to move one of the large pots of water to the brick floor surrounding the woodstove, replacing it on the burner with a tea kettle filled with potable water.

"If they have the moose under control, I think we are good. We have firewood and fires made in every room, mattresses in every room, fish for dinner." John let out a sigh. "I have earned a few hours on that comfortable couch. I'm too old to be lugging mattresses around." John sat with his elbows resting on the table and his hands clasped together. He stared out the window, watching Rebecca leave the storage room next door and walk towards Choate Road with an arm full of sheets.

"I like her. I like her a lot." John said out loud. He turned to his son. "You are lucky to have found her."

"We're all lucky I found her, but yes, I am especially lucky to have found her." Greg sat next to his father at the table. "We have a lot of work ahead of us, don't we, Dad." Greg changed the subject.

"Yes we do. Today is more like what we can expect from our new life, finding food, working in fields. I don't know, maybe there are other survivors, and we can grow, but if not, yeah, life might be kind of hard."

"Well." Greg put his hand on his father's shoulder. "I'm glad we're facing it together. We had some tough months, Dad, but we made it." He smiled at his father. "We made it."

They sat quietly until the tea kettle whistle blew. Greg jumped up and pulled the kettle off the stove, pouring water into two of the prepared cups. "I think Rebecca might be a while." He picked up the cups and sat back down next to his father.

"Do you miss Mom?" Greg asked. "Well, I know you miss her, that's a dumb question, but do you think about her? I think maybe it is because I was at school, and then on my own, and I didn't see any of you, but I keep expecting her to walk through the door."

"She's gone, Greg. Believe me. I think about her every day. I roll over to an empty bed every morning, and I wish she were there. I get in bed, and I sometimes still say 'I love you.' But there isn't anyone to hear it anymore. It has gotten easier. Taking care of your brothers, you, it keeps me focused on the good times, and my job ahead."

"I miss her. I think of her at least once a day. I think about her at a meal, or when I wake up a little late, or when I take too long in the bathtub, and I'm like 'Mom taught me better than this.' Not that she was a task master or anything, but you know, I don't want to disappoint her memory."

"I don't think you can, Greg. And you're definitely not disappointing her now." He patted his son's hand on the table. "You're a good kid, and a hard worker. I think you've even lightened up a little bit."

Greg laughed. "I kept telling Rebecca, I'm the serious one, wait until you meet my brothers and father."

"Your mother would like Rebecca." John grabbed his tea. "Now, I'm going to take a well deserved nap." He walked into the other room. "Try to keep things under control while I catch a few winks." John was exhausted. Between driving half of yesterday, staying up with his brothers, and working all morning, his body was done. He set the tea on the table, put his head on the pillow, and was asleep in seconds.

Greg went out of the kitchen through the back door and headed down to the other house to see the moose party.

41

"John? Are you there?" The radio crackled. "John, it's Todd. Are you there?"

The room was dim. John was disoriented as he opened his eyes. "What time is it?" He said out loud. He was on his side, a blanket placed over him while he slept on the couch. He sat up quickly to try and snap out of his haze. He was alone in the cottage.

"John?" The radio crackled again.

John grabbed the radio off of the table, looked at the time, 4:10pm, and pressed the talk button. "Todd? Hey, great to hear your voice."

"John! Where have you been, buddy? I've been calling you for 15 minutes. Did you have something more important to do?"

"I, uh, I've been busy." John was embarrassed. He had been asleep for almost two hours. "Where are you? What's your ETA?"

"We arrived at the Lebanon exit and pulled off about five minutes ago. I waited to hear from you, but got restless. We are getting close to Hanover. It's slow going, the snow is deeper in some of the shady spots, but we should be pulling up in about 10 minutes."

"Great! Go right to the old house. We have dinner caught, and beds for everyone. Talk to you then."

"Sounds good. I hope my bed is ready now. It was a long drive." Todd sounded exhausted.

"See you in a few." John jumped up. He was dizzy as the blood rushed back to his head. He called out. "Greg? Matt? Craig? Anyone?" The house was silent. "Where the heck is everyone?" He walked to the boot bin, pulled on his boots, grabbed his coat off the rack, and went outside. "They must be down at the other house." He mumbled. He turned and started a light jog down Choate Road.

There was smoke coming from the chimney of the big house. John opened the door and heard laughter. Light came from the living room on the left.

"There he is!" Paul announced. "How was the nap?"

Everyone was holding an insulated cup of steaming beverage. The room was warm from a fire roaring in the large fireplace. Paul, Hank, and Matt were in long, waffle knit underwear. There were two pots full of water sitting next to the fire.

Craig, Rebecca, and Greg sat on a couch pulled close to the flames.

"I heard from Todd. He just passed the soccer fields. He will be pulling up in five minutes."

There was silence as the room absorbed the news.

Hank, standing in his underwear next to the fire, spoke. "Well, I guess I have to get dressed to meet the new people." He nodded to Matt and Paul. "You guys want to head up and put some clothes on?"

"Why don't you guys have clothes on?" John asked. "Do I want to know?"

"Because we were covered in moose blood and needed new clothes, but someone's children outnumber the two of us, so we were forbidden from waking their father, who was taking an old man nap. All we could scrounge together were these thermals from the storage van." Paul explained. "Any other questions? You want to hear how I had to clean up in a cold room upstairs because you needed a nap?"

John laughed. "Thank you for your sacrifice. I do feel better." As the men left in their underwear, John addressed Greg, Craig, and Rebecca.

"Okay, now that the muscle is gone, I can work with the brains of the group. We have a giant grill in the U'Haul. We need to get that going as soon as we can and cook the fish for dinner. We can start the fire in the den to give people two places to warm up and congregate."

"I'll walk up the street and get the fish. Uncle Hank will help me with seasoning and other stuff." Craig got up from the couch. "We'll bring the food back."

"Hey, can you grab five boxes of the red beans and rice mix? That will go with the trout and be easy to make. It also has a lot of protein and calories." Greg asked.

"Red beans, trout, seasoning, got it." Craig ran out the door.

"Thank you for letting me sleep. I needed it." John confessed to his son. "I don't even remember falling asleep. I just conked out."

"We're pulling down Choate, just waved to Craig. Where is he going?" A voice asked through the radio on John's waist.

"I'll put more wood on this fire and start the one in the den. You two go and see your family." Rebecca volunteered. She was excited to meet the new people, but also a bit overwhelmed with the idea of fifteen more bodies invading her town.

Two car horns blared, announcing the arrival of the RV's. John and Greg rushed outside and waved. They saw Emily crying in the passenger's seat of the first vehicle. A young woman Greg did not know waved from the second RV. She was blonde and looked to be in her 20's. Every available window had little faces peaking through. The RV's came to a stop, and the side doors opened. People flooded out.

Greg recognized his cousins, but no one else.

"Greg!" Jay and Brian yelled. They ran to their cousin and engulfed him. "We just came from New York City. You won't believe how big that place is, it's HUGE! We saw the Statue of Liberty, and all these buildings." Jay told Greg all the things they saw. It did not occur to the young boy that he should be surprised or amazed to find Greg alive.

"Can I give you a hug to make sure you are real?" A woman's voice said from behind Greg. He turned and saw his aunt, tears rolling down her face. His uncle was next to her. They hugged him tightly. "How did you make it here by yourself? We had given up hope after seeing Baltimore and New York."

"I had a lot of help. Hank and Paul arrived a few months ago. They made it a lot easier." He told them during their tight embrace.

Todd let go and backed up. "Paul and Hank are here? Where?" He looked around wildly.

"There is a lot to catch up on. Let's introduce everyone to Greg. He met a girl on his adventures. She's inside lighting a fire and stoking another. Her name is Rebecca." John gave them a hug.

"I'm sorry I left in such a hurry yesterday. It's great to see you all again." John made his way around the group, shaking hands and rubbing kids' heads. When he met Solange she gave him a large hug and kiss on the cheek.

"It is good to see you again, John. I'm glad you found Greg safe. Would you introduce me?" She walked towards the boy.

"It's great to see you again too. I hope you understand why I left." He did not know why he was asking her forgiveness.

"I understood, but next time, I would love to join you on your adventures." She smiled at him as they walked to Greg. The boy was surrounded by people introducing themselves, patting him on the back, laughing at knowing he was alive.

"Dad, why do all the people act like they know me?" He asked his father.

"Because I talked about you a lot, we all talked about you. Greg, this is Solange, she was a sole survivor as well. We met her in Richmond, Virginia."

Solange ignored Greg's outstretched hand and gave him a hug. "It is very nice to meet you, Greg Dixon. You were missed by your father and brothers." She used his full name, like Rebecca.

"Nice to meet you, Solange." Greg did not know what to do other than return the beautiful woman's hug.

Greg was overwhelmed by the people. They were all around him, young kids, another girl that seemed to be his age, an older girl Matt's age, two older people, two women who were trying to corral the young children. The beautiful woman with a Latin accent trying to talk to him. He tried to listen to what his Uncle Todd and Aunt Emily were asking his father.

Greg looked for Rebecca. He wanted to introduce her to his Aunt, Uncle, and cousins. She was nowhere to be found. He politely excused himself from Solange and walked into the house. He found Rebecca in the study looking out the window.

"Is it as chaotic as it seems out there?" She asked. "We've gone from four to twenty-four in a day."

He walked to her and grabbed her hand. It was sweaty. He could tell she was nervous about the new people. "If it was easier with two, it has to be much easier with twenty-two." He touched her cheek and turned her towards him. "Come on, let me introduce you to my family from North Carolina. You'll like them."

She smiled nervously, but he could tell she trusted him.

"It is going to be better, isn't it." She stated rather than asked.

"Better is a relative term. Easier I'm positive. Better? We'll see how it goes, but we'll see together." She followed him out of the den and into the cool afternoon air.

Hank and Paul arrived with Matt. They were hugging Todd and Emily and crying. Jay and Brian were high fiving, and ran towards Craig when they saw him pulling a sled full of food.

There was confusion after Hank and Paul arrived, as people were introduced and stories of the drive were given. Once people realized they needed the grill to cook dinner, the storage cart was opened and the grill was ignited.

People continued to talk and make their way into the house and the fires. Greg and Rebecca wanted a tour of the RV's, which Jay and Brian were happy to give. Hank and Paul showed off their moose in the basement. When the grill was ready, everyone helped wrap trout in aluminum foil to grill for dinner.

Hank and Avery set up three folding tables in the living room. They instructed the younger kids on how to set the tables with plastic tablecloths, plastic ware, cups, and retrieve folding chairs from racks in the basement.

At 6:00pm the new tribe was seated at dinner. A hush fell over the room as people realized the magnitude of the moment.

Todd stood and held his cup of water in the air.

"Well, we're here, and we have a great meal in front of us. Thank you all for coming." There was a chuckle from the adults who understood the joke. "Thank you for joining our tribe or group or colony, whatever we want to call it. I think we have a great future ahead of us. I don't want to be melodramatic, but let's give thanks to whatever kept us alive and brought us together."

The table let out a cheer.

"And one more thing, just a request, not a command, let's enjoy tonight, tell fun stories, focus on being alive and here. We have plenty of time to discuss the future and the work ahead. We'll have another time to mourn our losses. It's been a long day and a long trip. Let's end it with a celebration."

Todd sat down. Emily was one seat over, Jay in between them. Todd leaned back and over to give his wife a kiss, something they did before every dinner together. "I love you." He whispered. Todd sat up and put his arms around his sons on either side of him. Their journey was not over, but he felt like Hanover was a milestone. The plan he set in motion eight months earlier was finally complete.

Everyone had half a fish and a large portion of rice and beans on their plates. There was wine, fruit punch, goat's milk, and water. As they ate, Solange told John about the previous night's dinner. "We had canned ham and beans. Please do not think I am ungrateful for the meal your brother made for us, but fresh trout is a step up, several steps up from last night."

"I don't know." Antonio cut in. "This fish is okay, but there's something about spiced ham and baked beans. Mmmm, man, the way you got a nice sear on the meat last night? It had some snap to it."

John was meeting the new Antonio for the first time. The gregarious and helpful teenager was very much in contrast to the loner he left the day before. He made a mental note to ask someone what the heck happened in the last day to change the boy so much.

"So you are comparing fresh fish, cooked with herbs on a grill to that meat you ate from a can?" Solange laughed.

"I'm with Tony." Ahmed cut in. "I grew up eating canned ham at least once a month. Eating it last night brought back some memories for me, took me back home for a minute. There are no bones in ham." He pulled a tiny pin bone from his mouth.

"Remember that crab boil from a week ago? Now that was food. Dumping Old Bay into a pot of water followed by dozens of crabs? Man, you can't beat that." Peter looked around the table at the people who did not enjoy it. "Then, the next night, he made Paella using crab stock made from the crab shells and leftover meat." He gave Todd a look. "I'm not saying you fell down last night, but you have to admit, crab boil to processed canned meat? Do I need to keep talking?"

"Look, I'm feeling a little anger towards the dinner last night. I was in New York. There was no food. It was a long day. I didn't have anything to work with. I fed all of you. Come on, ham and beans? That was comfort food, a warm meal for your empty bellies." Todd mock defended himself.

"Have you heard about how my dad fed us tuna mac for like two months?" Craig told the group. "I'll take crab or trout over tuna mac. You don't know what you're talking about until you face a 50th meal of tuna fish, macaroni, and Italian dressing."

Cameron raised his hand. Bernie sat next to him. "You don't have to raise your hand, dear. As long as you don't interrupt, you can speak up."

Cameron nodded. "I ate ten times last month. I counted. Ms. Bernie told me when months started and ended, and she told me it was March 1st, and I counted how many times I got to eat. I'd put a little pencil mark on my wall, really tiny, so no one would see and I wouldn't get in trouble for writing on the wall, and when she told me it was April 1st, I counted the marks, and I ate ten times. Then you all came. I liked the ham, and the meatballs, and this fish, even though I don't really like fish, I'll eat whatever you give me." He turned to Todd. "Thank you Mr. Todd." He lowered his head from shyness. He was a bold four year old, but even bold four year olds get nervous in front of crowds.

Todd, choked up like the other adults, cleared his throat to break the silence. "You are welcome, Cameron. Maybe one night you can tell me what you like, and I'll try to make it for you."

"As long as he doesn't ask for tuna mac." Craig cracked the much needed joke.

They ate and drank until 7:30. Exhaustion soon overwhelmed the children and most of the adults. The adrenaline they had upon arriving was gone, and the efforts of the last few days set into each of their bodies. A few of the kids yawned, despite the two packages of Oreos making their way around the table.

John stood. "I took a nap this afternoon. I volunteer to show people their sleeping quarters. Who would like to go to bed?"

Hands shot up around the table.

Todd's mouth fell open. "You were asleep? That's why you didn't pick up the radio? You were napping?"

John ignored the comment, and directed people towards their sleeping quarters. "Jay and Brian, you two are upstairs, not much of a walk for you. Your parents can start your fire and put you to bed whenever."

"Before we adjourn for the night," John continued. "Let's roll up the plastic tablecloths, and put them in trash bags. I'll take care of the pots in the RV later, and everyone can go to bed. The way we have things set up, Melanie is sleeping with Jacob, Jaclyn, and Casey in the cottage up the street. That's the house Greg and Rebecca used this winter. We have Wendy, Bridget, and Cameron in another room at the cottage with either Bernie or Kelly."

"I'm happy to stay with them tonight." Bernie answered quickly. "Particularly if it means I get to go to sleep right now." She nodded towards Bridget, who was already resting her head on the table with her eyes closed.

"Emily, can you put Jay and Brian down? I'll help John with the other kids." Todd offered. His wife nodded, noting that Jay was almost as asleep as Bridget.

Matt whispered to Ahmed and Avery. "You take the kids, there are enough of us to handle this mess."

Solange picked up Cameron, resting his head on her shoulder. "Let us get this little boy to bed." She told Bernie and John. Todd grabbed Wendy and John picked up Bridget in a similar fashion. Melanie had Casey over her shoulder. The twins, yawning, trailed behind her. Others in the group helped place coats over the children for the brief walk up the street. Greg opened the door and led the way to his house.

Bernie walked next to Greg. "You and that young woman lived up here, alone, for months? How old are you?"

"Rebecca and I make a good team, and work well beyond our age. It was tough, but never impossible." Greg explained.

"I can't wait to hear about your adventures." She said back.

"I'm sure you have a few of your own to share. I only saw a few people die during the rapture. New York City? You had to fight millions for food, water, supplies."

"I saw more than a few people taken." Bernie said gravely. "But I am here, and Todd has asked that we focus on the good tonight."

They came to the door of the cottage. Greg opened it for Bernie, "boots go in that bin. We try not to get muddy or dirty in here." He explained to her. It was his house after all.

The living room fire was smoldering, and the house was warmer than the outside. Greg turned on several lanterns to illuminate the home. He handed Bernie one, and led Melanie up the stairs with another. He showed Melanie, still carrying Casey, her room. He lit the fire for her. The starter log caught quickly, and Greg put a fire screen in front of it for her.

"There is wood in the bin. Unfortunately, you have to keep feeding the fire or it will get cold in here. It won't be too bad, but you won't want to get out of bed in the morning if the fire is all the way out." Melanie nodded as Greg gave her the instructions.

"Is there a way to restart it in the morning?" She asked him.

Greg shined his pocket light on the wood bin and starter log pack in the corner. "Just throw one of those in, paper and all, and you'll be fine. It will still take a minute to warm up the room, but you can curl up while the room heats." He addressed her in a low voice as not to wake Casey. Bernie listened. "These rooms are tiny, colonial, they heat quickly."

Greg gave additional instructions. "I am going to leave the lantern on low in the hallway. There is a bathroom out the back doorway of the house through the kitchen. I can show you each now if you like, or you can find it if needed. I'm sure the kids will wake you up if they have to go. You can show them."

"Let me put the kids down, and then you can take me." Melanie told him. "I want to use it before I go to bed."

Bernie nodded in agreement.

Bernie turned and walked into the other room. Her three roommates were on their mattresses, their fire was roaring. She felt the temperature of the bedroom rising. Solange was finishing with Cameron, making sure the little boy was tucked in.

Bernie followed the adults back down the stairs to see the bathroom. Todd and Solange looked around the house. It was their first time in the cottage.

"It is so clean and organized." She turned to Todd. "Two young children lived here for months?"

"Unbelievable." He agreed.

Greg led Bernie and Melanie to the back of the house, through the kitchen, out the back room, and down the steps to the bathroom. "It's not much, but it's better than the woods." He told them. "When you're in the kitchen, there are two doors. The other one leads to the chicken coop. You'll know right away you've made a mistake."

"You and that young woman have a chicken coop?" Bernie asked.

"We do. It was Rebecca's. She found a neighbor's chickens and coop, you know, after everyone died. We brought them up here with us last fall."

"Unreal." Bernie said out loud.

They made their way back into the house and the living room. Todd placed logs on the fire. "I don't know if you are going to bed or staying up to talk. I restarted the fire for you."

"Thank you, Todd. I think I will sit up for a minute. I want to relax and digest after a long day." Melanie sat down on one of the couches. "Oh my God. This is the most comfortable couch I have ever sat on in my life."

"I know, isn't it? We found that at a house over on the pond. It was a beast to get in here, but worth it." Greg told her. "Rebecca has vowed to take it with us when we leave."

"I agree with her." Melanie replied, closing her eyes and letting the comfort sink into her bones.

Solange was intrigued and took a seat next to Melanie. Her eyes closed as she leaned back into the couch. "Wow." She said to Melanie. "It is just the right depth for your legs, and the cushions are firm yet soft at the same time. It feels wonderful."

Bernie sat down in the third spot. "Even the middle spot feels great." She looked back and forth at Solange and Melanie. "Oh, this is coming with us, and if we can, we're going to find a few more."

Todd knelt next to the fire as it came back to life. He watched the women enjoy the couch. "Seriously?" He said to Greg.

"Uncle Todd, it's the couch. It's crazy. You aren't going to get a turn on it tonight, but when you do? You'll understand."

Todd stood, shaking his head. "Okay, I guess. You ladies need anything else? I am going to go back to my room and collapse."

"We're good." Melanie told him, not opening her eyes. "You can go." She gave him a motion with her hand, shooing him from the room.

"Are you staying here?" Todd asked his nephew.

"No, I'll come back and see what needs to be done. I didn't have that big a day. I mean, I didn't take a two hour nap like my father, but I also didn't drive through snow to get here." He started towards the door with his Uncle. When they got out to the street, Greg asked his uncle a question. "When did you know that Aunt Emily was going to make it? Of all the crazy things to happen, all the luck, all the beating of the odds."

"I know." Todd responded. "We both know. I know this will sound weird, but I knew right away. We were hungry. For some reason that gave me hope. Jay scared us with a flu bug that first week in Raleigh, but honestly, I believed we would survive from day one." He gave his nephew a pat.

"Are you and Rebecca an item? Am I allowed to ask that, you know, like it's high school or something?"

"I'd like to think it's more than a high school thing, but yes, we're kind of an item." Greg stopped. "I haven't really told my dad yet. Could you keep that between us? I mean, I'm not ashamed or anything, but it hasn't come up."

"I have your back, Greg. Don't worry. In this new world we live in, I'm not really your Uncle anymore. I'm your teammate or friend. We are going to rely on each other to survive. I think I can let you decide who and when you tell about your relationships." He waited a second before following up his comments. "So she's pretty special, huh?"

"You'll understand when you get to spend time with her. She's unbelievable. She's smart and funny, and caring." Greg gushed.

Todd was excited for his nephew, and looked forward to getting to know the young woman who had captured Greg's heart.

Greg and Todd looked at the houses on their right and saw fires burning in the windows. "It looks like everyone split up for the night." Greg observed. They continued to the main house, walking into the front room and finding all of the Dixons with Rebecca sitting in front of the fire.

"There they are." John said loudly. "You get everyone tucked in?"

"We left the three women sitting on 'the couch,' marveling at how comfortable it is. Melanie dismissed us."

"That's my couch, and it's coming with us." Rebecca said firmly.

"Relax." Hank said to her. "No one is stealing your couch or leaving it behind. Geesh, you and that couch."

"Is it the most comfortable couch you've ever sat on?" She asked him.

"Yes."

"So you understand why I'm attached." Rebecca turned to Emily for some female support. "Men think they understand, but they don't. Wait until you sit on it."

"I'm intrigued." Emily told her.

There was a pause in the conversation as Greg and Todd pulled up chairs to sit with the group by the fire. It was a large fireplace, and there were several logs burning, kicking off enough heat and light for the semi circle.

Paul broke the silence. "Well little brother. We're all here, just like you asked." He made a gesture with his hand, sweeping it around. "What now?"

"Funny." Todd said back.

"Seriously." Hank replied. "What's our plan? Rebecca has worked on best case locations and travel scenarios. It's early April. We probably need to get to where we want to go soon so we can plant, or build, or plan, or whatever we have to do to prepare for winter. We have to prepare for the current food stores to run out."

"We have two years of food left, minimum. Heck, we might have five years if we stay at less than 30 people." John told him.

"I agree, but it will take at least that long for us to figure out how to feed ourselves. Two growing seasons, two shots at learning how to can and dry cure things, two years at least." Hank explained.

"I can't think. I'm exhausted." Todd announced. "I'm sorry. It's been too long a day, too long a journey. I get it, Hank. We need to make a plan, or more importantly, execute a plan quickly, but tonight is done for me." He stood. "I'm going to bed." He turned to Emily. "Care to join me?"

"I'm always ready to hit the sack." She said goodnight to everyone.

Before leaving the room, Todd turned. "We have 1,000 pounds of moose meat downstairs. I propose we take the week, eat, get better acquainted with the New York crowd, study our options, and make a plan to move out in seven to ten days." He looked as exhausted as he sounded. "I need a week to recuperate from the trip here. I mean, look at poor Hubba, exhausted next to the fire. Two weeks isn't going to make or break us, Hank. We can spare two weeks." Todd took his wife's hand and left the living room. He turned left and walked up the stairs towards the bedroom where his kids were already sleeping on mattresses on the floor. A crackling fire warmed their room.

Emily and Todd quietly undressed and put on warm pajamas. "We made it hon, all of us, can you believe it?" He kissed his wife and climbed into a queen bed with an old four poster wood frame. "All the death and destruction, all the time between last fall and now, all the things that could have gone wrong. We made it to Hanover, as planned, ahead of schedule."

Todd leaned back into the pillow and closed his eyes. He thought he heard his wife respond, but she was too late. He drifted off to sleep instantly.

42

Todd's eyes opened as he heard a whisper. "Daddy, I need to go to the bathroom." The room was bright. Todd was disoriented and confused.

"Huh? What's going on?" He asked Brian, standing next to his bed. After a quick second of thought, Todd realized where he was, and how he could help his son. "Number one or number two?" He asked Brian.

"I have to pee really bad." His son pleaded.

There was a balcony off the back of the master bedroom. The door leading out to the balcony was next to the bed on Todd's side. Todd sat up, the fire was going nicely and the room was warm. He moved his feet to the floor and walked the few feet to the door. It was locked and jammed shut, but with some heavy shoulder leaning, Todd got the door open. Todd reconsidered. They were probably going to collect rainwater or melting snow from the downspouts around the house. If Brian peed on the deck, it would contaminate their water source.

"New plan, let's run to the RV's outside." Todd slipped on shoes. "Can you make it?"

"If we hurry." Brian told him.

"I have to go too!" Jay jumped out of his sleeping bag and put on his coat and shoes. They walked downstairs. Todd looked into the living room. The chairs were still arranged in a semi-circle around the fire, but the fire was out and the room was empty. The house was cold, warmer than the outside, but cold for a house.

The study door was open. Todd saw three empty mattresses on the floor.

"I think we're late for breakfast." Todd told his kids.

"I heard people leave a little while ago. I didn't want to wake you and Mom, but I had to go too bad." Brian told him. "I couldn't hold it."

"Don't ever worry about waking us up." Todd said to them. "It's not an issue. It's kind of our jobs to look after you." Todd opened the door and saw both RV's parked in front of the house. As cold as it was in the house, it was much colder outside. Southern living thinned Todd's blood. He was not prepared for a cold April morning in New Hampshire. His breath blew white out of his mouth.

"Wow is it chilly. Okay, this is going to be a cold bathroom stop. Let's run over to an RV and use the restroom."

The boys scampered ahead of him. Todd jogged behind. He needed to use the facilities too. Each boy, after finishing their business, ran out of the RV and towards the house and the warm bedroom upstairs. Todd was the last to use the toilet. He made a quick exit, opening RV door into the cold morning air.

Todd looked up the street and saw smoke rising from the chimneys of three houses.

"I might actually be the last one up." He mumbled. He was too cold to care, and quickly shuffled back into the house and up the stairs to the bedroom.

The boys were in bed with Emily. They were talking and giggling under the covers, trying to stay warm. "I have to go to the bathroom, but it's too cold." Emily told them.

"It's cold, colder than we've been in a while, but you'll survive." Todd looked at a chair in the corner of the room. There were two bathrobes made of thick fleece neatly placed across the back. "I wish I had seen these before I went." He picked up a robe and held it for Emily. "I believe you are in luck. Here is a robe for you, and it is thick and fuzzy."

She reluctantly got out from under the covers, slipped on her boots and the robe, and left the room. Todd debated whether or not to put another log on the fire when he heard a knock on the door.

"Uncle Todd?" It was Matt.

"Yes?"

"We have breakfast going at the other house. I can take Brian and Jay if you want to sleep in longer."

"Matt, come on in." Todd turned to the kids. "Why don't you two go up with your cousin and get some breakfast. I'll wait for your mother, and follow you in a second."

Matt opened the door and stood in the room next to the fire. The hallway was cold, and he warmed himself. "Everyone is there, and we have plenty of food." He turned to his cousins. "You should get your clothes on and we can go to Greg's cottage. It's pretty neat if you haven't seen it."

Jay and Brian had yet to see the mythical "cottage" and wanted a peak at the legendary abode. They were out of bed and into warm clothes in seconds.

"Be good, and I'll see you in a few minutes." Todd gave a nod to Matt. "Thanks, Matt, I appreciate it. Save me what you can, particularly some coffee."

"You got it. Come on guys." Matt and the two boys bounced down the stairs, passing a running Emily, hurrying to get back to the warm room.

"Get in here so I can shut the door." Todd called to her.

"Why do you think I'm running?" She said, slightly out of breath.

Emily hurried around her husband as he closed the door. Todd examined the room for the first time. There was a sitting bench at the end of their bed. "Let's pull that next to the fire, get warm before we go back outside and up to the cottage."

"I love you." Emily started. "And I realize it's been a while since we've been 'alone,' and while we have an opportunity right now," she paused again, "It's too cold."

"Okay, I wasn't thinking that, but then I was, and now I'm not again. Thank you. I assume we have to be in a warmer climate before we renew our marital relations?" Todd asked.

"At least 60 outside, and inside for that matter." Emily's comment highlighted that is was only in the low 60's in their room.

"Here's what I want to talk about quickly." Todd started, ignoring the other conversation. He sat down on the bench close to the fire. "Ah, it's a lot warmer when you are almost sitting in the fire." He patted the spot next to him, inviting Emily.

"So the way I see the dynamic, at least right now, you and I need to agree about where our family goes. I know that sounds obvious, but what I mean is,"

She cut him off, "You want to make sure you and I are on the same page before we speak to the other Dixon's at which point you want to approach the entire tribe, right?"

"I think so, don't you? I mean, in theory you and I could take the kids and the dog and go our separate way. I don't think we would do that, but if something weird happens, if the dynamic of the group turns into something we don't agree with, well, I want to make sure you and I are good."

She leaned over and kissed him. "We are going to be fine. I will formally state, I don't believe separating from your brothers is a good idea, and I will probably say the same for separating from Melanie and Solange. I cannot speak for them, maybe they want to leave. I wouldn't mind keeping Kelly around so she can take care of Hubba."

"Funny." Todd replied. "I'm starting to think it might be Hubba ahead of me."

"You'd be right some days." She stood. "Let's get some coffee and breakfast before it's all gone." She took off her robe and found her clothes. Emily brought in overnight bags when Todd went up to the cottage. "I have some clothes in here for you. Rebecca said it was going to warm up today, probably be in the high 40's, maybe even mid 50's. Maybe this sweater will work for later." She pulled a half zip cashmere sweater out of a bag and tossed it to him.

Todd sat on the bench, keeping warm by the fire.

"You believe Rebecca now too?" Todd asked her, standing up to take off his pajamas and dress for the day.

"I'm not sure what that means, but yes, talk to her for five minutes, you'll understand. She's working above our heads. She's a fantastic girl, and bright as hell doesn't begin to describe her intelligence. I wish you could have seen Ahmed try to talk quant with her. He was some high flying investment banker, talked about analytics, wanted to know her methodologies. She wasn't rude or condescending, but she politely destroyed him. She started talking about assumptions, parameters, working models, regression analysis, heck, I don't know what she was talking about, but Ahmed didn't either. After a minute, he smiled and threw up his hands in a mock bowing gesture."

"When did all this happen?" Todd appeared to have missed much of the evening.

"You were off making dinner or putting kids to bed. You know I'm the social one. You're always trying to avoid people through projects. I talk and listen." She dressed and sat on the bench by the fire. "Come on, let's go pokey."

Todd pulled on his socks and boots, and they made their way out of the house and to the cottage. When they walked out of the front door they saw John opening the driver's door to an RV.

"Want a ride up?" He waved to them. "We are moving one of these to the Cottage."

"Sure." Emily waved back. She and Todd jogged to the big vehicle. "What's up? Why are we moving it?"

"For the bathroom, we can move and empty these when the bathrooms are full. The port-o-john was fine for two people, a stretch for four people, but not practical for all of us." John turned the key and the engine fired up. "Plus, I think these bathrooms are more comfortable, and the kids feel safer using them."

"Sorry I bailed last night. I was exhausted." Todd said to John, putting his hand on his brother's shoulder.

"I made that drive. I understand. Besides, we have plenty of time to talk. There are expeditions out right now, fishing at the trout pond, checking traps, and finding a place for the kids to play." He looked at them and smiled. "You two are late to the party this morning."

"There better be coffee left." Emily said in a threatening tone.

"There is food and coffee. We have you covered. It's great to have milk and eggs to work with, particularly when cooking for such a large group. It is going to be a challenge keeping everyone fed unless we get to an ocean or find more game." The RV stopped in front of the cottage.

Emily looked out the window. "So this is it, the famous Webster Cottage." She turned to John. "How did Greg figure out to stay here? You have one smart and lucky kid."

"I have no idea. I had to find a house with solar power cells to keep myself going all winter. He and Rebecca lived colonial style. They even have a bathtub. She barely knows how to drive, and yet they brought a grocery van full of food and supplies from Concord, including chickens, and found this old home. They lived pretty well."

John turned the RV off and started to get out.

Todd grabbed his arm. "John, before we go into the house, what kind of long range plans do you have in mind?"

"Today? I'm going to relax a little."

"You know what I'm talking about, come on."

"Geesh, when did you get so sensitive?" John looked at Emily. "Maybe he needs the coffee more than you do."

"There are some mornings." Emily laughed. "Seriously, John. We know the situation. We can't settle in Hanover, but we can't force other people to do what they don't want to do. I'm sure that our family, the big family, can come to a decision on our next steps. How much are we considering the inclusion of outside people?"

"That's the question, isn't it?" John opened his arms in a fleeting gesture. "I'm not prepared to leave some of these people, but you're right, we can't force them to come with us. We can't force them to become farmers or fishermen. Maybe they have better ideas. I agree with you, the Dixon family will stay together."

Emily looked out the window at the cottage again. "I'm not sure the new people aren't Dixons at this point. You know?" She turned to look at her husband and brother in law.

"How about we decide this, we are open and forthright with our plans with everyone. We let the chips fall. I wouldn't call this a secret meeting, but let's limit these types of family only discussions, and try to treat this as an actual tribe." John shrugged his shoulders. "That might be the best way to handle this small a group."

Todd agreed. "Well, my short-term goal is to use our time in Hanover, however long that time is, a week, two weeks, the summer, whatever, to learn to be a tribe. To discover our skill sets, get stronger where we are weak, create a team. I don't like the politics or decision dynamics that might come into play. I am not a coward or spineless with my opinion, but I do not enjoy the discussions on our future when we splinter into groups." Todd paused.

"But you just brought it up with me behind closed doors." John replied.

"I know, and I shouldn't have, you can see how poorly I did it." Todd walked towards Emily and the side door of the RV. "Okay, coffee and breakfast, then let's see what needs to be done."

John sat in the driver's seat. He was not sure what just happened. "I could use some more coffee too, especially after that conversation." Before John jumped out of the driver's door, Jaclyn came in the side door.

"Hi Mr. John, just using the bathroom, if that's okay." She said politely. She was a great kid. John never had a daughter and did not know his nieces. Jaclyn was his first experience with a girl. He was enjoying it.

"That's why I brought it up here." He jumped down and walked around. There was a queue forming at the side of the RV. "Is everyone going to use the bathroom?" He asked.

"Yes." A chorus of children told him.

"Sounds good to me, I'll be inside." John strode passed the line of children and into the cottage for a fresh cup of coffee.

John heard Paul and Todd having an animated conversation in the kitchen. He walked through the living room, waving to Melanie sitting on the couch playing Go Fish with three of the kids. John found his brothers and Emily eating and talking. He entered the middle of the conversation.

"You never went there?" Todd asked.

"The roads just cleared, literally, just cleared this week. Not only did I not think about it, we had no way to get there. Let's try today. If there is anything to salvage, we need to salvage it before the thaw let's more critters into the supplies." Paul sat on a barstool sipping what John guessed was his fifth cup of coffee.

"Paul? Have you moved from that spot in the last two hours?" John asked him.

"I got up to get coffee when no one would get it for me. Does that count?"

"No." John told him. "Where did you not go? What is Todd talking about?"

"The flour company with its headquarters, factory, and factory store across the river in Norwich or White River. We might be able to find flour that will last us a long time." Paul took another sip. "We have to get the Suburban anyway. We'll make a side trip to find it. Can you imagine how much they might have there?" Paul looked over at Todd. "Scones, there might be boxes and boxes of scones mix."

"I don't like scones, too dry. They are like drop biscuits, not a fan." Todd told him. "Did you know I have a pizza oven in the trailer?"

"You have a pizza oven? When were you going to tell me?" Paul set his coffee down.

"I did just arrive yesterday afternoon, so I..." Todd was cut off before he could finish.

"Are there other secrets you've been keeping? What supplies do you have?"

"Well, I took some art from the Metropolitan, you would probably like the Van Gogh I have, and we picked up the Constitution and Declaration of Independence when we were in DC. Oh, and Peter, he's the older gentleman, he has a letter that the President wrote for survivors. It was on the desk in the Oval office." Todd stopped. "Does that sound about right, John?"

"Yeah, I think that's it for the big stuff. We have food and clothes and things like that, but the big things are the art, historical documents, and the pizza oven."

"Hank and I rode bikes across the country to get here. I'm sorry we didn't take more time to stop and sightsee like you did." Paul held up his hand in mock anger. "I'm going to get ready for the day. I'll talk to both of you later." He stomped out of the kitchen towards the bedroom to get dressed. He was sleeping at the old house, but his clothes were still at the cottage.

"Wow, he was so mad he left his barstool." Todd picked at the strata made from eggs, last night's bread, and some kind of sausage. "Where did we get sausage?" He asked John.

"Hank used the grinder on the leftover squirrel and rabbit. He's turned into quite a sausage maker. He was talking about making a bunch of moose sausage." John took another sip. "He's off fishing with a group that includes Antonio, if you can believe it. What did I miss that turned him around?"

"Solange." Emily said through a mouth full of breakfast casserole. She sat at the kitchen table enjoying the brother's conversation. "Tony, that's what he likes to be called, mouthed off to Todd in Spanish. She walked up to him and slapped him right across the face, went off on him in front of everyone. She told him to grow up or get the hell out. She spoke to him in Spanish, whispered into his ear, and he's been the new Tony ever since." She took another bite of food. "She's the big sister he never had, the big sister that would have kept him in line and not let him join a gang." Emily spoke with her mouth full of food. She was hungry. "Tony grew up on the water, his father was a ferry boat captain for New Jersey Transit. He's probably fished his whole life." She took a sip of coffee.

"Wow." John said with a smile. "That woman surprises me every day. Good for her and for him."

"I bet she does." Emily replied with an even larger smile.

"And what is that supposed to mean?" He asked her.

"Nothing, nothing, never mind." Emily put her head down, smiling from ear to ear, continuing with her breakfast.

"Where is Solange this morning?" Todd asked to break the silence.

"She went with Greg and Matt to check traps. Bernie, Peter, and Jamie are talking about finding a better place for the kids to play. With all of the snow, there's no open area. I told them to move some chairs and tables and use a room in the library. It will be cold, but it will be dry and snow free."

"Back to our earlier conversation, it appears we are settling into Hanover." Todd finished his last bite of strata.

"It's a great place, there's no doubt about it. It's beautiful and secure. We have access to water and food, and the climate is fantastic for about five months of the year, but the other 7 months are tough. Twenty-two mouths to feed for seven months on food stores alone?" John stood. "It's just like we said, let's take a break up here, learn to live and work as a tribe. We can decide upon and make a move to our final location later. If we spend a month up here, I think we'll be okay." He put his hand on Todd's shoulder. "I busted my ass to get here. I left a solar powered house on a bay brimming with fish. I've been tortured by the separation from my son, I deserve a few weeks of rest and relaxation."

John looked at Emily. "Would you like to come to the flour factory with us? I don't think we'll be doing that much heavy lifting even if we find a warehouse."

"I'd love to come." She pushed her chair back. "Do you have any idea where my two sons are? My dog has found a spot in the kitchen."

Hubba was on a small blanket next to the woodstove. "But I think I need to find my kids before I commit."

"They were outside with my twins that last time I saw them, waiting in line to use the bathroom. It looks like they are playing in the library. I saw them run out when the RV pulled up. Maybe Bernie was successful in her playground expedition. They're fine. I'll make sure they stay out of trouble." Melanie yelled from the other room. "You go have an adventure. Bring me back some cake mix or something sweet."

"Thanks, Mel!" Emily called back. She lowered her voice to reply to John. "Yes, I would love to go with you."

"Great, let's get Paul, and find a vehicle." John walked into the living room. Melanie was still playing cards with the girls. Paul sat on the couch next to her, looking at her cards, and pulling on his socks.

"I saw you speak once." Paul said to Melanie. "You were great. It was a lecture on new techniques for less invasive neurosurgery. You know your stuff." He paused. "That was you, right?"

"Oh my god, you attended one of those lectures? Which one?"

"Cincinnati, I was dean of admissions. I'm not a medical doctor, I'm a 'phony doctor' as the MD's used to call me." Paul grabbed his boot and laced it onto his foot.

"The things I had to do to keep on staff at Hopkins. Lectures and papers, that was the name of the game." She looked at Paul. "You really liked it? If you aren't a doctor, why would you care?"

"The surgery aspect was over my head, but I enjoyed seeing faculty from other schools, kept me up to date on the competition. Some places I could say 'have you ever seen Dr. Smith lecture, check it out on the web.' You know, if the surgeon was boring and flat, it might sway a recruit my way. You were tops. I didn't direct people towards your videos. Did you know Rebecca was accepted to John's Hopkins?"

"The girl that was here with John's son? She's thirteen. How was she coming to Hopkins?" Melanie did not know the young phenom yet. She was too occupied with her own brood to meet new people past handshakes and quick introductions.

"She wasn't necessarily going to Hopkins. I just said she was accepted." Paul had his boots on and stood. "I can't believe I know two of the people who survived the rapture. I admitted one to medical school, and saw another speak. I'm going to play the lottery today."

Paul, John, and Emily went out the front door in search of a vehicle and baking supplies.

Todd sat in the kitchen by himself, enjoying a few moments of quiet. He finished his breakfast and entered the living room to sit next to Melanie. He put his hands on the cushion. "This doesn't feel all that comfortable."

"That's the couch, not this one." Melanie motioned to the other sofa occupied by the three little girls. "I was listening to you and your brothers discuss Hanover. Aren't you the one who brought us up here? Why are you in such a hurry to leave?"

Bridget and Wendy were making bead necklaces on the other couch. They were not paying attention to the conversation.

"Sixes?" Casey asked Melanie. She focused on her cards.

"Go fish." Melanie told her. Casey frowned and started rooting around the pile of cards on the table.

"I'm just trying to get a handle on our situation. If we are leaving, I want to know when, who wants to come with us, and where do we all want to go?"

"Jacks?" Melanie asked Casey. Casey frowned again, pulling a Jack from her hand and giving it to Melanie. "Yes." Melanie said, accepting the pair and laying it next to her. "Sevens?"

"Go fish." Casey replied.

"Nuts, I thought she had a seven." Melanie reached into the card pile on the table in front of her.

"Competitive much?" Todd asked her. "Anyway, there was this big push to figure out our future, and now it has slowed down, or stopped. That's fine, I just want to know what is what."

"Nines?" Casey asked.

"Go Fish." Melanie turned to Todd. "Your brother found his son. He wants to take a break. I think we all deserve one. I can see how you don't need one, you've had your wife and children, heck you even had a dog this entire time. The rest of us want to take a breather, get to know each other, find out if we like each other, if we want to form this tribe your beautiful wife keeps talking about. Sixes?" Melanie had a smile on her face. Casey looked at her angrily. "I just pulled it." Melanie flipped the six of diamonds around to show the little girl.

"If you want to do something productive, try to figure out a better water situation for us. Maybe the town water tower has a valve at the bottom and we could fill up things from it. There has to be a better way than filling rain barrels or melting snow. Two's?"

"Go fish." Casey said happily.

Todd walked into the kitchen. There was one more piece of strata, but he was full. He looked around for something to cover the food. He found plastic wrap. He poured half a cup of coffee and sat down at the table to think.

"Water." He said to himself. He grew up in Hanover. He visited his parents for years. As he thought, he realized he had never noticed a water tower. "I guess the best place to start is the town hall." He was spoke to Hubba, curled up on his blanket next to the warm stove. "You up for a walk buddy?" The dog did not move.

"That dog is not going to talk back to you, and he's definitely not going on a walk with you." Melanie called from the living room.

Todd knew she was right, and was impressed with Melanie's hearing.

"Well, I guess I'm on my own." Todd said to Hubba. He drank his last bit of coffee, grabbed a bottle of water from the counter, and went in the other room to have an adventure. Melanie was playing a new game with Casey. Bridget and Wendy were still making bead jewelry. Meredith and Avery were sitting in chairs reading books. "Anyone want to walk downtown with me? I'm going to see if we have a water tower anywhere near us, or if there are other options for drinking water."

Avery lowered her book. "Sure, I'll go. Can we look at other stuff too?" She elbowed Meredith. "You want to come?"

Meredith shook her head, not lowering her book. "I'm at a good part, and the fire is warm. I'll catch you later."

"Looks like it's you and me." Avery said to Todd. She got out of her chair and moved towards the coat rack. "I should be good in this, right?" She held up a ski parka.

"That's all I'm wearing, plus a hat and gloves." Todd grabbed his boots out of the boot bin and pulled them on. "We can check out some of the stores in town if you like. I just need to look at the Town Hall map to see if we have a water tower anywhere near us."

Avery was dressed and at the door. She wore a cute pink knit winter cap with a pom pom top. "Every town has a water tower. It has to be somewhere."

"I hope." He replied. "We'll be back." He told Melanie.

"I'll probably be here." She did not look up from her cards, but put a hand in the air to wave.

Avery was a tall girl, almost a woman. She was thin from months of starvation in New York. The two days of full meals brought color back into her sunken cheeks. She had long sandy brown hair that she let fall out of the pink cap. She had beautiful brown eyes, and a wonderful smile.

Todd did not know much about Avery other than her striking physical appearance, and that she looked out for Meredith.

As they turned right towards town, Todd asked her basic questions. "So, Avery, what's your story?"

"Do you mean what is my tragic rapture story or what is my life's story?" She was more or less the same height as Todd, close to seeing eye to eye with him.

"Whichever you want to tell me. I can give you my story, or we can just walk into town and talk about whatever."

"I grew up in New York City. My parents were normal people. I was the oldest of three kids, and we lived in a three bedroom apartment, rent controlled on the upper west side of Manhattan, pretty far from the park, but a nice neighborhood. My dad was an IT guy for a big law firm, and my Mom worked as a teacher at a tawny private school, which is where I got to go. I am, or I guess I was, a tennis player. I was pretty good, not playing on the tour good, yet, but ranked in the top five in New York state good."

"John and his kids play tennis. I don't think they are close to your level, but they play. There are courts here."

"I am starting to miss it. I'm sure you had something in your life that was a grind. That's what tennis became for me. Pressure to play well for my team. Pressure to play well and get into a good college. It was a grind to practice all the time. Now that it's gone, I miss it. I miss playing for fun with some of my friends." She looked at Todd as they walked. "I wasn't a very nice person." She paused for a moment as they continued towards town. "I knew I wasn't nice, but when you're in a good high school, and you're pretty, and you're a tennis star, and you have a senior boyfriend, well, you just sort of evolve into this self-centered bad person. I was mean, and petty, and self important."

"High school, good times." He told her.

"Yeah, well, it was fine for me. My parents gave so much, and my brother and sister were such sweet kids, and I was this self-centered bitch that steam rolled their lives."

"I'm a parent. That's not how we feel."

"No, I was horrible. I've changed. You don't sit at the bedside of your brother while he dies, then your sister, then your mother, and finally your father, without becoming a bit introspective. I know what I was, and I know what I want to be."

They were to the corner of town, walking in a well worn path used by Rebecca or Greg hundreds of times. Someone had cleared the way with a snow thrower. Small banks arose on both sides of the path.

"I think about why I survived." Avery's voice was flat. "Was it some kind of punishment? A curse? Did some power make sure the selfish tennis bitch, who took her family and friends for granted, lived through their deaths. Did God keep me alive to make me realize how much I needed them? Is this a punishment for how I lived my short life? How I'd squandered my time with my family?"

"That's pretty harsh thinking for a young woman." Todd tried to console her.

"I don't know you, Todd. I see that you have your wife and kids, and you didn't go through the alone time that most of us did. I was alone in my apartment building for weeks. I stayed at my neighbor's apartment because they fled the city to try and escape the disease. My family was dead right next door for four weeks, and all I had was time to think about how shitty a person I was. How crappy a sister I was. How ungrateful and disrespectful a daughter I was." She stopped walking. "God, I don't even know you, but I'm rambling on about how horrible I was. And then I tell you that you don't understand because you are blessed with your family. I mean, all you asked me was 'what's your story?' and now you're probably like 'I'll never ask Avery a question like that again."

"I like talking to you, Avery. It's why I asked. I don't know you, but I want to know you. We're probably going to be together for the rest of my life, helping each other, our children, our grandchildren, survive whatever world we can carve out for them." He looked at her when he spoke. "You're right, I have a different perspective. I didn't lose my family or my brothers. I have people in my life that know me. I can't say I've experienced the gut wrenching loss that you did. Hank, my oldest brother, who you probably just met for a moment, he can talk to you about loss and despair. I can talk to you about hope, about fighting for the next chapter in my life. I do not have the opportunity or the curse that you do. I did not suffer through weeks of solitude or months of desperation and starvation, but I can help you think about where you want to go and help you become who you want to be."

They walked again, and Avery continued. "Well, to recap, I was a bitch, and my family died, and I'm stuck in an apartment in New York with not so much food. The stores were all looted weeks before, no more deliveries were being made to Manhattan. I was up a creek without a paddle or even a boat. I cried a lot. I kept waiting to get sick, hoping I would get sick. I didn't want to live and fight to survive. I'm seventeen, I'm a princess, I'm not a badass who takes on the world and kills animals to eat. Shit, I was a vegetarian."

Todd laughed.

"Yeah, that does deserve a laugh. I'm not a vegetarian anymore, I can tell you that much." She laughed too. "So, I'm into my third week of loneliness, the power is off, I'm trying to ration my food, my water, and I'm in a really bad place. I'm bored, and one of the things my mother always told me, 'you're never bored if you have a good book.' Totally a mom thing to say, right? Anyway, I find my neighbor's bookshelf, and they were Jewish, and I find *Night*, and I read it."

"Incredible, right?"

"I'm sitting on a couch, and I finish this book, and I'm crying, and I realize, I am going through something similar. I mean, not the horror of being murdered, but losing everything, losing my family, watching them die one by one as I'm helpless to do anything about it. I think, what the hell is wrong with me? I'm alive. I'm strong. Get the hell off the couch and do something."

"Pretty big stuff for a seventeen year old princess."

"You're not kidding. It was October, and cool in New York. I put on jeans and a warm coat. I pack a backpack full of stuff I can use, and I start walking. I don't even care where I'm walking, but I assume people might be near the park or the water. I'd heard rumors about the park, about fighting and guns, all before my dad died. I decided on the river. I walked west and south, and who do you think I run into?"

"Meredith?"

"Sal Torvale."

"No."

"Yes." They stood in front of the town hall. Avery's story was so riveting neither of them wanted it to stop. "I run into this absolute creep. The one thing I will say about Sal, he was not a pervert. He never once acted or spoke sexually towards me. He wasn't a gentleman, but he wasn't a perv. There, I said something nice about him. Now, the rest of his personality? I could tell he was high. I went to high school, I'd seen the stoners, the rich kids who took drugs. Sal was just floating along, and he didn't care about anything. He would smash windows and doors as if he liked it." She turned and looked at the town hall. "Like this glass door. He would pick up a rock and throw it through. Is that what you and I are going to do? Maybe, but he wouldn't even try the door first. It might be open, but he didn't care, he would smash it." She walked over and pulled on the door. It was locked, but she noticed the bolt was barely catching the hole to lock the door. Avery tugged and the door popped open.

"See? Sometimes you don't have to destroy things. Anyway, the problem with the rapture, as I'm sure you've realized, once you hook up with someone, you're stuck with them. I couldn't shake Sal, well, I could have, he got high and passed out a lot, but really I couldn't. How could I leave a person who was providing food and protection for me? It's like you said a few minutes ago. I'm stuck with this bum for the rest of my life."

Avery held the door open for him. A second door was also glass, but did not have a lock. He pushed it open and let her into the building.

"How long was it just the two of you?"

"A week. An entire week with just me and Sal. He's high almost all the time, but he's functional enough to get us food and shelter each day and night. It's funny, he was breaking into places to find drugs, while I hunt for food, water, blankets, a bed. I might have been helping him more than he helped me that first week. Anyway, I keep asking him, 'do you think we should settle somewhere, have you heard about other people?' but I don't ask too many times because, well, I'm afraid of the guy. The one thing I controlled was our direction. I keep moving west and south. We ran into Jaime a week later. She was a spitfire old woman, heavy, smart, funny."

"Heavy?" Todd asked, he looked at a large aerial map of Hanover Township hanging on a wall in the lobby, scanning water works notations.

"Yes, she was actually kind of fat. She was round and pissed off. She wasn't from New York. She got stuck there. Anyway, she meets us and says there is a group of survivors forming at a seminary in Chelsea. When Sal and I arrived, Cameron, Wendy, and Bridget already made their trek. I'm sure you've heard highlights of that, amazing. Ahmed was there. He acted very important, like he was trying to contact the Mayor and the President directly to see what the next steps for our country were. I did not have the heart to tell him everyone was dead. He kept dialing numbers on his phone. Meredith was in a corner, sitting in the fetal position. She wouldn't talk. She barely ate. She was a mess."

Todd made big red X's where he thought there might be water towers. None of the X's he drew were near town. "What woke her up?"

"Bernie pulled me aside and told me the girl's name was Meredith, and asked if I would take her under my wing. Bernie was too busy with the three little ones. Kelly wasn't around to help out yet. Jaime was too old to break through the wall Meredith built. I was enlisted to help." She stopped and pointed to a spot on the map. "There's one."

"Thanks."

"I was glad to have buffers between me and Sal. As I said, he never tried anything, or looked at me funny, I think because he had a daughter my age, but I was still creeped out by the guy. I told Bernie I would do whatever she needed, and I went around the room and introduced myself. I started with the kids, then Ahmed, who gave me his resume, and then sat down next to Meredith."

"And?"

"She was at a bad age. The little ones were too young to understand. Older people have seen or experienced death, and can digest it. She was old enough to understand, but too young to digest. I was sort of the same way, but maybe I was just old enough, anyway. You'll get to know her, she's a great kid. She was one of eight children, the fifth born. She lost everyone." Avery stopped. "And had to watch it happen. Her parents were Mormon, and her grandmother lived with them too. Can you imagine? Eleven people living in New York together? Anyway, they had a place in Queens, a house, and her father heard about Bernie, 'The Pastor Who Didn't Get Sick' was the blog article. He brought Meredith to the seminary on his deathbed. Their car was parked across the street from the seminary all winter. He went into an apartment building and died in the stairwell. I made it my mission to get her out of her cocoon."

"You did that and more." Todd looked at the map before turning to Avery. "I didn't see anyone die." Todd confessed to her.

"What do you mean?"

"You and everyone else, you talk about seeing someone die from the rapture, and, well, I never did."

"How is that possible? You have to have seen people dead. They're everywhere, even here in Hanover."

"I've seen the bodies. I saw the grave in Central Park, the gunfight at the Metropolitan. I've seen death, but everyone talks about watching parents, children and siblings die. Emily and I were in our house with Jay and Brian. We didn't lose anyone in the house. We lived our lives, shielded from it all. I don't know the despair you have experienced. I can guess what it's like, but I didn't have to deal with it myself."

"You didn't lose anyone in your life?"

"I lost three in-laws, four nieces, I lost plenty. Friends, probably all of my extended family, but I didn't watch anyone die. You talk about being there, next to the bed when your parents passed. That's unreal to me. My brother Hank held all of his girls' hands as they died. I can't believe he is recovering from that. Everyone in the group has experienced a level of pain I can only imagine."

"You know why Bernie snapped back in New York? She took in all of the orphans and needy, she watched people die over and over again. The morgue truck was parked outside her building for the first months. She buried her own family, tended to dozens, hundreds, thousands of other people who died in beds around the seminary." Avery looked down and shook her head. "I think it blew a fuse in her brain for a while. We are all excited about this second chance at life. We met about it after dinner that first night, talked about how incredible this opportunity is, to meet up with other normal people. You've saved us, helped us find our way."

"Don't give us too much credit. We are just as lucky to find you. Plus, I brought you to a frozen town in New Hampshire."

Todd shook his head. "There's nothing near us."

"I have an idea, I don't know if it will work." Avery said shyly.

"What is it?"

"My best friend's mother was a realtor. She had detailed files on houses she listed, and I think her office kept those files. She was older, so when I say files, she had paper files. They weren't computer files."

"Yes."

"Well, maybe there is a solar house or green house we could consider. When I was talking with Matt two days ago, he said he lived in a solar powered house in Charleston. What if we could find one here in Hanover, or some other town close by? I'm sure there was some environmental crazy who had solar cells and well water. I read about all of the green options in high school. They were expensive, but rich green-minded people didn't care."

Todd looked at her. "Avery, you are brilliant. What's even better? If it's a current listing, it might be empty. We won't find bodies."

"I didn't think of that." She agreed.

"This is why we have to think like a team. Everyone should voice their ideas. Don't hold back on me again." He mock scolded her while making his way towards the door. "There's a real estate office right across the street. Actually there are two or three." Todd stopped. "Before we try our next idea, you said you wanted to check out some other stores. Do you want to do that first?"

"I know there is a library, but can we find a bookstore? I want to pick up books for Meredith. I know Bernie is also struggling to find things for the kids to read or be read to."

"And maybe get a few books for yourself?" Todd smiled.

"I admit I have selfish motives. "

"We walked right passed a bookstore while we were talking. It's three stores back. Why don't we grab some books, use a basket or something to bring them with us, and we can cross the street to the real estate offices."

They walked back to the bookstore and picked out books for everyone on their list. "There's a library right down the road, and it has a fireplace. We will start school down there this week. I know Emily wants to get Brian and Jay back in the groove of school a few days a week."

"Meredith isn't going to like that idea, but it works for me." Avery held two plastic shopping baskets. "I don't need to learn Calculus, but I'd like to study solar energy, and maybe some house building and repair."

"I know my nephew, Matt, has been studying farming for the last five months. He is in the same boat as you, doesn't need to learn how to read and write, he needs practical skills. My sons need to learn how to read, write, and use math."

Todd held up his two baskets. "Let's take these with us. Leave them by the door at the real estate offices. My mother always told me, don't backtrack if you don't have to."

Avery followed Todd across the street to an office with house pictures taped to the windows. Todd tried the door. It was open. The bolt was broken and the wooden frame was splintered.

"If I had to guess, I would say someone tried this idea already." Todd said. "The office is not ransacked, but the files have been searched."

"Do you think this was our group?" Avery asked, looking around at stacks of papers neatly placed around the file cabinets.

"I do. They had the same idea as you, and went down this road already. It was a great idea, Avery, keep them coming." He leaned over and picked up his basket of books. "Looks like our mission is going to be shorter and less successful than we thought. We didn't find a water tower, and we didn't find an alternative source for water." He opened the door for Avery. "We did figure out one thing, though."

"What?" She asked as she walked passed him.

"We need to have a group meeting to set up daily chores, brainstorm about solutions to any problems we have found, and find out what has been tried already." He followed her out the door, letting it shut behind him.

"What was it like in Raleigh? The news reports were so strange." Avery asked.

"Raleigh?" He replied. It felt like he left the town a year ago. "How do you mean?"

"I don't know, the government was focused on your town for a few weeks, before the nationwide outbreaks. You were all people talked about. After the first deaths, and the mass exodus, no one had a way to get reports out of Raleigh. You were this black hole in the country. Reporters were not allowed in and did not want to risk getting the illness. You were a word and an arrow on a map. They ran footage of the traffic jams getting out of town over and over again."

"I was too worried on finding food and staying under the radar from the guys in yellow Hazmat suits to watch much television. I was lucky in more ways than one. Jay had the actual flu that week. He had a temperature, was flat on his back, so we didn't even try to leave town. We wouldn't have made it through the first check point. I lived in a nice neighborhood. Everyone bugged out, more or less. Some of people in my neighborhood died quickly, but most of the houses in my subdivision were empty after the first week. I had access to food that was left behind. There was no looting. Everything happened too fast and people left so early. The black hole on the map was just that, a void of activity. Once the government pulled out to try and contain the disease, Emily and I were alone."

"You had food, water, electricity?"

"We did, for the most part. The electricity went off in late September, but I had propane tanks to use on the grill. I had a generator to heat the house if I needed it. We had chickens and goats that we rounded up from farms. As I said, the level of despair and loss that you endured? Emily and I had our issues, but they did not compare to what everyone else in the country went through."

They were on the corner of Wheelock and Main Street when they heard a person yell, "Uncle Todd!" Avery and Todd looked left and saw Craig waving to them with his left hand. His right held a chain creel with 5 large trout. A group of people walked behind the boy, Hank, Antonio, Ahmed, and Rebecca.

"Hello!" Todd and Avery yelled and waved back. They held up their baskets full of books. "Need any help?"

"We have it." Antonio yelled back. "They want to carry the fish and take credit for our catches. No way." He smiled to the rest of the group.

Avery and Todd crossed Main Street and waited for the fishing group at the corner. When Craig reached his Uncle he held the chain up to show him the big rainbows. Avery stepped back, not happy about fish dangling near her face. "Um, they're nice."

"Did you not get to see fish on the upper west side, Avery?" Antonio laughed.

"I'm starting to get used to the new ways, Tony. Give me some time. I milked a goat this morning. I may be grossed out by fish, but I milked a goat."

"You milked the goat this morning?" Todd asked her. "And you didn't brag about it until now?"

"I know, right? I mean, that's pretty cool."

"You're cool, Avery, you know it. I'm just messing with you. You should come out fishing with us tomorrow or the next time we go. Craig will clean your fish. You just need to catch them." Antonio gave her a pat on the back.

"I'll clean your fish, I will." Craig agreed. "I don't mind." He was overly excited. He loved to fish, and he had a new friend in Antonio.

Rebecca was quietly pulling up the rear. Avery wanted to walk with her. "Rebecca, hi, I'm Avery."

"I know. We met last night." There was an awkward silence between the two. Rebecca was not intimidated by Avery, but she was not used to being friends with a girl like her, tall, pretty, most likely popular. Months after society's collapse, Rebecca found it difficult to deviate from social paradigms.

Despite her old tendency to ignore 'pretty people' like Avery, Rebecca understood when a person was making an effort.

"What books did you get? " Rebecca reached out.

"I picked up some picture books for the little kids, and some young adult junk for Meredith. Todd and I went to see if we could find a water tower. We couldn't find one close to town."

"That's a smart idea. With only two and then four people, we used rain barrels. Once it got too cold, and the water was freezing at night, we shoveled snow into them in the kitchen. It's a pain for not that much water."

"Yeah, well, we couldn't find a tower. Then we thought about looking for a solar house at a real estate office."

"We tried that. We couldn't find anything outside of 'solar water heater,' which didn't help." Rebecca was impressed. "You and Todd were smart to think of the real estate office so quickly."

"Todd thinks we should get our ideas and previous attempts down on paper or something, so that we can be more efficient as a team. Not that our time was wasted this morning, but maybe next time we try something that you and Greg didn't already attempt."

"I totally agree."

They fell behind the group, walking slowly as they talked.

"I like your hair and cap. It makes you look like a catalog model or something." Rebecca was sure Avery modeled in New York.

"Thanks. I got this at Barney's during one of my many 'shopping' trips this winter."

"Oh my god," Rebecca said loudly. "I made Greg go shopping at the stores here like fifty times, until the snow came and blocked us. You did that too?"

"Yeah, I mean, what teenage girl isn't going to love shopping? It's awesome." Avery paused. "So where are you from? What grade were you in?"

"I'm from Concord. My parents owned a grocery store. I just finished High School, well, I had another semester because I had to fulfill these stupid credits, but I was already accepted to a few colleges."

"Wait, what? How old are you?" Avery stopped.

"I just turned 13. I know, I sort of skipped some grades. I have book smarts."

"That is so cool. I worked hard in school, it was tough for me, but I made sure I got good grades. Wow, finished with high school already. So, where were you going to college?"

"I don't know. I hadn't decided. Greg and I fantasized about where I was going, used it as a game to pass the time. On the worst winter days we'd always default to Stanford."

"You got into Stanford? I thought young kids who graduated early always ended up going to some mediocre school."

"I don't know, I got into everywhere I applied. Maybe I was old enough so that they didn't think I was a freak or something." Rebecca remembered her interviews, and her ability to sway the committees towards admitting her. "What grade were you in? Were you a senior?"

"I was, but never got to that magical senior year." Avery told her. "I was a tennis player, pretty good for New York. I was riding that talent to get into a good college. I studied too, but if I was going to Stanford, it was to play tennis, not because of my grades and test scores."

"You know, I would not have spoken to a girl like you before the rapture." Rebecca admitted. "I saw you last night, and you're pretty, and you were probably popular, and I was this twelve year old brainy kid in high school. Our circles would not have intersected. I judged you, and I'm sorry."

"I wasn't a nice person a year ago, and I wouldn't have spoken to you either. You're right. I was the person you're talking about. I'm trying to be better. You know, Meredith? She's eleven. She's a great girl. You'll like her. She was only in sixth grade though."

"The rapture wasn't a blessing, it was a horrible thing, but I'm trying to take all the positives I can from the experience." Rebecca told her. "I didn't have any friends before. I was always younger than my classmates, and while people were nice to me, I didn't have friends. I'd never spoken to a boy before, not one like Greg. He's the boy I met last fall."

"Oh, I know who Greg is." Avery winked at her.

Rebecca blushed, "Yeah, well, I didn't have friends, I didn't talk to boys. I was happy. I did eighth grade volleyball. My parents pulled some strings to get me on an age-appropriate team, but I only saw those girls in the afternoons, and I was not really friends with them." Rebecca paused. "I guess I'm trying to say, I'm glad you stopped to talk to me. I'm glad I talked to you. I know we are going to be friends, and Meredith too. I'm not happy the rapture happened, but I'm learning to be happy for the things that come from it. Does that make sense?"

"It's so cliché to say that you are making lemonade, especially when the lemons were the total death and destruction of the human race, but yeah, I get it. You have to move on. I'm trying to do the same, to be a good person, to be kind to people. I was not a nice person ten months ago, and maybe I still have my moments." Avery stopped in front of the cottage. "We may not become friends, I'm okay with that, but it won't be because I'm mean. If we aren't friends it is because we don't click. Does that make sense?"

"Wait, you don't like me?" Rebecca asked in a serious tone.

"No, I mean, I didn't mean that." Avery was flustered, something she was not used to being.

"I'm just kidding. I've been living with a sarcastic boy for six months. He's rubbing off on me." Rebecca laughed.

"Not funny, well, kind of funny. I am never the butt of jokes." Avery feigned anger, but thought, 'I just met my new best friend.'

"Let's go see what's for lunch. You can introduce me to Meredith beyond the 'hello I'm Rebecca.'" Rebecca walked up the shoveled path. Melting snow ran down the concrete in small rivers.

"You got it." Avery told her.

Rebecca expected the cottage to be packed with people, particularly because it was lunch. She found only Hank. "There is a cookout at the other house, everyone is down there. Greg brought the meat grinder. They are grinding fresh moose burgers while the grill heats."

Avery set her books down.

"Sounds good to us." They said in unison.

Hank, having raised daughters, understood when two people clicked.

"I can walk down with you." He wore a light jacket, tan canvas on the outside, flannel lined on the inside. The weather was turning. Hank did not need the heavy coats he wore for the last five months. "Avery, isn't it? I met you last night for a second. You were with that other young girl, Mary? Is that your sister? My name is Hank."

"Her name is Meredith, and she's not my sister. She's a friend, a fellow survivor from New York. Actually she's from New Jersey."

"Meredith? I was close with Mary. Okay, thank you. I'm still trying to learn everyone's name. I'll get there. Let's head down for some food." He opened the back door for the two women and followed them out. "So what were you and my brother doing in town? Were you looking for books?"

"We were trying to find a better water source. We failed."

"Water is tough. We struggled with it all winter. Not locating it, but keeping it in drinkable form, plus having water on hand for dishes and bathing. It's a mystery we'll have to solve. We live by a river and a pond, and it rains here. We have to learn how to harness our sources better."

"We'll run out of chlorine at some point too." Rebecca noted. They used chlorine to purify the rain barrel water for drinking and washing dishes.

"We'll figure it out." They strolled at a leisurely pace. "You know, Avery, I spent two months here before you came, and I never stepped foot in the bookstore. We always went to the library, the college library. I guess I didn't do enough recreational reading. We've been busy reading statistics and things like that. My brain could use a break."

"Your brother talked about starting school for the kids down at the town's library. He said there is a fireplace." Avery liked Hank. He was a big, kindhearted man.

"It's a walk, but that's probably a good thing too, keep the muscles and the mind fit. Yeah, that will work well for the time we need it." He turned and looked at the young woman. "How old are you, Avery? Seventeen?"

"About to turn eighteen. Good guess."

"I had four daughters. One was your age." Hank looked at Rebecca. "You can go a little easier on the new guy. He doesn't understand what he's up against. I think he still believes he's a managing director."

"I don't know what that means." Rebecca replied defensively.

Avery laughed. "He means Ahmed still believes he's a big shot. That somehow his former life is going to come back into play." She looked at Hank. "Has Rebecca been mean to him?"

"He pressed me for details on my analysis. I gave them to him. He keeps saying things that are wrong, and I correct him." Rebecca answered flatly. "I am not being mean. He's being mean, talking to me like I'm in fifth grade."

"I know. I was just kidding. It's been interesting to watch. Ahmed is it?" Hank asked Avery. "He was probably a big shot analyst, or managed analysts, and he is used to beating people up with his intelligence. He's taking it well. I can tell he's a good person. He opened up when we were fishing. Yeah, he still thinks he's in charge of something."

"Well, I haven't been mean." Rebecca repeated.

"I know, I was just giving you some grief. Geesh." Hank put his arm around the girl and gave her a half hug as they walked down the road.

"Ahmed's a good person. He always ate last, always helped Bernie with the kids. It took a while for him to realize no one was coming to help us, that there was no one to 'call,' but after that, he settled down and worked really hard to keep us alive."

"He's out of his league with our champ here." Hank beamed about Rebecca. "Granite State represents."

"Oh my god, you're such a dork." Rebecca told him. "Represents? What are you talking about?"

They pulled up to a gathering of people near the RV and large grill. The adults stood around the burning charcoal and wood. The RV generator was running. Hank assumed the kids were watching a movie or playing video games. Greg and Matt tossed a baseball in the yard.

"What's the word?" Hank asked as he approached the grill. "Burgers coming up soon?"

Kelly offered her assessment. "We moved the moose into the wood room and shoveled ice and snow onto the ground in there. It will keep the meat the right temperature for a long time." She had blood on her clothes, signs that she helped move the large slabs of meat. "It was like an episode of the Flintstones, moving those giant moose legs, but we got them moved, hacked off some meat, and Peter is cranking the grinder while Jamie forms patties. I bet they come up with some meat in a few minutes."

Hank nodded, "okay then. What's the talk at the grill?"

"I want to have a meeting after lunch." Todd told him. "We should get together to discuss needs and chores. Maybe set up a schedule or chart. There are animals to feed, traps to tend, fishing to be done. We need to figure out a water solution, set up a school for the kids, find more supplies, stock the firewood bins. Let's spend a few minutes, or even hours, coordinating. We have a lot of people and a lot of moving parts.'

"Everyone okay with that?" Hank asked around the grill.

"It's the smart thing to do." Ahmed replied. "I totally agree."

Bernie nodded, "we need to get the kids back to school, but we also need to make sure someone is finding food and cooking for us." She took the conversation further. "We need to make bread every day, bread or rolls or some kind of food that can be used for lunches. We can't expect to have a big cookout every lunch. We have water to find and boil or purify. At some point we will have to tend gardens, can fruits and vegetables, the list isn't endless, but if we don't get on top of it, well, we might end up like we did in New York, lost and very hungry."

Hank was surprised. He expected tension from the new group, but they yearned for order and direction. He was all for setting up daily chores, not assignments, but a list of 'must get done' for each day. It was their initial roadmap towards a society.

"Okay then, sounds like a plan. Lunch and a meeting. Do we have a side dish?" Hank looked around.

"Solange is making pasta salad in the RV. Orzo mixed with veggies and lemon dressing." Melanie told him. "She's watching the kids too."

"Is there anything for me to do other than stand here?" Hank, in constant motion for months, was uncomfortable 'just standing around.'

"Relax, it's your turn to stand at the grill, make some conversation. Meet everyone. I'm Melanie." The doctor stuck out her hand. "I don't think we've spoken more than a few words."

"Are you a New Yorker?" Hank asked. He remembered her name was Melanie, and she looked after three of the kids.

"No, I met up with the group in D.C., just outside the White House."

"Melanie, I'm Hank, I am John and Todd's oldest brother. I rode over from Dayton, OH on a motorcycle last December, spent two months at a bed and breakfast in Vermont, true story, then arrived here on the snowmobiles parked by the cottage."

"You were in a bed and breakfast?" Melanie asked, shaking his hand. "It kind of makes your story seem less tough. If you say you road motorcycles, then snowmobiles, and leave out the B&B part, you will be cooler."

Rebecca snickered.

"Well, I wasn't trying to sound too tough, you just met me." Hank admitted. "I could tell you about how I lived in a burned out house for a few months, avoiding government capture. That is pretty cool."

"Why would you do that?" Avery asked him.

"Wait a second, I feel ganged up on." Hank put up his hands to signal 'enough.'

"Really, why were you in a burned out house? Was that in Vermont?" Avery asked again.

"Well, it seems kind of foolish now, since you all survived without moving into a hole, but, well I was worried about the government grabbing me for experiments or something nefarious. I had a friend that was snatched. I didn't want it to happen to me. I hid in the ground for a few months. I waited for everyone to die."

Ahmed jumped into the conversation. "I had a coworker get nabbed. He went to the food handouts at the Metropolitan Museum. He got snatched for not being sick. A bunch of us were supposed to go on a raid and get him, but I was too scared. Everyone else had fevers, weren't eating, they were dead people walking. I had my wife at home to care for, and I wasn't sick. I believe you. Roundups were happening everywhere."

"Don't encourage him." Todd said. "Please just roll your eyes."

Bernie shook her head. "They came to the seminary after the blog post about me and how I wasn't getting sick. They told me they needed people to derive a cure, maybe a vaccine. They asked me to turn people over to them."

"Oh my god, you didn't do it, did you?" Kelly covered her mouth.

"Does it look like I helped them?" Bernie responded. "I'd always shake my head when new people came into the seminary, lower my eyes to say 'fever' or 'no appetite.' They helped with supplies as long as I agreed to point them towards healthy people. The interesting thing? I was worried the officials would notice Ahmed and the children, you know, staying healthy, like me, day after day, but the clipboard holders died so rapidly I would get a new official every visit. They never had a memory of who was already at the seminary."

"Why didn't you tell me?" Ahmed was stunned by her admission. He was with Bernie before the blog post. He had a reporter friend write the article.

"Because you would have called someone, Ahmed, you know you would have. You were driven by a need to accomplish, a need to speak to someone in power. If I told you they were rounding up people, you would have called and probably gotten yourself taken. I accepted the risk alone."

Ahmed lowered his face. "You're right, that's exactly what I would have done. I can be a bit of a dumbass. Ask Rebecca." Ahmed was aware of his reputation. Like all of the survivors, he worked on fixing his faults.

"I didn't say anything." Rebecca replied.

"I know." Ahmed smiled at the girl. "I'm just saying you can back up my claim of being a dumbass, particularly when I question you about analytics."

Todd spoke. "Solange and I went to the Metropolitan. We took some of the art, but had to walk through hell to get t. It was a battle or a massacre or something in between. Horrible. Be thankful you made the right decision."

The door to the house opened and Jamie walked out with a platter of raw mooseburgers. "We ran the meat through the grinder three times. It's tough stuff, but we should have eatable burgers. Is the grill ready?"

"Yes!" was cheered in response.

Jamie placed twenty burgers on the grill. Peter was grinding another ten.

"We have to try and make cheese." Matt noted, coming over from his game of catch.

"I've made ricotta and mozzarella. It takes a lot of milk." Todd told him. "I'm not sure it's worth it. I mean, it's worth it, but I'm not sure it's worth the amount of milk we'd have to use. The kids need that milk."

"I need it for my coffee." Ahmed added.

"Amen." Bernie agreed.

There were no buns. Todd added the absence of buns to his list of comments for the meeting. If the group had a schedule, a plan each day, he would have made hamburger buns that morning.

Solange emerged with her orzo salad and several cans of fruit cocktail. Plastic plates were distributed. There was silence as most of the people enjoyed their first fresh meat in over six months.

"I forgot how great burgers are." Avery broke the silence. "I was a vegan before the rapture. It's been like four years since I've had a real burger from the grill. Oh my god is this delicious."

Hank suggested they make another round. "Did we even put a dent in that meat?" He asked Peter.

"No sir. This is five pounds off a hundred pound leg. There's a bone, but we used a tenth of the meat from just one of our four legs."

"Let's cook more. I'll work the grinder." Hank followed Peter into the house and down to the basement.

Jamie put the ten uncooked burgers on the grill.

The children were done eating, but the adults were not. As Peter and Hank returned from the house with another 20 burger patties, Paul, John, and Emily pulled down the road in a lime green Hummer.

The enormous SUV stopped behind the RV. "Are you kidding me?" John jumped out. "You had a cookout without us?" He watched Hank slap 20 burgers on the grill. "We went to a store to try and find supplies, and you party while we're gone?"

"Relax, these are for you, we've eaten. There is pasta salad and fruit salad right over there. The burgers should be done in a few minutes." Hank waved off his brother.

"How'd we do?" Todd asked his wife as she gave him a quick hug and kiss.

"Big score. Bags upon bags of flour sealed in a storage vault free of rodents. Boxes of cake, cookie, and bread mixes too. We are set for a year." She quickly pushed passed him and grabbed a plate. Emily piled the pasta salad into one of the plastic compartments. "I miss fresh fruit so much, but this will work." She spooned some of the peaches and pears into a second compartment.

"Hungry?" Todd asked her.

"We were surrounded by pictures of bread, cakes, and cookies, but there was nothing to eat. Yeah, I'm hungry. Hurry up with the burgers!"

Paul and John agreed with Emily, and piled the remaining side items on their plates. "You know." Paul said through a mouth full of food. "They had a huge commercial pizza oven. I know you have a home sized one, but seeing the larger oven got me thinking. It makes sense to tackle larger baking projects from the oven at that wood-fired pizza restaurant downtown. They have a commercial sized pizza oven. It would be a pain to walk down there all the time, but for big bakes, like a Monday when we cook loaves for the week. Or if we decide to do a group pizza night, that oven is much larger."

Todd pulled out his note pad from his back pocket and scribbled what Paul said.

"What is that? Are you a detective or a waiter?" Paul asked him through his mouth full of food.

"If you're a waiter, put me down for another burger. These are fantastic." John told him.

"We're having a meeting after lunch. I'm making notes."

John tone changed. "What kind of meeting?"

"I suggested the meeting, but the rest of the group agrees we need one. We need to set chore schedules, plan meals, assign larger and long term tasks. We need to hash out possible projects, discuss what Greg and Rebecca have already tried, what other people have tried when solving issues. We need to take stock of our supplies, food and intelligence."

"I agree." Paul voiced through his constantly full mouth. "That's a great idea. We're not electing anyone or voting on anything, we're just brain storming. I like it." He forked the last bit of orzo into his mouth.

"Alright, let's do it. Five minutes? Do we have a fire inside?" John looked at the chimney. "Looks like it. What's the plan with the kids?"

"They can play in the house, sit in on the meeting, or watch TV in the RV. Anyone can participate." Todd put the remaining burgers into a ziplock bag. "Hubba is going to eat well tonight." He scanned the lunch area. It was clean. He motioned towards the front door. "Let's move into the house and get started? I want to make sure we don't take all afternoon."

The afternoon sun shone into the windows on the south side of the house, warming the living room. A crackling fire brought the temperature up to a comfortable 60. People could remove their coats.

Todd placed legal pads of paper around the room with a few boxes of pens. Craig wandered over to his father, "do I have to be here or can I go play with J and J?"

"It's up to you. Matt, Greg, and I can handle it. Realize you will be placed on the food collection detail, or the 'fishing squad,' as we'll call it."

"I'm cool with that." Craig said, turning away from his father.

"Really? Because if it's raining, we still need to eat. If it's cold outside, and you're tired, we still need to eat. If it's hot, and the bugs are biting, and you only have three fish and you're tired of fishing, we still need to eat. This isn't just a fun fishing trip with Uncle Hank. It will be a job, a responsibility."

"I know, well, I didn't think of all of that, but I know. I'm good at fishing. It's the best way for me to help."

"Okay, go play." John grabbed his son by the arm. "Hey, can you be the adult out there? Keep things under control. Let us know if you need one of us to come out." He let go of Craig's arm.

"You got it, Dad." Craig grabbed his pullover from a pile of coats and ran towards the front door.

"Alright, let's start talking." Todd said. "While Avery and I were downtown today, she came up with a fantastic idea. She said we should go to real estate offices and try to find a solar powered house."

People turned and looked at Avery, who raised her hand and waved 'hi.'

"Yeah, it was smart thinking, so smart that Greg and Rebecca tried it already." There was additional muttering in the room. "I thought we could come together, I mean, we're not a large group, and share some ideas. We have chores or daily tasks that need to be handled. We need to milk the goats, collect the eggs, feed the animals, clean cages. We need to fish most days, check traps, set traps, collect water, purify water. We need to cook meals and clean up after meals. If we want bread, we need to make bread, even plan for bread. We need to collect and distribute firewood. We will have to cut down trees and create firewood for next fall."

"Are we writing this down?" Peter asked, interrupting Todd. "Some of us are older, and can't remember things off the top of our heads."

"Most of us." Hank joked.

"We can write on this wall." Solange said, taking a black marker in hand, and writing down the tasks Todd mentioned as well as ones she knew to be necessary.

"Thanks." Todd said to her.

Solange nodded back to him. "English is my second language. It makes sense for me to be the one to write the notes on the wall."

Todd waited for the laughter to subside before he lowered his voice. "This isn't summer camp or boarding school or the army. I don't expect to have a duties chart." Todd heard snickers from his brothers. "Yeah, yeah, I said duties. Anyway, I don't think we need a formal plan, but we need to make sure this stuff happens. There are 18 of us in the room right now. Everyone can contribute, even Cameron and Casey can collect eggs and feed the animals. I hope the first part of this meeting is used to formalize daily and weekly tasks. What I hope we can do as a second agenda item is brainstorm ways to do these chores more easily, and maybe consider projects that will make our lives better."

"If we knock these out quickly." John began, "we need to discuss long term plans."

"Take a look at this list." Solange said loudly. The chores were listed on the white wall. "What do we want to do with this list? Are we going to choose what we each do best? Are we allowed to pick what we enjoy doing, like Craig did with fishing? Are we going to assign particular tasks to people based on skills, regardless of desire?"

"I enjoy teaching the kids. I can formally accept that position, if people don't mind." Emily volunteered. "I'm not versed in every topic, but I can read, write, and do arithmetic. People can float in and out to help me, but I can accept education responsibilities."

"Done." Bernie said to her.

"Yes, done. I can help when possible, but thank you." Melanie told her friend.

"If it's okay with Tony, put us down for fishing. One of us will motivate each day to take a group." Hank looked towards Antonio with his chin up in a 'that okay?' pose.

"Yeah, I can do that. I can help with boats, cars, and engines too. I'm good with stuff like that, but I can fish too."

"Anyone want to accept the laundry?" Solange joked.

"I can make sure it gets done, but I don't know if I can do it all." Jamie sat next to Peter. "I had a lot of kids and grandkids, and I usually air dried my clothes, but I had a washing machine."

"I think everyone will help." Solange told her.

"Ahmed and I will cook, or make sure someone else volunteers. I know Greg is a fantastic cook, as are many others, but if it's okay with Ahmed, we will make sure a meal is prepared." Todd commented.

"I assume I will keep my managing director title." Ahmed drew a laugh.

"Matt and I will hunt and trap. Right?" Greg nodded to his brother.

"Water is too big a project for one person, but I'll try to set up a system." John announced. "We have water, and we have ways to collect it or get it, it's just a pain right now. I'll work on making it easier, and make sure we don't run out."

"I will do the same for firewood." Solange said. "I cannot carry all the wood, but I will make sure we find it when we need it."

"It makes sense that I will care for the animals. I'm a vet. I'll make sure the kids feed them, and we milk them." Kelly said.

"I'll do that too. I mean, if it's okay with you, I'd love to learn how to take care of them." Avery asked the young woman.

"Absolutely, I'd love the help, and to pass along knowledge. I paid a lot of money to learn how to care for a dozen chickens and goats." Another laugh came from the group.

Items were checked off the list Solange had on the wall.

Melanie stood. "I'm going to move on to the next topic. As some of you know, I am or I was a surgeon. I am a doctor, and I will continue to practice. I hope I can convince one of the younger people to work with me, learn some of the things we'll all need going forward. If Kelly thinks she paid a lot to care for chickens and goats, well, think how I feel right now." She paused, "I'm also an amateur botanist, and I'd like to talk about crops. If we stay here, even if it's just for the summer, we need to build a greenhouse and start our seedlings. We need to find some land that allows us to plant." She looked around the room. "If we aren't going to stay here, well, we can address the farming question when we get to our next home."

"Wait, you're a surgeon? Did we know this?" Ahmed turned to Bernie and Kelly.

"I didn't, Ahmed, but I don't know what most of these people did in their previous lives." Bernie replied.

"I asked everyone to keep it quiet, not to lie, but keep it quiet until we knew you better. Physicians are in short supply. I'm sorry if you feel deceived." Melanie told the three New York adults.

"No, I understand. I'm excited. You're right, we need a doctor. I think Kelly will be a fantastic resource for both human and animal well being, but to have a surgeon? Wow, it's like we lucked into an even better situation than we realized."

"I planned on attending medical school. I would love to learn from you if I can." Rebecca said from the back of the room. "I have little interest in farming. It's not a package deal, is it?"

Matt jumped in before Melanie could respond. "I am excited about the farming. I know I'm signed up to help Greg with the trapping and hunting, but I've been studying farming for the last few months."

"I'd be lucky to work with both of you." Melanie told them. "Did I raise the question none of us wanted to ask? How long are we going to stay here?" She looked around the room. "I'm tired. I've been fighting to survive and keep my kids alive for half a year. We lived through the stress of the rapture, through months of confusion and struggle. I want to settle down for a few weeks, get our bearings. I don't know how we decide where to go and when to go there, but I'd like to vote on staying here for at least two more weeks, maybe a month. We probably have enough moose meat to last us that long."

"Do we even have to vote?" John asked. "We all feel the same way. Two weeks is an easy decision. I think the bigger question is if we stay the summer."

"I don't know if gas will work at the end of the summer. You're talking another five or six maybe seven months? If we don't have gas, we have to walk out of New Hampshire. That will be a problem." Todd brought realism to the vacation plans.

"I don't want to discuss our next destination, I just want to talk about how long we stay here. We all okay with two weeks?" John asked. No one replied. "Anyone not want to stay here for two weeks?" The room was silent again.

"Okay." John said. "We stay, relax, get our energy, put some pounds on you New Yorkers, re-assess the situation in two weeks."

Everyone was quiet. The group had established daily tasks, assigned them to qualified people, decided on a short-term timeline. It was a good meeting. Todd, who sat down after the conversation began to flow, stood. "Does anyone have any additional business? Anything they want to talk about?"

"I want to lead a party down to Boston, look for survivors." John announced. "I was against approaching people, going to major cities. I was against finding all of you, and I was wrong. I want to give any survivors in Boston a chance to join us. I assume it will be a day trip, maybe overnight. I can take the Suburban."

"I would like to go with you." Solange said, standing up to join him. "Any long trip, or any task we do that is away from our home, we should do in pairs."

"Does anyone have a problem with us going down to Boston?" John asked again.

"If you can help people, it's the right thing to do. If you can save people like you saved us, I'll pack your food for you." Bernie gave John the support he was looking for.

"Okay, Solange and I will leave in two days. The snow might be off the highways by then."

Todd continued. "Well, that was productive and expedient. It's only been about an hour. Do we want to talk about long term plans? I know we just said we would hang out for two weeks, which is great, but do we want to discuss our long term goals?"

Rebecca raised her hand.

"You can just speak, Rebecca." Todd told her.

"Everyone knows I've run analysis of where we should go. Some of you know my findings, that the coast of Virginia is probably our best spot, except if we can get to Hawaii or some other tropical island. There are two ways we can get to the islands. We drive to California and figure out how to work a large boat, which I conclude is improbable." She paused and looked at Peter. "or we fly."

"Fly? How are we going to fly?" Ahmed asked.

"I'm a pilot, retired navy, retired commercial." Peter spoke loudly, clearly, and with the confidence expected from a pilot. "If there is a plane that works, I can get it in the air. Our issues are fuel and capacity; capacity for people and supplies as well as capacity for fuel and distance."

"You have a doctor and a pilot?" Ahmed asked.

"We have a doctor and a pilot." John emphasized the 'we.'

"I love that we are talking about this, and I want nothing more than to live in Hawaii, but let's also discuss a third capacity that Peter is not discussing, the capacity to land. What if we fly to Honolulu and the airport is in ruins or there are planes blocking the runways?"

"Honestly? I don't see that as an issue." Peter to d him. "I doubt the airports on every island will be destroyed or unavailable for landing. If they are, which again, is not realistic, there will be a stretch of highway somewhere we can use. Could we end up landing on the highway in the lava fields on Kona? Possibly, but there are three air strips on Oahu alone. The military would never leave the airstrip blocked. We can land at Pearl if we needed to. Is it a risk? Yes. Is it a big risk? No."

Paul nodded as Peter explained the options. "Okay, I'm appeased. You're good."

"Son, you have no idea." Peter winked at him.

"Seriously?" Rebecca said with exasperation. "I did all this work and the answer is Hawaii? Everyone in the room would have said Hawaii without turning on a computer. Unbelievable."

"We were bored, it kept us busy." Paul told her. He knew her venom was directed at him.

Kelly stood. "I like the idea, and I understand why Hawaii presents so many benefits to us; climate, water, food, safety, the list continues. Are we concerned about being stuck there? If we fly to Honolulu, I doubt there is a way to return. We are done. If supplies are not as abundant as we think they are, we're looking at New York City all over again."

Rebecca answered. "The ocean will not run out of fish. The tropical fruit alone can sustain us, but I assume we are going to bring seeds to plant, corn, wheat, rice, etc... I agree, flying to Hawaii means we are going there forever, for the rest of our lives, but you have to understand, if we settle in Virginia? We are making the same choice. Once our gas goes bad, we have to walk, bike, or ride a horse to get where we want to go." Rebecca looked around the room and could tell some of her audience was not convinced.

"I know it was two years ago, but think about the hurricane that plowed up the east coast and took out all of those bridges and homes. Remember when the Mississippi River flooded ten years ago? The water rushed over bridges and washed out roads. Just the freezing and thawing that occurs every year will ruin any bridge that was close to being replaced before all of this. In a few years I doubt the highway system will be available. Trees will have fallen across most if not all of the roads. Vegetation in the warmer climates will consume everything. In five years it will not be a simple feat to move. How do we get across the Connecticut River without a bridge? How do we get across the Mississippi? How do we traverse a highway littered with pine tree refuse?" She noticed nodding and mumbles of acceptance.

"Where ever we go? That is where we will stay." Rebecca did not mean to sound dour or foreboding, but the facts were the facts. "Is there a chance we could migrate from Virginia to some other place? Sure. But the odds would be small. Greater than if we move to Hawaii, but small none the less."

Todd waited before he spoke. "Look, this isn't a decision we need to make right now. Maybe we explore the options, see if there are any planes in Lebanon, have John and Solange check the planes at Logan and Manchester. I brought up our long term plans because I know we're all thinking about it. Kelly brings up a great point, Hawaii has finality to it. I'd like to drink cow's milk again at some point in my life. If we go to Hawaii, I'm not sure that is going to happen. Let's look into some of this stuff, maybe continue the conversations informally."

"I am a good resource for a lot of these questions. For one, there are cows on almost all of the islands. At least, there were cows eight months ago." Rebecca offered. "I've been studying Hawaii for a while. I can discuss Virginia and Northern California too. Thanks to Paul, I can discuss just about anywhere we would consider settling. I'm really not as mean as Ahmed makes me out to be."

Avery laughed to support her new friend.

"Okay, okay, that's enough laughing." Ahmed said. "And she is as mean as I think she is, smarty pants."

John walked over to Peter. "Should you come with us to Boston, or are there things you can tell us to look for with regards to the type of plane we need?"

People began to engage in side conversations. The meeting appeared to be over.

Rebecca spoke to Greg and Matt in the back of the room. Avery walked over to join them. "You go girl, look who's leading the group to paradise."

Rebecca blushed. "Thanks, and thanks for laughing at my lame joke."

"It wasn't lame. You were taking a beating from Ahmed and people who felt you should have humored him more. It's your time, Rebecca. It's our time. Teenagers rule."

Greg stared at Avery, "I'm Greg. I met you last night for like two seconds."

"Nice to meet to you again, Greg. I'm Avery. I met you with my friend Meredith, who is over talking to Kelly, the vet." Avery turned towards Matt. "Hi, Matt, nice to see you again."

Avery, pretty, and confident made shy Matt tongue tied.

Greg teased him. "Seriously bro? We're not at a dance. Yes, Avery, this is my shy brother Matt."

Matt managed a "hi" before elbowing Greg. "Dude, uncool."

Avery was used to boys being flustered around her. Matt was tall, thin, muscular, and handsome. She made sure to give him a smile to let him know it was okay he blushed. "So you are the other half of the team that lived up here?" She focused on Greg. "You have to tell me some stories. Did anything crazy happen? Did a bear chase you into a house? Did you see mountain lions or anything?"

"I take it you are one of the New York City people." Greg said with a smile. "Didn't get out of the city much, huh?"

"You're making fun of me."

"Yes, yes I am. No, we didn't have any wild animal encounters. We probably could have if we had been careless with food, but bears typically go to sleep in the winter."

"Greg tried to catch a turkey." Rebecca started.

"Seriously? Again with the turkey story? Come on, at some point I have to live that story down."

"Well it's not today." Rebecca recounted Greg's early adventures with hunting.

"Looks like two of us didn't get out of the city much." Avery said to him after they stopped laughing.

Greg did not mind the ribbing. He was now a capable hunter and trapper. His early attempts were amusing, even he laughed when Rebecca talked about running at a turkey with a hoe. "It's nice to be around other young people." Greg told them after a few minutes. "Rebecca and I were alone for a long time, and we couldn't be young, couldn't be kids, and then my uncles, man, they are old men. It's great to have my brothers and some other teenagers here."

"Do you guys play tennis?" Avery asked them.

"I do, but I was way more into baseball. Matt was the tennis player." Greg used his shoulder to push Matt forward.

"I played in my parent's club league, but that's about it."

"If we can find some rackets and get a court cleared off I'd love to play a few sets. You can show me your stuff." Avery winked at Rebecca to let her know not to tell the boys about her tennis past.

Matt, over his initial awkwardness, was excited to spend time with Avery. "Sure, hopefully in the next two weeks."

"What should we do with the rest of the daylight?" Avery asked them. "Is there anything that needs to get done?"

"Firewood." Greg and Matt said together.

"Greg had an idea of filling a pickup truck with firewood and parking it down here, making it easier for people to come out and collect wood when they need it."

"We have to find a pickup truck?" Avery asked.

"There are a bunch of pickup trucks parked behind one of the college buildings, a row of green utility vehicles just about a half mile from here. They will work, assuming they start. The keys are hanging in the office where they are parked. "

Antonio walked up to the group of young people and listened. "You should take one of the cars we have working, use it to jump the truck. No way it will start without a jump."

Matt did not know Antonio very well, and was happy for the advice. "Any chance you want to come along and help?"

"Yeah." Antonio stuck out his hand. "Tony." He said, introducing himself to Matt.

"Matt." taking Antonio's hand. "This is my brother Greg and our friend

Rebecca."

"Hey." Antonio flipped his head to Greg and shook his hand. "I know Rebecca from fishing. Her old man taught her how to fish just like mine. Hey." He said to her.

"Well, now that we know each other, let's get to it. I'll ask Meredith to come. She needs to get to know all of you." Avery waved to Meredith.

"Let's do it." Matt walked over to the coat pile before making his way to the adults on the other side of the room. "Dad? We're going to get some firewood for the houses. Anything else we should be thinking about?"

"Can you grab your brother? He should help."

"There are six of us already. Our plan is to fill a pickup bed with wood, park it down here. Craig and the other kids can distribute the wood to the fireplaces when we get back."

"I like the way you think. See you when you get back."

The young adults walked out of the house and towards the cottage. They needed gloves to avoid splinters.

Matt and Greg, reunited for three days, used much of their time together to catch up.

Rebecca was glad to have friends. She was never close to people her own age. It was amusing to her that Avery, a senior in high school, would be so friendly. The senior girls Rebecca met before would not acknowledge her. Rebecca was the curve buster, a freak blowing through their grade, a nerd. Today her intelligence was an asset, not a character flaw.

Rebecca knew the circle of kids she walked with today was her peer group for the rest of her life. Unless they started rounding up survivors, or found more teens in Boston, she was walking with the same people she would see in fifty years.   It was an odd realization.

"Thankfully, everyone is normal." She thought to herself.

43

The adults remained in the house after the kids left, enjoying the roaring fire.

Emily spoke to Bernie and Melanie about developing a routine for the children. Emily enjoyed the 'every other day' school system she used in Raleigh. Bernie and Melanie agreed to anything, as long as they did not have to teach.

"We should turn off the movie and video games. Take the kids over to the library, let them check out the building. Heck, it might not work for us. Better to find out this afternoon than to show up tomorrow expecting to have school. It's a beautiful day outside. Let's take a walk."

"I'm in." Melanie said, moving towards the shrinking pile of coats. "I could use a nice walk."

Bernie followed her over to the coats. "You are a doctor?"

"I'm a doctor from a hospital that had all the latest gadgets. I'm not sure I would know how to make a cast if we needed to. I am used to having 'people' do that for me, but I can diagnose the heck out of all of you." Melanie joked.

"How did this happen?" Bernie asked. "How did everyone die? Why couldn't you help?"

Melanie dropped her joke. "It was too fast. It was just too damn fast." She walked ahead of Bernie and out the front door before stopping. "As a person of God, I ask you the same question. Why was the world forsaken?"

Bernie shook her head, not offering an explanation.

They waited silently for Emily to guide them towards the library.

"We're taking the kids over to the library to scout out the school situation." Emily said to Todd, interrupting his conversation. "We'll be back at some point."

"Okay, I'll see you. Have fun." He gave her a kiss, and turned back to his circle.

"Our best case scenario is finding a loaded fuel truck. We will use it to fill the plane, but if the fuel is in a holding tank, we have to figure out a way to get power into that pump, get the fuel into the truck, and drive the truck to the plane." Peter explained airport fueling logistics to them. "If we don't find fuel, obviously, we're done."

Peter continued. "The issue is figuring out whether we land on the west coast to refuel. It will depend on the type of plane we find, and if we want to take the risk of not finding fuel out there. What if we land in San Francisco and cannot find a fuel truck or fuel?"

"We have dozens of airports to explore. I am positive we can find a plane and fuel. We might have to drive back to Raleigh to do it, but we can find something that will work." John assured everyone. "Seriously, Raleigh's airport is probably pristine, and definitely has fuel."

Hank turned to Paul, "remember that dairy farm we kept talking about going to after the thaw? The Hummer should be able to brave the trek, let's hit it tomorrow."

"The farm that ran tours? You expect to find something?" Todd knew the place. He took Jay and Brian there in the summer. The farm was a staple of his family visits to Hanover.

"If we don't find animals there, we can check the hundred dairy farms in and around here. Maybe some of the cows found hay stores. Maybe the grass poked through the snow in spots. I bet something survived."

Hank was convinced he could find livestock. "We should at least try."

"I'm up for a trip." Paul told his brother.

"I'd like to come along. I can help with any sick animals. I did a rotation on a dairy farm. I know how to get dairy cows producing again." Kelly looked at Todd. "We could be swimming in milk pretty quickly. One healthy cow, milked a few times each day, would give us four to six gallons of milk. That's just one cow."

"What are the odds we find a cow producing that much milk?" Hank asked her, skepticism in his voice.

"Depends on everything you just said. If we do find a cow, we can get one producing with the right nutrition and food. If we find a few cows? We'll have enough milk and cheese for our group, more than enough. You have to realize, cows today have been bred to give enough milk for millions of people. When you only have twenty people to feed? One cow would overwhelm us with milk."

"Speaking of feeding twenty some odd people, I'm going to grind some meat and make sausage for breakfast and dinner tomorrow." Hank gave the people on either side of him pats on the back as he headed towards the basement.

"I can help with that." Jamie called after him.

"I am going to get an early jump on dinner." Todd announced. "I'll light a fire in the oven and start on the bread. Fish stew is on the menu this evening. I want to make sure we mix up how we serve the trout."

"I'll join you. I can fillet a trout like nobody's business. You leave too many bones." Ahmed rubbed his hands in the fire, almost standing in the flames during the conversation. He, like the other New York people, was rail thin, and had a hard time keeping warm.

John, Solange, Peter, Paul, and Kelly remained in the living room.

"It's a little after three. I'm going to catch 40 winks. I'll need my strength for tomorrow." Peter said as he pushed himself out of his chair.

"What is tomorrow?" Solange asked him.

"You, John, and I are going to the airport in the next town to look at airplanes. I will show you what to look for at the airports Manchester and Boston. We might have what we need already, and a plane could be a few miles away." He waved, taking his coat and heading out the door to his bedroom in another house.

"No chance we can use a plane out of Lebanon. They are all turbo props. We'd have to land every hour to refuel, and it would only fit about twelve of us. It will be good for us to see what we need to look for in Manchester and Boston. I'm hoping Manchester will suit our needs." John grabbed the end of a couch. "Hey, help me move this in front of the fire?"

Paul grabbed the end, and the two men moved the couch to the fire. They repeated the procedure with a second couch. "Dinner's being made. Firewood is being collected. The kids are in school. I heard a vote about relaxing for the next two weeks. I might take another nap, or at the very least relax in front of the fire. I have a busy next few days."

John kicked off his shoes and sat on one of the couches. He looked at the fire and the pile of wood in a bin next to it and nodded. "Should be enough to keep me warm and happy for a few hours."

Solange and Kelly sat on the other couch. "You do not expect to find cows alive, do you? How can a cow live through winter with no building or food?"

"They are animals. They survive. It's what they do. I bet a couple figured it out. I really do." Kelly was confident they would find cows, cows that were alive and would serve them well.

The women started a long discussion, only part of which was heard by John. He was soon snoring next to them.

Paul was not tired, but he did not have anything to do. He walked back to the cottage to let Hubba out and read a book.

44

The Lebanon Airport was a bust. Not only were the planes too small to accommodate a group of their size, the planes only had a short fuel range. There was a fuel truck in Lebanon, but it was a small truck with limited capacity, not enough fuel to fill a large jet.

"It's a start." Peter said enthusiastically. "We have fuel, and we could drive this truck down to Manchester or Boston if needed. It works. We can use it to fill a jet if necessary. It will take a few loads from this tank to fill a jet, but we can do it. Not an optimal solution, but a solution." Peter was energized.

Peter told stories on the way back from the airport, old war and flying stories. He lived an interesting life. His wife was able to join him on many of his longer layover trips. They enjoyed traveling the world. He was not a chatty person, and his main point in telling the stories was to relay that he knew how to fly. He was good, and he could take them where they wanted to go. He needed the right equipment, and a whole bunch of fuel, but he would get them to Hawaii. Peter learned a long time ago that one of a pilot's jobs was sell confidence and security to passengers.

"How are we supposed to get into a plane that is parked? Is there a handle on the door? And how are we supposed to tell if it's a 777? Are there markings on the plane?" John drove back from Lebanon.

"The easiest way for you to tell, a 737 has ten wheels, the 777 has fourteen. There are always two for the front set, that tiny arm that drops down? The back of the 777 will have six on each side, and the 737 will have four on each side."

"Is that it?" Solange wrote down the tire numbers.

"The 777 is huge. It will be much, much bigger than any of the other planes. You're talking about a plane that can fly twice as far. It's going to be enormous next to the 737. Count the wheels, but really, you won't have to worry about figuring it out." Peter gave Solange a confident look. "Look for airlines from Asia, those will be 777's. Asia, the middle east, they used the big planes. Those planes should be in Manchester and Logan. I followed the airlines when the rapture began. Everything was grounded. We didn't want the plague over here, and they didn't want the plague over there. Instead of saying 'everyone get home, this is your last flight,' countries cancelled everything, didn't even let the pilots bring the airplanes home."

"Do not forget South America, they might have big planes too." Solange smiled at the older man, showing him her continental pride.

"You're right, there might be a Brazilian airplane at Logan. Look," Peter was sitting in the front seat, and swung his arm over the back to give attention to both John and Solange. "There are going to be planes there, at both airports. Don't worry. We'll be able to move anything that's in our way for takeoff. Our big question is fuel. How much will we find, and will it start the engines. I'm not worried about whether a 777 is available. I bet there are ten of them at Logan, and at least two of them in Manchester, maybe more."

They drove through the looted and destroyed stretch of Lebanon. "Reminds me of Philly." John said to them. "Amazing it is so close to Hanover, yet there is no looting there."

"Just like the countries, Hanover didn't let Lebanon in." Peter turned back around and faced forward. "The world was pretty selfish towards the end. Love thy neighbor became avoid thy neighbor."

They were quiet as they remembered the rapture. It was easy to not think about it as they moved forward with their lives, but impossible to forget as they looked at empty and vandalized streets.

"So," John broke the silence. "Which truck should we take tomorrow?

Our suburban or the new lime green Hummer? Both have the capacity to bring people back, but I think the Hummer sends more of a message. Makes me seem a little 'cooler' than the suburban does."

"I can pull off the Hummer. You cannot." Solange told him.

"What? Are you kidding me? I can certainly pull off the Hummer." John looked towards Peter for confirmation. Peter shook his head.

"What? You too?"

"John, you are a great man, but if I see you getting out of a truck that color, well, I would think you're having a mid-life crisis or you borrowed your wife's car." Peter put his arm on John's shoulder. "I see her getting out? I whistle."

The rest of the five minute drive home was spent arguing, John futilely defending his ability to 'pull off' a lime green car. Peter and Solange laughed at him. They drove up to the main house, and John got out and walked over to Matt.

"Matt. I'm thinking of taking the Hummer tomorrow. You think I can pull it off?"

"Ha! No." Matt tossed a nerf football with Craig, Avery, Meredith, and Greg.

"Dad? Come on, you are more of a suburban guy. Actually," Greg looked around. "A Volvo sedan."

Everyone nodded.

"I can't believe this. Solange, we are taking that Green Hummer, and I am driving."

"Okay, but if we find people, they will believe it is my car."

Ahmed, Hank, and Paul pulled up two hours later. They were grinning from ear to ear.

"We found cows. We found quite a few animals actually, some cows, pigs. Most of the animals starved, but a few were able to find enough food. They are thin and weak, but Kelly thinks she can save almost all of them." Hank beamed as he relayed the story. "We found some hay and grain that was not rotted, and we fed the animals. Kelly decided to stay. There was a farm house with a woodstove and plenty of canned food."

"Milk! Can you believe it? We have cows for milk! There's even a bull! We should be able to breed a herd." Paul crossed his arms in triumph.

The tribe enjoyed an Italian feast that night. Despite his previous concerns about the volume it took, Todd made goat's milk Ricotta cheese. They grilled Hank's moose sausage and cooked it in jarred marinara sauce with red wine. The pasta was finished in the sauce, and the entire dish was sprinkled with the homemade cheese.

The meal of homemade bread, sausage, pasta, sauce, and cheese lifted their spirits. The conversation was fun and lively. A warm breeze blew from the South, and the temperatures stayed in the forties the entire evening.

Spring was coming early to New England.

Rebecca told stories of watching plane after plane depart from Manchester at the height of the rapture. "There has to be fuel there, a lot of fuel, and I know there are Southwest planes."

"Those are 737's, they can go about 3,000 miles." Peter explained. "We would get to San Fran on fumes, then have to refuel and could get to Hawaii from San Fran. We'd have to find gas. What we are looking for, and what I need John and Solange to find if possible, is a big, big plane, a 777. We could also make it on a 767, that will give us about 1,000 miles or so to spare, but the triple 7? We could fly to Hawaii and back on a full tank of fuel."

"So you're saying we could get lost for a little while." Emily asked. "but if we take one of the smaller ones, we can't get lost for very long."

"Em, we can't get lost, period, but if we are in a 777, we'll have enough fuel to hit land on the other side of Hawaii. If we aren't in one? It will be close." The table went silent as they all digested their food and the thought of being lost high in the sky over the Pacific ocean.

45

John and Solange pulled away from Hanover at 6am the next morning.

They found plane fuel in Lebanon. Their group had livestock. Everything was breaking their way.

John road the accelerator hard on the almost snow free road, and they made the 65 mile drive to the Manchester, New Hampshire International Airport in 45 minutes. Two weeks earlier it was dark at 7am. Today the sun was over the mountains and warm light flooded the canyons and valleys. John stopped the car at the entrance to the airfield. He and Solange looked at an arch that spanned the three lane entrance, "Welcome to Manchester Airport." The airport sat on a plateau at the top of a hill. John and Solange sat in the running car at the bottom of the hill.

John landed and took off from this airport dozens of times, visiting his parents throughout the years. He knew the area well.

"There's a big stuffed moose in the lobby." He told Solange. "It was a clean and well run airport."

"I have never been this far north. New York City was as cold as I ever wanted to be." She replied.

"Should we just drive around the terminal? Bust through any gates we need to, and get over to the runways?" John looked at her with shrugged shoulders.

"I do not want to get out until we need to check the fuel trucks." The South American gave a faux shiver of her shoulders.

Rebecca told them about seeing planes take off in September, and how actively the military utilized this airport during the rapture. She did not go to the airport after the plane traffic stopped, and did not know the condition of the area.

A green military jeep sat at the bottom of the hill, parked in the middle of the road leading up to the airport. It looked like a checkpoint. There was a second jeep blocking the road leading out of the airport.

"It looks like they turned this place into a military base." John pulled around the checkpoint and headed up the hill. The road spiraled up the slope before straightening out at the top for a clear view of the terminal and the airstrip.

Large green military trucks littered the terminal pickup and drop off loop and were visible on the airfield.

"They must have been moving supplies and people. Look at all these transport trucks." John pointed his finger and moved it across the landscape. "What are there? 30? 40 trucks? This looks like a military base, not a civilian airport."

The left lane was clear for John to pull the Lime Green truck around the abandoned military transports.

"You know, you're not allowed to park in the passenger drop off lane. They are very strict about that." John threw Solange a smile.

She was not in a joking mood. The images of the Metropolitan Museum were fresh in her mind, and she anticipated a battle scene similar to the one in New York. She looked for bodies, broken terminal windows, fire damage, but no carnage appeared as they crept around the glass terminal building.

The airport consisted of two buildings, a terminal, which they passed on their right, and a parking garage to their left. The garage appeared to be a standard parking structure, five levels of concrete built for short term parking near the terminal.

A small parking lot for hourly or employee parking sat between the road and the garage. Large green military tents covered the open lot.

"It looks like MASH over there." John said out loud.

"What does that mean?" Solange asked him.

He stopped the slow moving car, slid it into park, and turned towards her. "What do you mean, 'what does that mean?' MASH, the television show."

"I have not seen it before." She continued to scan the area, not giving him her full attention.

"You've never seen or heard of the show MASH? It was the biggest show in the world. More people watched the finale than, like anything ever."

"When was that?" She asked, facing him.

"I guess it ended in 1983 or '84." He calculated her age in his head.

"I was born in 1985." She smiled. "I am also from Ecuador. It might not have been shown in my country."

"I forgot how young you are. But seriously, you should know what MASH is."

"If it makes you feel better." John's hand was resting on the gear shift handle between the two front seats as she moved her hand over his. "I do not think of your age either." She leaned towards him and kissed him on the mouth. Her eyes were closed as she leaned into him. He kissed her back, but his eyes stayed open.

It was not a long kiss, but it had passion and meaning.

Solange pulled away from him, keeping her face a few inches from his. She opened her eyes. "Do you think we should walk through the tents or terminal now that we know this is a military base?" She smiled with satisfaction.

John was in shock, and his mind was no longer at the airport.

"John, do you think we should explore the situation, or focus on finding airplanes and fuel?"

He looked into her brown eyes and beautiful face, still inches from his. "Why did you do that?"

"I am sorry," she started.

"No, no, I am glad you kissed me. I just didn't expect it, and I don't understand." Her hand still rested on his. He released his grip on the gear shift and interlocked their fingers.

"I am a woman who takes control of a situation. I like you. I am attracted to you. If this last year has taught me anything, it is that life is fragile, and we must seize opportunity. When you announced you were going to Boston, I decided it was my opportunty to show you how I feel."

They held hands and shared the moment before John replied. "As easy as it would be for me to kiss you back right now, we have a job to do. We can continue the conversation about 'us' throughout this trip. Let's focus on the task at hand?" John squeezed her hand before turning to look at the tents. "Let's get out and walk around. It's 42 degrees. It's practically summer temperatures in New Hampshire."

They slipped on their winter coats, gloves, and hats. John left the car running as they exited the truck and walked towards the tents. As soon as they opened their doors they could smell rotting death. The stench was similar to the Central Park grave.

"It's getting stronger the closer we get to the parking garage." John pointed as he wrapped a scarf tightly around his nose and mouth to minimize the impact.

John went ahead of Solange. He felt her hand on his arm and stopped.

"That is where the soldiers went to die." Solange held her left hand over her nose and mouth, pointing to the concrete building with her right index finger. Canvas draped from the top of the parking garage to the ground floor, tenting the entire structure as if they were fumigating for termites.

Corners of the canvas fell open in spots. Even from their distance Solange and John could see corpses ravaged by animals and birds.

"Okay, note to self, don't go in the garage." He nodded at her and gave a thumbs up. "Do you want to go back to the truck? You've seen this movie before. No need for you to deal with it again."

"I am okay, but yes, I am not going into the parking garage." John expected to see the corner of her eyes crinkled from a smile after her witty comment. Solange's face, blocked by a scarf in similar fashion to John's, did not move. She was not comfortable or happy.

John was not sure why he was outside of his truck. He had food. He had water. He did not need guns or ammunition. He was going to the tents to satisfy his curiosity. He yearned to know how the military handled the last few weeks. How close was the government to a cure? Could he decipher the last days of their world from what was behind the curtain? He reached the tent, looked at Solange, took a breath, and pulled back the flap.

It was another bunk house. The smell hit him in the face like a baseball bat. He dropped the tent canvas and stumbled back.

"More bodies." He gagged as he told her. "There's nothing here. Let's get back in the truck and get the hell out of here." He motioned with his hand for her to walk back to the truck. "Let's find a plane. Find available fuel, and let the dead rest in peace."

"You will get no argument from me." She said, her voice muffled by the scarf around her mouth.

They walked back to the Hummer quickly, jumping into the car as soon as they could. The air was fresher inside, but the rotting smell crept into the vehicle.

John let out a sigh. "I bet there are a couple of hundred people over there."

"We should get to the other side of the terminal." Solange recommended.

John put the Hummer into drive. They moved away from the garage, their eyes turned to the right, looking through the airport buildings glass walls for any clues, and averting their eyes from the mass grave that was the Manchester Parking area.

A "restricted access" sign stood on the right side of the road to the airfield at the end of the terminal building. A large metal gate swung from a pole on the right side, locking into a pole on the left. Today the gate was open.

John followed the road to the end of the terminal and out onto the tarmac. The military used armed guards in jeeps as sentries instead of gates and fences. With the people dead, the airstrip was open.

"Well, that was easy." John commented as they drove on the tarmac side of the airport. Empty terminal gates were giant rectangular holes in the glass walls. The passenger ramps were retracted and snug against the building.

"Lucky for us, no one was left to lock the door." She nodded.

"Lucky for us indeed." He pointed to four large fuel trucks with white cylinder tanks on their backs. John made his way to the vehicles.

The tarmac and runway were almost clear of snow. Puddles and islands of drifts dotted the concrete landscape, but the plateau of the airport and slanted design of the runway rid the area of snow naturally.

"I got this, you stay inside. No use both of us dealing with the cold and smelly air." He opened his door, jumped out quickly, and shut it before too much foul air could rush in.

The trucks were similar in look and shape to the one in Lebanon, but they were much larger, used for large commercial jets rather than commuter planes. John knew where to look for the fuel capacity gauge on the side of the white tanker. The gauges were not dependent on power. The first truck's needle was between half and three-quarters full. The other three trucks were full. As he checked each truck and found fuel, he gave thumbs up. When he saw the fourth truck was full, he put both of his arms in the air and danced in circles.

He jogged back over to the Hummer and hopped in quickly. "We are set. Three full, one two thirds, plenty of fuel."

"What was that?" Solange asked him with a frown.

"What was what?" John replied, confused.

"Your little dance. What was that?"

"Rocky Balboa at the top of the steps in Philly. It's cool."

"No." She said, sitting forward in her seat. "That was a bad Rocky. You looked like Mary Tyler Moore throwing her hat in the air. It was not what a man should do."

"You know Mary Tyler Moore but you don't know MASH? How is that possible?"

"My father liked strong female role models. He ordered Mary Tyler Moore tapes and we watched them together." She told him. "We still need to find a plane."

"I know there is a plane at Logan. I hope we can find one here, but finding fuel was the key. We can figure out the plane situation. You watched Mary Tyler Moore with your father?"

"I did." She scanned the horizon as he asked her the question. "Over there!" She pointed to a group of planes. "It looks like the military moved all of the commercial planes over there."

John followed her finger to a grouping of planes, a dozen white jets of various sizes rested near a few brown UPS planes.

"All right, let's go check it out." He slipped the Hummer into drive and headed towards the parking lot of planes at the end of the main runway a quarter of a mile away. Some of the planes were parked on the grass next to the security fence. As they drove closer, they noticed the size differences. There were two enormous jets, dwarfing the others. John and Solange assumed these two were the 777's needed for their trip. There were 8 smaller planes, the same size as the three UPS planes, parked towards the end of the fence. Seven smaller jets and turbo prop planes were further off the runway.

John pulled directly behind the behemoths.

"Three sets of wheels on each side. Exactly as Peter told us." Solange nodded to the landing gear.

"Well, if we want to go to Hawaii, it appears we have a way to get there." John put the Hummer in reverse, turned it around, and headed back down the runway. "Let's get out of here. This place is a giant graveyard."

"We can send Peter down with a group. He can see if the plane will start, and get it fueled." She paused. "If we decide we want to go to Hawaii."

"What's your take on that? What do you think we should do? Should we risk our lives on a plane to get to paradise?"

Solange took a deep breath, thinking about the question. "I think so, yes."

John gave her a quick glance. "That's it? Yes? You are cut and dry on your opinion?"

"I am. I believe we can thrive there. There are no predators. There is food, fish, vegetables, fruit, water. It is warm. It has rain. It has sun. I believe it is a risk, but the risk is worth the reward. Peter is confident and appears capable. If the fuel works, we should go while we can."

"I agree." John told her. "Did you ever watch any of the survivalist shows?"

"The reality show about people voting each other off?" She asked.

"No, the ones where they would drop people, usually one guy, maybe a couple of people, in a remote location and he or they would need to survive for a few days, maybe a week. Did you ever see those?"

"The man who fought the wild?" She replied back.

"Yes, those are the shows, exactly. Anyway, whenever they are on a tropical island where it isn't cold? It is child's play for those people. As long as they have water, they can go forever on a tropical island. There are fish, they catch crabs, they have bananas and pineapples. It was almost a joke." John left the runway area, travelling through the old checkpoint and back onto the public road leading out of the airport and to the highway.

"Put that against the ones where they are stuck in Canada in the winter? There is no food, there is almost no heat, they struggle to find firewood and fuel. It's scary to think about us trying to get through a harsh winter three of four years down the road. All of our canned or boxed food is gone, and we are relying on crops and canning, maybe hunting to feed a group of at least 22 people?" They turned out of the airport toward the highway to Boston. "Solange, I think we need to take this flight to Hawaii. I don't think it's a choice. In my mind, it is get to

Hawaii or die in five years."

He turned up the entrance ramp to the highway.

"As I said." Solange told him. "I think we need to go."

It was 7:30am as they made their way towards Boston. In just thirty minutes they had secured fuel and found two planes suitable for a flight to a Hawaiian island. The Manchester runway was clear, and their destiny would be set if the fuel worked.

"We have a few minutes." John said to her. "How about talking about 'us' for the rest of the trip?"

"I enjoy the sound of 'us.' What would you like to discuss?"

"You don't think the age difference is an issue?" John asked her, baffled that this beautiful woman in her twenties kissed him a half hour ago.

"I do not have many options. Your brother Todd is taken. You are the next logical choice."

"So I'm just a consolation prize?"

Solange laughed.

"You are a strong, confident man, who rescued me from a bad situation. You are a good leader for our group, and you give off a masculine quality that I find handsome. I have never dated an older man, but I find you interesting and attractive, and I want to spend more time with you. I find myself missing you when we are apart. I did not propose to you, but I would like to explore a relationship and see where we might go." She rested her hand on his thigh.

"I married the love of my life when I was in college. I haven't looked at another woman since then. I do like you, and I am attracted to you, and I find myself drawn to you when we are in the same company, but you have to take it slow with me. I'm not ready for anything fast, and I want to make sure my boys are ready for me to date."

"Of course." Solange said. "So if I asked you to pull the car over and fold down the backseats?"

John looked at her, his head turning away from the road. She rubbed his leg higher. He lifted his foot off the accelerator and the Hummer slowed to a stop on the highway.

30 minutes later the two lay together under a LL Bean flannel duvet cover, basking in the glow of their new relationship. "So that's what you consider taking it slow? Interesting."

"Life is too short for slow." She faced away from him, her naked body pressed against him. Her eyes were closed and she wore a grin. Her head was on a soft flannel pillow packed for their night in Boston. The car sat in the middle of highway 493 still running. John reached up and turned off the engine.

The sun was higher in the sky, but the outdoor temperature crept into to Hummer. Solange pulled him tightly around her to keep warm.

John was conflicted. He still wore his wedding ring, honoring his wife of over twenty years, but that life was gone. He felt a pull to Solange, a desire for her as a woman, but also for the new life she represented, a life of love, respect, and passion. He decided to enjoy the moment, to live in the now, and he squeezed her when she pulled him closer.

"Do you mind if we take a nap together? Just for a little while?" She asked him softly.

He kissed her on the back of her neck. "We have all the time in the world."

She gave a satisfied sound and drifted off to sleep.

They awoke an hour later, making love again in the cold car under a warm flannel blanket. After a few moments of tenderness, she asked him to start the car and heat the interior so she could get dressed.

"But I'm cold too, why do I have to start the car?" He asked her, as he slipped out from under the warmth of the double flannel sheet.

"Because you are the man, and that is what men do."

"I see how this relationship is going." He said, pulling on his clothes as quickly as he could to escape the cold air of the car.

"I think you will do just fine." She said from under the blanket.

He knew she was right, and he sat patiently as the inside warmed enough for her to climb out from under the covers. John watched her get dressed, looking at her body as it went from naked to wearing tight jeans and a cashmere sweater. He enjoyed watching her. Solange noticed and smiled, slowing down to let him soak it all in. She knew she was beautiful, desirable to men. She had always been, but she rarely returned affections. She was genuinely taken with this man, and she let him enjoy her however he wanted. If he liked watching her dress, she would dress slowly.

"Stop looking at me that way, unless you want to turn the car off again." She made her way from the back seat to the front.

"I'm sorry, it's just, you're very pretty, and I, well." He stammered like a teenager.

"I enjoy your gaze. I am just warning you that your gaze has consequences."

John took a moment to compose himself. "Okay, let's focus on our job for a moment. We need to get to Boston before dark." He put the Hummer into drive and pushed down on the gas. The tires squealed as the truck jumped out of their parking spot. A few minutes later they were on Interstate 93 South towards Boston.

"What do you think? Philadelphia or Washington D.C.?" She asked him, referencing a dead city in ruins and an intact metropolis with survivors.

"I think Washington. Judging from all the military we just saw, I bet they had Boston under wraps. I doubt it got out of control like Philly. Who knows, maybe that's why the military was staging up in Manchester instead of at Logan."

"I have never been to Boston, and know little about the city. Where should we go? Is there a good spot to light a fire and signal the rest of the city?"

"It's pretty spread out, but it's also flat. I've spent some time there. We can start in Beacon Hill or Back Bay. There is a big park with ponds for ducks, maybe lighting a fire will create a scene. We've gotten pretty lucky the last three times we've looked for people. Hopefully we haven't used up all of our luck." He drove quickly down the highway.

"Let me know when you are hungry for lunch. Todd made a large sausage sandwich for us to share." She drank from one of their water bottles and offered him a sip when she was done. He took the bottle and drank.

The drive from Manchester to Boston was quick. John unknowingly benefitted from the military keeping the highway clear to link the airports for troop and supply movement.

John and Solange used the car time to learn more about each other. John knew almost nothing about Ecuador. He asked about her life, her family, why she was in the U.S. to study. John wanted to know everything.

Solange was open about her life, her family's money, her privileged up-bringing. She talked about her siblings, her parents, her country. She had a softer side, one that John had not seen, and it came out as she spoke.

Her rapture story was similar to Jamie's. Solange was in school when the epidemic hit Brazil, and all intercontinental travel stopped. She was stuck in Richmond, Virginia at VCU, alone, separated from everyone and everything she loved.

"I'm sorry." John said to her, putting his hand on her leg as she talked about losing her family.

"I am too." She did not cry. "What makes me most sad, what keeps me up at night when I am not exhausted from the day, is the idea that I will never see any of it again. I will never step foot in my house. I will never see my dogs, or say hello to my Nana. I cannot play futbol with my brothers and sisters and cousins, and I will not hug my mother or father. I never got to say goodbye to anything. I was up here on an adventure, a six month trip for fun because I am a spoiled rich girl, and my decision to experience the United States at the wrong time means I lost the ability to see everything and everyone I loved ever again."

"I think about your son Greg. He was at school, and did not get to say goodbye to his mother, or his friends, but I am one step further. I did not get to say goodbye to my homeland, my country, my continent." She paused for a moment, sighing with a deep breath. "But I have made peace with it. I cannot change the way my life has gone. I am moving forward." She clasped his hand, still resting on her leg. "I have found you. I have found a new family, and we will make a new home. I decided to not feel sad about my loss, to only make my thoughts of my family and home happy thoughts, to make their memories happy memories, honoring the time. I had a truly great life, and while that part is over, I can be happy it was filled with love."

Solange's mixture of heartache for the past and hope for the future was the norm among tribe. She had her moments of sorrow, black hours of loss and depression, but as her time with the group continued, her optimism and spirit grew.

"How old are you again?" John asked in a tone that let her know it was a rhetorical question.

"Living alone in a strange city in a strange country adds years to your maturity. When I say alone, I mean there is literally no one else." She squeezed his hand.

Boston was on the horizon, still a few miles away, but getting larger in the windshield. There were neighborhoods on either side of the highway, and the landscape turned decidedly urban. John and Solange continued to talk until John noticed the "Copley Square/Back Bay" exit sign.

"That's our exit." He announced.

Solange looked to her left and saw a large monument on a hill in an open area. "What is that?" She asked. John slowed the Hummer to get a better look.

"It's Bunker Hill." He stopped the truck. "It's certainly the historical choice, and it looks like it might be the highest point in the area." He took the exit onto Route 1. John found Boston was easy to navigate when he did not have to obey the road and highway directions. Ignoring one-way streets and "do not enter" signs, they pulled up to Bunker Hill one minute later.

It was a beautiful spring day in Boston. The temperature was in the 50's and a slight breeze came off the water. They walked up the hill to the monument, taking stock of their situation and location.

"It's certainly high up, but I wouldn't live here. I'd be in Beacon Hill or Back Bay. There are larger homes, fireplaces, it's a lot closer to those buildings." John pointed towards downtown. Solange looked around the monument. The grass was overgrown and full of weeds, like every other location in the world.

"I can imagine how beautiful this area was." She swept her hand across the mangy hillside. There was trash on the sidewalks and thick rotting leaves covered the ground.

"It is going to get worse. The plants are going to consume everything. It's another reason we have to make our decision on where to go soon." He looked around the monument area. "We have two boxes of those starter logs, right?"

"Yes." She replied.

"Let's put a fire here, leaving a note to meet us over in the park I mentioned. We can start a fire in the park too. I like this spot for a fire, but we'll have more luck over there." He pointed towards the city. "We're not trying to signal a ship." He moved his head towards the water. "We're trying to find people."

They agreed on the plan, and looked for a way to start a signal fire.

John clapped his hands. "I've got it."

"What?" Solange asked him.

"Let's get one of the dumpsters that are behind a restaurant or building. We can set it out in the open, light it on fire. The metal will contain the flames, and hopefully there will be enough trash to sustain the fire for a while."

Solange nodded, smiling as he described his idea. It did not take them long to locate a dumpster. Solange wrapped a rope around the bin and secured it to their tow hitch. John eased the Hummer forward and towed the dumpster the short distance to the bottom of the monument.

"I'm not worried about being on top of the monument hill. The fire is going to smoke like crazy. I want to get it into an open area so we don't set the neighborhood on fire." John and Solange worked well together, methodically and intelligently. They knew they did not have a deadline for getting this fire started. It was only 11:30. John siphoned gas from a nearby car, and poured the gas into the dumpster. The trash was from a Bunker Hill museum located across the street from the monument. It contained boxes, wood frames, and plastic. The dumpster lid was shut, keeping out rain and snow. The trash had not decomposed over the winter. Solange lit a singles newspaper from a nearby machine and threw it into the gasoline soaked trash. The gas caught immediately, and the signal fire pumped thick black smoke into the air.

John put his arm around Solange. "Why don't you get lunch? I'm going to find a few chairs or tables from the museum to throw on the fire." He made his way over to a nearby building, smashing a window, and unlocking the door.

Solange pulled off her work gloves along with a pair of yellow latex gloves underneath. She tossed both sets of gloves into the trunk. She jumped in the Hummer and started the car. The sun was shining, and the interior was warm. She let the warmth soak into her bones. It may have been 50 outside, but it was still chilly to her. The warm car was a welcome change.

She pulled their lunch out of the backseat, a wicker picnic basket with a leather strap. She unhooked the strap and grabbed the large sausage sandwich made on a baguette. It was already sliced in half. She had a bag of potato chips, a chocolate bar, and two sodas.

John opened the door and got into the car. "Oh man does this feel good." He said to her. He flipped his gloves into the backseat and squirted sanitizer onto his hands. "Soda? How did you sneak two sodas?"

"The women are controlling the camp. Todd thinks he controls the food. I asked Emily for the chips and soda. It was easy."

John grabbed one of the plastic bottles. He twisted off the top and took a long drink. He closed his eyes and grinned with satisfaction. "I don't care that it's warm, that is delicious." Soda was a dwindling resource, and rarely used.

"I cannot get used to the U.S. version made with corn syrup. I enjoy the ones I used to have made with sugar." She popped a chip in her mouth, another soon to be lost luxury.

"Let's drive over to the other park while we eat." He put the car into drive. "There are better areas to sit outside and en oy our picnic."

"There may be better places, but I am not leaving this warm car. I do not like the cold." She buckled her seatbelt as they drove lazily towards Back Bay. They took a ramp up to the highway, over the bridge, and onto Cambridge Street.

"So that's why you want to go to Hawaii. You don't care about anything other than 'not being cold.'"

"It is a reason, just as valid as any other." She ate another chip and drank her soda.

46

Dan sat on the balcony of his house reading *Dubliners* by James Joyce. He tried to alternate his reading between popular less sophisticated novels, and ones he considered classics. The other people he lived with were inside arguing about when to leave Boston for a warmer climate. He wanted a break from the discussion. It was the same fight day in and day out. He excused himself and retired to the second story deck, outfitted with comfortable chairs and a dining table. The sun felt warm as he read. He was in jeans and a thick flannel shirt. He wore a red, white, and blue cotton knit stocking cap, a habit picked up over his last decade in New England.

It was not Dan's house. It was owned by a friend who died from the rapture while vacationing in Bali. Dan knew it had a half dozen fireplaces, heavy stone walls, and was a perfect place to ride out a New England winter while he and his new friends figured out how to survive the apocalypse.

Dan lost his wife and five children to the rapture. He worked part of the year in Boston and lived the rest of the year in Seattle. He and his family were in Rhode Island when the disease struck. Dan was a man of power and influence, but he could not save his family. His private plane was grounded. The hospitals were closed. When his family died like so many others, he was left to figure out how to survive a Boston winter without food, water, or electricity.

He was a laid back guy from Seattle, but possessed a work ethic that rivaled anyone alive. Blessed with a gift for leadership, and backed by a relentless pursuit of excellence, perfection, and knowledge, his talents and drive brought him unfathomable success, success that died with the rapture.

Stripped of his prestige and wealth, Dan focused on survival. He carefully studied potential houses and locations before choosing his friend's house in the Back Bay area of Boston. He learned how to fish and catch seafood in the abandoned Boston harbor. He kept physically fit without burning too many calories and jeopardizing his food. Dan managed every controllable aspect of his life.

The other people who survived and currently lived with Dan did not fall into the controllable category.

Dan met Ryan, a lawyer, after the military disappeared from Boston. The men decided to merge their survival operations. Those were the words Ryan used to describe the partnership. Dan, though he did not particularly like Ryan, knew two people had a better chance of surviving the winter than one.

The men met Karen, a pediatric nurse, several weeks later. She was wandering the streets, dehydrated, and hungry.

Lucinda was the fourth survivor. They did not know her last name, what she did, or from where she came. She had a Texas accent, but claimed to be from Medford, Massachusetts. She was sitting on their back steps one afternoon when the group returned from scavenging. She walked through the back door that afternoon, and had yet to leave the house since.

Dan spent most of his time looking for wood, fuel, water, and food. They had lobster traps set in the harbor. He checked the traps and fished when the weather agreed. He tried to stay out of the house as much as he could. When he was home, he read quietly in his room or outside.

He needed his alone time today. Five months cramped into a house with people he did not like was exhausting. Dan did not know what to do, but he would not accept a life with Lucinda and Ryan. He was going to break away. Karen was a good person, a hard worker, and did not bother him. He had already asked her to leave with him.

Dan finished the third short story in his new book, used a picture of his family as a bookmark, and looked at the city.

He saw a thick black stream of smoke billowing from across the Charles River. It was a clear day. The electricity had been off for months. There was no way a fire started spontaneously.

"Survivors," he muttered to himself.

Dan dropped the book on his chair and ran inside. "There are people in the city. They just started a fire across the river."

The group sitting at the table looked at him, mouths agape. Ryan was the first to stand. "Let's check it out." He walked to a closet and retrieved his coat and a gun. Karen and Lucinda remained seated.

"Do we know if they're friendly?" Lucinda asked in her heavy Texas accent.

"I see a fire burning. It might not be people at all, but there isn't any other explanation. No, I don't know if they are friend or foe." Dan told her. "Would you like to stay here while Ryan and I check it out?" It was not a real question. Lucinda was not leaving the house.

"I'd like to go." Karen stood, "but I understand if we leave Lucinda behind, you know, to be safe." Karen went to the closet. She was in her late twenties. Nine months ago she was a morbidly obese nightshift nurse at Boston Children's Hospital. Today she was down 120 pounds, and excited for an adventure with Dan and Ryan.

Lucinda was scared.

"Lucy, stay here, we got this." Dan grabbed a walkie talkie from the table next to the door, turned it on and set it in front of Lucinda. "We'll keep you up to date."

Lucinda's shoulders, tense with worry, eased slightly. "You don't mind?" She asked, calming at the prospect of staying in the house.

"We'll go, you stay here. I'd ask you to watch for more activity, but whatever." Ryan used a tone of derision and shame towards the woman. Lucinda barely stepped out on the balcony let alone the house.

They left Lucinda behind and headed to Dan's truck, a four door Ford pickup parked behind the house. It was four wheel drive, could haul or move anything, and the cab warmed faster than any car manufactured, at least Dan believed it warmed faster than any car he ever owned.

"I bet it's tourists. I could swear the fire is at Bunker Hill." Dan joked. He pulled the gear on the steering wheel and they drove towards the smoke. He headed onto Storrow Drive. The road gave them the best view up the river and the source of the smoke.

Ryan was looking towards the fire when he noticed a neon green vehicle on the highway bridge going south.

"Holy shit! Dan, Karen, it's a Hummer, a bright green Hummer." Ryan swore like a sailor.

Dan slammed on the breaks, swung the truck around, and tried to keep the glowing green vehicle in his sights. His truck was headed on an intercept pattern at North Station. Dan leaned on his horn, accelerating to get ahead of the slow moving Hummer.

Solange and John drove casually down the highway, enjoying their conversation, chips, and soda. "Did you hear that?" Solange asked. Her ears were younger than John's.

"What?"

She rolled down her window. The sound of a car horn blared. John slowed the Hummer to a stop. He was about to enter a tunnel, but stayed outside of the mouth and in the sunlight. He did not see another car, but he heard the horn.

"Do you see anyone?" He asked Solange. They were in an artificial valley, a walled part of the highway just before the tunnel. They had two ways to look, up or back.

John sat down in his seat. "Well, I'm going to eat my sandwich. Let's give them a little while. They saw us. They signaled us." He shrugged his shoulders and took a bite of the hoagie.

"It is delicious, right? Todd is becoming a master at the bread." She continued to enjoy her half of the sandwich. They ate their lunch in silence, waiting for whoever honked the car horn to find them.

Dan stopped the truck. Ryan stood in the flatbed looking over the edge of the road that entered the tunnel. Ryan's face appeared in the open driver's window.

"They're stopped at the entrance to the tunnel. I could swear they are eating lunch or something. If I had to guess, they heard the horn and are waiting for us."

"Get in and let's go meet our new friends." Dan looked at Karen as they waited for Ryan to get back into the truck. "Are you ready for this?" He asked her.

"I was getting a little tired of the three of you. It will be nice to meet new faces." She smiled.

Ryan got into the passenger's seat. He pulled a handgun from his jacket pocket and made sure the safety was off and a round was in the chamber.

"Seriously?" Dan asked him.

"I don't trust anyone." Ryan did not look at Dan when he replied, he continued to check his weapon. "We have food, water, heat. Those are things people might want to steal. They aren't taking them from me."

Dan shook his head. "What an idiot" he thought.

Dan put the car in reverse and drove backwards across the causeway.

He went up the exit ramp for 93S and hung a sharp right. He could see the green Hummer idling just outside of the tunnel. He accelerated to a moderate speed before parking next to a man and a woman eating sandwiches and drinking soda.

"Are they having a picnic?" Karen stuck her head between the front seats. She faced away from the green car so her lips could not be read. "I swear to god, they're having a picnic."

John waved and rolled down his window. The situation was surreal. John made the universal 'roll down your window' signal by twirling his hand in a circle. Ryan obliged, as did Karen from the rear seat.

"Hello. My name is John and this is my friend Solange. We came from New Hampshire looking for survivors. We represent a group of twenty some people."

"And a dog" Solange said behind him.

"Oh, and a dog, and we are hoping to meet people like you to invite you to join us." He took a quick bite of his sandwich. John had a feeling he would not have the opportunity to finish his lunch once they got out of the Hummer. He was starved from the morning, and wanted to eat as much of his sandwich as possible.

Karen spun around again. "Did he say they have a dog?"

Dan turned off the truck and opened his door. He walked around the front of both cars and towards Solange's side of the Hummer. She saw him coming to her door. She opened it and got out. John put his sandwich down. His jaw was on the floor when he recognized who was walking around the front of his car.

"Hello, my name is Dan." Solange accepted his handshake.

"Solange Wright. Very nice to meet you, Dan."

"You don't sound like you're from New Hampshire." He gave her a quizzical look.

"I am from Ecuador. I was studying at Virginia Commonwealth University and became stranded in Richmond, Virginia. I met John and his family as they made their way to New Hampshire."

"Well, again, my name is Dan. I have two friends, Karen and Ryan talking to John through the window. We have one more survivor named Lucinda. She is a shy, and decided to stay in our house until we discovered the source of the thick black smoke."

"We lit the fire. We were finishing our lunch and driving to Beacon Bay to start a similar signal fire."

"It's Back Bay or Beacon Hill." Dan corrected her with a smile, "Although I guess it's not really anything anymore." Dan took a step back, shook his head, and continued to smile. He was suddenly overwhelmed by the situation. "You're real, you're actually survivors, and there are over twenty of you?" He touched his fingers to his eyes. "I know it's not over, I know this is still a nightmare, but," Tears rolled down his face.

Solange opened her arms and stepped into the tall man's grasp. "So many times we debated leaving, debated trying to make a break for Florida or back to my home in Seattle." He squeezed her tightly. "But we stuck to our guns. We knew there have to be other people, and we gave it until May."

He stopped talking. Solange was a good judge of character, and she liked Dan instantly. She knew he needed a moment, a few seconds to absorb the realization that he was saved. She had been rescued herself, she knew the feeling. She understood his elation and relief.

Dan let her go. "Let's get you back to our house. I can jump in with, John is it? Ryan can drive the truck." Dan looked over the hood of the Hummer. "Hey Ryan, slide over and drive the truck back. I'll jump in here and get them over to the house."

Ryan grimaced.

"Well, John, I will see you in a second." Karen said to her new friend.

Solange got into the Hummer after waving to the truck.

Ryan had yet to say a word to John or Solange. He sat in the front seat, his eyes narrow. "I look forward to talking about options and making some decisions." He told John before rolling up his window and moving to the driver's seat. Karen waved from the back window.

The rear door of the Hummer opened and the tall man got in. His hand shot through the gap in the front seat. "John, very nice to meet you, Dan Couples."

"Hi, Dan." John tried to keep his cool as he shook the man's hand. "I am a big fan."

Solange gave John an odd look. "What do you mean?" She asked him, looking back at their passenger.

"Dan is a pretty famous person. He is the quarterback of the New England Patriots." John did not let go of Dan's hand. "Seriously, I'm a huge fan."

"Thank you, I appreciate it, but none of that means very much now. I'm just a survivor like the rest of you." He nodded at John, acknowledging the compliment.

John finally let go of Dan, turned around and caught his breath. He took a moment to compose himself. "Dan Couples! I'm in a car with Danny Couples!" He screamed in his head. John was like a little kid meeting one of his idols.

He calmed down enough to ask his new passenger, "Um, where am I going?" John tried to sound collected, but his voice cracked a bit from excitement.

"Pull a u-turn, we'll pick up the exit ramp a little ways back and take Storrow Drive to our house. Boston is pretty easy to get around when you don't have to follow the directional laws."

"That's what I said." John laughed. He actually giggled. Solange gave him a stern look, similar to the one she gave him after his bad dancing at the Manchester Airport.

"I know you are going to have to repeat this to our group, but what's your story? Where are you from? You've hooked up with other survivors in other cities?" Dan was ecstatic to meet new people. "This nightmare may be coming to an end after all."

Solange gave their background. She did not give details about their future plans, focusing instead on the events that led to today. She was at the part about meeting the group in Washington D.C. when John pulled up to a large stone house. He parked next to the truck Ryan drove.

"This is it." Dan said, waiting for Solange to finish. "I've been here since October. I gave serious consideration to driving across the country to get back home to Seattle, but the reports I read about the Midwest discouraged me. I knew the owner of this place, he and his wife were good friends. They got stuck in Bali. I had a place in Rhode Island, but it was huge, and there was no way I could keep it heated. I also wanted to find some people, any people, and I knew the city was the best place to do that." They exited the Hummer.

"Do you have food?" John asked him.

"Oh, yeah, we have plenty of food. We have some lobster traps we..."

"So will anyone be offended if I bring my lunch inside and finish eating? I am starving." John cut him off and held up the picnic basket.

"No." Dan shook his head and chuckled. "Don't worry about it. We have plenty of food. It might actually calm Ryan down. He is worried you are here to steal our supplies."

They went into the building through a back door. The house had a reverse floor plan. The first level was a four car garage. Stairs led to an empty floor that used to be a laundry, gym, home office, and a half bath. John and Solange followed Dan up the stairs to the true third floor, a beautiful room with a gigantic fireplace and open kitchen concept. The ceilings were low, and the room seemed warm, warmer than what a single fire, even the giant fireplace roaring in the wall, should have allowed.

"I picked this house because my friend was very into green energy. There are a few solar panels on the roof, and he had electric heat on this floor powered by the solar cells. I would have been dumb and made the ceiling vaulted in here, you know, create a dramatic effect. He kept them low with double insulation. The fire place, the heaters, we were comfortable during the harsh winter."

Ryan and Karen waited to speak, not wanting to be rude. "Hello." Karen said, rushing over to hug Solange. "Oh my god, this is incredible." She moved to John and gave him a hug.

Ryan was not as warm. He stepped forward to shake their hands. Lucinda stood alone, waiting for an introduction. She was shifting from one foot to the other nervously.

"Hello, John Dixon." John said to her, stretching out his hand.

"Lucinda. Danny calls me Lucy sometimes, but he's the only one I let do that." She looked down at the floor as she shook his hand. "Glad to meet ya'll. We have so much space, so please make yourselves at home." She shook Solange's hand. "I was tickled when Karen radioed me and said she'd found two more survivors. Ryan," She turned to him. "Why don't you check the lobster traps, let's have some lobster tonight. I know we're sick of it, but it's been a few days, and I bet these people would love some." She was frenetic in her mannerisms.

"Would you mind if we sat down and finished our lunch? John and I have been working all morning, either driving or trying to find you. We are very hungry." Solange looked towards John who held up their basket.

Five minutes later they were seated around a table, except for Lucinda, who would not sit down. She was too jumpy, and stood in the kitchen area. She prepared lunch for her group while John and Solange ate. John gave a quick recount of their tribe's story.

"So your three brothers survived?" Ryan asked. John could tell he was suspicious.

"Yes, and my three sons and two nephews." John told him.

"I don't buy it." Ryan said, leaning back in his chair. "None of that makes sense." The lawyer shook his head.

"So you think Solange and I are making up our story?" John asked him.

"I don't know, I'm just saying I have a hard time believing that an entire family survived. Ask Karen, she saw thousands of people die, tens of thousands. No way nine people from the same family lived."

Solange did not like Ryan. He was a rude bully. She did not have time for a person like him. "It is more amazing to me that John's sister in law, Emily, survived with her husband and sons. You could convince me that a group of brothers survived, and that maybe their children would be resistant, but for a husband and wife? Truly unbelievable."

Karen stared at John and Solange as they ate. "Where did you get that bread?" She had a tone in her voice that conveyed deep envy. "We don't have bread, or don't make much of it. Where did you get that? It looks so good."

John smiled. He could tell she would follow him to the northern provinces of Canada for bread. "My brother, Todd, has become a bit of an artisan bread baker. He has a pizza oven, makes different kinds every morning." He held the sandwich out to her, "would you like a bite? Honestly, it's too much food for me."

She shook her head. "I'm a little afraid of eating sausage that is probably a year old." She made a face.

Solange put her sandwich on her plate and used a nearby knife to cut the remainder in half. "It is fresh sausage made yesterday. We, or I should say Hank and Paul, John's other brothers, killed a moose a few days ago. We are curing most of the meat for steaks, letting it get tender, but we had moose burgers and moose sausage already."

Solange handed half of the sandwich to Karen. The nurse accepted the gesture without hesitation. "Oh my gawd!" She said in a thick Boston accent. "This is amazing! Can we go to your camp tonight? How far is it? Can I go there by myself? I'm there. I don't care if you have three fake brothers, and claim Paul Bunyan and Shrek are up there making these sandwiches. If there is more bread and sausage, wait a second, is this cheese? Dan, there is cheese on this sandwich."

"There is more, and we can leave whenever. Solange and I are just a search party, we do not plan on staying here more than one night."

"Whoa, whoa, whoa, Karen, you just met these people, and now you're willing to take your life in your own hands for a sandwich? I know you used to be fat, but come on." Ryan leaned forward in his chair and turned to John. "So that's your game. You come in and steal people from other groups? "

"Ryan, I am a direct person, so let me be as blunt with you as you appear to be with everyone else. We are a group of survivors. We are living in New Hampshire. We are making plans for our future. I," he paused. "Solange and I."

"Thank you." Solange said to him.

"Sure" he nodded to her. "Solange and I made a trip down here to find survivors and ask them to voluntarily join our group. If you do not want to come with us, okay. If you do, you are welcome. We don't have rules, we don't have a grand plan. We still need to figure out how to survive once the cans of soup and boxes of pasta run out. I don't have an agenda. If you don't trust me, I don't really care. Stay here. Live on your own. Drive to Florida. If a person chooses not to come with us, totally their decision, but please understand, it is anyone's individual decision to make. You make yours, she can make hers."

"Nice choice, join the cult or get left behind." Ryan narrowed his eyes again. His hands clenched.

"Okay, let's just calm down." Dan put his hands up. "Ryan, check the attitude. I understand you are leery of new people, but you have to at least be polite." He looked at Karen. "You're not fat, he didn't mean that." She nodded to Dan, who knew the fat comments from Ryan stung her. "I guess story time is over. We can catch up later. Let's eat, talk, find out more, then we can make a decision."

"I'm going." Karen said quickly. "I can't rot here anymore. They have children, they have families, I want to feel that again. I'm going. Dan, I respect you more than anyone I've ever met outside of my parents, but this isn't a group decision. This is my life."

"Fucking ingrate." Ryan spit at her.

"Ryan, calm down." Dan tried to stop him.

"No, no fucking way, Dan. We keep her alive, we find her, fat and helpless, and we give her a warm place, and food for what, six months? And now she finds a new sugar daddy and she walks away? You ungrateful bitch."

John's eyes narrowed. He gave Solange a look before turning towards Karen. "You are welcome to come with us, Karen. I am sorry I have caused an issue within your group."

"John, it's not your fault. We've been cooped up in this house for months. It's safe to say that we are four very different people from different walks of life, and our personalities don't mesh as well as they could." Dan put his hand over Karen's hand resting on the table. "I agree with Karen, I'm ready for a change, a life instead of survival."

"Are you out of your fucking head?" Ryan said to him.

Dan turned his full attention to Ryan, "I'm a laid back person, you know that, but you also know I'm not going to let you talk to me like that. Karen is right, this isn't a group decision. I speak for myself, and I want to leave this house. I can help these people, but not as much as they can help me. They are making the best of this horrible situation. It's time we started to do the same."

"Great, so my choice is to join a group I know nothing about, or stay here with Crazy Lucinda?" Ryan flipped his thumb over his shoulder towards the frail woman standing in the kitchen.

John's knuckles were white, his hands clasped in fists of anger. He did not understand who this person was, and he did not want Ryan's poison near his family.

Solange squeezed his leg tightly as Ryan threw insults around the room. She could tell John was ready to pop. She could also tell that neither of them wanted Ryan to come up to Hanover.

John stood up from the table. "I've caused a bad situation. I'm sorry. You need to talk as a group. You owe each other that."

"Who the fuck do you think you..."

John put up his hand as Ryan was talking. "I have no idea why you talk to people the way you do. Maybe you are lashing out because you are threatened, maybe you're just an asshole, I don't know, but I do understand your argument, and you're right. You all need to talk." He turned to Solange. "We'll figure out where to go for tonight, don't worry about us. There is a lot for you to digest. How about we come back tomorrow morning?"

"Did you seriously just call me an asshole?" Ryan pushed his chair back.

Dan stood too. "I think you're right, we could use some time. The four of us owe each other that much." Dan's eyes moved from Karen to Lucinda, then back to John and Solange. "Are you sure you can find somewhere to stay? "

"Dan? This guy comes in here..."

"Ryan, he's leaving, we can talk about it when they're gone. Let it go." He extended his hand to John. "We'll see you tomorrow."

John and Solange packed their basket and walked down the stairs with Dan. "Hey," the tall muscular man said to them at the car. "Karen and I are coming with you. I'm not sure what Lucinda will do, she has some issues."

"It was very nice to meet you, Dan Couples." Solange gave him a hug.

After the hug, Dan pointed down the road. "Lucinda mentioned our lobster traps. If you want a few, we're tired of eating them. Our traps are set in the harbor, near the aquarium. There are a bunch of big red buoys. You can't miss them. There are hooks on the pier, just haul them up using the pulley and crank." He pulled a walkie talkie out of his pocket. "Take this. I'll let you know if anything happens before tomorrow morning."

John shook his hand and thanked him. "Any advice on a cheap room for the night?"

"If it were me, I'd find a church. Most of the back offices have a fireplace. They were built of stone a long time ago, and should heat up nicely for the evening. Find a pot, boil some water, enjoy some lobster. I'll see you tomorrow. Hopefully we can talk in a more civil manner."

"Dan, I'm sorry we caused an argument. Solange and I have been through this before, and we've never had a negative reaction. The people we met in New York were starving, the people in D.C. were desperate for help with three kids under the age of eight. I did not expect to be such a problem."

Dan shook his head. "You hit the nail on the head. Ryan's a total asshole. I've had to live with him for six months. He's scared. Hopefully he'll figure it out, because he's a good worker and a strong set of hands."

John liked the way Dan thought.

"I can handle Ryan. We'll figure it out. Keep the radio on, find a warm room. I am excited to drive to New Hampshire and eat some steak." Dan went back into the house, but spun back around. "Where did you get cheese?"

"We have a few goats that give us milk. We also have chickens, and we just found some cows and pigs that survived the winter at a nearby farm. One of our members is a vet, she's confident we can get the cows healthy and producing."

"Unreal." Dan flashed a smile and slapped the top of the Hummer twice with his palm. He turned to walk inside. "We'll see you tomorrow morning. We'll be ready to roll." He yelled over his shoulder.

Solange and John got into the Hummer. As soon as the doors were shut, John spun his head to look at Solange. "This is unbelievable."

"I know, Ryan will not fit into our group."

"No, not that, I just met Dan Couples. Danny frickin' Couples! This is insane."

"Who is Dan Couples, other than the nice man I just met?"

"I can't talk about this with you." He thought for a second. "It's like I just met Pele, or, or, Maradona."

"I am from Ecuador. Maradona is Argentinean. Ugh, Americans." She shook her head. "I did meet Pele once, at a reception in Quito. I had a picture taken with him. It was in my bedroom on my desk. He was Brazilian, but I still liked the picture." She stopped for a moment. "You know, I do not have anything from my past life. I have some pictures on my tablet, but really I have nothing." Something triggered her sadness. "I miss my family. I loved them all, and I never got to see them in person to say goodbye. We did video chats, but I will never see my home again." She looked at John as he drove the truck towards the piers to get lobster. "It makes me sad."

"I know." He rubbed her shoulder. "I know. It's easy for me to forget that I have my sons, I said goodbye to Charleston, I was there when," he stopped. "I said goodbye to who I needed to."

They got lost on their way to the piers, but eventually pulled up to the water. Boston Harbor was enormous. Luckily, the large red buoys were easy to find. John used a nearby hook to grab the rope, and he wound the rope onto a pulley bolted to the pier. He brought the lobster trap to the surface.

"There are a dozen lobsters in there." He said excitedly. "Let's cook six of them and let the rest go."

"How are we going to get them out of the trap? Look at those claws." Solange took a step back from the edge of the pier. The pulley was on an arm that swung the trap onto the pier.

"You unhook the carabineer, and voila, the top opens and you grab the ones you want, toss the other ones back."

"And the claws?" Solange made a claw shape with her hand, two fingers on the bottom, three on top, and made a snipping gesture with the hand.

"Well, we have to be careful, that's for sure." John spun his head around in search of something. He walked down the pier to search the SUV's in the parking lot.

"What are you looking for?" She asked him curiously, rubbing her hands together. It was much cooler by the water. A stiff breeze blew from the ocean.

"We need a cooler or a bucket to put the lobsters in, maybe splash some water on them too." In the fourth SUV window he saw what he needed. John pulled a window hammer from his coat pocket, the kind found in car safety kits, and smashed the window of the SUV. He carried the hammer around with him for just such occasions. He pulled a blue cooler with wheels out of the broken back window and wheeled it down the pier.

Solange had not touched the lobster trap, not even the carabineer clasp. "Come on." He said to her. He undid the top and flipped it open. The lobsters were not friendly. Some of them began opening and closing their claws.

John used two sticks he found on the ground in a chopstick fashion to move eight large lobsters from the trap to the cooler. "I thought you said six?"

"I'm hungry"

"How can you be hungry after that big sandwich?"

"I don't know, I'm hungry, it's no big deal, there are two other traps." He used the giant chopsticks to free the five smaller lobsters in the trap. "Tomorrow we'll empty the other two traps, and bring the lobster up to Hanover for a lobster boil." He left the trap on the pier. "You know what? If this dries out, I think we should bring it with us. Maybe we can put it in the flatbed of their truck. We can use this to catch things in Hawaii. This is all coming together." He had his hands on his hips as he looked at the lobster trap on the pier and the red buoys in the water.

"If you are done being proud of yourself, can we find a place to light a fire? I am very cold." She hugged herself for warmth against the cold sea breeze.

They found a church close to the harbor. Dan was right, the office in the back had a large fireplace. It had a giant iron hook made specifically for a pot. Before Solange could ask what they would use for wood, John smashed a wooden pew with an axe from the Hummer. They lit two of the starter logs, heaped furniture wood on top, and their little room was warm within a few minutes.

"I saw some restaurants down the street. Maybe I can get a big pot or something to cook these in." He pointed to the cooler. "You stay here and keep the fire going. Get warm."

"You will get no argument from me." Solange pulled her chair close to the fire.

It did not take John long to find a restaurant, a pot, tongs, and a pan. He snagged a few bottles of white wine, a package of pasta, a jar of minced garlic, olive oil, and a case of Pellegrino sparkling water. He carried everything inside the big pot. He was excited to make lobster pasta, saving a few of the crustaceans for breakfast.

He strode into the church in a great mood. He had a beautiful woman, lobster, wine, and fire. What could go wrong?

"Dan radioed." Solange said solemnly. "Lucinda jumped off the porch. She is dead. Ryan stole their truck and fled. Dan and Karen would like to leave. We need to go back to the house."

"Damn." John lowered his head. "Damn, damn, damn."

They loaded the Hummer and drove to the house. Dan was standing by the back door. He had several boxes stacked, ready to move into the Hummer.

"It's not your fault, it's not our fault, she had issues." Dan said immediately. "I should have known. She hadn't left the house in five months. When you arrived, she panicked, and when you left? She got worse. She was pacing." Dan stopped to give Solange a quick hug. "Ryan went berserk, yelling and ranting, I don't know why, he was making less sense than she was. Anyway, he storms out, says he's taking the truck to Florida. Karen and I follow him nto his room where he starts throwing things in a duffel, then he storms down the back stairs. Lucy is just saying 'no, no' over and over again, her hand on her mouth. Karen tells her it's okay, we're all fine. I'm trying to keep Ryan from taking my truck, not that I cared about the truck, but it was our best vehicle, and well, I did kind of like the truck. He tries to shove me, he's yelling, I'm yelling, Karen is yelling, we heard a thud." Dan stopped. "Karen and I ran back upstairs, Ryan jumped in the truck and bolted." He dropped his head, shaking it slowly from side to side. "She didn't want to deal with it, you know, the new world, the way things are."

"I'm sorry." John offered. "I'm truly sorry."

"Karen and I spoke, and we decided we can't stay here. I mean, Lucy's body is sitting in the road out front. We have to get out of here." He bent down and picked up two boxes. "Do we have room in your truck for our stuff and us?"

"Yeah, here." John walked around the back and opened the tailgate. He pushed the blue cooler to the side. The salt air smell poured out of the trunk.

"You found the lobster." Dan noted, his voice flat.

Karen was in a fog, moving listlessly through the second floor. She did not have anything to bring other than clothes and a few pictures, but she seemed to be looking for something to pack. "Let's go Karen. This wasn't our house, it wasn't even our home, it was just some place we shared for a little while." Dan waved her over. "You have your pictures? Clothes?"

She nodded.

"Let's go." He put his arm around her and gave a squeeze. John thought he saw her wince. "Come on. There's nothing we can do here."

John felt odd asking, but he did anyway. "Do you have a big cooler? Maybe a few of them?"

"Sure, downstairs." Dan nodded. "What's up?"

"I know this is going to sound crass, thinking about food, but I want to stop and empty the lobster traps, bring the food to Hanover for dinner. We shouldn't waste it. The least we should do is let them all go."

"We can do that. I'll drive us over. It will be faster. I know a shortcut." Dan let go of Karen, picked up two more duffels, and walked down the stairs.

Solange followed him out. "Do we need gas? " Dan's hands were occupied with duffels, but he motioned with his head. "That SUV is full. Maybe we can siphon it over."

"Dan, are you okay? You are leaving very quickly." Solange showed concern for her new friends.

He threw the duffels in the back and looked at her. "Solange, I buried five children, my wife, and all of my family. I lost friends and teammates I've known for 15 to 20 years. That is loss, and I mourned when it happened. I'm still grieving. This place? I have no problem walking away. It's a thing, a place that kept me warm. Karen and I made our peace with Lucinda before we called you. I made this decision. I want to move." His eyes brightened. "But thank you for asking. You and John are good people, I can tell." He exhaled a quick sigh. "I can work with anyone, it's something I've had to do my entire life, work with whoever is put on my team, good person or bad, asshole or friend. I look forward to working with the two of you."

He pointed to the SUV. "I'll bring it next to the Hummer, gas tank to gas tank."

As Dan moved the SUV, Solange retrieved a tool from the backseat. It was a modified hand bailer from a boat. Matt called it 'the siphoner.' Tubes were used to extend both ends of the device, allowing the sucking tube to go to the bottom of the SUV's tank, and the bailing tube to go into the Hummer. Solange pulled the pump handled up and down, and watched the fuel flow from one vehicle to the other.

"You guys have done this before." The man from Seattle commented.

The Hummer was loaded and refueled, the lobsters were retrieved or freed, and the four survivors left for Hanover, N.H. at 3:30. Karen wept with Solange in the backseat. She lived in Boston her entire life, receiving her nursing degree from Simmons College, and working for Boston Children's. Boston was her home, and she never planned to leave. Solange kept an arm around her. Dan and John sat quietly.

"You driving fast enough?" Dan eyed the speedometer needle touching the 100 m.p.h. "Are we in a hurry or something?"

"No," John stammered. "I guess not." He dropped the speed to 75 and set the cruise. "You're right, as it gets closer to dark there might be deer. I'm used to driving as fast as I want. Sorry."

Dan sat comfortably in his seat. Solange and Karen chatted in the back, mostly about Lucinda. Dan put his arm on the seat back to look at them before turning to John. "So, John, tell me about yourself."

Maybe it was the fact that Lucinda's death was one more among the billions, or that Karen and Dan knew she was not destined to last very long in the new world, but whatever the reason, they moved on from Lucinda's suicide quickly. Dan talked about the nights he heard her pacing in her room, and the mumbling he could hear through his wall or vent. Karen brought up the days, usually several in a row, Lucinda would stay in her room, crying loudly and screaming if anyone tried to come inside. Lucinda was a mystery, a woman found sitting on their back porch one day like a stray cat, her thick Texas accent asking if they had seen her tour bus or cruise ship. Neither Dan nor Karen knew where she was from or anything about her. They admitted neither could recall Lucinda's last name. A woman they lived with for six months, and they did not know anything other than she was scared. Dan admitted he felt horrible, but relieved that Lucinda found peace. It was a hard peace, but not unexpected for a woman so troubled and sad.

John brought up Ryan. Neither Dan nor Karen would discuss him. "If he comes to his senses and shows up in Hanover? Well, we can figure out how to handle the situation. He helped me find fuel, food, and water. Everything else? He was probably one of the worst people I've met in my life."

Karen nodded. "If I never hear his name again, that will be fine with me. He was a misogynistic, mean, petty jerk, and I'm glad he's gone. He knew Dan loved that truck, but did he take the SUV or any of the other cars? Whatever, he's gone."

Ryan was dropped. Solange changed the subject and gave a rundown of the people in camp. She also discussed their plans to fly to Hawaii.

"You have a pilot?" Karen asked.

"We do." Solange told her.

"You think I can make chowdah with coconut milk, Dan?" She laughed.

"I bet you can." He told her. "I bet you can."

They pulled within radio distance of Hanover by 5:00. John called the house and asked if they had dinner made. When he was told "planned but not made," he asked them to get as many pots of water going as possible, and to prepare for two more mouths for dinner.

"Just two people?" Todd asked back.

"What do you mean 'just.' We found two people. That's great news.

One is a nurse. Tell Melanie we don't need her anymore." John smiled in the rearview at Karen.

"Yeah, she heard you, thanks for that, John." The radio clicked. "What about the other person?"

"He was a team leader, quarterback type." John laughed.

"Great, tell him we welcome another chief to our ever growing tribe of chiefs. We'll start the water boiling. You better not have forgotten tha steamuhs." The radio went off.

"Todd and his damn steamers. No, I did not get him steamers. Unbelievable. We have, what? Thirty lobsters and he's going to bitch about not having clams."

"I take it that's your brother." Karen asked. "He does a horrible New England accent."

"I know, and he's from Hanover." John continued to shake his head. "Steamers. That's going to burn my ass for the rest of our drive."

The mood in the car turned jovial as the somber events of the afternoon were put to rest. Karen's and Dan's relief and excitement were palpable. Locked up with a mentally unstable woman and a jerk for six months, they were starved for normal people and the bright future this new tribe offered.

John took the Lebanon exit to avoid the steep hill on Wheelock Street. He felt he needed to say something to Dan. "So, uh, you're probably used to people acting strange around you, right?"

"Yes, I get it. Don't worry." Dan was distracted by the carnage on the streets of Lebanon.

"Oh, don't worry, this looting is localized, it didn't get to Hanover." John assured the two of them. "So, anyway, please forgive my family and friends if it gets weird. I mean, we grew up in New England."

"I get it. Believe me, I get it." Dan looked at Karen. "Go ahead, tell them."

Karen blushed. "I had Dan's poster up in my bedroom." She turned to Solange and mouthed "ten posters" holding up all of her fingers. "I fainted when he and Ryan found me. Honestly, I fainted, and then I woke up, and fainted again. I couldn't stop smiling for like a week, and I giggled all the time. I don't think I said anything to Dan for the first month. I just giggled and blushed"

"See? I get it. It won't be worse that Karen, not a chance it's worse than Karen."

Solange did not understand. She sat in the backseat with a curious look on her face. She glanced at Dan and tilted her head. "Crazy Americans" she thought to herself.

They pulled down Main Street in Hanover. Dan was relieved to see the town was intact. He pointed to a restaurant. "I've eaten there. I came up and did a session with some medical group at Dartmouth. It was low key. No one knew I was in town. It's a nice place, but too landlocked for me. I need the ocean."

John turned left on Choate Road. There was still some daylight. Karen saw the kids running around the front yard of the big house. "Oh my gawd, you do have children! I didn't believe you, well I did, but I didn't. It's been half a year, maybe more, since I saw a child." She put her hands to her mouth and began to cry. "Dan, this is life again. Do you see it? It's life!"

The adults were in jackets standing next to the grill. Steam rose from a large silver pot on the fire. Todd waved, and everyone walked towards the Hummer. John put the car in park and got out.

"We've had a good trip. Some bad things happened, but some great things too." John announced.

"We thought you were staying another night." Emily asked, coming up from behind Todd.

The passenger door opened and Dan got out. The back doors opened too, but no one noticed. The men stopped talking. Emily, who was not much of a football fan, walked over to the tall stranger. "Hello, Emily Dixon. This is my husband, Todd." She turned, assuming Todd followed her to the new person. Todd had a look of wonder on his face. Emily ignored him and extended her hand.

"Hello, Dan Couples, very nice to meet you." He waved to the other people.

Emily moved to Karen. "Welcome, Emily Dixon."

"Karen Walker" Karen's bubbly personality emerged the further from her former living conditions she went. "I was a nurse at Children's, but I haven't seen a child in, well, you know." She admired the kids playing tag. "Are any of the little ones yours?"

"Yes, two," Emily cupped her hands around her mouth. "Jay, Brian, come over here! I want you to meet someone." The boys came over, as did the rest of the kids. "Hey everyone, this is Karen."

"Hello Karen!" The kids replied in unison. Jay walked up and touched her on the arm.

"You're it." He smiled.

"Oh no you didn't." Karen jumped into a squat, bending her knees and sticking her hands up. "It is on!" She yelled, giving the kids a head start before chasing a little girl. The kids screamed with excitement.

John waved Dan over to the group of men. "Hey, everyone, this is Dan."

Ahmed shot forward. "I had you and Randel in 2008, won my league."

"Glad I could help." Dan told him, shaking his hand. It had been a while since anyone had spoken about fantasy football with him.

"Seriously, I had no one else, but it didn't matter. Other than a bye week, I crushed everyone."

Dan nodded and smiled. He knew the excitement of meeting 'Dan Couples' would pass after a few days.

Melanie walked over. Jacob stood next to her. He was in 'timeout' for pushing his sister during the game of tag. Melanie gave Dan a hug. "I have no idea what Ahmed is talking about, but it is very nice to meet you." She turned to Jacob, elbowing him.

"Very nice to meet you sir." The young boy said. Dan towered over both of them.

"Very nice to meet both of you." He shook Jacob's hand, smiling at Melanie. "Do you like lobster Jacob?" He asked. "We brought a cooler full of lobster for dinner tonight."

"I like crab. Is it like crab? I'm from Maryland. I ate a lot of crab."

"Not as sweet, but there is more in each one, and it's not as much work to eat."

"Yeah, I'll try them." He looked at Melanie. "Can I go back? I won't push anyone, I promise."

"Go ahead." She said, smiling as Jacob ran to the kids and Karen.

"Let's get those lobsters going." Todd said, snapping out of his amazement. He stuck his hand out towards Dan. "Todd Dixon." They shook hands. "Let me help you get those puppies in the water." He stopped walking. "Butter! We should have tried to make butter. Damn it, we don't have any."

"We can do without." Dan consoled him. "I'm burned out on lobster, but the first few months I was eating it? I didn't miss the butter. You'll get through." They went to the back of the Hummer, each grabbing an end of the cooler.

"I enjoyed watching you play." Todd was not as rabid a football fan as his brothers, but he did enjoy watching Dan.

Kelly pulled up in an old red pickup truck as the last lobsters were dropped in the water. She had great news about the health of the cows, two of which were already strong enough to transport. She welcomed the new members. "How long was I gone?" She joked.

Everyone enjoyed the lobsters. Some dipped the pieces in garlic olive oil and salt, others used cocktail sauce, and three little kids made most of the adults gag by using ketchup.

Hank tried to take the lobster away when he saw them dipping it in ketchup, but he was talked down. "I'll make them burgers." He pleaded.

Dan and Karen were treated to moose burgers instead of lobsters.

At the end of the meal, Hank asked people to dump their lobster shells into a pot of water on the grill. He boiled the shells with a jar of minced garlic. "This is going to make the best lobster risotto tomorrow." There was a lot of lobster meat left. Hank put it in a bag and walked down to the moose meat locker. The room had a few feet of shoveled snow on the floor, and made a fantastic refrigerator.

People rolled into their already establish routines, leaving the dinner circle to start their fires and warm their bedrooms. Children were tucked into their beds. Todd and Ahmed spent an hour prepping bread dough for the next day.

Dan, Greg, and Rebecca sat in chairs next to fire pits. Rebecca was wrapped in a plaid cashmere blanket with frilly ends, her only visible appendage was an arm, sticking out of the chair to hold Greg's hand. The teens were on a folding loveseat. Dan sat in a green camp chair. He was fascinated by their story.

"If you had come south, you would have found me." He told Greg. "But it sounds like you did better going north."

John was exhausted. It had been a long day. He found Matt and asked him for a moment.

"Matt," he began, too serious for what he wanted to tell his son.

"Jesus, Dad, what is it?" Matt looked worried.

"No, no, well, this is going to sound weird, but Solange and I are going to start seeing each other." He put his hand on Matt's shoulder. "I wanted to tell you, because, well,"

"Seriously? She wants to date an old guy like you?" Matt could not keep a straight face.

"Now, wait a second."

"Dad, it's great. She's great. I hope you are happy. We all need to be happy, because I think our lives are going to be filled with a lot of work." He gave his dad a soft punch in the stomach. "Way to go. You are shooting well below your handicap with her."

"What is that supposed to mean?" John knew what it meant.

"I'm just kidding, well, not really, but you know. Hey, it's great. If Craig is upset, I'll set him straight." He gave his dad a hug. "Now go get some sleep, you look like hell."

"It's been a great day, but there were some lows as well. I will tell you it was long, very, very long. If you could make sure your brother doesn't stay up too late, I'm going to hit it." John slapped Matt on the back and walked up the road. Matt expected him to turn and go into the big house, sleeping in the study with Hank and Paul. His father walked two houses up and went into the one Solange was using.

"That sly dog." Matt mumbled. "Good for him." Matt saw the group moving from the fire pit into the house.

"Karen wants to go to sleep. We're moving the party inside." Greg told him. "Stay up a while."

"Did you see Dad? He and Solange are a 'thing' now." Matt replied.

Karen collapsed, fully dressed, on the queen bed in the RV. She tried to listen as the boys walked away, but she was too tired, and they walked too fast. She looked up at the stars through her little skylight, and thanked whatever brought her into her current situation. Her eyes fluttered, and she fell asleep instantly, barely pulling a comforter over herself to keep warm.

47

Karen woke up to voices outside her window. She was disoriented and looked around to find her bearings. She was in a large bed in a cold room. Her side and stomach ached. "I'm in an RV in New Hampshire." She said to herself. "Okay, it wasn't a dream, I'm really here." She often dreamt about escaping the house in Boston for a safe home away from Ryan.

She looked under the comforter and saw she was still fully dressed. She decided to change into sweats, ones she brought up from Boston in a duffel in the other room. She changed and went outside to see who the voices were coming from.

Todd and Ahmed were talking about bread, sports, and other meaningless things. "I hope we didn't wake you. I didn't know there was anyone in the RV." Ahmed apologized.

"That's okay." Karen paused, she was horrible with names.

"Ahmed, and this is Todd. I lobbied for name tags at one point, shirts with name badges sewn into them, but no one went for it." Ahmed took a sip of coffee.

"Where did you get that." Karen needed her coffee. "I so want that." She was forward, and funny. She fit into the group immediately.

"You need to walk up this street to the end. Take a right, second house is a white cottage, smoke coming out of the top, walk in, take off your shoes, put them in the bin, you'll be rewarded with coffee. Don't take off your shoes? Rebecca will throw you out. Drink all the coffee? Todd's wife will throw you out."

Todd laughed at Ahmed's directions.

"Rebecca is the girl, right? The teen? She's in charge?" Karen asked, confused.

"More than you know." Todd smiled at her, sipping his own coffee. "It's her house, kick the shoes into the bin."

Karen thanked both of them for the advice, and walked up to the cottage. The road was clear of snow, but wet from streams of thaw running down in all directions. She could see her breath as it blew into the morning air. She looked at the houses to her left, pale gray smoke puffed out of chimneys in the first four homes. Karen stopped at the top of the road, turned right, and walked to a sign that read Webster Cottage. She knocked meekly before opening the door. "Hello?" she asked.

"Come on in." Melanie called from the living room. "Shoes in the bin, coffee and eggs in the back. I'm Melanie, we met last night."

"Hello again, Melanie. " She nodded, "Karen. There really are eggs? OMG!" Karen put her shoes in an overflowing bin.

Melanie was surrounded. She had three kids on the couch with her, one still asleep holding a blanket, and two playing checkers. There were two older girls on the opposite couch reading. All of the kids looked up and said hello and waved. Karen remembered none of their names. She waved back with a broad smile. A fire burned in the fireplace. The chill Karen felt since she woke disappeared.

She walked through the living room and into a dining room area. There was a fire in a fireplace here too, and more young people sitting at a table. John and Solange were there, and they both said good morning. "Look who finally got up. You Boston people know how to sleep. You're the first one up of the two of you."

Karen spoke to them for a second, said good morning to the people around the table, a Tony, Greg, Matt, Rebecca, and Craig. "I wish I was better with names." Karen thought to herself. She pushed through the dining room and into the kitchen. It was also full of activity. The older woman Karen met briefly the night before was scrambling eggs in a giant caste iron skillet on a woodstove. There were two coffee makers working off of a solar panel charged electric hub. A tall older man, again, someone who Karen met the night before, was slicing bread for toast.

"Good morning Karen!" The older woman smiled. "You're just in time for some fresh eggs. Peter has a batch of toast in the woodstove. Grab a plate from the stack, come on over. Coffee cups are on the counter, milk and sugar are on the table. Don't miss the sausage patties." She pointed a large spatula towards a plate of cooked sausage.

There were people sitting at a table, John's brothers, Paul and Hank. "Yes!" Karen said to herself as she recalled their names. They had three very young children on a bench at the table with them, two girls and a boy. Karen assembled her breakfast and asked if she could join them.

"Of course," Hank told her. "We are explaining the weather to the kids, how snow is just cold rain. That sort of stuff."

Talking to kids was right up Karen's alley. "Why are you asking, honey?" She did not use the little girl's name. Karen depended on charts hooked to the foot of a bed for names.

"Rebecca said there might be some snow next week, that it was going to get cold again." The little boy who responded was sitting between two girls. Karen guessed he was between 4 and 5 years old, possible a very big 3.

"It's pretty late for snow, but it could happen." Karen said, nodding to the children.

Paul jumped in, "if Rebecca and Greg could live by themselves for the whole winter, we don't have to worry about some spring storm. You know what we call that? Snow day!"

The kids giggled. Karen noticed how thin they were.

"Peanut butter toast is coming up kids." Peter walked over with a plate of toast slathered in peanut butter. "Anyone need refills on milk?" There were headshakes of 'no' as each kid grabbed the toast.

The morning reminded Karen of her family reunions. The house was full of life, crowded with teens, pre-schoolers, and adults. She felt safe and happy for the first time in almost a year.

The kids finished their breakfast, said thank you to Jamie and Peter (Karen caught their names finally) and ran out. Karen turned to Paul. "Is this what mornings are like?"

"I'm not sure what you mean." He said back.

"Well, like, everyone eating together, and talking and working nicely. Everyone gets along so well."

"Yeah, it's been like this for a while. You have to realize, we've only been together for two or three weeks, but it seems to be working. Why?"

"We weren't like this in Boston." She did not say anything else.

Paul heard the story of Lucinda's suicide and Ryan's departure. It was a bad situation in Boston.

"Well, so far, that's how it is here. We have a task board, essential things that need to get done, along with a list of 'if you have time' things, longer term projects. It's up in the dining room. If there is anything that strikes your fancy, have at it. It's your first day, we'll let it slide if you don't milk the goats. Besides, that's already done." Paul gave her a pat on the back, and slid his chair away from the table. "Yep, you gotta get up early to milk the goats." He used his best farmer accent for the word 'goats.' "I'm heading over to the dairy farm to check on the cows and pigs with Kelly, the veterinarian, you are welcome to join us, or again, take a day to rest and get used to the area."

"You seem to enjoy children." Hank said from behind his mug of coffee. "Emily and Melanie use the town library for school, teaching the kids how to read and write. They love guest lecturers or permanent helpers. Melanie is switching to farm duty when the season changes."

Karen nodded at him.

"Do you think that other guy you lived with will show up?" Hank asked, curious for her perspective.

"No." Karen said quietly. "No, I don't, and I hope he stays away. He was mean, a rotten person, and while Dan told me we needed Ryan to survive, well, that's not true now. Even if he could help us, he's not worth the price."

"I agree." Hank let the topic die. He was there when Dan told the true story of their last hours at the Boston apartment. It was different than the one Karen wanted known.

"After John and Solange left it got ugly." Dan told the group in the living room when Karen had gone to bed. "I told them a lie this afternoon, when they came back, because Karen asked me to, but here is what happened. I went upstairs and Ryan has Karen up against a wall. He was yelling at her, screaming in her face." He took a sip of wine as he told the story. "When we first got together back in October, well, Ryan and I were talking about our survival strategy. Karen cut in on us, said something against Ryan. He slapped her across the face and told her to shut up."

Rebecca put her hand over her mouth and gasped.

"Is it okay if I tell this in front of her?" Dan looked to the adults.

"I'm okay, just stunned." Rebecca told him.

Hank and Paul nodded, giving the okay to continue.

"I was stunned too, and without hesitation I popped him one in the stomach. I don't punch people in the face, because I don't punch people, but also because it's a good way to break or injure my hand, and I was so used to taking care of my hands." Dan could tell he was getting off track. "Anyway, I punched him so hard he went to the ground. I didn't hold back. You don't slap anyone, but you definitely don't slap a woman for speaking. I picked him up. I could tell he was hurt, really hurt and it was killing him to stand up straight, but I held that bastard up and looked him in the eyes and said 'if you touch her again, I'll kill you. Do you understand? I won't kill you quickly, I'll beat you and leave you out in the cold to die like you deserve.'"

Dan shook his head. "I'm not a bully or even a violent person, but I could tell this Ryan was a piece of work. I kept him in line for the rest of the time. He still called Karen a fat bitch, or told her to shut up, and I'd ask him to stop, but really, what was I supposed to do? I needed him to survive, Karen needed him to survive. We were in hell. We're stuck with a total asshole who hates women, and our fourth group member is insane, literally mentally insane. Lucinda did not sleep at night. She'd wake me up thinking she'd heard something. She never left the apartment." He paused. "I debated leaving every single day. I wasn't living anymore, I was cobbling together a horrible existence, survival, but not life." He paused for another sip of wine.

"Back to yesterday, John and Solange leave, I come up stairs, Ryan's screaming at Karen, right in her face, calling her a traitor, bitch, ingrate, whatever. I pull him back, tell him to calm down. Lucinda is crying, screaming for us to stop. I get the situation under control, Lucy stays in the kitchen, like she always did. I'm on a couch with Karen. Ryan is in a chair. He doesn't want to go, doesn't trust Solange and John. I tell him I'm leaving, Karen agrees. Lucinda starts ranting about inviting John and Solange to live with us. She's telling us she won't go back to the cruise ship where all the people are dead, something so bizarre. How we can all stay here in Boston, how none of us will get sick if we just stay in Boston, I don't know, it didn't make any sense."

"Ryan is seething. All of a sudden he looks at Karen and says 'the next time we are alone, I'm going to kill you. You better pray Dan stays with you forever, cause I'm going to wring your fat neck.' I mean, seriously, he is looking right at her. Karen is one of the sweetest people, she was a pediatric nurse, who hates a pediatric nurse? I was floored. What the hell is wrong with this guy? Karen is done, she knew she was out, so she stood up and walked over to him, looked him square in the eye and said, 'I hope you try.' He kicked her right in the stomach. He was wearing socks. If he had boots on, Karen would be dead." He paused, everyone stared at him.

"I pointed my finger and told him to go. I told him to pack his things and get as far away from us as possible, to take one of the cars and leave. As I am talking, I feel a breeze from the balcony door being opened. I see Lucy walking towards the railing. She hadn't gone out there, ever. I knew this wasn't good. Karen was coughing on the floor. Ryan is looking at me like he is going to kill me. I jump up and run towards Lucy. She is at the rail of the balcony. She looks at me, and in the most even and rational voice I've ever heard her use she says,"

"Dan, thank you, but I'm done."

"She dove over the railing, kept her arms at her side, and she was gone. I was standing at the edge looking at her when I hear the door slam behind me. Ryan locked me out on the porch. He kicked Karen a few more times in the stomach and side until she passes out, and he leaves. Karen didn't wake up for a while. She crawled over and let me into the house. Thirty minutes later, when some of the pain pills kick in and Karen is able to stand, I radioed Solange."

Hank thought of the story as he watched Karen eat her breakfast. He thought about how excited she must feel to be out of that house in Boston, away from some random abuser with whom she had the misfortune of surviving a global plague.

Karen sat at the table, forking eggs and sausage into her mouth. She smiled. Smiling was part of her training. No matter what is happening, good news or bad news to the patient, painful procedure or taking a temperature, grin and put on a good face.

Tears welled in her eyes. The warm liquid dripped down her face on to her plate. She was finally safe. She was free of Ryan. There were good people around her, and there was a life ahead of her.

Hank drank his coffee and let her have the moment. He saw the tears. He leaned towards her and whispered. "This is real. We're real. You're safe. Enjoy it."

Karen put her hands to her mouth. She moved them to cover her eyes and wept. She laughed while she cried. Her tears were of joy and salvation.

"I guess she liked the eggs." Peter said to Jamie. Hank heard the comment, and laughed.

John popped through the door to see what was so funny. "What's going on in here?"

"It has been a while since Karen enjoyed eggs and sausage. She's a little emotional about it." Jamie told him.

"And she's realizing she doesn't have to live with an abusive asshole anymore." Hank added.

Karen was too overwhelmed to speak. She laughed and cried, waving to John. She mouthed "thank you" to him.

"Well, as long as I'm here, I'll take some more eggs. I think everyone is up that is going to get up." John let Jamie spoon more eggs on his plate. He forked two more sausage patties and took more toast.

Peter filled his cup with coffee and followed John back into the dining room. The kids had left to go on a firewood run, allowing Peter to join John and Solange at the table.

"You two went to bed so early, I didn't get a chance to hear the rundown of the airport. You found three fuel trucks? Two planes? That's the story?"

"We did." Solange confirmed. "The runway is clear."

"I will go down to take a look. If we get fuel in and the engines turn over, well, I bet we can extend our time here as long as we want, within reason of course." The old pilot sipped his coffee.

"I need a day before I go back down there." John told him. "I'm tired and sore." The eggs were fantastic, and he offered Solange some of his seconds. She shook her head. "One thing," John told him. "It's a mess at the airport. The parking garage was converted into a military barracks. There are tents full of bodies. There are scavenging birds and animals, it smells like rotting flesh. If Solange and I are not in the group, know that you want to avoid the front of the airport. Go straight to the planes and fuel trucks."

Peter nodded. He had seen some things in his life, he was not squeamish, but there was no need to invite those images into his memory.

"I'd take Tony. That kid knows how to jump start vehicles, and I bet you're going to have to jump the battery on that plane." John talked through his toast. "You are also going to have to figure out how to get into that monster."

"I know how to do that, don't worry. You found the plane and the fuel, the rest is up to me." Peter thought about the jumpstart. "You just leave the rest up to me." He leaned back in his chair, kicking his feet straight out in front of him. He was thinking about cows, pigs, goats, chickens, supplies, and most importantly, people. "I think I can give Antonio some flying lessons over the next few weeks, make him a pretty serviceable co-pilot."

A wry smile crept across Peter's face as a plan formed in his head.

48

Dan woke late. He rolled over and looked at his watch, placed neatly on his nightstand the night before.

10 a.m.

The fire he lit the night before was out long ago. His room was cold. He was warm under the covers of his bed, his knit cap securely on his head.

He faced two problems. He was hungry, and he had to go to the bathroom.

He ran to the bathroom outside of his room, and bolted back to his bed.

"One out of two isn't bad." He thought to himself.

Dan pulled a pillow over his head, rolled away from the bright sun streaming through the window, and went back to sleep.

49

The chores posted on the daily calendar in the dining room were done. The firewood truck was filled and parked on Choate Road. The goats were milked and fed. The chickens were fed and the eggs collected. Bread was baked and cooling. Water was boiled for drinking, and the tanks of the RV's were filled for showering. There was no fishing, hunting, or trapping expedition for the day, as there was lobster and moose for both meals. The kids were at the library until 12:30, free to enjoy the rest of the afternoon.

Matt and Avery used a snow blower to clear a set of tennis courts the day before. They left to play on the newly cleared and dry surface. Meredith was never far from Avery, and asked to tag along. A dozen people quickly planned to use the tennis courts or watch their friends play.

It was not the "date" Matt hoped it would be.

Lunch sizzled on the grill, thinly sliced moose steaks pounded tender and served in baguettes. Todd put out jars of roasted red peppers, homemade mayonnaise, and scavenged steak sauce.

Greg and Rebecca were early to lunch. They made a large sandwich, and snuck away before the crowd came from school and the cottage. They went to a one room coach house they kept secret from the rest of the survivors. Not even Paul or Hank knew about the private spot. It was a charming little place about a half of a mile away from Choate Road. It had a half bath, day bed, couch, desk, and fireplace that warmed the room. There was firewood neatly stacked against the side of the cottage next to the sliding glass door. Upon arrival, Greg lit the starter log he brought under his arm, and loaded the wood box next to the fireplace with the wood from outside.

"It's not too bad in here." Rebecca said to Greg as he made his second trip in from the wood pile. "I think the skylight let's enough sun in to warm it up a bit." She looked at him. "I still want the fire."

"No kidding." He replied.

She took off her backpack and emptied the contents of their picnic on the coffee table in front of the couch. They had the steak sandwich and two bottles of water. Not a huge offering, but certainly enough for the two of them. Instead of sitting down, she pulled a few logs from the wood bin and placed them on the now burning starter log. The dry wood caught immediately, popping as it burned.

Greg dropped a third armload of wood into the bin, an adequate supply for their picnic lunch and an afternoon of relaxation. He pulled off his work gloves and set them down next to the bin. He walked over to the sliding door and shut it. He untied his boots, set them by the door, and finally sat down next to Rebecca on the couch.

He leaned over and kissed her. They embraced for a few moments. Their lips unlocked and she buried her face into his shoulder. "I miss you." She said into his sweater, a blue cashmere she picked out for him at one of the stores in town.

"I know. I miss you too. I miss us." They leaned back in the couch, holding hands. They enjoyed being together, alone together. It had been a week since they were alone.

"I love your family." She sat up after a few minutes. "They are great. Your uncles are cool. Your dad is nice. Your brothers and cousins are awesome. I like everyone. I love everyone." She bit into her sandwich. "I especially love Todd's cooking." She said.

"But you don't love them all the time." He added.

"It's not even that, it's like we're all together all the time. We sleep in a house with 10 people." She ate more sandwich. "I'm a kid, I get it, they look at me like I'm 13, which I am, but you and I were alone for a long time. We were on our own for months before we found each other, and months before anyone else came."

"I know."

"And, well, I was alone a lot before the death. My parents both worked at the store, and some days I would be by myself, and I got used to that lifestyle."

"Yep." He ate his sandwich as she spoke.

"So I don't know how you feel, I usually do, but I don't right now." She paused as she chewed. "I'm usually much more in control of a situation." She put down her sandwich and looked at him. "I, I'm hoping we, but I'll start with I, need to figure out a long term solution to our living situation."

"I agree." He said through a mouth full of moose.

Greg put his sandwich on the paper plate she had brought for him, and finished the bite in his mouth. He touched her hand, sliding his fingers into hers so their hands became one. "It's we. Don't think it's ever not we. I love you. Yes, I'm a 15 year old kid. Yes, to all the things you just mentioned, and yes, we have to figure out how the "we" fits into the "tribe" my aunt Emily keeps talking about." He looked at her. She was a confident woman, not so much the young girl he met skipping out to her trashcan six months ago. Her hair was long, and hung down her shoulders and back. Greg used his free hand to touch the back of her head and run his fingers through the auburn locks. She closed her eyes, and leaned forward so her head was resting on his shoulder again.

She kept her eyes closed. "I know everything I want to do. I can see how we are going to get the tribe to Hawaii, how we are going to make a life there, but it has to be on our terms when we get to Hawaii. We have to be able to live our own life, two of us, not eight of us sleeping in a room together."

"It will be." He stroked her hair. "We won't let them control us." He leaned back on the couch, putting his legs up. She snuggled on top of him, her eyes still closed, his arm around her. They enjoyed the moment, lying together, breathing together.

"So you seem to be hitting it off with Avery." Greg said, breaking the silence.

"I know, isn't that funny? She is not my type, but maybe I don't have a type anymore. I mean, you're not my type."

"I am so your type." He said, lifting his head off the pillow to look at her.

"No, you're not. You're a jock, a popular kid. Sure, you're smart, but you're not the level of smart that I hung out with."

"First of all, let's be honest, your level of smart is kind of its own level." He chuckled at her false modesty. "How many boyfriends did you have before me?"

"None." She sat up with her elbows on his chest, her chin in her hands.

"And I didn't have a girlfriend, at least a serious one before you, so that means we're perfect for each other, and therefore, as you smart kids would say, each other's type."

"Really? Okay." She kissed him on the nose before sitting up. "I'm finishing this sandwich."

Greg sat up too. He picked up his lunch. "You think we can get to Hawaii?"

"Yes. No question." She chewed and looked at the fire.

"Really? That simple?"

"I pulled the specs on the Boeing 777. Peter is right, it has the capacity and the range. Your father found fuel. Peter is licensed to fly that jet.

We are good."

"How do you know he's licensed?"

"I asked him. He has his license for both a 747 and a 777. Either plane will work. I think he'd rather find a 747, it's smaller and probably easier for one man to handle, but again, either will work. The fuel should be fine. We are going to Hawaii."

"See, one hour with me, alone, and you're back to the old, confident Rebecca." Greg smiled at her, putting the last bite in his mouth. "That steak tasted so good. I had no idea how much I missed red meat. Squirrel and rabbits aren't the same thing. And Uncle Todd knows how to make bread." He sat back and rubbed his belly.

"You're not my type, because I didn't have a type." She said to him, still looking at the fire.

"I didn't have a lot of friends, Greg. You know that. I was too different, and that horrible disease took everything away. I gave up my childhood to be smart, to do well, to move on to medical school or get an engineering degree. Probably both, actually, I could handle the load." She turned to look at him. "I sacrificed more than any 7 year old should be asked to, but I did it, and I didn't mind, because I knew what was at the end, but look what happened. I don't have an ending, do I? I threw away being a third grader, skipping rope and playing with dolls. I lost all of that for nothing."

"Come on." He rubbed her back.

"No, it's fine, it's upsetting, but I get it. Life is like that." She put her hand on his leg. "I got you. Whatever took everything away from me gave me you to make up for it. That sounds insane for a rational fact based person like me to say, but I think I believe that through all this death and destruction and pain, we got each other." She fell into his arms. "I love you, Greg. I didn't have a type, and if I did, it wasn't a handsome, baseball playing, good grade getting, hardworking boy like you, but you're my type now, and I'm getting tired of sharing our time with everyone else."

He held her, and they watched the fire getting low. Greg stood to put a log on.

"What if we promise each other this." He asked. "When we get to Hawaii, we find a place, a little house, maybe close enough to everyone else, but still just ours, and we live like we're supposed to live, together, the two of us. We are part of the tribe, but we get to be alone when we want to be."

"I love your family, but I can't live with them n the same house. I accept your offer." She was exhausted, her words were coming slowly, her eyelids fluttered, and there was a yawn at the end of her sentence. Rebecca let herself fall sideways onto the couch. Greg placed a soft blanket from a nearby chair over her.

"Sleep tight." He kissed her cheek.

Rebecca awoke to the sound of Greg placing another log on the fire. "What time is it?" She asked him, stretching her arms and watching him head back to a big leather reclining chair. "That was the best sleep I've had in a week."

"It's 4:30 sleepy head." He sat in the chair reading old magazines. "I mean, fun afternoon away you planned for me. 'Why don't we sneak off so I can take a four hour nap.'"

"I can't help it if you don't take naps. Mine was great. It was just what I needed." She sat up. "You promised me a bungalow in Hawaii, and you guarded me for a nap. Rebecca wins."

He gave her a look from his chair. "Are you ready to go? We should get back."

"You know what I'd like to do? I'd like to spend the days working with the group, doing our tasks, helping out, then come back here and be alone for the night."

"I don't know." Greg replied. "The Boston people just got here. That's a bold move."

"I know it's not going to happen, but it's what I would like. I'm just saying it to you. I'm not asking you to do it."

"It has been nice to sit down and read a magazine again." He held up a tabloid. "Do you remember when we cared about all of this stuff?" A celebrity couple smiled on the cover. The woman was pregnant, and there was a fake tear between the two people signaling a break-up. "It's weird to think all of these people are dead."

"Maybe they aren't dead." Rebecca told him. "If Dan Couples is alive, maybe one of them made it."

Greg nodded. "You know, if we do stay here for a while, more than two weeks. I will move over here with you. I can't take the summer camp lodging we have. Yes, I'm 15, but does that mean I get put in the kids' house with everyone else? Matt must feel the same way. Sure, fun to see him, love him and Craig, but we didn't share a room in Charleston. Why am I sharing a room now?"

She stood and walked over to his chair, sitting on his lap and cuddling. "It's just the way it is right now. This is all temporary."

"I know." He put his arms around her. "You understand, I love a lot of the things we have with the new people, but I miss some of the things you and I enjoyed when it was just us."

"Now you sound like me. This is your family. Snap out of it Dixon." She enjoyed his embrace for a few minutes.

"Okay, time to get back." She got up from his lap. "We probably need to help distribute firewood or make dinner or something. Let's not become freeloaders."

"Alright, just let me run through this one more time. I've had a few hours to stare at this half bath. The sewer system is still there, right? If we can figure out a way to have water in the toilets, if the pipes running to the sewers aren't frozen or did not burst this winter, we should be able to use the toilets, right?" Greg was determined to restore modern conveniences.

"Yes." She told him, pulling on her shoes.

"What if I redirect the gutters on the houses into rain barrels, and we have the rain barrels fill the backs of the toilets after flushing. Sure, we'll have to fill the toilets manually with a spigot, but it's still better than going outside."

"See, I knew I liked you for your brains."

He looked through the door of the half bath. "I could run a hose or gutter through the window and use the sink for a stand." He thought out loud. "I'm going to try it here first, maybe tomorrow. There are some rain barrels along the big house."

"You are overlooking a bigger issue on the horizon." Rebecca grinned wryly.

"What?" Greg replied, true concern in his voice. "Are you afraid the sewage is emptying into the river or pond?"

"At some point we are going to run out of toilet paper. You should focus your attention on learning how to make soft, pliable tissue rather than worrying about a toilet."

"Oh my god, you're right." Greg had not considered toilet paper, tissues, paper towels, or even diapers as a fleeting resource.

"Okay, Greg, let's get our shoes on and go." She waited for him by the door.

He walked over to his boots. "When did you plan on moving over here?

Was it when my Uncles arrived? I bet you've been thinking about coming over her for months."

"You know I'm a girl with a plan." She flashed her confident smile.

"It would be a hard winter here, but not too bad a spring, summer, or fall." He laced his second boot. "I know how you work. You can't fool me." He grabbed his coat and gave her one more hug and kiss before opening the door.

"I'll never lie to you, but that doesn't mean I'm looping you in on all of my decisions." She gripped his hand as they walked outside. It was cold. The wind shifted from a southern breeze to a northern gale. "Brrr." She said. "I told everyone it was going to get cold again."

Patchy black clouds blew across the sky at a rapid pace. The sun was shining, but the temperature was dropping despite the sunshine. Greg and Rebecca planned a leisurely walk back to the house. Their plan changed to a quick trot.

There was no one at the Choate Road house. Greg and Rebecca went to the Cottage. Everyone was inside, crammed into the small building. Screams came from kids upstairs. Bernie was talking to Karen in the living room while Jamie and Peter sat next to each other on a couch. The older kids were playing cards in the dining room. The kitchen was full of adults.

"Welcome back." Matt said to both of them. He sat at the table, a smartass grin on his face. "I hope you two had a nice afternoon."

"I appreciate that, Matt." Rebecca said to him. She was not embarrassed or ashamed of her alone time. "What are you up to?"

"We're playing spades, trying to pass the time. It's freezing outside. It cut our tennis game short, but not short enough that Avery didn't crush me in humiliating fashion."

Now it was Rebecca's turn to smile. "She didn't tell you she played?"

"Must have slipped my mind." Avery winked at her friend.

"The jokes on the two of you." Matt told them. "I had fun anyway." He stuck his tongue out at Avery.

"Why are we all inside?" Greg asked.

Tony put his cards on the table, making sure no one could see them. "It got cold and everyone freaked. We ended up in here. Hank had plans for some big pan on the grill, but now he's in there making dinner on the woodstove. I think everyone wants to eat so they can get out of here and go back to their own places." He picked up his cards. "Now can we get back to me winning at cards?" He looked around the table.

"Thanks for the update." Greg gave Antonio a pat on the shoulder.

"Dad was looking for you." Matt told him, still grinning.

Rebecca noticed Avery was not playing. She was just watching the card game. "How was tennis, really?" She asked her. Avery got up and walked over to Rebecca.

"Forget tennis, where were you two? It was the talk of the house for a little while, you two sneaking off for the afternoon and not telling anyone."

"Really?" Rebecca feigned surprised. "I guess. You know how it is. We lived alone for months, then we only had Paul and Hank, who gave us space for the next two months. I'm not used to sharing a house with twelve people. I needed a break. It's my fault, I asked Greg to sneak off with me."

"Hey, don't apologize to me. You're right. I'm not in your boat, they gave me my own room, well, sort of, I do share it with Meredith, but she's cool. We have a house we can go to." Avery gave her a small punch in the shoulder. "Nice work, girlfriend, raising some heck in the house."

Rebecca blushed, "whatever." She replied. "Can you keep a secret?"

"You know I can."

"I fell asleep and napped the entire time."

"What?" Avery said loudly, getting looks from the spades game table. She said it softly. "What? You sneak away, and all you did was fall asleep?"

"Yes, honestly, it was the best nap I've had in a week, but that was it. We went to this little coach house we know about, lit a fire, ate the steak sandwich, and I passed out. How sad is that? I needed some space, some alone time, and I blew it on a nap."

Avery laughed. "Tennis was fun. I like Matt. He's funny, and pretty easy on the eyes." She looked over at him. "I'm going to see where it goes. I met him like a week ago. I don't have many options, but still, I don't want to start seeing a guy on the first day at a new school, right?"

"I think you have some time. You know his Dad is seeing Solange now?"

"Get out!" Avery said loudly again. This time the conversation in the living room stopped and people turned.

"Subtle." Rebecca told her. "Anyway, yeah, they are staying in the same house. I saw him go into her place last night, and he told Matt about it after dinner. Wild, huh?"

The girls gossiped while the other teens played cards.

Greg's conversation with his father did not go as Greg expected.

"Look," John said. "You are your own man now. I stopped being your boss when I hung up the phone last August. All I want you to do, and this is a request rather than an order, is to tell someone, anyone, Cameron if you want, where you are going and how long you'll be gone. You can even grab a radio, just give us a way to connect with you if there is an emergency." John sat at the kitchen table with Paul and Ahmed. They each had a glass of wine.

Hank cooked dinner in a fantastically large pan he found at a restaurant in town.

"Okay, you're right. Rebecca, and I won't lay blame on her because I went on my own, wanted some alone time, a few hours without a crowd. I know you care, and I should have told you. It won't happen again."

"Where did you go, anyway? Did you two keep some spot secret from me and Hank?" Paul asked.

Greg smiled. "You know we did." He blushed. "There is a coach house behind one of the big houses on Balch Street. It's like an office or something, but it has a fireplace and a couch. We considered it for a living space, but it's just one room and a half bath."

"That half bath would have been nice in the winter." Paul mumbled, more to himself than Greg.

"Alright, so if we can't find you, will it be safe to assume you are there?" John asked.

"It would be the first place you should look." Greg answered. "And it's not that we don't like everyone, we love everyone, we like that everyone is here, but," He paused, "well, I'm used to being on my own, not sleeping in a house with twelve people, most of them under the age of eleven. Matt, Rebecca, and I are the only older kids in the cottage."

John looked surprised, not because Greg was wrong, but because he had not thought about it. "You're right. I lumped you in with the kids, and you three aren't kids. Whatever you want to do is fine with all of us. Let me know, let any of us know, and we can help you find a bedroom with a fireplace, get you set up. You've earned it."

"Well, this conversation didn't go as I thought it was going to." Greg admitted. "I knew I was in the wrong when I snuck away, but sometimes, you know, kids do things. I didn't realize I wasn't a kid anymore."

John smiled. "Yeah. I was mad. Your brother set me straight." He stood up and walked over to Greg, wrapping his arms around him. "I'm your dad, that's never going to change, but now I'm your friend slash dad. That doesn't mean I want to know specifics of what you were doing at your coach house, but it means I am not your boss. You are an equal in this tribe or group, or whatever the hell we are."

They released their hug. Greg turned to his Uncle Hank at the stove. "What is that? It smells incredible?"

"Lobster risotto with roasted red pepper. Tastes better than it smells. I'll admit, it's turning out damn good." Sweat beads dripped down Hank's forehead from the heat of the woodstove. He wore a look of pride as he stirred his masterpiece.

Paul asked Greg a natural follow up question. "Do you and Rebecca want to move over to the coach house?" The question was met with silence from the room. Paul looked around. "Hey, we're all adults, and he's earned it, you just said it yourself, John. I am opening the door for him to walk through."

"I appreciate that, Uncle Paul, I really do. Here is my honest answer. If we plan on staying in Hanover for a long time, yes. If we are here for another two or three weeks, no. We don't want to fracture the group, have us start pairing or even singling off until we're at our final location. Rebecca and I talked about it. She has a plan."

Paul and Hank laughed.

"What?" John asked.

Paul clued his brother in on the comment. "Well, as you spend more time with Rebecca, you'll realize she always has a plan, typically she is several steps ahead of you with her plan. Also, she's always prepared. Your son was making a joke."

"Okay Mr. Jokester, why don't you feed and clean the animals this afternoon, since you decided to take the day for yourself." John threw his thumb towards the fenced in back barnyard.

"I collected firewood this morning. It's not like I slacked off."

"Greg, it's filling a trough with water and making sure they have food, maybe shoveling some crap into the trashcan. Man up." Ahmed spoke for the first time. "You know what? Dan wants to see how it is done. Grab him from upstairs. He's reading books or playing nerf basketball up there."

"I'll just do it while there's still sunlight." Greg shuffled out the back door. Ahmed was right, it was not a hard job. The tough job was milking the goats in the morning, and even that was not difficult. Greg slipped on the pair of communal rubber work boots and barn coat they kept by the back door, and made quick work of the chores.

The converted barnyard had a fence running around a small perimeter, and a ramp running into the screened in porch on the side of the house. There were nesting spots for the chickens, and hay beds for the goats to use at night. The afternoon animal shift was easy and basic. Clean up poop, make sure the animals have clean hay for the night, check their water, and spread food on the ground for the chickens. Not much to it, but essential to keeping the animals happy and producing.

Greg heard the back door shut. Dan stood on the small landing. "Hey, Greg, I wanted to see what the job was back here. Okay if I help or watch?"

"Sure, I was just shoveling poop. If you want to put on some gloves, you can spread the feed, maybe check the water?" Greg pointed towards a box of work gloves by the back door.

"How was your first day with us?" Greg asked.

"Let's see," Dan started as he walked over to the feed pail. "I slept until noon, came out and enjoyed a steak sandwich, played tennis. Living here isn't too bad."

Greg chuckled. "You should try it in December. Not as much steak and tennis, and it feels like it gets dark at noon."

"I was down the road a few miles, I know what you're talking about. From what I've been told, we are kicking back and enjoying a vacation before we move to Hawaii. New Hampshire in April is our vacation before we start our life in Hawaii."

Dan looked around the small yard. "I threw the feed. The water looks cleanish and full. Anything else?"

"If you open the door, at the top of that ramp? See if I need to clean up in there, and make sure the goats haven't eaten their beds and the chickens' beds. If they have, just throw some more hay down from one of the bails on the other side of the fence under that tarp." Dan followed Greg's orders.

A few minutes later they were sitting on the back porch steps watching chickens eat feed off the ground. The goats milled about.

"You and I are lucky people." Dan said to the boy. "Not because we survived the rapture. That wasn't lucky, it was torture." He put his elbow on Greg's shoulder . "This is lucky, living like this, having potential again, having possibility again."

"What do you mean?"

"I was living with two people that were driving me crazy. I was going to leave and try to survive on my own. How long would you give me? A year? If my car breaks down and I don't find water? A week?"

"Maybe."

"Yeah, well, I give you and Rebecca a year up here. I've heard you developed some fantastic trapping skills, and she is whip smart, but seriously, two more winters? If one of you gets sick, gets hurt." He looked at Greg. "We were rescued. That's damn lucky."

"Did my Dad send you out here?" Greg gave Dan a sideways look.

"No." He held up his hands. "Honest, I am just making conversation."

"We did get lucky." Greg looked back to the goats. "Do you think they wonder how they went from North Carolina, where it's warm, to New England, where it snows? You think the goats are like 'What the heck is this?'"

"The goats aren't from here?" Tom did not know the back story.

"I guess it makes the joke hard to understand if you don't know where the goats are from. No, my aunt and uncle had them in Raleigh, along with two thirds of the chickens. Rebecca and I had ten this winter, well, we started with ten, went down to five, but that was more than enough to keep us in eggs."

"We had fish and lobster, lots of lobster. I would have killed for some eggs or meat. Once the snow flew, we didn't do much by way of hunting or fishing." He put his hand on Greg's leg, gave it a pat and stood up. "Like I said, we are two lucky guys to get rounded up like we did."

"I'll tell you the story of my month in my school dorm, or the two weeks it took me to find Rebecca. I was one meal away from eating cat food. It confirms your belief that I am lucky."

"I'd like that. Maybe we can share stories about our initial weeks during the flight."

"Did you hear the one about the two little girls and boy walking half of Manhattan?" Greg heard the story second hand from Matt.

"Like I said, we can compare notes during the flight. Let's go in and see how long before we eat. The house smells wonderful." Dan opened the door and went inside. He kicked off his boots by the back door, and started talking to people as soon as he got to the kitchen. He was a social person, fun, nice, and his true personality was bottled up for months in Boston. He felt joy around the new people and families.

The weather turned worse, and temperatures dropped back into the thirties. A needed reminder of how fickle and harsh New England weather is. The rain and sleet made it impossible to use the outdoor pizza oven. Todd and Ahmed moved their production into the Italian restaurant downtown Hanover, lighting the commercial brick oven and inviting everyone to join them for pizza night. They made goat's milk mozzarella cheese, and found canisters of grated parmesan cheese in pantries around the town. People enjoyed sausage and cheese pizzas for the first time in close to a year.

Kelly and Hank spent the day tending to the animals at the dairy farm. They were back in time for pizzas and wine. They reported that one cow was producing milk again, not in any quantity, but producing none the less.

Dinosaur rock, controlled by the adults, played from speakers, and candles lit the building. The little kids danced and laughed, and the adults drank a few too many glasses of wine. People were happy and comfortable in Hanover.

Peter approached Antonio at the party. "Tony, I need to ask for your help."

Antonio and Peter had only exchanged cordial hellos up to this point in their relationship.

"I want to go to the airport, the one an hour away? I was hoping tomorrow or the next, and I think I might need help getting the plane started. I heard about how great a job you did with the boats, and, well."

"Road trip. Nice!" Antonio stuck out his hand and shook Peter's. "Yeah, I'm in, anything I can do to help. I don't know anything about airplanes, but if an engine is an engine, I'll give it a go."

"Great." Peter turned to walk away before spinning around. "You know, I want to teach someone how to fly, just some basics in case I need help. Any chance you want to log some time with me? Get some flying lessons over the next week or so?"

"That would be crazy. Yeah, hell yeah. Give it up, Peter." Antonio put his hand out again, but this time his elbow was bent so his hand was more at chest level. Peter imitated the motion, and shook hands awkwardly. Their chests were inches apart. Antonio smiled and nodded his head. "Pilot Antonio, damn does that sound good." He walked off to tell the other teens.

Rebecca found Peter later in the evening. "You should go tomorrow, you know, to Manchester. The snow will start to fly on Wednesday. you don't want to drive in the snow, or on slick, icy, roads."

"That's good advice. I didn't have any plans tomorrow anyway, might as well knock it out." Peter went off to find Paul and Todd to see if they were interested in going.

50

The rain stopped the next morning, but the clouds remained as Peter, Antonio, Emily, Meredith, and Paul raced down the highway towards Manchester. Meredith wanted an adventure, and asked if she could tag along. It was her first time away from Avery since her family died.

"Why not?" Was Peter's response to her request to join him.

They pulled into the airport, speeding away from the parking garage and parking lot tents, straight to the backside of the terminal. Emily stopped the Suburban once she was through the open gate and onto the runway. The fuel trucks were to her right. The planes were off in the distance on her left.

"Which way?" She asked Peter.

Peter pointed left. "Drive down to the planes. Let's see if there is a stair truck. Pilots had to get out of those planes somehow once they drove them down there."

"We're looking for a pickup with a set of stairs on it?" Meredith asked, poking her head between the front seats. "Like that one?" She pointed to the right, next the fuel trucks. Parked beside the last terminal gate was a truck with stairs running up the back of the cab.

"Exactly." Peter said. "Like I said, let's go over there and get that truck started. One of us can drive it to the planes."

Emily turned the SUV right instead of left and drove to the stair truck. The door to the truck was unlocked and the keys were in the ignition. It did not turn over.

"Do we want to use the new battery or jump the old one?" Emily asked

Antonio through the window.

"Let's jump it if we can. I like keeping a spare in case our battery dies. Roadside assistance isn't all that reliable anymore." The new Antonio was intelligent, practical, and a hard worker. Emily wondered why his attitude and work ethic had done such a one eighty. What made him join a gang in the first place? He appeared to have a loving father, a good family, siblings he cared about. Maybe one day she would ask him. She also thought about letting the past go, and enjoying the new man blossoming in front of her.

She popped the hood for Antonio. He pulled twelve foot jumper cables out of the back of the SUV. He connected the batteries, waited a few seconds, and the stair truck came to life. It had plenty of gas.

"You mind if I take it over? I like driving things like this." Antonio asked hopefully.

"Just don't get close to the plane until I get out and direct you." Peter asked him. "I don't want you breaking the plane or this truck."

"I wanted to drive the stair truck." Paul said from the back seat.

"Well, you should have gotten out to jumpstart it then. You don't get the fun when you don't put in the work." Emily mock chastised him. "Maybe Tony will let you drive it when we're done."

"Funny." Paul replied. "Very funny."

She followed Antonio's stairs down the runway towards the large grouping of planes.

"John and Solange are right. We have two planes. Hopefully one of them will work." Peter said upon seeing the two 777's.

Instead of backing the truck against the plane, Peter suggested they park the stairs parallel to the door. He did not want to take a chance of hitting or denting the plane or ruining the stair truck. He could get into the cabin from the side of the stairs. He directed Antonio to the right spot before running up the stairs to the jet's door.

"Do we need a key or something?" Paul asked, coming up behind Peter.

Peter looked at him with as close to a 'really?' expression as the polite man could give. "No, these do not get stolen very often. We need to use our muscles and twist this handle."

A circle with a bar running through it, similar to a Greek letter Theta, was recessed into the side. Paul noticed a metal catch that held the handle into a "locked" position. He pushed the catch up, like he would the safety on a gun, and turned the circular handle to his left for half a rotation. The safety button clicked back into place and the seal on the door made a noise like opening a new jar of pickles.

"Nice work. We're in." Peter patted him on the back.

The door pulled out a few inches and slid to the side. They were next to the cockpit. Peter saw the rubber floor of the steward's area. "It smells a little stale, but other than that..."

The level of the stairs was equal to the floor of the plane. One by one they stepped into the cabin.

Peter went to the cockpit with Antonio. The others checked the cabin areas. "Holy moly this plane is big." Emily said. "I mean, seriously, we should have enough room, don't you think?"

"Yeah, we are good." Paul looked around the steward's cabin. It was fully stocked. "I bet this plane was supposed to take off and was grounded. It probably has a full tank." He looked at Meredith. She sat in a first class seat. "Meredith, let's go in the back and check the cargo hold. Anyone want to see if there is luggage back there? This plane might have been boarded or had people sitting in the terminal waiting to board."

Meredith jumped out of her chair and made her way to the back. She had flown before, but only to Orlando from Newark. She had never been on a plane this large. She eyed the next area of seats. "If that was first class, what is this?" She asked.

"Business class." Emily told her.

"What does that mean?"

"Another way for the airlines to make money." Paul told her.

The cabin lights came on. Paul and Emily cheered. They yelled louder when the engines started. They were in the back and did not see Antonio jump out of the plane to move the stair truck and drive the Suburban towards the terminal.

Paul, Meredith, and Emily were searching the cargo hold when Peter stuck his head through the door. "They were going to leave, must have been stopped." There were hundreds of stowed bags. "Why wouldn't they give people their stuff back I wonder?"

"It was a weird time. I would have gotten out of Dodge, not cared about my luggage." Paul told him. "I know the Cincinnati Airport was closed. It just closed. I read on a blog it was nasty, armed troops in hazmat masks throwing everyone out. People were told to leave without their things."

"We can go through the luggage if you like, but I'd just as soon lighten our load, particularly if we are taking cows. Cows are heavy."

"We aren't taking the cows, are we?" Paul asked.

"We're not? Then why is Kelly trying to save them?" Emily asked back.

"Because that is what she does, at least that's what I assumed. I mean, I guess we can take the cows. Dairy is a good thing. We know there are cows in Hawaii, right?"

"There are wild pigs and chickens too." Meredith chimed in. "I was reading a book about Kauai at the library during school yesterday." She continued to give facts, and grinned as she talked about the island.

Emily enjoyed seeing her smile. Like so many of the tribe, Meredith emerged from her shell the longer she was in Hanover.

"The reason I came back here was to tell you that I am putting the plane in reverse to jockey down the runway towards the terminal. You need to find a seat and buckle up. It might be a little bumpy as I take this baby over grass and up and down the runway edge." He looked at Meredith. "I need a co-pilot."

"Okay." She said, dropping her head from shyness. Meredith looked over to Emily. The young girl's eyes blazed with excitement. She followed Peter up front. The old man moved quickly, and Meredith had to hurry to keep up.

"Well Emily, I suggest taking our seats in first class." They shut the cargo door and walked back towards the front of the plane. "I didn't realize we were taking the cows. That was dumb of me. Are they going to walk up the stairs and onto the plane? Are they going to walk down the stairs in Hawaii?" Paul had logistical questions, which he continued to ask Emily after they took their seats.

"You worried at all about this?" Emily asked him, ignoring most of Paul's questions.

"About taxiing to the terminal? I question why we are taxiing to the terminal when we can just leave the plane here."

"No, about flying to Hawaii."

"Yes. I'm scared, but it's the right thing to do. If it works out half as well as we think, we'll be able to survive. If things work out half as well as we think in Hanover? We die. If they work out half as well as we think in Virginia? We are barely eking out an existence."

"How do you mean?" The plane bumped up and down as Peter pulled backwards and jumped the runway curb.

"Let's say we get to Hawaii. It's warm, all the time, so we don't have to worry about weather. There is water, there are animals. Hawaii presents a lot of givens. There are some variables, like can we grow crops or catch enough fish, but the givens are tropical fruit trees, tropical vegetables, things that are already there. Right? We can't screw that up. We can't stop avocados from growing all over the place."

"Okay," Emily replied in a leading voice.

"In Virginia? It gets cold and things die. We'd have to can and cure for the winter months. We have to figure out how to fish all year around. We get a blizzard or something? We could be socked in, screwed. Do we survive? Yes. Does it suck? A whole bunch. Those things won't happen in Hawaii. It would be, and I say this with complete confidence, impossible for us to starve to death in Hawaii. Literally, impossible for us to starve. In Virginia? We could starve. Up here? It's a better bet we starve than don't starve, particularly in three to five years. In five years? We have to be able to grow and kill all our food. How are we going to do that in New Hampshire?"

"That makes sense." She agreed.

"I am afraid. I'm afraid we'll fall out of the sky. 'm afraid we won't be able to land over there, or we'll have to land in the water, or we'll meet a number of bad scenarios, but once we get there, once my fears have come unrealized, we have set ourselves up for thrivival."

"Thrivival?" She asked.

"You like it? Combining Thriving and Survival? It's my word. Hawaii is thrivival, Virginia is survival, and New Hampshire is most likely death."

"Why do you need to make up a word?" Emily and Paul thrust forward ever so slightly as Peter put on the breaks.

The intercom buzzed, "sorry about that folks, came in a little hot. Welcome to Manchester International Airport. It is 10am local time. If you don't mind, I'm going to run a few quick tests on the engines. You'll hear some revving and it might get a little loud. I'll let you know when I am done."

"He's funny." Emily commented.

"I think he wants us to trust that he is a real pilot. I hope to God he's a real pilot. Shit, I could do the pilot impression."

They heard the engines come up, revving loudly. They were halfway down the runway, still a hundred yards from the terminal. The plane moved forward and began to pick up speed. The engines revved down and the plane slowed. Peter kept a steady pace until they arrived at the terminal.

"This concludes our flight for today. Thank you for flying Reinhart Air."

Paul yelled towards the cockpit. "Peter, don't turn the plane off yet, I have an idea I'd like to run by you." He unbuckled and walked to the front. Meredith and Peter wore giant headphones. "Nice." Paul told them.

"Peter," he continued. "How hard would it be to get the plane up against a gate at the terminal?"

"Pretty easy, but we still need to move the bridge from the terminal to the side of the plane."

"If we want cows and pigs and goats and supplies, all those things will be easier to load from a ramp than a staircase. If we can get a ramp over to the side, like we are truly boarding this plane, well, that will be a great thing. Plus, we can pull back and take off, not worry about a chair truck sitting next to us."

"The chair truck would not be an issue, but I get where you are going. Most of your scenario depends on us being able to get power to the terminal, and to one of those telescoping ramps to the plane."

"We can get a generator to make the telescoping happen. Just park the plane where you would normally put it." Paul gave Meredith a thumbs up. "And you keep doing what you're doing, great work." She giggled. The oversized headphones slipped off her ears.

"You got it. Hold on. I might bump into something I don't see on the ground, but that's okay. Typically a jumbo jet wins confrontations." Peter pulled the jet towards the last terminal spot ten yards from a telescoping ramp.

Antonio retrieved the stair truck, jogging all the way back to the end of the runaway. He parked near the plane door.

"Before we get out, let's check supplies. We have enough chips, crackers, and cookies to hold us for a while." Emily spoke from the first class steward closet. "We also have booze, water, soda, and orange juice."

"The fuel gage reads full." Peter added. "We have enough to get us to Hawaii and back to the California if we needed."

"Let's unload the luggage and head back home. This was a successful trip." He shook Peter's hand, and gave Meredith and Emily high fives. "Based on your opinion, we could leave tomorrow?" He asked Peter.

"We could leave tomorrow. I want to get a good night's sleep, it's been a long time since I flew for 12 hours, but yes, we could go wheels up tomorrow if we needed to do it."

"Do you know how to open the luggage door to get the bags out?" Emily asked him as they made their way to the back of the plane.

"I do, but we're going to need a little luggage ramp car to access it."

"I love those things." Meredith laughed. "It will be just like Toy Story 2."

51

"We have a pilot, a plane, fuel, and a clear runway." Emily ceded the return driving to Paul. Antonio assumed shotgun. Peter was curled up in the backseat for a nap. Meredith sat next to Emily and listened.

"Check." she responded.

"It's supposed to snow tomorrow." Gray clouds hung low over the area and the air felt heavy. Rebecca's prediction was going to come true.

"Check."

Emily enjoyed the 'check' responses. "We have to move supplies and what we want to take. We have to move the animals. And we leave."

"Check." Meredith nodded with finality.

Emily pulled a notebook from the pocket in front of her seat. She made a list of supply items. There were three lists; Wants, Needs, Haves.

"Peter?" She asked, knowing he was still awake. "If we can get into a warehouse and find food, how much weight can the jet handle?"

"With no people? Unless you're putting the entire warehouse in, I don't see a problem. If we get a herd of cattle, then we have another conversation."

"Thank you." Emily made notes. She wanted rice, beans, pasta, and canned food. Similar lists were being made by everyone in the tribe. It helped them pass the time.

Meredith read the list from the next seat. "We need seeds."

Emily looked at her. "I'm sorry, honey, what was that?"

"Most of what you are writing should be in the 'wants' category. We need seeds more than anything else. We have to grow things, lots of things. Cans are heavy and will go bad. We need to learn how to live off the land."

"We have to survive once we get there." Emily told her. "We need to take as much food as we can."

"Sure, but not so much that we need a warehouse. There is going to be food there. Craig can catch fish for us." She giggled, Craig had the reputation of being the best angler. "We should take livestock and food, but not so much food that we raid a warehouse. We can't live like the past, we need to look at the future. We need to grow, hunt, harvest, fish." The young girl stopped talking. She felt uncomfortable speaking to an adult so candidly.

Emily looked at the young woman. There was silence in a car. Paul and Antonio glanced at each other with a look men have when they are uncomfortable, particularly when the situation involves two women.

"You're right. You're absolutely right." Emily balled up her piece of paper. "We need seeds and livestock. We probably need a month of food to take, and maybe a little more to help us on days we don't catch fish, but Meredith is right. I need to start thinking like it is, not how I want it to be, or how I've been living for the last few months." She winked at Meredith. "You keep telling me when I'm wrong, when I'm living in the past."

Meredith gave her a simple "check," in reply.

"You gonna tell her the other problem?" Antonio spoke over his shoulder to Meredith. "About the talk we all had?"

Emily looked up from her pad and faced her young friend. "What is it?"

"Some of us don't want to go." Meredith admitted.

"What?" Paul responded from the driver's seat. "We have to go. Our lives depend on going."

"Dude, it's not like we don't want to go to Hawaii. I want to lie in the sun and catch fish and crap, but you're old. You're goin' there to retire. I'm seventeen. Who I gonna be with? How am I gonna live my life once the old are a lot older? We don't have enough people."

"Who doesn't want to go?" Emily asked Meredith.

"Avery, Antonio, and I have talked about it. It's like he just said. I want to stay with the group, but my prospects are rotten if we don't find other survivors. I'm not sure Bernie wants to go either. Kelly is getting the cows healthy in hopes it will convince people to stay here. I don't know Dan and Karen well enough yet."

"Tell you what we can do." Peter yelled from the back. "We can go over, and if we think it makes sense, I can fly back to San Francisco, Los Angeles, or Tokyo for that matter. We aren't just considering Americans, right?"

Antonio yelled back. "What do you mean we can come back?"

Emily turned around in her seat to see Peter. "Would it be possible to drop paper from a 777 flying over cities?"

"Possible or advisable?" Was his response.

"Maybe we can fly over cities and drop paper, notes to have people meet us in San Francisco or Los Angeles to get picked up in a month."

"Let me think about it. We might be able to find Antonio some women yet." Peter worked the problem in his head. Maybe they could put leaflets in the landing gear and fly low over Chicago, opening the landing gear to release the notes. He smiled as he formed the plan in his head. "We need to decide what cities. I'll make it work." He said to Emily and Meredith.

"I wouldn't mind finding some additional women." Antonio cracked a smile. "I always want to increase my odds." He may have matured, but he still relied on occasional swagger. "You know what I mean, Paul?" He gave the driver a punch on his upper arm.

"I think we all know what you mean, Tony." Paul did not comment beyond the acknowledgement.

"You know what we need to do? We don't want to land, we just want people to figure out how to join us. Right? We should drop leaflets or something, and tell people where we're going." Antonio paused. "If you can't figure out how to get to us, I'm not sure I want you joining the tribe, right? You got to earn your spot on Team Antonio."

"We're not calling it Team Antonio." Paul said to him immediately. "There aren't any proposed tribe names, but if there are, Team Antonio would not make it on the list."

"You know it would." Antonio backed up his comment.

"No, it wouldn't. I'd vote for The Lollipop Guild before Team Antonio."

"You'd rather be the Lollipop Guild? Some Wizard of Oz crap before Team Antonio? That's cold, damn cold, Paul."

Paul drove quickly towards Hanover. Small flakes of snow fell, melting on the windshield.

"I miss NPR." Paul said, as the conversation paused for a few minutes. "It was great to drive and listen to stories about beavers or religion."

"I liked "All Things Considered", but their weekend shows were horrible. Who could listen to that "Wait, Wait, Don't Tell Me" crap?" Antonio shook his head as he mentioned the show.

"You liked NPR?" Paul looked over at him.

"I'm supposed to be ignorant on national and world topics just because I'm in a gang? Some of those stories were good."

"Tony, you are a man of surprising depth and intelligence." Paul complimented him.

"Yes I am." He told Paul. "Yes I am."

They rolled into Hanover at 2pm during a driving snowstorm. It hit early, a day before Rebecca forecast. She saw potential for an early storm, but the models presented a low probability for Tuesday and higher for Wednesday.

"Weather is an imperfect science." She told them, her hands upturned and out to her side.

52

"Snow in April. Why did you bring us here Todd?" Melanie was not happy. Neither was Solange. The temperature was back in the low 30's.

"It will all be gone by Thursday, don't worry. It should warm up." Rebecca assured everyone. "Until then, we can hunker down. Cozy up next to the fires."

During the scouting trip to the airport, the Hanover group made plans for the spring snowstorm. They acquired and set up two ping pong tables in the basement of the Choate Road house.

Teams were drawn at random, and a tournament bracket was put on the wall. The games ran all day Wednesday. There were singles and doubles divisions, and an under twelve age group.

It was not a fair tournament. Avery dominated the singles side of the competition, and carried her partner, Jamie, through the doubles. There was outcry throughout the house, accusations of sandbagging the event, withholding information, but in the end, Avery was declared the singles and doubles ping pong champion.

"Next time you have to play left-handed or something like that." Dan said to her after his drubbing in the semifinals.

"I could use my backhand exclusively, but wouldn't it humiliate you more when I still win?" She had her paddle facing down, making a sweeping motion towards him, shoeing him away.

"You just made an enemy." He put two fingers pointed towards his eyes, then pointed them back at her. "Watch your back next tournament."

Dan was her most competitive match, which Avery still won 21-11. Regardless of the domination by one player, the event was successful and fun. The twelve and under bracket used a smaller table. Jacob and Brian played a thriller in the final match, with Brian winning 21-19.

"We have to get a pool table." Paul told John as they sat and watched Rebecca play Matt. "We need a pool table, maybe a dart board, some backgammon. We should make a true rec room."

"We're not staying here that long, remember? Maybe you can find a pool table and use it at that location. It would be a lot easier than hauling one in here." John's head bobbed back and forth with the ball.

"We're so busy too, would be hard to find time to help me." Paul replied sarcastically. "Did you know the young people are reluctant to move? Meredith, of all people, talked to us about it in the car. It's not that they don't want to move to Hawaii, it's the finality of their numbers. They want more of an effort put into finding survivors before we isolate the tribe."

"What did you tell her?" John asked him before yelling. "Oh! Nice point Matt." It was not a close match. Matt was better than Rebecca.

"I did not answer. Emily suggested a plan on our way to Hawaii. We will fly over large cities and drop fliers from the landing gear."

John nodded, still watching the game. Paul was surprised his brother was blasé about the idea of losing half of the tribe, particularly the younger half.

"I completely agree with them. We need more people, but we are up against a clock. I have no idea how long the plane will work. I don't know how long the cars will work. We have to get to Hawaii before the end of summer. We've travelled up and down the east coast. I've made a specific trip to Boston. If they still want to leave, we can't stop them." John turned away from the match. "But I'll do everything I possibly can to appease their concerns, help them find additional survivors, and convince them that we are executing the best and only option for survival by going."

Paul nodded. "Hey, did you know we were taking the cows with us?"

"Yeah, why wouldn't we take the cows? What did you think Kelly was doing over there the last five days?"

"Apparently she is one of the dissenters with regards to leaving and is possibly creating a food source for the people who stay here, but, I also just assumed she is a vet and vets heal animals."

"Do you not want to take the animals?"

"I do, it just seems funny, very Noah's ark. We have a dog, chickens, goats, cows, pigs, and people, and we're all flying to paradise."

"So we hope." John told him. "So we hope."

Matt won match point. John screamed, "yes!"

It was early in the tournament, Paul turned to his brother. "Have you seen Avery play?"

"No." John said, standing up to congratulate his son. "Why? She as good as Matt?"

"Save me a seat if they play each other. I want to make sure I'm next to you for that one." Paul put his hand on John's back and gave him a pat.

John looked at the board. "Actually, I'm playing her next. Maybe you want to stick around and watch me?"

Paul smiled. "I wouldn't miss it, John, wouldn't miss it for the world." Paul sat back down and watched the match. It asted less than ten minutes, 21 – 3. John's three points came on Avery's double faults.

The temperature rose in the late afternoon. The snow became a drizzling rain. Fog and mist enveloped the roads and landscape. A pot of moose chili bubbled on the sun porch woodstove and cornbread baked quickly in a cast iron skillet..

"Do you have any idea how tired of moose meat we are going to be in another few days." Hank ate his chili next to Kelly.

"Well, it's food, it's good food, and there aren't any moose in Hawaii, so realize this is the last time in your life you will ever have moose meat. I'm upset we wasted the smell of cornbread and chili on a screened porch." She took another bite. The chili was delicious, regardless of it being the sixth meal in a row of red meat. "It might be the last red meat you have in a long time too. There are pigs, fish, and fowl in Hawaii. I know there are cows, but cows don't go feral as well as the other animals. I'll try to breed, but, you know."

"So you're telling me to eat up." Hank pushed another spoonful into his mouth.

"More telling you to stop complaining." Kelly laughed as she watched a fake smile spread across Hank's face while he ate. They worked together at the dairy farm over the last few days, getting to know each other better. She was fast friends with the older man. They both enjoyed punk music in its many versions. Double Nickels on the Dime by The Minutemen was Kelly's favorite album. Hank had nothing but respect for her after she told him.

"When do you think we'll leave? I heard the plane works and is full of fuel." Kelly switched topics.

"I don't know. You and I have to get those cows healthy. Probably another week or two, right?" He ate some of his cornbread.

"Yeah, I'd say. They don't have to be 100%, but I want them a little stronger before we move them. The pigs are probably fine, they'll sleep like Hubba. No worries." She paused. "So I'm the hold up, or do you think people still want to stay and relax?"

"A little of both. Don't rush, we have nothing but time. Did you hear the latest plan?" Hank tore into his second triangle of bread. "To eject pamphlets from the plane, fly over most of the major cities?"

"I've heard pieces. If we can make it happen, sounds good to me. I'm one of the people voicing concerns about the small size of our tribe, and how we need more young people. Once I get to Hawaii, I don't plan on coming back. If this helps us ease our conscience, possibly rescue some people by setting them on a path towards us, I'm all for it."

"Yeah, I agree on all fronts." Hank finished his meal. "There's cake tonight, want me to grab you a piece?" Pockets of people ate and spoke in groups around the Choate Road mansion.

"Who doesn't like cake?" Kelly asked rhetorically.

Todd watched the rain wash away the snow. Emily came up behind him and slipped her arm around his back. He looked through a window in the den converted into Hank and Paul's bedroom. The fire smoldered behind them.

"Whatcha thinkin'?" She asked him.

"That this is the last snowfall I will ever see. I always thought, or dreamed at least, that you and I would spend some of our retirement in New England, that we would enjoy the leaves changing color, that our grandchildren would go sledding on the same hill I used as a boy." He turned to look at her, kissing her. "But I will have grandchildren, so I'm not sad. I'm just enjoying the last snow."

She put her other arm around his front, hugging him from the side. She watched the rain with her husband. "You know, I was never going to retire to New England, right?"

"Yes." He said back.

"I hate the cold."

"I know."

"I love you." Emily squeezed him tightly, "I love you so much. It was a great idea for us to come up here. We found family and new friends. You saved us."

"I know." He said jokingly and without modesty. "I did it for selfish reasons too. I didn't know at the time why I was sending us here. It was a bad idea, believing we could live in Hanover forever, but it has let me say goodbye to my town. It's brought us friends and a path to our new life. I can leave Hanover in a few weeks remembering my childhood, my boyhood home fondly. I'll always remember it like this, beautiful." He turned and kissed her again. "And I'll always remember our last snowfall."

Todd smiled as he turned and looked back out the window.

53

The weather turned warm, just as Rebecca forecast.

Antonio was able to hotwire a car battery to the ramp extension near their airplane. He moved the walkway and attached it to the side of the plane. He would pull it back a few feet just before takeoff, and use a board to walk across the gap.

With the ramp attached, and a conveyor truck in place to load the cargo/luggage hold, tribe members made trips to Manchester to load items. They packed seeds, fishing gear, feed for the livestock, rice, pasta, canned goods. They took clothing and shoes, blankets and sheets, bleach, water, soda, and batteries.

Peter gave parameters on weight, but the load limit he set was high. He, Jamie, and Hubba never left Hanover.

Seats were removed from coach to accommodate the animals. Metal fencing was installed to keep the different species corralled.

Dan was the only tribe member to spend time in Hawaii. He went every year for vacation, but his family stayed on Maui, with only a few day trips to Kauai. He admitted that he did not know much about Kauai specifically, other than seeing a Walmart, walking around a few downtowns, and remembering there were two different climates. The north was green and cool, the south was sunny and hot.

"Not much help, am I?" He asked Rebecca as she read through books and asked him questions about the area.

"No, but that's okay. We'll figure it out. It's great to have you as a resource."

Tribe members not packing and traveling to Manchester fulfilled the daily chores necessary to keep the group alive. They fished, purified water, cooked bread, and figured out new and inventive ways to serve moose.

Paul, having tired of moose more quickly than the rest, decided to make moose jerky from as much of the remaining meat as he could. He dried and packaged relentlessly. Jerky was easy to store, had a decent shelf life, and it was light in weight. It took him the entire two weeks, but he managed to "jerkify" as he called it, the last one and a half moose legs.

He personally drove the hundred bags of moose jerky to Manchester.

Peter confirmed their plan to spread notes across the country. They would stuff the fliers, thousands of them, near the landing gear. Peter would fly low into the city, let the gear down, and the pamphlets would drop to the ground.

They could repeat the procedure as necessary, loading the wheel well in flight.

A favorite pastime became running the copiers at the local print shop. A gas generator powered the industrial copier. They created more than 100,000 fliers, all shipped to Manchester and placed near the landing gear wheel well.

After a visit to an office supply warehouse in Lebanon, Avery and Meredith took an added step of laminating several hundred copies of the note. Rebecca took great pleasure in calling them nerds.

They planned to fly over Chicago, St. Louis, Dallas, Houston, San Antonio, San Diego, Los Angeles, San Francisco, and Seattle before turning for the Hawaiian Islands.

The note was written in English and Spanish: 20+ survivors, men, women, and children. We are starting a colony on the island of Kauai, Hawaii. Join us. We will return on August 1st to the San Diego Airport to meet survivors. Gather as many people as possible.

Hank joked that he wanted to include a phone number and email address.

John toyed with adding the line 'No assholes allowed.'

Days were productive, busy, yet relaxing. If people wanted to take a day off from packing, loading, or working, they did.

Jamie was not strong enough to load the plane. She helped with meals, fed the animals, and made herself useful. She read stories to the children at school, giving Emily much needed breaks.

Ten days after the snowstorm, it was close to 60 degrees, and the sun shone brightly. Light puffy clouds drifted across the pale blue New England sky. Kelly and Hank arrived at the RV for lunch, after spending another night at the dairy farm.

"Milk!" She said, jumping out of the pickup truck and announcing their latest prize to the group. "Three gallons of real milk! The cows are ready to go." She walked to the tables near the grill in front of the main house and placed a large metal milk jug on top.

Todd turned to John and said three simple words.

"Time to go."

He put his arms out and patted his brother and wife on their backs before walking to the table to congratulate Kelly and Hank for their hard work.

John looked at Emily. She nodded. He turned to Solange. She wore a smile on her face.

"You heard him. It is time." Solange walked towards the table to have a glass of cow's milk.

Most of the preparation for the flight was done. The plane was loaded with supplies. The coach section was converted into a barn with pens and feed for the animals. There were 100,000 copies of their flier ready to distribute.

Even with the massive transfer of supplies to the plane, the Hanover camp did not suffer from lack of food or clothing. The only key piece of equipment missing was Todd's pizza oven, forcing him and Ahmed to use the commercial wood-fired oven in town.

"Let's talk timeframe and logistics." Hank sat at a large table in the restaurant that night. The sunny start to their day turned cloudy, and a light rain drizzled outside. The tribe enjoyed brick oven baked fish, French bread baguettes, and roasted canned asparagus.

"Kelly and I will make sure the animals get to Manchester and on the plane. We measured the width of the cows, and since they are all pretty skinny right now, they will make it through the jet doorway with room to spare." Hank prepped a trailer to bring the five cows, one bull, and 8 hogs to the airport. He and Kelly would get them on the plane, sedate the cows and hogs, tranquilize the bull, and be ready to go at least an hour before the proposed takeoff.

"I don't want them on the plane too long before us. You know they are going to stink up the place." Melanie did not like the smell of animals. It was a necessary evil for the trip, but she wanted to minimize the problem.

"Don't worry. We'll take care of it." Hank assured her. "Sorry a few hours of smell might save your life with food and dairy down the road." Sarcasm was common among tribe conversations, particularly involving Hank.

"I'm paying for a first class ticket. I expect an odorless flight." She smiled.

"I'll keep my animals under control, you just keep your kids out of my section." Hank knew it was going to be more difficult to entertain the children for twelve hours, than keep the animals at bay.

"We all want to go, right?" John asked. "So let's go. Two days. We'll run through our checklist of supplies tomorrow, and leave the next day." John turned to Peter. Peter was the lynchpin, the key to their journey. He made the final decision.

"I'm ready. The plane checks out. The supplies are well under weight even with the livestock. I feel good, strong, well rested. Let's fly."

The group did not cheer. They nodded in agreement. Their die was cast. They were leaving Hanover, even though it had become comfortable over the last three weeks.

The mutiny of young people planning to stay behind in North America was quelled by the flier dropping plan. Other ideas emerged to grow the tribe. Ahmed volunteered to remain in North America, zig zagging across the country until August 1st when he would meet the rescue plane in San Diego. Antonio and Meredith offered to stay behind with him.

Rebecca met with them. "Ahmed, even your limited understanding of mathematics must understand that three people represents more than 10% of the current tribe. What if you break down and cannot make the August 1st deadline in San Diego? What if the tribe makes a water landing or lands on a highway landing in Hawaii and cannot find another plane?"

Ahmed respected intelligence and rational arguments. He could not refute Rebecca's final statement. "The best and safest way to increase the tribe's numbers, without risking our current members, is to drop leaflets across the country, have all of us fly over, and have Peter return in August."

"I'll fly until the fuel goes bad or we run out, but we'll find more young people for you." Peter assured them.

Peter was in his late sixties, and while strong for his age, he knew his limitations. He used the ten days to develop a serviceable co-pilot. Flying a plane for twelve hours was not something he wanted to try, particularly with a potentially tricky landing on the backend of the flight. He would need bathroom breaks, and a nap. He wanted Antonio to sit in the cockpit while Peter curled up and slept for a few minutes, possibly an hour.

Antonio was mechanical and understood gauges and dials. He knew about longitude and latitude beyond the lines on a globe. His years of deep sea fishing with his father taught him to trust readings rather than his eyes out the window. Antonio could read the instruments, adjust their heading when needed, and keep his cool if any lights came on.

Peter took him to Lebanon airport and sat in the cockpit of the largest available plane, an eighteen seat turbo prop.

"Okay Tony, this will be my version of a pool certification for SCUBA diving you might receive at a resort. It's going to be fast. It's going to be effective. It by no means certifies you to fly a plane without me, and you will most likely forget everything you've learned a week after we land in Hawaii." Antonio nodded. "I am going to take off and land the plane. We can talk about landing, but if there is an issue with me on the way over, and you have to try and land a 777 without me?" Peter paused. "Yeah, let's just move on from that scenario. The other thing I want to drum into your head, the plane is going to be on autopilot. The 777 has a system that is advanced, safe, and almost foolproof. It could potentially land the plane for us if needed. I will show you how that works when we get up in the air, but I will be landing the plane myself. All I want you to learn over the next few hours is what to do if the autopilot fails and I am asleep or in the bathroom." He paused again for emphasis. "The autopilot is not going to fail, it just won't, but in the one in a million chance that it does, I need you to be able to grab the controls and keep us in the air. That's all we're trying to do here, nothing more. You shouldn't feel any pressure to have to learn how to fly a plane or land a plane. Please just focus on being able to grab the handle and keep us steady until I can get back."

Antonio nodded again. His typical swagger and verbal bravado was noticeably absent. "I'll say this a few more times, just to make you comfortable. You are completely unnecessary. The autopilot on these planes is incredible. Other than taking the plane out to the end of the runway, I am almost unnecessary. The computer can do everything. I'm the backup for the computer, you're the backup for me. Double redundancy, and you're the redundant backup. It never gets to you. Got it?"

Antonio listened, took some notes, and quizzed himself throughout the week. He had fun taxiing the plane around the little airport, paying attention to which levers did what. Peter was confident he could handle the plane for the minute it might be necessary.

Peter sat with Antonio at dinner. "You ready?"

"Ready to do nothing?" Antonio replied.

"Exactly." Peter grinned. "You catch on quickly."

Greg and Rebecca left the dinner together, Greg holding a large umbrella in his left hand, his right arm swung around Rebecca to keep her warm. He enjoyed holding her. They left to spend the night at the coach house. One last night alone in Hanover, the way they started their journey.

"I'm getting excited about the trip." Rebecca told him. "I know you think I'm sad to leave New England, my home, but I'm not. I'm excited to start something fresh."

"Really? Aren't you scared?" He was scared. Scared of the flight, scared of what they might find or not find on the islands. His stomach did back flips with increasing speed over the last week.

"I'm not." Her left arm was around his waist. "These are good people, great people. We are going to build a fantastic tribe that can accomplish anything, overcome any shortcomings we might find." She continued talking as they walked.

"I'm a planner, you know that, you probably think I am uncomfortable in a situation I can't control or plan, and normally you'd be right, but not today. I'm ready. I'm an optimist for the first time in my life. I'm looking at the next week as a positive, not a set of odds that I need to calculate." Rebecca's voice was filled with enthusiasm.

"Your family created this excitement for me. They are so full of hope, so full of life. They are taking this journey by the horns, accepting the downside that might occur, and meeting it head on. I sound like a sports metaphor for the first time in my life. I never talk or think like this, but today? We're ready, we as a group, we as a couple, me as a person. Ready to go."

"Wow." Greg replied after her speech. "It's hard to argue with you when you have this much passion. I'm scared, scared like I was when I decided to leave the dorm last year. I have no idea how this trip is going to go, the actual trip over to the island, and the life we create. I am going to do it. I'm getting on the plane. It's the right thing to do, but I am going to hold your hand when the wheels go up."

"Greg and Rebecca." She said to him quietly.

"Greg and Rebecca." He said back, pulling her towards him as they walked.

"Do you think we'll find anyone alive over there? Will someone see our plane in Honolulu and try to come over to Kauai? Do you think anyone will be on Kauai?" Greg read the travel guides for the islands, but he did not know the islands population before the plague. What were the odds they found people or even a person?

"There should be a person alive. The population is over one million three hundred thousand. I don't know if that means two people made it. We are going to Kauai. Its population is sixty thousand. That island should be empty, but you never know. We fly low over Honolulu, drop some flyers, make it known we are going to Kauai. I bet Peter will find a small plane he can pilot over to Pearl or something, if he wants to pick up a survivor. Antonio can take a boat."

"Could you imagine being alone in Hawaii, literally alone like you and I were, only for almost a year, then a plane flies over your head? If it were me, I would think it was a dream." Greg opened the front door of the coach house and let Rebecca walk through. There was a pre-made fire in the fireplace. She lit it while Greg shook out the umbrella and took off his boots. They had a solar lantern, one of the few left in town that wasn't packed on the plane in Manchester. The fire cast enough light for the room, and Greg clicked it off.

It was cool in the room, the evening temperatures were still in the low 50's. Rebecca kept her sweater on until the fire brought up the heat. Greg had a flannel shirt unbuttoned over his long sleeved crew neck shirt. He sat down on the couch with her. She cuddled into his arm and chest. The fire danced in front of them. They sat quietly, and relished their time together. She fell asleep on his chest, and he enjoyed her feeling against him. Greg let her sleep while he watched the fire, and worried about the flight.

54

"You're sure this bull isn't going to fall asleep before we get it on the plane? We aren't going to wait for it to wake up, and I don't think we can carry it." Hank pulled an increasingly groggy black male steer through the Manchester Airport.

"He'll make it, don't worry. We need to get him on the plane though, so stop complaining and keep pulling." Kelly was walking next to the animal, coaxing it along. Hank made it to the gate and walked down the corridor. The bull snorted, raised its head, resisted the enclosed space for a second, and moved forward.

"It's okay big fella, you're doing great, keep walking." The bull slowed to a painstaking trot, but made it to the door of the plane. It pulled its head back, but was drugged enough to be led forward through the door. Hank turned the beast towards the pen in the back of the plane, and after fifteen minutes of handling, the large animal was in a chain linked fence. It blinked a few times, bent its legs to lie down on the ground, and its eyes rolled into its head. His side moved up and down as he breathed. Kelly checked its heartbeat and pulse, and gave Hank a thumbs up.

"He's going to be out for a long time, and I mean a long time. If he opens his eyes, I'll hit him up again, but even if he wakes up, he'll be in a daze."

"Let's get the cows, the pigs, goats, and chickens." Hank looked at Kelly. "I cannot believe I just said that, both from the standpoint of me, a non-farm type person, and because we are loading a plane to Hawaii full of farm animals."

The cows loaded easily, as long as the first one walked the others followed. Hank put them in an area next to the sleeping bull. The pigs came in a herd to their pen. The goats and chickens were on their way down from Hanover.

With their animals loaded, Hank and Kelly sat in first class chairs, sweaty and ready for a break.

"When do we take off?" Kelly asked, exhausted.

"I asked Todd to have the water filled and hot in the RV so we could shower before the flight. I plan on sleeping as soon as we are in the air." Hank put his hands behind his head. "Everyone should be here soon."

Todd pulled up in the RV fifteen minutes later. He called Hank on a handheld to say he was outside of the terminal.

Todd did not want to expose the kids to the noxious smell from the parking area. He told them to hold their noses and run into the terminal once they saw Hank or Kelly spinning the large revolving door.

"They'll come out, and you go in." He told the ten kids with him. Bernie, Emily, and Melanie nodded in agreement.

Hank and Kelly appeared on the other side of the glass windows. They spun the door, and Emily took a big breath, picked up the sleeping bulldog laying at her feet, let Todd open the door for her, and ran the ten feet into the terminal. The children did the same. Bernie and Melanie went last.

Hank and Kelly ran from the terminal into the RV once the kids were inside with Emily.

"Shut the door!" Todd yelled. "The smell is incredible."

"Sorry." Hank was sweaty and panting. "It might be a little from us too. We've been sleeping with and moving farm animals for twelve hours."

"Are they all set?" Todd asked.

"The bull is out, and the rest are sedated for the flight. We are good to go." Kelly looked at Hank. "I'm going to jump in the shower if you don't mind. I'm calling 'girls first' on you."

"Please." Hank told her, sitting down on the couch in the RV.

"You do smell." Todd told him. "Dan is driving the other RV with the adults and animals. They were supposed to leave within ten minutes of me."

"All going as planned? Any problems?" Hank had been at the farm with Kelly.

"We are amazingly problem free. I was sad leaving Hanover, but we're all excited for the journey. It's time to start our lives." Todd looked towards the terminal. "I better get in there to see if Emily needs any help. Did you get breakfast?"

"Not really." Hank admitted. "I was planning on chips and cookies on the plane."

Todd gave him a wink. "You think I'd let my brother go out like that? We had steak and eggs this morning. I saved you and Kelly some steak, the last of the moose, sliced it with some fresh mozzarella and basil mayonnaise on a baguette I made last night." He pointed to the oven. "I hid it in there so no one would find it before you two got to eat."

"I love you, man. I really do. I think I might cry." Hank walked to the oven and claimed his prize, biting into his half of the sandwich as soon as he exposed an end from the plastic bag.

"Don't forget there is a piece for Kelly. It's not all for you." Todd waited for Hank to nod. "Okay, I'll see you in a few." Todd took a breath, opened the door, and ran for the terminal.

"What's for me?" Kelly asked, coming out of the master bedroom in a senior citizen style sweat suit for the flight.

Hank held up her half of the sandwich. No words were exchanged, she accepted the food and began to eat. They were ravenous. After a few bites and swallows Kelly managed a "oh my god this is so damn good." Hank nodded. He was slowing down, his belly full for the first time since he awoke five hours earlier.

"I'll be in the shower, out in a minute." He said getting up from his seat.

"I'm not going to lie to you, it feels as great as this sandwich tastes." Kelly ran a brush through her hair with one hand and held the sandwich in the other.

She was right. Hank washed the grime from his body, and enjoyed a minute of happiness in the warm water. He turned off the shower, dried himself with a towel, and put on his own senior leisure suit. When he emerged into the main part of the RV, Kelly was gone. Hank ate the last bites of his sandwich as the other RV pulled up behind him. He took a gulp of water from a bottle on the table, and ran into the terminal.

Hank did not go to the plane. He waited for the people to come out of the RV. Peter ran into the airport first. He said hello, and made his way down to the plane for his pre-flight systems check. One by one the people came out of the RV and into the terminal.

John, a bandana wrapped around his nose and mouth, opened the animal trailer, and led the goats into the terminal.

Solange, also sporting a bandana, ran to the animal trailer and grabbed two cages of chickens. She handed a cage to Avery.

"It's not as bad as I remember." John said to Hank as he waited with the three goats. "But it's still pretty damn bad. There are ten chicken cages. Everyone needs to grab one." John grasped Solange's empty hand, and they walked towards the ramp leading the goats.

Hank, Paul, Dan, and Ahmed took turns running out to the trailer for chicken cages. Once inside, they handed the cages to a waiting person. Dan came back with the last cage.

"That's it." He said, gasping from holding his breath. "It's empty."

The chickens beat their wings against the cages. The rooster crowed. Paul looked at his brother, Hank. "Nice sweat suit grandpa."

"I bet I can sell this to you in six hours. Comfort is key on a long flight." He showed off his moccasin slippers.

"I have a set on the plane. I'm making fun of you while I can." Paul picked up a chicken cage and walked towards the plane. Hank fell in step next to him. "We've come a long way from me finding you in a hole."

"We have." Hank put his free arm around him. "I know we aren't there yet, but." There was a tear in his eye. "I feel like we made it, Paul. We made it through this whole damn mess."

"From a hole in Ohio, to a snowy bed and breakfast in Vermont, we made our way onto a plane bound for Hawaii." Paul shared his brother's sentiment. "The ticket price was too damn high, but we made it."

Dan walked behind them, chicken cages held out to his sides in each hand.

"We're going to get a ticket leaving those RV's in the fire lane." Ahmed said to the men.

"I can get you out of most tickets in New England." Dan replied over his shoulder. "I'm pretty popular with law enforcement."

They walked up stairs to their gait at the end of the terminal.

"I swear, I'm always the last gate." Dan shook his head in mock anger.

"Could be worse, we could be in Minneapolis or Atlanta." Paul responded. "Honestly, Dan, when was the last time you were in the public side of an airport?"

"It's been a while. I remember them being more crowded, and the security being tighter." He smiled at his own joke.

They arrived to a plane full of noisy children, adults, and animals.

Peter greeted them, escorting Dan and Paul towards the back. "Hand the chickens to Avery and Matt. I want to show you my plan for the flyers."

The adults were in first class. The children occupied business class, and the animals crowed, oinked, bayed, and mooed in coach. Peter walked through a door to the cargo area and stopped when he reached a door handle in the floor.

"See this?" Peter twisted the handle and opened the trap door. Light from the outside glowed from below. "This is the access panel to the landing gear, which is down, obviously. You can see the outside at the bottom of the wheel well. When we're in flight, the wheels will tuck in here." Peter pointed towards the stacks of printed paper in piles next to the trap door. "When the wheels are up, put fliers in here, not too many, but you know, a couple of thousand or so. It's going to be very cold in this cargo hold when we reach cruising altitude, but you'll manage. I'll drop the landing gear over the cities, the papers will drop, rinse and repeat, easy peasy."

"And we know it will work?" Hank asked.

"No, but it's the only option. I give it a 90% chance of success. Do I think all the flyers will go out? No. Will most of them? Yes. I have no idea what the coverage will be. Chicago is a big place. People could be on the North Shore, the Southside, or any of the suburbs around the city. We have a very small shot of landing flyers on people. We do a pass, we drop the flyers, hope the sound of a plane alerts people, they find the instructions, it's all we can do." Peter shut the door and twisted the handle. "Any of you want to try it?"

They each took turns opening the door and shutting it. Thick winter gloves and hats sat in a pile next to the door along with several noise suppression headphones.

"You think Chicago is big, what is our plan for the other places? Houston? Dallas? San Antonio? Los Angeles is massive." Dan shook his head. "Needle in a haystack to find people."

"We give it a try because it's the right thing." Hank gave Dan's arm a pat. "As Peter says, it's all we can do."

The men stood in the cargo hold. "Are you ready, Ahmed? Let's get this show on the road. The rest of you? Seat belts on and seats in their full and upright positions."

"Yes sir." Paul told him, falling in line behind Ahmed.

Antonio backed the accordion gate away from the plane door before jumping the two foot gap to get back on the plane. He gave his ever present cocky smile after landing the jump.

"Never in doubt." He said.

"Next time, wait for one of us to be by the door to catch you." John told the young man. "We can't afford to lose you."

"Next time?" Solange asked him.

"Yeah, next time he's jumping from a ramp onto a 777 bound for Lihue." John replied sarcastically. "You know what I mean."

Antonio shut the door and locked it into place. "The trick is going to be getting off this thing on the other end." He said.

"Emergency slide." John told him. "You get to push the cows."

"Emergency slide." Antonio said back, realization in his voice. "Yeah, that makes sense."

"Stick with us, Tony. We've got your back." John joked as Antonio walked into the cockpit.

There were four seats in the cockpit. Peter motioned Antonio to the other front seat. Ahmed sat behind Antonio. Ahmed had not trained with Peter, but his previous experience as an investment banker, a job with extreme hours and pressure, made him a nice third person in the cockpit.

"I guess it's time to leave." Peter said to them. He pressed the button to start the plane.

Cheers erupted from the cabin.

"Next stop, Lihue, Kauai." He backed the plane away from the terminal and started towards the runway.

Peter picked up the intercom, "We are currently first in line for takeoff. Please secure any farm animals that may be loose among the cabin, and get a good hold of your dog. We should be off the ground shortly." He set the intercom down and drove to the end of the runway, turning the plane at the top of the strip, and directing it into takeoff position.

Peter undid his buckle and got out of his seat. "Come on." He said to Ahmed and Antonio as he walked to the first class cabin.

"This is it." Peter said loudly, addressing the group with purpose in his voice. "I'm not saying we can't change our minds and land back here, because we can, but this is it. Once we hit water, or maybe even when we drop our first set of flyers, we're committed." He clapped his hands together. "Is this our final unanimous decision?"

The plane was quiet. Emily, sitting in the second row aisle with Jay in the window seat on one side and Brian across the aisle on the other, was the only one to reply. "Let's go to Hawaii and restart our lives, Peter."

The old man nodded with finality, and said. "Okay, let's do it. Come on guys." He directed Antonio and Ahmed back into the cockpit. They sat down in their seats, and Peter revved the engines.

Without fanfare or another announcement, Peter pushed the controls forward and the plane sped down the runway. Peter adjusted the flaps. The front wheels came off the ground, the back wheels lifted, and they cleared the trees at the end of the runway by several hundred feet. They were in flight and headed west.

Dan leaned towards Brian. "Pretty exciting, huh?"

"Flying is boring. You have to sit in your seat the whole time, and my mom told me this flight is for like two days." Brian crossed his arms, lamenting the next twelve to fourteen hours.

"We'll figure out how to make it fun. Don't worry." Dan assured him. "We hooked the gaming gear up to the big television in business class, and we can run movies back there. You kids can have your run of that section."

"Can I go now?" Brian's arms uncrossed.

"Let's give it a few minutes." Todd told him. "You have a long time to have fun."

"I know we are free to do what we want." Peter crackled over the intercom. "But stay buckled for a few minutes while I get up to the correct altitude. It can be bumpy at these lower levels. Dan, if you want to load the flyers while that room isn't cold, you can get up, but everyone else should stay seated for a few minutes." The intercom clicked off.

Peter put the microphone down. "This is going to be an adventure, fellas. I don't have a weather report. For all we know, we could be running into a huge tropical storm in Hawaii, or a spring storm in any of our cities. We'll play it by ear." Peter settled into his chair. He had flown for over fifty years, and never lost the thrill and love of being in the air. It was in his blood. He knew this was close to his last flight, and he soaked in every minute.

"Do you need me to stay up here?" Antonio enjoyed the takeoff, but was more interested in seeing a movie or gaming in the back of the plane.

"No." Peter told him. "If Ahmed will stay, I should be good. I'll call you if I need a break or the rest room."

Antonio jumped up and went in the back. "If you can get another person to sit up here, you can take breaks." Peter told Ahmed. "I just want someone with me to make sure I don't fall asleep."

"The computer is flying us, right?" Ahmed scanned the controls.

"Yep, but I don't want to risk not having two people up here."

"Well then, what do you want to talk about?" Ahmed asked, his aviator sunglasses reflecting the blue sky and clouds.

"Warm water." Peter replied. "The warm ocean water I am going to dive into when we get to Hawaii. Sandy beaches, empty from one end to the other, and beautiful blue warm water."

Ahmed and Peter discussed the joys of tropical living, and their anticipation for sweating under a hot sun for the first time in months. Peter missed fresh fruit more than any other food. He could take or leave steak, but bananas? They were his favorite. Their conversation lasted into Chicago's airspace.

Peter kept the cabin door open during the flight. He turned and yelled for Dan as the plane approached Chicago.

"Yes?" Dan replied, poking his head through the door a second later.

"Are we locked and loaded with the flyers?" Peter asked.

"We've been good since we left."

Peter picked up the intercom. "If everyone could sit down, I'm going to give our operation paper drop a try in the Chicagoland area. It might get a little bumpy while I'm descending, so buckle your belts for a few minutes." He looked at Ahmed. "Where should we go? We only get one shot at this."

"I would guess people would stay by the lake for food, but I have no idea. We can't drop the paper by the lake, that would be a waste." Ahmed laughed. "We should have discussed this earlier. Maybe it wasn't a game time decision."

Todd snuck up to the cockpit and strapped into one of the empty seats. "We lived in Chicago for five years. Let's go up to Evanston by Northwestern. It's near the lake. Some of the paper might blow into the lake, but it's a chance we have to take, right? That's why Avery laminated a few. I know you are probably thinking people might live right on Lake Michigan to fish, but I doubt it, not in the winter. They would go to the suburbs. There are plenty of small ponds to fish. There are deer and game to hunt. West and north of the city is the place to drop."

Peter descended at a comfortable pace. There was a little turbulence, but no big drops or jolts. The enormous plane absorbed most of the turbulence bumps. "I'll fly straight up the city, drop the leaflets coming from the south. When I see the football stadium I'll bank west, open the gear, and we'll give it a try."

"All we can do." Todd was curious to see if the flyer program worked.

"I'm going to put it on the screen for everyone to see." Peter smiled, his teeth were white under his three day salt and pepper stubble and dark sunglasses. He pointed to a button that read 'rear camera.' "This plane has a camera on the belly. You can watch the landing gear go down. A fun gimmick to keep the passengers occupied."

"Nice." Ahmed duplicated the old man's grin while nodding in approval.

Chicago loomed in their front window. Peter was down to 5,000 feet, and the ride was choppy. He buzzed over the Sears Tower heading north. Todd watched as they passed over a noticeably brown Wrigley Field. The normally green ivy appeared dead.

"I miss baseball. I didn't go to many games, but it was a big part of my life. I never saw the Cubs win the World Series. Damn."

"Like the rapture had anything to do with that." Ahmed replied sarcastically.

"That's the place you're talking about, right?" Peter pointed towards the football stadium at Northwestern.

"Yes, go up a little bit more, turn and drop." Todd's face was glued to the window to see the flyers.

Peter waited a few seconds, turned the plane west in a wide bank, and announced to the cabin. "Well folks, pardon the interruption, but if you would please focus your attention on the viewing screens, you'll see our first attempt to contact other survivors." Peter flicked the camera button to "on" and dropped the landing gear.

The passengers watched their television screens as papers flew out of the bottom of the plane. The kids screamed.

"It sounds like it worked, at least from our end." Peter said to Ahmed and Todd. He kept the landing gear down for a few minutes before raising the wheels. Peter set the altitude to 36,000 feet, and sat back as the plane ascended. When the plane was back to appropriate altitude, he noticed the fuel gauge needled was down a notch.

"We have a problem." Peter reported to Todd. "We can only drop leaflets one more time, maybe twice."

"What's wrong?" Ahmed asked from the co-pilot seat.

"It's eating up too much fuel. We burn more at the lower altitudes, and climbing back up to 36,000 is almost like taking off again. If we fly to Texas, drop fliers three times, maybe hit St. Louis going there, Los Angeles, San Diego, San Francisco on the way up the coast? We'll crash in the Pacific before we get to Hawaii."

"Holy shit." Todd said.

"Don't panic, we're fine, but we can't drop fliers from here to Honolulu. Pick two more cities, and we go from there. I suggest L.A. We drop as many as we can, then we fly to our new home."

"I'll discuss it with everyone. Damn. Well, it was a 'nice if we can.' I'll let Antonio know he might not get a bump in his female population." Todd unbuckled and went into the back.

"You need anything?" Ahmed asked. "I'm going to use the restroom, grab a drink and some crackers."

"I'd love a water, thank you." Peter sat comfortably in his seat. The plane was on auto-pilot towards Dallas. Peter took a guess and changed the destination to San Francisco. The plane altered course, steering ever so slightly towards the west. "We'll hit San Francisco and L.A. Anyone who stayed in Texas in July probably died from dehydration or heatstroke." He mumbled to himself. "Or they made the smart move towards the coast and are in Mexico or Los Angeles."

Todd relayed the fuel concern to the group. "Doing it two more times would not be a risk, but that's it. We can fly low through San Francisco, L.A. then it's off to paradise."

"You really think people are in San Francisco?" Avery asked.

"It's a big area. Oakland is there, San Francisco, Sacramento. They could fish for food. The climate is nice. Yes, probably a better bet than L.A. L.A. is hot. People in California would migrate north to escape the desert." John answered.

"I'll report to the captain." Todd walked towards Peter, meeting Ahmed in the steward's cabin. "We vote for San Fran and L.A."

"I thought as much." Peter replied. "I set the location to San Fran. We can drop the paper and fly down the coast to L.A. at a lower altitude before climbing back up and out to Hawaii." Peter looked down at the computer. "We have three hours before the drop. Can you let Dan know he can reload whenever." Peter remembered their confusion about where to drop in Chicago. "And ask if anyone has a suggestion on where to drop in San Francisco. I've been a few times, but only as a tourist. Am I dropping on Nob Hill and calling it a day?" Peter

"I'll check, and if you need relief, I can send Tony up here. He's playing games and watching videos with the other kids."

"I will stretch my legs and walk back with you. Ahmed, you okay for a second?"

"To just sit here, right? I don't do anything?" Ahmed had mild concern in his voice.

"Just sit back, enjoy the view of nothing, and eat your crackers." Peter told him. "I'll come back with some Milano cookies." He gave Ahmed a pat on the shoulder.

Peter used the facilities and came back to the cabin. "Has anyone spent any time in San Francisco?"

"I went to Stanford." Dan told him, raising his hand. "It's a complicated area. San Francisco is big. Oakland is big, Sacramento is big, and there are sizable towns up and down the coast. All of the areas are suitable for people." He thought for a minute. "Let's descend over Oakland, drop fliers on San Francisco, keep low, and I'll throw leaflets all down the coast. We have more than enough papers. I'll save a thousand for Honolulu."

"I don't want to raise and lower the gear. Can you not get sucked out the trap door hole if I leave the gear down?" Peter was weary of playing up and down with the landing gear.

"I hope." Dan laughed. "L.A. is a desert. No one could stay there. They'd die. Any survivors would migrate to Malibu for food, water, and vegetation." Dan shook his head. "California and L.A. had so many people, I bet there are fifty survivors down there." He paused. "Let's fly to San Diego, keep the landing gear down to Malibu. The odds are high a group of people are down there."

"I can do that." Peter told him. "We'll make it work. We have plenty of fuel with our revised plan."

"How about this?" Dan continued. "I'll work with the door open in SoCal. If I don't get sucked out and can drop fliers to the ground effectively, I'll pepper Northern California the same way. As a favor to me, let's add Seattle before we bank west to Hawaii."

A smile crept across Peter's face. "That is a great plan. I'll call you when we're close. You have two and a half hours until we hit San Diego." Peter walked back to the cockpit and sat in his chair. He checked the instrument panel, adjusted their heading from San Francisco to San Diego, and settled back in his seat to talk to Ahmed.

Dan stood to load fliers into the landing gear. He watched the group from the door of the steward's pantry. Despite the total collapse of society, people still followed established rules with regards to plane travel. Seat belts were fastened, and his friends remained in their seats.

"What's the story?" Bernie asked. She was on a break from the kids, who did not need the chaperoning she anticipated. The children watched movies and played games happily and without incident.

"We are going to fly over California, drop leaflets from San Diego to Seattle. We have about two and a half hours." Dan explained. "I'm going to load fliers. I want a movie rolling when I get back."

55

Dan and Paul wore gloves, ear protection, and coats as they stuffed rescue letters through the jet's floor open to clouds. Their ears stung from the noise despite their protection. They let go of the bundles of notes above the opening and watched the papers get sucked to the ground. Peter assumed the cold would be unbearable, but the noise trumped any discomfort the sub-zero temperatures posed.

Paul grabbed the trapdoor handle and shut the hole. "That's enough, I can't take anymore. I want to hear when I get old." He screamed to his friend. They had thick rope wrapped around their waists, safety lines preventing them from getting closer than a foot to the opening. The lines were not to help them if they fell out of the hole. The lines prevented them from getting anywhere near the hole.

The noise was deafening until the landing gear was raised and the outer doors thumped shut.

Dan sat with his legs stretched out ahead of him. He panted. It was not hard work, but it was exhausting to stare into a 5,000 foot abyss, throw papers, and make sure you do not go with them. He used his hands to keep himself up, his palms on the ground just behind him.

"You think there was anyone down there?" Dan asked with a yell.

"I don't know. You stayed in Boston, and that place was freezing. I bet survivors stayed. Where would they go?" Paul stood and reached his hand out to help Dan off the ground. "We're doing what we can, what we know is right." Paul grunted as he helped the large man to his feet.

"Thanks for the help." Dan pulled off his gloves. "You're right, all we can do is what we can." The plane ascended slightly. Paul opened the trapdoor and threw two thousand notes into the wheel well for the last west coast drop in Seattle.

"You should go up front to see the space needle one more time." Paul told him.

"It shouldn't be too long, maybe another four hours before Hawaii." The stack of was down to a less than a thousand. Dan and Paul peppered California with close to 80,000 rescue pages.

"I hope Peter takes a break. He's been sitting up there all day." Paul unzipped his coat and placed it on a pile of luggage.

"He won't. You can tell, this is what he does. He flies planes. If you were doing the thing you loved for the very last time, wouldn't you soak it in? I would." Dan placed his jacket with Paul's.

Dan enjoyed the Seattle skyline one last time. It was raining. Peter opened the landing gear over the Space Needle before banking west towards Hawaii. He hoped the rain would not destroy all of the fliers, though he knew fifty of them were laminated.

Peter made an announcement as Dan and Paul walked towards the cargo hold to dump papers in the wheel well for the drop over Honolulu.

"Ladies and gentlemen, we have begun our final ascent towards Lihue International Airport. Kick back. According to the navigation computer we'll be landing in approximately three hours and forty two minutes. The next land you see will be the beautiful island of Oahu."

Dan and Paul shook hands after the final loading of fliers into the landing gear well. "Let's get back to our seats before they put a rom-com on the screen." Paul looked at the animals. He nodded to Kelly and Karen, playing Gin on the ground next to the cows.

"To be honest, I didn't go to many movies. I'll watch pretty much anything." Dan did not rush like Paul asked.

"You have to back me up on this one. I can't watch another romantic movie, I just can't." Paul pleaded.

"Okay, I'm just saying, I haven't seen it, so it wouldn't be the worst pick." Dan raised his hands in mock surrender.

"Just work with me, okay?" Paul parted the curtain into first class. "When Harry Met Sally" was on the screen. He dropped his head.

"Awesome, I haven't seen this before." Dan said, sitting next to Todd. "Paul, can you look for some popcorn like you said you would? Thanks."

"Popcorn sounds great! Thanks Paul." Emily told her brother in law. "Maybe pass around some drinks too?"

Paul's mouth opened slightly in disbelief. He risked his life to throw fliers out of the plane, and now he was relegated to steward duties.

Dan did not make eye contact with him.

"I'll take a Sprite." Jamie called out, eyes glued to the screen.

"Coke!" Todd raised his hand.

Orders continued. Paul was in a no win situation. He went to the pantry for popcorn and soda.

56

Peter's voice interrupted the movie. "About an hour, stretch your legs if you need to."

The adults were antsy and nervous. The kids, entering their twelfth hour of media, were ready to get off the plane. Even the animals in the back grew increasingly restless.

Kelly did not want to use additional tranquilizers or sedatives on the animals. She was sure she could manage them for another hour, probably close to three hours at their current doses. Her biggest concern was the bull. If he woke, he would get rowdy with the cows and surrounding animals. She assured those who came to see the animals, that the bull would be asleep for several more hours. Secretly, Kelly was not as confident. She had tranquilized horses, but never a bull. In theory the weight to sedative ratio should be the same, but theory and practice? Kelly prayed the big animal with horns and a temper would stay asleep.

Greg and Rebecca sat quietly for most of the flight. They occupied seats in the last row of first class next to a window. Matt and Avery sat in front of them, and turned around often to pester the couple. Greg and Rebecca played cards, a travel version of scrabble, or talked quietly. Rebecca was the only one who knew Greg was secretly afraid to fly.

Towards the middle of the flight Matt goaded the teens into playing Monopoly. The game lasted over three hours, and most of the plane watched parts of the match. The long flight reminded Greg of the days he spent stuck in the Webster cottage, snowed in or weather bound by negative temperatures. If he had not been afraid of flying, the twelve hours would have been a breeze.

Towards the end of the flight, even the stoic Greg felt the excitement of landing.

"I can't believe we are going to make it." He gripped Rebecca's hand tightly.

Matt turned around and put his palm in the air for a high five. Greg released Rebecca's hand and slapped his brother's. Avery knelt backwards in her chair to face them.

"This is so exciting!" She practically yelled.

Craig wandered into first class from the video game marathon.

"Are we almost there?" He asked. His eyes were wide open and bloodshot as if he had watched television for a week.

"Better grab a seat, Craig. We are about to land." Matt pointed to the aisle seat next to Rebecca.

"Do we know what we are going to do when we land? Are there going to be cars? Do we know where we're going to stay the first night? I'm hungry. Can someone get me a drink?"

Rebecca stared at the boy. He was young, but should not have whined like a four year old. "You can go grab some chips or crackers up there." Rebecca pointed towards the steward's area. She had never been as helpless as Craig appeared to be.

Craig asked if others would like something, and despite the 'no' replies, he brought back two boxes of goldfish, an assortment of chips, and bottles of water.

"So what are we going to do when we land?" He asked again.

Matt put a chip in his mouth. "Well, we've done some advanced planning. Don't get too worried. Tony was smart enough to load five new car batteries into the hold. We will swap out dead batteries and get cars or vans working. We have studied guide books and found several places for tonight. It's going to be afternoon when we arrive, but we'll be exhausted. We just want beds for the night. Food? Eat what you can right now. I believe we are hoping for fruit and other things to materialize tomorrow. I doubt we'll do dinner tonight."

Peter's voice came over the speaker again. "If you look out your window, you'll be able to see the islands of Hawaii. We'll fly lower over Honolulu. We should be on the ground in less than 20 minutes. I have received clearance from the tower. We are number one to land."

Some of the adults chuckled. Craig did not understand. "But there aren't any other planes." He said to Matt.

"That's the joke." Matt told him. "Anyway, yes, we are ready for when we land. I'm not sure it's going to be a bang bang operation, but we know what we're doing." He looked at Avery. "You have any idea how excited I am to be warm? I haven't been warm in like six months."

"You've been cold? I was in New York, you were in South Carolina." Avery rolled her eyes at him. "It's going to be incredible. I might run into the ocean with all my clothes on." she had a grin on her face, as did everyone in the first class section.

The excitement was palpable.

Peter looked out the window. An hour ago he was exhausted, falling asleep in his chair. Now he was full of energy, ready to land the bird. "You see anyone?" He asked Ahmed.

"No smoke, no cars moving. Nothing." Ahmed slept for most of the trip from Los Angeles to Seattle to be rested and ready to help while they were over the ocean. He looked out the window at the large city. Honolulu was below them as Peter had brought the plane in low. He dropped the landing gear and the last fliers fell from the plane.

Peter brought the plane higher to allow him to see the Lihue runway from an appropriate distance. He pointed to the island. "There she is." Peter grabbed Ahmed's upper arm and began shaking it back and forth. "God damn, there she is. We made it. I had my doubts, but we god damn made it!"

Ahmed turned. "Wait, what? You had your doubts? What do you mean?"

"Nothing, never mind, I'll tell you over a tall glass of pineapple juice, just get ready to pull the cord on that emergency door and feel the heat of the sun." Peter studied the maps of Kauai and knew the location of the airport, as well as the direction of the runway. It cid not matter which end of the runway he started his landing, those rules were gone. Peter knew Lihue was equipped to handle 777 landings, but he was not sure how much wiggle room he had to stop the plane. There was a difference between 'you can' land the plane and 'it's easy' to land the plane.

The runway stretched ahead of them. It was clear of planes and apparent obstacles. "I'm glad we timed this correctly. Arriving at night would have been problem." He chuckled.

Ahmed was not amused. "Exactly how many concerns did you have that you did not voice?"

Peter touched down as close to the beginning of the runway as possible. When all of the wheels were on solid ground, he slowed the plane. He did not stop at the end of the runway. He turned the jumbo jet towards the airport.

Screams of joy erupted from the cabin.

Ahmed patted Peter's shoulder. "Great landing, Captain. Great flying."

"Thank you Ahmed. It was my pleasure." He steered the plane next to a stair truck, parking a few feet from a gate ramp.

The strong and stoic pilot powered down the engines, put his face in his hands, and sobbed.

57

Antonio opened the door of the plane. Hot air blew inside and hit him in the face.

"Damn, it's hot here. I mean, it's like 80 or 85." He pulled an emergency handle, inflating a giant yellow slide from the doorway, and creating a path to the ground. He cradled a car battery tightly on his chest, both of his arms curled around it like he was holding a baby. He sat down on the side of the plane, extended his feet out, and inched his behind onto the slide. When his butt was off the end, he slowly made his way down. He used his feet to moderate his speed. He set the battery on the ground and turned around.

John and Hank looked down at him.

"It's all good." Antonio yelled to them. "Let me get the truck started and I'll bring the stairs over."

John jumped out and slid down to the tarmac. "You think you get all the fun?" They made their way over to the stair truck. "What do you want to do, get the stairs over and then see if we can get the ramp?"

"Yeah, let me get the truck going. We can get everyone off, and I'll move the ramp over so Kelly can walk the animals into the terminal." The keys were in the stair truck ignition. Antonio expected them to be. He turned the key, and got a respectable light up of the dash, but the truck did not turn over. He popped the hood, and installed the new battery. The truck turned over immediately. With John's direction, Antonio guided the stairs flush against the rear door of the plane.

John ran up the stairs and knocked on the door. It popped open with Emily's smiling face on the other side.

"Welcome to paradise, ma'am. Please watch your step."

Emily nodded to her brother in law. She held a second battery and wore a set of jumper cables around her heck neck like a scarf. She walked down the stairs towards Antonio.

"Tony!" She yelled over the wind on the tarmac. "Let's find a vehicle!"

Antonio got out of the truck and met her for the walk. "Are we looking for a big hotel van? Maybe two vans?" He asked her.

"We're looking for something that will start. That's the first priority, Tony. A vehicle we can get started after it's been sitting in the sun and salt air."

Antonio took the battery from her. It was the chivalrous thing to do. Lihue was a small airport, closer in size to Lebanon than Manchester or Boston.

Emily found it was too hot to exert herself beyond walking quickly.

"It's warm, huh? I'm not used to this much heat." Beads of sweat formed on her forehead. They made their way to a large parking area. There were rental cars, rental vans, hotel vans, and a local shuttle van. Emily pointed to the shuttle. It was large enough to bring the entire group. "Can we start one car and jump a few more off of that battery? I know we'll probably take two or three groups from here."

"It's all about finding the keys." He told her. They walked to the shuttle. It was parked in the fire lane, left in what appeared to be a hurry. Antonio pried the bus doors open and searched for keys. He came up empty. He was drenched in sweat. "Let's go with our first plan, hit the rental counter where we know there are car keys. It's too hot to mess around like this."

"I agree." Emily was in shorts and a tee shirt, and was still warm. The sudden climate change was too much for her body to handle. She followed Antonio towards the terminal, leaving the jumper cables next to the car battery he put down on the sidewalk.

They approached the rental car area. Antonic walked behind the counter and opened a cabinet holding dozens of car keys.

"We want SUV's, right?"

"Yeah, for now." She answered, wiping her forehead again.

Antonio pawed through a cabinet of keys on the wall, pulling off chains with SUV models scribbled on the white tabs; Tahoe, Escalade, Explorer, Expedition. He handed the keys to Emily.

"That's seven, good enough for now." She flicked her head in a 'let's go back out' motion. Emily looked around the airport. It was empty. There were no bodies, no bags, nothing.

Antonio put one set of keys in his pocket, a mustang convertible. He was going to drive the car until it stopped working. Emily was already outside, and he hurried to catch up with her.

Dan and Ahmed stood on the curb waiting for them.

"How incredible is this?" Dan asked. "No humidity, 80 degrees, unbelievable!"

"I thought there might be bodies or something, out this place is empty, deserted. Now that I think of it, I didn't see any planes."

Antonio looked at her. "What's the first vehicle?"

She held up a set of keys and clicked the panic button. Lights on an SUV in the second row flashed weakly, the horn gave a half hearted blare before stopping.

"I'd say that battery is dead." Antonio picked up their new battery and walked to the vehicle.

Emily used the key to unlock the door. She popped the hood and waited for the boy to do his magic.

"Try it." He told her after a minute under the hood.

Emily turned the key, and the SUV came to life. "Yes." She said to herself. The fuel tank was full, as they hoped all of the rental cars would to be. She cranked the air conditioning, and waited to see what Antonio wanted to do.

"Keys?" He asked her. "I want to see if we have the ones for the trucks on either side of this one, you know, make it easy to jump."

"I'll go back inside and get them." Dan walked behind the two trucks and noted the license plates, makes, and models. "I'll be right back."

Antonio took a spot in the air conditioned car until he saw the lights flicker in the SUV to his left. He got out and opened its door, popped the hood, and jump started the car. With a system developed, they soon had seven SUV's running.

Antonio pulled the new battery from the first SUV, inserted the old battery, and jumped it from one of the running vehicles. He walked the new battery into the terminal to use on the telescoping ramp.

From the windows in the terminal he saw everyone was off the plane. Supplies, food, and water brought for their initial days, were rolled down the yellow inflatable slide. Antonio watched three SUV's drive onto the tarmac. The little kids jumped in the air with excitement and the adults clapped.

Antonio looked down at his watch, already switched it to local time. It was 5:30. He was exhausted, but like the rest, he had work to do. He had to get the gate door open, the ramp motor working, and the ramp over to the plane for Kelly to walk the animals off the jet.

They also had to find a place to sleep tonight.

Despite the work ahead of him, Antonio was excited and happy. He did not believe they would make it to the island. He was prepared to die in the air, or have the plane land in a city somewhere other than Lihue. He never believed he would be standing on a tropical island at the end of their day. Antonio was a pessimist, often proven wrong, but correct enough times to believe he was 'unlucky.' His pessimism led him to 'just join a gang and get it over with, you're screwed anyway.'

He was happy to be wrong. The scene on the tarmac, watching Cameron, Wendy, and Bridget jumping up and down, clapping their hands, made him feel warm inside. He banged on the windows from the terminal until the people turned and looked at him. Antonio began to dance a goofy, out of character happy dance. Within seconds the young kids emulated his moves and the adults smiled and laughed.

His dance over, Antonio returned to his task at hand. He turned the handle on the gate door, expecting to find it locked. It was open.

"This must be my day." He said aloud.

He walked down the corridor to the telescoping booth close to his plane. He was four feet away from the door. He could have jumped, but the cows and pigs needed to walk. He popped open the access panel on the control system, finding the same red and green wires he identified in Manchester. He hooked the wires to the battery. There were no lights or sounds letting him know he had power. Antonio grabbed the control knob, said a quick prayer, and pushed it in the direction of the plane. The compartment moved.

When the ramp was against the plane, Antonio knocked on the door. He heard the lock click and levers turn on the other side. He could have opened the door himself, but it was easier to unlock from inside. The door popped open and Peter stuck out his hand.

"Great work, son. Great work."

Peter looked exhausted. The adrenaline rush that carried the old man through the last hours of the flight was gone, leaving the 68 year old haggard and tired.

"You're the hero, Pete. You the man today." Antonio displayed rare emotion, wrapping his arms around Peter in an unsolicited hug. "You earned the king size bed tonight."

Peter hugged the boy back. He hoped to stay awake long enough to find a bed, any bed, let alone a king sized bed.

"Follow me, Peter, I'll take you to one of the cars, drive you around to the group. You've done enough driving for one day." Antonio kept his arm around the tall man, letting Peter shift some of his weight to him. Antonio could tell the man was almost asleep on his feet. They walked through the airport and towards the largest of their SUV's available.

"Jump in the backseat and lay down. We've been napping all day. You take a break."

Peter did exactly that. He was a former soldier and long haul commercial pilot. His body was used to exerting itself up to and beyond the point of exhaustion, then collapsing for recovery. Peter climbed into the third row of the large SUV, used his hands for a pillow, and fell asleep within seconds.

Antonio jumped into the driver's seat and brought the car around to the airplane. He exited the SUV quietly, pushing the door shut softly. He let everyone know that Peter was asleep in the back.

The group stuck to their plan; get off the plane, get the animals off the plane and somewhere near the airport with food and water, find shelter, sleep.

The road system on Kauai was not intricate. The adults studied and memorized the area while in Hanover. Six SUV's pulled away from the jumbo jet, four trunks carried chickens, one trunk had goats, and the last brought food and water. Hubba sat between Emily and Todd in a front seat.

Hank, Kelly, Paul, Karen, and Dan remained at the airport to tend to the cows, bull, and hogs. They waved as the SUV's pulled away, promising to be close behind.

Kelly led the groggy bull off of the plane and towards baggage claim. The animals were spending the night free range in Lihue's empty airport. It was an open area that did not have glass windows. A breeze blew through the transoms. The area was warm, but would be fine for the evening.

"We're going to be back tomorrow. These animals aren't going anywhere." Kelly pointed towards benches and tables, directing the construction of makeshift pens to segregate the pigs from the cows and the bull.

"Anyone want to hit the beach?" Dan wore a smile and a bathing suit. His sweat soaked shirt clutched in his left hand.

"Hell yes!" Hank replied, pulling off his sweaty t-shirt.

They jumped into the last SUV, rolled down the windows, and headed towards the initial meeting spot, a beach resort near the airport. The survivors banked on finding a few empty rooms in the massive hotel.

Dan pointed to black smoke rising in the distance. He drove towards the smoke and they pulled up to the resort within a few minutes.

Dan drove up to the check-in circle, jumped the curb, and steered towards the beach. He used sidewalks and open areas, passed a black muck filled pool, and stopped at the top of the sard. A bonfire blazed on the beach while everyone swam or waded in the ocean.

"It looks like they started without us." Paul unbuttoned his madras shirt.

"So much for our list of priorities." Kelly opened her door and walked towards the water.

The latecomers nodded to Peter, resting comfortably in a lounge chair near the fire, and waded towards a gathering of people.

"Welcome to your new home." Bernie said to Kelly, putting her arms around her in a hug. "It's been a long trip."

"So the whole idea of finding beds for the night? We'll do that when?" Hank asked Todd, standing with Emily and watching the children splash around in the water.

"See those cabanas? We can sleep in those." Todd pointed to a dozen beach cabanas with fabric draping down their sides. Hank was about to respond before Todd started again. "I know, I know, we're being the grasshopper and not the ant. Look, it's been a long day. We're in Hawaii. Tomorrow is going to be another long day of hard work. Let's blow off some steam."

Hank looked at the beautiful sandy beach and the inviting Pacific ocean. An abandoned resort sat behind them. The goats were tied to a tree and munching on tropical plants. Hank gave his brother a pat on the back before diving into the water. He popped out of the water and waded towards the goats. He wanted to see what they were eating.

"Pineapples." Hank said to himself when he got close enough to the plants. "Son of a gun, there are pineapples everywhere." He scanned the area and saw that coconuts littered the ground around the palm trees, while bunches of green orbs hung high above the ground, below the fronds.

"Todd!" He yelled back to the ocean. "You have a chef's knife in one of the trucks?"

"The one without chickens. It's in the box with the cookware. Why?" Todd cupped his hands around his mouth to cut through the noise of a stiff breeze.

"Pineapples! Lots of ripe pineapples right here! Fruit!" Hank turned to go to the cars when he realized he did not know where the cars were. "Hey, where are the trucks?"

Todd was halfway to the beach after he heard the word fruit. "I'll help. We didn't even think about food, just ran to the water." He pointed towards the parking lot on the other side of the hotel. "We obeyed pedestrian traffic laws."

They ran barefooted, using the balls of their feet and trying to not step on anything sharp. The light was fading slightly as the sun approached the horizon behind the east facing resort.

Six SUV's were parked in a row next to the front of the resort. Wild chickens surrounded the open trunks, inspecting their caged brethren.

"This is mildly off putting." Todd said as he shooed chickens away from his car.

"Sorry the chickens scare you." Hank pulled a plastic box from the back of the truck and removed a large cleaver. "Nice!"

"Yeah, I picked that one up at the mall in Raleigh. Sweet, huh?" Todd pulled a chef's knife from the box along with a flashlight. They walked back to the beach. Hank carried the entire plastic box filled with dinner supplies and cooking implements. Faint shades of orange and red filled the sky behind them. It was officially dusk.

"If we are going to find places to sleep other than the huts on the beach..." Hank said to him.

"Yeah, I know." Todd looked towards the lobby of the hotel. "I'll see if I can find a master key or something to open doors. We might have to kick doors down to get in." He held up the chef's knife, handing it to Hank to put back into the plastic bin.

Todd went to find room keys. He hoped the batteries powering the room locks still worked. Salt air and eight months of time were not on his side.

58

During the early stages of the plague, when the disease was ravaging South America, Europe, and Asia, there were few travel restrictions for U.S. citizens within the U.S. Still, no one made trips to resort islands like Kauai. Tourists already on the island quickly departed. International travel was suspended, but European and Asian tourists fled the small island for the international airport on Oahu. Almost every plane in Hawaii was at the Honolulu airport. The handful of tourists who remained on Kauai died in the hospitals. Locals passed in their beds. The island was deserted and pristine.

A stand at the front door of the lobby, printed in large red letters read, 'No Vacancy.' The wording of the sign was a trick devised by a hotel manager. She argued that a 'Closed' sign would invite looting and squatting, while a 'No Vacancy' sign would fool potential squatters into believing the hotel was occupied and full.

Todd, a potential squatter, fell for the trick and believed every room in the hotel contained a corpse or had dirty linen.

Regardless, he scoured the front desk for a log book or list that might indicate empty rooms.

The front desk was clean of papers. There were six check-in stations with six computers. There were no log books or keys hanging from a peg board, similar to the system they found at the car rental agencies at the airport. The information Todd needed was locked away on a dead server, only accessible from the dead computers in the dead hotel lobby.

Three drawers fell below each of the computer stations. Todd opened each drawer and found blank key cards, but there were no cards with room numbers or the words 'master key.'

"Think Todd" he muttered to himself. He looked at a door behind the front desk. He walked over and opened it. The back room did not have windows and was pitch black. He flashed his light on a small desk and saw a clipboard with papers clipped to the top. Todd walked closer and saw room numbers, dates, and check marks to indicate the last cleaning day.

"Cleaning staff." He mumbled. Todd opened one of the desk drawers and found several cards on wrist lanyards.

"Bingo." He grabbed all of the lanyards and keys and left the backroom for the beach.

Todd approached the first room on the first floor next to the lobby. The key box had a yellow light on the top that was still illuminated. He slipped one of the cleaning staff's keys in the card slot on the door. It flashed green, and he heard the sound of a sliding bolt.

He pushed the door open. He did not look into the room. He lifted his nose for the smell, the horrible putrid rotting smell he met at the Manchester airport, or the houses in Raleigh and Hanover he scavenged for food. Other than a hint of mildew, the room was clean. Todd flashed his light and saw the bed was made. He flipped the deadbolt slider from the inside, assuring the door would stay open, and moved to the next door. Room after room was empty and contained clean linens. Todd unlocked the entire first floor.

He walked out to the bonfire. Hubba rested in the sand next to Peter and Jamie in lounge chairs. A paper plate filled with pineapple, moose jerky, and gold fish crackers rested between them.

"How did you do with the rooms?" Jamie asked.

"See that building?" The resort had several buildings. Todd pointed to one behind him on the left side of the beach. "The entire first floor, twenty or so rooms, are all unlocked, unoccupied, and have clean linen. I can't speak for bugs, but we are good to go for mattresses and sheets."

"You're kidding." Jamie said back. "There aren't any bodies? How can that be?"

"Jamie? I just flew on a jumbo jet from New Hampshire to Hawaii eight months after a plague killed every living soul on the planet. I have a dog when no other dogs or cats survived. I stopped asking questions like 'how can that be' a long time ago." Todd held his hands out to his side and shook his head.

"Would you mind if I went ahead and used one of the rooms?" Peter asked, sitting up. "I need to get some sleep."

"You can do whatever you want, Peter. Here is a lanyard with a key, but I will probably sleep with my door open or unlocked." Todd tossed him a pink wrist lanyard with a key card.

"I will too." He stood up carefully. "It's been a long day." Peter said goodnight to Jamie. Hubba lifted his head and watched the tall old man walk towards the hotel. The sun was not down, but daylight was almost gone. There were millions of stars lighting the sky. A full moon reflected off the ocean.

The bonfire made enough light for them to eat their fruit and enjoy the warm breeze coming off the water. The adrenaline loss Peter experienced swept through the group. The children were groggy, adults felt tired and sluggish, and the tribe made their way to the bedrooms.

John and Solange were the only two left on the beach. He placed another piece of wood on the fire. They did not need the warmth, just the light the fire provided.

Solange pushed two chaise lounge chairs together to snuggle with John. "Finally, weather I can enjoy." She said to him as he sat down next to her.

"It does feel nice to not have on long pants and a flannel shirt even when inside." He put his arm under her back, and she shimmied next to him. They lay together, under the Hawaiian sky next to a fire on the tropical beach.

"We have a lot of work ahead of us, but not as much as I thought." John said to her. "There is food hanging from the trees and growing up from the ground. If we can catch fish and find water, we can survive here."

Solange had both arms around him, one under his back and the other across his chest. "It is incredible. Just the idea that we are not cold, that we can eat food without setting traps far from camp." She looked up at him, her chin on his chest. "It is like this in Ecuador, but the snakes and bugs would swarm us off the plane, and the humidity, you would not like the humidity."

John did not reply, he held her and enjoyed the moment. There were towels hanging on the back of the chaise. John pulled them down to cover himself and Solange. He closed his eyes and drifted off to sleep.

Solange continued to talk about Ecuador until she saw that he was asleep, his chest lifted and fell in a slow easy rhythm. He had a satisfied smile on his face, a tiny grin that told her he was having nice dreams. Solange put her head back on his chest. She did not fall asleep immediately. She listened to the waves lap the shore of the cove, and watched the fire dance in the night.

59

John and Solange were on the beach under half a dozen beach towels and next to a pit of smoldering black logs, when the roosters began to crow. It was in the low 70's. The rising sun added degrees to the temperature every hour.

Rooster after rooster crowed at the light.

"Should we catch and eat one of them?" Solange asked without sarcasm. Her belly rumbled.

"If you can, we'll need more than one." They spooned on the lounge chair. "I bet we have at least a few eggs from our own chickens. Maybe we start our breakfast with those."

"I do not want to get up." She squeezed him. "But I will light the fire." She stretched her arms out to the side. Solange went to where the bonfire had been, looking for embers she might bring to life. The fire was red in one spot. She used dry coconut husk to kick start the flame.

John walked towards the parked SUV's to check for eggs in the chicken cages. He pulled a dozen fresh eggs out of the cages, shooing away the native chickens that gathered around the cars. "I bet a few well placed kicks and I could have chickens for breakfast."

John believed a little hunger might motivate the younger people in the group to focus on work, instead of lounging on the beach like they did last night.

The roosters brought the camp to life. People staggered out of the hotel and made their way to the beach. It was early, only a few minutes after sunrise, and while they had adjourned at 9pm, getting up at 5:45 was still painful.

"How are we going to make coffee?" Melanie was a bear without her coffee.

"I bet we can figure something out with the pouches in the rooms. We can use them like tea bags in a pot of water." Paul needed his coffee too. Necessity was breeding invention.

The sporadic crowing of roosters filled the air.

Paul collected the one shot coffee pouches made for single serving coffee pots in the hotel rooms. He looked at the eight quart pot of water resting on the fire, and judged eight pouches would make strong coffee.

"It's a start." He told Melanie.

The famous fireplace grill set Rebecca and Greg used in their first house straddled the small beach fire, and easily accommodated the water pot and a giant caste iron skillet. John cracked the eggs into the skillet, and began to scramble.

"There isn't a lot, but you can supplement with all the fruit you can find." John did not inspire the group.

Weak coffee from stale hotel pouches and half an egg each was a bad start to the day. Todd could not sit idle and watch it happen.

"I love you, John, but please move aside." He pulled two zip lock bags full of cooked rice out of the plastic bin. He seized the metal spatula from his brother. "Ahmed, can you tear some of this jerky into small pieces?" Todd used the spatula to finish scrambling the eggs and set them aside on a paper plate.

Todd had small jars of olive oil and soy sauce in the bin too. He added oil to the skillet, dumped the cooked rice onto the oil, and fried the breakfast. "Throw the moose in as soon as it's ready. Emily?" He looked at his wife. "Could you get some pineapple? It will add a lot of flavor."

"How about mango?" Avery asked as she chewed a ripe fruit. She held another mango in her other hand.

"Perfect." Todd accepted the fruit from her, tearing pieces of the mango with his finger and dropping it into the sizzling rice. When the rice and jerky were reheated, Todd dumped the eggs into the concoction, drizzled some soy sauce, and announced breakfast was ready.

"That's how we stretch our eggs." Todd prepared for the first meal two days earlier, cooking the rice, and bagging the jerky, oil, and soy sauce.

Despite his desire for motivational hunger, John was pleased with the larger meal.

"It's a little spicy." Meredith said as she fanned her mouth. She was not used to flavorful foods. Her family stuck to a bland diet.

"I mixed some garlic chili paste into the soy sauce to give it a little kick." Todd was proud of himself, the fried rice was excellent. "I thought the mango would mellow the heat enough for you."

"It's good." The girl told him. "I'm still getting used to spicy."

Hank was the first to mention work. "We need to go to the plane and unload our supplies while it's morning and not blazing hot. I bet it get's over 85 by 10am. We don't have to get it all unloaded this morning, but we need to start."

"We have to find a place to live, maybe get some larger vehicles. The livestock, they need food and water. Let's focus our efforts on finding a farm, some houses, water."

Kelly wanted to move her animals to a comfortable, permanent place with food and water. The shock of their new environment along with the trauma of flying was a lot for an animal to take.

"Okay." Hank conceded. "I don't mind shifting our priorities, but we need to motivate. We just used our rice. Our current cooking situation is crappy. Let's get to the real estate office in town and move along with our plans. We have our entire lives to play in the water."

"Tony and I are going to catch some fish for lunch." Craig announced.

"We are?" Antonio looked at him.

"Yeah, let's go back to the airport, get the fish ng stuff, start that Mustang you were talking about, and catch some fish." Craig was eager to try out the new waters.

"Okay, hold on." John cut in. "We have to figure out where to meet. This is not a huge island, but it's big enough that we could lose each other for a few days. Where are you going fishing, and where are you bringing all the fish you catch?" He was proud of Craig for taking initiative.

Todd jumped up. "Hold on, you keep talking, I have an idea." He ran back to the SUV's.

"If we are going to fish off the shore, we can throw lines in right here." Antonio told John. "We just have to get the gear from the plane or try to find an outfitter here in town."

John nodded. "Okay, if you stay here, we won't have to scour the beaches for you. Don't forget to wear sun block and hats. This sun will burn the skin right off of you."

Todd came back to the beach carrying a large plastic container and what looked like a big walnut cracker. "Here's what I need you to do." He looked at Antonio and Craig. "I noticed a few lime trees. When you catch the fish, please fillet and chunk the meat into here, which I will have filled with lime juice and spices. It will cook the meat."

"Ceviche." Solange announced.

"Yeah, under the current conditions, it seems like the best plan." Todd replied. "So, put the fish in here. At lunch, I'll toss in avocado, mango, whatever else I can find, and we'll have a great meal. If you get really lucky with the fishing, don't put it all in here, save some for dinner, but put enough so we can all eat."

"Are you sure? We won't get sick?" Antonio asked, skeptical of the plan.

"It's fresh fish, we aren't going to get sick, and the acid from the lime cooks the meat. You'll see. All the fish meat will be white. They do this off the coasts in Florida, Mexico, Central and South America. It's great food."

"Whatever we catch?" Craig asked.

"Whatever. Shrimp, lobster, fish, it all goes in here."

"Let's do it little bro'." Antonio scooped the last spoonfuls of fried rice into his mouth and walked towards the parking lot. Craig followed him, talking a mile a minute.

Todd went to a grove of trees. He plucked limes and juiced them into the plastic container using the fancy lime juicer he acquired at a cooking store in Raleigh.

"Alright, we have lunch squared away, hopefully. What else do we have to do?"

"Mel and I will take the kids into town to walk around, find items we might need. Tropical clothing is first on our list." Emily gave Melanie and Bernie a head nod.

"Okay, the rest of us will hit the real estate office, and split up to find a farm or place to live. Kelly, are you going to tend to the animals?" Hank looked at the vet as she nodded in response.

"Well, if no one else has anything to say, let's rock." Hank finished his food and put his plate in the plastic bag held by Rebecca.

Peter walked towards him. "Do you mind if I superv se Tony and Craig. I am still run down." The man looked exhausted.

"The rest of us sat around while you flew the plane, take all the time you need."

Jamie stood behind him. "Peter, I'm going shopping with the gals, but I'll bring you back something nice. Maybe a new hat." She hugged Peter. Jamie made sure he had a few large bottles of water for himself and the fishermen. She told him to watch the sun, and go back to the room if he needed to.

Paul got into Dan's SUV. It was still parked right on the beach. Greg and Rebecca jumped into the backseat. "Hold on." Dan advised them. He pushed the gas down and shot the big truck onto the sand. He turned left and gunned it, tearing down the beach with all of the windows down. Dan and Paul squealed with excitement. There was a small access path at the end of the beach. Dan turned the SUV onto it and soon found a paved road back to town.

"Having fun?" Greg asked the men in the front seat.

"You need to lighten up." Rebecca told him. "You're too serious."

Paul pulled a cd out of his backpack and slid it into the player. He and Dan turned the volume up when the first song played. They sang the entire 15 minute ride into town.

The other people arrived at the parked SUV's and had to figure out what to do with the chickens? Kelly suggested putting them in one of the hotel rooms with the door propped open and the cages blocking the entrance.

Within minutes the chickens enjoyed scattered feed off the floor of a Hawaiian resort beachside bungalow. The wild local fowl strutted and clucked on the free side of a wire cage wall.

The local real estate office kept detailed paper files on current listing.

Folders contained residential descriptions and color photographs. A special 'green' section highlighted homes with alternative energy options. Farm files were in manila folders with tabs denoting crops and animals.

The office had a large map of Kauai on the wall. John took the map down to use as a reference. He wanted to triangulate a living zone based on the farming areas and coastal fishing access. Walking and biking would soon be their mode of transportation. They could not live all over the island, and had to find a small area that fulfilled all of their needs.

Rebecca researched Kauai while in Hanover. She drew a square on the map in an area on the northern shore.

"It receives consistent rainfall, and the temperatures are warm but mild." She explained. "The forest has wild pigs to hunt. We can fish on the coast, and the farmland is the best on the islands."

Rebecca knew finding empty homes from real estate listings was a short term solution. They needed to pick one area and clear the bodies out of the neighborhood. Sometimes, even though she knew the outcome, she let other people figure out the solution.

Rebecca felt it was important for John to make the settlement decision. She put the square on the map and let him get to a solution on his own. She was reluctant to accept the mantle of tribe leader, though many of the members looked to her for answers and final decisions already.

"Dad." Matt said to his father. "We have too many people in here. You can handle this, and no offense, but Rebecca seems to have the solution already." He looked towards the red headed genius. "The rest of us want to do some exploring, maybe find more lunch, get fishing tackle, towels, whatever."

John looked up from his stack of listings. "Just be back at the hotel for lunch."

"Dad, it's not even 7am. How long do you think we could possibly take? It's a tiny island. We'll be there by 9am at the latest." Matt and the other kids chuckled. Everyone was disoriented from the time change and the early morning wake up.

"Oh, yeah, right, okay." He waved them off, returning his attention to the farm listings. John spoke to Hank and Dan. "Let's take a ride up to these farms, see if we can find any equipment that we can use to haul the cows and hogs." He looked over to Paul, Ahmed, and Rebecca. "You three okay to keep working? We're going to try and get a trailer for the livestock, get them to a cooler climate today."

"I already know where I'm going to live." Rebecca told him. "But I'm happy to search for other places if you would like me to." She had picked her street while in Hanover, and it was easy for her to find the best home from the few listings in that area. Rebecca did her research, as always, so the actual work was quick and easy.

Solange lifted her head. "Which one is for you and Greg?"

Rebecca held up a listing brochure for an estate in Hanalei. She handed it to Solange.

Paul checked the address, and put a red dot on the map with a marker he found on the table. "Okay, let's see what's near Rebecca's house."

John looked up. "So she picks and we work off of her?"

"Why not? We need a starting point. She's the most versed on the island. I say we go with it." Paul put down the marker.

Solange flipped through the listing. "It is a perfect estate. Our next step is to visit this house and see what our options are around it. I know it will not be a pleasant job, but we should clear out the occupied homes in the entire area."

"So what you're saying is, now that we have a house, we need to go up there and figure out all our other options. We have to find the nearest farms, fresh water, fishing spots, everything." Dan was on board with going up to Hanalei. "I am all for book work when necessary, but it seems like an expedition would be more effective."

Everyone put down the listings.

Rebecca asked a simple question. "Why don't we take the farm listings, take the giant map, and see if everyone wants to head up to the new location? It is much cooler up there, and if we want a resort, Princeville is beautiful. We can fish just as easily on those shores."

John picked up his walkie-talkie. "Hey, Matt, we're done here. We're going to the hotel, pick up our stuff, and move to the north."

"We're moving already? Rebecca found our spot?" Matt radioed back.

"Yes, we'll get up there and find a trailer, come back for the animals today. Let's make our move this morning. " John smiled when Matt referenced Rebecca. As much as he tried to lead, she was the default oracle. John was a fantastic field general, but Rebecca was clearly in charge.

"We found a Walmart. We're going to grab some stuff. We'll see you back at the beach." Matt replied.

John switched radio channels and had the identical conversation with Emily. When they arrived back at the beach, Craig and Antonio were sitting next to Peter and Todd. They were talking and laughing as Hubba lay in the sand at the old man's feet.

"What's with the laying around?" John asked.

"It's like fishin' with dynamite. We couldn't get them off our lines fast enough. I bet we have four pounds of fish in the container, filleted and chunked." Antonio pointed to the plastic bin.

"Seriously, it was like the fish wanted to get caught. They had six good sized fish in less than a half hour. Tony would cast, hook a fish, hand it to Craig to clean, and I would fillet. I couldn't keep up."

Todd explained with amazement how easy it was to catch the fish. "Even Peter was yanking them out like it was a cartoon."

"I may have kept my angling skills a secret until now, so I wouldn't have to walk that hill in Hanover every day. My wife and I had a condo in the Marathon, Florida for years." Peter said coyly.

"You old dog." Antonio chided him. "You sandbagged us, and stayed off fishing detail."

Everyone smiled at the old codger. "Well pack up." Dan announced. "We're moving north. Now that we have lunch, our decision is that much easier. All we have to do is cage the chickens again." He turned to Paul. "I hate catching those chickens."

The plan was relayed to the fishing group, and they prepared for the trip. Instead of caging the chickens, Dan backed his SUV up to the door of the chicken room, and a few of the men went into the room and tossed the chickens directly into the back of the SUV. Dan and Paul volunteered to drive the truck north. A few cages tied to the headrests separated them from the free roaming fowl.

"You can listen to your loud dinosaur music with the chickens." Rebecca told them.

The SUV already smelled. "Sunroof open, windows down, we'll be fine." Dan assured Paul.

As the tribe pulled away from the beach resort, the temperature was already climbing into the low 80's. Matt's group had the find of the morning, a large moving van acquired from a rental agency near the stores downtown.

Emily radioed Kelly with the news of their departure for Hanalei and the discovery of a van. "I can drive it." She crackled back over the walkie-talkie.

Antonio and the van were dropped off at the airport rental lot. He sat in his Mustang convertible, and waved goodbye to the others.

Kelly herded the cattle into the back of the truck. She brought the cows during this trip, and would make two more with the hogs, and the bull. She drove the Kauai coast towards the lush green farmlands on the north shore. Antonio drove his convertible behind the truck. The convertible top was down so he could enjoy the sun and the salt air.

Forty-five minutes after shutting the doors at the airport, the van pulled into rich, fertile farmland at the top of the Hanalei wildlife preserve. John gave Kelly a map with a red circle around a farm. She stopped the van in a driveway and saw their goats munching happily on overgrown vegetation.

Fences surrounded the property. The goats stood in one section of a large pen area. A stream ran through the farm, and Kelly walked the livestock down the ramp of the truck and into a beautiful grazing field. Wild chickens and roosters ran about. Kelly saw birds flying in and out of the trees to the south.

"Welcome to your new home." She said. The cows grazed immediately. Some drank from a large water trough filled from a hand pump tapping an underwater spring.

The temperature was moderate. Livestock shelters were built up around the fields for relief from the sun. Some of the shelters were in disrepair, but with only a few cows, Kelly knew this farm would work perfectly. She pumped water into a trough in a different paddock, preparing for the arrival of the pigs later that day.

There was a farmhouse near the barn. Antonio sat in his car listening to music. Kelly pointed to the house, then to herself, letting him know she was going inside. He nodded and did not turn down his music.

Both the screen and storm front doors were unlocked. Kelly took a step inside and into a good sized first floor. The house was nice but not extravagant. A living room to the right was bright with sunlight from a bank of windows running the south side of the house. The air was stale and smelled of death. Kelly did not have to look, she knew there were bodies upstairs. She opened all of the windows on the first floor, and propped the storm door open for a breeze to flow in and out of the home.

Kelly found two fireplaces in the house, one in the kitchen and one in the living room.

"I could live here." She said to herself. "I hope I don't live alone, but if I do, I can make it work." She opened a back door and walked onto a lanai on the field side of the house overlooking the farm. It had an outdoor shower that worked off a cistern next to the house. She pulled a chain and cold water rained out of a round showerhead.

Done exploring, she made her way back to Antonio.

"Is it going to work?" He asked her, yelling the question over his music.

"Yeah, once we get rid of the previous family."

"Damn, I knew you were going to say that." He shook his head in disgust. "I have a feeling we'll be doing a lot of that over the next week."

Kelly agreed and slid into the passenger's seat. "Let's see what this thing can do."

Antonio grinned and hit the gas. Both of their heads shot back as the car flew down the dirt road. Antonio spun the wheel and turned them around towards the coastal highway.

As they passed the farm, Kelly waved to the grazing cows. The van was parked in the road. Antonio avoided an accident, but came closer than Kelly would have liked.

60

It was noon and a temperate 82 degrees. Soft puffy white clouds drifted across the blue sky as a stiff breeze blew from the ocean. Antonio screeched to a halt at a semi-circle driveway filled with six SUV's in front of a seaside estate. A realtor's sign stood next to the mailbox.

Kelly and Antonio walked through the front door into a gorgeous, fully furnished house.

"This is a nice place." Kelly said to the young man. Antonio was struck dumb by the opulence.

Neither of them had been in a house of this expense or quality. They heard voices and continued through the home towards a beautiful lanai with a saltwater pool and panoramic views.

"You made it!" Bernie yelled. "Wash your hands before you eat. There is water! It comes from a natural spring, and solar cells power a pump. How crazy is that? You can wash your hands in a sink with a faucet and not from a rain barrel or bucket of icy snow water. There is even an electric on demand water heater, so, get ready, there is hot water." Bernie gave Kelly a hug, grabbing Antonio's shirt and pulling him towards them.

"Bernie, calm down. Where can I go wash my hands and eat. I'm starving, and I'm the one who caught the damn fish. Am I the only one who works around here? Tony, start the cars. Tony, catch the fish. Tony this, Tony that."

Bernie gave him a stern look. "You need to watch your language around the children." She pointed towards a half bath near the pool.

"I'm sorry." Antonio replied. He walked towards the bathroom muttering under his breath about all of the work he was doing. When he returned, he went straight for the food. The ceviche was in a large serving bowl with a ladle to spoon out individual portions onto plates stacked on the table. A bag of tortilla chips and boxes of saltine and melba crackers we open to accompany the meal.

Todd added fresh avocado, mango, and cilantro to the fish.

A platter of sliced pineapple, star fruit, and bananas was also available. Antonio grabbed two bananas and a several slices of star fruit.

"Are we all going to live here?" Kelly asked. She was not up to speed on the living arrangements.

"Rebecca picked this place for herself." Bernie told her. "We have to find our own slices of paradise."

"What is she going to do with all this space?" Kelly looked around in wonder at the enormous home.

"Location, location, location." Rebecca said to Kelly before enjoying a tortilla chip covered in fresh fish. "We are close to a bay for fishing. We are within a mile of the farmland. We are on springs for fresh water. There are a dozen homes on this road. We will stay close without crowding each other." She ate another bite of food. "This is the place for us. This is where we should settle. I mean, why not?" She pointed towards the private beach.

"And you get this great house." Kelly said to her, a knowing smile on her face.

"Well, I may have selfish reasons." Rebecca was not embarrassed about her selection, and the other houses on the road were of similar grandeur.

"Okay." Todd said behind them. "It's lunch on day one. We've accomplished a lot already, but we have work to do. Dan, Hank, and I are going through the houses along this road for removal. We'll do the same down at the farm houses. We will be busy for the rest of today and maybe tomorrow." He took a drink of water. He enjoyed the water from the tap, a pre-rapture luxury taken for granted.

"We need to retrieve the supplies from the plane. We need to figure out a system of distributing food. We need to figure out how to split up the chickens or if we are going to keep the chickens in one location. I know there are only 24 of us, but this is also a society. We should decide how it is going to work."

Kelly ate her food, and chimed into the conversation. "I need to eat, I'm famished, but then I am making a swing down to the plane. I need to get the hogs and the bull. You can have the truck when I have finished moving our animals."

"I don't want to concern anyone, but we need to think about our next meals. Sure, we have food we can scavenge or that we brought, but I was thinking of throwing down some traps or trying to find something that we can cook." Greg's traps were in the airplane, but he thought about using his bow to snag a few of the chickens running around.

"You just want to get out of working in the hot sun unloading the plane. I can walk outside and kill a few of the chickens at sundown." Matt eyed his brother with skepticism.

"You plan on catching, cleaning, plucking enough chickens to feed everyone as the sun goes down? If it was just you and me, sure, but we've got Craig, Jaclyn, Jacob."

"Greg's right. He's on food for tonight, protein at least. Everyone else should go down to the plane, help with the animals, or help watch the kids." John had no desire to go to the plane and unload, but it had to get done.

Melanie found Kelly. "Were the farm homes nice? I know my kids will want to live on the ocean, but I am excited to start a farm."

"The one I put the animals next to is very nice. We'll have to clean it out first." Kelly made a face, "but it's a beautiful home with a spectacular lanai. It might be a better home for you and the kids than just me." She described the farm and home in detail.

"I doubt we'll get our own places, do you?" Melanie was feeling the young veterinarian out. "I know Rebecca enjoys her space, but I don't want to live on a farm by myself. If the house is as big as you say, I hope you would consider staying there. You don't have to raise my children, but we'd love to include you as part of the family, even more than we already do."

"If it doesn't work," Kelly told her. "I can always move."

Kelly did not live alone before the rapture, and the few weeks she hid in her building were not pleasant. She did not hesitate to accept Melanie's offer.

"I'll make sure the men get those bodies out today or tomorrow." Melanie gave her a wink.

Todd, Dan, and Hank assembled for a walk through the neighborhood homes. The afternoon would be spent opening houses and determining which ones were available for immediate occupancy, and which ones needed to be cleared. Tomorrow they would find a pickup truck or van to use for clean-up duty.

Melanie approached their strategy conversation. "The farmhouse needs to be taken care of. I'm not telling you to do it right now, I'm just telling you so you know it has to get done."

"Noted." Dan nodded.

"If you need any help, I can't lift as much as you burly men, but I have a strong stomach from working at the hospital." Melanie did not mind dead bodies. She had no love for the smell, but could handle the task.

"You take care of your kids, we'll get your house cleaned. We are going to wrap the bodies in sheets and take the mattresses out too. Everything goes into a van or truck, and we'll find a place to bury or burn it all." Todd hoped to be as brave as he sounded when he encountered the bodies.

"Just thought I'd offer, but you have it under control. The kids and I will be down at the plane loading the supplies." Melanie rubbed Todd's back and walked towards the porch.

"Let's start on the ocean side of the road, cross the street and come back the other way." Dan pointed west, and the men walked off the back lanai towards the road. "Princeville is that way." Dan pointed toward the town. "Let's see how far we get."

They each had a backpack filled with snacks and water. They wore yellow latex gloves and white mouth and nose shields.

"Let's do it." Hank walked between the two men as they approached the front door of the house neighboring Rebecca's. "I put the over under at 3 homes with people."

"Pretty low, what's your theory?" Todd asked as he tried the front door. It was locked.

"These are expensive homes, probably second or third homes. The rapture hit in July. If you live in Hawaii, and there are a few months you decide to go somewhere else? It's the summer. Maybe ski season, but really, if you have to go back to the continental U.S. it's in the summer. If this is your vacation home, you're not coming in July. These places are empty."

"I stayed at the Princeville resort for a few days. It was before I was married. Nice place." Dan made a move towards the beach side of the home.

Most of the ocean view houses had open floor plans and large lanais. This house was no exception. The back lanai was open into the living room. There were plantation shutters, but they were not pulled shut. Todd jumped over the knee wall and into the house.

"I don't smell anything." He gave a thumbs up. "I'll walk around to the front door and open it. Meet you up there to move to the next home."

They spent two hours walking up and down the road, breaking into houses when necessary. They found one set of corpses on the entire street. From the pictures in the home, it was a retired couple, older, living alone. They were decomposing in a large bed in the master bedroom. An open bottle of pills on the nightstand led the men to theorize the one died of the rapture and the second committed suicide. The couple would receive a burial on the central part of the island.

The farmhouses were occupied by dead families. It was bad work, but the men used a pickup truck they found near the Princeville Resort to clear out the bodies. Instead of two days, they were done in one afternoon. Todd, Hank, and Dan agreed to meet at sunrise to bury the bodies.

"Let's see how long the walk to the ocean is. If walking is our mode of transportation, it will be good to know how long it takes us to get fish." Todd was tired, but knew he would be making this walk for the rest of his life, and he would often be tired while doing it.

It took them twelve minutes to get to the first house on Anini Road. They guessed it would take twenty minutes at a leisurely stroll, but the men were hungry and thirsty, and ready to dive into the water.

"About a mile?" Dan said when they were in sight of the house.

"Yeah, that's what I'd guess, maybe a little more, but a mile give or take." Hank felt better after the walk. The fresh air helped him forget the rancid smells at the farmhouses. The walk stretched his legs and back, both tight from the twelve hour flight the day before.

They walked down the road to Rebecca's house. She and Avery were in a discussion. The men waved, and went into the water, clothes and all.

"It's the way it is Rebecca. I'm sorry. This isn't a private Greg and Rebecca vacation. We are all in this together. Living in a big house by yourself, well, it's not happening. I know you and Greg love each other." The comment made Rebecca blush, but she did not drop her gaze from Avery. "And I know you value your privacy, but we are part of a cooperative now. You can have the first floor master. Hole up in there whenever you want, but you have to live with people. Unless you start your own family, and even then you'll probably want people to help you, you have to accept all of us are in your life. We are part of your family. You're not an only child." Avery made it clear to her friend that other people were going to live in her house. Meredith and Avery were definitely moving into the home.

"But there are homes right next door. Why do you have to live with us, when you can live in the same community, but in a different house? That doesn't make sense." Rebecca did not argue as fiercely as Avery expected.

"We need to eat meals together, work together, help each other. I can't be there for you if I'm living ten homes down the road by myself. That's not a community. No walls like the old days. No locking yourself in your house and shutting out the world." Avery put her hand on her new friend's arm. "Besides, I'm moving in. You want this house? You'll share it with me and Meredith, and anyone else who wants to live here. You don't want to live with me? Move, but I'll probably move with you."

Rebecca believed Avery, that she would follow Rebecca and Greg from house to house. Rebecca also believed in the fundamentals of Avery's position. This was a community. Moving into twenty different homes was against the fabric of what the tribe was trying to build.

"We get the big bedroom on the first floor, and if one of you is a slob, you're out, or I'm out. I will live with people happily. I will not live with a slob."

"Deal. Believe me, you're making the right decision." Avery was used to getting what she wanted. It might take more tenacity now that she was not the beautiful tennis princess, but Avery had plenty of tenacity.

Hank came up from the water. He felt refreshed from the awful job he just completed. "How did you two get out of unloading?"

"I don't know." Rebecca told him. "Honestly, we were just standing here, talking, and everyone left, and Ahmed told us to stay here and keep things under control. We were both like, 'okay.'"

"We didn't want to be total slackers, so we gathered fruits and vegetables from all around the homes. We started a map of the local fruit." Avery pointed towards a table with a bounty of fruits, peppers, avocados, and a large white paper. "Then we became slackers."

"We even found some onions." Rebecca added.

Hank walked to the table and looked through the vegetables and at the map. He could not believe how much food was available. Flocks of wild chickens wandered around, fruit fell off the trees, fish almost jumped into the nets. Kauai was a Godsend for their group.

"We cleared the homes. The farmhouses might take a few days to air out, and we'll have to move new beds into the bedrooms, but everything is done." Hank sat down at the table, grabbing a banana from the basket. "What are you two talking about?"

"Community." Rebecca said. "Avery convinced me of the idea that we need to stay close, live in a tight community rather than spread out. I'm willing to give it a try."

"So you aren't keeping the big house for just you and Greg?" Hank looked at Avery. "You're good, well done."

"I usually get what I want." Avery put her hands behind her head as she lay back in the chair and closed her eyes.

"Well, I'm still impressed. We looked at the houses on either side of this house. Each home has a separate guest house and four or five bedrooms. We can all live very comfortably in this area. The farmhouses are more spread out, but the people who want to live down in the fields will be happy in two of those homes. They are just down the road from each other."

"Hello!" Greg said, rounding the corner of the house and into the backyard. He was dirty with green flora stains, dirt, and what appeared to be blood. "I need a little help. Mighty hunter bagged himself a pig, or a boar, or something that resembles a pig but with tusks. It was mean." He held up his hand and showed a cut running across the back. The cut was not deep, but it looked painful.

"How big?" Hank asked. He walked towards Greg and made a motion that he would help, holding his arm up above his head and pointing to the front yard.

"It's going to feed us." Greg assured him. "For a few days I suspect."

A large hairy beast lay in the back of the truck. "I would guess it weighs at least forty pounds, maybe fifty on a good day. I had a rough time getting it into the truck by myself."

"Holy crap, Greg." Hank was stunned. He did not expect the boar to be so big.

"I know. I've gotten pretty good with the bow. It still came at me, so I hacked it down with my machete, right in the head, like it was a zombie or something." There was pride in Greg's voice. "I cleaned it in the woods, which lowered the weight enough so I could pick it up and put it in the truck."

Hank put his arm around his nephew. "Well, it's not as big as the moose Paul and I killed, but it's a nice sized animal for you."

"You mean the moose that wandered into town and stood still while you and Paul shot it twice?"

"Yes, Greg. The ton of animal with large antlers that I killed. The animal that fed all of us for weeks, and is still feeding us, like the moose fried rice you had this morning." Hank could one up the kid all day.

"I give." Greg said. "Unless I catch a great white shark, I'm never going to out do you and Paul. You win." Greg did not care about the good natured ribbing. The boar was a prized kill. Like the fruit around them, and the fish they so easily pulled from the ocean, this boar was proof that they would not just live on the island. The group was going to thrive on the island.

The airplane unloading party pulled up an hour later. Tired, sweaty people poured out of their SUV's. Emily was at the head of the pack. "It is five degrees cooler up here, maybe ten degrees cooler." She found her husband on a lounge chair.

"It's done." She told him. "Half of us probably have heat stroke, but it's done. All the supplies are in the truck." She sat down on the foot part of his chair. Todd sat up and crossed his legs in front of himself.

"The houses are cleared of bodies. Greg killed a wild boar. Avery and Rebecca gathered fruit. I think we can relax, if we can figure out where we are sleeping tonight."

"Where do you want to live?" Emily was a mess. Her hair was pulled back into a tight pony tail that stuck through the back of a baseball cap she wore to block the sun. The cap was soaked with sweat. A thin white line of salt ran across the brim at the top of the sweat. A few strands of her hair stuck to her forehead. Her arms were streaked with grease and dirt, as were her legs.

"Hawaii?" Todd replied. "Kauai?"

Emily ignored him. "John is going to live here, by the water for Craig.

Solange and he are going to stay together, obviously. Matt wants to live on the farm. Mel is going to live on the farm with Cameron, Jackie, and Jacob. Kelly is joining them to care for her animals. I am leaning towards living down in the valley."

Todd looked behind his wife to the ocean. "All of this is new. The way we're going to live will be new too. I understand your need for stability. I know you want a permanent room for the kids. You want them to grow up with friends their own age. What is Bernie going to do? She has little ones too." Todd thought for a second before continuing.

"Maybe we live both places. Maybe the village is where we end up some nights. If Craig has a big haul, the farmers will come up here, and instead of walking down the road in the dark, they stay in this location. Maybe when Greg kills another boar, instead of walking it all the way to the ocean, we cook it at the farms, and the ocean people stay down there. Jay and Brian need to know how to fish, hunt, and farm, and be comfortable in both locales."

"We can't move them around every day or week." Emily did not like Todd's answer.

"Then my answer is I don't know." He took her grimy hand. He flipped it over and saw blisters on her palm and fingers. "Ouch." He said to her. "I might not like the farm. I might not like the sea. The great thing is, I'm telling you we don't have to make a firm decision. We won't have a mortgage. We can move."

"I'd like to try the valley first." Emily took hold of his hand. She squeezed it like a person in love.

"Works for me. The real question is. Will it work for Hubba?"

Emily leaned in to give Todd a hug.

"Are you nuts?" He said, pulling away from her advance. "You're filthy. Go in the ocean or take a shower." Todd let go of her hand. "Yuck."

Emily did not back away. She pushed her husband onto the lounge chair, grabbing his hands and pinning him down. She kissed him. Todd feigned a struggle, but kissed her back.

"Get a room." Melanie said a few feet away as she toweled off from her swim. "There are impressionable children and jealous widows nearby."

The house was equipped with a grill, and like the other high end furnishing, it was a top of the line wood drawer model.

Ahmed flipped pork chops, now sizzling above the flames.

"Fried mango rice for breakfast. Ceviche for lunch. Pork for dinner. I think we've adapted to life in Hawaii quite nicely." Ahmed took a sip from his glass of water. He held the glass up to the group sitting in front of him. "To our first full day."

"Hear hear!" Was the loud reply.

"Our first crop should be rice. If corn is possible, we do corn, but I know we can grow rice here. Right? We're practically in Asia." Matt strategized with Melanie.

"We need a grain, that's for sure. We can grow sweet potatoes or something easy like that in pots. We'll check the books at the library. It should have local knowledge and information we could not access in Hanover." Melanie listened to Matt while combing Casey's hair. She liked Matt, and knew he would be a great partner. She needed to harness his enthusiasm. Farming was a long term project. Matt wanted crops to grow 'tomorrow.'

Similar conversations occurred across the lanai, decisions about where people would sleep that night and live the next day, decisions about what supplies needed to go to the farms and what stayed at the beach, decisions about how often the groups would gather.

At 6:30 the sun was still high in the sky, but everyone was exhausted. The early wakeup by the roosters at dawn, working in the heat and sun, and the five hour time shift caught up with the tribe. Cameron, Bridget, and Wendy were curled up on couches, taking quick naps before dinner.

"We need tables." Bernie said to Kelly and Jamie.

"There is one inside." Jamie pointed to the dining room table visible from their seats.

"No, we need a couple of long tables, and we need a few sets, one set for here and one set for the farm. We need to eat together at tables." Bernie referred to an ongoing communal eating area, not their immediate dinner plans. "I'll ask Ahmed to find a library or high school to locate long tables and chairs. We need our dinners to be social and in one locale."

Kelly described the lanai at the farmhouse. "It will accommodate tables for all of us, and enforce rule number two."

Jamie looked puzzled. "What is rule two? And what is rule one for that matter?"

"Rule two is never go two days without eating together. John and Paul are setting up loose tribe rules, and they want to make sure we stay unified. We never go more than one day without gathering for a meal. We always come together every other dinner or lunch. We can eat every meal together if we want, but never two days apart."

Jamie was tickled. "I could not agree more with rule number two. What's rule one?"

"It's more of a way of life than a rule." Bernie told her. "Rule one is to always remember that we are in this together. I believe it is being referred to as the 'thick or thin' rule."

Jamie understood rule one. She survived a bleak and hungry winter in New York City because of rule one. Her eyes filled with tears. She raised her water glass and barely got out an "amen."

"That's my line." Bernie chuckled, clinking Jamie's glass in agreement.

61

Rebecca woke to the sound of roosters. A week had passed, and she still had no idea how to get rid of the roosters, or keep them from crowing at sunrise. She did not move. She was on her side in a king bed with her eyes open, staring at the wall. Greg lay next to her. "Just go back to sleep." He mumbled. "They'll stop in a little while." He pulled a pillow over his head.

"You know I can't fall back asleep once I'm up." Rebecca sat up in their bed. She wore a U.N.H t-shirt. She brought several of them to remind her of her home. She put her feet in slippers next to the bed and left the room.

It was cool in the mornings, dropping into the high 60's overnight. Rebecca poured herself a glass of water and walked out onto the Lanai. She sat in a chaise lounge chair. The pillow was cool, but not wet from dew. She made sure to keep the chairs under the roof so they were dry in the morning. The coop she brought from Concord was in the yard, and several roosters strolled around the fence surrounding her mainland chickens. They kept eight chickens at the house for eggs. She planned to incubate and hatch dozens of chickens. She wanted fresh eggs each morning without making the long walk to the farm.

"Morning." She nodded to the roosters. One crowed at her before strutting away. Greg came outside and sat down in the chair beside her. He wore an orange hooded sweatshirt. The hood was up to keep his head warm.

Lapping waves and an ever present wind created a constant din. The price they paid for living less than twenty-five yards from the ocean.

He put his hand out, and she took it, intertwining their fingers. He leaned back in his chair. Rebecca and Greg sat and watched the roosters walk around the yard.

"I believed you when you told me we'd make it, that you'd keep me alive." Greg's head was turned, looking at her. She focused on the chickens.

"I know." She squeezed his hand.

"I don't know why I did. You were some teeny bopper, skipping back and forth from your house to the trash cans on the street, but for some reason, I believed you."

She looked at him. His skin was a dark tan from the week under the tropical sun.

"Thank you." He said to her.

"Anytime." She smiled.

They heard footsteps come down the stairs in the front hall. The roosters claimed other victims. Rebecca and Greg did not move. They held hands and watched the Pacific Ocean break against the sandy Hawaiian shore.

ABOUT THE AUTHOR

Brad lives in Raleigh, NC with his wonderful wife and two sons. The Last Tribe is his first novel.

Printed in Great Britain
by Amazon